Legend of Siljatjern Seter:

Love, life and faith on a Norwegian mountain dairy

By Gunlaug Nøkland

Beste hilsen Gunlaug Nøkland

English translated by Liv Nordem Lyons

English edited by Jo Ann B. Winistorfer

Published by Deb Nelson Gourley, Astri My Astri Publishing

Lunde Forlag, Oslo, Norway, grants to Deb Nelson Gourley, Astri My Astri Publishing, USA, exclusive license to publish in book form in the English language and the Norwegian language the following two books by author Gunlaug Nøkland: *Setra,* copyright © 2002, and *Amerikabrevene,* copyright © 2003.

Library of Congress Control Number: 2007932660

ISBN: 978-0-9760541-3-9

Published and marketed by:
Astri My Astri Publishing
Deb Nelson Gourley
602 3rd Ave SW
Waukon, IA 52172 USA
Phone: 563-568-6229
Fax: 563-568-5377
deb@astrimyastri.com
http://www.astrimyastri.com

Printed by:
Sheridan Books, Inc., MI

Cover art by:
Anders Kvåle Rue, 3841 Flatdal, Norway

Cover layout by:
Chris Shelton, Waukon, IA

First printing
2007
Made in USA

PREFACE · ACKNOWLEDGMENTS

In Norway as in America, the old traditions are slipping away. It's rare today to find farms where everything is done by hand—from the fields to the kitchen. Author Gunlaug Nøkland, a Norwegian wife, mother and textile enthusiast, was lucky to learn the old methods of running a household from her maternal grandmother. As a girl, Gunlaug watched her *Bestemor* Astri card, spin and dye wool, weaving it into fabric. Over the years, Gunlaug learned to prepare foods as her ancestors did. From her parents, Olav and Marta Skuland, she learned the skills needed to manage a dairy farm.

Gunlaug's book preserves these nearly forgotten traditions for future generations. She tells the story through her main character, Mette, who faces modern-day challenges in her new job as a *budeie* (dairy maid) on Siljatjern Seter, an old Norwegian mountain dairy-turned-museum. There, Mette falls in love, uncovers the truth about an ancient legend, and renews her faith in God.

In writing about Mette's experiences, Gunlaug has woven together the skeins of her grandmother's handicrafts, cooking traditions (including recipes in both English and Norwegian), memories of life on the seter, and a family history that includes finding long-lost relatives in the United States. Throughout ripple the threads of a mystery, a dead woman whose legend will not die. Completing the rich tapestry is Gunlaug's wish to share her strong faith in God with her readers.

Two books by Gunlaug, *Setra (The Seter)* and *Amerikabrevene (The America Letters),* published in Norwegian by Lunde Forlag in 2002 and 2003, make up the second half of *Legend of Siljatjern Seter.* The first half contains the brand-new English translation of the original two books. Readers should note that the English is not a word-for-word translation; some chapters have been shortened and revised. The book is enhanced with historic photos of seter scenes and items used on the seter. A pedigree chart on the last page helps identify six generations of family members featured in the book.

We hope you will enjoy this glimpse of life on a Norwegian mountain dairy.

—Jo Ann Winistorfer, editor
—Deb Nelson Gourley, publisher

There are many to thank for their assistance with this book, including my family. I especially thank my husband, Alf-Torgny Nøkland, and our oldest son, Audun, for their support and encouragement. I'm grateful to Rolf Steinar Bergli of Lindesnes bygdemuseum, who offered assistance and supplied many of the photographs used in this book. I also wish to acknowledge Liv Nordem Lyons for translating the book into English; artist Anders Kvåle Rue, who brought the book's characters to life with his cover art; and Chris Shelton, who did the cover layout. My heartfelt appreciation to Deb Nelson Gourley, Astri My Astri Publishing, for suggesting the use of historic photographs (which she processed in Adobe Photoshop), for promoting the addition of bilingual recipes, for creating the pedigree chart, and for recommending the cover artwork. Special thanks go to Jo Ann Winistorfer for her creativity in designing and laying out the pages, and for editing the English portion of the book.

—Gunlaug Nøkland, author

CONTENTS · ENGLISH

PART 1:
THE SETER

PART 2:
THE AMERICA LETTERS

INNHOLD · NORSK

DEDICATION · PHOTO CREDITS

This book is dedicated to Andrea Ritchie and Ed Hansen, my two second cousins in the United States. After many years of separation and no contact, we now enjoy a renewed relationship, including visits in person.

Aase Gurine Aurebekk (Gurine), an older sister of my grandmother, immigrated to America over a hundred years ago. She then married Martin Hansen from Denmark. They had one son, Edward (born in 1919). In 1929, the Hansen family visited their relatives in Norway. Edward got to know his grandparents, aunts and uncles (see photo). Gurine's siblings continued contact with her until she and her husband passed away.

In 1979, Jens Aurebekk, the only remaining sibling, died. Having no direct heirs, he left a monetary legacy to be shared by his relatives, including his unknown family in America. An intensive search ensued, and a year later, thanks to the efforts of the Salvation Army, they were located.

At that time, Edward Hansen and his wife, Cynthia, lived in Connecticut; they had a son, Ed, and a daughter, Andrea.

While this book is not about my family roots, this experience inspired me to include a fictional account of their story in these pages.

I also want to offer my heartfelt thanks to the Salvation Army for the help they gave us in locating our American relatives.

—Gunlaug Nøkland

Edward Hansen, age 10 (right), proudly displays one of the birds he shot while on his trip to Norway in 1929. His uncle, Jens Aurebekk, is in the middle. To the left is Lars Lohne, his hunting buddy and local schoolteacher.

Historic photographs courtesy of:
- Rolf Steinar Bergli, Lindesnes bygdemuseum, Vest-Agder
  *(For these and other historic photographs,
  visit www.lindesnes-bygdemuseum.net)*
- Hægebostad kommune, Vest-Agder
- Leonhard B. Jansen, Setesdalsmuseet, Aust-Agder
- Gunlaug Nøkland family

· PART 1 ·
THE SETER

1 • A surprise meeting

The sun beat mercilessly down on the figure trudging along the narrow dirt road. The backpack was big and weighed more than she would have liked. But she didn't feel like sitting down to rest quite yet. She still had a long way to go, so it was best to press on. Sweating a little actually felt good after all the hours she had spent behind a desk back in Oslo.

It was a lovely day. Birds chirped above her head. The bogs along the road, encircled by gnarled birch trees, gave her a sense of the higher elevation of this part of Vest-Agder *Fylke*—administrative district—in southern Norway. The fresh air created a sensation of well-being that flowed through her entire body.

Yes, Mette was altogether in a great mood. Not even the heavy backpack was able to take that away from her. Far ahead she could make out high, bare mountaintops, some with white areas around their summits. She wondered if the snow up there would disappear completely during the summer.

When she took in this marvelous landscape, her spine tingled at the thought of all the weeks she was going to spend here in Indre Agder. (Indre Agder includes the *kommuner*—municipalities—of Sirdal, Kvinesdal, Hægebostad and Åseral and the valley called Setesdal.) But she had not realized that it could be so warm up in these heights. She had celebrated Midsummer Night in Oslo two days ago. There, she had shivered from the cold air and drawn closer to the bonfire as the evening progressed.

The road meandered between outcroppings, bogs and small lakes. It seemed to be in pretty bad shape, but it was still negotiable for cars. Now and then she got to stretches where the road widened to allow for oncoming traffic to pass.

After passing a large outcropping, she discovered an idyllic little lake right by the road. A big, flat rock jutted into the water.

This has to be the perfect rest stop, thought Mette, and she proceeded down to the water's edge. Further along the bank stood some big birches. She took off her backpack and sat down in the shade under the trees. It felt great to get rid of the heavy weight on her back. She almost regretted stuffing so much into it when she left the railroad station down in the mountain town. A lot of it should have been left behind in the storage locker there, along with her suitcase.

She had arrived by train much earlier than she had planned. The train she was supposed to take was scheduled to arrive at the railroad station at 5 o'clock in the afternoon. But for some reason it was cancelled, so she had to take an earlier train. Thus, she had arrived at noon.

Mette looked at her watch. It was almost 1:30. She didn't quite know how much further she would have to walk. She might be about halfway there. Regardless, she wanted to take a good rest. In her backpack she found the brown bag lunch she didn't eat on the train and half a bottle of lukewarm soda. Food would really taste great now.

While she ate, she enjoyed the view of the mirror-like lake. Now and then a faint breeze swept across and rippled the surface. The thought of the adventure she was about to embark on made her body tingle again.

Right after Christmas, she had started thinking about making some much-needed changes in her life. She worked for a missionary organization. For eight years she had worked there. She was in charge of organizing events and other missionary activities at home and abroad.

She traveled a lot. Almost every summer she visited missionary stations around the world. She had always felt her work was fulfilling and rewarding. And she was grateful for the opportunity to see so many exotic places.

But as time went by, she began to feel run down. The hustle and bustle she had originally enjoyed had started to make her feel more and more drained. She had seen many alarming examples of preachers and missionaries who crashed and burned and needed long periods in recovery before they were able to return to their duties. She realized that she was in danger of ending up in the same predicament.

Another thing that had become a problem for Mette lately was her relationship with Tore, one of her co-workers. They didn't get along. Certain episodes had taken their toll on her. That, too, had been part of why she felt so run down. So she decided to do something about it before things went too far. She would take some time off and do something totally different.

Then, while visiting another community for a meeting, she saw an ad in a local paper. A farmer was looking for help on his farm. It was *seter** work he needed help with. He simply needed a *budeie*—a dairymaid.

Mette had laughed when she read it. So there were still people around who were looking for dairymaids in this country. She didn't know that. But she grew up on a farm, so this was work she knew. Yes, thinking it over, she felt more and more attracted to the idea of applying for the job. After all, it was only for a few months. And this had to be the perfect change from the stress that troubled her more and more.

And so it happened that she applied. But first, she called the farmer to find out about the nature of the work. She got the impression that this seter was run by an elderly couple. And it wasn't just ordinary seter work. It was based on tourism. In the spring and fall, the couple hosted groups from camp schools and taught them how the seter work was done in times past.

The farmer, whose name was Morten, talked about an Anna, who would be able to tell her about the work, based on her experience as a dairymaid when she was younger. Mette assumed Anna was his wife. The work Mette would be required to do was simple enough. She certainly was used to regular farm chores. Only three or four cows to milk, some heifers and sheep to look after, and some hay to hang to dry. Then she would have to help Anna now and then when she had presentations scheduled.

When she got the message that the job was hers, she became wildly excited. She took time off from her job in the city, which didn't pose much of a problem.

And now she was here, on her way to her new job. No one met her at the station, for which she was fully prepared. She had tried to call Morten several times, but didn't get an answer. Consequently she wasn't able to let him know that she would arrive earlier than planned. But at the station she met someone who was able to tell her where this seter was located. She could put her luggage in storage to be picked up later. It was that simple. That's why she had set out on her own.

Mette finished eating. She should get up and move on. But the lake, mirror-like and tempting, inspired in her an intense desire to get cleaned up. It would be so wonderful to take a short swim. Certainly she had time for that. Quickly, she fished out her swimsuit from the backpack. Changing was quick, too. After all, there was no one to hide from up here, desolate and empty as the landscape seemed for miles around.

When she jumped in, shock waves ripped through her body. The water was much colder than she had imagined. She swam only a few quick strokes before she climbed back onto the flat stone. But it felt good to cool off. She sat down and allowed the sun to warm her body.

Then she jumped to her feet. It was best to move on. She wanted to get there before the old man left to pick her up at the station. Hastily, she pulled off her swimsuit and reached for a towel. At the same moment she heard a sound coming from some bushes nearby. Surprised, she turned to investigate what kind of animal might be there.

But there was no animal. Stupefied, she stood there looking into the most wonderful, deep, dark eyes she had ever seen. A remarkably handsome face with a well-trimmed beard and a dark brown, neatly styled shock of hair was looking back at her. Suddenly he turned and disappeared behind the underbrush and rocky knolls.

Mette suddenly realized the state she was in. Quick as lightning, she grabbed the towel and covered herself up. What must this man think of her? Never in her life had she felt this embarrassed. He would have to think she was standing there, exposing herself. How awkward. She dressed in a hurry, but this time there was no way she was doing it without covering up.

Back on the road on her way up the slope, Mette thought a lot about this man. How could she exhibit such frivolous behavior? Her only consolation was that she surely would never meet him again. Still, a feeling of shame ached like an abscess in her body. She should have realized there would be people around in the mountains. Morten had even told her about all the tourists who went hiking there.

From now on she would watch her behavior, even if she thought she was all alone.

3

2 • *The seter* *

Mette was surprised to note there was so much forest this high up in the mountains. She had reached an area where there were lots of pine tree.

She hiked along a valley. To judge by the sun, she was heading north. Far ahead and on both sides, mountain peaks towered against the sky. The terrain was too hilly to be called a mountain plateau. But she would likely reach the plateau when she had continued on far enough.

Suddenly, she was out of the forest. The road made a turn around some knolls, and the terrain opened up into a wide plain. Mette just stood there looking. The road continued straight across the plain, which sloped slightly upward and ended near a group of small buildings nestled at the foot of a steep, rocky slope.

Behind it the terrain rose considerably. On the right was a long, narrow field, stretching far toward the east and ending by a large lake. The field was cultivated, its grass already long and lush. A fence ran along the left side of the road, and a few cows grazed on a hilly slope a little farther away.

Mette had never seen a more idyllic place. She realized she had now reached her destination. So this was the seter where she was going to work for the next three months. The sight filled her with an indescribable joy. This beautiful little place, ringed by the mountains to the north, the forest to the south and the alluring lake to the east was more than she had ever dared hope for. To the west, sloping pastures flowed into mountains and plains.

I am going to like it here, she thought, continuing her walk toward the seter building. A car parked outside indicated someone must be home.

From the seter house a trail ran along the long field down toward the lake. On the upper side, between the trail and the mountain, was a relatively wide, open area. The grass was cut short and a few RVs were parked there.

To the left of the seter house, across the fence, was another building that had to be the cow barn. And behind it, very close to the rocky slope, was a small shed — maybe a sheep shed. All the buildings looked like they were being used.

When Mette got up to the house, she noticed that the door was left half-open, but she didn't see anyone anywhere. She knocked cautiously, but there was no response. She took off her backpack and placed it against the wall. Then she walked over to the cow barn and peeked in. She saw tools and buckets in there, and some feed sacks in the corner. But no living creature was to be found.

Well, then, she thought. She could just take it easy and wait. Sooner or later some-

---

A seter * *is a seasonal farm in the Norwegian mountains used only in the summer in order to utilize the resources of marginal land. It is an ancient agricultural tradition. The primary purpose is grazing, but with milk-producing livestock in a place of geographic isolation, the perishable milk is converted to less perishable butter and cheese, although in modern time it is mostly brought to a local dairy. A whole range of dairy products emerged from the seter tradition. A third purpose of the seter is cultivation of hay, which was brought back to the main farm and used at a later date. A cherished cultural treasure of legends, music and poetry grew out of the seter tradition, and the life at the seter is portrayed extensively in Norwegian literature.*

one had to appear because of the livestock grazing nearby. She returned to the seter house and tiptoed through the open door.

Inside, she stood there, looking around. It was evident that time had stood still here. Everything was orderly, clean and tidy. But there were few modern implements. A large wood stove stood by one wall—a stove like the one she had seen in her grandparents' old home when she was young. Used mostly for cooking and less for heating, it featured a flat metal top with many rings. These rings were removed until they fit the cooking vessel to be placed on the burner. Mette smiled to herself. It would be fun to try out these old implements.

Nearby, she noticed a modern gas burner. So they were not entirely dependent on old-fashioned procedures.

A distance away, on the same wall, a steep, ladder-like flight of stairs led to a loft under the ridge of the roof. At the far end of the room stood a sofa-like bench. In the corner right next to it was a beautiful, carved cabinet.

To her left, she noticed a large, wooden table, which was pushed all the way up against the wall below a window. On each side of the table a wooden bench provided seating. Above the table hung a beautiful kerosene lamp. It was evident there was no electricity in the house at all.

Suddenly, she felt uneasy. What had she gotten herself into? When she thought about it, she knew next to nothing about the activities she was about to get involved in. The short conversations she had with the farmer didn't provide her with that much information. And she hadn't thought about asking that many questions. The whole thing had seemed so incredible. Was this something that would turn into a bad dream rather than a beautiful fairy tale? No … she wouldn't allow herself to think like that. She was here, and she wanted to make the best of it.

A sound coming from somewhere behind one of the doors in the room made her jump. Might there be someone here after all?

"Hello, is anyone here?" she called.

At the same moment a door opened and a rotund little woman appeared.

"What in the world, are there people here?" she exclaimed, alarmed. "I was just getting a room ready for someone who is coming to help us here at the seter this summer, so I didn't hear that you were here."

She talked away, so it took a while before Mette could introduce herself. The woman became even more alarmed, but also enthusiastic, when she learned who was standing there in the seter house with the big backpack, and why she was there and not at the station.

"I never heard the likes of it. Did you really walk all that way? And Morten, who was to pick you up at the station! Well, will he be surprised! It probably won't be long before he gets here." She glanced at her watch. "His car is outside, so he will have to stop by here first. He is just out to look to some of the animals grazing around here. Apparently there were some fences that needed mending."

She looked at Mette inquisitively, and then she laughed again.

"And we thought we were expecting an elderly lady, and then this young beauty shows up. Yes, yes, age doesn't mean that much. In any case, you are welcome. Well, here I am prattling away without introducing myself at all. I am Aunt Anna. Everybody calls me Aunt Anna, regardless of whether I'm their real aunt. Actually, that's what I prefer to be called. Just plain Anna seems so stilted and serious. No, you call me

Aunt Anna, too. That's what I would like the best."

Mette had to smile. She already liked this talkative, older lady. It was funny the way her entire rotund body portrayed what she was talking about. And her eyes disappeared almost completely in her big, fat cheeks when she laughed. It was a wonder she was able to see anything at all, for she laughed almost all the time.

Her catching laughter made Mette relax and the unease she felt just a moment before vanished as completely as dew before the sun. She wouldn't have any problems getting along with this woman. She was sure of that. And if her husband were as nice as she was, this would turn into a good experience.

She knew Morten wouldn't be as talkative as Aunt Anna. Rather, she thought he had seemed a little taciturn and quiet on the phone, but he had also seemed nice.

"Now come along and see your room," Aunt Anna said, walking with a rolling gait back across the floor.

Mette was delighted right away when she saw the small, narrow room that was to be hers. The view from the window wasn't exactly the best. She looked right into the rocky slope behind the house. Rather, it was the log walls and the old-fashioned furniture that gave the room such a special and romantic touch. The ceiling sloped toward the outer wall, so the window wasn't large. Perhaps this part had been added on some time after the house itself was built, Mette mused.

Two beds stood in the room, one at each end. Made of solid wood, they could be pulled out into the room for sleeping. One pulled out lengthwise, while the other one could be pulled out and widened. They might serve as a double bed and a child's bed. Between the beds along the outer wall sat a bureau—a magnificent piece of handmade furniture with beautiful carvings. On the wall above it, next to the window, hung a mirror. Its frame, too, was carved wood.

There were no closets in the room. If Mette wanted to hang her clothes, she would have to hang them from the wooden pegs pinned between the logs in the wall. Apart from two small nightstands and a few woven rugs on the floor, there was nothing else in the room.

"Do you think you'll like it here?" asked Aunt Anna. "It is not a large room, but I have cleaned everything and put new sheets on the bed."

"This is absolutely great," Mette answered enthusiastically. She pulled out one of the heavy drawers in the bureau. There was plenty of room, she noticed. "Yes, I will definitely enjoy staying here," she said.

Aunt Anna's smile widened even more. "But now you need some food," she said. "You have to be starving after that long hike."

Mette realized that she was indeed hungry. Some food would really taste great. She was thirsty, too. Aunt Anna ordered her to sit down on a chair. There Mette sat studying the friendly lady she already had started to appreciate so much.

Aunt Anna talked a mile a minute while she worked. In the short time it took for her to prepare the meal, she had time to tell about the job the new dairymaid was about to tackle. She talked about the cows that needed milking. The farm didn't have many animals, just some sheep and four cows, including two that were milking at the moment. The other two were *gjellkyr,* said Aunt Anna, taking it as a matter of course that Mette understood it meant they were *kalv*—pregnant—and had stopped milking for a while. And then there were two heifers, grazing further into the mountains, that would have calves later.

Farm tourism was their business at the seter, so the milk wasn't shipped to the dairy. They fed to the farm animals what they didn't use for demonstrations aimed at tourists and school children, showing them how butter and cheese were made in the old days.

Morten had started running the farm this way when he got permanent employment at the town bank. And, according to Aunt Anna, it was only in the summer and fall that he worked on the farm. He had an arrangement with the bank in which he took four months off at this time of year.

Mette was puzzled. Morten had to be ⸻ ⸻hat younger than Aunt Anna, she reasoned, for the older women had to be ⸻ 70s.

Suddenly the door opened. A ⸻ walked quickly over to a bench, poured water in a basin and s⸻ Mette felt herself tense immediately where she sat. The ⸻ he way out to the roots of her hair. The man turned ⸻ everything stopped. Even Aunt Anna was s⸻ hear her.

For there ⸻ beautiful eyes she had ever seen ⸻ e lake. Here was the man ⸻ ⸻ad seen her while she ⸻

⸻ength.

Magnar Undheim
Sinnes
4443 Tjørhom
Norway
E-mail: magnar.undheim@sirdal.kommune.no
0047383703
HAYMAKING IN SIRDAL

• The farmer

To Mette ⸻ ⸻e an eternity, but it probably lasted only a minute. Aunt Anna's voice brok⸻ ⸻ough, and then everything seemed normal again. Maybe to the others, the passing moment had seemed normal. Maybe it was just Mette who experienced a moment of intense excitement. The man didn't seem to recognize her at all.

In Mette, the excitement was replaced by confusion. Her confusion didn't diminish when Aunt Anna resumed her stream of words:

"Well, there you are, Morten. Now you can save yourself the trip down to the village this afternoon, for here is the lady we have been waiting for. Not at all an old biddy, like we thought. Can you imagine! She walked all the way up here from the station!"

Aunt Anna recounted the whole story before either of the other two were able to get in a word.

Mette looked from Aunt Anna to the man and back at Aunt Anna again. What was this? She had called this man Morten. Was this the farmer? Mette's confusion was complete. He had to be in his 30s. Not all that much older than she. And what was this about their assuming she was an old biddy? She certainly had penciled in her date of birth and the year in her application. And Aunt Anna … Mette was all mixed up.

As usual, she didn't have to wait long for an explanation when Aunt Anna had the floor: "I would like to introduce my nephew."

Mockingly solemn, she addressed Mette. Morten came over and shook her hand as if he had never seen her before. This made Mette relax a little. He didn't recognize her. That would explain it, then. She forced a cautious smile as he shook her hand. She

7

looked at him searchingly one more time, but there was no sign of recognition as far as she could see.

So this was the farmer and her boss. This was the man she was going to work for this summer. She sensed a slight shiver going through her body as she studied the agile man facing her. His tanned face revealed that he had spent a lot of time outdoors in the sun.

Suddenly she straightened. What was she standing there shivering for? She usually didn't react like this when meeting a man for the first time. He would certainly not knock her off her perch. Firmly determined to start her vocation as dairymaid and nothing else, she returned the handshake and introduced herself.

After Mette got over her initial alarm, she dedicated all her time getting acquainted with her tasks. They sat for quite a while at the large dining table, talking about her job.

Morten explained about the tourists they were expecting the first week. He had prepared the agenda and planned a strategy. Aunt Anna played an important role in it all. She was to demonstrate the separation of milk and the churning of cream. Then there was cheese-making and the preparation of a number of old, traditional foods. Mette was to help with whatever was needed.

In addition, Mette was responsible for the daily care of the seter livestock. While the groups of tourists were there, she would likely be surrounded by children and adults alike when she worked.

Mette listened in delight. This sounded exciting.

"Let's take a walk to look around," said Morten suddenly.

Mette jumped to her feet. "Yes, let's," she quickly answered.

She looked forward to getting outside and giving her surroundings a closer inspection.

The new dairymaid found the tour both fascinating and helpful. Morten talked eagerly and with commitment about everything they saw and what had to be done. From the cow barn they walked over to some grazing sheep. The lambs came running over to them and lifted their muzzles up to Morten's hand. He laughed and scratched them behind their ears.

"I think they're looking for treats," he said. "Usually we give them something so they stay by the seter. They are here because the tourists come to see them, so they shouldn't stray too far into the mountains."

Mette noticed a rock fire pit behind the seter shed. Morten said it was used when it was dry and too risky to start a campfire anywhere else. It was normally used when school camp groups visited. And Aunt Anna used it for some of her demonstrations.

Morten also showed her the tenting and camping area. It was located at the end of the seter house, where the grass was cut short. Presently, there weren't many campers around, but the area would soon be full, he told her. One of the campers that was there now, he told Mette, belonged to his sister. She and her family used it to stay there as often as they could.

They continued down the path toward the lake.

"You really have an idyllic lake here," said Mette.

As they walked along, they could see a valley stretching eastward on the other side of the lake. They also caught a glimpse of some faraway buildings on the hillside.

"What are those buildings?" she asked, pointing.

"That is the Fjellbu Seter," answered Morten. "It is not in operation anymore, but it is now used as a vacation home both in the summer and the winter."

Soon they reached the bank of the lake. A nice swimming area had been cleared there. They sat down on a rock that formed a natural bench on the bank.

"I think I will spend a lot of time here," said Mette, laughing.

Morten laughed, too. "Knowing myself and all the others here, you won't be the only one."

For a while they just sat there, watching the beautiful landscape. At the end of the lake to the north, a narrow valley stretched into the mountains. In the middle of the lake was a small island where some gnarled bushes had dug in their roots. The sunshine made the surface of the lake appear to be made of glass. Only a few ripples from the weak mountain breeze ruffled the idyllic, mirror-like water.

The sunshine was still bright and scorching. Mette noticed she had gotten just about as much sun as she could tolerate in a day on her bare arms and face. Her short haircut didn't provide any protection for her neck, which was now exposed to the burning rays. Her fair, blond hair made it obvious that her skin was not the most robust for such weather conditions. But the stunning view and the peaceful atmosphere made her reluctant to leave.

"Do you own all of this?" Mette was completely captivated by what she saw.

"The lake here and the areas within viewing range on this side are mine," answered Morten. "But the hillside and valley over on the other side belong to the owners of the Fjellbu seter."

"Does the lake have a name? And your seter, what it is called?" Mette swept her arm toward the meadow and the buildings they had just left behind.

Morten smiled. "Obviously it never dawned on us to let you know. The lake here is called the Siljatjern. And so it stands to reason that the seter is called the Siljatjern Seter."

"Siljatjern …" Mette tested the name. "It sounds so Swedish or Finnish."

"Yes, it may seem that way. But the origin of the name is as Norwegian as it gets," answered Morten. "The name is derived from a legend that has been known in this area for ages."

"A legend? How thrilling. How does the legend go?" Mette looked over at him.

He sat with his elbows on his knees and his head in his hands, while his eyes gazed across the still, dark surface of the lake. For a moment it was as if he were completely entrenched in a long-gone past. But then he started recounting the story.

"Many years ago, at least 200 or 300, it is said that a dairymaid working at this seter got into big trouble. She came from a cotter's farm in town, and was employed at our place. It turned out she was pregnant. It was said that the father was the son of a well-to-do farmer in one of the neighboring communities. But he didn't want to admit to the relationship. A rather classic story, as you can see.

"The girl's parents feared there would be a scandal. And more than anything, they feared the farmer, who was an influential man. So the girl was sent off to the mountains as a dairymaid. In that way she would be out of sight for a while.

"One morning her small sheepdog arrived down in town. It was absolutely wild, so they understood something was wrong up at the seter. When they got up here, they found the cows outside the door to the barn. They were bellowing, obviously upset. It wasn't hard to figure out that they hadn't been milked. But the dairymaid was nowhere to be seen.

9

"Shortly thereafter, they found her drowned in this lake. The strange thing was that there was no fetus in her body. After that, rumors and speculations started going around. Some thought she had given birth to the child and killed it. Then she had buried it and drowned herself. Others thought that the father of the child had been seeing the girl while she was up here, and that when the child was born, he took it away and gave it to foster parents in another town. The poor girl couldn't handle losing her child, so she jumped in the lake and drowned herself. This story and its many versions have been told around here ever since. The girl's name was Silja, and the seter got her name."

Mette shuddered. Suddenly the idyll in front of her seemed sinister.

"Do you think it is a true story?" Her eyes, too, gazed across the still, dark surface of the lake.

Morten laughed. "I don't know. But in any event, that incident has not been the only bad thing to happen around here throughout the centuries. We just haven't preserved all the other stories like that particular one. And that is probably just as well."

Mette, too, had to smile. Of course there was no reason to allow this sinister story from the past to leave its mark on this beautiful day. Every place had its legends. What they did was make the past a little more colorful.

Morten stood up. "I figure it is best to start the evening milking. I will come with you until you have gotten acquainted with the animals and the work itself."

Mette got up too and they both returned to the cow barn.

4 • City girl

The sun had not risen far in the sky when Mette woke up on the first morning of her new job. She peeked out of the small window. Today, too, seemed to be warm and pleasant. Two small lambs scampered around one of the sheep in the farmyard. Obviously, they were looking for breakfast. They both found a teat and started their meal, their little tails swirling around in the air. Mette had to smile. What a carefree world theirs was.

She got dressed and joined Aunt Anna, who was busy making coffee for breakfast.

"Good morning. Did you sleep well? Look what a nice day we'll have today. That's great, considering that we'll be starting the haying …"

As usual, words poured out of her. If she asked a question, she didn't always expect an answer. Mette tried to respond when the opportunity was there; otherwise, she let her talk without stressing out about it.

But she had discovered that the old, kind woman could listen quietly, too. The evening before, the three of them sat together and talked some. Mette then told them about her childhood at home on the little farm where she grew up. She also talked about her job and all the traveling she used to do. Aunt Anna had listened silently for long periods of time.

It was only when Mette talked about her Christian faith that the old woman's enthusiasm started bubbling again. Morten, too, obviously appreciated that. The fact that the three of them shared such a significant interest made them suddenly feel closer.

10

Breakfast was put on the table and Mette learned where to locate dinnerware and utensils. Next to her bedroom was a sizeable dairy room where most of the food was kept. When she entered, she stood looking around, surprised. Over in a corner was a large refrigerator. A light bulb hung from the ceiling, and on the wall above a bench she could see an outlet. This didn't fit with the rest of the house. Obviously there was power here, but where did it come from? She would have to ask Aunt Anna.

"Morten installed a solar panel so we can get some power in here," she explained. "After a while, it became difficult to preserve all the dairy products without being able to cool them. And it happens now and then that we have a need for something that requires power. But Morten is adamant that this should remain the only room where we have electricity. The rest of the seter is kept like it used to be in the old days."

A while later, Morten got up, too. His room was up in the loft.

"Today we'll get a visit from a group of American tourists," he said while they were having breakfast. "They are staying for three days. During that time we will mostly do regular, old-fashioned seter work. The tourists will hang around watching what is going on."

"When are they coming?" Mette was eager to get going for real.

"I will go to town to help transport the campers," Morten answered. "They rented some campers to use for lodging. The deal is that we'll meet down there at 11 this morning. Then I can get your suitcase from the station, too. I can imagine that you miss it."

After breakfast, they went to tend to the animals. Morten called the cows, which were grazing over on the hillside. When they heard his voice, they started walking toward the cow barn.

"I can see they know your voice," said Mette.

"You should do some calling yourself," he said. "They will have to get to know your voice, too."

"Yes, I imagine I will have to practice on some fancy cow calls," she said, and laughed.

When the two milking cows were tied up in their stalls, Mette sat down on a small stool with the pail between her knees. The cow shifted restlessly, sensing there was a stranger in the cow barn. But when Morten scratched the cow behind her ear and talked to her soothingly, she immediately calmed down.

The milking went well. Mette discovered she hadn't completely forgotten the skills of her childhood. With even and measured strokes, she squeezed the milk out of the teats. It flowed into the pail in long, thick streams.

It was the first time she tried this method of milking here. The evening before, Morten had shown her how to use the gasoline-powered milking machine, so then they had done the milking by machine. They practiced both methods there at the seter, but when they had tourists visiting, they almost always used the old hand method.

Soon the pail was full. There was no more milk left in the cow, either. Mette proudly carried two pails of milk into the dairy room.

Aunt Anna readied the separator. "It is best to separate it right away," she said. "If we're going to get the cream out properly, the milk should still be a little warm."

Mette poured the milk from one of the pails into the large container on top of the separator. Aunt Anna started turning the crank slowly. It took a while for her to get up to speed, but soon two thin streams flowed out. A pale white, strong jet ran back down into the pail. That was the skim milk. From another spout, a thinner stream flowed into a bowl. It was much whiter in color and appeared much thicker. That was the cream.

"It is important that we work at the appropriate speed so the cream acquires the right thickness," said Aunt Anna. "You may try your hand with the other pail."

With proper instruction from Aunt Anna, Mette was able to separate the entire pail. Afterward, they brought the skim milk outside to feed to the animals.

Behind the seter house, a door led directly to the dairy room. This was the door they used when they carried the milk in and out. A practical and good solution, thought Mette, so they didn't have to go all the way through the house with the pails.

There was also a water pump and a big sink in the dairy room.

"We do all the washing up here," said Aunt Anna. "It makes it easy to keep all the mess away from the main room in there, for we often have to use it for demonstrations when we have visitors here."

Soon, Morten arrived with the group of tourists, consisting of four families with children of different ages. In addition, there were several couples and single individuals, for a total of 25 people. Mette wondered how they would be able to drive their big campers on the narrow road.

Soon the campers were in place at the campground and the children ran around exploring the area. The lambs were the first to get visitors. They tumbled and jumped excitedly around in the meadow.

Mette had to laugh as she stood watching them. She recalled her own childhood. She had played with the animals in exactly the same manner at their family farm. She remembered well their behavior when they were allowed outside for the first time in the spring. Cows and calves raced around the field in ferocious gallops, their tails pointing straight toward the sky. The children had joined them in their happy dance. Often they pretended they were in the Wild West of America, rounding up the animals.

Mette didn't have much time to stand there watching them. She had to get back inside to help Aunt Anna. Part of the welcoming ceremony involved introducing the guests to good, old-fashioned seter fare. The tourists were actually responsible for their own food; this was just another occasion to introduce some traditional dishes.

A large table was placed in front of the house. Mette and Aunt Anna started bringing out flatbread, lefse and regular, homemade, whole-grain bread. There was *eggost**, *gome**, *dravle**, *prim** and other dairy products. And then there was a big platter of home-churned butter. Everything was made from seter milk.

Aunt Anna had prepared everything well in advance. There was *fenalår*—salt brine and air-cured leg of lamb—and *spekeskinke*—leg of pork cured in the same manner.

The food was greeted with enthusiasm and delight. One platter after another was scraped completely clean.

Mette and Aunt Anna watched the guests, who sat around in the meadow, eating.

"Is all of this food traditional here in northern Vest-Agder?" asked Mette.

"Oh, no." Aunt Anna rocked her big body back and forth. "I have picked up a few things from all parts of the country. If I run into something new, I can't rest until I have tried it."

Again they sat watching the guests.

"This is what inspires me to keep going," she said later when they looked at the

---

Footnote: *Authentic Norwegian recipes for foods marked with asterisks throughout the book can be found following the English and Norwegian sections.

empty platters. "The gratitude and excitement these people show makes me want to do even more."

She smiled so broadly that her eyes completely disappeared in her face. But the red spots in her cheeks revealed she had done enough, at least for today. Mette urged her to go to her room and rest for a while. She would be able to wash the dishes without any help. Reluctantly, she was taken up on her offer. It was clear that she felt tired.

Aunt Anna had a big room under the loft. She also used it for storing wool and yarn and other materials she used for her demonstrations. Mette had seen an old spinning wheel there, too. She looked forward to seeing all this in use.

Later that afternoon, Morten grabbed a scythe and walked toward the part of the meadow that was closest to the lake. Mette followed with a rake. The grass was not long enough to be cut, but he wanted some sweet, good hay for the sheep. And it had to be cut fairly early, he said.

Morten started cutting the grass in the meadow with long, assured sweeps of the scythe. Mette followed him, raking away the newly cut grass so it would be out of the way when he started on the next row. In this manner they cut and raked one row after another.

Soon, tourists surrounded them. Cameras and camcorders hummed and clicked. They obviously associated this work with old-fashioned farming.

The children were asked to stay at a safe distance from the scythe.

"When these people leave, will another group come?" asked Mette as they returned to the cow barn with their farm implements.

"No," said Morten. "This weekend I want as few tents and campers as possible at the campground. We're having a revival meeting here."

"Revival?" Mette looked at him in surprise.

"Yes, every year we organize a meeting here. It has been a tradition for years."

"Do you get a big crowd for these meetings?" asked Mette eagerly.

"Oh, yes, it is a very popular event. You can count on preparing lots of food."

"Food! Are we feeding all of them?" Mette looked at him in shock.

Morten had to laugh. "Aunt Anna always makes *rømmegrøt*—sour cream porridge—for this meeting. And then she makes pancakes during the breaks so people can get them piping hot."

Mette was relieved. It didn't sound quite so dreadful after all.

"It will be fun," she said. "I must say that this seter is used in a variety of ways. I only wish we had more livestock. It looks to me like hanging out with the animals is what the youngest of the tourists enjoy the most."

"We'll get more animals up here over time," Morten said. "After this weekend I will get some goats, but I don't want them around until the meeting is over. There will be a lot of cars, and I don't want the goats to bump up against them. Those animals are not easy to corral.

"And there will be some calves here soon. I expect one of the cows up here to calve at any time now. And there will be more births throughout the summer. I always make sure that some of the cows will give birth while they stay at the seter. It is a very special experience for the tourists who happen to be here when a calf is born."

Walking toward the seter house, Mette stopped to talk to some children who were playing in the meadow. Morten continued toward the cow barn with the implements. All at once, she noticed some men walking across the pasture. They carried backpacks, so it was clear these people had been hiking in the mountains. Mette walked over and opened the gate for them.

One of the men stopped and looked at her.

"My, my," he said, an odd smile playing on his lips. Then he continued in the same tone: "I say, Morten knows how to set things up for himself, up here in the middle of nowhere, far from people!" A little laugh escaped him at the same time.

The others turned around and laughed when they heard what he said. They seemed to understand the hidden meaning of the remark.

Mette felt her face get hot. What were these men implying? The confusion she felt for a moment was replaced by a feeling of something starting to boil in her gut. She didn't answer, but stood there staring at him with an intense and challenging glare.

The man didn't seem to be alarmed by her flashing eyes. He continued as if nothing had happened.

"Yes, this is really a magnificent specimen of a dairymaid."

This again evoked whoops of laughter from his buddies.

"And someone from the city, I was told. Didn't know that city girls could find the teats on a cow. But there may be other, weightier qualifications. Yes, I'm sure that Morten knows …"

He didn't get any further, for Mette felt that something was about to burst inside her. Never in her life had she met a more disgusting and obnoxious guy. She didn't take time to analyze his remarks, but interrupted him with such a force and intensity that he backed off in alarm.

"I have no intention of standing here listening to such filth from an animal who obviously is only concerned with following his primitive instincts," she hissed. "We have no use for such people at this seter. The road to town is in that direction."

She pointed a shaking finger at the road. Then she turned around and marched toward the seter house. If any of them were still laughing she would never know, for she was too mad to regale them with another look.

Aunt Anna looked up in alarm when Mette stormed in. But she didn't stop to offer an explanation, just went directly to her room. There she sat for a long while. Her heart beat hard and fast while she clenched her fists in her lap. To speak to someone like that! She was so furious she was tempted to tear him to pieces. City girl—was that what she was called! And in the most negative context possible.

But she would show them. They would see she was no newcomer to this field. No one would be given any reason to say that she shied away from the tough chores of farm life. She would certainly make sure of that.

Nor was she going to become too dependent on this farmer. No, she had taken this job, and she would perform it to the best of her abilities. That was all.

It took a while for her to calm down enough to go out and face the others again. But finally she felt her intense agitation abate. She decided not to tell anyone about the episode. It was probably best not to make a big deal of it.

5 • Excitement in the cow barn

When Morten started calling the cows to get them home for milking time, the visiting children got excited. The adults joined them to watch the milking, too. The cows grazed high up on the hillside, so it took them a while to get home.

But the two that were to be milked reacted quickly when they heard Morten's voice. Mette called them a couple of times, too. It was best that they got used to her, since milking was her job from now on.

"We're a little bit early tonight," said Morten. He looked at his watch. "They always drift toward the cow barn when it gets close to milking time. It almost seems as if they can tell time."

Morten chuckled as he watched the two cows ambling toward them. A little farther away the third cow was coming along as well. Even if she wouldn't get milked, she knew there were treats to be had in the cow barn. But she took her time. None of the animals allowed themselves to get stressed out by the presence of so many people. They were used to all kinds of visitors.

"This is odd." Morten shaded his eyes with his hand and looked up the hillside. Cow number 4 was nowhere to be seen. "That is the cow that's going to calve soon," he said. "I hope she isn't hiding away up there somewhere in order to do her thing. I better go check on her."

Morten took off right away. Some of the older children followed right behind him.

When the cows had found their stalls and Mette had given them some feed concentrate, she took the pail and the milking stool and sat down to milk. Again there was videotaping and the blinking of flashbulbs. The tourists formed a tight circle around her, asking her questions while she milked. Now she was glad she had grown up on a farm. It made her able to answer most of the questions.

She also understood why Morten had been so adamant that she be well versed in languages for this job. He had told her she had to be able to speak English and German fairly well. And Mette's knowledge of just those languages happened to be good. Because of her work and all the travel that went with it, she had made a point of learning English well. But she knew German fairly well, too. And she could make herself understood in French and Spanish.

Some of the people around her wrinkled their noses and left the cow barn early, probably finding the smell from the animals a bit strong for their liking. One of the smallest boys took off in a hurry, too. He was standing close behind one of the cows. Suddenly she lifted her tail and a strong jet shot out from her behind. The little boy was hit right in the side. With howls and cries for his mommy, he stormed out—while the rest of the crowd doubled over with laughter.

When the worst laughing was over, Mette asked the children to each fetch a cup so they could taste the milk. Several of them did what she told them at once. They came right back. With eager eyes they watched Mette, who took cup after cup and filled them with milk directly from the cow's teat.

The taste of the warm milk was a big surprise for most of them. "But this is really good," said one little girl. She emptied her cup and asked for more.

Mette laughed and filled it up again. "Fresher milk than this you will never get," she said.

But not everyone was that excited. Some thought the warm milk was icky, and spat it out again.

While Mette was on her way to the dairy room with the pails, she saw Morten coming down the hillside with the missing cow. She breathed a sigh of relief. So the heifer didn't stray that far. And it didn't look like she had had her calf.

She returned right away and let the cows out of the barn. The cow that Morten brought home looked big and round because of the calf she carried. Her udder was extremely large and swollen.

"Look," said one of the boys and pointed at the bristling teats. "It looks like an airfilled rubber glove." Everybody laughed at the striking description.

"It won't be long before her calf is born," Morten said. "The birth process has already started. That's probably why she didn't come along with the others tonight. She tried to find a place where she could have her calf in peace and quiet."

He tied the heifer up in one of the stalls in the barn. He then gave her some food. He also picked up an armful of old hay in the hayloft above the cow barn. This he scattered in the stall so it would be clean and dry.

"Now we have to leave her alone as much as possible, and then the calf will be here before we know it."

"Is the calf coming now?" One of the boys stood staring at Morten with big eyes. Then he looked over at the heifer.

Morten had to laugh when he saw all the eager eyes following everything he said and did. "We can count on it. There will be another little one in this cow barn tonight," he answered.

"May we stay and watch?" one of the boys who had gone along to find the cow was asking.

"I don't know when the calf will be born," answered Morten. "It may happen in the middle of the night."

"That doesn't matter," several of them cried with one voice. "We will manage to stay awake."

Morten looked a little concerned. He looked from one to the other. The eager, alert eyes of the children made it impossible for him to deny them this.

"Then you have to promise me one thing," he said in a serious voice. "The cow needs peace and quiet. You have to promise to keep quiet when you are with her in the cow barn."

Eager nods promised that they understood.

"And if you notice anything unusual about her," he continued, "then you have to come and let me know."

The children took their task very seriously. It was as if they had been given a great responsibility. After a while, the older ones made sure that the younger ones were quiet as they tiptoed into the barn.

Throughout the evening Mette noticed that the children kept slipping through the door to the cow barn. Sometimes a few of them stayed for a long time before they returned to their families in the campers.

Mette went to check on the heifer herself. She was lying on the dry hay in the stall. Her udder was so swollen that it seemed painful for her to lie down. It can't be long before the calf is born now, she thought. The tendons at the base of her tail were all relaxed and slackened; it was a sure sign she was about to calve.

16

Suddenly she stopped chewing her cud. She gave a couple of stifled cries while spasms racked her huge body.

"Now the birth contractions have started," Mette said to the two children, who at the moment shared the milk stool in order to watch over the creature about to give birth.

They jumped up as on command. "Is it coming now?"

"No, no." Mette had to laugh. "It can still be quite a while before anything happens. But at least the birthing process has started." She could see how excitement built in the two of them. "But you have to remember that she needs to rest," she continued.

The two of them just nodded in reply. They were so caught up in the significance of the moment that they didn't dare raise their voices in order to answer her.

Mette returned to the house and left the watch to the eager children. She found Morten engrossed in something over by the dining table.

He looked up at her as she entered. "How are things in the cow barn?" he asked.

"The process seems to have started," she answered, "but the calf is nowhere to be seen yet." She walked over to the burner and poured herself a cup of coffee from the pot. "Now we have so many people to keep vigil that we don't have to fear anything will happen without us knowing."

Morten laughed, too. "I'll say, all the kids got busy all of a sudden when they heard there was about to be a birth in the cow barn," he said.

Her cup of coffee filled to the rim, Mette sat down at the table, facing Morten. Then she noticed that he was reading the Bible.

To answer the question in her eyes he said: "I was thinking of getting ready for the meeting on Sunday. Then I came across something here that grabbed me with its relevance. It is from the prophet Isaiah, Chapter 56, Verse 9. Listen to what it says:

" 'Come, all you beasts of the field, come and devour, all you beasts of the forest! Israel's watchmen are blind, they all lack knowledge; they are all mute dogs, they cannot bark; they lie around and dream, they love to sleep. They are dogs with mighty appetites; they never have enough. They are shepherds who lack understanding; they all turn to their own way, each seeks his own gain.' "

Mette sat listening while he read to her. But she didn't understand what was so relevant about it.

He continued, "I have read this before, but now its meaning is revealed to me for the first time. I see it in light of the kind of situation we, too, may find ourselves in. Here it says that the watchmen of Israel are blind. They are compared to watchdogs that don't do their job — watchdogs preoccupied with their own enjoyment and gain. The dogs here are clearly a metaphor for spiritual leaders, including spiritual leaders today."

She started to catch his excitement now, for it dawned on her what he meant. "You mean this situation exists among some of the spiritual leaders in our time and in our country?"

"Yes," he said. "I believe this is a serious warning to all Christians. We all are responsible for speaking up if things that may contribute to leading us away from God threaten to sneak in among us."

Mette looked worried. "The Bible often urges us to keep watch, but how do you think we are supposed to do that?"

Morten considered this before he answered. "I really don't think we humans possess that much of what is required for this kind of watch. But I do believe the Word of

17

God may give us the right qualifications if we allow ourselves to be influenced by it. I think this is something for which we need help from God Himself. If we study the Bible, we will get the direction we need."

"Yes, you are probably right," said Mette, still studying the verses. "Probably the devil is calling his army, described as the beasts of the field. They do not sleep. They see the situation just as it is. They must realize when the watch command is alert, too. When they know that, then the attacks won't be carried out?"

"I think it is an illusion to believe that the ones who are alert won't be attacked," Morten said. "It isn't that easy to be on the alert on all fronts at all times. I believe this watch is most easily kept through prayer. It may be that the problem lies with the interceders when we have a leader who clearly acts and teaches against the Word of God."

They sat discussing this for some time. The reason Morten had conceived this as such a serious matter was that he saw himself as a spiritual leader in his community. He was both on the church council and the meetinghouse board. In addition to that, over the years he had been on numerous boards and councils in important leadership roles.

"Well, I know at least one thing," he said after a while. " I think the most important thing is to work through prayer, and deal with things as they happen. When we pray for wisdom, I believe God will counsel us in each separate situation we might be in."

It was clear this was something that had fired him up. But Mette was not able to determine from what he said whether he was thinking of any situation in particular.

Suddenly the door was yanked open and a boy came rushing in. "Something is happening in the cow barn now!" he yelled. His excited eyes almost popped out of his head.

Morten jumped to his feet and was out the door in a moment. Mette found her camera and followed. She wanted to preserve this moment for posterity. She might not be able to experience such an event again.

It looked as though all the children had been notified, for now they came running— at least, the older ones who had not gone to sleep.

A few red rays painted the sky in the west in a last greeting from a day slipping toward night. Dusk started to descend on the mountains. But no one had time to watch the beautiful scenery. A line of excited children and some adults, too, headed hastily for the door to the cow barn.

Inside the barn it was obvious that someone was going through a great struggle. Loud moans and hoarse bellows were heard in the still of the night. As quietly as possible, one after the other slipped in through the door. Still, there was some commotion as the crowd around the cow grew bigger.

"Now you have to try to be completely still," whispered Morten. "She is resting comfortably now, but it won't take much for her to get unsettled and scramble to her feet, and we don't want her to do that, for the birthing will be so much harder."

He talked to the cow to calm her down and patted her gently on her back. Behind, below her tail, some small, white hooves had emerged. The cow lay quite still for a while, breathing in great heaves.

Suddenly the huge creature started convulsing again. Again, birth contractions set in. A long cry escaped from her foaming mouth. The small hooves worked their way farther out, and a pair of skinny calf's legs appeared. A thick membrane covered them.

Again and again, birth contractions racked the laboring animal. The minutes passed, but no one thought about checking the time. Everyone followed, as if hypnotized, what was taking place right there on the floor of the cow barn.

"Don't we have to get a vet?" asked a small, unsteady voice. The pain reflected above the foaming mouth of the cow brought tears to the child's eyes.

Morten looked over at him and smiled. "She'll be all right," he said soothingly. "She is having a hard time now, but that will be over as soon as the calf is born. It is a natural thing. We just have to be patient and wait it out."

Suddenly a sack full of water emerged. At the same time, the cow bellowed and the water splashed across the floor. A scream rose from the crowd of spectators. A girl disappeared out the door. Several others followed. This was too much for some of them, while others became even more interested in what was going on.

When the cow had calmed down, Morten addressed one of the boys, who had followed the process eagerly.

"Can you give me a hand?" he asked.

The boy was ready for action right away.

"Grab this little calf's foot here. I will hold on to the other. When the cow starts pushing again, you tug it carefully toward you. We have to help her a bit at the end. The calf is coming soon now."

With shaking but determined hands, the boy took a firm hold around the wet and slimy hoof. They waited in silence for a few minutes. Now they also could see a small muzzle clearly working its way into the day.

Soon the cow started laboring again. Slowly, more of the small head came into view. Morten and the boy tugged gently at the calf. Suddenly they heard a pop and the entire head was out. The boy almost fell on his back in amazement. Morten had to laugh.

There were not that many spectators left, but the ones who were there stood spellbound by the powerful experience. A camcorder whizzed and rolled the entire time. And now and then, cameras flashed. This was an event they might never experience again. Mette didn't save her film, either.

Morten cleaned out mucus and membrane from the mouth of the little calf. Mette found a towel so he could dry it off a little.

The cow had calmed down again. She had put her head on the floor and breathed hard from exhaustion.

"Poor cow," the little boy repeated in a shaky voice. He still had tears in his eyes. But he bravely prevailed. Obviously, he wanted to see the end of this.

The cow wasn't allowed to rest for long. Soon contractions racked her anew. Again Morten and the boy took hold of the calf's feet. A loud and prolonged bellow burst out of the cow as the rest of the calf slid out. It landed in the hay with a thud. It all happened so quickly that the boy fell on the floor. He breathed heavily as if he had been holding his breath for a long time.

Water and blood squirted around them. The spectators had to jump aside to avoid getting soiled. A heavy spray doused Mette's leg, for she was more intent on taking photos than getting out of the way. The two birthing assistants weren't able to avoid getting soiled, either. They had mucus and specks of blood all over. The boy didn't seem to mind, but the excitement and his reaction to the strong experience made his entire body shake.

Morten began rubbing the calf with some hay. Soon the disheveled creature on the

19

floor gave a weak little sound. Trembling, it lifted its head and shook it without much control.

Morten laughed. "The newborn seems to have some life in it," he said. "It is big, too; no wonder the birth was a little rough."

Carefully he lifted the calf over to the cow so she could lick it clean. He loosened the rope that tied her to the stall so she could get at the calf. Mette scraped away membranes and water from the floor and put down new hay.

"Now these two can cuddle up here in the cow barn tonight," said Morten. The cow was on her feet and busy cleaning up her calf.

"Are we going to milk her now?" asked Mette.

"No," said Morten. "I will leave that job to the calf tonight. Then we'll see if there is anything left to milk in the morning. I may just allow the calf to suckle her. That is the easiest thing to do. And it is nice for the tourists to watch, too."

They all left the cow barn, but evidence of their powerful experience was written all over their faces. When they came outside it was dark, but over the mountains to the east the sky brought tidings of a new day. The short night would soon be over.

Now, Mette could feel that she was really tired. It would be good to get to bed. Far too soon it would be morning—and another workday.

6 • *Kalvedans and licorice lozenges*

The next morning several of the children got up early, even if they had gone to bed late the night before. Everybody was excited to find out how the newborn in the cow barn was doing. When Mette got there, four boys and a girl were sitting on some hay in a corner, watching the little calf. It was stalking around on its long, skinny legs, searching for its mother's teats. It was a heifer.

"That is a little girl," Morten told them the night before. So they named her "Missi."

Now and then some of the braver children went over to pat her gently on the neck. But as long as the mother cow remained so close, they mostly left her calf alone.

The other cows waited outside to get into the cow barn. Mette let in the two that were to be milked and tied each one up in a stall.

The cow barn started getting crowded again. Quite a few people wanted to watch. Morten arrived, too. After the calf had its fill, he emptied what was left in the udder of the new mother.

"It seems she can't drink it all," he said, "so we'll get some *råmelkspudding** (pudding made from first milk) as well."

Mette smiled delightedly. "That will be delicious," she said. "I can remember my mother making a pudding from first milk. She called it *kalvedans*. We kids loved it. I haven't had that kind of pudding for years."

Morten laughed a little. "I will ask Aunt Anna if she can make some today. Then all these inquisitive kids can have a taste, too."

Aunt Anna loved the idea of making kalvedans. She filled a jar with the thick, yellow first milk and placed it in a big pot, to which she added some water. She placed the

20

pot on the stove.

"Now it has to simmer in this water bath until the milk is completely thickened," she said. "It will probably take a while. This milk is so 'first' that I'm sure it will be nice and thick. But it won't take many days for the milk from the new mother to turn much thinner and get back to normal. Then thickening it by this method won't work anymore."

While the milk simmered, she showed the tourists both how to separate the other milk and how to churn butter. She explained and demonstrated, nonstop. Mette had her work cut out for her translating it all, for Aunt Anna was only speaking Norwegian.

The cooking process mainly interested the adults. The children watched for a while, but then they ran out to play with the lambs and Missi.

Throughout the day Mette got plenty of time to talk to the tourists. She wasn't that busy. It was so hot that working too hard simply made her feel uncomfortable. She discovered that a lot of people really enjoyed talking to her. The children, too, asked questions eagerly.

"Now it's time to take a swim in the lake," she called out after a while, as she noticed people beginning to move into the shade behind the seter house. "Who wants to come along?"

Cheers from all over told her she wouldn't be alone in the swimming area.

Soon a big crowd of adults and children gathered down by the lake. Mette was one of the first to jump in. Ice cold, she thought as she went in. But it didn't take long for her to get used to the difference in temperature. Then it just felt wonderfully cool.

Playful splashing and ecstatic shouting grew louder and louder as more people jumped in the water. Mette returned to the bank. She sat down on the stone bench and watched the enthusiastic children. Some of the adults had joined in, too. A man crouched down under water while one of the kids stood on his shoulders. Then he straightened up quickly. The boy was thrown up in the air and landed in the water with a splash. More kids gathered around for the same kind of treatment.

Morten came over and sat down next to her. "Are you sitting here?" he asked. "Don't you want to join in the play?"

Mette shook her head. "I ..." she hesitated. "I'm not very comfortable in the water," she said, laughing self-consciously.

"Are you a sissy, too?" Morten responded with a laugh. "I really don't think about you that way. Obviously you can handle most of what's going on here at the seter. Is there anything at all you don't have the competency to do?"

Mette laughed a little at the friendly teasing. But then she turned earnest again.

"You have to understand," she said. "I had a bad experience as a child, and it won't let go of me. Many years ago I went fishing with my father. We had a small boat. The sea was rough, but not so bad that Father thought it was unsafe to go out. Suddenly there was a great blast of wind and the rocking of the boat took us by surprise. I was totally unprepared and fell back against the railing. And before we knew it, I was in the water.

"Father pulled me out right away, but the moments I found myself in the churning sea I though I was going to die. I remember it as if it happened yesterday. Since then, when I go swimming and the sea gets rough and agitated around me, I relive the panic I felt that day. My body tenses up and I feel that I am about to drown again. I thought I would grow out of it, but it hasn't happened yet."

Morten turned earnest now. "You are not the only one to feel that way," he said. "I haven't experienced anything exactly like that myself, but I have heard of many others, who have. Being afraid of water is no joke. I am sorry for what I said. It was inconsiderate of me."

"It doesn't matter," Mette smiled. "But now you have to jump in the water so you can join the fun."

He got up and walked over to a rock a short distance away. From there he made an elegant dive into the deeper water on the far side of the rock. With long, strong strokes he swam toward the islet in the middle of the lake. Several of the tourists followed in his wake. Mette watched him as he swam. His dark hair was slicked back on his head. But even now it looked nice and well groomed. As she followed the swimming man with her eyes, she felt a few shivers going through her body.

Suddenly she straightened up. She scolded herself. What was she sitting there fantasizing about? No, she was working here, nothing else. She shouldn't forget that.

She stayed for a while, watching the swimmers. Everyone appeared to be having a good time in the invigorating waters of the mountain lake. She was pleased to have found this swimming area. Since the seter had no shower or bathtub, this was a great substitute.

Again she had to think about the big difference between the life she was used to in the city and this. There, she had everything she needed in terms of resources and convenience. Here, she had to make do with the lake as a bathtub and the old-fashioned outhouse over by the cow barn for a bathroom. She might even take a swim every day in this cool lake, for chores involving the farm animals called for a little extra hygiene.

Little by little, the guests started moving toward the seter meadow again. Mette followed, too.

When everybody was back, Aunt Anna took out her spinning wheel to demonstrate carding and spinning to the tourists. She sat outside in the meadow, surrounded by big baskets filled with wool and yarn.

First she carded the wool so it plumped up, light and fluffy, without any knots or lumps. With a practiced hand she quickly made a neat little "sausage," which she placed in a basket. Then she put some new wool on the carding combs and, presto, she had a new sausage. Soon she had a stack of woolen sausages in her basket.

Then she moved over to the spinning wheel. She used her hand to get the big wheel going. She stepped on the pedal and the wheel spun around at great speed. It looked like magic to some of the kids, as they watched the wool sausages being transformed into a long, thin thread. One sausage after another was fastened to the thread, which twisted around and around as quick as lightning.

Aunt Anna worked steadily. Her feet, fingers and mouth were in perpetual motion. It was incredible that she was able to concentrate on everything at the same time. Again, Mette had a challenging task just translating for her. The bystanders received all kinds of information about how to work with wool. In addition, they got one story after another about life at the seter in the old days. Afterward, they each received a small ball of wool as a souvenir.

Mette helped Aunt Anna carry all the baskets inside again. She studied the beautiful colors of the wool and the yarn. Some was yellow and some was green. There was blue and brown yarn as well.

"Is this wool that you bought?" she asked.

"Oh, no." Aunt Anna chuckled as she walked toward the seter house with her spinning wheel. "This is wool from our own sheep here at the seter."

Mette looked at her in surprise. "But all these beautiful colors, how do you get them?"

"I use plant dyes," she answered. Aunt Anna continued before Mette had time to ask any further: "I'm giving a class later, but not to this group. Next week a home craft organization will be here to learn about natural plant dyes. They are going to participate in the entire process, so it will be an all-day event."

"I'm really looking forward to that," said Mette excitedly. She studied closely the woolen balls of yarn with their clear, intense colors.

"You are welcome to take some of this yarn if you can use it for something," said Aunt Anna, noticing Mette's interest.

"May I?" Mette looked eagerly from Aunt Anna to the pretty balls of yarn. "May I take some of this and knit something I can keep as a remembrance of this summer?"

"Just help yourself," answered the chipper lady. "I won't be able to use everything I make. I have to give away most of it anyway."

Thrilled, Mette picked out a couple of balls of yarn before she returned the baskets to Aunt Anna's room. She picked colors she thought blended together well. She could hardly wait until she got a chance to sit down with her knitting.

A while later, Aunt Anna asked Mette to go out and invite their guests for some kalvedans. The pudding was ready and waiting, piping hot, on a table in the meadow.

Soon a large group gathered around the jar with plates and spoons. Aunt Anna happily started to hand out servings.

Suddenly a small boy came running through the gate over by the cow barn.

"Someone gave the lambs licorice lozenges. I found a whole bunch of them over by the lambs." He showed them something he held in his hand. "Look, and there is a lot more over there."

Mette looked into his little hand. "But honey, these are not licorice lozenges. Did you try to taste them?" She looked worriedly at the eager boy.

"No, I just tried to give some to the lambs, but they didn't want them."

"I bet they didn't," said Mette, laughing merrily, "for this is sheep dung. Just watch next time they poop."

Quick as lightning, he threw all the small, black pellets to the ground and rubbed his hand frantically on the seat of his pants. Two huge eyes stared at her in terror. The roars from the others made the little fellow feel embarrassed and shy.

"No wonder you mistook them." Mette felt he needed a little comfort. "They look exactly the same. Anyone could have made that mistake. But come over here so you can taste the kalvedans."

The råmelkspudding was a new taste sensation for the guests. Aunt Anna sprinkled sugar and cinnamon on their plates as she handed them out. The light, yellow pudding disappeared quickly from the plates. Some asked for extras.

"This almost tastes like *flan*," said a girl, who had downed her second helping.

Soon Aunt Anna's jar was empty. Mette was not at all sure whether Aunt Anna herself got any, but it didn't seem to bother her at all. She smiled contentedly. Her main satisfaction came from watching the delighted faces of the guests as they tasted something she had prepared and that they obviously enjoyed.

7 • Revival meeting

Mette stood watching the scenery around the seter house. The sun was about to break completely through the cloud layer. It actually looked as if it might be a nice day in spite of the dreary morning. It seemed as if the revival meeting might take place without any serious weather problems.

This morning she woke up early and noticed the drumming of rain on the roof. And when she got outside, a heavy fog looming over the lake greeted her. She was worried about the event they were planning in the seter meadow. Morten had put up some canopies in the camping area, but it would still be a wet experience if the rain were to continue.

But now it seemed as if the sun was getting the upper hand. The rain had ended a while ago, and big breaks in the cloud layer allowed the rays to shine through.

Mette noticed that the disappointment and gloom from earlier that morning was about to be replaced with the anticipation and excitement she had felt the day before. She had especially looked forward to participate in serving the great seter fare that Aunt Anna had prepared. And, she looked forward to meeting people from town. She hadn't yet had the opportunity to get to know many of them.

But what she looked forward to the most was listening to the preachers. She hadn't been to church or to a prayer meeting in quite a long time. The spiritual need she sensed in her inner being fueled her strong expectations for the day.

Aunt Anna was busy preparing the *rømmegrøt*—the sour cream porridge. It had to be the real thing, made from scratch. She accepted no semi-prepared foods from the shopping center. And she was a great cook. The porridge would be perfect, Mette was sure of that.

Mette went back in the house to make the batter for the *lappekaker**—small pancakes. They planned to make them inside, on the large stone griddle, during the break. They were going to be served up piping hot.

Morten drove up. He had been down in town to borrow a speaker system and some chairs from the meetinghouse. While Mette and Aunt Anna prepared the food, Morten set up all the equipment in the campground. He wired the speaker system to a small truck. The chairs were set out and he also had brought a podium.

Soon everything was ready for the crowd. It didn't take long before the first cars started to arrive. For many, this revival meeting at the Siljatjern Seter was a tradition they didn't want to miss. Some came early to get set up in a good spot. The old-timers knew the area might get a little crowded. It was a popular event, partly because of Aunt Anna's great seter fare.

Soon the heat in the seter house became oppressive, so Mette was happy when they finished what needed to be done and could go outside. Two tables were placed along the seter wall, where the food would be served when the first session was over.

Mette sat down in an empty chair in the shade under one of the canopies. Morten had asked her to say a few words at the opening of the meeting. She was prepared, but she felt the need to settle down a little before it all started.

From her seat, Mette could see most of the crowd. There were not many faces she knew. But still, she had a feeling of contentment. The song of the choir swept enchantingly from the powerful speakers across the mountain area.

Next, Morten stepped forward and welcomed the assembly to yet another revival meeting at the Siljatjern seter. Then Mette was introduced, and she had the floor. She didn't take up much time with what she had prepared. She said a deeply felt prayer, thanking God for the lovely day and for everyone who was there for the meeting.

The first session went as planned. The preacher who spoke was young and energetic. Mette knew him slightly from her days working with the missionary organization. The sun rose steadily in the sky. It was fortunate they had the canopies for shelter, she thought, or the sunshine would soon have become unbearable.

She wasn't able to concentrate properly on the preacher's message, for after a while she felt she should go inside to help Aunt Anna with the food.

As the choir performed its last song, Mette began carrying out the pot of rømmegrøt and the flatbread. Aunt Anna was in full swing making pancakes. Soon people were lined up to help themselves. She had set out home-churned butter arranged on a platter and two large jars of jam for the pancakes. The blueberry jam and raspberry jam, too, she had made herself. On a stand was a *fenalår*—cured leg of lamb—from which people could cut off pieces to eat with the porridge and the flatbread.

Everyone enjoyed the food and camaraderie. The children played in the meadow while some of the people walked over to the hillside to watch the animals grazing.

Suddenly Mette became aware that a gate was open. The farm animals might quickly slip out and bump against the cars that were parked close together along the road. The children wouldn't realize the importance of keeping the gates shut on a day like this. She ran over and secured it firmly. It was best to keep an eye on it, at least during the lunch break while people were milling around in the area, she thought.

When she turned to go back, a man was walking slowly toward her. She didn't know him, but she had seen him with some other people from town, so she assumed that he was a local. He stopped in front of her. He seemed to be about to say something, but he just looked at her, a look of concern in his eyes.

Mette felt uneasy. There was something about him she couldn't define. Her first thought was: *Not again!* His intense eyes made shivers run down her spine. What did this man want?

Suddenly he started speaking. His voice was strained. "You have to watch out for yourself." He bent a little closer and lowered his voice: "You should understand that the way Morten goes about things ..."

He stopped abruptly when he noticed that Morten stood talking to an elderly couple close enough to hear what was said. The perplexity reflected in the man's shifty eye gave her an even stronger feeling of unease.

Abruptly he turned and walked back to the others. Mette stood there staring after him. This time it was not anger that overwhelmed her, but unease and bewilderment. What was going on here? What were these men insinuating; was there something weird about Morten? What was it this man implied Morten was up to?

Slowly she walked back to the assembly, her thoughts tumbling around in her head. She kicked the dust in disgust. Why did these unsettling incidents occur when she just wanted to enjoy herself and experience peace and blessing?

No, she wouldn't allow this to ruin such a fine day. She prayed silently for help to concentrate on good things, and not on the unease that now threatened to invade her spirit. As she busied herself with her work and interacted with their guests, the episode gradually faded. Peace was again allowed to fill her inner being.

8 • *Come unto Me...*

Morten called for people to gather again. The campground was even more crowded, for several more people had arrived during the break. It took a while before the hum of conversation died down, but finally it was quiet enough for the meeting to start.

After the choir again performed a couple of songs, the next preacher came forward. He was a short, slight man, somewhat on in years. But when he started speaking, the assembly was struck by the power and intensity that characterized his voice. He began his talk without any kind of introduction. He went straight to the heart of the matter.

"Jesus said, 'Come unto Me, all ye that labor and are heavy-laden,'" began the preacher, citing the theme of his sermon. His words echoed across the mountain landscape. He stood there for a few seconds looking out over the crowd.

When he commenced speaking, his voice was softer but more intense: "Is something burdening you … something heavy, something you carry alone, something you can't ask your neighbor or family to help you with? How are you really … today?"

Everyone sat in breathless silence, eyes fastened upon the podium.

"Then listen to these words from Matthew, Chapter 11, Verse 28," he said, citing the familiar passage from beginning to end: "Come unto Me, all ye that labor and are heavy-laden, and I will give you rest."

After a pause, he continued: "In the following verses are hidden some deep truths. 'Take my yoke upon you and learn from me, for I am gentle and humble in heart, and you will find rest for your souls. For my yoke is easy and my burden is light.'

"We know that a yoke has always been interpreted as something heavy. So God asks us to assume a burden … a burden that is from Him. This will provide us with the insight we need.

"I am afraid that today a lot of people ask God to take away the burdens that come upon them instead of taking the yoke upon themselves and thus gaining the insight that this provides.

"But how can this be? Wasn't it just that which we were encouraged to do … to come to Him with our burden? Isn't that what is written here?

"Yes, it is written that we should bring our burdens to Him. But notice what His promise is: 'I will give you rest.'" He paused slightly after his last word, as if he wanted the word "rest" to sink into his listeners' hearts.

"Rest," he continued, "is what God promises us here. And rest is what people like us need more than anything. This is just what God sees. It is the burden of the yoke that He will help us with.

"In Verse 30 it also says: 'For my yoke is easy and my burden is light.'

"How can God say that the burden is light? Such a statement may provoke many of us who have experienced hardship. Or perhaps they instead experience it as relief and comfort, because they realize what it means—namely, that we are allowed to take our burden to God and then He will help us carry it.

"It is obvious that when someone who has the power in Heaven and Earth carries our burden with us, then the part we have to endure isn't necessarily that heavy. At least, it is not too heavy for us to manage. But in order for us to achieve the insight He wishes us to have, or for others to achieve insight through what we have to carry, He gives us a few burdens and yokes throughout our lives.

"What He would like to teach us the most is just this: that we are to come to Him. It is characteristic for us humans to feel we are fully capable of managing on our own when things are fine. But when we face adversity, then we pray. God wants us to pray. In order to get us to that point, he often uses some mysterious (to us) means."

There was again a moment's silence. The eyes of the preacher drifted away, an expression of pain on his face. Yet when he continued, his words were delivered with an intensity that seemed to come from his innermost soul:

"Here in this world we will have to take into consideration all kinds of hardship and suffering. But there is a place we can go to for help. And it is this place that I want to point out to you today. This place is Jesus. Use this place. You find it here." He lifted his big Bible high above his head. "Here in the Word you will find rest.

"Now obviously we are not supposed to believe that all suffering is bestowed upon us by God in order for us to endure it. No, what we read today is about leaving our matters completely in the hands of the Lord. And then He will deal with them as He sees fit. He relieves much of our suffering when we bring it to Him, for He sees that otherwise we will not become the tool for Him that He wants us to be.

"Yes, sometimes He takes our troubles away without our knowing why. And at other times we have to carry our burden without knowing why. Illness, for instance ..."

He stopped for a while, seeming to consider something before he continued.

"In regard to illness, we should take into account the words and promises of the Bible. The letter to James, Chapter 5, has a description of just how to act in regard to this. We can experience healing today just as much as people in biblical times experienced it. But sometimes I'm afraid we have to count on enduring illness, too."

Mette sat listening with increasing interest. She experienced an atmosphere of spirituality that made her think she was at the podium of the Master, the slight preacher up there a tool to spread God's message to people.

At the end of his speech, the preacher spoke about God's concern and love for each individual. As he stepped down, the choir lined up again to sing. The first song was introduced as a text inspired by the verses in Job, Chapter 36, Verses 15 and 16.

When their voices started drifting out over the audience, Mette again felt the tremendous peace that the holy atmosphere created. The words of the song were completely appropriate in the context of what the preacher had talked about.

Is it dark in your heaven? Is it dark in your home?
Is it dark in your innermost soul?
Have you felt that your life is turned inside out,
So your thoughts all are far from whole?
Have you asked a question and looked for a nod,
But felt nothing but silence from God?

Your questions are many. Your powers are faint.
Your hands, they are folded in prayer.
And those hands reach out toward Him who has promised
To help all His children out there.
"Just wait now, my child, I have something to say.
Soon your trials will all go away."

27

See the clouds breaking up, see the light in the east.
See the end of the longest of nights.
For the light from the Word is a promise to you,
As to Job in his terrible plight.
Through your trials your mind opens up to the new.
God's Lamb is there waiting for you.

Soon your mind will awaken, soon a new day will dawn
Soon the rays from the sun you will feel.
You will see that the promise made you in the Book
Is a truth that is fully revealed.
He your trials will soothe, you will get your reward,
Thank your Savior, your Heavenly Lord.

9 • *Conversation under six eyes*

For the audience, this song and the speech of the elderly preacher had hit home. Many asked to be allowed to speak afterward. One by one they gave moving witness. By now it was getting late, and the preachers had a long drive home. In the end, Morten had to break it up and allow the meeting to come to an end.

The crowd grew restive. Some got up and started packing up their gear. Others picked up conversations they started during the lunch break. And some took the opportunity to visit with people they hadn't seen for a while. Many were touched by the sincere nature of the meeting and wanted to share their thoughts with others.

Soon, Mette became aware of a woman who walked over to Morten. He greeted her with delight. Mette was clearing a table close by, so she heard very well what was said. The two clearly knew each other.

"Boy, it is a long time since I saw you last," said Morten. "Do you still live in the city?"

"No," the woman answered. "I lived in Oslo for several years, but now I have moved to my sister's. You know she lives in our family's old house here in town."

"So that's what you did," said Morten. "I suppose that means we'll see more of each other in the time to come. That's great."

The woman didn't answer. She hesitated and looked down at the grass. Morten studied her in silence for a moment.

Mette, too, studied the two of them as they talked. There was something odd about this woman. She was extremely thin. The fact that she was petite probably made her look especially frail. But the most noticeable thing about her was her expression. Her eyes seemed enormous in her pale face. Also, something watchful in her eyes gave her an air of anxiousness. She seemed haggard—as if she were tired and weary.

It was also obvious that the main purpose of this conversation wasn't to refresh childhood memories. No, there had to be something in particular that this woman wanted. Morten seemed to have noticed, too, for his demeanor indicated that he was

28

waiting for her to bring up whatever she really wanted to talk about.

She straightened and then continued the conversation by saying: "There is some-thing specific I wanted to talk to you about, just the two of us." She hesitated a little. "I didn't have the courage to contact the preachers, and they have left now, anyway. But it shouldn't matter who it is."

She stopped and didn't complete the sentence. "Since I used to know you," she continued a little shakily, "I thought that maybe we could talk."

Morten looked at her intently. He seemed to sense there was something special she wanted to discuss.

"Yes, of course we can talk. That will be great," he said. "We can go to the seter house. We won't get interrupted there. But we have a principle that I would prefer that we follow. When we have a talk like this, we always are three people present. Do you mind if my assistant, Mette, joins us?"

"No, that's perfectly all right," the woman answered a little absently.

Morten signaled to Mette that she was to follow them, and so the three of them went inside. He fastened the hasp on the inside of the door so they wouldn't risk get-ting interrupted while they talked.

The woman was asked to take a seat at the table. He placed himself on a bench, fac-ing her. Mette sat down with her knitting and removed herself a little. She tried to seem preoccupied with her knitting so her presence wouldn't be an impediment. For it was Morten this women wanted to talk to, not her.

The woman squirmed in her chair. "It is so good to be in a place where the Word of God is preached," she started. "It is so good to be reassured that we have a God who listens to us when we pray and cares about us, regardless of the circumstances."

"Yes," said Morten. "That is really good to hear. And it is good to know."

"Yes," the woman replied a little hesitantly. Her entire face demonstrated anxiety. She wrung her hands in her lap. The huge eyes had a blank stare, not looking at any-thing in particular.

Mette looked over at her. What was troubling this frail woman? Never had she seen anyone so dispirited. She talked about how it was good to hear about a God who lis-tened to one's prayers, but it didn't at all seem as if she were convinced this was really the case.

Almost as if answering Mette's thoughts, the women suddenly said: "Do you be-lieve that God hears all our prayers—regardless of what we pray for?"

Morten hesitated a little. He seemed to realize there was something more behind this question than what she let on.

"Is there a specific thing you have prayed for without feeling that you were an-swered?

The woman looked down at her hands and wrung them even harder. "Yes ... no ... I don't know," she whispered.

Morten bent across the table and looked her directly in the eye. "My dear Solfrid," he said in a gentle voice, "What is troubling you?"

She looked at him for a moment before she looked down again. The twitching of her lips revealed that she was about to cry. "It is just that I am so scared," she whispered.

And then it was as if a dam broke. Tears streaming down her cheeks, she started to explain: "I have cancer. It was discovered a few weeks ago. For a long time I had no energy and felt tired. I lost weight, too. But I wasn't in any pain. My physician thought it was due to a virus or anemia, but he did some tests, just in case. And that's when it was discovered. I had surgery, and a tumor was removed from my abdomen, but it turned out that it has spread throughout my entire body. There is no hope for me to get well. I just get some treatment that may slow down the spreading of the disease."

Her voice shook, and now and then shivers coursed through her entire body. She couldn't stop crying. "And then there are these treatments," she continued. "At times they are a nightmare to me. Sometimes I think of them as the last straw. You know, it might just so happen that they work and that I will have many good years left. But then there are times when I think of them as prolonged torture. If I can't get well and the disease just keeps progressing, then it is much better to go quickly so the suffering doesn't go on forever."

Mette's knitting needles had stopped moving. The entire idea about keeping her presence low key was forgotten. She sat staring at Solfrid, which she understood was the woman's name. But it didn't seem as if the two over there noticed her.

At the table, Morten covered Solfrid's hand with his. And his dark eyes showed deep compassion. "What you are telling me pains me deeply," he said.

Solfrid sobbed as she continued: "I am so scared." The words burst from a throat that was strained to the limit. Suddenly it was as if her eyes lit up. "God," she said. "God, He is almighty—isn't He?"

"Yes," Morten nodded a little hesitantly. He sensed they were getting into something that would require him to choose his words carefully.

"Yes," she continued, forcing an excitement that wasn't there. "That is really why I am here now. God can heal, I know that. Would you please pray for me? Maybe you can anoint me like the preacher talked about. For God can heal," she repeated. "Don't you, too, believe that? It is my only hope!"

Morten paused before he answered. It was obvious he ached for this desperate woman. Solfrid's entire tense body demonstrated her need for assurance.

"Do you have faith that you will be healed?" asked Morten gently.

"Faith!" The word erupted from her. She jumped up from her seat. "So you, too, are one of those who believe you can't be healed if your faith isn't strong enough. Don't you understand …" Her wild eyes looked in Morten's direction without really seeing him. "Don't you understand … I can't handle this … this thing about faith. I am so sick … I can't take it anymore." As she spoke, her voice changed gradually from rage to tears.

Now Morten got to his feet, too. He took her gently by the arm and sat her gently down on the chair again.

"No, my dear Solfrid," he said. "Now you misunderstand me." Her frantic stare met his calm, caring eyes. "Allow me to explain something. Faith is not something you have to work at to achieve. Faith is a gift given us by God Himself. He recognizes your predicament and He understands your needs. But He also knows His own position and His own needs. These two matters—our own predicament and God's position—may often look like conflicting issues. But God sees the whole situation in a different light from what we do. This light belongs in a different dimension, in another world.

"We humans are not capable of seeing or understanding this. We don't have the mechanisms in place to fully understand the nature of this light. We have to go on living in this world as if in some kind of haze. But we have the Word of God. And the Word of God helps us find what we need in order to live our lives in this haze. God thus looks at our situation in an entirely different way. What disappears from our world does not disappear from His.

"We cling to life; no wonder, for that is a part of Creation. It is completely natural. Everybody does. But God is the Lord of life and death. When a person who is saved in the name of Jesus Christ dies, it shouldn't be considered a tragedy. It is just a transfer in His eyes. 'Promoted to glory,' as we sometimes hear at funerals.

"But it is also so that God has given us another option in regard to the sick. That is what the preacher spoke about out there today. In James, Chapter 5, it says we should anoint them and offer our prayers. It goes on to say that prayers offered in faith will help the sick person get well. At least, that is the wording of the Bible translation I have here."

Morten retrieved his Bible and looked up the passage he was talking about. "Look here," he said. "It says 'help the sick person,' not 'heal the sick.'"

Solfrid bent eagerly over the Bible and read the entire verse to herself. She was a little calmer, but still seemed anxious and tense. "But God heals, doesn't He?"

"Yes, of course," answered Morten. "That's what is so incomprehensible to us. Yes, God heals. He heals a lot of us, even in this day and time. But He doesn't always enlighten us as to whom—and why.

"Nevertheless, God bestows upon people who experience this healing a special kind of faith. Some receive it as an inner confidence, maybe because of something they read in the Bible. Or they get it by preaching the Word. Others may get it through a subconscious inspiration. Yes, there are many ways in which this may happen. The point is that they do what the Bible tells them and seek intercession for their problem."

"But that is exactly what I'm doing right now," said Solfrid.

"Yes," said Morten. "And you are quite right. I just wanted to discuss this with you first, for it is so easy to mistake faith for our own fervent wishes."

Solfrid shrank a little on her chair again. Her tears started anew. "But how in the world am I to know the difference?" she asked, completely devastated.

Mette followed the conversation with great interest while appearing to be preoccupied with her knitting. Her needles worked energetically, but she would have to unravel some of it later, for she was unable to concentrate on the pattern.

"My dear," said Morten. "I hope what I said didn't confuse you. Of course, in many circumstances it is impossible to understand the difference. But it doesn't really matter that much. For God does not depend on your full comprehension in order to heal you. This is not at all contingent upon any kind of performance on your part. All that needs to be done has already been done. Jesus did that once upon a time on the cross.

"The only thing He asks of you is that you ask for intercession. And if you don't know which category you fall into, asking for it is still the only thing you have to do. Never be afraid of asking for intercession, for His promise applies to everybody. Intercession will help the sick. And if God has given you faith that you will be healed, you will be, whether you understand it or not.

"The reason I tell you all this is that some people get so disappointed after intercession if nothing happens. Yes, I would say that sometimes it even affects their peace of mind. I don't want that happening to you. I want to anoint you and pray for you now. But I also want you to trust that you are in God's hands—regardless of what happens. I want you to understand that the ways of God are not always our ways. Sometimes we just have to accept that, without ever being able to understand it. But healing is a fantastic thing that God allows to happen. And we will now ask Him to do that."

31

Morten looked at her sitting over there on the chair. She was very pale, but her tense body seemed more relaxed.

"Yes," she said calmly. "Let us do it. And in regard to acceptance, you will have to ask for a miracle, too."

"Well," Morten said. "We need a lot of miracles from God. And I am convinced He will spare no effort when it comes to you."

Morten got to his feet. He took out the small bottle of oil tucked into the cover of his Bible. "Maybe you, too, would like to participate in this?" he asked, directed at Mette.

She quickly put aside her knitting and walked over to Solfrid. They stood next to her, one on each side.

"May we lay our hands on you?" asked Morten. Solfrid nodded.

He poured a drop of oil on a finger and rubbed it across Solfrid's brow. Then he prayed sincerely for help and comfort for the sick. He prayed that, if it were God's will Solfrid be healed, He would make it happen according to the pledges and promises that are stated in His Word. But if it were so that God wanted to take her home, Morten prayed that the Lord would give her the strength to accept that. He prayed with sincerity that she would experience God's care and love.

Mette prayed, too. She prayed that Solfrid would serve as a light for Him, either through healing or through her illness. In the end, she prayed that the name of God would be glorified through this woman. As they prayed, Solfrid hid her face in her hands. Her shoulders shook while she wept quietly.

After their prayers, the room fell silent. No one wanted to break the holy atmosphere that filled the room. In the end, Solfrid rose and walked quietly toward the door. "Thank you," she simply said. Then she left.

They didn't know exactly what her feelings were now, but they let her go. Now it was up to God to do His work on her according to His plan and will.

As Solfrid closed the door behind her, Morten sat down on the bench and buried his face in his hands. Mette sat down, too. No one said anything for a while.

Suddenly Morten looked up at her. His face seemed haggard. Deep furrows creased his brow. It was clear that the episode had made a deep impression on him.

"I probably talked way too much for her." His expression showed that he was deeply concerned.

"I don't think so," said Mette. "Obviously, a long speech like that may not be quite the right thing for such an ill person, but I think what you said was appropriate in this particular situation."

Morten continued, more to himself than to her: "I just got this notion that her strong desire for healing was a result of her dread for the disease, and not some kind of admonition from God. But, of course, I may be wrong. Strong admonitions are not always needed in order for God to heal."

"It is not easy to be able to help people in such a deep crisis as Solfrid finds herself in now," said Mette. "I just think we have to trust that God will take care of her. We have placed her in His hands. I don't think we can do any more than that right now."

"Yes." Morten nodded and got to his feet. "This is His business now."

Then he left to start cleaning up after the meeting.

10 • Mountain hike

Morten stood in the doorway to the cow barn and looked up the hillside toward the west. A brisk breeze played with his dark hair. In the east, the sun struggled to overpower the cool mist left behind by the night. Some clouds blocked it from growing as strong as it would like to. The fragile tinkling of sheep bells and the customary sounds from the milk pail disrupted the calm as Mette was about to finish up with the last cow to be milked. A few clear, flute-like notes from a bird up on the hill also wafted through the air from time to time.

Mette, too, went over to the door. For a while both of them stood there in silence. She felt a wonderful peace and quiet descend on her soul and mind, inspired by the serenity and harmony, the farm animals and nature itself here at the seter. She felt she was about to become one with it all. This filled her with an inner joy and happiness that she could hardly describe.

Suddenly Morten turned and looked at her. "I wonder …" He stopped and looked searchingly at the hillside. "… I don't know where they could be."

Mette looked at him and noticed he seemed worried. She wondered if what he said was directed at her or if he were speaking to himself.

"Who is it you think will appear up there?" she asked.

Morten looked at her and smiled. He got the joke in her question and answered in a mockingly grave voice: "I thought I saw Trylska put her porridge pot on the fire up there where you can see the smoke drifting up from the mountain. But then, she sort of disappeared for me."

"Trylska?" Mette looked bewildered. She realized he was joking, but still she didn't understand what he meant.

"Yes," he laughed. "We kids always used to say that the trolls were cooking dinner whenever we saw foggy patches on the hillsides. And Trylska is, of course, the wife of the troll."

Mette had to laugh, too. "It is easy to understand how these mountains can fuel people's imagination."

"But," she said earnestly, "I doubt that it was Trylska you were searching for a minute ago."

"No, it wasn't." Morten sobered, too. "I don't understand where our two heifers are. Usually they come down to visit with the other cows now and then, but I haven't seen them for several days. A couple of times I have hiked a little way into the mountains, but I haven't come across them there, either. Sure, grazing has been great while it's been so warm, so they would have found a lot to eat. But I am worried about one of the heifers. She will be calving soon, and I'd rather have her back here in the cow barn when it happens."

Again he stood studying the landscape. "In any case, they are nowhere to be seen around here," he said after a while.

Then he grabbed the milk pails and carried them to the dairy room. Mette let the cows out to pasture again before she went inside.

Morten poured the milk into a big container and carried it over to a pool in the stream by the rocky slope. There it would be left to cool in the cold well water.

"You may take today and tomorrow off if you want," said Morten when they got back to the dairy room. "There won't be much going on here during the next few days, and you'll have to spend your time off doing something worthwhile now and then. You may use the car if you want. I don't need it, for I have to look for the two heifers in the mountains. It may be that I'll spend the night and return tomorrow. The weather is so nice that I'm sure it will be all right to sleep under the skies. I do that in the summer all the time."

Mette looked at him with interest. "It must be fantastic to be able to roam around in the mountains."

For a moment his eyes met hers. A tiny smile played on his lips. "Do you want to come with me?" His eyes lit up expectantly.

"May I?" Excitement was written all over her face.

"Sure, but bring appropriate gear. If we have to sleep outside, it might get cold at night."

Now they busily made preparations for the trip. Morten got hold of Petter, his neighbor down in town, on his cell phone. They had an agreement that Petter would pitch in if they needed extra help at the seter. It was he who took care of Morten's animals during the winter. Now he promised to take care of the animals until they returned.

Aunt Anna was down in town, too. She wasn't expected to return until she was to teach the class for the home craft organization, scheduled at the end of the week.

Mette stuffed her backpack with extra clothes, food and some gear that Morten suggested they bring. "Sleeping bags will be too heavy to carry," he said. "I usually do fine with just a blanket."

Mette was glad to hear that. She thought her backpack was full enough as it was. Morten also brought a large coil of rope that he put over his shoulder. "When you go looking for livestock like this, you usually will need a lot of rope," he said when he noticed that Mette looked curiously at his gear.

Soon they were on their way, hiking up the hillside at a brisk pace. The air was getting quite warm, so Mette had packed most of her clothes in her backpack. T-shirt and shorts were more than adequate for someone who was out hiking in this summer heat. And luckily, she was wearing comfortable shoes.

The first leg was pretty steep. Mette was glad she was in good physical shape. She wasn't exactly a bundle of muscles; on the contrary, she was slender. But neither was she frail. She liked exercising and hiking. Oslo offered lots of opportunities for outdoor activities, so she didn't have a problem following Morten.

Before they reached the top of the hill, Mette felt sweat running down her back. Actually, it felt good to be able to use her strength like this. She continued doggedly at the same speed. They didn't talk much as they hiked. The terrain was so rugged that they often had to walk in a single file.

When they reached the top, Mette noticed how the landscape widened and seemed to go on forever. Far ahead were towering mountains. Around them were hills with wide bogs in between. "I would think there are lots of *multer*—cloudberries—here in the fall," said Mette as they stopped for a moment to catch their breath.

"Sure," said Morten, pointing toward some marshland to the southwest. "Over there are some of our best cloudberry bogs. If it doesn't get below freezing during the night in late spring, the area is teeming with berries when fall comes around."

"Do you think they will ripen before I leave?" asked Mette eagerly.

"Yes, I would think so," he answered. "But we have to be careful not to pick them too early. If we pick the unripe berries, the plants we pick them from won't bear fruit for five to seven years."

Mette looked at him in astonishment. "I didn't know that. Is that why they always tell you not to pick unripe cloudberries?"

"Yes." Morten was serious. "A lot of people don't understand that. Some years there's a veritable race here to be the first to get to the best berry-picking areas. Often, the cloudberries are still red when they start picking them."

"How do you know when it is all right to pick them?" asked Mette.

"They should not be picked before they let go of their husk. At that point they are juicy and yellow. Those are the berries that give the best jam and the best dessert," answered Morten.

They continued their hike along a stream running toward the northwest. Mette noticed that in some places there were long stretches of fencing. Morten explained that he and other property owners up there had worked together on the project. It was a measure of safety for their livestock while grazing in the mountains. But it was impossible to fence in everything, so they had used natural barriers as much as they could. Mountains and streams were adequate fences, at least for the heifers.

They got close to a small hill, and Morten said he wanted to climb to the top. Maybe they would be able to spot the missing animals from up there.

Again, the climbing was tough. In some spots it was steep. Morten had to help Mette several times so she could get up the steepest parts of the terrain. It took them a while to get up there. But finally they could sit down and relax and take in the magnificent scenery that met them at the top.

The view was incredible. Mette gazed about her in silent appreciation. The open mountain plateau stretched for miles and miles in all directions. Farther away on the horizon, towering peaks almost disappeared in a faint, blue haze. In other areas where the peaks were closer, she could see white, snowy blankets around the summits. Tenacious snow clung to the deepest crevasses facing north. The brisk breeze that swept across the mountains probably did its share to make them last.

Bushes and lush mountain grass grew down in the valleys. Small streams meandered in complex patterns along the valley floor. In between, small blue mountain lakes twinkled in the sunshine.

Mette breathed deeply. The fresh air and the magnificent panorama almost made her feel intoxicated. How glad she was she was able to come along on this trip. She found her camera and took several pictures.

Morten had retrieved the binoculars he wore on a cord around his neck. Through it, he scrutinized the plains around them. But as thoroughly as he studied the area, he didn't see the animals anywhere.

"I guess we just have to keep on looking," he said and lowered his binoculars. "I don't even see the shadow of any heifers here."

Morten knew the mountains well, so it was obvious the route he took was not accidental. Resolutely, he continued toward the high mountains on the horizon. Now and then they climbed to the top of hills to check the area anew. But the result was negative every time; they spotted no heifers. They came upon both sheep and goats grazing on the hillsides. But the animals they were looking for were nowhere to be seen.

Later in the day they decided to take a rest by a lake. Morten started a campfire between some rocks by the edge of the water. Mette took out the food she had brought.

A big chunk of cured leg of lamb was cut into strips. Morten cut some wooden sticks for skewering the meat. Then he grilled them over the fire.

They also had brought some potato *lefse**. As the skewered meat was done, he wrapped them in lefse pieces, and then they ate the freshly grilled meat. Mette had never tasted anything so delicious.

"As children, my parents used to grill cured lamb ribs in the fireplace on Christmas Eve," said Morten. "My father used to do it sometimes on winter nights when I was a child. The memories of those evenings around the fireplace are among my most precious," he said and looked dreamily ahead of him. A tiny smile was on his lips.

For Mette, the taste and the tradition were completely new, but she would definitely like to try this again. The strong, salty taste of the lamb lingered in her mouth long after she swallowed it.

After the meal, they sat looking over the lake. They found a shady place behind some rocks. The sun was quite hot, so they enjoyed the shade they were able to find.

Suddenly Morten turned to Mette and looked searchingly into her eyes. An amused expression sparkled in his dark brown eyes. Mette felt embarrassed by his intense stare.

"I have never ever seen such blue eyes," he said after a while.

Mette was completely taken aback by this personal remark.

He burst out laughing. "It is just that I have noticed. Sorry if I was too personal." He looked away and continued to watch the lake.

It took a few seconds for Mette to be able to speak.

"Yes, I guess I am pretty blue-eyed, I have gotten comments on that quite often," she finally said. They both laughed. "I inherited it from my father," she continued. "He, too, has intensely blue eyes. Actually, much lighter than mine. Sometimes people who don't know him wonder if he is drunk, for his eyes appear rather unfocused."

"I didn't mean it like that," said Morten quickly. "Your eyes are definitely beautiful. Why don't you tell me a little bit about yourself?" he continued. "For example, how old are you? One is not supposed to ask a woman about her age, but I thought …"

He stopped and looked searchingly at her again.

Again Mette felt herself blush. But she answered as light-heartedly as possible. "I will be 32 this fall." Suddenly she turned around and looked at him challengingly. "If you read my job application, you would have noticed that my birthday was listed there."

"But that was just it," he answered, frowning. "I thought it said you were born in '42. But it was '72, then?"

Yet again Mette felt herself blush, this time to the roots of her hair.

"Sorry," she said quietly while looking down at the ground. "I was traveling when I filled out that application, and I didn't have access to a PC. I know that my handwriting is awful. The number '7' may easily look like the number '4' when I have to write by hand."

"So that explains that," laughed Morten. "I have really been wondering about it. But that doesn't matter. So then you are a year younger than I."

Mette didn't let on that she was pleased to get that information. But she had guessed he was about her age.

"Maybe you have siblings, too?" he continued.

Mette started talking about her family. She told him about her parents, who lived in a small town called Grimstad in Aust-Agder Fylke, and about her sister, who was married and lived in the same town. She talked about the three little nephews she tried

36

to visit as often as she could. Then she reminisced about the farm where she grew up. It was now sold to one of her father's younger brothers. She had talked a lot about her childhood days there the first evening at the seter, so she didn't go into much of that again.

Morten listened intently. Now and then he asked a question and Mette went on with her story. Soon she felt he knew everything about her and her family, her Christian upbringing, and the safe home where she grew up. Few problems had troubled her adolescent days.

"Maybe this will bring me problems later?" she ended. "You need some adversity in your life in order to grow."

Morten smiled. "I think you should be grateful for all the good things, and then take on hardships as they come."

A shadow crossed his face. For a while he sat still, as if engrossed in old memories.

Suddenly he started talking about his own family. He talked about his father, who had suddenly died of heart failure eight years before. He also mentioned his mother, who had been sickly over a long period of time before she, too, died. That was a couple of years ago.

Then he spoke about his two sisters. Marit was married and lived in the same town, and then there was Siri, who lived in Trondheim with her family.

Mette listened with interest. Aunt Anna had also mentioned a few things about the family, but it was really nice, she thought, that Morten volunteered the information. Usually he wasn't that talkative in regard to personal matters.

Still, he didn't spend much time on his account of his family before he looked at his watch. "I think we have to get going if we hope to track down our fugitives today," he said, getting to his feet.

Quickly they packed their things. Then they were off again.

11 • The log in the water

They clambered up another hill. They had realized their search was easier from an elevation where they were able to overlook the mountains and the plains.

Finally reaching the top, Morten again brought out his binoculars and checked out every hill and valley. Mette sat down on the flat bedrock. She was tired after having climbed all those steep slopes. It felt good to take a rest at the top.

"I really don't understand this." Morten examined the area again and again. "Where could they be?" He lowered his binoculars and looked into the distance. "Where should we go now? We have walked around these plateaus almost in a circle. If we now continue toward the south, we will be back at the seter within an hour or two."

He looked at his watch. It was almost five in the afternoon. "What do you think?" He looked directly at Mette. "Should we head back? Then we will be back at the seter well before dark. Or should we hike a little farther to the east? Maybe they managed to cross the stream over there in that valley."

He pointed toward a valley east of where they stood. It would be a tough climb to get up those hillsides. "Do you think the heifers could have climbed up there, even if they managed to get across the stream?"

Mette looked doubtful. Morten, too, looked hesitant.

They discussed the various possibilities. It was impossible to know exactly where to search. Even if Mette felt tired after hiking all day, she didn't want to return to the seter yet. The weather was ideal. The clouds in the sky hadn't blocked the sunshine for some time now. But neither was the heat too oppressive, for a brisk breeze swept across the mountains and cooled their sweaty bodies. At least, it felt good at this elevation.

After a rest, Morten took his binoculars and walked a little way across the flat bedrock. Mette rose, too, and followed him.

Suddenly he stopped with a jerk. "What was that?" He stood still, listening.

Then Mette also heard a sound. It came from somewhere far below. Quickly they put on their backpacks and headed in the direction of the sound. Soon they reached an area where the mountain ended in a cliff overlooking a valley. They stood at the edge of the cliff, looking down. Below them they saw a sparkling little mountain lake almost abutting the side of the cliff.

Again they heard the odd sound. Now they were able to make out the short bellow of a cow.

"Look over there!" Morten called out in alarm, pointing to some bushes at the water's edge. There was a cow, staring anxiously at the lake. Now it moved to one side, now to another. It looked as if it might jump into the water at any time.

"Is that one of your heifers?" Mette studied its strange behavior with increasing concern.

"I'm pretty sure it is." Morten studied her through his binoculars.

"It looks as if she is interested in the log out there in the water," said Mette, point-ing toward something floating, almost immersed, in the lake.

Morten let his binoculars sweep across the surface of the water. Suddenly he called out again. "Log? Did you say log?"

Mette looked at him in alarm. Why the urgency in his voice over a mere log?

"I tell you, that is no log!" he cried in distress. "That is the other heifer. It is almost completely submerged in the lake down there. I am pretty sure those are my heifers."

They both took off in a hurry. Farther on stretched a crevasse where the mountain slope was a little less steep. "I think we'll be able to get down here," said Morten. They were straight above the location where the heifer lay.

"Look here!" He pointed down the slope in amazement. Mette came closer. She no-ticed that moss and lichen had been torn off in big sheets. They continued downward. And all the way down there was clear evidence of someone being there before them.

"The heifer must have fallen down here," Morten said.

"But how in the world did she manage to get up here?" Mette looked at the steep ravines in bewilderment.

Morten stopped and pointed toward the south. "Over there it is not that steep. She probably came up over there."

Every so often, Mette had to get down on her backside to keep from sliding down too fast. Her backpack was difficult to control, too.

Continued nervous lowing was heard from the distressed heifer at the edge of the lake. The "log" in the water also emitted some anguished sounds.

When they reached the edge of the lake, the gravity of the situation revealed itself to Mette in all its horror. She felt herself tremble as she stood watching the animal that was almost submerged in the water. Only a head and parts of a back were visible.

"How did she get so far out?" she wondered.

"She probably struggled to get up," offered Morten. "That probably moved her farther out. The water is quite shallow here, but the bottom is a thick layer of mud. She's probably stuck in the mud."

He tore off his backpack and started digging out some of the gear he had brought along. "Fortunately I brought a lot of rope. I reckon we're going to put it to good use now."

When the other heifer spotted them, she greeted them with long bellows. Then she came running and almost knocked Morten to the ground.

Mette had to laugh. "At least there is no doubt these are your heifers," she said. "This one obviously knows you very well."

Morten looked at the anxious animal. Then he looked at the lake again. "The one out there is the one about to have her calf," he said, his voice worried.

"How are we going to get her back up?" asked Mette. She watched the poor animal doubtfully.

After some planning, they agreed to try to pull her toward the bank with the rope. If they both swam out, they would figure out what had to be done.

Quickly, they changed into their swimsuits. For Mette this was an easy task, for she was wearing hers under her other clothes. She had hoped to get a swim in a lake or some other suitable place during their hike. Never did she imagine that it would happen under such traumatic circumstances.

With the coil of rope over his shoulder, Morten started swimming out to the heifer. Mette needed a little more time to get into the chilly water. But soon she was on her way out, too. Swimming in this lake wasn't easy. She hit the muddy bottom often with her legs, sending black clouds of sediment billowing to the surface.

When Morten reached the heifer, he fastened the rope around her neck. "Can you hold this?" he asked when Mette got close enough. He handed her the coil of rope. She grasped it while struggling to keep her legs out of the heaviest mud.

Suddenly the heifer started thrashing with her entire body. She swept her head about her, water splashing around them. It caught Morten unprepared, so he fell on his back and disappeared under water. He waved his arms and created a huge spray. For a chaotic moment, the entire lake around them was in turmoil. Waves hit Mette's face. She breathed in quickly and swallowed a big gulp of water.

She felt as though a moist, cold claw were gripping her. Panic engulfed her. What happened in her childhood again became vivid in her mind. Her entire body went rigid, and she wasn't able to think clearly. Another breath forced another gulp of water into her throat. Her arms struck frantically against the surface. The mud whirled around her and splashed up in the air. "I'm dying!" The thought was there all at once.

Then she felt an arm around her shoulders. Gently but firmly, she was pulled against a strong shoulder. Morten's calm voice whispered against her hair: "It is all right. Just take it easy."

Slowly she felt the panic let go of her. Her muscles gradually relaxed and she allowed her head to rest against his reassuring form. She gasped, and a shiver went through her entire body. It lasted only for a moment. Then Morten gently let go of her and everything was as before.

"Can you take this rope and swim toward land?" Morten handed her the rope as if nothing had happened. "If you swim over there," he said, pointing to an area where a promontory stretched into the lake, "then we can try to pull her in over there. The water is a little deeper over by those rocks, and the bottom by the bank there is a bit firmer."

Mette took the rope and swam toward land. Morten had tied two ropes together, making one long rope.

"When I let you know, you have to pull gently at the rope," he called when he saw she was safely on land.

Mette fetched a towel and laid it across her shoulders, then sat down to wait for her cue. She looked around her. There was more space where she now sat, although it was within seven or eight yards of the area where the cliff rose almost vertically. The bank of the lake was grassy, with occasional rocks. She looked up at the crevasse where they had come down. The lush grass growing there probably had tempted the heifer, and then she had slipped and gone down.

It was a beautiful place. The lake looked idyllic in its mountainous surroundings. Some small, straggly birches grew around the banks. The entire area around the lake was accessible, so they wouldn't have any problems getting out of there with the animals.

If the circumstances weren't so dramatic, she would have enjoyed the scenery by the lake. But now she wasn't able to concentrate on anything but what was going on at the other end of the rope. She could see that Morten had his work cut out for him out there with the heifer. Again and again he dived under water. He pushed and lifted, but the poor animal remained nearly submerged in the lake. Now he was on one side of the heifer, now on the other.

"You have to try to pull now," he suddenly called.

Mette scrambled to her feet and pulled the rope taut. But there was no sign that the heavy body was moving. Rather, the heifer's head was being pulled under water.

Again Morten disappeared. Mette thought it took forever before he reappeared. But finally his head broke the surface.

"I can't see a thing in this mud," he called. "But she seems to have hurt her leg. It is completely stuck in the mud. Obviously she hasn't been able to move it. I think I was able to loosen it a little. Now try pulling again."

Once more she pulled the rope. First, nothing seemed to happen. But then there was a tug at the rope, and slowly the heavy animal body moved closer to land. Morten pushed as much as he could. Little by little, they got into deeper water. From there, everything was easier.

The heifer wasn't able to move much. She didn't make much noise, either. Looking completely exhausted, she must have been struggling for a long time.

When they approached the bank where the bottom was firmer, it became obvious to them that she had injured her leg. She couldn't put any weight on it at all. Exhaustion was probably part of the reason. She tried to get her forelegs on firm ground, but fell forward in the water. For a moment, she struggled frantically to support herself with her good leg.

It was a battle, both for the heifer and her two helpers, to get her on land. But with great effort, they succeeded. Almost lifeless, the injured animal lay on the ground with her leg sticking straight out from her body. Her head rested on the ground and her tongue hung out of her mouth.

"Poor animal." Mette bent over and stroked her head and neck. The heifer didn't pay any attention to her at all.

Morten found his blanket and placed it over the soaking wet animal before he changed into dry, warm clothes. Mette got dressed, too. She noticed that Morten was shivering after his long stay in the water. It was obvious that the struggle had worn him out, too.

She filled a cup with coffee from the thermos and handed it to him.

"How are you doing?" she asked, sitting down next to him on the grass.

"Thank you," he said, grabbing the hot coffee cup. "I'm doing fine." He smiled a little wearily. "I just have to get my breath back. This was a tough job."

They sat in silence for a while. The other heifer had calmed down and was grazing farther from the bank. The lake was again quiet and still. Only a few muddy tracks told about the hard struggle they just had been through together.

12 • *Caesar*

Morten drank his coffee while he continued to study the animal lying on the ground. He was still quiet, but Mette noticed there was a lot going on in his mind. The deep creases between his eyes revealed that he was facing an important decision.

Mette didn't say anything, either. In a way, there were no words for the situation in which they found themselves. Nor did she know what to say. She had never experienced a more desperate situation.

So there they were. For more than an hour they worked on the heifer. They had managed to get her back on land, but her condition was as bad as it could be. In any case, it was impossible to bring her back home in her current condition. It was already after 6, and soon it would be nightfall. Mette sighed to herself. The situation was desperate. She didn't know what to say.

Suddenly Morten stood up. He lifted the blanket aside and started examining the seemingly lifeless body. A small movement of the head told them the animal was still alive after all. Time and again, convulsions racked her huge body. Morten put his ear to her chest to listen to her heartbeat. Then he stroked the large middle part of her body with both hands. Again and again, he let his hands glide across the heifer's belly.

When he sat down again, the creases between his eyes were if possible even deeper. "She is alive," he said, "But I don't think she will last long. She probably has hurt more than her leg. She will probably have to be put down. What worries me is that we then will kill the calf inside her, too. I clearly could feel that it is alive, and it is nearly fully developed."

He stared ahead while he talked. Mette felt something knotting inside her. She was no stranger to animals being put to sleep. She had experienced that many times during her childhood at their home farm. But this was somewhat different. The heifer would suffer if she was just left there. The best thing they could possibly do for her would be to put her down. But the calf … It seemed so senseless.

She got to her feet and walked over to take a closer look at her. "When is the calf

41

due?" she asked.

Morten came over, too. "It would have been born within a week," he said.

Carefully, Mette placed her hand on the big belly.

"Feel here," said Morten.

Mette allowed her hand to slide down to the spot he pointed out to her. There she could feel movement. A deep compassion for the little unborn creature filled her.

"Is there anything we can do?" Her tears were not far away. She had to swallow a couple of times to make her voice sound normal.

Morten wasn't unaffected, either. He didn't reply right away, but examined the spot thoroughly for a while.

Finally he straightened and looked directly at Mette. "If you will help me, we can give it a try."

"Yes …" She hesitated a little. "What do you want me to do?" Her voice had turned almost to a whisper. She trembled slightly. What was he planning that required her help?

Morten walked around the heifer a couple of times, studying her from all angles before he continued. "We have to try to cut out the calf."

Mette gave a sob.

Morten looked directly at her again. "Do you think you will be able to help me?"

Two terrified eyes met his. She wasn't able to answer. She trembled even more.

Morten lowered his eyes again. It was as if all strength and courage left him. His voice, too, was only a whisper as he continued. "Of course, it is too much to ask. Sorry. There probably isn't much we can do here."

Then Mette felt her courage rise and experienced a strength from a source she couldn't name. She straightened.

In a clear, firm voice she said: "Of course, I'm going to help you. If there is something we can do to save the calf, then let's do it."

Morten looked at her in surprise. A flicker of renewed hope instantly lit up his eyes. "Do you think we can do it?" His words still came out in a whisper.

"Just tell me what to do, and we'll give it a try." Her body wouldn't quite stop shaking, but she was determined to do her best.

Morten stood up quickly. Again he started examining the heifer.

"Her pulse is weak, but she is still alive," he said. "Did you bring a knife in your backpack?"

Mette thought about it for a moment. "I have the knife that we used to cut up our food. I'm afraid it's just a bread knife."

"That will have to do," said Morten. He was busy examining the heifer's belly. "I have a sheath knife in my backpack. We'll have to try working with what we have."

Mette found the knives and Morten rubbed them against each other to sharpen them as much as possible. Mette tensed with anticipation.

Morten gave her the bread knife and crouched down by the heifer's head.

"When I let you know, can you plunge the knife deeply in there?" He pointed to a spot on the animal's neck.

Mette felt something roiling somewhere deep in her belly. But she swallowed hard and sat resolutely down next to him.

"Was it there?" she pointed to make sure that she had gotten it right. Morten nodded and turned toward the middle section of the animal. Again he explored her belly with his hand. Mette was so preoccupied focusing on the point on the neck she was about to puncture that she didn't even notice what Morten was doing.

"Are you ready?" Morten's voice was strained to the limit.

"Yes, I am ready." Mette's entire body was tense. With every fiber of her body she was concentrating on the small point there on the neck.

"Do it!"

In the same instant, the long blade of the knife sank deep into the animal's neck. She was totally unprepared for what happened next. The heifer shivered and jerked while the blood spurted straight up in the air. A muffled scream escaped her as her entire arm, face and parts of her chest were colored red by the thick, warm liquid.

She rose quickly and wiped her eyes, removing enough blood to be able to see clearly again. For a moment she stood swaying. The contents of her stomach didn't want to stay down. But a couple of deep breaths of brisk mountain air seemed to settle things down.

Finally, she was able to turn her attention to what was going on next to her. She looked at Morten. He was on his knees, both arms buried deeply in the dead animal's body. Quickly, he pulled out a big sack consisting of bloody membranes. He cut open the birth sack, and a disheveled, wet calf appeared.

He worked quickly and with great concentration. Soon, all traces of its former protected existence were removed from the calf. Mette drew closer and examined the little one lying on the grass. It appeared to be completely lifeless. Morten gave it a few slaps and tried to clean out more mucus and membranes from its mouth and nose. It didn't seem to help much. It was still as lifeless as before.

Mette felt the lump in her throat was about to burst. Was it all in vain? It had been alive a minute ago; she had registered that herself.

Then Morten bent over and put his lips on the muzzle of the calf. With long breaths, he forced air into the mucus-filled nostrils. Mette grabbed her towel and with shaking hands started massaging the wet body. They worked in silence for a while, both of them concentrating on their job.

Suddenly a gurgling sound escaped the calf, and they heard a weak sound from its mouth. They both stared at it in breathless suspense. Another little "moo" sounded, while it weakly shook its head.

"It is alive!" exclaimed Mette.

At this point the other heifer joined them. She obviously had registered that something was going on down by the bank of the lake and wanted to join in. She didn't seem to notice her dead friend at all. But she showed great interest in the newborn calf. She sniffed it a little. Then she started getting excited. With quick nods, she nuzzled the little wet bundle. Her long, rough tongue quickly started an efficient cleaning process.

"She doesn't think I did a good job," Mette said with a shaky laughter.

Morten pulled back, too. "I think she knows how to do this better than we do," he said.

Now the calf lifted its head and shook it, ears flying. Mette laughed. She could feel that her face was completely wet. She also realized that it was due neither to the blood from the dead heifer nor the water she had been swimming in. The lump in her throat had simply burst without her noticing. Her entire face was drenched with tears.

"It is alive!" Her feeling of joy increased her flow of tears even more. Morten smiled, too. They looked at each other.

43

For an instant they stood there in stunned surprise. Then they both burst out laughing. What a sight! Mette spotted with blood everywhere. Down her face, her tears had made stripes in the clotted blood. Clothes and hair looked as if she had been swimming in a pool of blood.

Morten didn't look much better. His arms and chest were covered with mucus and blood. All of it had ended up in his lap. Mette thought he was never going to get those pants clean again.

"I had to put on whatever clothes I could find before I started this job," said Morten. "I didn't have time to bring my washing board, either."

Again they were overcome with laughter. They went over to the bank of the lake and washed the worst of it off their faces and arms. Then they sat down on the grass. They looked at the heifer, which painstakingly licked the calf all over. Soon, though, she seemed to feel enough was enough, for she went down to the lake to take a drink.

The calf lay motionless on the ground. It lifted its head now and then, so there was life in it. But otherwise, it looked weak. Morten fetched the blanket he had used on its mother. He wrapped it carefully around the newborn.

"Do you think it will make it?" Mette looked worriedly at the little bundle.

"I don't know." Morten looked worried, too. "It depends on whether we will be able to feed it."

"Feed it!" Mette looked at him in consternation. "What kind of food can we find for it here?"

"The way it looks now, we won't be able to feed it at all," offered Morten. "It's too weak to be moved, too. I think we just have to stay here for a while and watch how it is doing. Then we have to carry it down to the seter. We have plenty of milk for it there."

Again they sat watching the little creature lying on the blanket, fighting a battle of life and death.

"It is so cute," said Mette after a while. "Is it a boy or a girl?"

Morten smiled. "It is a boy. That much I was able to figure out. But he is very small. That, by the way, can be a plus on our way back. If we have to carry him all the way home, he will certainly be heavy enough."

He turned to Mette. Now he looked earnest again. "You did a great job today. Thank you so much!"

Mette smiled. A feeling of joy filled her. They did it! Even if the calf wouldn't make it, at least they had done what they could.

"You were an excellent surgeon," she laughed. "Imagine, a Caesarean section in the middle of the wilderness!" Suddenly she stopped and looked excitedly at him. "Do you know what I think? If this little creature survives, he should be named Caesar."

Morten laughed. "That is a most suitable name. Let's call him that."

13 • Sunrise

Mette twisted and turned. Never had she slept on a worse mattress. It was absolutely impossible to sleep. Darkness had descended on mountains and plateaus some time ago. From somewhere nearby, she heard the faint sound of waves splashing against the rocks along the bank. She also heard Morten's easy breathing. He was asleep, no doubt about it. If there was anything he needed now, it was sleep. The events of the day had worn him out, that much she knew.

She turned again. The branches she had broken up to fashion a bed for herself felt like knives on her sore back. It might have been better to sleep directly on the ground like Morten did. She glimpsed his outline nearby in the dark. He had placed himself up against the calf, to keep the newborn warm and to share the blanket that was draped around him.

Mette had snuggled close to the cliff wall as shelter against any wind that should kick up during the night. But she needn't have worried; the night was warm and calm for this altitude. Morten had mentioned to her that they had experienced a surprisingly warm period during the time she had been at the seter. Evidently it wasn't always this nice. In any case, she was grateful they didn't have weather-related problems in addition to everything else on this trip. They had troubles enough already.

So here she was, in the middle of the night, at the foot of a cliff wall. On one side of her were a dead heifer and a newborn calf. On the other, the living heifer had bedded down. Every living being in this mountainous void seemed to be sleeping—except Mette.

After adjusting the birch branches under her, she closed her eyes again in a brave attempt to get some sleep. But then all the thoughts came.

The events of the night churned around in her head: the heifer out in the water, the terrible moment when her fear of water overwhelmed her, and the wonderful feeling that replaced her terror—the moment she rested against Morten's safe shoulder. She could still feel the warmth deep inside when she thought about it.

Then there was the heifer, the blood, the calf. She was determined to write it all down in her diary as soon as she got back to the seter. Every night she had recorded in that book the events in which she had participated. Her experiences on this trip would provide material for several pages.

As the minutes turned into hours, Mette's body grew stiffer and sorer.

Finally, she sat up. If sleep didn't come, it would be no use trying. Over toward the east she could see the sky growing lighter. The darkness surrounding her wasn't that dense any more. Wearily, she got up. The uncomfortable bed was not the only thing making her so stiff; the soreness also came from her exertions the day before.

Cautiously she started climbing the crevasse she and Morten had come down. The sky looked completely clear, and Mette thought a sunrise above these mountains would surely be a fantastic experience. The view would be incredible.

The climb took some time, for she had to position her feet carefully in the dim light. There was little to hold on to if she were to slip.

When she finally reached the top, her efforts were rewarded with a panorama that made her gasp. The sun was still not visible above the mountains to the east, but the long rays of daybreak created an extraordinary shadow effect over the mountainous landscape.

She stood watching the awe-inspiring scenery for a long time. Slowly, the peaks took on a golden hue in the bright glow from the horizon. The mountain slopes and valleys were still sheathed in muted shadows.

In several places, a woolly fog covered the streams and lakes. Columns of fog rose in several areas along the mountain slopes as well. She smiled as she remembered Morten's explanation for this phenomenon the previous morning. No wonder humans of the past were trapped in a world of their imagination. Living so close to nature, they probably experienced similar phenomena often. And imagination might play tricks on anyone under such circumstances.

She sat down on a flat rock resting on the mountain plateau while a strange emotion filled her. The air was cooler up here than down by the lake. It was windier as well, so she pulled her jacket more tightly around her. But the feeling of being a tiny part of this immensity gave wings to her thoughts.

The shadows shifted as the light grew stronger and brighter. The golden peaks contrasted sharply with the dark mountain slopes and valleys.

As she sat there watching the ever-changing effect of the light, she understood the fears this might cause in people who believed in creatures from the netherworld and supernatural phenomena. It must have seemed so real for people who believed, for example, that the *hulder*—beautiful women with cows' tails—might appear in a place like this and lure some miserable wretch into the mountain. It wouldn't be hard to convince someone who didn't know better, that this was a fact of life.

A peaceful smile drifted across her face. She was so grateful hers was a different truth. She knew of Someone who had conquered all those evil forces and horrors. Someone who had risen on a bright morning after having been entombed for a dark day and night, dead in a grave. This man was Jesus Christ. Because of His victory over darkness, she had nothing to fear. Without realizing it, she burst into song:

Jesus lever, graven brast!
Han sto opp med guddoms velde.
Trøsten står som klippen fast
at Hans død og blod skal gjede.
Lynet blinker, Jorden bever.
Graven brast, og Jesus lever!

Jeg har vunnet, Jesus vant,
døden oppslukt er til seier.
Jesus mørkets fyrste bandt,
jeg den kjøpte frihet eier.
Åpen har jeg Himlen funnet,
Jesus vant og jeg har vunnet!

Jesus lives! The victory's won!
Death no longer can appall me;
Jesus lives! Death's reign is done!
From the grave Christ will recall me.
Brighter scenes will then commence;
This shall be my confidence.

46

Jesus lives! I know full well
Naught from me His love shall sever;
Life nor death nor powers of hell
Part me now from Christ forever.
God will be a sure Defense;
This shall be my confidence.

The words came so wonderfully alive. It was as if in that precise moment, she experienced its reality. The clear rays of the rising sun were a monumental symbol of Jesus' divine powers over darkness and evil forces, represented by the fog and the dark shadows between the mountains.

Little by little, the light gained the upper hand. The minutes passed, but she sat watching the transformation without paying attention to the time. She wanted to drink in every ray and allow it to bring life and warmth to her frozen body.

She sat there, enjoying her feeling of absolute tranquility. This moment she would carry with her forever. It was as if Jesus were with her in the light and gave her a glimpse of eternal truths. The peace she felt filled her with an incredible joy.

Suddenly a sound rose up to her. It was the long lowing from a cow. Mette stood up quickly. It was as if she were awakened from a dream, yet the peace and the truths that were revealed to her still seemed real.

When she reached the edge of the cliff, she saw the heifer grazing along the edge of the lake. Morten sat upright, but she wasn't able to clearly see what he was doing. Quickly, she started her descent. Several times she wondered how she had managed to climb this crevasse in the dark. Once she had almost fallen, clinging to some heather to keep from sliding.

When she got back down by the lake, she saw that Morten was tending to the calf. The animal lay in Morten's lap while he petted the newborn's head and neck. The calf had three of Morten's fingers in his mouth and was sucking hungrily.

Morten looked up at her and smiled as she came closer. "What do you say, doesn't he look frisky now?" he said.

Mette looked at them in astonishment. Then she fell on her knees next to them and put her head against the neck of the little animal.

"How beautiful you are, Caesar," she whispered in his little ear.

Morten laughed. "It really looks like he is going to make it," he said. "Now we just have to get him down to the seter so he can enjoy some life-giving drops of milk. Missi's mother can probably spare a few."

Mette looked at her watch. It was just past 6 a.m. "When do you think we'll be down there?" she asked.

"I'm not really sure," Morten looked a little concerned. "It depends on how often we have to take a rest. But I hope we'll make it in a couple of hours."

They started getting ready for their return trip.

"We'll only bring what's absolutely necessary," he said. "I will have to come up here again to bury the dead heifer. Then I can bring back the stuff we won't be able to carry now."

They put what they thought they would need into Mette's backpack. Morten emptied his completely. "We have to try to put the calf in it," he said.

It was quite a job to get Caeser into the backpack, but they soon managed. Mette

47

helped Morten get the knapsack onto his back. The front part of the calf stuck up over the rim. They placed the baby's forelegs across Morten's shoulders so he could hold on to them across his chest. They also tied a rope around the calf so he wouldn't fall out if he started struggling. Then they set off for the seter.

They walked along the edge of the lake toward the east. "Over there at the end of the lake is a sloping valley," said Morten. "It's the same one that goes down to the Siljatjern. We can just follow it. Walking is pretty easy down there."

Morten walked in front with the calf on his back. The heifer followed him. Mette finished up the parade. She had to make sure the heifer followed them and stayed on the trail.

The return hike went well. The calf kept still, inspecting his new surroundings. Now and then he made a leap, but being unable to get out, he soon lay quietly again.

Abruptly, Morten stopped and cried out in surprise. Then he started laughing. Wet spots appeared on his behind and trousers.

"I didn't know that anything wet could come out of this poor little creature. After all, he still hasn't gotten anything on board."

Mette had to laugh, too. "Nature takes its toll, you know," she said.

The pair didn't take many breaks. They wanted to reach the seter as soon as possible. It was also easier to guide the heifer when they kept going.

They followed an old path. Morten said it was often used in the past when the seters in the area kept lots of livestock. Herders from various areas used it for bringing their livestock to the mountain pastures. In later years, it was mostly used during the hunting season.

Mette didn't get much of an opportunity to enjoy the landscape around her. She was occupied with keeping the heifer on the trail. A couple of times the heifer tried to veer off the path, so Mette had to scramble to turn her around.

When they finally caught sight of the Siljatjern between some bushes and trees, Mette took a breath of relief. The effects of her sleepless night were beginning to take their toll. It would feel good to curl up under a soft comforter. After all, it was her day off. So she didn't have to worry about her chores.

The heifer bellowed several times as they got closer to the cow barn. She obviously knew she was close to other specimens of her race. At the same time, Petter appeared in the door to the cow barn. He carried milk pails in both hands. When he saw the approaching party, he stopped so abruptly that milk splashed out of the pails. Two horrified eyes stared at them. Mette looked down at her clothes and quickly realized what had shocked him so much. No wretch should be exposed to such a gory sight that early in the morning. They had to laugh.

"What on earth has happened to you?" he cried when they got closer. Morten walked over to the cow barn to put down his load, then started recounting events. Mette realized she was no longer needed. Relieved, she entered the seter house.

After a quick cleanup, she dived into bed. She had completely forgotten that she hadn't eaten anything since the night before. Sleep overcame her before she had time to turn to the wall.

14 • Chamber-pot blue

Early on Friday morning, Aunt Anna was back at her post at the seter house. She had gotten word about their adventure in the mountains, so her mouth worked harder than ever. Mette was glad the older woman was so skilled at combining her talking with the work at hand. If not, Mette feared they wouldn't get much done that day. Still, it was enjoyable to have her back. She had missed her cheerful laughter and quick replies the last few days.

On the agenda for the day was working with wool and, in particular, demonstrating the dyeing process to their guests. Aunt Anna had prepared a huge pile of wool. It was lying in the middle of the floor. Several large pots were placed by the fire pit near the steep rocky slope behind the seter house. Mette brought over several armfuls of wood. The grate covering the fire pit was large enough to hold three to four pots at the same time. Aunt Anna stretched a clothesline between the seter house and a tree by the rocky slope.

"Here we can hang the wool out to dry after the dyeing," she said. "It will be nice and shady here in the afternoon."

They heated water and poured it into a big tub. In it, Aunt Anna placed an armful of wool.

"Are the people we're expecting today from town?" Mette asked as they sat down with a cup of coffee after all the preparations were finished.

"No," said Aunt Anna. "They are from another community, but it is not very far from here. We may expect them at any time now. I believe we have the first ones already."

She rose in a hurry and walked over to meet the car that drove up to the house as she spoke. Mette followed. Warm greetings were exchanged between Aunt Anna and the two women who exited the car. It was obvious they knew each other well.

"Come on and meet our dairymaid," she said.

When Mette was introduced to the two newcomers, she found out they were not from the home craft organization. One was Morten's sister, Marit; the other was her friend, Ellen. Marit owned one of the campers that was parked in the campground. The two of them wanted to spend some vacation time at the seter.

Mette and the two women soon found common ground. Before long they were all eagerly chatting away.

It didn't take long before the guests from the neighboring community arrived. Fourteen women and a few kids poured out of the cars now parked in the campground. Mette had set out some tables and chairs in the meadow. Everyone was invited to have a cup of coffee and get some in-depth information before they got on with the work.

Aunt Anna obviously enjoyed immensely the opportunity to be able to talk incessantly to such a large group of interested listeners. First she talked about her childhood at the farm. Her mother had been especially interested in this kind of work. From her she had learnt everything she now was about to show them.

Then she talked a little about caring for and shearing sheep.

When spinning the wool, she told them, it should always be done before it was washed. The wool fat, lanolin, helped make the spinning much easier, she said. Thus her mother always used to spin the wool before she dyed it. Now Aunt Anna hadn't managed to spin as much wool as they would need for the dyeing, so today they were just going to dye wool that had not yet been spun. And if they wanted to use the wool for felting, it shouldn't be spun anyway.

She had washed the wool very carefully. This was important for all kinds of dyeing. She explained what kind of detergent should be used, and how the water had to be prepared both in terms of temperature and calcium carbonate ratio.

Everybody listened closely. Sometimes a question was interposed, and Aunt Anna gladly told them anything they wanted to know. There wasn't a thing she didn't know.

"Before we start the work, I would like to explain a little bit about the process," she continued. "It is always important to use young plants. Down at the farm we used to say they had to be collected before St. John's Day—the first day of summer. The young shoots contain the freshest and most concentrated dyeing compound. Up here we can probably wait until later in the summer, for spring arrives considerably later here. You may, of course, pick the plants in the spring and dry them for use later in the year, but then the colors don't turn out quite the same. Most of the plants should be picked in dry weather, so we have ideal conditions right now.

"The first thing we have to do is to *mordant* the wool. I have bought something called *alum mordant*. It has to simmer slowly with the wool for an hour. This mordant helps fix the color to the wool fibers. While it simmers, you may set out to find plants for the dyeing. Actually, the wool needs to soak for quite a long time in the mordant. It has to be cooled in the water in which it was boiled. We'll see how long we'll be able to allow it to soak today, since we only have this one day available to us."

This was a lot of information at once. Some made notes in order to get it all.

Aunt Anna separated them into four smaller groups. Each group was told what kind of plant they were to look for. One group was to gather birch leaves and another to find some juniper. She reminded them that it was important that they only pick the young juniper shoots.

Another group was to locate a certain type of moss. She had a small clump of moss lying on the table to show them what kind of moss they would be looking for. The fourth group was to pick heather.

The entire group trekked over to the pots to watch how the mordant was applied. Aunt Anna measured up the alum and dissolved it in one of the pots of water. Then she placed the soaked wool in the water with the added mordant. She made sure the new water was the same temperature as the water in which the wool had been soaking. She cautioned against adding too much wool to the pot, as it needed to float freely.

"We mustn't pack it in," she said. "Then the coloring may turn out to be uneven. Now this has to be heated up slowly."

After they had prepared the wool for the mordant, everybody spread out to find the required plants. Some set off toward the lake, while others hiked up the hill. Mette stayed behind to help Aunt Anna. She followed everything with growing interest. Frequently she had to bring out pen and paper. She wanted to make sure she got the entire procedure. Aunt Anna chirped along the entire time. There were so many details to remember that Mette became disoriented now and then. She had to ask repeatedly.

"You keep saying we have to boil this wool," she said, watching the large pots in puzzlement. "I didn't know you could boil wool at all."

Aunt Anna laughed while she stirred the pot. "If you boil your woolen sweater, you will get an unpleasant surprise," she said. "But this wool is to be carded afterward.

Then it will get back its fluffiness. And if we boil the spun yarn, it will turn out all right, we just have to be careful with the heating and cooling. It has to be done slowly. We shouldn't work it too much while it's in the pot, either. And the drying process must be slow. That is why we hang it to dry in the shade. Especially the last part of the drying process must be done slowly."

While they waited for the plant gatherers to return, Mette took a stroll around the meadow. One of the lambs came running over to the fence when it discovered her. Obviously it hoped to be fed something good from her hand. She hadn't brought anything, but she went in and lifted the soft animal into her lap. With one hand she patted its curly wool while scratching behind its ears with the other. They sat on the grass, enjoying each other's company for a long time. It was hard to say whether Mette or the lamb enjoyed this the most. Again, she felt the wonderful satisfaction of being surrounded by such a harmonious atmosphere. She had rarely experienced such peace.

Over by the tables she saw Morten visiting with Ellen. It was obvious they knew each other well. They laughed and seemed to enjoy each other's company immensely.

A shadow passed over Mette's face. Who was this Ellen, anyway? A friend of Marit's, they told her. But what about Morten? Maybe it was … No, he had never said anything about having a girlfriend.

Mette thought about this some more. What did she really know about Morten? He had told her a great deal about his family, the seter and the farm animals, but he never said much about himself. She knew he was a Christian, but little about him personally. What he felt and thought, he kept pretty much to himself.

The day they hiked the mountains they had talked comfortably while they stopped for their lunch break, but it was mostly she who did the talking. Morten had listened with interest to everything she told him. What little he told her was mostly about his parents and his family. And she didn't have the gall to ask him close, personal questions if he didn't volunteer information.

He was in no way like Aunt Anna. One didn't have to spend much time with her before one knew precisely what was going on under her headscarf. No, Morten was very different.

Mette looked at them as they sat together. They didn't seem to notice their surroundings. Both demonstrated a vivid interest in what the other was saying. They appeared to discuss something very special.

"Morten has never shown such confidence in me," she suddenly thought, but felt ashamed of herself right away. Why in the world would he do that? She was just the dairymaid at his seter. Their only connection was work.

Slowly she rose and joined Aunt Anna in the seter house. She was anxious to get some information from her about this Ellen, but didn't dare say anything. Besides, Aunt Anna talked non-stop about the food they were to prepare for the guests upon their return. They would serve the usual *rømmegrøt*—sour cream porridge. Mette soon realized she had better concentrate on that. She would figure things out as time went by.

Soon, one guest after another returned with shopping bags filled with plants. The birch leaves and chopped heather were both placed in pots and set to boil. Aunt Anna had also put some wool in water that already had mordant added to it.

"This wool we can start to dye right away," she said. "By the way, the wool that is to be dyed with juniper doesn't need the mordant. The color of the juniper fixes itself to the fibers as it is, so we can start dyeing it right away."

The juniper was chopped and layered with the wool in a huge copper pot. This was also placed over the fire right away. "Now it can sit here and boil while we eat," said Aunt Anna.

During the meal, Mette frequently had to check that the pots kept a steady simmer. The pile of wood she had carried over in the morning was steadily getting smaller. Soon she would have to get a few more armfuls.

They all enjoyed themselves out in the meadow. The children went repeatedly over to the lambs. The calves got visits, too. Caesar had recovered remarkably during the days he had stayed at the seter. He and Missi got along well, and Missi's mother took care of the new calf as if he were her own. Both were allowed to suckle the old cow. The children loved the animals.

After the meal, Aunt Anna showed them samples of wool she had dyed at an earlier date. Most were balls of yarn, but she also had some wool. Her students were surprised at the clarity of the colors she had produced.

"This is dyed with alder bark," she said, holding up a ball of yarn with a sharp, greenish color. "For this I used lichen from firs," she said, holding up a light yellow ball of yarn.

A girl of around 10 buried herself in the basket, checking out the beautiful hues. She lifted out one with a clear, blue color. "Did you use blueberries to dye this?" she asked.

Aunt Anna laughed. "No, I didn't use blueberries," she answered. "That color is not found outside in nature. It is a color that I bought. In order to get that color blue, I have to use a mineral called *indigo*. It has to be dissolved in chemicals before it is added to the wool. But in the old days they used another method."

She rocked back and forth and laughed. "You may try it if you want. You would have to purchase the mineral. But in order to dissolve it, they used regular urine. That is why the color still is called 'chamber-pot blue.'"

The girl stared in horror at the old lady. "Did you try it?"

"Oh, yes. Of course, I had to try."

The blue ball of yarn fell to the ground immediately. "Yuck," she said, wrinkling her nose. She rubbed her hand intensely against her trouser leg.

Aunt Anna's cheerful laughter sounded again. "You can rest easy. I didn't pee on that particular yarn."

Everybody laughed. The girl breathed in relief, but didn't volunteer to pick up the yarn again.

It was an unusually pleasant afternoon. No one had problems passing the time while the wool and dyes boiled as long as required. They chatted continuously. Mette helped watch the timing of the various pots. After birch leaves and heather had finished boiling, the liquid was strained. In the resulting "soup," they placed the wool treated with mordant. Then this had to boil for another hour.

After everything had finished boiling, the wool had to be completely rinsed. Everybody worked hard. Aunt Anna talked about the modifications they could make to the process in order to bring out different hues. For instance, they would get different hues depending on whether they used a pot made of iron, aluminum or copper. They could also change a color by dipping the wool in a different "soup" when it was finished boiling in one.

Both Mette and the others took a lot of notes. Little by little, the questions turned more and more specific and complex. Several people expressed their wish to try this at home. They asked for Aunt Anna's phone number so they could call her if they had trouble with something.

As evening came around, several tufts of wool were still hanging on the clothesline behind the seter house. Aunt Anna said members of the class were welcome to take all the wool home. They might share it, and finish drying it at home.

It was late at night before the last guests left the seter. Mette noticed that Aunt Anna was tired, so she told her to just go to bed. Mette could clean up the rest on her own.

15 • *Wrong chemistry*

Morten stuck his head in the doorway to the cow barn. "Can you manage the seter chores on your own today?" he asked. "A friend of mine has come to see me. We would like to go fishing in the mountains."

"Sure," replied Mette. She stood petting Caesar with one hand while he eagerly sucked the fingers of the other. "There isn't much going on today, so that will be fine. You just go."

She continued to putter around the animals before she let them out. It was always such a joy to listen to their contented stirring and moaning as she tended to them.

When she finished her chores and the animals were grazing outside, Mette went over to the meadow and sat down in a chair to relax in the warm sun. She never tired of watching the scenic landscape surrounding the seter. The lake glittered as invitingly as the first time she saw it.

Up on the hillside behind the seter house she discovered some ptarmigans. When they became aware of her, they flapped their wings and took off toward the mountains and plateaus. A few woolly clouds floated in the blue sky. With her eyes she followed an eagle sailing on outstretched wings toward the mountains on the other side of the lake. Perhaps it had its nest there, she thought. She had noticed it circling the area several times, hunting for food.

With a contented sigh, she sat back in her chair. A comfortable drowsiness came over her. The sound of bells and the bleating of the sheep grazing peacefully on the hillside once again made her experience the complete contentment and harmony that she so often had felt here in the mountains.

Suddenly she sat up with a jerk. She had caught sight of two men coming down the trail. One was Morten; she recognized him. But the other one had something familiar about him, too. Suddenly the men stopped. Morten pointed toward the valley at the end of the lake. He was probably explaining which direction to take. So this was his friend. Yet there was something familiar about him …

Both men turned around while Morten continued to point along the mountains to the north. Mette felt herself stiffen. Now she saw his face, and there was no doubt about it. It was Tore. So Morten and Tore were friends …

A moment later the two men continued their hike and disappeared behind scrubs and underbrush by the edge of the lake.

Thoughts and feelings rushed through Mette's mind. Her main reason for getting away from the office for a while was Tore, her co-worker. The tense relationship that had developed between them had worn on her. She simply couldn't stand his arrogant way of dealing with her. And if he found that she had made an error, he never neglected to let her know. And now this man was here.

Quickly she got up and entered the seter house. She was alone, so she was free to plan her day and her work as she pleased. Although there were some tourists in the campground, they weren't scheduled for any demonstrations or programs that day. Thus the only thing she had to do was prepare for the next day.

Resolutely, she started what she needed to do. She wanted to get done as soon as possible. Then she would take the car and go to town. She wanted to be gone when they returned. She simply couldn't handle meeting Tore up here.

○ ○ ○

It was already later than the regular milking hour when she drove the car up in front of the seter house. Relieved, she registered that the visitor was gone, for there was no car outside. She found Morten inside behind a newspaper. He looked up as she entered. Mette didn't say anything at first. But her curiosity about how the two came to be friends soon made her ask that question. "So, I understand that you know Tore?"

Morten smiled in surprise. "So he is an acquaintance of yours?"

She didn't return his smile. Instead a sullen expression clouded her face. "Yes, and he is the most obnoxious man I know." An angry stamp of her foot revealed that she meant what she said.

Morten's smile disappeared slowly while he raised his eyebrows. The newspaper sank into his lap. "Oh, my," he said in his calm and deliberate manner. "He is actually one of my best friends. We got to know each other in the military, and since then we have kept in touch. How do you know him, since you have such a bad impression of him?"

"We actually work together," she said. And then everything she had been experiencing and feeling came out of her in a rush. How he carped at her if she made the slightest error, and the arrogant manner with which he treated her. She explained how this, in addition to their busy working environment, had been wearing her down to the point where she felt she couldn't take it anymore.

Morten sat listening in silence. When she finished venting, there was a moment of silence. Morten cleared his throat before he started speaking again. "I really think you must have misunderstood him. He is a picture of goodness. You are right in thinking he seems a little arrogant, but you shouldn't pay attention to it. It's just the way he is. Yes, it's simply his nature."

Mette felt something starting to boil inside her. She stepped closer and leaned toward him. Her light blue eyes flashed and her normally full lips were pressed together, forming a white line.

"Just the way he is?" her words rung out in a dangerously low range. "I'll tell you," she continued with considerably more intensity, "if you knew how it feels to always be reminded of how useless you are, I think you would say otherwise. To make excuses for a person by claiming he 'is just that way,' when he is out to destroy another person, is simply not acceptable."

She stopped momentarily. Morten fell silent, but he had a concerned look on his face. For a moment she glared at him with a ferocious look in her eye. Then she continued: "I really don't understand how you can be friends with such a guy."

Then she turned abruptly and stormed out the door.

In a second, she had the cows in the barn. The fury she felt made her work with a hurried intensity. She sat down on the stool and started milking. Fortunately, no tourists were there to watch. She didn't feel like company just then.

Suddenly, tears started streaming down her face and she was overcome by weeping. All the bad feelings returned: the feeling of inadequacy, the hurt of the repeated jabs at her sore points, the humiliation of being the target of taunts and patronizing, and now the feeling of not being understood by someone who had shown her understanding, warmth and respect.

Another feeling that bothered her was her own strong reaction to this. Why did she always get so angry? She was just creating trouble for herself. How many times had she been forced to go and ask someone's forgiveness just because of her fiery temperament? And now there was Morten …

She rested her head against the cow and allowed her tears to dampen the animal's warm belly. Useless, her hands fell into her lap. The pail was only half full, but she wasn't able to concentrate on her work anymore.

Now she became aware of something moving over by the door. It was Morten entering the cow barn silently. She looked up for a minute, but then sank back against the cow again.

"I just want to apologize for my clumsy behavior," he said quietly.

Mette looked at him in surprise. "You shouldn't be the one to apologize. It was I who overreacted," she said, perplexed.

"No," said Morten. "I didn't understand how deeply hurt you were. You and Tore are very different personalities, and it is not unheard of for disagreements to arise. It is something that should not be taken too lightly."

His words felt good to Mette. So he was capable of understanding, after all.

The cow moved softly. She clearly had noticed that the milking wasn't progressing according to custom. Without further warning, she kicked out with her leg and hit the pail so it rolled across the floor, spattering the milk in all directions.

Mette jumped to her feet in dismay. Her inner tension made her boil over again. "Can't you stand still, you miserable cow?" she cried, slapping her hand against the animal's behind. "That milk was for Aunt Anna to make *gome**."

"Yes, you just blame the cow," said Morten.

Mette noticed he was almost doubled over with laughter. But there was no irony or mockery in his voice. On the contrary, it sounded friendly and caring.

Mette sank down on the milking stool again. "Why can I never curb my temper?" she sighed. "Now I have to ask forgiveness of the cow, too."

Again Morten roared with laughter. She had to smile, too. How comfortable and liberating his laughter was.

Morten helped her finish the evening milking. Afterward, they sat down in the meadow. Mette still hurt from thinking of Tore's mistreatment. The days she had spent at the seter had helped her distance herself from the problem, but now everything came back, full force.

Morten was the first to break the silence. He talked about Tore, how they got to know each other, and how they had kept up their friendship ever since.

Mette listened in surprise while he described Tore as a somewhat touchy and easily wounded person. He usually compensated for this by being arrogant and abrupt. He was a good administrator and organizer of complicated projects. But in regard to meticulousness and accuracy in more detailed work, he probably felt inadequate.

He stopped for a moment and looked searchingly at Mette. She sat there in silence. It was hard for her to make this description fit Tore.

"You are probably Tore's opposite," Morten continued. "I can imagine he has felt inadequate and clumsy compared to your competence and meticulousness. Probably he felt that all his weaknesses were highlighted working with you. I can easily believe this would have led him to treat you that way."

"But I am neither meticulous nor very competent," said Mette, looking at him in shock. "That's the problem. He is always pointing out my shortcomings. I simply feel I'm unable to do anything right when I'm around him. He actually seems to gloat every time he catches me in a mistake."

"I really think he realizes that you are more competent than he is. That would be difficult for him to handle. That's why he probably gets some satisfaction from pointing out your mistakes."

They both sat quietly for a while. Mette understood what Morten was saying. When she thought about it, she had to admit he was right. But it was maddening to have to make excuses for this man who had upset her so often. She could point to innumerable instances when he had hurt her.

"If he really is the way you describe him, why is he behaving this way?" sighed Mette in despair.

Morten smiled. "This is what they mean when they talk about wrong chemistry," he said. "Sometimes this can cause great conflicts. And it isn't always easy to do anything about it except accepting each other as we are. I'm not so sure he has any idea that he has hurt you. Or maybe you have spoken to him about it?"

"No." Mette shook her head weakly. Just the thought of doing so freaked her out.

"It may be that it is wise not to have to deal with each other too much," Morten continued. "I don't think it is wrong to try to avoid conflicts and hurt feelings. But if you were able to stop taking to heart what he says, then I am sure the problem will diminish. It isn't always easy to try to change a person, you know. It is easier to do something about oneself."

Again they sat in silence.

Soon Mette rose to her feet. "I want to thank you for your patience," she said shyly. "I will think about what you said, but I need some time …" She stopped abruptly. Then she turned around and entered the seter house in a hurry.

16 • The meetinghouse chairman

Morten entered and kicked his shoes off by the door. He seemed tired and preoccupied as he dropped down on the bench by the table. Mette poured him a cup of coffee, but she didn't say anything. His silence didn't invite conversation, so she continued what she was doing over by the counter. Still, it was not an oppressive silence. The atmosphere was comfortable. They could be in the same room without necessarily having to talk that much.

After a while, Mette turned and looked at Morten. He seemed to be studying some oddity down there in his coffee cup, his thoughts seemed far removed from what was going on around him. Mette wanted to ask what was bothering him, but she didn't have the courage. If he didn't want to share his thoughts with her, he shouldn't have to. She didn't want to interfere with something that was none of her business. But she had never seen him so pensive. And this, without doubt, aroused her curiosity. She put bread, butter and some cold cuts on the table. Then she poured herself a cup of coffee and joined him.

Suddenly Morten seemed to wake up. "Oh, some food would really taste great now," he said. "I'm starved."

They ate together in silence. Mette looked out of the window, and soon her thoughts drifted far away, too. She was startled when Morten talked to her.

He laughed. "You were far away now," he said.

"Yes, about as far away as you have been since you came in," she answered and smiled back at him.

"Uff, yes," he said, his smile wiped out in an instant. "There are so many problems you can get yourself into. And it looks like I'm getting into most of them." He sighed and took a big gulp of his coffee. "Do you know what? Sometimes I get so frustrated that I feel like holing up at the seter and never showing my face again."

Mette's eyes widened at this outburst from such a normally calm and collected man.

"But what has upset you this much?" she asked curiously.

He laughed a little and shook his head in dismay. "It is just these attitudes and opinions that collide completely between generations," he replied.

"Oh?" Mette lifted her eyebrows, looking at him in bewilderment.

"I was down in town today," he continued. "At the store I noticed a new poster that had been put up after I was there last. Or rather, a quite upset elderly gentleman made me aware of it. Then I was told what kind of moral deterioration the meetinghouse now was about to support. The poster was an invitation to join a dance group at the meetinghouse."

"Dance group?" Mette looked at him in surprise. "Are they going to start a dance group at the meetinghouse?"

"Yes," laughed Morten. "According to this man, who obviously read only two of the words on the poster—namely, 'dance' and 'meetinghouse,' that's what it is about. And I happen to be the one who has the full and complete responsibility for this 'abomination,' since I am chairman of the meetinghouse council."

Mette continued to stare at him. "But what did the poster say?" she asked.

"Well, that was the problem. Before I could defend or explain anything, I had to go over and see what it actually said. And then I realized what it was all about.

"We had it on the council agenda early this spring. Some girls, probably around 10 or 12, wanted to start *tria dancing*. They gave us a demonstration, and we decided it was innocent enough. It was just movement to music.

"The whole thing reminded me of the movement to songs that we used to do in Sunday school. I suppose the girls' dancing was a little more advanced and the music a little more lively. But what I liked was the enthusiasm they demonstrated. For them, it was not only movement to rhythm. They wanted to emphasize the message in the songs through movement. They actually wanted to portray the gospel.

"This form of dance wasn't like anything like what you would see at discos or similar party places. This was entirely different. It's just the word 'dance' that causes some people to make the association."

Mette smiled. "This is probably not the only place where this subject has made waves," she said.

"We have run into this several times at work, too. But what do you think?"

She frowned and said seriously: "I'm thinking about what you read from Isaiah the night before the revival meeting. Do you remember the watchmen who were blind and so the enemy was allowed to enter the herd?"

Morten nodded.

Mette continued: "I know some groups have a strong wish to make the activities at the meetinghouse as much like a disco as possible in order to get more people involved. They want to blur the distinction as much as they can, and that often detracts from the preaching of the Word of God."

"Yes, I know," said Morten. "But what I'm talking about here has nothing at all to do with that kind of thing. On the contrary. Here, dance is used to emphasize the message. That's a big difference. People who shut their eyes as soon as they hear the word 'dance' will never learn anything about the difference. As they learn more about the Christian form of dance, though, they will understand that it has nothing to do with their past life. The Spirit will help them realize that.

"What I fight for is that we don't reject anything that is from God. He wants to bring us all with Him to Heaven. And to accomplish that, He will use all means available to Him. His love for us is that great. Now He notices that some young people have the inclination to preach His Word in this way, and He won't hesitate to use it."

Mette thought over what he said. Then she said: "You don't think this can push some away? I'm thinking about the older ones …"

Morten, too, had to consider the question before he answered. "I would rather turn the question around: Might it be that we push away some people by the way we practice religion today? I'm thinking about young people."

Mette had to laugh. Morten laughed, too.

"The one thing we have to remember is what I said at the beginning. Dance is many different things. There is a world of difference between this *tria dance* and the couple's dances they do at the disco."

There was a short pause. Both sat thinking about what they had discussed.

Mette suddenly smiled again. "We got quite serious today, didn't we. I don't think you should take this criticism that seriously. I think we should focus on preaching what God bestows on us, and we will best be heard in the manner He shows us. I believe His Word will triumph in the end, regardless of dissent."

Morten looked at her, and the smile he sent her was filled with warmth and gratitude. "I really think you are right. Now we'll forget this entire episode, and you have to join me in praying that I don't do any harm expressing my opinion. Could you do that? Even I might be wrong now and then?"

The facetious glimpse in his eye made her laugh aloud. But she knew that the promise she made, to pray for him, she was going to keep.

After Morten left, Mette stayed on for a while, nursing her coffee. They had had a deep conversation. Ordinarily, she didn't like to discuss such complex and controversial subjects. She was so easily carried away and apt to say things she would regret later. But this was different. With Morten, she felt so relaxed and free. She could say exactly what she meant without being taken the wrong way.

They often had similar conversations and discussions, especially in the evenings, when they had finished their chores. Sometimes it could get late before they went to bed. These conversations would surely be what she would miss the most when she had to leave the seter.

17 • Visit from Russia

The days went by, turning into weeks. In the campground, new campers and tenters arrived steadily, while others packed up and left. Morten often took tourists on hikes into the mountains. Mette had children and adults around almost all the time while she tended to the animals and demonstrated farm and household chores done the old-fashion way. Aunt Anna kept busy as well, but she didn't stay at it as long these days. Mette and Morten tried to ease Aunt Anna's workload as much as they could. She didn't want to admit it, but she often appeared tired and weary. She was no longer as spry as she once was. But Mette had learned so much from the older woman that she was soon able to cope quite well on her own.

Now and then Mette made the trip down to town. Sometimes she shopped for supplies, but most of her time was spent up there at the remote seter. She smiled when she thought about it. She didn't have television or Internet access. The battery-powered radio in the seter house was used mostly to hear the news and weather forecasts. It would be strange to return to civilization, she thought. True enough, she had her cell phone so she could keep in touch with family and friends, but she didn't use it that much.

But she didn't feel lonely. She now knew many of the seter's visitors and planned to keep in touch with some of them in time to come. And then, Marit and Ellen were still at the farm. She got along well with them, even if she still had questions about Ellen's relationship to the family.

The weather had been mostly warm and pleasant. The effects of the long, dry period were plainly visible. Morten was worried. "We need some rain," he said one morning as he stood in the doorway, studying the brown patches that had started to show up in the meadow.

Although Mette had enjoyed the nice weather, she understood the problem. The

59

farmers needed rain for their next crop. The grass at the seter was only cut once a year, so it wasn't that important to them, but they needed good pasture for their livestock.

The meadow had been cut a while ago. Mette was overjoyed to take part in a familiar and cherished activity as she and Morten raked the hay together and dried it on the rack. She associated this chore with the summers of her childhood. True, she hadn't enjoyed it that much as a child. Back then, she often found it tedious and boring to go out in the field day after day, hanging the grass on the steel wires. But now it was different.

The same job at the seter involved only a single field, easily done in a day. One of the tourists had helped out as well. What the children liked best was to transport the hay to the hayloft. Morten had borrowed a wagon and a placid, good-natured horse from town. The horse didn't mind being surrounded by running and jumping children. Now and then Morten allowed one of them to ride horseback when heading for the barn with a load. The children discovered a new playground in the hay in the barn. They had a great time bouncing around in there.

The animals roamed freely outside in the meadow. Their number actually increased: Petter brought up a couple of cows and some more goats, so now Mette had more animals that needed milking. Missi and Caesar were still suckling their cow, which meant she didn't need milking. But Mette loved the work, so even if her job in the cow barn were busier, she still would have enjoyed it just as much.

"Tomorrow we'll have a special group of visitors," said Morten as they sat down to breakfast. There were just the two of them. Aunt Anna had left for town the day before, and Marit and Ellen were staying out in their camper. "We'll have some Russian tourists here," he continued excitedly.

"A group from our community visited there a few years ago. Ellen and I went on that trip, too. We visited a church there. It was incredibly interesting to get to know the people. Last year, a group from there came to visit our town, and they spent some of that time here at the seter. Many good relationships were established, and that's why they asked to come back this year. I believe their trip was partly sponsored by some of our local organizations. Ellen has been heading up that effort. It was she who asked if we would host the group for a couple of days this year, too."

Mette listened with interest as Morten continued his account of their trip to Russia. Ellen's name was brought up as a natural part of the story. Again Mette wondered: Were they more than friends? No, now she was speculating again. Why was she so hung up on this? Morten should be able to live his life as he wished without her making it her business.

She concentrated on paying attention to his conversation. The pair did some planning for the visit, but the guests mostly wanted to just hang out and take part in the daily routines at the seter. People from town would come up to visit. They probably would arrange some special events on occasion of the visit, too.

The next day they woke up to cloudy skies and light rain, the first such day in some time. The 19 guests in the Russian group, most of them women, were lodged in rented campers. Being reunited with these return visitors was a joyous occasion for the seter folks. Ellen was especially excited about their visit. The weather didn't dampen the guests' spirits, although they were used to neither mountains nor plains nor livestock.

It didn't take Mette long to get to know them, either.

Now and then language problems occurred, but most of the Russians knew some

English, so they managed to make themselves understood.

Some people from town arrived in the evening, crowding the seter house. Morten had picked the site, since it was the only place where everybody could be together under one roof. Despite the crowding, the evening was unforgettable. A member of the Russian group served as interpreter for the ones who didn't know much English, and Morten interpreted from English to Norwegian for the Norwegians who didn't understand much English. They told stories all night.

The Russians stayed at the seter for nearly a week. All during that time, people from town and from other nearby communities came to visit. Many times they picked up the visitors and took them to events around the district. Morten participated in most of them. Now and then Mette came along, but usually she stayed behind at the seter. She was responsible for the livestock, and the animals couldn't be left on their own for long periods.

When the week ended, the seter folks bid their guests an emotional farewell. Mette and Morten stood waving them off as the cars started down the road. Ellen went with them to town, to make sure their departure went well, she said. A bus was waiting for them there.

Later in the day. Ellen returned. She seemed worried and upset as she entered the seter house. "Where is Morten?" she asked.

Mette had just picked up the milk pails. She was heading for the cow barn and the milking. "He went over to visit with Marit in the camper," she answered. "I'm sure you'll find him there."

Mette walked toward the cow barn while Ellen ran across the meadow. Mette stopped for a minute, watching Ellen and wondering what had upset her.

After Mette had finished her barn chores and placed the milk in the well for cooling, she returned to the seter house. No one was there. She made coffee and set out the evening meal, but no one came to eat. Puzzled, she looked out of the window. Then she discovered that Morten's car was gone. Even more puzzled, she walked over to the table. There was nothing else for her to do but sit down to eat by herself.

When Mette went to the cow barn the next morning, Morten still had not returned. She finished her chores quickly and walked over to Marit's camper to see if someone might offer her an explanation. She was even more puzzled when she found it locked and empty. So all three of them had gone to town. What could have happened? Why did they leave in such a hurry without letting her know? Mette felt her anxiety grow. She knew Morten was expecting a group of tourists that afternoon. He had to be back by then … if only an accident weren't the reason for his absence, she worried, picturing a worst-case scenario in her mind.

A good deal of preparation was needed before the scheduled afternoon visitors arrived. She started working automatically, but her thoughts were far away. The thoughts she never allowed herself to think emerged all of a sudden. Morten and Ellen … Ellen and Morten … Her thoughts wouldn't let go, ruining her concentration. She returned to reality just in time to snatch a pan of porridge from the burner, barely saving it from scorching.

Suddenly she heard the sound of cars from the road. She rushed to the window. The tourists were arriving.

Soon the meadow was full of cars and people. She went out to greet them. Then she spotted Morten, right in the middle of a group. She wanted to run over and ask him what

61

had happened, but she contained herself. He was engaged in spirited conversation, so this was probably not the right time for explanations.

All afternoon, both Morten and Mette were busy with their own chores. They didn't get a moment to talk in private. Mette noticed that Morten acted completely normal. Now and then he joked and laughed, so whatever had happened couldn't be that serious.

Not until late at night did she manage to exchange a couple of words with him. He had come in to pick up some gear he had left on the bench. "I have to go back to town," he said.

"Did anything happen?" Mette looked at him curiously.

He shook his head and laughed.

In that same moment, a boy came running through the door. "You have to come!" he yelled. "One of the goats has gotten into our camper. Mom is going nuts!"

Morten ran out. Mette stumbled into a pair of shoes and followed. Over by the camper, a screaming woman was pacing back and forth in front of the door. A small group of tourists had gathered by the camper. Inside was one of the goats, his head buried in a cooler, helping himself to the contents. A loaf of bread lay on the floor, a substantial chunk missing. A man was trying to push the animal toward the door, but the billy goat didn't want to let go of the goodies he had found.

Morten leaped inside the camper. With concerted effort, the two men managed to push the stubborn goat outside.

"I'm not quite sure what to do with him," he said to Mette. "I think we'll have to put him in the barn for the night. Then we'll see how he behaves in the morning."

"I'll take him over there," said Mette. She took a firm hold of the goat's shaggy hair and pulled him along with her. The boy who had alerted them came along, too.

"He is really a good goat," the boy said as they were heading for the cow barn. "I'm sure I would have gotten him out if Mom hadn't been so hysterical."

Mette had to laugh. "If she's not used to animals, this would have been a little overwhelming for her." Mette felt she had to defend the poor mom.

"Now you have to close the door behind us so he doesn't run off again," said Mette to the boy as they entered the cow barn. She brought an armful of hay and some feed concentrate, which she gave the goat to get him settled down.

When they left the barn, Morten was already gone. The boy ran back to the camper while Mette returned to the seter house.

That evening, Mette sat in bed for a long time, her diary in her lap. The eerie light from the oil lamp she had placed on her nightstand fell on the old walls. It was pitch dark outside. She would never allow anyone to read what she wrote in her diary. Maybe she would never even dare read it herself.

She felt a strange unease building inside of her. How would this end? Suddenly she remembered what the strange man had said on the day of the revival meeting. She had to watch out, he said. Might there be something about Morten she had to watch out for? But what in the world might that be? She had always seen him as a picture of decency.

She put her diary away and blew out the lamp. She didn't want to think anymore. Now she just wanted to sleep.

18 • *Conversation by the fire pit*

With great effort, Mette tried to get a good fire going in the fire pit. If they were going to grill sausages there soon, the heat had to be stronger. She added some more dry wood she had brought over from the seter.

A camp school group was visiting the seter today. Now the entire group—including two camp schoolteachers—sat by the lake bank while Morten told them about the old legend and the old way of life at the seter. They all sat listening to what Morten told them.

The sausages were ready for grilling. Morten had cut a pile of wooden sticks to serve as skewers. Soon the fire blazed and sparks started leaping between the logs. Morten finished his presentation and invited his audience over to grill their sausages. A circle of young people gathered around the fire, each boy and girl with a sausage speared on a stick. Mette poured fruit juice in paper cups and handed them out to the students. Talk and laughter rang throughout the area.

Mette moved away from the crowd. Her eyes drifted past the group of lively boys and girls, stopping at Morten. He was talking to one of the teachers. The two were laughing and seeming to enjoy themselves. In no way did he seem to be struggling with any kind of problem.

Since the day when they had to remove the billy goat from the camper, they hadn't had many opportunities to talk. Nor did Morten seem to have a need to tell her anything. Mette didn't dare ask about it. If he didn't want to say anything, then it was none of her business.

Over a week had gone by. Their open, comfortable way of communicating with each other was in some ways still there, but Mette felt something had closed between them. Yet she was not able to share with him the unease that had come upon her.

She hadn't seen Ellen, either. Morten had been in town several times, but she knew little of what he was doing down there.

She looked up at the clouds. If it would only stay dry until this day was over. The sky was already gray and the air much cooler. They were already well into August. A twinge of melancholy swept over her when she realized she had only a little more than three weeks left on this job. But maybe it was best for her to return to the city. Here a lot of strange thoughts had started bothering her.

The routine had changed slightly after the camp school groups had begun coming. The agenda included more teaching and fewer demonstrations of daily seter chores. In some ways, Mette had been looking forward to fall. It would be a new challenge with all the youngsters from school.

Interrupting her thoughts, a boy walked over to her and sat down next to her. He bit off a chunk of a rather scorched sausage. Silently, he studied the small gold cross that she wore on a chain around her neck.

"I like your pendant," he said in a moment.

Mette smiled. "You like it? In any case, it is precious to me," she answered.

"Are you, like, a Christian?"

The question came naturally and Mette had to smile again. "Yes, I am a Christian."

The boy continued to study her cross while he chewed avidly on his sausage. He looked directly at her and said: "I am going to be confirmed next spring. But I don't know if that's what I want."

Mette grew concerned. The boy lowered his eyes as if he had said something wrong. "Why is it you think you don't want to?" she asked.

He didn't answer right away. He studied some moss on the ground while kicking the dirt absently with his shoe. Mette sensed he might be shy, but that there was something he needed to talk about.

"Do you have a particular reason?" she continued.

"I want to be confirmed, but I don't know if I want to do it in the church," he answered after a while.

Mette noticed a worried crease between his brows.

"Are you baptized?" Mette felt she had to ask him that before saying any more on the subject.

The boy looked up at her in alarm. "Of course I am," he said. "You have to be baptized with the kind of parents I have. They're not cool."

Mette had to smile again. She recognized herself in this boy. "Do you know what?" she said, looking into his eyes, a smile on her face. "I also thought my parents were the opposite of cool when I was your age. But now, what they say actually makes sense."

The boy had to smile, too. Obviously he got her point. "So you think there's hope for my parents, too?" They both laughed.

But soon he was serious again. "They want so very much for me to be confirmed in the church, but I don't know if it is right. I have a friend who belongs to 'The Free.' We have talked a lot about God and Jesus and stuff. What he says seems so right, and he's going to have a different kind of confirmation."

Mette gathered her thoughts before she answered. "I know there are alternatives to both baptism and confirmation," she started. "I don't think we should spend much time trying to figure out whether one is right and the other wrong. What we have to consider is, 'Is this right for me? How do I interpret the Bible in regard to those questions?' "

The boy answered impatiently: "How in the world am I to figure it out? There are so many different opinions about it."

"You're right about that," Mette continued. "This is not easy to understand. But you said you were baptized. Maybe you also went to Sunday school or were introduced to the Bible in other ways?"

"Sure. But different people have their own way of interpreting the Bible. That's what's so confusing."

Mette thought again. "Is there something you find especially hard to understand?" she asked.

"There is this thing about whether we want to belong to Jesus and how we become Christians," he said quickly.

"Do you want to belong to Jesus?" Mette looked searchingly at him.

"Sure, I want to. But I want it to be proper. In church they say we become God's children when we are baptized, but how in the world can that be, when we are so young that we can't make any decisions for ourselves?"

"May I try to explain it to you?" She looked at him in earnest, but also in a friendly manner. They were so focused on their conversation that they didn't notice the others, laughing and talking around the fire. They both understood that this was an important moment.

"Salvation," started Mette, "is a two-part thing. It is baptism, and then there is faith.

As I understand it, you have a problem regarding faith. You can't believe that a little child can have faith."

"Yes, exactly," he responded eagerly. "That's just it."

"Listen up," said Mette and continued. "Baptism is like a pact between an individual and God. It is a pact about belonging together. This faith is grounded in a very young child as well. Faith is a gift from God. The only thing we need to do to receive this gift, is to accept it. A very young child has no problems with this. A baby accepts all gifts, faith as well. It is much more difficult for us adults. We don't accept just anything without questions.

"But this faith needs nourishment in order to grow and develop. When a small child is baptized, the parents and sponsors promise to make sure that the child is taught about the Word of God. This is so that the child's faith can grow."

Now the boy fidgeted, as if he were protesting with his body. "Well, then, it just doesn't work," he said in a huff. "Just look at all the people who have been baptized, but how many are still Christians as adults?"

Mette smiled at his excitement. "Of course, we see a lot of people who bring their children to be baptized without attaching any deeper meaning to it. It happens far too often that the promise to teach the child the Christian faith is not kept. And just as often, we see that many choose to walk away from God, even if they were introduced to faith as children. This is probably the greatest cause of grief for us Christians. But their baptism is still valid throughout their lives.

"We can lose our faith if we choose to live our lives away from Jesus and His salvation. And then the power of baptism loses its influence on our lives. But if a person is saved later, then the faith returns. And it is then that the miracle happens. Baptism again becomes a force in your life. Full power is restored to the covenant that we established with God when we were little children. We don't have to re-establish it."

Mette halted her monologue. She was in doubt as to how to continue, or if the boy grasped any of what she was talking about.

He sat silently for a while. But then, looking thoughtfully at the ground, he said: "How would you know? I mean, how can you be sure that the covenant of baptism really still stands when we again choose to embrace the Christian faith, after maybe having been away from Jesus for years? How can I be sure that my baptism still works when I'm an adult?"

His question told Mette that he understood her message. Now she must try to explain so he would get the entire context.

"In the Old Testament of the Bible, we find a lot of mystifying stories," she continued. "It tells about kings and prophets and many mysterious happenings. It also contains the history of the Israeli people. I assume you have heard some of this?"

The boy looked at her and nodded cautiously. "Of course, I have heard about Abraham and Moses and them. But when I read that part of the Bible, I don't understand that much."

Mette smiled, delighted by this youth who was opening up to her so candidly. "You have heard about Abraham," she continued. "Can you remember whether you have heard the story about Abraham, who had to go out and count the stars? When God spoke to him and told him that his descendants would be as numerous as the stars in the sky?"

The boy nodded. "I remember that story," he answered.

"God established a covenant with Abraham and his descendants," she continued. "The covenant also included his people as long as they lived on earth. It was a covenant between God and the people to belong together. It is still valid for the ones who receive Christ and live as His children today.

"We can liken this covenant to a representation of baptism. Through that covenant, God's people came into being with Abraham. They didn't always live as God wanted them to live. We see that especially in the story about Moses and their wandering in the desert. You remember that, don't you?"

The boy nodded knowingly.

"You may also remember that they often defied God," she continued, "and He had to punish them. When they showed remorse and returned to God, they experienced His forgiveness. They were welcomed back into the fold again. But they didn't have to renew the covenant. It was still binding. It didn't help them when they were disobedient and refused to walk the path of God. But once they returned, it was there, and they were able to experience its blessings.

"It is the same way with the covenant of baptism. Once we return to Jesus and are saved, the covenant is there for us and as binding as when it was established when you were a little child."

"Oooh …" An expression of wonder lit up the face of the avid listener. But then it darkened a little again. "But …" the boy hemmed and hawed. "The people who rebelled against God in the Old Testament … You said God had to punish them for their wrongdoings. Doesn't He have to punish us, too, when we do something wrong—for example, leaving His path?"

"Yes," said Mette eagerly. "He really must. But do you know what? We don't have to suffer His punishment. For Jesus took that punishment upon Himself when He died on the cross."

Suddenly the face of the youth next to her lit up again. "But that is true! Now I understand." A smile spread across his entire face. "Then my baptism is just as good as the baptism of those people who get baptized as adults?" The statement shone as a question toward Mette. It was obviously a statement he wanted confirmed.

"Yes, you can be sure of that." Mette returned the bright smile. And then she continued: "Now, you must have experienced that there are different opinions about this. What I just explained to you is the Lutheran doctrine. That's what you are brought up in. I think it is important that we are firm in our own beliefs, and that we also respect others' beliefs, even if we can't always understand them."

He nodded eagerly, turning toward her. "Thank you. This was a good talk."

Mette smiled at his grown-up way of expressing himself. But she was glad that what she had explained to him, obviously had been of help.

When he rose, Mette pulled a pen out of her pocket. She also found a piece of paper. On it she wrote a Bible passage. "Read this when you get home," she said.

The boy took the scrap of paper eagerly and looked at it. "Yes, I'll do that," he said. Then he stuffed the paper in his pocket and walked back to the others.

Mette looked after him. The passage she had written down for him had once been of great help to her, too, regarding these questions. It was from Paul's second letter to Timothy, Chapter 3, Verses 14-15.

She quoted the verses to herself from memory: *"But as for you, continue in what you have learned and have become convinced of, because you know those from whom*

66

you learned it, and how from infancy you have known the holy Scriptures, which are able to make you wise for salvation through faith in Christ Jesus."

Now the group was making its way toward the seter meadow. Mette had been so preoccupied with her own thoughts, it hadn't registered in her mind that the students had received new directions. She rose quickly and began cleaning up the leftovers. She bent over, collecting paper cups and other trash that had been thrown on the ground. When she straightened, she was taken aback by meeting Morten's intense eyes. He had stayed behind when the others left. Abruptly, he turned around and followed the youth group.

Mette looked at him in bewilderment. He had been staring at her. Again, something stirred in her. Why did he do that?

19 • *The nature of God*

It was Saturday, Mette's day off. She had a hectic week behind her, so she looked forward to taking it easy again. Today she wanted to do some shopping and maybe take a drive around town. Morten had told her she could use the car all day if she wanted to. He was in town, too. She would pick him up on her way back.

First she drove to the shopping center. It wasn't a big center, but the town wasn't big, either. She knew her way around after having been there a few times during the summer. Some people greeted her when she got there. Most people knew that she worked at the Siljatjern Seter.

Further into the store, she passed two men engrossed in conversation. As she passed them, an odd expression came over their faces. They stopped talking and eyed her strangely. She walked around a rack and began looking for something on a shelf. From where she stood she wasn't able to see the men, but she could hear them.

They snickered. "That was the lady from the seter," she heard one of them say. "I'll say, she has things going on." Both chuckled again.

Mette was startled. It was clear the words were not for her ears. It was also obvious they were implying something dirty.

Not wanting to hear more, she hurried away. Why were they talking about her like that? She walked for a while, trying to figure it out. Again, she remembered her meeting with the men at the seter earlier that summer. At that time, she had been furious. Now she just felt uneasy and uncertain.

She also remembered the man who had tried to warn her at the revival meeting. What was this all about? As much as she racked her brain, she wasn't able to figure out what they alluded to. But she realized that some people had dirty minds. It was best to forget about it.

The men were gone when she made her way out. She felt relieved. It was a great day. She stood for a while outside the store, enjoying the beautiful scenery. The farms were laid out on both sides of the main road. The store, which was part of a larger complex with bank, post office, a physician and some public offices, was close to the road

The road cut through town from east to west. She was on the south side of the road.

The meetinghouse was on that side, too, just a little farther east. The church was in the same area, but on the other side of the road. From where she was standing, she could see the road leading up to the seter. It ran straight north. The turnoff was just a short distance past the store. That's where Morten's farm was located.

The town was surrounded on the north and west by wide plains and mountains. To the east lay a valley, and to the south, woodlands. The railroad ran through the south end of town.

What a scenic town, thought Mette. Farms and houses were bathed in sunshine below the majestic mountains and plains. Her eyes sought Morten's farm. She wasn't quite able to see it, but the big, beautiful main house peeked through some trees. She knew the barn was right behind it. Mette smiled to herself. Imagine living alone with so much space.

"Hello, if it isn't Mette."

The sudden interruption startled her. She turned around and saw a woman on her way from the store. Mette was confused, for she couldn't remember having met this person before.

The woman noticed her puzzlement and laughed. "I remember you from the revival meeting you hosted at the seter this summer," she explained as she came closer. "By the way, I'm Solfrid's sister. I know you talked to her that day."

Mette greeted her warmly. It was impossible to believe that this heavy-set woman was the frail Solfrid's sister. Then she remembered Solfrid's condition. "How is your sister?" she asked. "I have thought about her so often."

A painful expression appeared on the woman's face. "I'm afraid she is not doing well. She is in a lot of pain, and the treatment is rough on her. Right now she is in the hospital. I don't think the treatment is helping much, either. The cancer has gone too far. But they are doing what they can," she said, sighing. "I'm not even sure she'll ever leave the hospital," she continued, her voice barely a whisper.

Mette remembered the anguished face of the suffering woman on the day of the meeting. She cringed with pity. For a moment they stood together in silence. Mette didn't know what to say. The other woman seemed to look at something far away. It was easy to see that her sister's illness had affected her deeply.

Suddenly, she looked at Mette again. "It is so hard ..." She stopped and looked down. There was another pause. Then she continued: "I don't know how I'm going to bear it."

Mette wished there was something she could do to help ease her pain, but she didn't know what it would be. "I understand very well how terribly painful it must be for you to watch your sister suffer in this way," she said.

The woman continued to look down. The deep creases on her brow seemed to be ingrained there. She spoke again, her voice weak and shaky. "It is so hard ... it is so hard to think about ..." Obviously, she wanted to say something that was difficult to express.

When she looked up at Mette again, her voice grew more intense. "Who can understand it? There she was. Going week after week, yes, month after month, while the tumors grew and spread in her body. And she didn't notice anything. She didn't have any more trouble than I do when I'm tired after work. When they discovered the disease, it was gone too far for them to do anything about it."

Tears began running down her face. "What's scaring me is that I might get it, too."

68

Her voice rose gradually as she talked, her eyes taking on a feverish look. "How can I be sure this won't happen to me, too?"

Mette realized the terrified woman needed comfort and peace. Her fear for this disease was crushing her. Gently, she placed her hand on the shoulder of the anguished woman. "I understand that you are a Christian?" she asked in a gentle voice.

The woman nodded.

"In a crisis like this," continued Mette, "it may be hard to believe God is there for us. But I am sure you know something about the nature of God?"

The woman looked at her inquiringly. "Yes?" She sounded uncertain about what Mette wanted to say.

Mette smiled at her puzzled look. "Yes, I believe you know the nature of God, so I want to ask you this: Is it the nature of God to think: 'Now, I want this woman to experience every detail of this horrible disease to show her what kind of illness she will die from later! I want to put her there by her sister's bedside and show her every grimace of pain and panic attack in her tortured body, so her anguish, too, may become complete'?"

Mette felt the intensity of her own words, which just came to her as if it was the most natural thing in the world for her to say them.

The woman stared at her with her mouth open. She didn't answer.

Mette continued even more urgently: "Do you think this is the nature of God?"

The woman slowly shook her head. "No," she said. "No, absolutely not. But ..."

Another pained expression passed over the woman's face. "So many people get cancer, even those who know exactly what it entails. Nurses and others who know a lot about it, get cancer too, don't they?"

"Oh yes," said Mette, "but your problem is that you fear this cancer. There is really nothing saying that you, too, will get the same disease as your sister. How horrible it must be to carry around a fear about something that will probably never happen. I cannot believe that God wants you to have to go through that. Now He wants you to be of support and help to Solfrid, so you have to regard it as her disease. I understand that your fear is real. God sees that, too, and I think that's what He wants to tell you right now."

A smile appeared on the heavy-set woman's face. Mette could see her body relax gradually. For a while longer she stood there, mulling over what she had been told.

Suddenly she put both arms around Mette's neck and gave her a hug. "Thank you," she whispered in her ear. "I never thought about that. You're right. God doesn't want me to be paralyzed by fear." She let go of Mette and stepped back. "Do you know what?" She looked at Mette with an earnest expression. "This was about to cripple me completely. I haven't been able to visit my sister for several days. But now I feel that the terrible fear is about to let go of me." A smile appeared on her face again.

"Oh, by the way," she continued, "Solfrid asked me to ask Morten, if I met him, if you and he would come to visit her sometime. She is so grateful for the intercession she had from you."

Mette was puzzled. She really didn't know the woman. But her hopeful eyes made it impossible to turn her down. "I will speak to Morten about it," she answered.

Then the woman turned around and walked toward one of the parked cars.

Mette placed her shopping in the car and sat down behind the steering wheel. For a while she sat there immersed in thought. With determination, she started the car and drove over to Morten's farm.

She found him out in the yard. He looked surprised when she got out. "Are you heading back already? I thought you really wanted to make the most of the day and get away from your enslavement up there." His eyes twinkled teasingly.

Mette smiled. But then she turned serious again. She told him about the meeting at the store.

Morten looked serious, too. "It may be that she won't live that long," he said quietly. "Maybe it's best that we go to the hospital as soon as possible."

"That's what I thought, too," said Mette.

"If you can wait a few minutes so I can change, we can go right away," he said.

Mette smiled. "Pull on your rags and let's go!"

Morten disappeared quickly into the house, laughing at her quick reply.

20 • Visit to the hospital

The hospital was located in a city some distance away. It took them almost two hours to get there. Morten drove. Mette was glad she didn't have to, for she didn't know the road that well. Nor did she know where the hospital was located. While driving, Morten talked about his childhood when the kids played together at school. Solfrid was one of the cheerful and happy girls he remembered from those days. It was unbelievable that she was now on her deathbed.

When they left the car in the parking lot, they stopped for a moment. Neither of them felt especially confident. How would they handle the serious situation they now were about to face? How was Solfrid today? The many questions they had made them feel insecure.

Morten started walking toward the entrance with determined steps. "Now we are here, so we really don't have a choice but to go in," he said. Mette followed close behind him.

One of the nurses showed them to her room. "She may be sleeping," she said before they entered, "but she will probably wake up soon. She is quite heavily medicated, so she is a little disoriented at times. But I don't think you'll have problems communicating with her. Just don't stay too long. She tires easily."

Mette and Morten walked quietly through the doorway. At first sight, there didn't seem to be anyone under the big comforter. But then they saw a pale, tiny face on the pillow. Her eyes were closed as though she was sleeping. Next to her bed was a stand from which some bags were hanging. Tubes snaked down to needles that were attached to her thin arms and hands. Everything sitting on the nightstand revealed that it belonged to a desperately ill person.

For a while they just stood there, looking at her. Neither of them said a word. They didn't want to wake her if she was asleep.

Mette remembered her well from the meeting, but if she was small and frail then, she was even thinner now. Her cheeks were hollow and her shoulders looked as if her skin was pulled tightly over her bones. Her hair was almost gone, too. Mette felt a growing lump in her throat. Poor little woman, she thought.

Slowly, the eyelids of the person in the bed opened. For a moment she just lay there, staring at the two standing next to her bed.

Morten took her hand and shook it gently. "Hello, Solfrid," he said. "We just wanted to see how you are doing. Your sister said you were here."

A smile spread across the tiny face. Her voice was weak but surprisingly clear when she answered: "How kind of you to come. I so much wanted to thank you for what you did for me that day at the seter." Her eyes moved and she looked over at Mette. "I was so afraid I would die before I had a chance to talk to you, so I asked her to give you my message. Thank you so much for coming."

Both looked at her in puzzlement. What was she thanking them for? What in the world had they done to help her? Mette didn't understand. She had asked them for intercession at the seter because she wanted to be healed, but it didn't happen. So then, what was it she was so grateful for?

Solfrid seemed to notice their bewilderment. She smiled quietly and then closed her eyes. The smile still lingered on her lips, so they knew that she was not asleep.

"You seem to be surprised that I want to thank you," she continued, her eyes closed. Then she opened them again and looked directly at Morten. "When I saw you up there, I found myself in a horrible crisis. I realized this disease would kill me. Even if I was certain that I was a Child of God, I was still terrified. I didn't want to die. At that point, there was nothing I wanted more than to live. And I knew that the only chance I had was to be healed. I was actually desperate. I needed to be healed. I was in such a state then that I tried to force God to heal me. When I asked for intercession, that's what I was really trying to do. But you, Morten, caught on to what I was up to."

Questioning eyes looked at him. He sat down on a chair by her bed.

"I don't know," he said. "But I was afraid you would be disappointed if what you wished for didn't happen. So that's why I gave you that long lecture. Afterward, I thought it was way too much for a sick person."

Solfrid smiled as her eyes closed again. "There and then I wasn't able to take it all in, but later, what you said came back to me and gave me peace." She looked at him again. "The speech that the preacher gave us …" She stopped a little as if trying to remember his name, but then she gave it up and continued: "… and what you told me have been of incredible help to me."

Now her voice was weaker, and Mette was afraid she had talked too much. Maybe it had worn her out. Worried, she stood there following the conversation. For a while, the patient lay motionless in bed with her eyes closed. Maybe she had fallen asleep? Mette sat down quietly in a chair at the foot of the bed. Morten, too, sat quietly, holding Solfrid's hand.

It didn't take long before Solfrid's eyes opened again. She continued as if there had been no interruption. "You both quoted the verses of the fifth chapter of the letter from James in the Bible. You told me it says that we should anoint the sick and offer our prayers, and then the prayers offered in faith will help the sick person." She emphasized the last part of what she said.

"And would you know! That's exactly what I experienced!" Her entire being radiated peace. "I got to experience it!" Her voice was clear and intense. "Time after time I experienced that my fear just disappeared when I though about that verse. Other verses in the Bible came to me, too. Such did the ones that the preacher quoted … about bringing to Him all the burdens we carry … and then He will give us rest. Yes, rest is what

I found. It is absolutely incredible that it works. I would never have believed it if I hadn't experienced it directly."

Again there was a pause. Mette was moved to her innermost core. Morten was affected, too, she could see that. But they didn't say anything. Now it was Solfrid's time to speak. That much was clear.

Soon she started speaking again. "How many times have I lain here in bed, apprehensive about some test I had to go through ..." Her voice was weaker now. She didn't look directly at any of them, but her eyes were open. "Then I reminded Him about those verses. I don't always have the strength to pray, but it doesn't look as if God really minds. It is enough that I just remind Him about those verses, and then the feeling of peace returns. Sometimes I have even been able to sleep until I was taken down to the lab. Yes ... the prayer of faith helps the sick!"

The last words were uttered with conviction. Then she seemed to shrink on her pillow. It was clear the conversation had worn her out. Mette and Morten looked at each other. Had they stayed with her too long? Maybe their visit had tired her too much? But they couldn't bring themselves to leave just yet. It seemed as if she still had something important to put into words.

For a long while she just lay quietly on her pillow. No one said anything. Then she opened her eyes again. Her smile was back. "It was so good to see you," she said.

They realized that the visit was over. Morten rose cautiously.

All at once, she gripped his hand more firmly. "Now, don't you think that I'm lying here, resting in absolute peace all the time," she said. "The fear always returns. Sometimes I have to ask the nurses for some Valium, too. But I know this: God is here all the time, whether I am at peace or I'm afraid. I am in the Lord's hands, I know that. And then there are all these blessed medications and treatments. I have often thanked God for the Valium."

Her eyes bored into Morten's. "Please continue to pray for me. I know I still need that more than anything else."

Morten nodded. "That we can promise you for sure," he said.

"Yes ... my fear keeps returning," she said, sinking back into the pillows. "You know ... if I didn't get restless and anxious, then I wouldn't be able to experience how wonderful His peace really is," she ended with a pale smile.

Mette wiped away a tear that had found its way all the way down to her chin. Morten stroked the emaciated woman's cheek as he said goodbye.

Solfrid turned to Mette. "Thank you both for coming. Then we'll meet again ..." She pointed upward with a weak hand while a spark of humor twinkled in her dull eyes.

"Yes, we'll meet again," said Morten, great emotion filling his voice. Mette just nodded. Then they left.

They didn't talk much on their way out, not until they got to the car. The visit had made a strong impression on both of them. But when they drove out from the parking lot, Morten said: "At least this gives me a greater confidence in praying for the sick. It seems as though it helps, regardless. And how mysterious His ways are. I'm glad He doesn't require me to understand everything He does or why He acts as He does."

Mette didn't answer right away. Frenzied thoughts were racing through her mind. "I thought we were going to see a dying person and offer some consolation," she said after a while. "I didn't get to say much."

Morten smiled. "Someone was there before us, comforting her. We would never have been able to help her find that kind of peace."

"No," said Mette. "It is good to know we have a God who has the power to help all the way into death."

They talked for some time about what they had experienced there at Solfrid's sick bed. Both felt as though they had been on holy ground. The atmosphere in her hospital room had radiated such a wonderful peace, although tragedy was there as well. The line between life and death suddenly seemed so frail. They felt close to heaven.

Even though they were strongly affected by their experience, they had to go on with their daily chores. Morten had business he wanted to take care of since he was in the city already, and Mette wanted to look around some of the stores. They parted after agreeing to meet several hours later.

21 • Visit in the night

Sunday was a quiet day at the seter. Morten left early for the mountains with some men. Mette took the car and went to church in the morning. Later she went home with Aunt Anna for dinner. In the afternoon they both drove back to the seter.

Aunt Anna chatted away as usual. Mette wondered why she didn't get tired of her continuous flow of words. She always seemed to have something to talk about. But she never gossiped or made negative comments about other people. She always managed to talk about something positive and interesting. One felt lifted up in soul and spirit just being around the cheerful woman.

This particular Sunday turned out to be especially nice—just the two of them together, all day. Mette was overjoyed. It was so great to be able to relax without having to deal with the thoughts that had bothered her lately, hints and reactions she was unable to understand. Nothing could be more frustrating.

They expected a new group of school children the next day. Aunt Anna had to make some preparations for the visit, and Mette had to take care of the livestock. They both puttered around, minding their own business in peace and quiet. Afterward, they set the table for an evening meal rife with goodies from Aunt Anna's refrigerator. They sat around for a long time, enjoying the meal and each other's company.

"It's great to see how well Morten has managed," Aunt Anna said while chewing on a thick slice of whole-grain bread topped with *gome**. The golden, curdled cheese was piled high on her slice of bread. It was a miracle she was able to get her mouth around the whole thing. But Mette didn't dwell long on the cheese-covered slice, for the remark she just heard interested her more. Before Mette had time to ask any more about it, Aunt Anna continued giving voice to her thoughts.

"It was hard for him after his parents died. He had the sole responsibility for the farm and all the livestock. But Marit has been of incredible help to him. She seemed to feel responsible for her little brother. And then he had Ellen ..."

Mette felt a sting in her chest as she heard that name. Aunt Anna seemed to know about most things going on within the family, and it seemed as if Ellen was almost a family member.

Mette sighed. Her face took on a serious expression. Might Aunt Anna know about the things she had heard such strange hints about? No. She abandoned the thought right away. This expressive woman would never be able to keep quiet about secrets of that nature. If there were some "dirt" here, it would have to be something she didn't know about. Mette was sure about that.

When Aunt Anna said she wanted to withdraw to her own room, Mette headed for bed, too. The golden glow from the lamp created a cozy atmosphere in the room as she sat in bed with her diary, but she wasn't quite able to enjoy it. She thought about Ellen and the rest of Morten's family. She felt that all the vagueness and hints had started to wear on her.

No, she didn't want to think about it. Sleep had begun taking effect, so she put her diary on the nightstand and turned off the lamp. Not long after, she was sleeping soundly.

Suddenly she woke up and sat up in bed. An icy fear crept down her spine. There was someone in the main room. She had heard a sound. Mystified, she turned on the flashlight on her nightstand and checked the time. It was 1:30 in the morning. It was pitch dark outside her window. Breathlessly she sat there, listening. Who was talking out there? There, she heard it again. A strong, male voice boomed away: "You must understand the way everything is …" The rest of the sentence was drowned out by the sound of something being pushed across the floor.

She wasn't able to distinguish the answer, but she heard Morten's voice. So it was Morten who was addressed in this forceful manner. Again she heard the agitated male voice: "You should have anticipated the consequences." She heard just fragments of the rest of the outburst: "… no one would know … false or truth …"

Morten's voice was again very subdued. It was as if he were cringing at a deserved reprimand.

Suddenly a third voice joined the conversation. It was not quite as upset, but it was serious. She could distinctly hear the clear voice: "It may have to be reported to the police."

Then there was some talk she couldn't discern. The voices were softer for a while, but then the first one cut through again. "You should have thought about this before you hired her!"

Mette felt her anxiety was about to paralyze her. They were talking about her. What was it about? She wanted to get up and listen closer to the door, but she didn't dare move. What would happen if they found out she was awake and had heard what they said?

Then she heard the front door open and shut again. The sound of a car revealed that someone was leaving the seter. Mette relaxed a little. But her unease and fear wouldn't let go of her. She couldn't figure this out. Now she had undeniable proof that Morten was mixed up in something. But she wasn't able to understand what it could be. He was so helpful in every way. Never did she get the feeling that he had something unresolved with people or with God. She had felt his inner strength on more than one occasion, and she herself had been strengthened by it. His calm and harmonious nature always created a comfortable atmosphere for people around him.

Mette was completely confused. And then the remark that clearly had something to do with her.

Her worries troubled her and swept away all notions of sleep. She felt herself trembling. Tense, she pulled her comforter closer to her chin, but her fear made her rigid body shake even more.

She sat up and lit the lamp. "Dear God," she prayed while reaching for the Bible on her nightstand. "Help me. I am so scared!"

She opened her Bible to find a word that would calm her down and comfort her. In the flickering lamplight, she looked down at the page she had opened arbitrarily and started to read. It took a while for her to be able to concentrate on the words. But then she sat staring in amazement. What was it she was reading? "You will not fear the terror of night, nor the arrow that flies by day." Her eyes sought the top of the page. "Psalms," it said. So she was reading from the Psalms. Psalm 91, it said.

Never had she been more amazed at something she read in the Bible. It was as if God had answered her immediately as she cried out for Him. Yes, she was convinced that was exactly what He did. She felt her inner being fill with complete peace. Her anxiety was gone.

The words were from Verse 5. Curiously, she checked Verse 4. In order to see the entire verse, she had to turn the page.

"He will cover you with His feathers, under His wings you will find refuge. His faithfulness will be your shield and rampart."

A peaceful smile came over her face. She was safe, for she had found refuge under the protective wings of God. She lay down on her pillow and sent heartfelt thanks to her Heavenly Father. He saw her anxiety. And He cared about her. What comfort was hers!

But she was still bewildered. She had questions about what she had just heard. There was something she didn't understand ... something that wasn't right. But this was obviously something she didn't need to fear. She could relax completely.

Quickly, she turned out the light. Now she could go to sleep safely. And soon she was fast asleep again.

Even though her sleep had been interrupted, Mette woke up early the next morning. Aunt Anna wasn't up yet when she entered the main room. Morten was nowhere to be seen. She remembered clearly what had happened last night. She was no longer anxious, but her curiosity had been piqued immensely.

She finished her barn chores as fast as she could. The animals seemed surprised that she arrived so early. They were good at telling time. They noticed very well that Mette arrived almost an hour earlier than usual.

She knew that Aunt Anna was planning to use a lot of milk that day, so she brought a big pail to the dairy room. The goats trotted at her heels as usual. Wherever she went, she could count on them to be hanging around. They had become especially affectionate and attracted to people after being coddled by the tourists all summer. She gave them some feed before she went back inside.

"You're up early today," said Aunt Anna when she saw Mette returning from the cow barn, fresh as a daisy. "I woke up early," she said, "so I thought I could just as well finish my morning chores."

It took a while for Mette to ask the question she had been dying to ask all this time. Aunt Anna had a lot to convey before she stopped long enough for Mette to get a word in. But finally she did. "Did you hear anyone here last night?" Mette looked anxiously at the old lady. She stared back at her in surprise. "Was there someone here last night?

No, I didn't hear anything. Did you hear someone?"

Mette told her about the voices she had heard, but she didn't say anything about what was actually said.

"It was probably Morten and the guys returning from the mountains," she calmly concluded. "I see his car is gone, so they probably all left for town. He should be back soon, for our guests will be here shortly."

Mette didn't say any more. It was obvious that Aunt Anna wasn't the least worried about Morten, and then Mette wouldn't cause her any extra consternation. It was probably best she bring this up with Morten himself.

She sat for a while, lost in her own thoughts. Aunt Anna went to the dairy room, so Mette was able to focus on her own thoughts for a moment. She was not sure she would bring this up with Morten after all. It might be this was something he wouldn't want to discuss with her. Maybe she should just give it a rest for a while. It might be that he would bring it up himself later.

It still took a while before they heard the sound of a car coming up the road. Aunt Anna was busy with something in her room, so Mette was alone when Morten entered. He greeted her absently and went over to the stove to pour himself a cup of coffee.

With cup in one hand and newspaper in the other, he went over to the table and sat down. Mette studied him in silence. He opened the paper, but soon he allowed it to fall into his lap again. His eyes seemed to look at something far away, outside the window. Deep creases had formed between his dark eyes.

Mette resumed what she was doing when he entered. Again he had this distant look that didn't invite any kind of conversation. She didn't dare ask the questions she was dying to get answered.

All of once he rested his elbows on the edge of the table and his chin in his hands. A heavy sigh sounded from him. When he started talking, his voice was as distant as his eyes. It was also marked by deep seriousness and gloom. "I've done something incredibly stupid …

He stopped again and looked at Mette. With bated breath, she waited for him to continue. But then he seemed to change his mind. With a shake of his head that showed her how deeply upset he was, he rose abruptly and left.

Suddenly, the despair Mette had seen in Morten's eyes enveloped her, too. All her questions came back to her. Would she never get them answered? So Morten had done something stupid. She had made a note of the way he phrased it. He didn't say "wrong;" he said "stupid." Might that be of significance? She fervently hoped that was the case.

In the same moment, Aunt Anna returned. She hadn't noticed a thing of what had been going on in there. She was talking a mile a minute as usual. Neither did she seem to notice that Mette was extraordinarily quiet.

Soon the group from school arrived. Immediately, everyone was involved in a frenzy of activity. But Mette had problems concentrating on her chores. Her thoughts kept scattering in all directions.

When evening arrived, she felt exhausted. She just wanted to dive into bed. Still, she lingered at the table with her cup of coffee. Morten was not back yet. She hoped they would be able to talk, just the two of them. Aunt Anna had left for town with the group from school, so they were the only ones up there.

After a while Morten arrived, but he stopped right inside the door. "I'm afraid I have to go back to town," he said. "Do you mind staying here alone tonight?"

"No." She hesitated. She wasn't afraid of being alone at night, but she had really hoped to speak to him. Neither could she imagine why he had to go back to town. Her disappointment felt like a physical pain. There was so much she wanted to talk to him about.

Morten didn't seem to notice her disappointment. Rather, he seemed to be relieved that it was all right with her to stay there by herself. Then he turned, said goodbye, and went to the car. Mette stood at the window and looked after him with tears burning in her eyes.

Well. Now, at least, she could go to bed.

22 • New horrors

Dazed and shaking, Mette sat up in bed. Bewildered, she looked around the room. What was that? What was it that woke her up? She felt completely disoriented. Sleep still had its hold on her. A sound caused her to feel an icy fear. Dazed, she rubbed her eyes in order to wake up. The room was pitch dark, so she realized it was the middle of the night. This time it wasn't voices that had awakened her, she was sure of that. But what could it be?

A loud bang made her jump in her bed. At the same time she relaxed a little. It was a mighty clap of thunder. So there she had her explanation. Even if a thunderstorm might be scary enough, at least it was something natural. Evidently she was to be bothered by annoying noises yet another night.

It didn't take long before she heard the next clap of thunder. It was even stronger than the first one; at least that was her impression. For a while, she sat upright in bed and listened to the thunder rolling between the mountains. Then came a tremendous lightning flash that lit up her entire room in the fraction of a second. Not long after, another thunderclap followed.

Shaking, Mette sat counting the seconds between the lightning and the thunder. She knew that with more than a seven-second interval, there was no danger that the lightning would hit too close. But she only got to four before she heard the thunder. And a stronger flash and bang than this she had rarely experienced.

Soon a new sound filled the air. Heavy raindrops splashed against the roof and her window. Actually, it couldn't be rain making that much noise. There was no doubt that it was hail.

The noise made it impossible to go back to sleep. She fumbled for her flashlight to check the time. How irritating that she didn't have a watch with hands that glowed in the dark.

When she finally found the flashlight, she noted that it was almost 3 in the morning. An oppressive pain in her head told her she sorely needed a good night's sleep. Soon the sound from the roof grew softer, but the intensity of it just seemed to increase. The rain poured down in buckets.

Suddenly she jumped where she sat. The animals … how did they manage in this weather? They had to be terrified. The sheep could take shelter in the sheep shed. But the others were outside, and the door to the cow barn was closed.

Quickly, she jumped out of bed and put on shoes and a jacket. In her haste, she didn't find her rain slicker. Flashlight in hand, she opened the door and hurried outside in the pouring rain. Before she reached the cow barn, she was soaking wet.

The cows and calves were huddled in front of the barn door. They lowered their heads against the rain and mooed uneasily. Fortunately, everybody was there. She opened the door, and soon the doorway was congested with animals, all wanting in at the same time. It took a while for her to separate them so they could enter one by one.

Aided by the weak beam from her flashlight, she began tying them up, one at a time. The goats came in, too. It was best to tie them up, she thought. If they were scared even more, they might create quite a commotion in there.

As she left the barn, she could see the sheep clustered together in the sheep shed. Since she was already soaking wet, she might just as well go over and check on them, too. They had to be scared, but it was nice and dry in there. Every one of them was there. Fortunately, none had taken off in panic.

She ran quickly over to the seter house again. Before she got to the door, she heard a bang again. This time the lightning and thunder happened simultaneously. Mette stopped for a moment, paralyzed with fear. This bang was different from the others. It was more like the sound from a gunshot, closely followed by a splintering, scraping sound. That was a hit, she thought and looked around in panic. She wasn't able to see anything. Darkness surrounded her, for the beam from her flashlight didn't reach very far. At least the building wasn't hit; she was able to register that.

She hurriedly slipped through the door. Shivering with cold, she tore off her wet clothes. After drying herself thoroughly with a towel, she put her nightgown back on and jumped into bed again.

The bad weather continued. She could just forget about sleep tonight.

Soon another worry started nagging her. What if the cow barn was hit by lightning? All the dry hay in the hayloft would easily ignite from a spark. Even if it rained heavily, it might burn for a long time before the raindrops managed to put out the fire.

She swung her feet out of bed again and put on a pair of slippers. Then she pulled a knit sweater over her nightgown and left the bedroom. In the main room, she wrapped herself in a blanket and sat down at the table. The cow barn was in the line of sight from the window above the table, so she could safely keep watch from there.

While she sat staring into the dark, she again felt an eerie feeling creep into her. This was no fun. Lightning stroke after lightning stroke was succeeded by thunderclap after thunderclap. The storm raged furiously above. The thunder created extraordinary echo effects between the high mountains. She was scared. Yes, she was really scared.

Then she remembered the Bible verse she had read the night before. Aided by her flashlight, she opened Morten's Bible, which was lying on the table. Quickly, she leafed through it to Psalm 91. Slowly she read the fifth verse. Again she felt how the blessed words gave her peace and comfort. "You will not fear the terror of night …" She folded her hands on the open Bible and thanked God for being with her.

When she again opened her eyes, she looked at the ninth verse. She read: "… the Lord, who is my refuge." Her tears started running in gratitude. She had nothing to fear. The tremendous forces that raged out there, no human could ever control. But she also knew that lightning and thunder had to submit to the hand of God. Even those enormous powers were mere trifles compared to His omnipotence. No, she didn't really have anything to fear this night, either.

A thump over by the door made her jump on the bench where she sat. Perplexed, she looked around her. Daylight filled the room. Mette realized it was morning. She had fallen asleep there at the table. Outside, everything was quiet. The terrible weather had been replaced by fluffy clouds drifting along in the brisk breeze; she could see them through the window.

Suddenly Morten was standing next to her. In shock, he stared at the rumpled person sitting at the table. At first, Mette felt embarrassed. She really didn't want him to see her like this, dressed just in her nightgown. But Morten didn't notice. All he did was show real concern for her.

"Did anything happen?" he asked, and sat down at the table, facing her.

Mette smiled shyly. Then she told him about the events of the previous night.

Morten listened closely. A look of despair appeared on his face when he realized what a night she had been through.

But Mette smiled again. Then she pushed the Bible over at him. It was still open at Psalm 91. She pointed to Verse 5 and said in a cheerful voice: "I had nothing to fear. Look here. God showed me this last night. She almost said 'again last night,' but stopped herself. It was better to hold off bringing up the events of the night before last.

Deeply solemn, Morten read the short verse. His voice was almost inaudible when he said: "So someone takes care of His own when others fail."

Mette felt terribly sorry for him, but she didn't know what to say. A lot of unresolved issues had come between them, she thought. The closeness they once had wasn't quite there any more. At least, she felt sufficiently insecure not to be able to speak as openly as she used to.

"You just take it easy," said Morten as he rose to get dressed. "I'll tend to the animals today."

She looked at him gratefully. "Thank you. My head doesn't seem to enjoy nights like that," she answered and went to her room. The thudding pain was getting stronger.

The day was no longer young when Mette woke up again. Rested and chipper, she jumped out of bed. Soon all this excitement would be history and she could enjoy the last few weeks of her stay to the fullest. If she would only get a chance to speak to Morten soon, then everything would be fine.

Mette didn't see much of Morten that day, either. He had lots of things to take care of outside. Up on the steep rocky slope behind the seter house he discovered a tree that was completely splintered. That's where the lightning had hit.

Mette shivered when she realized how close she had been. She really had been watched over by angels that night. Morten came over to her as she stood looking at the demolished tree. For a while they stood there together, studying what easily might have been a tragedy. Then he suddenly turned toward her.

"You cannot be alone up here at night. That's for sure." The tone of his voice showed great concern. "I will ask Ellen to come up here tonight."

Mette didn't answer. She just looked at him, confused. Again, a feeling of unease came over her. Was he heading down to town again tonight? She didn't have the courage to ask. And then this Ellen ...

Nothing more was said between them. Morten turned and went back to what he was doing.

When Mette again entered the seter house, she had only one thing on her mind.

She had to get rid of all her worries. They just made her feel bad. This was really none of her business. If it were, Morten probably would have brought it up with her. She was so irritated she stamped her foot. Why was she always so sensitive? Why did she worry about everything?

She didn't see Morten again that day. A while later, she heard his car disappear down the road.

Sure enough, Ellen arrived a while later. Mette didn't feel very sociable that night. After their evening meal, she excused herself, said she had a headache and went to her room. And that was no lie. The heavy thudding had increased, so she really felt like going to bed.

23 • What the moon revealed

Ellen was as nice as she could possibly be. Mette was ashamed that she wasn't able to be more cordial to her. Ellen helped with the chores both in the cow barn and the dairy room in an easy manner. Mette didn't have to tell her how to do things. She seemed to know what to do. This, too, gave Mette an urgent feeling of unease. She thought this confirmed her suspicion that there might be a closer relationship between Ellen and Morten than either let on.

As they were having breakfast, Ellen suddenly turned somber. "This has really gotten awkward." She looked ahead of her, hesitating. Mette felt herself tense up. Would Ellen now shed some light on what was going on? Mette wasn't sure she wanted to hear the truth. Ellen didn't seem to notice.

When she continued, Mette realized that Ellen thought she knew more than she did. "I've ended up in the middle of this," she continued.

Then she looked directly at Mette. "I really think it would be best if you left soon. It would probably be best for everybody, not in the least for you. If that's what you choose to do, I'll be glad to take over for you for the rest of the season. You know I'm used to this kind of work."

Mette felt as if knives were piercing her chest. What was this woman saying to her? Did she want to get rid of her? Mette was unable to see that she had behaved in any way that might have made Ellen feel threatened. A thousand questions raced through her mind. She didn't know what to say. In the end she was able to stammer an answer: "If … that's what you think is best, then …"

Ellen was caught up in her thoughts again. "I don't know," she said. "I really don't know."

They didn't discuss the matter any further. Mette felt she had to be alone. As soon as it seemed the natural thing to do, she said she wanted to hike up the hillside to see if she might find some berries. They weren't expecting any visitors that day, so there wasn't much for her to do before the barn chores in the evening.

Never had she felt more miserable than she did as she climbed, bucket and berry picker in hand, up the hillside. Missi and Caesar came running when they saw her go. How wonderful it was to be around these animals. In their daily life, there were no difficult questions asked or impossible decisions to be made. If they got their food and care and a good portion of petting, they were happy.

Mette put down her bucket and put both her arms around Caesar's soft neck. This calf was special to her. In a way, she felt she was his mother. He seemed to regard her in the same way. He licked her hand and snuggled against her. He awoke so many thoughts and feelings in her. His birth was fresh in her mind. The way she and Morten had fought together to save this little creature's life. Other feelings came to her as well. The moment in the water …

She put her head close to the calf's, her tears dripping onto his soft fur. "Soon I'll have to leave you," she sobbed, "but I don't know how I'm going to bear it."

Missi came over to her as well. She licked the tears off her cheeks. Mette had to smile. The heifer seemed to want to comfort her in her distress.

For a long time she sat with the calves. They didn't seem to tire of her company.

When she finally rose and continued on, both of them followed her. It was fine with her. It felt good to have them there. They were a great comfort.

At the top of the hill she found a place where the blueberry plants were chock-full of berries. Over and over again she filled up her berry picker. The bucket was full too soon. "Why didn't I bring another bucket?" she thought. She didn't feel like going back yet.

She sat down on a rock and looked around her. Down below, she could see the entire seter area. One thing was for sure. She had never seen a more beautiful place. The sun twinkled in the lake. Around her she could see that Nature was getting ready for fall. Even if there were no striking colors to be seen yet, the birches had already turned yellow. Where she sat, the air felt brisk, but the sun warmed her enough to keep her from feeling cold. The temperature was not what it had been just a few weeks earlier.

She turned slightly, looking at the bogs and plateaus reaching toward the majestic mountains on the horizon. Some hills in between stopped her from taking in the entirety of the wide-reaching beauty.

A little further away, she heard the bubbling of a small mountain stream running between the hills. Some ptarmigans took off in alarm as Missi and Caesar got too close, kicking and frolicking.

Time seemed to stand still as she sat watching her spectacular surroundings. She didn't bother to check her watch.

But in the end, she rose reluctantly and started on her trip back. She had to walk carefully, for berries filled her bucket to the rim. The calves were still hanging around, so she had to watch out for them, too.

Everything seemed empty and deserted when she arrived back down at the seter. She noticed that Morten's car was there, so he had to be somewhere nearby.

She found herself a sheltered spot by the sunny wall of the seter house. She sat down to clean the berries. Then she discovered Ellen and Morten. They were engrossed in spirited conversation over by Marit's camper. Morten pointed toward the lake. Both looked in agreement in that direction. Mette turned her attention to the berries again. What they were up to over there was none of her business, she reminded herself.

They had dinner together in the afternoon. If either of them noticed that Mette was unusually quiet, they didn't comment on it. The two were engrossed in a conversation concerning some tourists they had met in the mountains—people they hadn't seen for years, but who had lived in their town when they were young. They both had played with them in those days. One story after another was brought up. If Mette hadn't felt so down, the meal would have been a pleasant one.

As soon as they had finished their meal, Mette went to see the animals. She brought special treats for all of them. The lambs had grown so big. They were no longer as playful as they were when she arrived right after St. John's Day, but they knew her so much better. As soon as they saw her, they came running. She took her time with each one of them today, not knowing when she would be leaving the seter. What Ellen alluded to might have been her own wish, but Mette couldn't let go of the notion that it was her honest opinion. If only she could have a word with Morten …

She took her time finishing the milking. She went from one cow to another, scratching them behind their ears and patting their necks. They knew her so well. They seemed to like the dairymaid who had taken care of them this summer.

After she finished her barn chores, she took her time preparing the milk. She both separated and made *eggost**—egg cheese. She didn't see the others and was actually relieved. The car was there, so she knew they had to be around somewhere. Maybe they had gone for a hike or sat talking in Marit's camper. For Ellen used it as her sleeping quarters when she stayed at the seter.

That evening, Mette twisted and turned back and forth in bed. Sleep made itself scarce. Thoughts raced through her mind and turned into complete chaos. Everything was quiet in the house. Outside her window, dusk had turned into night. With her eyes open, Mette stared around her room. Soon it would be so dark that she wouldn't be able to see any of the cherished things she had come to know so well. The bed at the other end of the room was full of items she had brought in her suitcase. The dresser was full, too. Outside she could hear the bells of the sheep as they moved around in their shed. The sound had always filled her with deep contentment. Tonight it just made her feel sad.

She lit her lamp and opened her Bible. She might find some words of comfort there. For a while she lay flipping through the pages. In the end she put it away again. She was incapable of concentrating on what she was reading.

Time went by. Minutes turned into hours, but Mette was still wide awake.

She threw aside her comforter and placed her feet on the floor. She might just as well get up. Trying to sleep was a complete waste of time. Quickly, she put a jacket over her nightgown, slid her shoes onto her bare feet and walked out to the meadow.

She shivered as she stepped out the door. The air was cooler than she expected. Up in the sky, the moon had risen over the mountains to the east. It gave enough light for Mette to see where she was going. The grass was wet from the dew. She walked along the path down to the lake. All was still. The animals were probably asleep, each in their own spot. Only the wind whispered faintly in the treetops to the south.

Mette stood by the lake while her memories came back to her. All the good times she had had by these banks, sometimes with Morten and other times with visitors. She shivered, realizing it was not caused by the chill in the air. She would always remember this summer as one of the most fantastic experiences of her life.

Slowly the moon drifted behind some clouds. Complete darkness fell around her. Only a weak glow lingered above the mountains. The cold starting creeping inside her shoes and along her bare legs under the long nightgown.

Suddenly Mette heard a sound. It came from the other side of the lake.

She peered intently into the dark, but was unable to see anything at all. It was probably an animal moving along the bank.

There, she heard something again. Now it came from the water. Might it be an animal taking a swim? The moon was still hidden behind the clouds. She looked up at the sky. If it would just reappear, then she would probably be able to see what it was. Slowly the clouds drifted by, but it still would take a few minutes before the moon cast its glow over the landscape.

The sounds of measured splashing coming from the water were getting closer and closer. For a moment, she considered turning around and running back to the seter house. But curiosity got the better of her. What could this be?

She listened to the splashing, and suddenly she realized that what she heard, had to be the strokes of the oars in a boat. So there were people out on the lake in the middle of the night. Quick as lightning, she crept behind some nearby bushes. She didn't want to be seen there, dressed only in her nightgown. Whoever it was would probably think she was sleepwalking. She also worried about what kind of people would be out and about at this time of night.

She heard the boat bump against the bank just a little way from where she was hiding. Quiet as a mouse, she huddled behind the bushes. At the same time, the moon came out, bathing the bank in bright moonlight. Then she clearly saw two people step out of the boat and moor it by the bank. Waves of shock went through her when she realized who they were. One had Morten's unmistakable shape. The other, who he gently helped out of the boat, was also soon recognizable. A ringing laughter revealed that it was Ellen whom Morten was with on this night out on the lake. The two of them seemed to be enjoying each other's company a lot. Again and again, they both laughed happily.

Mette stayed long after they had disappeared up the path. Never, ever, would she want them to discover her there. She had to make sure they were safely inside before she returned. Soon she saw a weak light in the window up by the gable. Then she realized that Morten was up in his loft. She stayed there for a while longer. She could hardly feel her toes. The rest of her body was ice cold, too.

Finally, she dared come out. As quietly as possible, she ran along the path. Just to make sure, she took a detour to the outhouse by the cow barn before she entered the house. If she met someone, they would think she just had some business out there.

It took a long time for Mette to get the warmth back in her body. And it took even longer before she was able to sleep. A boundless despair welled up in her.

Suddenly it was as if everything became clear in her mind. "You can't go on like this," she said to herself. "Now you have to acknowledge this and do something about it." It became suddenly clear to her … the reason she felt so uneasy … why she was so devastated by what she saw in the moonlight out there that night.

Mechanically, she lit her lamp. She grabbed a piece of paper from her nightstand — a receipt from when she last went to the store. With the pen she kept in her diary, she quickly wrote down four words:

"I love you, Morten …"

For a long time, she stared at what she had written, tears running down her cheeks. Now it was spoken and put in print. So this was her problem. Finally she dared admit it to herself. She knew right away this wasn't something that had happened there and then. No, she had felt this way since the first day … when she saw him down by the other lake.

She was about to be overcome by tears. What use was it to admit to this? The whole

83

thing was hopeless. Could she get stronger evidence of a relationship between the two of them than the fact they had been out on the lake together in the dark?

It was completely clear that she had to leave as soon as possible. She would never be able to function in her job with those kinds of feelings, now that she had admitted them to herself. All she would accomplish was to hurt the relationship between Morten and Ellen, and obviously, she didn't want that to happen. No, she had to get away, and it had to happen fast. She was determined to talk to Morten the next day. Her mind was made up.

All this time, she still had a tiny hope she might be wrong. It might just be a misunderstanding. If that were the case, she would find out tomorrow, she thought.

After making her decision, she was able to relax a little more. She placed the little receipt on which she had written the four words, into her diary. No one would ever see it. She might burn it soon … but not quite yet.

Little by little she drifted into an uneasy sleep.

24 • *Departure*

Mette had never felt as exhausted as she did when she woke up the next morning. Her body was stiff after her chilly walk in the moonlight the night before. Her lack of sleep was best measured by the degree of her thudding headache. Her dreams had been troubling and depressing. It was as if she had been sleeping all tensed up the entire night. Still, the decision she had made, stood. She just had to get out of bed and get it over with. She also realized she would have to explain everything to Morten, humiliating as it might be. He had to know the full, complete truth.

With this decision in mind, she got up and dressed. When she came outside, she didn't see any of the others. One thing she was going to insist on: When talking to Morten, she had to make sure they were alone. This was not for other people's ears.

"I can just as well start the milking," she thought as she stood there. "Then it's done."

The entire time she worked in the cow barn she fought back a big lump in her throat. Time and time again, she realized this might be the last time she did her barn chores. The worst moment came as she was petting Caesar. "I don't know how I will make it in the city without you," she said, pulling the warm animal body against her as closely as she could. A few large teardrops fell on his little muzzle.

Before she returned to the house, she walked over to the well by the rocky slope to wash her face in the cold water. Maybe this would wipe away some of the traces of her emotional farewell to the animals.

Morten was at the table drinking coffee when she entered. Ellen was nowhere to be seen, so Mette assumed she was still out in the camper. She had a late night the day before. The first thing that struck her was that this was the time to do it. The situation was ideal, and it was best to get it over with.

She started a little falteringly, and had to stop. How in the world was she going to explain this? Morten looked at her, puzzled. She was obviously nervous.

"I have though it over and think it's best that I leave …" No, uff. This wasn't the way she meant to say it. Mette looked down.

Morten stared at her. Then a dark shadow drifted across his face. He cringed as if experiencing physical pain. His voice sounded considerable stressed when he answered: "Yes, maybe it's for the best. I can understand why you must feel that way."

Mette looked at him in bewilderment. Could he understand it? Was it that obvious? Did this mean that her suspicions were correct? Her tiny hope vanished right away.

Morten clenched his hands and took a deep breath before he continued. "I can take you to the station. You just get ready and I will check the train schedule."

Mette felt she was about to faint. She wasn't able to say any more. If she opened her mouth now, she would break into tears, guaranteed. A stiff nod signified that she accepted the offer. Then she went quickly to her room.

Never had she packed this hurriedly. Clothes and other belongings were stuffed into her suitcase and backpack. She didn't take the time to worry about folding her things as neatly as she should. When she went to fetch some warm water to clean herself up, she noticed that Morten had left. She was greatly relieved that she didn't have to face him again just yet. He still hadn't returned when she sat down at the table to eat some breakfast.

Not until she had finished doing the dishes did he return.

"The train leaves in two hours," he said without looking at her. "Will you manage to get ready by then?"

"I'm ready right now," answered Mette, straining herself to the limit in an attempt to make her voice seem relatively normal.

"That's good," said Morten. "If you get your luggage, I'll carry it out for you."

Mette went back to her room. She stopped for an instant inside the door and took a deep breath. Then she scanned the room quickly to see if she had left anything behind. That's when she discovered her diary on the nightstand. A shiver went through her as she grabbed it by the cover and tossed it into her bag, pages aflutter. Wouldn't it be embarrassing if she'd left it behind!

She didn't seem to have forgotten anything else. If they found something after she was gone, they could just send it to her. Quickly, she wrote her address on a note and left it on the nightstand. She would tell Morten why she had left it on their way down.

The drive to town was a nightmare for her. Not much was said. Morten had never been talkative. But still, they had always been able to talk easily and comfortably. Today, he hardly answered when she addressed him. His face was a picture of gloom and his dark eyes were completely black. Deep creases lined his forehead. His expression worried her. He looked almost 10 years older.

Mette couldn't think of much to say, either. Throughout the entire trip she fought to control the storm raging inside her. She felt as though she were about to erupt any time. And what the outcome would be, she had no idea.

She didn't notice at all the scenery along the road. Only as they drove by the lake where she took that swim on her way up, did she turn and look. Morten turned around, too, and glanced toward the lake. A grimace drifted across his face at the same time. Maybe they were thinking the same thing? Not once this summer had he hinted about that meeting … when he had seen her naked while she was about to get dressed. Mette still cringed at the thought.

That this wonderful summer would end in this way felt like a catastrophe. The worst thing was, all this time she had a feeling there was some kind of misunderstanding involved. But she had no idea how to clear it up. Too many unresolved matters stopped her from bringing things up. What bothered her the most was the suspicion there was some nastiness going on that shouldn't be brought to light. It was just so unfathomable that Morten would be involved in something like that. All this time she had known him as honesty itself. A more morally upright man she had never met. Nor had she seen a better minister. No, this was too complicated. She couldn't bring it up. It was impossible.

The railroad station was located a little west of the shopping center, but not that far away. Morten stopped when they arrived and put her luggage down on the platform. Mette exited the car. She didn't quite know what to do or say. There was still some time before the train would leave. For a moment Morten stood looking at her. She looked directly into his somber face. Time and time again she swallowed, but still wasn't able to say anything. The lump in her throat made everything choke up down there. And she didn't want to cry. No, that must not happen.

Morten was struggling with something, too, but she didn't understand quite what it could be. It seemed as if he wanted to say something. But he didn't make a sound. His face just took on a pained look. Mette was unable to interpret it. She wasn't able to think clearly enough to even try.

When he finally opened his mouth, he simply shook her hand and said: "Thank you for this summer and goodbye ..."

He paused. Mette, too, managed to whisper a goodbye.

Suddenly, he turned and left. Not even for a moment did he look back ... just turned the car around and took off. Then he was gone.

Never in her life had she felt as lost as she did standing there, all alone, on the platform. The lump in her throat threatened to burst. She fought and fought. She just didn't want to cry. Ohhh, how she wished for the luxury of a good cry all by herself. Scream ... yell ... shout ...

If she did what she felt right there at the station, her arrest would be guaranteed, she was sure of that.

Finally, the train arrived. As swiftly as possible, she boarded and found a seat as far away from other passengers as possible. She had no idea how to get through the hours ahead.

Later, she remembered this trip as a never-ending agony. The lump in her throat felt like an abscess that was just growing and growing. She was afraid it would burst at even the smallest trace of emotion. Now and then she tried to read, but she wasn't able to concentrate. She finally had to put away newspapers and books. She also tried to sleep, but that, too, proved impossible. Food she wasn't able to think about at all. She had brought some food for the road, but she didn't touch it.

She arrived safely at the Sentralbane Station in central Oslo, hailed a cab and soon was back in her apartment.

Cold and stale air greeted her when she unlocked the door and let herself in. It was obvious the place had been unoccupied for a whole, long summer. She opened a window in the living room, but soon shut it again. It was too cold to air out the room. The weather in the city was gray and melancholy. It fit her mood to a tee. The temperature outside had fallen considerably since the calendar went from August to September. Besides, the exhaust-filled air outside was nothing she wanted to let into her living room.

Mette noticed very well the difference from the fresh mountain air she had grown used to.

After turning on the heat, she went to her bedroom. Her bed was made up, just like she had left it.

Finally, she thought, "Now I'm alone. No one knows that I'm back. No one will ring the doorbell." Her cell phone was turned off. She was alone … all alone. Now she could … With a sob she flung herself on the bed. And then the tears came.

She stayed there for a long time. Accompanied by uncontrolled sobs and wails, her tears streamed and dampened her pillow. She didn't mind, just continued to cry. How wonderful it was to finally have this painful abscess lanced. But it was also painful to allow all those hurt feelings to emerge anew.

Her thoughts whirled back and forth. At that moment, she mostly felt sorry for herself. The worst part was that she couldn't find anyone to blame for her misery. Who might she really blame for all this pain? When she started thinking about it, she choked. Everything was confusing and chaotic.

No, she didn't want to think about it. She could only blame this on herself. Why in the world would she go and fall in love with this man? If she hadn't done that, the entire situation would have been different. In any case, she wouldn't have had to be this miserable.

At long last her tears ran out, and exhausted, she fell asleep.

25 • *Alone with tears*

Confused, Mette sat up in bed. Where was she? Her woozy head wasn't able to sort out her thoughts. She heard the sounds of traffic from the outside, but how could that be? Where were the sheep … and the sound of their bells? And the mooing of the cows eagerly waiting to get inside to be milked? The room was pitch dark, but where was she?

Slowly, the events of the previous day came back to her. She was back in the city. For how long might she have been asleep? It took her a minute to find the switch to the lamp on her nightstand. When she finally managed to turn it on, she saw that it was only 3 a.m. There was no sense in getting up yet. She shivered a little, for she had fallen asleep on top of her comforter. She lay there fully dressed.

Awkwardly, she undressed and crept under the covers. It was best to get some more sleep. But she felt completely miserable. Her headache throbbed steadily. All thoughts of the days ahead distressed her: How would she be able to tackle her job at the office again, or answer the questions that would be asked? She though of the expectations of her friends and co-workers. They probably were just about to burst with anticipation. When she left, they had chided her in a friendly manner about her returning in a *bunad*—a folk costume—with a headscarf covering her hair. Maybe she had brought a billy goat or two in her luggage. She had enjoyed their jokes then. She had even promised to arrive in full dairymaid costume on her first day back.

And then there was Tore … She sank into her pillow again. Did he now know where she had been this summer? She had actually decided to take Morten's advice and not pay much attention to what he said, but rather compliment him now and then. But now her good intentions seemed as futile as trying to cross an impassable mountain.

Again she started to cry. It was unbelievable that she could possess so many tears. Fortunately, she wouldn't have to go back to work for another week. She was also relieved that she didn't have to worry about someone showing up at her door. No one knew she was back.

As morning approached, she fell asleep again and didn't wake up until later in the day. A gnawing feeling in her stomach told her she needed some breakfast.

With an effort, she sat up and rubbed her eyes. Her entire face felt stiff and strange. "I need a good cleanup," she thought and went to her bathroom.

The shocking sight that met her in the mirror made her wish she had just stayed in bed. What a sight! Her entire face was swollen, with red spots all over. Her eyes were red, too—at least, what she was able to see from between her swollen eyelids. Her hair was a mess. It probably got wet from lying on the damp pillow and then it had dried in the shape in which it had been molded.

Never in her life had she seen anything this repulsive. She had probably been crying in her sleep, too. If everything hadn't been so tragic, she would have laughed. But one thing was for sure; she couldn't be seen like this. She was completely isolated in her lonely existence in her apartment.

Showering didn't help her appearance much. Still, she felt better afterward. It was just her inner being that didn't improve much from soap and water.

Then there was breakfast. It didn't take long for her to realize the consequences of her hasty return back home. She didn't have time to plan anything. The only edibles in the house were the sandwiches she had brought along for the trip and a bag of rolled oats sitting in her cupboard. And then she had water from the tap. She didn't even have coffee.

While she ate her sandwiches, she started wondering about when she last had something to eat. It had to be more than 24 hours ago. She didn't have a bite on the trip. And when she got back to her apartment, she had just gone directly to bed.

Still, she wasn't hungry. But the gnawing in her stomach told her that she had better eat something. The way she looked, she couldn't go shopping, so there would be oatmeal porridge for supper.

An inexplicable feeling of despondency came over her as she sat there. If only she had someone to confide in. Maybe a friend or relative, but no one came to mind. There were probably several in her circle of friends that she might have talked to, but she couldn't stomach the thought of opening up to someone. It was entirely too humiliating.

While she considered this, her tears started anew. She wasn't able to stop them. She didn't see a reason for it, either. She just let them run. Where was her zest for life and her enthusiasm? She always used to have something she enjoyed doing. It might be some hobby, crafts or simply something work-related. Now everything seemed hopeless. Nothing seemed to entice her to get on with her business. The only thing she wanted was to sit there and cry. Never in her life had she experienced something like this.

She took her Bible from her suitcase. Maybe it would have an encouraging word for her. Apathetically, she leafed back and forth, but she still was unable to concentrate on any kind of reading. In the end, she put it down. "Maybe God, too, has left me," she thought. "He probably thinks I'm a fool, sitting here with my sorrows." Her tears kept running.

Suddenly, she remembered some lines from a song. "Tell Him everything, then it's no longer yours …"

"Tell Him everything" … could she possibly do that? Might God care about this? She gave it a thought for a moment. She might try, but …

Doubtfully, she folded her hands and started giving words to her thoughts. "Dear Jesus, I'm in such pain. I feel completely …" Stumblingly she began describing everything as she saw and felt it. For a long while, she sat deeply concentrating on her prayer. Slowly, she started to relax.

But then it came over her again. It was as if a red-hot fury started welling up inside her. "Why did it have to be this way? Why didn't You stop this from happening? You are almighty. This is not especially hard for You. At least You might have made sure that I didn't fall in love with this guy. Why didn't You?"

A violent anger filled her. She fell on her knees by the chair and gave her fury free rein. Again and again she cried out her questions. "Why … why … Maybe You don't exist? Maybe I have staked my life on something that doesn't exist …?"

Slowly, her anger abated. Soon she sat there in complete exhaustion. She didn't have any more to say. No more questions. Everything had sort of run out of her. Her thoughts were a jumble. She just stayed there on her knees in front of the chair.

Then it was as though she felt a hand gently stroking her hair. She looked up quickly, but no one was there. Of course, it was just her imagination. Her tears continued to flow and she collapsed again.

There it was again. She felt the gentle touch. Puzzled, she slowly rose to her feet. Then she felt, more than heard, a voice saying: "Read Psalm 91."

Unsteady, she reached for her Bible. It took her a while to find the passage, for her hands never stopped shaking.

Finally, Psalm 91 was displayed in her lap. Her eyes fastened on Verse 15. She started reading. "He will call upon me, and I will answer Him; I will be with Him in trouble, I will deliver Him and honor Him."

For a long while she just sat there, staring. She had called out to God. Never in her life had she called out more fervently for her Maker. But she had just felt she was calling out to her walls. She had felt completely alone and isolated.

But that had not been the case. God had been present between these walls. He had actually been there with her. The undeniable proof was there. She had called out to Him … and He had responded to her … His Word in the Bible was the truth. She knew … yes, she was convinced …

And then the rest had to be true, too. He was with her in her misery. She was not alone. Why He hadn't helped her avoid this predicament, she was unable to fathom. Nor did she understand why she had to go through all this uncertainty in regard to Morten. But she knew this: This was not something that had passed God by. It was something He noticed and that He wanted to take care of in one way or another.

There was also a promise in the passage. There was a promise about deliverance and glory. It was more than she was able to understand, but it gave her some of her courage back. Maybe there was a way out of this.

Her wonderment filled her more and more. She thought about the prayer she said. It wasn't exactly a humble and appreciative prayer. It was actually full of rage. As she thought about this, an incredible feeling of peace filled her. God had heard her prayer and He had answered it. But His answer wasn't in the same tone of voice. His answer had been filled with the most wonderful love. So then, God tolerated it when people raged against Him when life appeared to turn against them?

Yes ... this was the nature of God. She knew it so well, but in this particular situation, she hadn't been able to see it. She had to smile to herself. How could she forget so quickly. Not long ago, she had clearly experienced that her prayers were heard. God had answered her ever as clearly the night at the seter when she was so frightened.

And He didn't just listen to timid and mild prayers. No, He listened just as closely to the ones who came to Him in their most fervent need. And He was able to handle the strongest emotional eruptions.

Little by little, her body relaxed. Her sorrow and uncertainty were still there, but the peace that her experience had given her made it possible for her to think clearly again. The tears that threatened to well up the entire time seemed to be drying up, too.

She spent the rest of the day unpacking her luggage. Some clothes needed washing while others could just be put away. She could no longer wear her summer clothes. It was already fall, and winter was knocking at the door. She noticed that it lifted her spirit to keep busy with something. So she looked around for more things to do. Her windows needed washing, and the refrigerator needed cleaning before she started filling it up again.

When evening arrived, she felt her dark mood still buried deep inside her. Now and then she noticed that her thoughts returned to that painful place. She shed a few tears as well. But the peace from Psalm 91 was still there. This helped her go to bed feeling considerably calmer.

26 • *From dream to reality*

The following days were sad and miserable. She obviously had to start getting back into her social and work-related life again. On Sunday, she went to see some friends. They were puzzled by her somber mood. She tried to explain enough for them to understand there had been some kind of problem. But still, it wasn't easy. She didn't want to tell them anything about Morten and her feelings toward him. And regarding the rest of the problem, there was so much she herself didn't understand.

On Monday morning, she called her office. She wanted to know if they were really busy. If so, she could return to work a few days earlier than planned, she said. The idea of being shut up in her apartment, crying and harboring all kinds of notions, scared her. She would be much better to get back to work and concentrate on something else.

Her proposition was greeted with enthusiasm. They were really busy. It would be great if she could come right away. Grateful, she got ready and went to work.

If she had thought working would solve all her problems, she was wrong. Obviously, it was great to see her co-workers again, and Tore was—to her great relief—traveling. Thus, she didn't have to deal with him for a while.

But she had trouble concentrating. Time and time again, she caught herself staring at nothing. The letters she wrote had to be started over again several times. It was almost impossible for her to get her act together for planning the upcoming fall programs.

Her day turned out to be more of a struggle than actual diversion.

At lunch, she found herself alone for a while with one of the women from work. She looked at Mette with real concern. "What is bothering you?" she asked. "Your face is all white." She had also noticed Mette's absent-mindedness.

"I had some problems before I left my last job, but it will be all right soon." Mette didn't want to say any more. She didn't have the stomach to start on any kind of explanation. It was so hopeless anyway. Her co-worker looked at her searchingly for a moment, but didn't ask any more questions.

After work, she went directly home. She felt absolutely exhausted. Where in the world was her zest for life or her enthusiasm for her job? And the strength she had built up this summer—where was it?

The next day didn't turn out much better. She had to pull herself together and mobilize all the strength she had in order to concentrate on even the smallest task. More than once, she experienced that ordinary things had simply disappeared from her memory. And appointments she made had to be written down immediately, or the same thing happened with them.

"This is an impossible situation," she told herself as she dropped into her chair after work. "This can't go on." A small spark of determination and defiance still burned in her. "I have to do something about it. I can't go on like this." But then her resolve faded away, for what could she do?

She knew that she could call Morten and make him explain all the issues that bothered her so much—all the inexplicable events and hints that had caused her so much bewilderment. But she couldn't bring herself to do it. In no way did she possess the courage she might need to face the answers she anticipated.

Completely out of it, she leaned back in her chair. She looked at her watch. It was getting close to milking time now. She wondered if Ellen treated the sheep like they had come to expect at this time of day. And Caesar … did she spend enough time with him? He loved being petted and scratched behind his ears. And then he always wanted to suck on her fingers. Then there were the goats. Did Ellen make sure they didn't get into the dairy room? With horror, she thought about all the mischief they might get themselves into in there with all the dairy products.

She got up and went over to her cupboard. She took out the stack of photographs she had taken during the summer. Not once had she looked at them after she returned. Now, she wanted to go through them. Maybe something would come to her that would make her feel better inside.

She didn't look at many photos before she realized this was not the way to forget her woes. Feelings and thoughts washed over her again. There were the pictures she took when Missi was born. The boy who fell on his back in the hay on the barn floor as the calf suddenly popped out. She had managed to catch a moment of astonishment and mirth when a miracle happened. A small creature was born … It was as if she could hear Morten's cheerful laughter next to her.

Then there was Aunt Anna. Her round face shone toward her from the pictures. Far into the furrows of her face, Mette glimpsed two eyes that portrayed goodness itself. She also took a look at the pictures from the revival meeting and other events.

Strange how many pictures she had of Morten. His tanned skin made her seem pale in comparison. Actually, she had quite a few pictures of him and her together. It was never hard to find someone to help take pictures of them. The way he smiled at her in the pictures made her shiver inside again. She was about to burst into tears.

Slowly, the stack of photos sank into her lap. Her thoughts began wandering. Soon they drifted on wings spread wide. She was back at the seter. The sound of the bells and the whisper of the wind sweeping down from the mountain filled her with the serenity she wished for. There, Caesar came running toward her. She caught him in her arms and they tumbled around in the meadow. The goats, too, wanted to join in the fun. Aunt Anna stood in the doorway, beaming toward them. Soon a bunch of kids cheerfully joined in the game, too.

Then a car came up the road. It was Morten. As he saw them romping around in ecstasy, he had a mind to join in as well. He sounded his horn, causing animals and kids to jump to heaven high. With resounding laughter, he sounded the horn again.

Suddenly the blaring of the horn didn't sound that pleasant any more. Dazed, Mette shook her head. Where was she? She wasn't at the seter at all. On the contrary, she was asleep in her chair at home. The wonderful feeling she just had were starting to fade. So it was just a dream.

There was the loud noise again, but it was no car horn. It was her doorbell. Alarmed, she picked up the pictures and put them on the table. Some of them fell to the floor. As she passed the mirror, she turned to check if she was in any shape to see anyone at all. Her appearance wasn't much to write home about. Assuming that one of her neighbors was paying her a visit, she took the chance of answering the door despite her frazzled look.

Her face fell when she opened the door. Was she dreaming? She had to blink her eyes a couple of times to be sure. No, she was right. Morten was standing there.

A few long seconds they just stood there looking at each other. Then he gave her an uncertain smile and said: "May I come in?"

"Sure ..." Mette cleared her throat. Her voice wouldn't work. She tried again: "Yes, come in." Her voice was no more than a whisper. She opened the door wide and let him in.

After regaining her composure she showed Morten to the chair she had been sitting in. She seated herself in the sofa next to it. A fleeting thought suggested that she ought to make some coffee ... But she let it go. Never in her life would she be able to make coffee under such circumstances.

For a while, they just sat there. No one said anything. Thoughts swirled around in Mette's head. What had made Morten travel all these miles and hours in order to see her? Was there anything wrong? If so, it had to be something awful.

An icy feeling of fear started spreading throughout her body.

Finally, Morten cleared his throat. Obviously, this moment was hard for him, too. "I just wanted to talk to you," he started. "I'm afraid there might have been some kind of misunderstanding before you left."

Mette stared at him in surprise. What was this? She wasn't able to say anything ... just waited for him to continue.

He looked down at his hands, clenched in his lap, as he continued. "We talked about it after you left ... that is, Ellen and I ... There might have been a misunderstanding. She told me she had advised you to leave. I didn't know anything about it. I thought you felt the gossip was so hard to handle that you couldn't bear to stay any longer." His voice was soft and strained. Bringing this up at all seemed to take its toll on him.

Mette stared at him in even greater puzzlement. Her confusion was now complete. What was he talking about? Finally she was able to tweak a sound out of her throat. "Gossip?"

Morten gave her a pallid smile. "So you didn't know anything about it?"

She just shook her head. This was completely bizarre.

Suddenly his smile disappeared and deep creases dug in between his eyes. "But then, why did you leave?" His dark eyes looked at her with intensity.

Mette felt paralyzed. What would she tell him? His look demanded an answer, right now. She cleared her throat. Her voice still wasn't working quite right. There was nothing else to do but tell him everything. She wasn't going to hide anything. It would just lead to more misery. No, the truth had to come out.

She composed herself and mobilized all her strength before she answered. "I assumed that Ellen wanted me to leave."

Morten's eyes reflected great surprise as soon as the words were out. "Why in the world would she want that?"

Now it was Mette's turn to clench her hands in her lap. Her eyes seemed to study their movement in detail. When she continued, her voice was almost inaudible. "I assumed she wasn't pleased that I …" She stopped. But then she regained her composure. She just had to get this over with. "I mean, I assumed she didn't like me to be around … when you were there." Everything was tangling up for her now.

Morten sat forward, resting his elbows on his knees. His raised eyebrows coached her to continue. Again Mette composed herself. This was a mess. In a voice sharper than intended, she said: "I understood that you were in a relationship, and then you can't blame her for thinking it was foolish to leave you alone with another woman." Now it was said. Mette shrank a little and looked cautiously up at him.

The shock expressed in his eyes made her feel completely befuddled again. "How in the world did you come to think that?" He almost shouted the words at her.

Again Mette realized everything had to come out now. She started telling him about how she had noticed their close relationship. The manner in which they talked to each other and the interest they showed in each other. She ended by telling him what had confirmed her impression: the episode by the lake that night.

Morten listened in silence. Nothing revealed what he really felt. When she was finished and had told him everything, she stopped and sat there, hands still in her lap.

Morten, too, was quiet for a while. Then he roared with laughter. Mette felt like slapping him. So it was all a joke to him. Her indignant expression made him shut up in an instant.

Then it was Morten's time to talk. He explained to her that Ellen was his hometown neighbor. She had been around for as long as he remembered. They played together as children. One year, when Ellen was quite young, she had helped his mother for an entire summer, working as a dairymaid at the seter. And she still helped out Aunt Anna now and then as needed. She knew very well how to do the chores up there. If they had wanted to get married, they would have done so years ago. No, they had never considered it. They were just close friends.

Mette looked a little ashamed. "But what about the night on the lake?" She had to ask about it …

Morten laughed again. "Do you remember we were talking about meeting some old friends in the mountains?"

Mette nodded.

"They were renting the Fjellbu seter. You know, the place on the other side of the lake. That night we decided to go over to visit them. It was late before we left for home, so we borrowed a rowboat. In the intermittent moonlight, it was easier to row across the lake than try to find our way around it."

Mette felt a great relief—and at the same time a growing excitement—that made her tremble. It was good to get an explanation of his relationship to Ellen, but there was more. There still were unanswered questions.

"I realize that I jumped to conclusions," she said. "I'm sorry if I made things harder for you." Then she looked up at him again. "You said something about gossip. What did you mean by that?"

Morten's face turned gloomier in an instant. "Do you remember that Ellen was terribly upset when she returned from town after the Russians left?"

Mette nodded. She remembered it well. That's when everybody disappeared all of a sudden. That was actually when all the bad things had started to happen.

"As they boarded the bus, they discovered that one of the ladies in their party wasn't there," he continued. "They couldn't locate her, so the bus just had to leave. In a hurry, we organized a search operation. We found the woman at the home of one of the men who was a frequent visitor while they stayed at the seter. It turned out that they had made some kind of connection the first time they visited. Actually, they had kept in touch since that time. Now he offered to marry her, and she assumed that she just could stay.

"This created a lot of problems, not in the least because it turned out that this man treated her badly. We had to help this woman out in a lot of ways. The whole thing looked pretty grim for a while. Ellen took it especially hard. For it was she who invited these people to come in the first place. Fortunately, we were able to straighten things out after a while. But this incident caused all kinds of gossip.

"It actually started when the Russians visited the first time, for several people knew about the two of them. The whole business was rumored to be really dirty. My seter operations, too, were seen in a negative light. Some people seemed to think that I was running a bordello up there. I didn't know anything about this until after that particular episode."

Suddenly he stopped. He sighed and shook his head. "It is unbelievable what people can make of things when they allow their imaginations to run wild," he said quietly.

For a while they sat without saying anything. Mette thought about what he had told her. The pieces of the puzzle started to fall into place, but still there was something she didn't understand. She still didn't have an explanation for the conversation she overheard that night. That's when she realized she was somehow involved as well. And the next day Morten had told her that he had done something stupid. What might that mean? She had to ask.

Morten smiled crookedly. It took a while before he answered. It looked as if he was trying to figure out what to say. Mette waited in suspense. Was there still something dirty? She just had to know.

Morten cleared his throat. When he started speaking, he sounded as if he would rather not talk about it just that. But Mette's eyes pressed him on. "The rumors didn't improve when I hired a dairymaid. Some people were quite preoccupied with that, especially when she turned out to be a young, beautiful woman, and not the elderly lady we first thought we hired. And after the episode with the Russian woman, the rumors

94

took off completely.

"Late one night I had a visit from some members of the meetinghouse group. They were adamant that I resign from the board. No one knew what was true and what was false. They even thought there might eventually be police involvement in the matter. Those were some awful days." Morten looked ahead of him and shook his head.

So Mette finally had an explanation for what she had heard about him.

"I made up my mind to stay in town as much as possible," Morten continued. "I thought the gossip would die down if they saw I was never at the seter unless other people were there as well." He smiled a little shyly before he added: "It was noticed immediately if you and I were up there by ourselves."

What agony he had been through. Suddenly, Mette felt terribly sorry for him.

Morten continued his story: "There were times when I regretted hiring you. I took for granted that I had made things unbearable for you, too. That's why I said I had done something stupid."

Suddenly a spark of humor flashed in his earnest eyes. "But I don't regret it that much. It was great to get to know you, too."

Mette had to laugh. She breathed in relief. Now, she finally had explanations for everything that bothered her. She understood it all. The insinuations of the men she confronted up there early in the summer, and the warning from the man she met at the revival meeting. The conversation she heard at the store. And finally Ellen's statement that it was best for her if she left.

Oh, what a relief. Now that part of the problem was resolved.

27 • From darkness to light

They sat for a long time talking about what had happened. Mette was able to relax a little more and Morten obviously relaxed, too. He continued to tell her about what had happened after she left. He and Ellen had a long talk. It became clear that Mette's reason for leaving in such haste might be based on a misunderstanding. That evening, Morten took his Bible and looked up the verse in Psalm 91 that Mette showed him the morning after the thunderstorm. But it wasn't the words about not fearing the terror of the night that had stayed with him. It was the last part of Verse 5 that spoke to him so strongly. It said: "… for the arrow that flies by day …"

So he should not fear the arrow that flies by day. For him, the arrow had become a symbol of the gossip. He really had his share of rumors … the arrow … And he became worried. He tried to make the gossip go away by staying away from the seter as much as possible. And then he tried to quell the rumors by keeping mum about it. If he didn't mention any of this to anyone, maybe it would stop. But that didn't happen.

When he read that verse, he realized he was held captive to the rumors as long as he shied away from them and tried to run away. No, he had to face them bravely and with honesty. So he called a meeting of the meetinghouse council and informed everybody of the facts. He told them everything, and all present had an opportunity to express their feelings regarding the whole business. Many emotions and opinions were

95

put on the table that evening. But this also cleared the air. He had told them he intended to go to the city to talk to Mette. "Actually, I was completely honest even about that," he ended and looked bashfully down at the floor.

Mette listened in amazement. He was really incredibly brave. If she only had just a smidgeon of that bravery herself. Then she wouldn't have had to suffer all this time. Not once had she mustered the courage to speak to Morten about what bothered her up at the seter.

They both grew silent again. They looked at each other. Mette felt her heart beating hard. Morten looked as if he wanted to say something, but then seemed to change his mind. A faint blush spread across his face. There was something more … Mette could see it. She gave him a little smile in order to encourage him to continue.

"The real reason I came …" He cleared his throat before he continued. "The real reason I came is that I found something you left behind."

Mette looked at him in surprise. "But why didn't you just send it to me by mail? That's why I left my address."

Morten shifted in his chair. "That was not an option," he said. "I had to see to you, for there was something I wanted to ask you in person."

Then he pulled something out of his pocket and handed it to her. Mette tensed up when she recognized the small, white receipt. In a flash, she recalled tossing her diary, pages fluttering, into her suitcase. Not for a moment did she consider the small piece of paper tucked inside it.

He didn't need to show it to her. She knew too well the four words written on it. She just wished that the floor would open and she could disappear. She wasn't able to speak a word.

Morten looked nervous. "I just had to ask you if what the note says is true," he said in a voice that seemed about to break at any moment.

Again, Mette realized she had to tell him the truth. But she wasn't able to speak in an audible voice. Her answer was just a small nod. Morten got up, moved over to her and sat down.

"This is the thing," he continued. "If what's written on this note is the truth, then I want to ask you if you might consider returning … as my wife …"

Mette stared at him for a moment, tense and excited. Was he joking? No. His wonderful eyes were filled with great anticipation. It was as if her answer to his question meant more to him than anything in this world.

A bright smile appeared on her face while her tears started flowing. Slowly, her head sank down to rest on his shoulder. The words she whispered against his neck were not to be misunderstood. Gently, his arm closed around her shoulders, staying that way for a long time. Little by little her tears soaked her collar. But this time they were not tears of sorrow. If so, these were the last of that flavor flowing from her. After this moment there would only be tears of joy. Mette was sure of that.

Suddenly, Morten pushed her away from him and looked into her eyes. "There is one thing I have to say." Behind his serious expression was a flash of humor. Mette held her breath waiting for whatever confessions still remained. "I have to ask your forgiveness for watching you swimming in the lake that time … I have been ashamed of it all summer."

First Mette stared at him, then she started laughing. "And here I've felt so ashamed that I behaved so frivolously!" They both laughed.

96

"But I know this," said Mette. "That's when it happened, as far as I'm concerned." She pointed to the receipt on the table. "Something happened to this guy, too," said Morten and chuckled.

Then he sobered and looked at her again. "I thought I was going to die when I left you at the station. It is the worst thing I ever experienced. I didn't think I was ever going to see you again. That's why I had to hurry away so no one would see ..." he stopped for a moment before he continued in a much weaker voice ... "that I was crying."

Mette drew closer to him. Again they just sat there, cherishing each other's presence.

"Oooh, how I've missed it ..." Mette looked dreamily ahead of her, "the seter ... and the animals ..."

Morten looked at her, pretending to be offended. "The animals!?"

Mette's laughter rang out. "Yes, them, too ..." •

Haying on Aurebekk Farm, 1930's-style: Author Gunlaug Nøkland's relatives and their friends pose for a photo during the busy haying season on their farm in Holum, Vest-Agder. Pictured are, left to right: Front row—the author's grandparents, Amalie and Gunvald Skuland; Gunlaug's father, Olav Skuland; and a friend, Torvald Andås. Back row—a cousin, Karen Haus (in the hay); and Åse Andås and Karen Skuland, Gunlaug's aunt, astride the horse.

PHOTO ON PAGE 319: Around 1890, a Swedish photographer named Axel Lindahl took this photograph of the little village of Homme in Valle parish, Setesdal. The mountain in the background is named Einang.

PART 2

THE AMERICA LETTERS

28 • Uncle Torkel

A strong wind battered against the window, accompanied by dense snowfall. Mette stretched and peeked over the top of her warm comforter. With a little shudder she rolled up again, grateful she wouldn't have to go outside in this dreadful weather. Actually, she didn't have to get up yet at all. No job was waiting for her out there in the winter storm. She could just stay in her warm bed and relax for as long as she wanted. What a great life, she thought, and smiled to herself while snuggling in the warmth under the cozy comforter. Morten had left for work a while ago. He usually didn't wake her up before he left in the morning. Since she didn't have to get up to make it to work in time, he felt she should be allowed to enjoy these mornings in peace and quiet for as long as it lasted. Things had been stressful enough for her lately.

Mette checked the time. It was soon 8:30 a.m. She stretched again, but wasn't at all tempted to get up on such a cold and dark day. Instead, she stayed in bed while she allowed her thoughts to drift back to the events of the last weeks.

It was almost impossible to conceive that she was now married to the wonderful man she had fallen in love with at the seter where she worked last summer. She took that job to get a change of pace—away from the stress that had started to wear her down. She had fully intended to return to work in the office of the Christian organization that had employed her before her summer at the seter. But the feelings evoked that summer didn't go away easily.

The somewhat introverted and quiet, but gentle and kind, Morten, had now been her husband for two weeks already. They lived in the big main house on his farm near the small mountain town in Vest-Agder *Fylke* that had become so dear and familiar to Mette during the time she took care of the livestock at his seter.

After they decided to get married, it didn't take long for them to start planning their wedding. Neither of them wanted to prolong the wait. They lived so far apart and didn't get to see each other as often as they wished. The organization Mette worked for had a branch operation in town, and when it turned out that Mette would be able to work there, both she and Morten felt there was no reason why they shouldn't start planning their wedding. They decided that Easter would be an ideal time for the event. They chose the Saturday before Palm Sunday for their wedding day.

On their big day, Mette arrived with a large group of family and friends who had all been invited to the wedding. The early spring day was lovely and clear, even if the air was still chilly. Mette had nothing to do with the wedding preparations. Marit, Morten's sister, and her friend, Ellen, had insisted on taking care of everything. The lavish and lovely party had been a surprise for her. The celebration took place in the house that now was her home. Over 50 guests were seated for their wedding dinner in the large living room.

Mette smiled to herself as she lay in the wide old double bed and thought back to that day. Her parents had been there. Her sister and her family were present, too, and some aunts, uncles and friends from her hometown in Sørlandet in southern Norway. Some friends and co-workers from the Oslo office were invited as well. And then there were a few of Morten's family and friends from the community. It was a fantastic day that she was thrilled to reminisce about.

She almost had to laugh to herself when she thought about Morten's best man. Morten had a hard time figuring out who he would ask to do him the honor. They had a long phone call regarding the matter. Morten had so many friends in town, but he didn't feel he could single out any one person. That's when Mette suggested he ask Ellen to be his best "man." Morten had a good laugh at her suggestion, but Mette insisted. In the end he gave in, if Mette would be the one to ask her.

Mette assumed the task with great enthusiasm. Morten knew the reasoning behind Mette's suggestion. This was her way of asking for forgiveness because she had acted a reserved toward Ellen last summer. Mette had believed Morten and Ellen were in a relationship, and Mette couldn't handle it, though she wasn't yet willing to admit that she herself was in love with Morten. When she realized that kind of relationship between Morten and Ellen didn't exist, she was embarrassed for jumping to conclusions. Mette felt this would be a way to make everything all right.

Ellen got a good laugh when Mette asked her. And she had been a good sport and replied with a hint of humor that she would be glad to do Morten the favor. Mette was happy that Ellen accepted, feeling this cemented a good and close relationship to Ellen. They lived so close that they would have a lot to do with each other in time to come. All three of them were about the same age, in their early 30s.

Reluctantly, Mette sat up on the edge of the bed. She'd better get up. There was no sense in staying in bed all day. There were things to do in the house, so she wasn't out of work even if she didn't have to think about a regular job yet. She had a couple weeks off after Easter in order to get properly settled in her new home.

Shivering, she put on her slippers and walked to the bathroom. The big house had six bedrooms on the second floor. In addition, there was a large bathroom and a storage room. She never had this much space anywhere she had ever lived. It was a dream home, she thought. Even if it was an older home, it was well maintained and had been restored and modernized not long ago.

After a quick shower, Mette went down to the kitchen for breakfast. A comfortable heat greeted her as she opened the kitchen door. Morten had started a fire before he left, so she would get up to a comfortable temperature, despite the cold outside. The coffeepot was full of hot coffee, too. Quickly she made a couple of open-face sandwiches and sat down to eat.

Suddenly, she heard the doorbell. Mette jumped in her chair, splashing coffee out of the cup she held in her hand. Who might it be this early in the morning, and in this kind of weather? She rose quickly and went to answer the door. Outside stood a rather shivering and snowy Marit.

"Come in," said Mette, concerned. "What brings you out in this dreadful storm this early in the morning?"

Marit stepped inside the door, but made no attempt to take off her outerwear. Instead, Mette noticed a worried expression on Marit's red-spotted face. "I have to leave again," she said, "I have to be at school at 10 a.m., but I just had to talk to you."

Mette knew that Marit taught school in the next town. If she had to be there at 10, she couldn't stop for long. It would be hard to drive in this weather, so Marit would need plenty of time for the trip.

"It's about Uncle Torkel," Marit hurried to explain. "I looked in on him yesterday, and he didn't feel well at all. He didn't look well, either, but he insisted it was just a cold and that there was nothing to worry about. I thought I would see how he was this morning, so I called him. And this is what worries me: I didn't get an answer. I can't imagine that he has gone out in this storm, as weak as he was yesterday. I tried to call him twice, but no one picked up the phone. I'm worried. Even if he has always been healthy and in good shape, after all, he is 85 years old … no, I don't like it."

It was obvious the woman at the door was greatly concerned. "If it weren't that I absolutely have to be at school today, I would have taken the day off and gone up to see him. But I really can't do that right now. So I thought maybe you could go up there and check up on him." She looked inquiringly at Mette.

"Of course I can," answered Mette, glad to be asked. There was no question; she, with no responsibilities at the moment, would be happy to take the time to go and check on this old uncle. She knew where he lived. Morten had pointed the place out to her once when they drove around in the community to help Mette get more acquainted with her new hometown. She had also met the old man a couple of times, but Morten hadn't told her much about him. Neither had Mette thought of asking much.

"I can go right away," she told Marit, who obviously wanted to be on her way as soon as possible.

"Thank you," said Marit, relieved. "It's not that easy to have to look after a man like Uncle Torkel." She gave a little laugh and shook her head. "You know how stubborn he can be. But if he is sick, I don't think we can just let him sit up there on his farm, Lia, all by himself. At least we should keep an eye on him."

Mette nodded. She had no idea how stubborn Uncle Torkel might be. Morten hadn't mentioned anything about it, but she didn't think this was the time to bring that up. Marit had to get to work, and she had to take the trip up to Lia. It was best to get going.

Marit ran into the snowstorm again. She had parked her car by the main road. Full of snow, she had walked over to the house, for the driveway had not been cleared. Mette noticed it would be quite a job to clear the snow so she could get her car out, but she would manage, she thought.

Morten didn't have to think about clearing the driveway in the morning, for usually he walked to the office. The bank where he worked was so close to their home. And most of the snow had fallen since he left.

29 • The silent house

Mette drove at a snail's pace up the county road. The snowplow hadn't been there in a while, so the snow cover on the road made it slippery. The wind had increased as well, so even though the snow had tapered off, the drifting snow made it hard to navigate. A couple of times she thought she might have missed the driveway to Uncle Torkel's little farm. But then she drove past places she recognized, and she realized she wasn't there yet.

Mette guessed this type of weather must be common in this area, even though it was now well into April. In Sørlandet, her old home in southern Vest-Agder, she was used to daffodils and crocuses in their finest bloom at this time of the year. But she realized that the altitude of this mountainous area could make for very different conditions.

She tried to remember what Morten had told her about the old man and the farm on which he lived. She knew Uncle Torkel was the brother of Morten's maternal grandfather. So that meant that Torkel was Morten's mother's uncle. Apparently, in this district, uncles and aunts of parents were also called so by their children—at least, unmarried uncles and aunts—even though Torkel was actually Morten's great-uncle. Evidently Uncle Torkel had never been married, living alone in the house where Morten's mother grew up. If Mette wasn't mistaken, Torkel had taken over the farm after his brother died. She couldn't remember having been told anything else about Uncle Torkel.

All at once she stopped the car and stared through the windshield. The driveway had to be over there. A little distance from the road sat a small, older house. It had to be the house where Uncle Torkel lived. But the driveway to the house wasn't cleared, which meant that if she wanted to get there, she had to do some legwork.

With difficulty, she parked the car far enough off the road for the snowplow to pass. Then she was off. She was glad she had worn rubber boots, but even those occasionally proved to be too short. The fluffy snow whirled up at her every step. Lumps of snow found their way into her boots.

The almost 200 yards she had to walk seemed to go on forever. The snow and the wind whipped her face, making it difficult for her to see anything at all.

When she got close enough to take a better look at the place, she stopped and looked worriedly at the old house. Nothing indicated that someone had been out in the snow that day. Neither the path to the outbuilding nor the steps were cleared. The windows were dark, and there was no sign of smoke drifting from the chimney.

A shiver went through her. What had she gotten herself into? What would she encounter in there? Gripped by a sudden panic, she felt like turning back and getting someone to go in with her. But then she started thinking: Whom could she ask? Morten was at work, and it probably wouldn't be easy for him to leave the office. Neither Marit nor her husband was home. Aunt Anna, Morten's old, friendly aunt, wouldn't be able to get around in this weather, that much was obvious. Who in the world would she turn to for help?

She simply had to do this on her own. She couldn't run and hide now.

With determined steps, she walked toward the entryway at the back of the house. Cautiously she knocked on the door. Then she waited for a moment with bated breath. There was no reaction in there. She knocked again. This time a little harder, but it was still completely quiet. She peeked through a window. It had to be the kitchen window, she realized. It didn't look like anyone had been in there today.

Her uneasiness grew. Her heart beat faster and anxiety began setting in. He had to be in there. If he had been outside today, she would have noticed his tracks in the snow. And there was no sign that anyone had been outside the door after the snow started. The ground had been bare the day before, but then Marit had been there and seen that he was actually home.

Carefully, she pushed down the door handle. The door swung open right away. So it wasn't locked. Quickly, she slipped into the entryway and shut the door behind her. Then she opened the kitchen door and went in. She saw no sign of life anywhere. There were some unwashed cups on the kitchen counter, but she could see they hadn't been used that day. In the corner on the opposite wall sat a wood stove. She walked over and put her hand on it. Just as she thought, it was completely cold. And the woodbin next to it was empty, and she could feel that the temperature in the house was cool.

There were two more doors in the room. Right across from the door to the entry-way was one she assumed led to a hallway. Most houses of this type were built on the same pattern—two rooms with a hallway in the middle, then a kitchen and usually a small bedroom in the back. The entryway was an add-on with a lower roofline on the wall to the kitchen.

Mette looked at the door at the end of the kitchen. Maybe Uncle Torkel used the room beyond as a bedroom. As quietly as possible, she crossed the floor and knocked on the door. For a minute she stood there, listening. Then she heard a sound from within. Someone was coughing. Relief mixed with concern filled her when she realized there was life in the house after all.

Gently, she pushed the door open and peeked in. A strong, heavy odor greeted her. She could see a bed with a pile of bedding in it.

"Hello! Is someone here?" she asked. A movement over in the bed proved that there was more than bedding in it.

"Who's coming into my house this way?" said a hoarse and tense voice, as a tou-sled head rose from the pillow. Mette had to smile at the gruff greeting. But she also felt somewhat like a rude intruder, so she answered in a cautious and soft voice:

"It's just me, Mette. Marit was a little worried about you. I promised to look in to see how you are."

Two dark eyes stared up at her as she got closer to the bed. The expression on his face told her she shouldn't count on being especially welcome. The first thought that struck her was that the dark eyes had to run in the family. Morten would probably look like this, too, at 85, for it was his eyes and facial features on the damp pillow.

If the situation hadn't been so serious, she probably would have laughed at such thoughts and observations. But she wasn't there to observe a pair of dark eyes below bushy, gray eyebrows in a lean face. The situation might actually be serious. It was best she found out more about his condition before she was thrown out.

"How are you?" she asked worriedly. "You don't look too good."

A grunt was heard from the bed. "A little cold has never killed anyone, as far as I know," he answered grumpily.

"But … this has to be more than just a cold." Mette looked worriedly at the yellow face on the pillow.

"You tell Marit that I'll be back on my feet in a couple of days. The flu never hung around any longer than that before, so I suppose it will be the same this time."

His tone of voice indicated to Mette that he wanted to end their conversation, and that she should leave. But Mette wasn't that easily dismissed. She could clearly see the man was not well. Maybe he couldn't even get out of bed. How would he find something to eat, not to mention drink?

"It's cold here," she said. "Wouldn't you like me to start a fire before I leave?"

Again, just a grunt from the bed. He would have preferred to protest, but for some reason, nothing more was said. Mette didn't wait for an answer. She simply turned around and went outside to get some firewood.

She found a snow shovel in the entryway. It took her a while to clear the path to the woodshed, which she assumed had to be in the outbuilding. It wasn't much of a path, but she didn't stop until she had carried in enough wood to start a fire, both in the wood stove in the kitchen and in the bedroom. She also filled up the woodbins to feed the fire later. Soon, both stoves had a good fire going.

Over in the bed, there was little noticeable movement. For a moment Mette thought he had fallen asleep. But then came another spell of coughing. Mette went to the kitchen and filled a glass with water. Maybe it might help him a little. And she knew he needed to drink something anyway.

"Here is something for you to drink," she said as she entered the bedroom. A shaky hand reached for the glass. He didn't reply, but she sensed some kind of gratitude on his part.

When he pulled himself up on the pillow to drink, she noticed that he was fully dressed. She didn't say anything, just registered it with surprise. Maybe he was cold. His pale face, spotted with red, could indicate he was running a fever. Or maybe he simply hadn't been able to undress before he went to bed. There didn't seem to be much strength in the gaunt body under the comforter.

She noticed a phone on the small table that served as a nightstand. Again she wondered about what Marit told her, that she didn't get an answer when she called him that morning. He could easily reach the receiver from his bed. So how ill was he, really? Again, she felt uneasy. Could she leave him like that? No, she decided quickly. He needed help. But what could she do?

"Marit told me she tried to call you this morning?" She made it sound like a question in order to find out what might have happened that morning.

Frowning, he glanced up at her. "Yes, I figured it was her," he said brusquely. "You can't talk on the phone while your supper is about to leave you." A nod of his head indicated a bucket under the table.

All right, thought Mette. There's the explanation. He was throwing up when the phone rang. That also explained the heavy odor in the room. She felt like opening a window, but didn't dare. It would just make the room even colder for the sick man. Instead, she left the door to the kitchen open.

"Is there anything else I can do for you?" asked Mette. "Maybe I should call ...?"

She was interrupted by an incensed protest from the bed. "I haven't asked you to do anything, and I don't intend to, either. I said a couple of days. You tell that to Marit. Then I'm back on my feet again. Goodbye!"

The message was clear enough. She had to leave now. But could she just leave him here? She looked for a moment at the frail old man in the bed. He looked weak. That's probably exactly what he was, too, so in a way she could understand that he wanted her

103

out of there. She wanted to take the phone on the table and call Morten, but didn't dare. His message to her was unmistakable. Maybe she would make it worse for him by pushing him. No, she would rather not aggravate the old man more than necessary.

Without saying any more, she left the room. Regardless, it was no use to continue the discussion. Now she at least understood what Marit meant when she said he was somewhat stubborn and difficult to deal with. If she had known more about nursing she might have been able to evaluate his condition better. The only sensible thing to do now was to leave. But she would drive directly over to the bank and ask Morten what they should do.

As Mette rounded the corner of the house, heading back to her car, she saw the snow plow speeding by on the road. She was grateful that now her return trip would be easier. It wasn't snowing quite so much, but the wind was just as strong as before. Leaning into the drifting snow, she fought her way back to the car.

The trip back was indeed much easier. Soon, she stopped outside the shopping center of which the bank was a part. For a moment, she stopped and looked around. How often she had come here last summer when she worked as a dairymaid at Morten's seter. Back then, the weather was warm, with grass and flowers and leaves on the trees. Now it was snowy and cold. She thought the town looked just as beautiful in its winter shroud as it had in the enchanted splendor of summer. At that time, she had no idea this would be her permanent home. How different everything was now!

Because of the weather, she couldn't see her own farm. Neither could she see Petter's farm. Petter, their neighbor, helped Morten with his barn chores in the morning before work. He had helped them out at the seter last summer, too, so Mette knew him well. For a moment she wondered if she should drive over to see if he was home. She was sure he could help her. But then she made up her mind to go and talk to Morten instead.

Quickly, she walked into the warm and cozy bank. Morten looked up in surprise as she entered. He smiled at her, but then continued to address the customer he was helping. Mette sat down in a chair a little distance away. It was best to wait until he was done.

After a couple of minutes, the customer turned around and left. Mette saw that she would be able to speak with Morten in private now, so she stood up and walked over to the counter.

"What can I do for this lovely lady?" he asked with a fake seriousness in his voice.

Mette played the game, too. "I just would like to withdraw a couple of millions from an account," she said in her most sincere voice.

Morten lifted his eyebrows and looked at her in shock. "And from what account would do you like to withdraw it?" he asked while he tried to hide the fact that he was laughing.

Mette kept her straight face. "Naturally it would be from my husband's account," she answered quickly.

A man who worked nearby had heard the entire exchange. Now he started to laugh and said: "There you go, Morten. Remember what I told you. You jumped into marriage too soon. And there you are. Don't tell me that I didn't warn you. Women ..."

Then they all three started laughing.

After catching his breath and again able to speak, Morten asked: "Well, I assume you wanted something other than that. Or maybe you just wanted to see me ... just like that … in the middle of the day?" He winked at her with a big grin on his face.

Mette smiled back. "Yes, of course I want to see you," she answered. "Except today I have to talk to you about something in particular." At that point, he turned serious.

"Marit stopped by this morning before she went to work. She was very worried about Uncle Torkel. She visited him yesterday. Then he wasn't feeling well. But when she called him, he didn't answer. She wasn't able to stop by again, so she asked if I …"

She stopped abruptly and looked, puzzled, at Morten. Tense, he sat in his chair with a blank stare. All color had drained from his face. His jaw muscles bunched up on both sides of his face because of his clenched teeth. His right hand gripped a ballpoint pen so tightly she was afraid it might break. An icy cold shiver of alarm ran down her back. What was this about?

Suddenly, Morten straightened in his chair and put the pen down on the desk with a bang. His dark hair, which was always so well groomed, got a wild look to it. It was as if he were waking from a dream.

When he spoke again, he seemed almost the same once more. "Have you been to see him?"

Mette nodded. "He looked pretty bad," she said.

Morten checked the time. "I'll go over to see him as soon as I can get away."

Mette breathed in relief. "Then I'll leave the car, so you can take it when you go," she said, placing the keys on the desk. With a grateful smile, she turned around and headed for the door. Another customer had entered while they were talking. He stood by the counter, waiting for Morten to help him.

Mette looked over at Morten again before she left. A deep crease had appeared between his eyes. Something was bothering him, but she didn't know what it might be.

Worried thoughts churned around in her mind as she tramped toward home in the icy wind. She had already experienced, to her distress, that Morten was a quiet man who kept his thoughts and feelings buried deep inside. How many times had she suffered in agony up there at the seter last summer because of this?

But she also knew she shouldn't really blame him too much, for it was a part of his personality. If she hadn't been so sensitive and thin-skinned, this probably wouldn't bother her at all. But she was unable to distance herself from her feelings when she sensed something bad was going on.

And now it had happened again. If only she had been able to talk to him there at the bank, but with customers and other employees around him, she couldn't bring herself to ask about anything.

Uneasiness started churning inside her again. There was something … but what was it? No, she had no idea.

30 • Dark clouds

The minutes went by at a snail's pace and turned into hours. Mette couldn't stop thinking about the sick old man up at Lia. How was he doing? Several times she was tempted to bundle up and go up there to check on him. But then she remembered his negative reaction to her visit. It was probably better that Morten went. Uncle Torkel knew him better, so Morten was probably easier for him to accept.

She tried to do something useful to pass the time, but it was difficult to concentrate on the tasks at hand. She checked the time over and over. When would Morten be able to get away?

Outside, the wind was just as bad as before. The drifting snow seemed heavier now, and ever-growing drifts piled up, higher and higher. The snowplow swept by regularly, but driving conditions were not the best.

Suddenly, she heard a car stop by the driveway to the farm. Quickly, she walked to the door to see who it might be. She caught sight of a figure running toward the barn. It was Morten. After a couple of minutes, she heard a tractor starting. Soon after that, he drove off with it. He seemed to be in a hurry, for he drove faster than she thought was safe on the slick road. So what was going on now? Why did Morten need the tractor? She tried to reach him on his cell phone several times, but didn't get an answer.

A sudden impulse made her call Marit. The oldest son answered the phone. Marit was at Lia with Uncle Torkel. She had come home early from work and gone straight to his house. So then, at least something was happening.

Mette started dinner just to have something to do. Every so often, she would stop what she was doing and stand looking out the window.

A sharp, howling sound cut through the silence. A car with flashing blue lights sped by. An ambulance! Mette felt herself shiver. The situation must have been worse than she feared. Maybe she did the wrong thing. Maybe she should have called the doctor right away, without listening to the headstrong old man. She paced the floor, wringing her hands and worrying about the situation.

After about half an hour, the ambulance returned. It still had the blue light on, but the siren was turned off. Maybe this meant that the situation wasn't that bad … or … might it mean that there was nothing more to do …

"No, it wasn't that bad!" she said aloud, grabbing the coffeepot on the kitchen table. She poured herself a cup and sat down, trying to calm down.

Not long afterward, she heard Morten's tractor again. Weak with anticipation, she waited for him to come in. But it wasn't until he had shoveled the entire front yard that he finally entered the warm kitchen. He appeared to be in a somber mood, and his entire countenance showed that he had been involved in a bad situation.

"How is he?" asked Mette anxiously.

Morten didn't answer right away, seeming not to hear what she was saying. Mette looked at him with alarm. He sat down heavily on a chair, looking distant.

"I understand he had to go to the hospital?" Mette tried again.

Morten looked at her. It was as if he suddenly realized she was there. "Yes," he said. "Yes, he wasn't very well …" He sighed. She could see that his hands were shaking and his face was pale.

Again she was puzzled at his reaction. Usually he never got this upset, even in critical situations. She could hardly recognize her sensible and steady husband.

Soon he seemed to calm down and started talking to her. "When I got over there, I could see that his temperature was running quite high. He almost seemed to be asleep. In any case, he was almost unconscious. I called the doctor right away. Marit came as soon as she could, too. When the doctor arrived, he diagnosed him with pneumonia right away, which shouldn't be taken too lightly at his age. There was nothing else to do but get him to the hospital."

"What did you use the tractor for?" asked Mette after a while. "It looked like you were in a great hurry, you were going so fast."

"Yes, I had to hurry up and clear the driveway so the ambulance crew wouldn't have to carry the sick man all the way out to the road. It was hard enough to get him in the car in the middle of the snowstorm."

"Do you know anything about his prognosis?" Mette was worried.

Morten shook his head hesitantly. "It didn't look good, but at least he's getting good care now. We just have to hope that he'll be all right."

Mette was still troubled. Would she have been able to ease the situation if she had called the doctor right away? She had to ask Morten what he thought about it.

"No," he answered when she asked. His face took on a gentle expression when he saw how anxious she was. "You did a good job." He smiled at her. "You have to know Uncle Torkel in order to stand up to him. Even people who do know him have problems with that. I can imagine you weren't exactly greeted warmly. You did the right thing. Don't think any different."

Mette breathed in relief, grateful for what he said. It wasn't something she would have to blame herself for. And she would have had to clear the driveway in order to get the patient out. Mette would have had to deal with that, regardless. No, she couldn't have done it differently.

"Is it Marit who usually looks after him?" asked Mette. She walked over to the stove to dish up their dinner. He answered with a curt "yes." Puzzled, Mette stopped what she was doing and looked at him. The dark, withdrawn expression was back. He just sat there without saying any more.

Mette stood for a moment, staring at him. "Is there anything wrong?" Her anxious voice made Morten sit up with a jerk. Their eyes met in an intense stare.

Then a smile appeared on Morten's face and his expression became more relaxed. "No ... no, there is nothing wrong. It's just me being a little ... little stupid," he said with a strained laugh.

Mette saw that he didn't want to talk any more about it. Maybe he had problems dealing with illness this close to home. Apparently a lot of people were that way. No, there was nothing to worry about.

Even if the atmosphere in the kitchen was subdued and a little gloomy, it was not tense, or at least there was no tension between them. There wasn't really that much she could do for Uncle Torkel. Except for one thing, and she was going to do that, often. She could pray, especially if Uncle Torkel needed intercession.

She was tempted to ask about the old man and his spiritual state, but she decided not to bring that up now. All in all, there wasn't that much more to say about the situation, she realized. It was best to leave well enough alone until they heard from the hospital.

31 • On slick ice again

The snowstorm passed quickly. Everyone hoped it was just winter's last gasp before yielding to spring with its warmth, life and fertility. The next day it rained, transforming the snow into soggy, slushy puddles. The road became even more slick and hard to navigate. Mette was glad she didn't have to drive anywhere. With these road conditions, she could easily end up in the ditch.

Instead, she turned her attention to boxes of items she had brought with her from the city but hadn't taken the time to put away. The big house had plenty of room; it was just a matter of finding a convenient, practical place for everything.

Mette had to consider all this before deciding where to store her belongings. The living room contained some old furniture. A large hutch, part of an oak dining room set Morten had inherited from his parents, held most of her good dishes. The hutch, along with the massive table and the solid chairs, gave the dining room a stately appearance. The legs and backs were intricately carved. With its ample cupboards and drawers, the hutch covered almost half the end wall in the large living room.

At the other end of the room sat a leather sofa set. Everything blended well together, with no clash of styles between new and old. Morten had seen to that whenever he selected new things for the house.

Mette had sold the furniture she had in her city apartment. It wouldn't have looked good in such a graceful home. It was easier just to get rid of it and save the moving expenses. Morten had what they needed, anyway.

A big double door stood right in the center of the long outer wall in the living room. Earlier, the house had two living rooms with a hallway between them. At that time, that door had been the entrance from the garden. Later, the two rooms and the hallway were combined into a single, large room.

Formerly, the living room had been even bigger, for later a bedroom had been put in at one end. This was done when Morten's mother became ill. It was difficult to care for a bedridden person whose bedroom was in the attic. Thus, they created a room for her next to the kitchen. Morten had made this room into an office, and Mette thought it was a practical and convenient solution.

On the other outside wall sat the kitchen. That, too, was a relatively recent upgrade, with plenty of room in cupboards and drawers. At the end of the kitchen, a big hallway featured a staircase leading to the loft and the main entrance to the house. A recently added, modern bathroom was located next to the main entrance.

Mette went from room to room and from cupboard to cupboard. Little by little, she emptied one box after another. She put everything away, busily filling closets in the hallway downstairs and in the attic and humming and singing while she worked.

Suddenly she jumped. The phone rang. Surrounded by silence and in deep concentration, she wasn't prepared for signals from the outer world. But when she lifted the receiver and heard it was from the hospital, she felt her heart beat faster. Uncle Torkel was worse, they told her. His condition was now critical.

Mette thanked them for letting her know and told them she and Morten would be at the hospital as soon as possible.

After hanging up, she stopped to get her bearings. She shivered slightly. What should she do? She realized she had to get hold of Marit. She would have to tell Morten, too, but she wasn't looking forward to it. His strange reactions worried her. But what else could she do? No, he had to be told.

To her great surprise, there was no trace of an emotional reaction in Morten's voice when she called him. He had nothing but great concern for his old uncle. "I'll leave right away," he said.

They agreed that he and Marit should go to the hospital. He would call her right away. Mette was glad she didn't have to drive on the slick roads, but she was also worried about Morten, even if she knew he was more used to driving during these types of road conditions than she was. She was also worried about Uncle Torkel, but she realized there wasn't a whole lot she could do there. It was best that he didn't get too many visitors, for it might tire him out.

The rest of the day, Mette had a hard time concentrating on the tasks at hand. Her thoughts were constantly with the old man in the hospital. How critical was he, really? Was he in pain? Was he conscious at all? She hadn't remembered to ask about any of this when they called from the hospital.

And how was his spiritual status? She hadn't been able to talk to Morten about this. Was Uncle Torkel prepared for death? Pacing the floor, she pondered this question over and over. She folded her hands, her prayers and thoughts mingling.

She had been led to understand that Uncle Torkel was a somewhat gruff and stubborn person. But that didn't necessarily mean he had a strained and gruff relationship to his God. True enough, the Bible encourages people to be kind and considerate toward each other. But it is also the case that people are all different from one another.

And regarding the matter of salvation and eternal life, we are not judged by our performance. No, our relationship to Jesus Christ is the only thing that counts. People who have received Him and believe what the Bible says about Him are allowed to partake in the glory that we are granted after our life on earth is over.

But what if Uncle Torkel hadn't sorted this out? What if he had no relationship to Jesus, and has now slipped into unconsciousness. Maybe he wouldn't regain consciousness at all. Then what? Mette shuddered as she paced. She had heard a lot of grotesque representations of hell, but she wasn't sure of the correct description. But that hell was real, she knew from the Bible. Exactly what it meant was hard to understand. But she knew one fact that was stated clearly in the Bible: One would be separated from God forever.

Mette was certain of one thing, that it was important for people to define their relationship to God while they still were in this world. If this hadn't been important, then God wouldn't have gone through so much to establish the road to salvation discussed in the Bible. He wouldn't have had to send His son to His death to suffer the death sentence people brought upon themselves through their sins and wrongdoings toward God.

A wave of gratitude washed through her as she thought about this. Imagine, there wasn't anything she needed to do to be saved other than to accept what was done for her that day on the cross. Her transgressions, her sins, all had caused her to deserve the death sentence in the eyes of God. She knew this punishment was absolute, for no sin is allowed in the Kingdom of God. But Jesus was willing to take her death sentence upon Him. Everything that needed to be done, Jesus had done. If only Uncle Torkel also had realized this and accepted it!

Her thoughts continued to spin as time crept by. Soon, she started preparing dinner. But she had no idea when Morten would be back.

32 • Hidden pain

It was past 8 in the evening before the sound of a car outside the house announced that Morten was back from the hospital. He seemed tired when he entered and sat down at the kitchen table. With a weary gesture, he brushed his hand through his thick, black hair. Deep creases appeared above his almost black eyes.

Mette looked at him anxiously. "How is Uncle Torkel?" she asked, concerned. Morten shook his head slowly. "It doesn't look good. Marit will stay with him tonight, but he may not last many hours. It turned out to be cancer that had spread to his lungs that caused the pneumonia. He must have had it for a while without knowing it. When it turned into pneumonia, there wasn't much they could do."

The mood in the kitchen was one of deep concern. Mette didn't say any more. She just brought out some food for Morten to eat. For a long time they sat in silence. There wasn't much to say. Death comes to everybody at some point, but when it finally comes, it isn't anticipated, even if age tells a different story.

Not until they were about to go to bed, did Mette manage to bring up the question that had been on her mind all day: the spiritual status of the old man.

Morten thought about it for a while before he answered. "I really don't know. He wasn't exactly open about his personal business, but I do think he had respect for what he considered sacred. At least, he grew up in a Christian home, and was taught according to that. But, no ... I'm afraid I don't know much more. Today he was unable to speak at all. I don't even know if he knew we were there, so we had no opportunity to talk to him about things like that."

Mette didn't say anything. She was filled with an acute sadness. How important it was that such affairs be settled before things got too far. She sighed. But, of course, there was a chance that he had settled this already. For this was a business between him and God.

Marit returned early the next morning. She had had a long night behind her, watching the sick man. The fact that it was such a grim situation didn't make things easier. And now she had to tell them that Uncle Torkel had passed away quietly, close to dawn.

At once there was a frenzy of activity. The family had a lot of things to taken care of, including informing lots of people. They also had to make arrangements with the funeral home and the pastor. Fortunately, it was Saturday, so no one had to worry about getting to work.

The funeral was set for Wednesday the following week. Marit did most of the planning, but Mette and Morten helped as much as they could.

The funeral took place in the traditional manner, but they didn't have a gathering afterward. The ceremony ended by the gravesite. The day was cool, but the snow and slush from the last snowstorm had almost disappeared. The fields and the forest brought tidings of the impending spring, even if nothing had started to grow yet. The migratory birds were back, singing euphorically around in the hills. Swollen streams rushed down from the mountains. Thought there was still a lot of snow up there, it melted rapidly day by day.

When they returned from church, Mette stood for a while, looking toward the mountains to the north. Up there was the seter. She tingled with excitement and anticipation, knowing that it was getting closer to the time when they would start preparing for their seter operations again. They had talked about it now and then, and Mette looked forward to it with childlike anticipation. The somber and sad situation they just now had put behind them couldn't quell the exultant joy she felt at the thought of the coming summer. She had a deal with her employer that she would take a leave of absence for the time she was needed at the seter. She especially looked forward to working with Aunt Anna again.

She knew that Aunt Anna was just as enthusiastic about it. Mette had gone to visit with her quite often. Luckily, they didn't live far from each other. Aunt Anna talked a mile a minute as usual, and Mette had a great time. They had already made a lot of plans for the upcoming season. The food they would prepare and the kind of demonstrations they would give to the tourists visiting the seter were all worked out.

Over time, Mette had noticed that the old woman was less spry than she had been early last summer. And she wasn't getting any younger this year. But now Mette had learned so much from her that she would be able to do a lot of the work on her own. She planned to keep an eye on her so her chores wouldn't be too much for her. In many cases, it was enough that Aunt Anna was there to provide instruction and advice. And if there was anything Aunt Anna was good at, it was that. There was nothing wrong with her ability to talk or the agility of her mind.

During the next days, the family returned to their usual routines. Mette went back to work. She was often involved in meetings, or helping to organize some type of festivity or an event for children at some meetinghouse in the district. Every day, the air turned warmer and the evenings lighter. When Mette went for a walk, she often stopped to breathe in the refreshing spring air. Spring flowers started showing up in people's gardens. Back home in Sørlandet, they probably had been in full bloom for a while. Here everything was much later, naturally. But then, everything here happened faster when it once got started, she thought.

One afternoon she met Marit at the store. They talked for a while.

"It's probably best that we get started on cleaning out Lia," said Marit, as she was about to leave. "I've talked to Ellen, and she is willing to help me. I think we'll go up there on Saturday to look through the house. The estate has to be settled, but I'm sure we can handle that as we go …" She hesitated before she continued: "… but I'll take care of this." The last words were spoken quickly and with determination.

"But of course we will help out, that's a given." Mette was enthusiastic.

"No, no, we'll handle it. Don't worry about it," said Marit almost aggressively.

For a moment, they stood there staring at each other. It seemed as if Marit would rather not ask Mette and Morten to help out. But this was certainly just as much her and Morten's job as Marit's. The three siblings, Marit, Morten and Siri, were the first in line to inherit, Mette knew. Siri lived in Trondheim with her family, so it wasn't easy for her to help out much. Morten and Marit had to take care of most of it. But this shouldn't mean that Marit had to do everything by herself.

"I'll talk to Morten about it," said Mette at last.

Marit became visibly uneasy again. "You don't have to …" Then she stopped and thought about it. "Yes, well, do as you please," she said tiredly. Then she turned and left.

For a while Mette looked after her in bewilderment. Her behavior was strange. What might it mean? It was probably best that she go home and speak with Morten about it. Maybe he could explain it.

It took Mette longer than she thought to get a chance to bring the matter up with him. They were organizing a service for St. Thomas at the church that Saturday night, and Morten, who was on the church council, had scheduled a planning session for the event. Not until he got home from work on Friday did she get an opportunity to mention the cleaning at Lia. They had dinner at the kitchen table when she suddenly remembered.

"Marit wants to go over to Lia to do some cleaning there. I suggested that we go over to help. It has to be done soon."

Morten had piled up a big helping of *lapskaus**—meat and potato stew—on his plate. His fork stopped halfway to his mouth and dropped down on the plate again. "Yes ... we'll have to ... soon." His voice was almost unrecognizable, ragged and pained. In an instant his face went almost completely white. He took a couple of deep breaths before he stood up and almost ran into his office.

Mette was left at the table, shocked and confused. Her lapskaus was forgotten, too. From the office she could hear the sound of quick steps pacing back and forth across the floor. Something was wrong ... terribly wrong. But she had no idea what it was. He was greatly distressed, she understood that much. But he never said a word about what was troubling him so much. It seemed almost as if he was terribly afraid of something.

Marit would know about this. Maybe she thought that Mette knew as well.

Suddenly she felt insignificant and left out. Helpless, she remained seated at the table. She was no longer hungry. The minutes passed and she just sat there. The situation was so strange, it was frightening.

Suddenly she got to her feet. "No, this can't go on," she told herself with determination. Gingerly, she opened the door to the office. Morten stood in front of the window, but she was not at all sure that he saw anything outside. His face, his entire body, seemed to have aged 30 years in a few minutes. The pain stamped on his every feature and in his every muscle looked like it might overwhelm him at any minute.

"What is it?" Her voice came out as a whisper. Still, it expressed an intensity emerging from her innermost being.

Morten reacted immediately and came over to her. He placed both hands on her shoulders and looked deeply into her eyes. It was as if his eyes begged her for something ... for help?

"Mette ...!" The single word came out as a moan. Before she had time to say anything, he put a shaking arm around her and escorted her back to the kitchen. There he sat down heavily at the table again. Mette sat down next to him.

He didn't start eating. The food was probably cold now, too.

When he started speaking, it was almost as if he were transported to a different world. His eyes were distant and his voice soft and unsteady.

"It's almost 14 years ago ... we were going to help Uncle with some hay. Everybody was there, Mother, Father, Siri, Marit, I and Even ..." His voice tapered off. The muscles in his jaw worked frantically.

Mette felt herself shiver. "Even ...?" Her question was a mere whisper. She wasn't able to say any more. Morten breathed heavily. Then he gathered himself and started again. She didn't know if he had heard her question, for he continued as if there had been no interruption.

"It was hot, and all of us worked hard. No one noticed that Even disappeared. Not until some time had passed ... I don't know how long.

"When we had called him several times without getting an answer, we started searching for him. An 11-year-old boy couldn't just disappear in thin air …

"I was the one who found him." Two big tears started rolling down his agonized face. Knife and fork were clutched in his hands until his knuckles had turned white. Mette swallowed, but didn't say anything.

When Morten continued, it was as if he were a little more relaxed. His voice was stronger, but it shook, and he cried openly. "It was my fault. I should have warned him, for I knew the cover on the old well was rotten. He fell through. As he fell, he probably struck his head against a rock and fainted, for otherwise he would have been able to get up. At least, he would have been able to call for help.

"His head was under water. I got him out of there pretty soon, but it was too late …"

Mette was on her feet. She gently put her arms around her beloved husband's neck and sank down in his lap. He put his arms around her waist, burying his face against her shaking body while he sobbed, heartbroken.

Oh, what pain he had endured for all those years. Not even to her had he talked about Even. This was the first time she heard about him. No other family members had mentioned him either … not even the talkative Aunt Anna. Mette felt a deep pain inside. Her tears dampened his hair.

Soon, she felt his body relax. "Maybe we should try to eat something," he said with a shaky smile. Mette smiled back at him. "Yes, let's." She stroked his cheek and his short beard, and kissed his eyes tenderly before she got up and took a seat again. She had never seen him as handsome as he was this very moment. His revelation had brought them closer together. Mette knew her husband well enough to know what it had cost him to talk about this. But was she ever glad he had.

It was as if a wall had come down, not only between them, but also inside Morten. While they ate their cold lapskaus, Morten continued his story. He talked about his parents, who grieved deeply after Even's death, and how he had felt ever since that it was his fault because he hadn't warned Even about the dangerous well. After that, he could hardly bear to visit Lia at all. Just thinking about the little farm over there made him choke.

He also talked about his father, who died far too young from a heart attack, and his mother, who was ailing for a long time afterward, until she, too, died a few years back. "I think she became ill with grief," he finished quietly.

Even though Morten had finally been able to talk about this, Mette could see that he still felt the pain. She suffered with him, but didn't know what to do or say. That Marit, too, was in pain, she could well understand. But she didn't seem to relate her pain directly to the incident at Lia. Still, she obviously knew how it affected Morten. Now Mette understood perfectly why Marit reacted the way she did.

No, Mette wasn't going to insist that Morten take part in the cleaning over at Lia. He had to do whatever he felt was right for him. But it pained her to think about his long suffering. He ought to find a way to work through his grief.

33 • The dark hole

Mette woke up early the next morning, but Morten was up even earlier. She didn't know if it was because it was Saturday, his day to tackle the barn chores, or if there were other reasons why he couldn't sleep.

She dressed in a hurry and went down to the kitchen. Morten sat there with his cup of coffee, looking out the window. He looked at her and smiled as she entered, but then he drifted back to his own thoughts. Mette didn't say anything. She just started making herself some breakfast. She noticed that Morten had already eaten. He was obviously trying to work something out. The dark clouds on his face were not completely gone. No, he was probably still deeply affected by yesterday's events.

How important it is, thought Mette, that we work through our grief as soon as possible. Unresolved issues can often have dire consequences. If they are simply locked away or suppressed in silence, they continue to appear fresh in your mind. It's like a tin can. As long as it is unopened, it might seem completely lifeless. But as soon as you pick a small hole in it, the contents are as fresh as when they were first canned. Morten's feelings were as raw and painful when "picked at" now as they were at the time the tragedy happened.

Suddenly, Morten stood up. He emptied the last dregs of his coffee and headed for the door. "I'm coming with you to Lia today," he said as he opened the door. "I just have to finish my barn chores first." Then he shut the door and went outside.

Mette was left to wonder, but she was glad he wanted to do this. Maybe it would help ease the pain from all that had bothered him for so long. Or … she worried again. Maybe it would just make things even worse for him. No, he would have to follow his instincts. She had no idea what would be best for him. Tense, she began doing the dishes after breakfast while she waited for Morten to return from the cow barn.

On days he wasn't working in town, he took care of the animals in the cow barn. In addition, they still had their working arrangement with their neighbor, Petter. When Morten was at work, Petter cared for Morten's livestock. Or rather, Petter's son did. Mette had told him she would be happy to do it when she was home; she was in the cow barn so often anyway. Time and again she would go out to see the animals and pet them. And if she had some leftovers she knew they liked, it didn't take her long to get out there and give them a treat. But Morten had told her that Petter's son would very much like to keep the job, for it made him some extra cash.

Mette thought back to when she had taken the job at the seter last year. The newspaper ad she had answered had led her to believe she was going to work for an old couple. But the "old farmer" had turned out to be Morten, whose seter operation involved showing tourists what seter life was like in the old days. Hordes of tourists, school children and camp school groups came up during the summer and well into the fall.

And then there was Aunt Anna, who was responsible for a good deal of the programs. Aunt Anna had been getting old and frail and had been having problems managing everything on her own. Mette had been hired to tend to the animals, do demonstrations for tourists and prepare the food.

And then this had happened. She smiled to herself. She had managed to fall in love with that farmer the first time she set eyes on him.

But she didn't want to think about those dramatic events right now. It had been

114

both good and bad. Now, at least, everything was great between them. If only Morten, too, could get to the point where he felt more relaxed about certain painful events in his past.

Later in the morning, Mette and Morten left for Lia. They drove in silence. Mette felt tense. It was obvious that it was hard for Morten, too.

Now that the snow was gone, they could drive all the way up to the house. There was a car there already, so they knew that Marit and Ellen had arrived.

Morten got out of the car quickly, but he didn't head directly for the door to the kitchen. Instead, he walked toward the woods at the end of the outbuilding. Mette followed close behind him. Under some trees down the hill she saw a big pile of rocks and timber. Morten started moving rock after rock. Trembling, Mette stood watching him in silence. She realized only too well what it was. There was the well . . .

Soon, some panels of corrugated iron appeared. Several of them were stacked on top of each other. That well was certainly firmly secured … but she surely understood why. Morten started lifting away the panels. Before he removed the last ones, he stopped for a minute. Mette swallowed. More than anything, she felt like running away. Soon a dark hole would appear … would she be able to handle it? And Morten, how would he react?

Rigid with anticipation, she watched him remove the last panel. She stepped closer. A dark hole gaped below them. She started feeling sick. Morten stood still, staring into the dark. She saw him shiver. A couple of sniffles made her aware that tears were streaming down his face. Nor was she able to stop hers.

The sun shone over the treetops. They didn't have eyes for the beautiful spring day with birdsong from the hill and an abundance of life all around them, sprouting and growing. A frog croaked and jumped away amid fallen leaves. A teeming sea of ants was hard at work on their hill nearby. None of this—the miracle of spring with new life and growth—registered with the two who stood there staring down into the black hole. They saw death. Their minds, thoughts and feelings converged on death. An 11-year-old boy who had played there and enjoyed himself on a beautiful summer day, and all of a sudden it ended … the fresh, joyful life of youth … it ended abruptly, down there in the dark.

Morten started moving again. Slowly, he stepped over to the edge of the well and began climbing down. He climbed all the way to the bottom. He was down there once before.

Mette held her breath. For a few long seconds, she just saw his head down there. His eyes seemed to scrutinize every rock and nook in the bleak grave … grave, yes, that's exactly what she felt it was.

A gust of wet, musty soil hit her as she bent over the edge in an attempt to see. As she moved, a shower of dry leaves and dirt clattered into the pit and hit Morten on the shoulder, but he never noticed. He bent down and stroked his hand across a rock. She could barely see the outline of the well bottom and the rocks lining the sides, but Morten obviously didn't have any problems distinguishing one detail from another.

That rock …

Once upon a time it was covered with blood. Something solid had struck against it. The result was fatal. At that time, there was water down there. But that particular rock was above the waterline. It clearly bore marks from the impact. Morten recalled everything in detail. He remembered it as if it were yesterday. It seemed like the scene from the deep well was fixed to his retina in clear, vibrant colors, and in great detail.

This was an important moment. Mette knew it. She wanted to remain completely quiet and not allow a sound to interfere with what he was going through. How did he experience it? Mette pulled cautiously away and waited in anticipation. The seconds ticked by, but she seemed to have no sense of time. The silence was interrupted only by a soft whisper in the tree canopy above them and the joyful chirping of birds from the hill.

She felt as if the world had stopped for a few timeless moments, before she heard Morten climbing back up the well.

When he got up, he sat down on the ground a little distance away from the well. Mette sat down next to him. He put his arm around her, but the expression in his eyes was no longer as dark. He turned his eyes toward the dense canopy above their heads. A few bright rays of sun found their way between the jumble of branches and touched them.

"Up there ... somewhere above the sunshine ... that's where Even is now." Morten's voice was soft, but also bright and steady. "He is with Jesus now. He wasn't down in the well. I saw it ... his blood was gone, too."

An amazed smile spread across his face while his tears streamed. "There seems to be no reason to fear it any more." The last words came out like a sigh, more to himself than to her.

He slowly shook his head while he scratched the ground with a stick. "I thought death belonged to old people. The young ones, at least the children, should live." His words ran out of him. Mette didn't say anything. She just rested her head on his shoulder and squeezed his hand between both of hers, while her tears continued to run.

"I couldn't understand," he continued, "that God could condone something like that. No, for a long time I believed that He had nothing to do with it. It happened just because I was so careless and didn't warn Even about the danger that lurked here among the trees.

"And when I saw how Mother and Father grieved ... yes, my siblings, too, for that matter, then ..." His voice died. His eyes turned to the well again. Silence was all around them.

Mette looked at him. The profound love she felt for this man made her follow what he said with every fiber in her body. His words affected her like an intense physical pain.

Carefully she stroked his cheek and asked: "Do you still think what happened was your fault?"

He didn't answer right away but just sat staring blankly for a while. Then he turned abruptly toward her and answered with a little smile: "No. I don't think it was my fault. I know it wasn't. It just feels that way. But now I will try to allow what I know to take over my feelings. I just hope I will succeed." The last words came out like a sigh.

They sat there for a few minutes before they got up and started to cover up the well with the panels and the pile of rocks and timber. No one would ever again fall into it by accident, neither people nor animals.

After the job was done, they looked at the big pile of rocks and timber. Mette clung to Morten. He held her tightly, too. They seemed to seek comfort and security from each other as they stood looking at the big pile in front of them. They felt weak and helpless. But they also stood there with the knowledge that they, in their weakness, were in the hands of an almighty God. They had no doubt that He was a good and deeply loving God. But his ways were sometimes incomprehensible to mortals.

Morten turned. "I'm going to get my act together and fill up this hole," he said with determination. "It isn't used any more, anyway." They turned around and started back to the house.

They became aware of two figures standing on the back steps. It was Marit and Ellen. They didn't move. But as Mette and Morten got closer, they saw that their faces, too, were completely dissolved in tears. They understood well what had taken place over there at the edge of the forest this morning.

It had been a momentous event, not only for Morten, but also for his sister and her friend. Both of them had been deeply involved in the tragedy. Maybe this was a sign of brighter and better times ahead for them all, especially regarding their memories of Even.

The three of them sat talking in the kitchen for a long time. There was so much that needed to be said. Finally there had been an attempt to lance the painful boil. Maybe the pus that had been building inside it for all these years would finally be cleaned out. The memories of Even would always be there as something painful and sad, but their repressed and walled-up emotions might be easier to bear now.

Mette busied herself looking around the house. She wanted them to have this moment to themselves. They needed to talk … the three of them, alone.

34 • Final goodbye

The old house was worth exploring. Even if her thoughts were affected by the upsetting events that morning, she quickly became absorbed with all the interesting things at Lia. Old, beautifully crafted furniture graced all the rooms, undoubtedly handmade sometime in the past. Included were chests, cabinets and chairs in solid wood. One of the rooms on the upper floor had a large canopy bed with a matching dresser next to it. A washstand alongside the bed held a basin and beaker made of delicately patterned china. Under the bed sat a chamber pot in the same style. Mette had to smile. Everything was certainly in its place here.

In the next room she found a large rosemaled chest. Curious, she opened the heavy, curved lid. It was full of bed linens and old tablecloths. Carefully she lifted out a big white linen cloth. It was a delicate handmade piece of Hardanger embroidery. She rolled it out, admiring its beauty. Industrious hands had worked patiently and with great accuracy on this one. Cutouts and tiny knots were widely distributed throughout the material. She sighed. If only she had learned to master this art. Yet she realized she probably wouldn't have had the patience to complete this kind of work.

She refolded it and put it back in its place. Then she opened the lid of the *leddik,* the little tray at one end of the chest. Curiosity growing, she stooped and checked it out. It contained a stack of old, yellowing letters. She held up a few and looked at the address. "To Maren Lia," it read. Mette knew that Maren was Morten's maternal grandmother, wife of Uncle Torkel's brother.

Carefully she turned over the fragile envelope to see who the sender was. "Gunhild," it said. She wasn't able to make out the last name, but in any case saw that it had been sent from America.

Gently she lifted out a stack of letters. There had to be close to a hundred of them. All were sent from America, but some were addressed to Berte Maria. Mette didn't know who that might be, but the postmark showed that the oldest letters were about 80 years old.

Mette completely forgot time and place. Letter by letter, she placed them on a small table next to the chest. At the bottom of the leddik was a stack tied together with a piece of string. Those letters seemed to be even older than the first ones. She didn't untie the string, but looked only at the address. These, too, had come from America, but the names were not the same. "To Gunhild," it said, but it had to be a different Gunhild, for the postmark date was much older. The sender of the bottom letter was Theodor Evensen Lia. And it was sent from North Dakota.

How exciting! She hadn't heard anything about family in America. She had to speak to Morten and Marit about this. She gathered all the letters and wrapped them carefully in a towel she found in the chest, for she wanted to bring them back home and study them more closely.

When she came back downstairs, the other three were in full swing with their tasks. Ellen dug out old food and kitchen items that would be thrown away. Marit was busy with some clothes. Most of those would have to be thrown out, too. Morten was in the living room going through some papers in an old secretary.

"I have to look through this. Maybe there are valuables and papers that we need to keep," he said as Mette entered. "Settlement of the estate, distribution of assets and things like that will have to wait. Siri has to be here for that, too."

"How many heirs are there?" asked Mette.

"It's just we three siblings," he replied. "Uncle Torkel didn't have children. And his brother—that is, my maternal grandfather—had only my mother. There are no other descendants."

It was a hectic day. They lit a fire out in the yard and burned things that had no use or value. All valuables both in the house and in the outbuilding were carefully stored in places where they could be locked up. Everybody worked diligently, so they were tired when they drove back home in the afternoon.

Not until they were back in their own living room did Mette get a chance to mention the letters. She had brought with her the towel wrap containing the letters. Morten, too, was surprised when he saw all the old letters from America.

Mette spread the towel out on the dining room table. Morten took a letter and studied it in silence. Then he took another letter and turned it over several times before he pulled out the sheet of paper inside.

"This is surprising," he said after reading for a while. "When I think back, I seem to remember that my mother told me about some old relatives who emigrated to America at the beginning of the century, but I don't think she ever was in contact with anyone over there. This is a letter from her aunt. Her name was said to be Gunhild. Actually, I thought Gunhild had a twin sister who also emigrated, but I don't remember her name.

"In any case, these letters are so old that none of the people who wrote them are still living. We'll investigate this further at a later time. I'm tired now. If I'm going to make it to the mass for St. Thomas, I better lie down for a little bit."

Mette also felt she needed to rest after the day's efforts. The service didn't start until 8 in the evening.

118

Mette filled her lungs with deep breaths of fresh spring air as she walked with Morten along the country road toward the church. They walked hand in hand and enjoyed the peace and quiet around them. The night was light and calm. Along the road, *hvitveis*—white anemones—nodded their pale heads, and the willows rose from the underbrush in a shower of yellow-gray catkins. The buds on the birches were about to burst, just waiting for the thermometer to creep up a few more degrees. The peaks to the north, still covered by blankets of white snow, reflected the last rays from a sun, which was looking for a suitable crevice to set in far out there in the west.

The entire community seemed to be waiting anxiously for the great transformation soon to come. Life in forest and fields as well as in gardens and meadows would soon change these surroundings into a fantastic, bountiful land of plenty.

Car after car drove past them as they walked. It appeared that there would be a lot of people in church this beautiful spring day. Suddenly, she became aware of the expression on Morten's face. Some of his gloom and sadness was back. Poor man, he probably was still thinking about what happened over at Lia. Things of that nature didn't just go away at once. It would take time, but she was convinced he would feel better now that he had been able to open up a little.

Inside the church, the sacred, peaceful atmosphere was obvious to all. The organ played while people gathered together. In the center of the chancel stood a large globe of light. A tall candle burned in the middle, wreathed by smaller candles, ready to be lit by those who wished to express their feelings for God.

Candles glowed from the altar as well. Their light fell on the antique altarpiece that had decorated the old, cruciform log church for almost two centuries. Here Morten had been baptized and confirmed, and here he and Mette were married just a few weeks earlier. But these thick log walls had witnessed a lot more events over the years. Morten's mother and father had both been baptized and confirmed, and later, married here. Mette assumed that the people who emigrated to America more than 80 years ago had been carried to their christening in this church, too. In one way or another, most people in the community had been inside these doors on some occasion that was especially meaningful to them.

And from the chancel up front, Even had been carried out nearly 14 years ago to a grave somewhere outside the church. She had to ask Morten where he was buried. Perhaps they could visit the grave together sometime … at least, she hoped so.

Silently, they sat down in a pew toward the middle of the church's nave. The ceremony began. The congregation rose when the pastor, along with some helpers, entered in ceremonial procession. The music from the organ swelled, and the congregation joined in the opening hymn. Their song filled the room and soared up toward the mighty arch crowning the church.

As the last note died away, the pastor strode over to the chancel arch and welcomed the congregation. He explained how the service would be conducted. They would be spending more time on the intercession part, he told them. Then the congregation would move freely around in the church. In several places, stations had been set up where people could pray or ask for intercession. In one area, they were invited to write down suggestions for prayer themes and put their notes in a bowl. Later, the pastor would pray for what was written on the notes. Then the notes would be burned.

At the globe of light, they could light a candle and pray for whatever was on their mind. They could also kneel down at the altar, where the pastor would lay hands on them and pray for them. Those who wished to could stay in their pews and pray on their own.

The interaction between liturgist and congregation that followed gave parishioners a feeling of peace. Mette felt it was good to sit there and receive the glorious promise of help and comfort for people in need. Suffering was something she felt had touched her a little too closely on this day. How Morten felt, she didn't know. His facial expression appeared serious.

When it came time for the intercession, some people arose and walked over to the globe of light. In silence, each lit the small candles in their turn. Soon, more people followed them. A procession of people began moving about the room. The soft music of the organ seemed to flow around and between them all. Mette sat with folded hands. She wasn't quite able to shape her thoughts into concrete prayers, but her inner being was turned toward God in a single cry—a cry for help and comfort.

Now Morten stood up, slowly moving toward the globe of light. Mette rose, too, following him. He stopped in front of the candles, his face showing that he was struggling with something painful. With a shaking hand, he took a small candle and tipped it against the tall one, borrowing its flame. Mette knew so well what was going on inside him. She just stood there, next to him. She just wanted to be there now, close to him. After lighting the candle, he stood for a while. He took her hand and squeezed it hard, but his eyes were steadily fastened on the flame. His lips shook and his eyebrows were pulled completely together in a heavy frown.

Morten began walking as he continued holding onto her hand. She followed him. He didn't let go of her hand until he kneeled down at the altar railing. There he bent over and hid his face in his hands. Mette knelt quietly next to him.

In an instant, the pastor appeared. "Do you want me to pray for anything in particular?" he asked in a soft voice. It took a while before Morten was able to reply. But then it came as a sob: "Even …" It was the only thing he managed to say.

At the same time, Mette noticed a figure kneeling down next to Morten on the other side. It was Marit. She didn't try to conceal her tears.

Out of the corner of her eye, Mette glimpsed the pastor's face. The single word from Morten was obviously more than enough. The pastor, now an elderly man, had served the congregation for many years. He knew Morten and his family well. He knew about the tragedy involving Even. He had officiated at Even's funeral.

Clearly moved, he fought back something in his throat. His eyes were wet and his lips shivered. Morten shivered, too. Mette felt something tremble deep inside. Her tears were already soaking the leather that padded the altar railing.

When the pastor finally gained control of his voice, he began a prayer of comfort, care and compassion. Mette felt as if it were God Himself who spoke the comforting words. Yes, that was probably true. God was with them at that moment. He was close, not because they were in church, but because they had brought to Him their sorrow and need. He didn't reject them or stay silent and indifferent. No, He was there … and He suffered with them, she was sure of that.

The three of them knelt together and cried out their grief to God. But Mette was certain that they were not the only ones who cried. She remembered the story of Martha, Mary and Lazarus. When Jesus came to them, Lazarus was already dead, and his sisters cried. Jesus came to bring Lazarus back to life, but He still shared in the grief of the two sisters. Jesus cried with them.

Now Even was in Heaven with Jesus, and he was well. But Jesus still looked out for the ones who were left behind in their grief and loss. He felt for them, she was convinced of that, and she was sure that He now cried with them.

When they got up after the prayer, Morten put his arms around Mette and Marit, hugging them both. Then they went back to their seats.

Later, they took communion. It felt so good to receive the bread and the wine—another sign that Jesus was near. Mette looked at the circle of people taking communion. They formed a half-arc in front of the altar railing. In that moment, there was a full circle of kneeling people, taking communion. She knew this was a symbol of their unity with everyone before them who had passed on to eternity with Jesus. The other part of the circle was in Heaven, and Even was there. He was there … with them … in communion.

When the service was over, they stopped outside the church. Marit was there with them, but no one said much. They were still affected by the powerful experience. It was as if they were afraid the feeling of holiness would disappear if they started talking.

Suddenly Morten started walking across the cemetery. He stopped at a grave over by the wall. Mette and Marit followed. It was Even's burial site. Morten knelt and tidied up the already spotless grave. "Now I think I can finally say goodbye to Even," he said.

Although the words were spoken carefully and softly, the way he said them sounded firm and grounded. He wasn't crying anymore, and his face had a brighter, more carefree expression.

Marit dried her tears and sniffled. "Oh, I'm so happy about this," she said. "It has hurt me so much to see you suffer."

Not much was said on their way home, but they felt that the air had been cleared, that better times lay ahead, and that their renewed strength would support them if new hardships were to come.

35 • The America letters

The old letters from America lay sprawled across the big dining room table. Mette had sorted them by date and sender. Gunhild had written most of them. But some were from someone named Tomine, or "Mina," as she called herself at times. Mette assumed this was the twin sister Morten had mentioned. She had not yet untied the bundle containing the oldest letters. It was best to do this systematically, little by little, she thought.

Mette sat on the sofa, reading with deep concentration. Almost at once she was transported more than 80 years back in time. The history of a whole life spread out before her eyes as she put pored over one letter after another. The writing wasn't easy to understand, but most of the time she understood the meaning based on the context.

A strange feeling filled her. All these letters had been carefully read and preserved. Most of them were addressed to Berte Maria, or Mother, as she wrote—a mother who had experienced two of her children leaving her. The ones who stayed back home knew they probably would never see them again.

It was hard to imagine what might go on in a mother's heart. No wonder this treasure of correspondence was preserved so carefully and lovingly. This was the only thing left from her children, the only evidence that there was life, full and active, far away on the other side of the big ocean. But life … Mette wondered about it. What was the status of that after some time had passed?

When she spoke to Morten about it the day before, he said he thought they probably were dead and that they didn't have any descendants, since the letters stopped completely with time. Mette assumed that Tomine (Mina) and Gunhild were dead. Otherwise, they would be in their 100s now. But could they really be sure they didn't have children … or grandchildren?

Morten's reasoning was probably correct, but Mette couldn't let go of the notion there might be other answers. That's why she wanted to go through these letters systematically. This is where the answer would be found.

Mette wasn't doing this just to satisfy her curiosity. It was just as much to clarify the family relations. What if they later found out they had made a mistake, for if there were relatives in America, they would be entitled to inherit from Uncle Torkel. And based on what Morten had told her, she knew that the estate was not insignificant. It was not only the value of his farm and belongings, but also cash that he had accumulated. The sale of some attractive mountain lots to cabin owners had left him with a good chunk, and as he was a healthy and active man until his last days, he had chopped large amounts of firewood, which he sold every year. He hadn't been able to spend much of his income. The single old man at Lia was not only known for his stubbornness and obstinacy, he was also known to be rather stingy. He didn't spend more than what was absolutely necessary on himself.

As Mette read on, a new world and a different existence revealed themselves to her. Tomine (Mina) and Gunhild emigrated to America in 1921. The situation at home was hard for young people, and word about the great adventures on the vast American continent seemed to have tempted them. The two girls had left as 18-year-olds. But they didn't leave everything to chance when they left. Mette hadn't read far before she understood that they had two uncles who had emigrated more than 20 years earlier. They lived in North Dakota, and this was the girls' destination.

Mette was even more captivated when she read about the sea voyage and the big liner going to America. The letters conveyed the anticipation of all the people on board, of all ages and all walks of life—the dreams of a future filled with success and happiness. Maybe not everyone was that unrealistic, but they had high hopes for a life that would have more to offer than what they could expect home in Norway.

"The voyage went pretty well," she read, "even if we now and then got wind of what a sea voyage can be like, especially in regard to the weather. But now the sun is shining, and we know that we are approaching New York. It will be good to set foot on land again. But it will be a little sad to part from all the people on board we have come to know so well during our voyage.

"The worst part will be to say goodbye to the family that Mina has spent so much time with. It is a couple with five children. Things have not been easy for them on this trip. The youngest child is only 2 years old, and the oldest is 9. The needs of the littlest one have been hard on the mother all this time. She looks completely exhausted. The third child, who is only 5, has also been sick a lot. She doesn't handle the sea very well. But Mina has spent a lot of time caring for her. Almost all day, every day, little Karen has been in her lap. Mina has become very fond of the frail little girl. You know how she is, so caring and warm. I reckon there will be quite a few tears when it's time to say goodbye."

The rest of the letter, written after they landed in New York, followed as a new paragraph. The date was June 5, 1921:

"Mina is dissolved in tears today. Parting from little Karen and her family turned out to be much more dramatic than we thought. All of us traveled third class, so we weren't checked out on board like the passengers on first and second class. We had to go through immigration on Ellis Island. It turned out that the little one had tuberculosis. And they don't allow people with that kind of disease into the country just like that. The future looks dark for this family. We don't know how things will turn out for them, and we won't be able to do much for them, either, for we have to leave right away. We will travel with a group of Norwegians, who are also on their way west."

The rest of the letter described the docks, teeming with activity, and their own process through immigration. They came through it all without any problems.

Then they asked their mother to greet everyone at home. They sent special greetings to *Gomo*—grandmother—Gunhild and *Gofar*—grandfather—Even. Now they would soon be with Uncle Wilhelm and Uncle Theodor in North Dakota.

So the names of the girl's grandparents were Gunhild and Even. That explained to whom the bundled letters were sent. They were obviously sent by their sons, who emigrated to America before the turn of the century.

The route west that the twin sisters traveled was easy to follow. Mette took out a map she had of America. They had sent letters home from several of the cities where the train stopped along the way. Mina wrote a little, too, but usually it was Gunhild who was responsible for the correspondence. Gunhild seemed to be the practical one who explained how they were doing and how their journey was progressing. She wrote about the cities that they passed on their way west—Albany, Rochester, Buffalo and Cleveland.

Mina seemed to be more of a dreamer. She preferred to describe what they saw on their trip, or episodes that took place, or things that fascinated her. Once, in a long letter, she described a fight they had witnessed. Both knives and guns had been involved—a frightening experience that had made them realize they were getting closer to the real Wild West.

"Our next stop is Chicago," Gunhild wrote in a letter. "We're going to stay there for a few days. Our party is going to split up there, too. Some will stay, and some will continue on to Iowa and Nebraska. But fortunately, several others are going all the way to North Dakota, so we will still have company. The bad thing is that I'm worried about Mina. She doesn't say much, but I understand that she isn't well. It looks like she is coming down with the flu. I hope all this traveling won't be too hard on her."

The next letter was also written from Chicago, but it was dated three weeks later. Then Gunhild told that Mina had been very ill. She had been sick, too. They had to stay behind in the city while the rest of their party continued their journey. They were too ill to continue.

It had been a difficult time, but fortunately they got help from some Norwegians they met at a Norwegian church in town. They hoped they would soon be able to move

123

on. But Mina was still very weak. So they would wait a little longer.

As Mette read on, she became more and more engrossed in the story. She now noticed that several more letters were sent from Chicago, but not as frequently as the first ones. The two girls had a lengthy stay in the big city. Mina didn't seem to fully recover, so they decided not to make it even harder for her by continuing their journey. They rented a room, and Gunhild got a job as a kitchen maid at a hotel.

They stayed there all winter. Mina grew steadily worse, and soon it became clear that she had contracted tuberculosis. There was no doubt that she had caught it from little Karen on the ship. It must have been a difficult time for both women, but they didn't complain that much to their parents back home in Norway. They probably didn't want to worry them.

Then there was a letter from Mina. Mette was moved when she read it. "Today I feel a little better, so I will try to write to you, my dear parents. I realize now that we are never going to see each other again on this earth. Throughout this entire journey I have carried a seed of hope in my heart, the hope that we would get an opportunity to return to you some time in the future.

"Our home there at Lia is for me the dearest place on earth. But now I have started longing for a different home—a home that actually has come much closer. It is that glorious home in Heaven. Last night I thought Jesus was coming for me. I heard angels sing so beautifully, a wonderful peace filled my soul, and everything bad seemed to be gone. There was also a voice speaking to me. It said: 'I'll come soon!' Then my heart was filled with a single cry: 'Yes, come, Lord Christ.' Now I'll soon be home, I thought, and I can still feel the joy that filled me then.

"At first I didn't understand what it was—if it were a dream, or if Jesus wanted to tell me something so I wouldn't lie here fearing death. In any case, this gave me a strong longing for Heaven … a longing for Heaven that took away all my fears of death. But today, when I read Revelation 22:20, I realized that it was the Word of God. It was He who spoke to me. How wonderful. Soon Jesus will be here to get me.

"Promise me one thing, you, my dearest ones at home. Make sure that nothing will stop you from following me. We will meet again up there. And little Torkel … I miss him so. Show him this letter when he is old enough to understand, and show him the right path.

"Now I'm too tired to write any more. Goodbye, dear Mother and Father, and my dear brothers, Even and Torkel. We'll meet again."

With shaking hands, Mette put the letter back in the stack. She sat engrossed in thought. Little Torkel that Mina wrote about had to be the Uncle Torkel they had just buried. What love and care Mina had for him! But then, he was only 3 or 4 years old when they left. Their longing for their little brother probably affected them deeply. Again Mette wondered about his spiritual state when he died. Was he now reunited with his sister "back home"?

The next letter she read was dated just a few weeks later. It was Gunhild informing them that Mina was dead. She didn't describe her last days in detail, but it was obvious they had been hard, both for the dying woman and her sister, who watched her suffer.

Regarding the funeral, Gunhild had a lot of support from the pastor and her friends at church. Everything was taken care of in the best way possible. Now her dear sister was buried in the Norwegian cemetery in Chicago.

It seemed Gunhild had contemplated returning to Norway, but in the end she decided to continue on to her destination.

After this, the letters were infrequent. Gunhild seemed to have settled more and more into her new life. She got a warm reception from her relatives in North Dakota. Uncles, aunts and cousins welcomed her with warmth and love. She was considered a natural part of the family, but she also had her share of the hard life on the prairie. Hard work and many deprivations were things she had to accept.

After a while, new letters told about happier times. The name Nils was mentioned often, a handsome Norwegian and the owner of a farm somewhere west of the capital, Bismarck. Then there was a marriage and a change of circumstances for the Norwegian girl. From now on, her letters usually came at Christmastime and on special occasions. Soon there was an announcement that little Robert was born.

The letter fell into Mette's lap when she read this. This was critical information. This already confirmed her suspicions. She didn't know if the child lived or if they had more children, but the possibility was there.

They might have relatives in America who were legitimate heirs. They had to study this more closely and try to figure it out.

36 • *Greetings from your little brother*

Although spring seemed to be right around the corner, warm weather had not yet arrived. One cold spell after another brought snow from the sky and frost on the ground. There was still snow in the mountains, even though it was well into May. Not once had Mette been able to visit the seter. The road was still impassable. Of course, they might have gone by snow scooter, but Morten had been too busy lately. He was responsible for events both at the church and at the meetinghouse. Meetings and other work-related tasks took up his time. Mette was dependent on his coming along if she wanted to go, for she wasn't used to this kind of vehicle.

They hadn't been married long before they realized that the demands of everyday life had caught up with them again. She was busy with work-related tasks as well. She enjoyed the work, but soon felt an intense longing for the seter again. She often went to see Aunt Anna to talk about the upcoming summer. Even if Aunt Anna wasn't as spry as she used to be, she was determined to come along. Cooking was in her blood. Mette thought Aunt Anna would surely end her days stirring a pot full of porridge. Mette had to smile to herself. Knowing what she did about Aunt Anna, she realized the old lady probably couldn't think of a better way to end her life.

In Aunt Anna's cozy kitchen, they planned the dishes they would make for the tourists and what recipes to use. The enthusiastic lady constantly had new ideas and recipes she wanted to try out right away. Aunt Anna had collected recipes for traditional Norwegian food from different parts of the country.

One day the two of them worked together in Aunt Anna's basement, making *flatbrød**—flatbread. "We need to bring a lot of flatbrød," said Aunt Anna. "It goes with most of the dairy foods we serve."

Mette wasn't able to help her much, for this took great expertise, but she tried to learn. Aunt Anna was an excellent teacher. She talked continuously while she worked. Everything she did was explained in detail, and many a story from the old days was thrown into the bargain. It was incredible how much knowledge this woman possessed.

Mette was just as excited as she had been last summer, when they worked together in the same way. That this woman had the ability to work with great efficiency while words continuously poured out of her had surprised Mette more than once.

Often, Aunt Anna started Mette out on new tasks. The best way to learn is by doing it yourself, she would say. So Mette had to try rolling out the flatbread, but she felt clumsy and soon left the rolling pin to the old woman again. The only thing she did with confidence was peeling potatoes and pureeing the big batch of boiled potatoes they needed for the flatbread recipe.

A stack of thin, crispy flatbread sat on the basement table when the day was over. Aunt Anna and Mette sat down to take a breath at the kitchen table. They had hot coffee and freshly made flatbread. Aunt Anna served butter and homemade *gome** that they layered lavishly on their flatbread.

Aunt Anna told Mette that she had prepared for summer by baking *lefse**. "The whole freezer is full," she said, shaking with laughter. Mette had watched her bake lefse earlier. She couldn't think of anything more delicious than Aunt Anna's thin, soft potato lefse.

"Yes, I'm really looking forward to summer," Mette said, laughing along with her.

Suddenly Mette remembered the old letters from America she had gone through. Maybe Aunt Anna knew about these people. Just the day before, she had read some more and learned that Gunhild and Nils had two more children. One was named Willy and the other Mical. The youngest one apparently was sickly. It sounded as if he was significantly disabled.

Aunt Anna was enthusiastic when Mette brought this up. "Of course, I have heard about them," she said. "Berte Maria, Torkel's mother, often talked about their relatives in America. Apparently her grief was almost unbearable when one of the twins died. Yes ..." she stared blankly, consumed by thoughts, "you can understand that it must have been a blow to get that kind of message. Imagine, your 19-year-old daughter gets ill and then dies, far away in a foreign country. And you have no chance to even visit her grave. Yes, that poor Berte Maria, it wasn't easy for her."

They sat for a moment in silence thinking about the mother's grief, the sad outcome affecting them both. The hard realities of the past now seemed so close. And the brutal existence of those days seemed even closer as Aunt Anna continued her story:

"I think they were really struggling over there at Lia at the beginning of the century. The farm was not a large one, and they didn't have other sources of income. Not until Even, Morten's maternal grandfather, took over did they do a little better. He was able to make some more money by making furniture and selling it. He was an excellent cabinetmaker."

"So was he the one who made all the beautiful old furniture over there at the house?" asked Mette eagerly.

"Yes, that is truly a treasure that has to be preserved," answered Aunt Anna. "But before he started making furniture, things didn't go well over there. I remember my mother telling me that one day she had to go over to see Berte Maria. She was wondering why the children were nowhere to be seen. She was there for quite a while, but

126

she didn't see any of them. Later she found out that Berte Maria often told the children to hide in the attic when strangers came to visit, for she didn't want the town to know how poor their clothes were."

Mette shuddered. Imagine living in such poverty. No wonder so many immigrated to America. Over there at least they had some hope that there might be a better life in the future, even if the work was no less grueling than what they were used to from the Old Country.

"But," continued Aunt Anna, "they were not the only ones to suffer hard times. Our family struggled, too. But somehow we were always able to manage without having to set out for the unknown.

"The girls left before I was born, so I don't remember them. But I understand that Maren, Morten's maternal grandmother, kept in touch with their American relatives. Why they stopped writing each other I really don't know. Probably there is no family left over there. At least I never heard that Torkel was ever in touch with them."

Mette pondered this for a while. "Do you think the language problem made it difficult for them to keep in touch?" she asked, a little disheartened. She wasn't willing to give up the idea that they might have relatives in America.

Aunt Anna shook her head slightly. "I really don't know." She thought about it before she continued. "But of course, it's possible that was the problem."

They stayed for a while discussing the old letters, but then Mette had to leave. She didn't have much time before starting dinner, and later that evening she had a meeting.

A sudden impulse made her turn up toward Lia as she left Aunt Anna's yard. "Just a little peek," she thought. The house key was on her key ring, so she would be able to get in when she got there. She was not sure what she expected to find in the old house, but she wanted to see if there might be something that would provide new clues.

This time she studied the old furniture in the house with even greater interest. Spellbound, she examined the big secretary in the living room. Its four legs were carved in the shape of an S, its doors adorned by what looked like spiraling columns made of wood. The doors of the top hutch were made up of thin, square strips of wood. Red cloth lined the back of the doors, creating a luxurious effect when combined with the yellow-brown wood. Two balls, pointed at the top, adorned the front corners.

"Imagine making something this beautiful," thought Mette. "And he probably did it with just a knife, lathe and saw."

She moved from one piece of furniture to another, running her hand carefully across moldings and surfaces. She walked from room to room. She probably shouldn't go through the contents of drawers and boxes. That had to wait until they divided the assets. But first they had to figure out whether there might be other legitimate heirs in addition to Morten and his two sisters.

For a moment she again wondered why she came. It was impossible to know where to look for something that would provide more information about their American family. Discouraged, she went to the bedroom where she had found Uncle Torkel so ill that day. His bed was still there, but the bedding was gone. Marit had probably brought it home to wash it.

Up against one wall was a credenza with a bookshelf on top. It, too, was the same refined style as the rest of the furniture in the house. She became aware of an old Bible among the books on the shelf. Carefully, she took the book down and placed it over on the table. She noticed it had been well used, but the leather-bound covers still held the precious pages firmly in place. Despite its obvious wear, much of its original gold lettering still adhered to its spine.

Carefully she opened the Bible, sensing the odor of old paper. The cover page read, *"Bibelen eller Den Hellige Skrift indeholdende det Gamle og Nye Testamentes kanoniske Bøger"* (The Bible or The Holy Book containing the canons of the Old and New Testament) in elegant, gothic print. At the bottom was printed the year 1876.

So this was the family Bible that had followed this family through generations. She began leafing through the brittle pages. In some places they were almost worn to pieces. Here and there the worst damage had been repaired with needle and thread.

She became aware of something written on the first page. In fact, writing covered the page completely. The last page had writing on it, too. Although it was difficult to read, she could make out names and dates. Eagerly, she started reading. The entire family was recorded here. Maybe this would provide her with an answer.

She looked at her watch. Was it that late? Dinner should have been cooking a long time ago. It was best to leave as soon as possible.

Quickly, she shut the Bible and put it under her arm. She wanted to study this more closely when she got home.

They had a simple dinner that day. Morten was just as curious as she was to learn more about the old family.

After dinner, they both sat in the sofa with the old Bible in their laps. With joint effort, they were able to decipher name after name. The Bible seemed to have belonged to someone by the name of Even Lia. He was married to someone called Gunhild.

"A lot of the names are repeats," said Mette.

"Yes," Morten smiled. "They don't seem to have used their imagination in regard to names. But such were the naming traditions at that time. Children were named after their parents and grandparents. In a way, they didn't have a choice."

Their children were listed as Theodor, born in 1877, and Vilhelm, born in 1878; both had immigrated to America in 1898.

"Here it is," cried Mette eagerly.

Morten read on. Ola, born in 1880, married to Berte Maria, born 1882. They took over the farm. Then there were Berta and Matilde. They, too, emigrated, but there were no birth dates listed for them.

The next entries were Ola and Berte Maria's children. First there were the twins, Gunhild and Tomine (Mina). They were born in 1903, but immigrated to America in 1921. Next to their names, some information was added in smaller print. It was Tomine's date of death. The year was 1922. Then there was Gunhild's husband, whose name was Nils. Then followed three names: Robert, Willy and Mical.

Disappointed, Mette looked up at Morten. "This doesn't tells us anything we don't know," she said.

"No," said Morten, "but it is interesting anyway. For my part, I didn't know much about my family before. Look, here is some information about my maternal grandfather. He was brother of the twins, and he was the one who took over at Lia. His name was Even, and he was born in 1905. His wife, Maren, was born in 1908. Then there was Torkel, who was born in 1917. He took over the farm when my maternal grandfather died in 1966.

"Even and Maren had only one child, a girl, and that was my mother, Berta. She married Sivert, my father, and he was Aunt Anna's brother."

128

"This is a lot of names," said Mette with a sigh. "I'll have to study them for a while before I'll manage to keep track of everything."

Morten pulled the Bible closer and started turning the pages. "Look how worn it is. I would think this is a passage they have returned to often. Let's see what it is."

He started reading a page where a passage had been heavily underlined: *"Herre! Hør min Røst naar jeg raaber, og vær meg naadig og bønhør meg!"* (Hear my voice when I call, O Lord, be merciful to me and answer me.) It was Psalms 27:7.

Again, Mette felt she heard the echo of poverty from a distant past. Here a cry of distress rose up to God. A cry for help, maybe—help they sorely needed in order to sustain their life in the poor mountain community.

And how was their prayer answered? At least their family persevered; Morten was proof of that. But the ones over in America, what about them? They had no information about them. Would they ever know?

Suddenly something fell out of the Bible and landed in Morten's lap. Gingerly, he lifted up a white envelope. There was no address on it, but inside were two large sheets of paper. Morten pulled them out and started to read:

"Dear Mina. I'll never be able to send you this letter, but I have thought so much about you lately. I was only 4 years old when you left, but I remember it as if it were yesterday that we stood by the cart saying goodbye. The pain is with me still.

"You didn't get much to bring with you to the New World, but then, you never needed much. Now you are in a different world, where the things that we almost work ourselves to death for here are no longer needed. Neither will you have to suffer the broken heart that most people in this world rarely are allowed to escape.

"You don't have to watch Mother's tears, and you don't have to watch Father's worried eyes. You are now together in happiness. Oh, how I long to meet you all.

"You sent me a greeting before you left for the place you are now. Mother and Father were asked to tell me about it when I was old enough to understand. They did as you asked, but I probably didn't understand much of it then. Only now, lately, have my thoughts gone back to that greeting.

"Dear Sister, I would so very much like to see you again. All these years I have missed everybody, especially you, almost to the point of getting sick. You were always so kind to me. Even when we had so little that we had to go hungry, you always managed to find a treat for me. I suspect that you starved even more in order to give me something.

"Yes, I miss you, but lately I have longed even more to meet someone else, and that is Jesus. While I'm probably the greatest sinner in our entire mountain town, I was given a new start. Jesus took all the misery contained in my scrawny body and carried it away. Now the path is ready for me, too.

"I don't know how much longer I'll live. My health has been exceptionally good, I'll have to say, but I never thought about thanking Jesus for that. Not until now, when I desperately wish to go Home. I'm getting close to 80 now, so God probably won't wait too long to come for me, I reckon. I have nothing more to do here at Lia. And I don't think the town will miss me that much. I'm not able to live the way I should. The old is still too much a part of me, but fortunately I have met a merciful God.

"I just wanted to write this letter, I really don't know why. But I look forward to see both you and Gunhild again, and poor Nils, who was so unfortunate. It will be nice to meet Willy and Mical, too. I hope we will be able to understand each other up there in

Heaven, even if we didn't here on earth.

"Warmest greetings from your Little Brother."

They sat quietly for a long time. Mette had to wipe away some tears, and Morten's voice wasn't all that steady, either.

"Well, this answered an important question," said Mette, her voice shaking. "Uncle Torkel is in Heaven, no doubt about it."

"Yes," replied Morten, "and we also found out that both Willy and Mical are dead."

"But Robert?" Mette started blankly.

Morten looked thoughtful, too. "No, we can't give up yet," he said. "There is a possibility that Robert or his descendants are still living."

37 • The old box

A mild wind swept the yard and tousled Mette's short, blonde hair. She stood on the front steps and looked up the hill toward the north and the road to the seter. Finally spring was here with sun and mild weather, but the snow on the heights was tenacious. On the mountain peaks, white blankets reached far down the slopes. Now it might finally be possible to get up to the seter, thought Mette. The warm sunshine made her especially homesick for the way of life up there.

The warm weather had arrived at full force just a couple of days earlier. Down in the valley, buds had started forming on the naked birch twigs, and the birds were all busily occupied with their hectic spring life, building nests and looking for food. The sounds of their chirping filled the air from morning until far into night. Rushing streams tumbled down from the mountains in torrents of gray, muddy water. The river ran wide and mighty past the farm and thundered into the pools below the tall rapids. The snowmelt in the mountains made a great impact in town. Spring came almost like an explosion, Mette noted to herself.

They had celebrated *Syttende Mai* the day before. This was the first time she had participated in the 17th of May celebration in this community. She noticed with appreciation how everybody did their best to make it a remarkably festive day. The personal, friendly atmosphere made her feel welcome, even if the children's parade and the assembly hall at the school had fewer people than she was used to in Oslo.

Morten walked toward her across the yard. He smiled and followed the direction of her eyes up toward the mountain. "Are you soon ready to go?" he asked teasingly when he saw the longing in her eyes.

"Yes," said Mette. "How long do you think it will be before we can get up there?"

"I hoped we could go up there today," he said. "There's probably some road damage after the ravages of winter, but hopefully it will be passable by car. A man who wants to rent the seter house for the next couple of weeks has contacted me. We won't be able to start our seter operations yet, since spring is so late this year, so I thought we might as well make some money by renting it out."

"But then we have to get it ready," said Mette eagerly.

"Yes, that's why I thought we would try to get up there today," answered Morten.

Suddenly, Mette shifted into full swing. Quickly, she fetched what she thought they needed to bring, and soon they were on their way in the car.

Steadily and evenly, Morten's sturdy four-wheel drive climbed up the steep rocky slopes toward the bogs that reached for miles into the mountains. The road base turned out to be soft, and in several places there was still snow on the road, but no worse than they could manage. Not until they got to the last curve, where the landscape opened up toward the seter area, did they have to stop. A stream had jumped its banks and dug a big hole in the road.

"Looks like I have to do some roadwork here," said Morten.

But Mette didn't hear. She was already out of the car. She stood watching the marvelous scenery that had enthralled her so much the previous summer. There was the seter, so peacefully nestled under the steep rocky slope to the north. And then the meadow that stretched up toward the hillside to the west and down toward the sparkling but mystical lake to the east. To the south, where she now stood, the pine forest reached down the hill for quite a distance. Across the open grounds, the driveway went all the way to the seter house. On the east side of it was the campground where tourists stayed in the summer.

Now the entire area was drenched in sunlight. Mette caught her breath. She was finally here, and the place was as beautiful as she remembered it from last summer. The only difference were patches of snow along the field to the right where they had dried the hay, and the naked deciduous trees up the slope to the north, which last year still had all their leaves.

Slowly she walked up toward the house while breathing in the fresh mountain air in big gulps. Here, too, the birds were hard at work.

Time and time again, she would stop to look more closely at something. The cow barn and the sheep shed were still there, to the left of the seter house. The fence that stretched from the road by the pines and up to the barn was mostly in good repair. A few posts needed fixing here and there.

A musty, moldy smell greeted her as she opened the door to the seter house. The old log house was in good shape after the winter, or rather, after quite a few winters up here in the mountains. But the odor from the rough-hewn wood bore evidence of its age.

Everything was as she had left it last fall. A twinge of pain went through her, thinking about that episode. Misunderstanding, gossip and bad feelings had made the farewell both dramatic and painful for her. But fortunately, everything had worked out with time. She didn't want to think more about it. Now was a new time and a new year.

She looked quickly around the room. Over there to the right was the big wood stove. There they had made *lapper**—small pancakes—on the stone griddle as well as porridge and other dishes. The gas-burning stove was a little further away. That's where they used to make coffee in the morning.

Then there were the steps up to the loft that had been Morten's bedroom. The steps were no more than a ladder, but Morten had no problems getting up and down. He had used the ladder since he was a little boy.

To the left of the window sat the dining room table. Mette thought about all the conversations they had there over steaming cups of coffee. She remembered especially the night of the storm when she sat watching over the cow barn, which she could see from the window. Lightning and thunder had scared both her and the animals. She had been scared to death that lightning would hit the dry hay in the hayloft. She had to smile a little at the memories. But the experience had been dramatic enough. In the middle of the night, as she had to run outside to bring in the livestock in the terrible rainstorm, lightning hit the rocky slope behind the seter house. A tree was completely shattered. The fear had held its grip on her for a long time.

There were three more rooms in the house. Under the loft, Aunt Anna had her bedroom. There she kept all the wool and other material she needed for the tourist demonstrations. Then there was the bedroom in the back, the one Mette had used. The dairy room was located next to her bedroom.

Mette crossed the floor and entered the dairy room. It was the only room at the seter that had electric power, which came from a solar panel outside on the wall of the house. They needed power to keep milk and other food fresh. She noticed that the seter house had not been completely unoccupied during the winter. Some small, black grains on the counters revealed that mice had visited frequently. "I'll have to clean here for sure," she told herself as she shook mouse droppings out of a bowl.

But first she wanted to look around some more. She left through the back door and stood there for a while, closely studying the steep rocky slope. The tree that the lightning destroyed was now on the ground. Its sprawling roots looked like antennas, pointing straight up in the air. The snow had probably helped tear it apart even more.

She began climbing up the slope. That tree surely isn't far from the house, she thought as she looked down from where the lightning hit. "There I was, between the house and the barn," she said in a low voice. She shuddered at the thought of having been so close to a catastrophe.

Where the root of the fallen tree had been, she could see the stripped bedrock. Both moss and heather had been ripped away when it fell.

Suddenly she noticed a deep depression next to the root. She bent down to check it out more closely. There she saw a cavity starting in the depression and disappearing horizontally into the bedrock. The opening was actually quite large. Mette crept down and put her hand into the cavity to see how deep it was. But she wasn't able to feel the end, not even with most of her arm inside it.

"This is strange," she thought, examining the walls. Then her hand touched an object that scraped against the rock. Something was inside. Carefully, she explored the cavity again. There it was. Gently, she pulled something out. When she got it out into the daylight, she saw that it was an old chest or box, about the size of an ice cream container. Made of metal, it had managed to rust during the time it had been inside the cavity. She stood for a while, studying it. She noticed that it held something inside, something that wasn't heavy and didn't rattle.

The lid was stuck tight, so she decided she would have to bring it back to the house. Maybe Morten would be able to open it when he came back in.

The box turned out to be more difficult to open than they thought.

Morten, too, was filled with wonder about what might be hidden inside. "Maybe it's some papers," he said.

"Or money," Mette suggested eagerly.

Morten laughed. "Yes, that could be, but then, it isn't money that will benefit us. I'm guessing this box has been there for a long time."

"Do you think it can be that old?" Surprised, Mette looked at the rusty box.

Morten turned it over several times. "I don't know, but seeing how big that root is, it has to have been there for quite a while."

They were unable to do any more about the box. So as not to damage the contents, they decided to delay opening it until they had more suitable tools. They placed it in a corner of the cupboard and started cleaning.

It was late in the day before they could go back home, tired and weary, and then the box in the cupboard was entirely forgotten.

38 • The first tourist

A week of great weather had transformed the town from a cold, exposed winter place with snow and ice up the hillsides to a warm and lush summer paradise. The leaves were almost completely out on the birch twigs, and the grass grew green in the fields. Mette had never seen the likes of it. Several days ago, she had thought about this spring as an explosion, but it was even more than that. It almost took her breath away when she thought of all the things that had to happen during such a short season. The farmers were already fertilizing and plowing their fields, day and night.

Morten also had his hands full. Even if he didn't operate his farm the same way other farmers did, he still had many of the same chores. The property had to be maintained, work that was usually done during this short period of the year.

The road to the seter had dried up considerably, and Morten had fixed all the bad potholes, so now there was no problem getting there.

Mette sat on the porch and soaked up the pleasant temperature. Above her head a wagtail was busily working on its nest. Now and then it swept across the yard, flying so low that it almost touched Truls, the big tomcat that now kept watching it intently. Now and then Truls leaped into the air. He probably hoped to get himself a treat in a hurry, but it looked like he might have problems. The wagtail was always high up in the air again before the fat tomcat even got going.

Mette laughed as she sat watching their game. "No, you'll have to wait until we get to the seter. Then you're going to get as much cream and goodies as you can possibly eat," she called after him.

Come to think of it, Truls didn't really need any more treats than what he already got. His size was ample proof. But Mette still liked the idea that the very best things around, especially for an animal, were to be found up there at the seter.

Suddenly a car drove into the yard. A man got out and walked toward her. He greeted her, introducing himself as Arvid. Mette realized this was probably the fellow who was renting the seter. Morten was at work, so she would have to show him the way up there. "I'll drive ahead of you, so you can just follow," said Mette after they had exchanged a couple of words. "We'll be there in about 15 minutes, I would think."

She jumped in the car and drove quickly onto the road.

Up at the seter, everything looked much more lush than when they were there last, even if it wasn't as green as it was in town. But at least the snow in the meadow was gone. Only on the tallest peaks far away could they still see some white patches.

The guest was obviously excited about his new accommodations. He could hardly have found a more idyllic place. Mette showed him around in the seter house and its surroundings. Afterward, they sat down on a bench outside in the sun and talked.

Mette guessed Arvid was probably in his 30s. She observed that he was the complete opposite of Morten; he was almost as blond as she was, and his face was heavy-set but well formed. His hair was wavy across the crown of his head, but cut short at the neck. Otherwise, he was fairly tall and slender. His eyes were a mixture of green and brown. He was a handsome man.

The thought hit her so unexpectedly that she turned beet red and shifted her eyes toward the lake. What was she thinking? She scolded herself silently before she got her balance back and continued the conversation.

Arvid turned out to be a pleasant person who was easy to talk to. "Have you heard about the legend," she asked after a while, "that gave this seter its name?"

"No, I haven't heard much about this seter at all," he answered. "Is there a legend about this place? That sounds interesting."

Mette then she told him about Silja, who once upon a time was banished to this seter by her family because she was pregnant without being married. They wanted to hide their shame as long as possible, not in the least because of rumors that the son of one of the big farmers in the next town was the father. But he didn't want to acknowledge the relationship, and her family feared they might be in for severe repercussions.

That fall, something went wrong at the seter. One of the dogs showed up at the farm, acting strange. People set out immediately to find out what might have happened. There they found an flock of agitated farm animals outside the door to the cow barn, but no dairymaid.

"They did a thorough search," Mette continued. "In the end, they found her in the lake. She had drowned. But the strange thing was that she was no longer pregnant. After that day, the legend has stayed with this seter. That's why the lake is called the Siljatjern and the place is called the Siljatjern Seter," she ended.

Arvid listened raptly to the entire story. "That's quite a tale," he said, laughing. For a while they sat silently looking over at the dark surface. It was as if shadows from the past were reflected in its deep.

"No, don't let us sit here moping about old yarns that probably exist only in the fertile minds of the gossip mongers in town." Mette emphasized the last words. Last summer she had experienced what gossip could do, so she didn't have much patience for that type of conversation. "So what brought you up here in the wilderness all by yourself?" she asked with a smile.

The smile disappeared from his lips and a shadow came over his face. He kept looking at the lake. When he started speaking, his voice sounded sad, almost bitter. "I'm recently separated," he said simply. "My wife left me for another guy. That's it. I just had to get away."

"Oh, I'm sorry." Mette looked at him with deep concern. "That must hurt terribly. I'm sorry I asked …"

"No, it doesn't matter," he said in a brighter voice. Only now did he look directly at her again. A sad smile appeared on his lips.

"It's just as well that I talk about it. You had to know sooner or later, I thought. I hoped to be able to get my bearings again up here in the mountains. Hiking in fresh air and great scenery has always refreshed and relaxed me. And if I can also bring my fishing pole along, then everything is in place for the kind of therapy I need."

He stopped and shook his head slowly. His voice was almost inaudible when he started speaking again: "Lately, things have been so bad that I didn't know if I would be able to get through it. The answer to her troubles that Silja found has occurred to me now and then, too."

Mette shivered. "Poor man," she thought. There and then she decided to try to make life as pleasant for him as possible … if there was something she could do.

Not much more was said between them. Arvid thanked her for her help, and Mette said goodbye after impressing upon him that he had to let them know if there was anything they could help him with.

"Do you have a cell phone?" she asked as she got in the car.

"Yes …" He hesitated a little. "But can I get a signal up here?"

"Yes," said Mette. "At least it seems to work right here around the seter. Give me your number. Then we can get in touch with you if something is going on. I assume that you have ours?"

He nodded and wrote down his number on a piece of paper Mette found in her car.

It was a thoughtful Mette who drove down the road toward town that afternoon. She was filled with compassion for the greatly tried man. To have to deal with such misery. Might he really have contemplated suicide? How awful things must have been for him.

She was so consumed by all the things he had told her that she didn't quite concentrate on her driving. Without noticing, she pushed the gas pedal down another notch. As the speed increased, she became aware of a fox that jumped down from a hill and landed in the road right in front of the car.

For one chaotic moment, she had no idea what happened. The car spun around and landed in a bog well off the road, wheels in the air. Only for a fraction of a second did she catch a glimpse of the fox that jumped, quick as lightning, over some tufts on the bog and disappeared through the underbrush on the other side. It took a few more seconds before she collected herself and was able to assess the predicament she was in. There she hung, suspended by the seat belt, her head down, and with intense pain in her left shoulder.

39 • A single fox

"I have to get out of here, but how?" Mette felt she was about to panic. She could hardly move her left arm. At the slightest movement, pain ran through her body.

After working at it for a while, she was able to slide around until her head, at least, was upright. Also, she soon realized that none of the doors would open, but the windshield was broken. "Maybe I can get out through there," she mumbled, looking for something to help her remove the broken glass. The only thing she found was her shoe. Armed with that, she managed to clear an opening through which to crawl out.

After some more work and many painful moans, she was finally able to sit down on a tuft in the bog.

What now? She was filled with an intense rage. What was that darn, mangy fur ball of a fox doing in the road? Foxes were supposed to run away from people, to be shy … Yes, they were supposed to be shy. It must have heard her coming. And then it

135

wasn't even hurt. It was supposed to have been lying there dead as a doornail in the road. Yes, that was it … dead, as a cured leg of lamb. If she only had a shotgun, she would blast away at the first fox she saw. Yes, she would do it in a minute, even if she had never fired a shot in her life. And it would be dead, she would make sure of that.

In the same instant, she swung her good arm as if hurling something after it over there between the bushes. The result of her abrupt move was a howl of pain, followed by a few long, hopeless sobs.

"Oh, what am I going to do?" she cried. Her anger dissipated, transformed into despair. "Here I am, the car is totaled. I can't use my left arm and …" She groaned again. It was hard to breathe. How badly was she hurt? She felt sore all over.

Soon she was able to think almost normally. "I have to get help … the cell phone!"

With some effort, she got to her feet and soon found her cell phone. But no one picked up the phone at home. "Morten probably isn't home yet …" She looked at her watch. "Maybe he works overtime. I'll call the bank." But what was the number to the bank? As much as she racked her brain, she couldn't remember. Her thoughts were completely jumbled. She started to shiver. Even if the air was warm, she was shaking as if from severe cold. The pain in her shoulder was so intense that she had trouble concentrating.

"Who can I call?" She couldn't remember anyone at all. At least, not someone whose number she remembered. Of course, she had the numbers for emergency and police, but surely she couldn't bother them with this.

Suddenly she remembered the piece of paper where Arvid wrote down his cell phone number. Arvid, yes, he had to be the closest one she should call. But where was the note? She didn't want to climb through the window again to look for it.

After a while she saw it through the window. She wasn't able to reach it, but she could make out the numbers.

Arvid answered almost right away, and he grasped the situation quickly. It didn't take him many minutes to get to the accident site.

"What in the world happened here?" he asked, shocked, as he climbed down the slope to the bog. Mette was unable to answer. She was shaking so hard. Quickly, he realized that her shoulder was hurt. Her arm hung at a weird angle. "You have to get to a doctor," he said. "I'll help you."

Gently, he helped her onto the road and into his car. Mette still trembled, but it was great not to have to think about anything but sitting there.

Not much was said on the trip, but she noticed that Arvid looked searchingly over at her many times. Everything he said and did demonstrated great concern. Mette noticed that his kindness felt incredibly good. She now worried that she might have other injuries as well, for she had greater and greater difficulty breathing. She felt a sting in her side every time she drew her breath.

Suddenly her tears started running again. The notion that maybe the entire summer would be ruined made her body shake even more, increasing the pain.

"You seem to be in real pain," said Arvid in a worried voice.

Mette wanted to smile at him, but she wasn't able to. Her despair was too overwhelming. "Why did this have to happen?" A new fit of rage started brewing in her. "God, why didn't you stop this from happening?" She didn't say it aloud, but felt like screaming: "Couldn't you have stopped that fox from jumping into the road?"

In the same moment, a new thought came to her. Yes, it was almost like a voice from the outside: "Yes, I could have stopped the fox, but could I have stopped you from stepping on the gas pedal? What about concentrating on your driving?"

Mette shook her head and a new wave of pain racked her body. She sank back into the seat with a moan. Concentration? ... thoughts? ... She didn't want to think any more. She didn't want to hear more voices.

Arvid looked at her with even greater concern and increased the speed. He didn't speak, but probably interpreted her moans to mean that she needed the attention of a physician, right away.

Soon they were down in town. Morten was at home, and the shock of what had happened was written all over Arvid's face. After thanking Arvid profusely for his help, Morten took over the responsibility for his injured wife.

It was an incredible relief for Mette to get to the hospital and be taken care of. It turned out that her collarbone was broken, as well as some ribs. Nothing serious, fortunately. But she would need complete rest for a while.

"I'm sure you'll be all right again before you go to the seter," the physician told her when she voiced her concern. "You'll be as good as new in a couple of weeks."

It was a quiet time for Mette. But she enjoyed the peace and quiet after the mad rush she had been caught up in for so long. Arvid stopped by now and then to see how she was doing. For long periods of time, they could sit over a cup of coffee in the kitchen and talk. They got to know each other well during that time.

Morten, too, liked their new tenant. A couple of times they went fishing together in the mountains. But it was mostly when Arvid and Mette were by themselves that Arvid opened up and talked about his personal problems. Mette felt sorry for him. She understood that he needed to talk about them now and then, and she was more than willing to let him.

During this period, Mette also had plenty of time to study the old letters from America. Some more information came to light. She found out that Robert had studied to be a doctor in Minneapolis and worked at a hospital there. Eventually, Gunhild ended up in a nursing home in Bismarck. She died there in 1967. After that time, the communication with America seemed to have stopped.

It was only Maren, Morten's maternal grandmother, who kept in touch with the family over there at that time.

Now there was a possibility Morten might have relatives over there after all. Morten worked on the case for a full afternoon over at the bank. He contacted several banking operations affiliated with his bank, both in Minneapolis and Bismarck, in an attempt to get more information. But it was a futile exercise. He called the nursing home where Gunhild had stayed. They were able to confirm that a woman by the name of Gunhild Ånensen had been a resident there, but they didn't know anything about her family.

Mette felt an unspeakable hopelessness when Morten came home and told her about the negative result of his search. How in the world would they find this man if they didn't know anything about him?

"Did you check to see if he was married?" Morten interrupted her thoughts.

"Yes, I think I saw that somewhere." She went to the living room and returned right away with a letter. "I think there is something in this letter that confirms that." Silently, she stood for a while, scanning the lines to find the right paragraph.

"This has to be it," she said eagerly. She began reading:

"I don't get many visits now. After Carl sold the farm and went west, there is no one

137

left of Nils' family here. But Robert and Nancy were here a week ago. It was good to see them, even if they didn't bring the children. He doesn't get a chance to visit me very often. He is so busy at the hospital, and Nancy works so much at the office that they don't have much time off. But the other residents here and the staff are pleasant."

"Nancy has to be his wife." Mette continued to scan the lines to see if there might be more important information. In the end, she put the letter down and shook her head. "I haven't found out much more about them. I haven't figured out who this Carl is, but he seems to be a relative on Nils' side."

"It looks like they have children, too, but I haven't seen their names mentioned."

"Maybe we can contact the Salvation Army. They are good at finding people all over the world." She looked eagerly at Morten.

He smiled, but shook his head slightly. For a moment he was deep in thought, a smile still on his lips. At last he looked over at her. "Maybe we should take a trip over there to see what we can find out."

Mette sunk down into her chair, her blue eyes looking as if they would pop out of her head. "What are you saying? We … are we going to look around over there in that enormous country for a man we don't know anything about? Have you gone crazy?"

Morten laughed. "Why not? We have some very pertinent information. The hospital in Minneapolis will have records of their employees, or …" he thought for a while …"former employees. For this man might already be retired."

"I don't know at what age doctors retire over there," answered Mette, somewhat resigned. "But he has to be in his 70s now. Maybe he already has passed away."

"Yes." Morten still had his good-natured smile. "Maybe he is dead, but wouldn't the trip be fun?"

Mette had to smile, too. At that moment, she agreed with him completely.

They didn't discuss the matter further that day.

40 • Putting the cows out to pasture

"I have to get back." Arvid put his head in the kitchen door. "I just stopped by to say goodbye. My sick leave is almost over, so I have to get back to work again."

He seemed to be genuinely sorry. Mette, too, felt sad about his leaving, at first. It had been so nice to have him up there. And she would miss all the meaningful conversations they had. She didn't want to dwell on the fact that, with time, he made sure he stopped by when he knew Morten was at work. It was probably just a coincidence. Anyway, it had been enjoyable.

"How sad," she answered. "Then I suppose we won't see you any more?"

He stood for a while, studying her. There was something in his eyes that she couldn't quite define—a hint of an inner pain, and at the same time something that looked like admiration. But he had endured so much misery, poor thing. No wonder his eyes would be full of pain.

She went over to him and said goodbye by shaking his hand. Impulsively, she gave him a hug. She felt him twitch at the same instant, but he returned her goodbye hug.

"I've thought about maybe spending my summer vacation up there at the seter," he said suddenly as he was about to leave. "Maybe you could fit in another camper in the grounds up there?"

"Oh, yes." Mette showed considerable enthusiasm at his proposition. "You are most welcome!"

Arvid smiled and waved at her as he headed for the car. "I'll stop at the bank and say goodbye to Morten," he called back. "Then I can pay my rent at the same time."

Mette was left with a strange feeling of unease. She was going to miss this man. But ... could there be something wrong in it? No, she had done nothing she might regret in her relationship with Arvid. Still, she felt uncomfortable. But they had such a good time together, and he really needed someone to talk to, since he was in such a difficult situation. No, she didn't want to think about it any more. Now he was gone. And if he came back this summer, he probably would be over the whole thing.

○ ○ ○

The days became progressively warmer. The grass grew tall and lush in the meadow behind the barn. The farmers in town had already sent their sheep to the mountains. There was sprouting and growing going on all over—you could almost hear it! Mette's arm felt much better. Soon it would be as good as new. Morten had told her that they might expect the first tourists at the seter before St. John's Day, and that was next week. Mette looked forward to it with childlike anticipation. She had gone over to Aunt Anna's several times during the last days. Everything was ready for a new season. Now it was just a question of getting up there and settling in with people and livestock.

Morten had a deal with Petter that worked well for both of them. When the season was over at the seter, Petter bought the cows that gave milk. Morten couldn't keep milking cows in the winter because he wouldn't be able to fill the required milk quota. And when a new season started, Morten bought the cows back.

He didn't always get the same cows. Petter usually picked out some that he thought would do well up there. It was important that they were calm and friendly animals, since they were supposed to be around the tourists as much as possible. And it also served Petter's purpose well that they wanted cows that didn't give too much milk. Most of the time it was hard enough to find a use for all the milk, since they couldn't ship anything to the local dairy.

Two of the cows from last year were coming to the seter this summer, too. They were calm and gentle and accepted being milked by hand. Most of Petter's cows didn't put up with anything but the milking machine.

They had also agreed to take along a heifer that was about to calve. "It is her first calf," said Petter, "so the cow has never been milked before. But she is gentle as a lamb, and I really think she will be perfect for you. My kids have petted her all winter, so she is comfortable with both children and adults."

Morten was pleased with his purchase and felt that everything was now in place for a new season.

What bothered Mette the most was that Caesar couldn't come up with them. He was the precious bull, born last summer, that she had helped him into this world. She thought of the incident: They had found his mother in a lake; she had fallen down a rocky slope and was seriously injured. After a lot of effort, they finally got her back on land, but they had to put her down. However, Morten was able to save the calf by performing a Caesarian section on the dead heifer. Thus the name, Caesar.

139

Afterward, the calf was a special and loving friend for them all, especially for Mette. It was she who named him, too. Every so often Mette would stop by the cow barn during spring to talk to him and scratch him behind the ears.

Even though she had been gone for quite some time during the winter, she was convinced that he recognized her when she came to the farm.

Now Caesar was a big, strong bullock. Since they were not allowed to put such big bulls out to pasture in the summer, he had to stay home. But Missi was coming with them. She was housed in their own cow barn. She was the second calf to be born last summer. Now she had grown to be a good-sized heifer.

Mette knew one thing: The heifers wouldn't be allowed to roam too far into the mountains. She would make sure of that. She didn't want anything to happen to them.

Then there were the sheep and goats. That they were coming with them was a given. Of course, they had to come. Six sheep and 11 lambs were waiting impatiently in the barn, longing for the juicy, lush mountain pasture. So far they had been out in the fields by the barn, but it was the mountains that attracted them the most. And the two lively goats that made such a racket the year before would get another chance this year.

Mette smiled to herself when she thought about the times she had to chase them out of the dairy room or away from the campground when they became too assertive.

o o o

On Saturday morning, Morten and Mette were ready for the move up to the seter. Mette had brought up some supplies the day before. They needed clean towels and bedding, as well as items to be used for cooking. Now, both the drawers and cupboards were full.

Today they would move the livestock. Morten had borrowed a horse trailer to transport the animals. It was a great improvement that they no longer had to chase them up along the paths, over bogs and mountains, to get them to the seter. Morten had told her how this was done in the old days. He himself had never had to walk all day long, clogs on his feet and stick in his hand, following the flock of animals when they moved to the seter. But his father had told him how they did it in his childhood.

Back then, they carried their supplies up on horseback, while people and livestock had to walk. This moving day was a special day of the year, a day that many looked forward to and longed for. But it was also a day that was dreaded by some. Not everybody was happy about herding animals and hiking around in the mountains. In those days, this move happened much later in the spring. But these days, the deciding factor at Siljatern Seter was not the timing of cutting and drying hay or consideration for the rest of the work down on the farm. The tourists were now the only factor that determined their schedule.

Aunt Anna and Mette left first. They had to be there to help get the newly arriving animals settled in.

When the women got to the seter, Mette stopped to look at the meadow in speechless awe. Summer had cloaked both fields and mountains with a vibrant green. Again, she was struck by the intense colors displayed in the magnificent mountain scenery. Grass and leaves seemed so much greener and the glittering lake so much bluer. Even the sky seemed higher and clearer than down in town, she thought. The seter meadow had filled in well, but the grass wasn't tall yet. It would take a while before they could cut it. But they had to mow the camping area soon, for there they wanted to maintain a lawn. Standing there, Mette could feel the warmth of the sun, but there was still a nippy chill in the air. She was glad she brought a lot of clothes.

Suddenly, Aunt Anna's voice cut through the silence. She had already brought in a load of household items. Now she came out to the car to get some more: "I'll say you've made it look cozy in here. And it smells so clean and fresh! Yes, we'll really have a good time here this summer. I just hope the goats won't eat too much of the stuff in the dairy room." The last words were spoken with a rolling laughter that made her big, round body shake. Her eyes almost disappeared in her round cheeks.

Mette laughed, too. She was continuously surprised at how many words rolled off Aunt Anna's smiling lips when she was excited. But it wasn't just when Aunt Anna was excited that she talked a mile a minute. She did it all the time.

Not much later, Morten and Petter arrived in the meadow with the first animals. Good old "Plum" was the first to be brought over to the cow barn. Morten had named her that because he thought she was so round around the middle and the color of a plum. The year before, they didn't use names for the older animals, but Mette thought it was so much more personal if they did. So she decided that this year, the cows' names were going to be used more.

It was obvious that Plum knew where she was. She walked obediently over to the cow barn, but she also clearly realized that this was the beginning of freedom and bliss. Every so often she made a couple of excited leaps. Head pointed toward the ground and hind legs in the air, she waved her tail ecstatically.

Mette watched Plum with delight. "I'll leave her here so she can tire herself out," said Morten, leaving to get the other cow they brought—the new heifer. Petter untied the rope that held her, and then he pulled to make her leave the trailer. But it didn't look like she had any intention of moving. Instead, she fought back as hard as she could.

"Come on, now!" cried Petter. Morten walked around and slapped her on her neck to get her to turn around, but nothing seemed to help. The heifer was not moving.

Petter yelled and Morten slapped while constantly pulling at the rope, but the heifer was persistent. She wouldn't even move a leg.

Suddenly an intense and piercing sound cut through the air. It was Aunt Anna, yelling her "cow call" at high frequency. Startled, Mette almost fell on her back. The same happened to Petter and Morten. But what the yelling and kicking of the men didn't accomplish, Aunt Anna did with her well-trained voice. In a second, the heifer was off the trailer. Before Petter realized what had happened, the heifer was far down in the field. With lifted head and raised tail, she galloped straight for the woods. The rope trailed behind her, sweeping the ground.

"We have to get her before she disappears behind the hill," yelled Morten, running after her at top speed. Petter took off after them as fast as his knotty farmer's legs would carry him.

Mette noticed that Morten was considerably faster. With his slim and athletic body, he quickly put the green meadow behind him. It looked much harder for Petter. Both his behind and his tummy obviously had been sitting too long behind the tractor wheel, she thought with a smile. His overalls and rubber boots didn't help him much, either.

The heifer disappeared behind the trees at the edge of the field. But they soon spotted her again. This time she came rushing out of the underbrush much further up. With lifted head and ears, she headed straight for the seter house. Mette ran for the car in an effort to get out of her way. She noticed the expression in the eyes of the bolting animal. She looked wild. Mette could see the whites of her eyes, and vapor and foam

141

squirting from her nose. In the same moment Mette jumped into the car, they all heard another piercing sound, but this time it was more of a death wail. The wail came from Aunt Anna, who suddenly realized what danger she was in.

Mette would never have believed that the round, rocking body would be able to move that fast. In a second, Aunt Anna was inside the seter house. The door banged shut and Mette could hear the latch on the inside slide into place.

The heifer continued her wild run toward the cow barn. She jumped the fence, but wasn't quite able to clear it. Two posts flew in the air and the wire snapped as she went over. Plum stood watching the mayhem. With a terrified bellow, she took off. Four posts were pulled across the meadow as the cow jumped the fence in the opposite direction.

Now Morten and Petter were on their way back, panting. They stopped for a moment to catch their breath while watching the wild dash of the animals. Plum heading for the lake, and the heifer was already over on the hill to the west. She turned around as the slope got too steep, but she didn't reduce her speed. Before the two animal-control men knew it, the heifer ran past them. The fence was almost completely down now. Plum now stood by the lake, panting. Then she spotted the heifer that was heading in her direction again. A new bellow and some vigorous kicks made the heifer turn on her heels, and soon she was on her way back to the cow barn again.

Mette sneaked out of the car and walked over to the men. "What are we going to do?" she asked in despair.

Morten scratched his head. His dark eyes searched for the heifer. A resolute and firm expression appeared on his face. "If you two go over toward the lake, one on each side of the meadow, I'll see if I can chase her down to the bank. Bring some sturdy twigs so you can steer her in the right direction if she wants to turn. The heifer goes in the lake!" The last words were pronounced with clenched teeth.

Mette and Petter were already on their way over. Quickly, they both snapped off a twig from a birch at the edge of the field. Mette went to the left and Petter to the right. Not far from the bank, they aligned themselves, ready to chase the crazed animal into the lake. Meanwhile, the heifer had turned around on the hillside again and was on her way back. Plum was nowhere to be seen. She had probably gone into hiding somewhere between the trees.

Immovable, Morten stood firm, looking the bolting animal straight in the eye as she closed in on him at a furious pace. The two down by the water's edge weren't able to see what actually happened, but Morten had managed to get hold of the rope that dangled behind the heifer. Determined not to let go, he trailed behind her in an insane race.

"This isn't going to work!" Mette screamed, scared out of her mind. At the same time they saw Morten stumble and fall forward, but he didn't let go of the rope. He was being dragged behind the cow on his stomach.

As the heifer saw the water, she tried to turn to the left. But Mette was there, screaming and waving both arms and legs, so the animal didn't dare go in that direction. She turned quickly to the right, but there was Petter. She didn't fancy the sturdy, red-haired man with the booming voice, either. Now she didn't have that many options left. And her speed didn't give her time to consider what else to do. With a thundering splash, she rushed into the lake with Morten hanging on right behind her.

The impact nearly knocked the wind out of them both, but soon everything calmed down. Morten crawled quickly onto the bank and pulled on the rope. The heifer responded right away.

The animal they pulled out of the lake seemed completely different. Exhausted, she lay on the ground. She stayed down, panting, steam rising from her body.

"Gotcha," said Morten between chattering teeth. His swim in the cold lake hadn't exactly been pleasant.

"You better take this heifer back home again," he said to Petter. "I don't think I can take any more battles like this."

It wasn't long before the heifer was back in the trailer again. Petter backed it up as close to the lake as he could. With a concerted effort, they were able to load the exhausted animal. Plum came sneaking back after a while. Soon she grazed peacefully in the meadow.

After Morten had changed into dry clothes, he stood with Mette and studied the flattened fence.

"I thought Petter said this was a calm and peaceful heifer," said Mette, puzzled. "Why would she behave like that?"

Morten shook his head. "It isn't always easy to understand these animals. Sometimes they behave differently from what you expect. And if you run into that kind of problem with an animal once, you can be sure that the problems will not go away. I, for one, will not take a chance on it. But now I better get back down to the farm to help Petter with the rest of the animals. Hope we won't have more episodes like this."

He jumped in the car that Mette and Aunt Anna had used, and soon he disappeared down the road.

41 • Rest

Aunt Anna hummed and sang in the dairy room. Mette wasn't sure what she was doing, but in any case it was nice to listen to the familiar sounds. Outside it was cool, with fog and some rain in the air. Morten had left for town to pick up a group of tourists they were expecting today.

Both people and animals had settled in at the seter after the strenuous move. They had a new heifer that was much calmer. She too would calve, but not until later in the summer. Petter's children had named her "Silkedokk," probably because they thought she was so silky and soft. The other old cow was called "Stjerna," meaning "Star." She was black with a white star on her forehead. They also brought with them a 4-month-old calf called "Pia." They didn't buy it; they just kept it so the tourists would be able to enjoy its company. Petter was glad he didn't have to care for it during the summer. And young animals were always popular among the tourists.

Mette sat at the window of the seter house. For a moment she allowed her eyes to take in the herd of animals grazing so peacefully in the meadow. The sheep, too, seemed to feel at home. She could hear the brittle tinkling of their bells, even from in the house. They had found a good, juicy pasture up on the hill. The familiar sounds made her sigh contentedly. "How wonderful it is to be here," she said, smiling to herself.

None of the animals appeared to be bothered by the lousy weather. If they were allowed to stay in the mountains and gorge themselves on the lush mountain grass, that was the only thing they seemed to care about. The lambs scurried around their mothers while their tails whirled behind them like little propellers. There, under their mothers' newly sheared bellies, they found everything they needed; their happiness seemed to be complete.

But Mette didn't allow herself to get carried away watching the animals for too long. Her attention was focused on what she had in front of her on the table. It was the old box she had found in the cave up on the hillside. Because of the moving and everything else going on, she had completely forgotten about it. Not until she needed something from the cupboard in the corner did she remember, and there it was. Now she had it in front of her, trying to figure out how to open it. She was bursting with curiosity. What might be hiding under the stuck lid? She had tried to put oil around the edges, and then she picked and scraped away at it with a sharp knife. But nothing seemed to work. It was still completely stuck.

Aunt Anna came in from the dairy room. "What are you working on so hard?" she asked when she noticed Mette's concentration.

It's this box," said Mette, showing her the tin box. "I have no idea how to get the lid off."

Aunt Anna came closer, peering at it curiously. "Where did you find this?" she asked. Mette told her about the cave she discovered up there underneath the fallen root. Carefully Aunt Anna lifted the box and shook it. "There's something inside," she said. "This is strange. I never knew there was a cave up there, even if I crawled around in these hills a lot as a kid. This has to be really old."

Mette felt her excitement go up a few notches. If only she could figure out how to get the lid off without damaging the contents!

Just then they heard the sound of vehicles outside. Several cars and campers were on their way to the camping area. "There are the tourists," Mette called. Quickly, she put the box back in the cupboard and ran out.

All at once there was frantic activity outside. A group of German families would be staying at the seter for several days. They were responsible for their own food, but Aunt Anna always served something good, either as a welcome, or for the special events they organized up there. Now she had prepared flatbread, cured meats and other good things. She had churned butter early in the morning, and *gome**, *dravle**, *søtost** and several other cheeses were ready for serving.

Mette helped Aunt Anna set everything out. They had to put it on the table in the seter house because of the unpredictable weather. The tourists were invited to come in and help themselves after they were settled in the campground.

Theirs wasn't a traditional campground. Morten had just made a clearing so campers could park there. The only bathroom on the seter was the outhouse by the barn, while the lake served as a bathtub. But most of the campers the tourists brought with them were so well equipped that this usually didn't pose a problem. The main reason they were there was to participate in the daily life at the seter. In addition, they had the opportunity to go hiking, fishing and to just roam around in the mountains.

Now, eight families lined up in the seter house to taste the good food. Aunt Anna smiled from ear to ear as the diners complimented her profusely. Everything they served their guests was received with enthusiasm and ravenous appetites. Several foods weren't that popular with the youngest ones, tasting too sharp or too unfamiliar to young taste buds. Out in the meadow the children tumbled around in happy play. Life at the

144

seter was a special and exotic experience for them.

After the meal, Mette told them they were allowed to visit the animals, but they had to be certain to close the gates behind them. A flock of children soon ran across the pasture. Most of the animals liked to be petted and were friendly to people, so they came over to the youngsters right away. Some of the smaller children felt intimidated by the big cows. Two little girls ran screaming back, calling for their mothers. Mette took them and their mothers over to see the smallest lambs, which they deemed much safer.

With joyful squeals, the youngsters ran from sheep to cows. The animals were more than willing to play along, at least the youngest ones. Pia soon became their favorite playmate. She followed them wherever they went. Some of the children were simply spellbound, petting and stroking the soft animal fur. The lambs were especially fun to touch, and they didn't seem to get tired of the treatment.

In the afternoon, the weather improved. The fog lifted gradually, and the sun peeped out now and then between the fleeing clouds. The temperature wasn't typical for summer, being cooler than usual, but no one seemed to care.

When Mette took out her pails and headed for the cow barn to do the milking, she soon had a crowd around her. "You have to help me get the cows inside," she said. In an instant, the crowd went into action. Among yells and jumps, soon all the cows were in the barn. Mette tied them up, one in each stall. Then she brought out some feed concentrate for them. The children were allowed to feed them the concentrate. Immediately, they were fighting over who got to do the job.

"Quiet down, now," she said as she sat down on the stool to milk. "The cows may not let down their milk if there is too much commotion around them."

Mette was glad she spoke German so well. Morten had stressed language skills as a requirement for the job when he hired her last year. That she mastered English, German and a good deal of French probably contributed greatly to her being hired.

The children calmed down, but they were so eager and excited that it was almost impossible for them to stand still. Mette had to laugh at the eager look in their eyes as they followed closely everything she was doing.

The big tomcat, Truls, also an annual seter resident, came slinking through the barn door at the same moment.

"Pus, pus." Mette called the cat. He immediately came over to her stool. "Watch," she told the children, and then she squeezed a long stream of milk into the air. Truls immediately leaped forward and caught the lovely, warm milk with his tongue. Time after time she squeezed milk at the cat, and every time he caught it. The children laughed in surprise and excitement. Soon the cat had all their attention.

That evening they heard children laughing and shouting well into the night. Mette and Aunt Anna sat for a long while with their coffee after supper. They enjoyed hearing the commotion out in the meadow.

Morten went to bed early. He had been up at dawn, so as they had supper, his eyes almost fell shut.

Mette tiptoed quietly into the bedroom as it started to get dark outside. To her great surprise, she saw that Morten was still awake. The kerosene lamp on the nightstand was lit, and he was obviously engrossed in something he was reading.

"Aren't you asleep? You seemed to be bone tired at supper." Mette sat down on the edge of the bed and started to undress.

Morten looked up at her and smiled. "Yes, that's for sure," he said, "but I started reading this, and it woke me up again." Then Mette saw that he was lying there reading the Bible. "Listen to what it says in Exodus: 17."

He started reading about a skirmish the Israelites had with the Amalekites, led by Joshua. Moses, along with Aaron and Hur, climbed to the top of a hill where they had a good view of the fight.

Listening, Mette pulled on her nightgown and crept under the comforter.

"Listen to the rest of the story." The eagerness in his voice made Mette listen raptly. "As long as Moses held up his hands, the Israelites were winning, but whenever he lowered his hands, the Amalekites were winning. When Moses' hands grew tired, they took a stone and put it under him and he sat on it. Aaron and Hur held his hands up, one on one side, one on the other, so that his hands remained steady till sunset. So Joshua overcame the Amalekite army with the sword."

Morten stopped and looked at her. His eyes had a bright cast to them, as if he had seen something beautiful. Mette was puzzled. She didn't understand what he had seen in those verses.

Suddenly he sank back on the pillow and looked thoughtfully up at the ceiling. His voice was tired when he again started to talk:

"I've felt so tired this spring. Part of it was all the work that had to be finished during the short weeks from snowmelt to summer, but I don't think that was the only reason. This thing about Even and all the feelings that resurfaced over there at Lia have been harder on me than I realized. It has been extra difficult to fulfill my responsibilities at the meetinghouse and the church in addition to everything else.

"And then I started feeling guilty. I want very much to take part in our work for Christianity, but when I really don't feel I'm up to fulfilling all my responsibilities, then I think that whatever else is going on shouldn't detract from my work for the Kingdom of God."

He sighed. Mette stroked his head. Poor man. She had no idea he had worn himself out to this point. But then, it was Morten's nature to rarely show what went on inside him.

"Haven't you mentioned this to others in the congregation?" she asked softly. "There must be a way you can get help with some of this."

"Yes …" Morten hesitated. "I have mentioned it, but I don't know if I want to be replaced. I have felt my service was a calling, so I wasn't sure if it was God's will that I ask to be relieved of my duties."

He was silent for a moment. Then he gave another sigh before he continued: "Even praying was too much for me. I didn't even manage to find a quiet moment in my 'private chamber.' Often I cried to God for the strength to manage, but that prayer hasn't really been answered.

"The verses I read here in Exodus have been plaguing me like a scourge. Here we see how important prayer is. If Moses allowed his arms to sink down, the enemy would get the upper hand. As I see it, this is a clear example of how important it is to persevere in our prayers. If we fail or skip our silent prayers, then we can expect that our work for the Kingdom of God will stagnate. Yes, it may even dwindle and die."

"But …" Mette raised herself up on her elbows and looked into his dark eyes. "This can't mean we are supposed to wear ourselves out. We are only human; God knows that, too. Surely we must be allowed to take a break and get some rest?"

Suddenly eagerness was back in Morten's eyes. "Yes, that's just what I realized, reading these verses in the Bible. Moses was tired, too. Yes, he was so tired that he couldn't take it any more. But then what happens? His two helpers might have fallen on their knees and asked God to give Moses the strength to keep his hands up. And I don't doubt for a minute that He could have done it, too. He could have made Moses' arms stronger so he would have been able to stand, back straight, all day without even feeling it in his muscles. But Aaron and Hur didn't pray for more strength for Moses. No, instead they made arrangements for him to get some rest while he served. And those two friends of his also assumed a great deal of his burden."

Mette smiled as she lay next to him, feeling the warmth from her dear husband's body. Finally she understood what had made sleep elude him this late night. God had started talking to him about rest. Morten needed rest ... and most of all, rest from his spiritual responsibilities—the responsibilities that God Himself had given to this exceptionally dutiful man.

"This became such a relief for me," continued Morten while Mette nestled in the nook of his arm. "Rest, that's what I'll find up here at the seter. I'm not really looking for rest in regard to work, but rather rest from steadily increasing stress. Up here I can go for long hikes in the mountains, often with tourists. Such hikes have always had a relaxing and calming effect on me. And while I hike along, alone if possible, I can talk to my Heavenly Father. I will never find a better time or more strength for that. My best 'private chapel' has always been the mountains. And then the other members of the congregation can take care of practical matters down in town."

Mette was filled with an indescribable peace and happiness. How fantastic that they had a living God, one who looked after His children in all circumstances, and didn't demand more of people than they were able to contribute.

True enough, it was vital work they were doing. The work to win over souls, to which they were both so committed, was in their eyes the most important thing they could be involved in. And they were convinced that God, too, saw that as the most important. But what was so fantastic was the fact that He had ways and means in His work that weren't at all aimed at taking heart and strength away from His workers. All this comfort and help was written in the Word.

"His hands remained steady till sunset," quoted Morten softly by heart. "It seems to be a life-long service we're in, but He will make sure that our hands are steady until sunset, and we are home in Heaven."

"Yes," said Mette. Let us take one day at a time, and you'll see we'll get through this."

"And we have to pay attention to the voice that speaks to us from these pages," added Morten, patting the black leather covers. "We have to allow Him to guide us in all things."

The bedroom grew quiet. Peace filled the room. God was with them, they had no doubt about that. And if He was with them, then they could handle anything, thought Mette before her eyes fell shut.

Soon they both slept soundly.

42 • With horse and buggy

The German tourists seemed to be having a great time at the seter. Several of the adults often went hiking in the mountains with Morten, while Mette and Aunt Anna kept the children busy in the meadow. Aunt Anna had a lot of fun stories on tap. Though she needed Mette to interpret, she was able to fascinate even the youngest one by the engaging way in which she told her stories. Wherever she went, there was a constant tail of children behind her. She allowed them to try both the separator and the churn. The dairy room had a lot of gadgets that were exciting for them to study.

But the animals got the most attention. Truls the cat was petted constantly. Now and then Mette found him way under the dining table. He was in hiding, trying to get a few moments of peace. Although he was extraordinarily friendly and fond of people, it got to be too much for him at times.

The lambs were also visited frequently, but they didn't seem to get enough. They scampered around excitedly as soon as someone was willing to play with them. It was the same with the goats. The children followed them everywhere. The fence, which now was as good as new, didn't faze the lively rascals at all. And every so often they could see the goats way up on the mountain slopes. But they were never far away. They were far too fond of company. Soon they ambled back again to the area where they were normally fed. They knew exactly when that was; they had a good sense of time.

One day Morten brought a fjord horse, an ancient Norwegian breed, up to the seter. He had been able to borrow the calm and gentle horse from a farmer down in town. The animal had been ridden by both children and adults. It was also a good worker, used in the fields in the summer and in the logging industry in the forest in the winter. Petter had often borrowed the horse for farm work that was difficult to tackle with a tractor.

Morten thought it might be interesting for the tourists to see how farm work was done in the old days before they had tractors and other machines to help them. He also thought it might be fun for both children and adults to ride in the buggy. The owner of the horse had sent a buggy with him so they could make trips down the road.

Mette wasn't used to horses at all, but she soon felt comfortable with this one. It didn't take her long to learn how to put on the harness and steer the horse around.

Often, they took trips down the road with the buggy full of children. Usually, Morten held the reins. The horse always walked calmly and steadily along the road. Soon it knew the route so well that it didn't need direction. When it got to the driveway where they had to turn back, it stopped automatically.

It was getting close to the time when the Germans would leave. The children were sad to leave their beloved animals. Several of the Siljatjern Seter menagerie members clearly recognized the children when they came running down the pasture. It was heartening to notice how close they had become.

"Can't we take a last trip with the horse before we leave?" begged one of the boys. He was a lively 8-year-old who had taken a special interest in the horse the entire time. "Sure," said Morten, tousling the eager boy's hair.

In a short while, Morten started harnessing the horse. The boy jumped excitedly up and down, waiting impatiently for them to get ready for the drive.

"I just have to go inside to get my cell phone and take care of a couple of things," said Morten when he was done. "I'll be back in a moment. Just stay here."

He tied the horse to a fence post and ran to the dairy room. The boy, who was just about ready to burst with anticipation, ran over and grabbed the reins. "I can watch the horse!" he yelled eagerly. But Morten had already disappeared through the door, so he didn't hear what he said.

Now the boy quickly untied the knot around the post. Soon he was in the buggy, tugging on the reins. He had seen Morten do it that way, so he felt he knew how to handle a horse. What he *didn't* know was that this was the sign Morten gave the horse when he wanted him to get going. With a jerk, both horse and buggy were moving.

"Stop!" cried the boy, tugging the reins even more. The horse, thinking it was supposed to go even faster, sped up. Before anyone knew it, horse, buggy and boy disappeared around the curve down by the woods.

Morten came running out when he realized what had happened, but he quickly saw that he would never catch up with them by running after them. Now Mette also noticed that both horse and buggy were gone without the driver. Morten ran to the car and started it. Mette jumped in beside him. As they drove onto the road they could hear the screams of the boy's mother, who had just become aware that the horse and the boy were gone.

They didn't have to drive far before they saw the horse and buggy ahead of them. A chaotic scene was playing out on the road. The boy stood almost upright while slapping the reins against the horse's back. The horse, assuming it was constantly encouraged to increase its speed, was almost in full gallop.

"This is an accident about to happen," said Mette fearfully. "What can we do?"

She tried to call to the boy through the open car window, but he didn't seem to hear anything at all. Morten didn't say anything. He was deeply concentrated on what was going on in front of them, while trying to get the car as close to the boy and the horse as possible.

Soon they came to a curve. At that point the horse became aware of the car following it. It gave an extra kick and shook its head, veering closer to the ditch.

Morten slowed down immediately. "We mustn't get so close that we scare the horse," he said. "If we could only get the boy's attention, but he doesn't seem to be open for any kind of instructions." Deep furrows creased Morten's brow, and he pressed his lips tightly together while his mind worked furiously on finding a way out of this.

Mette was on the brink of hysteria. She leaned forward, her head almost touching the windshield. She had removed her safety belt, ready to jump out if the opportunity presented itself. But it didn't look like she would get a chance, for the horse was becoming increasingly agitated, shaking its head. Its confusion about the unfamiliar handling caused it to get more and more out of control. The speed was dangerously high. Nothing seemed able to stop the wild ride.

"We have to do something!" yelled Mette. "He'll get killed. Imagine what can happen when they get to the steep hills. They will never be able to stay on the road at this speed!"

"If I only could get past him," said Morten. "Then I'll be able to stop them, but the road is too narrow here."

"Maybe we could get someone from town to meet them," said Mette, a hint of hope in her eye.

Morten shook his head doubtfully. "It will really take something for them to get to the hills before the horse gets there."

"At least it's worth a try," said Mette, grabbing the cell phone.

"Try Petter," said Morten, giving her the number.

"Dad isn't home," said the child who answered when Mette asked for Petter.

"Are there other adults there?" Her voice was almost feverish. At a furious pace, she explained the situation and what they needed.

She could clearly hear that the boy was upset. "It's just Birger and me at home," he said, "but I will ask Birger." Then the connection was cut. Obviously he had hung up.

"It doesn't look like we'll find help," said Mette, bursting into tears. The horse and buggy ahead of them continued at the same, crazy speed.

Morten braked. "I'm afraid we're scaring the horse even more by following it in this way," he said, "but I would like to be close by ..." He stopped, an expression of pain showing on his face. After a sigh, he continued: "... in case something should happen."

They noticed the boy turning toward them. Terror in his eyes, he cried and waved his arms.

"Hilfe, Mutti, Mutti ... hilfe ..." The German words burst out of him. But Mette and Morten were not able to help him. Several times they feared the buggy was about to roll over. Mette screamed and grabbed the car door in an effort to get out. But somehow the rig still managed to trail the wild horse, wheels on the ground. Curve after curve zipped past them as the two in the car, their concern rising, followed the buggy. They realized the ride might soon be over, and they dared not think about what might happen.

"We're soon at the place where the hills are steepest," said Mette. Her voice was strained to the limit, and her tears kept running.

"If only they don't go off by the steepest part of the road," said Morten.

Mette shuddered. She imagined the rocky slope going down from the ditch. It was steep, too. In that particular place the curves were extra tight. The image of what could happen came to her in a flash.

A strange calm came over her in the middle of her panic. "God, I'm leaving this child in Your hands." She didn't know if she had prayed aloud, or if it was just a sigh from her inner being. She didn't have the strength to elaborate on the prayer.

Then she imagined that she saw a divine manifestation. The next moment she realized it was no supernatural apparition there ahead of them. Calm and steady, he stood planted in the middle of the road, his arms held high. The horse whinnied and shook its head, but soon the person standing there had it under control. Foaming with sweat, the horse stood there snorting while its rescuer petted and calmly talked to it.

Mette was out of the car before Morten was able to break to a full stop. In a moment she ran over to the boy who had fallen, crying and shaking, into her arms. She carried him over to the car while talking to him in a soothing voice. They both had tears streaming down their faces.

When Mette had put the boy in the car, she was finally able to get a look at the rescuer. Morten was already standing next to him. It was Birger, Petter's 12-year-old son. Parked over by the side of the road was a four-wheeler. A feeling of awe and admiration filled Mette. There was no doubt the boy had saved a life on this day. Probably he also saved the life of the horse. She could see Morten patting him on the shoulder. Knowing Morten, this wouldn't be the only thanks Birger would get for his brave action.

The horse had calmed down, but still showed signs of its wild run. Birger and the horse seemed to know each other well. With confident moves, he took care of the exhausted horse.

Morten came over to the car. "Birger wants to take the horse up to the seter, so then we can go back right away," he said, getting in.

They were met with great joy when they returned with the boy, even though the people up at the seter hadn't seen for themselves the danger he had been in. Morten tried, ever so cautiously, to make sure the parents realized how dangerous the episode had been. He wanted them to understand the significance of what Birger had done. Later in the day, Mette heard that the boy's parents had given Birger a large amount of money to thank him.

As evening came around, Mette felt that the stress of the day had been hard on her. But still, she was happy that everything ended so well. Birger did a great job, but she saw clearly that he had been guided by a higher power. She still had the strange feeling that came over her in the car at the very moment when she turned the entire problem over to God. It lifted her feeling of complete despair, facing an unavoidable catastrophe, by putting her trust in a power stronger than any natural force. She had turned the problem over to that power, and God had taken charge.

She knew perfectly well that He didn't always take charge this directly in all bad situations. Even was a good example of that. So many people were suffering from sorrow and pain, and in many such situations, people prayed for help. But help didn't always come. This is a difficult problem, thought Mette as she tended to the animals that evening. But she knew this: Today, God had intervened in a miraculous way, and she thanked Him for it.

Then she prayed for help to accept that He didn't stop all accidents that might happen to people. There was so much that was hard to understand. Again, it was clear to her that God's thoughts are often very different from the thoughts of people. What people saw as misfortune might not necessarily be bad in the eyes of God. Maybe it was just a matter of being "promoted to glory." Again, her thoughts turned to Even.

43 • Church outing

The number of tourists coming to the seter increased as the days went by. The warm weather had also arrived. Some came in groups, having made arrangements for various kinds of programs in advance. But many came just to see the seter and the farm animals. And if there was an open spot where a place could be found for a camper or a tent, they were allowed to stay for as long as they wanted. The rent might be a little steep, but on the other hand they got a lot for their money. They watched demonstrations of the old seter ways every day. Aunt Anna made cheese in a big pot on the wood stove in the seter house, frying both small and regular pancakes on the griddle. She showed the visitors how to card and spin wool. In addition, the tourists got to see many kinds of old farm implements and objects.

Mette usually had a flock of children and adults around her when she sat with the pail between her knees to milk the good-natured cows. Some of the children were allowed to try, too, but it wasn't easy to get any milk out of the teats.

One Sunday they were expecting a crowd. A church group from a neighboring town was having an outing at the seter. Morten was setting up for a service over by the lake. They had neither altar nor pulpit, and no pews to sit in. Instead, people were encouraged to bring something to sit on. Down by the water's edge, Morten had set up speakers, wired to a small truck he had borrowed. He was able to drive the truck almost to the lake bank.

The day before, Mette had cleared away debris that had gathered along the banks during spring, and now it looked as clean as a church floor. The water had warmed up during the last days, too. She had already tested it several times. Since they didn't have a shower in the seter house, they had to take advantage of the lake when they needed a bath. The first days up there, the water had been too cold to swim in, so for a while they went back home to the farm when they needed a shower.

The goats came leaping over to Mette as she sat on the big, rectangular stone that served as a bench on the bank. They put their muzzles in her lap. "Do you think I have treats for you?" she asked, scratching their shaggy hair. They always enjoyed kind words and petting. But more than anything, they liked getting something good to eat, and she probably indulged them far too often.

Morten had worried about having two such bold and curious animals running around among people and cars. But Mette suggested they put them in the barn during the service so they wouldn't pose a problem.

The year before, when they had also had a revival meeting at the seter, Morten didn't want the goats there at all. But this year Mette insisted on having them at the seter from the very beginning. She felt she would be able to control them.

They had planned a revival meeting this year, too, but it rained so much the day of the meeting that they had had to cancel. So they were glad to get another chance to have people gathered at the seter to hear the Word of God.

"I'd better get you in the cow barn, for soon the cars will be here," said Mette, giving the goats a last pat before she got up. As soon as she started back, the lively goats followed her willingly.

This day, at least, seemed to be warm and pleasant. The wind was not as chilly as it had been some days before. Walking along, she noticed that the grass in meadow had gotten much longer since the last time they had been there.

No sooner were the goats in the barn than cars began to arrive. One by one they parked in the meadow and down along the road. The crowd by the lake became larger and more rambunctious. Many of the children started running around and playing. They were told they might go over to the animals when the service was over.

The pastor was a sincere, elderly man. He stood up in his elegant robe and welcomed the congregation. They followed the liturgy from church, but had to do without an organ. Instead, two people played the accordion.

The open-air service was a fresh, positive experience, Mette thought. The pastor spoke so warmly about God's care and love. But he stressed that if people were to benefit from the good things Jesus had secured for them by taking their place at Golgotha, they had to accept it. This was not automatically given to people at the moment they came into this world. No, they had to accept Jesus Christ as their Lord and Savior. Not only that, but they had to include Him in their lives and allow Him to take away all their sins. This was the reason Jesus had come to earth, and this is what He wanted so much to do for each and every person on this day, too.

The sermon wasn't long, but the message was simple and understandable.

After the sermon, the program turned even more solemn for Mette, for a little baby was going to be baptized. Visibly moved, she sat watching the pastor pouring water from the lake on the child's head. Imagine that, a small child was being baptized in their very own lake. What a momentous occasion!

The fact that these parents brought their baby to be baptized demonstrated that they wanted the child to rest in the hands of the Lord. The parents' way of life would later demonstrate that this was what they wanted, keeping to the faith themselves so the child could get to know the Lord Jesus on a daily basis.

Mette knew all too well this was not always why people decided to baptize their children. Often, it was just a tradition. Still, she knew that God's involvement at baptism was just as important for the child. Through baptism, the child was received in Heaven. If this were not followed up with instruction in the Christian faith, baptism wouldn't do the child much good later in life.

Faith, too, was required for baptism to take effect. And if the grown child should receive God later in life, then what happened today by the banks of the lake would regain its full significance and implication.

While the baptism hymn rang across the water toward the mountains to the east, Mette's thoughts took their own course. She remembered the conversation she had by same lake the year before with someone about to be confirmed. It was about baptism at that time, too.

If this child were to die before baptism, what would happen then? Her thoughts continued to spin. The answer became clear to her in a moment. She remembered a verse from the Bible—Psalm 139, Verse 16. "Your eyes saw my unformed body. All the days ordained for me were written in your book before one of them came to be."

It says clearly that God is involved in everything that happens to a person from conception—yes, before birth. He has a plan for each person. But at the fall of man, people bungled His plan. When original sin came into the world, it applied to all people, even little children.

But if parents deliver their children into the hands of God from the beginning, God will have mercy on them because of the faith of their parents. They demonstrate that faith by bringing their child to be christened. Baptism is prescribed by God Himself, but He is not dependent on a certain time and place for the child to have its name written in the Book of Heaven. His grace is so all-encompassing that He is not dependent on our managing to get the child baptized. What counts is our faith—that is, the faith of the parents and their wishes for their child. God instills this faith in the child, too, as a gift.

But if the parents should say they don't wish to bring their child to be baptized because God will receive the child anyway, then this is a sign of unbelief and distrust in God's ordinance.

Mette thought as she sat there. She knew that many people practiced baptism in different ways. She had no doubt that they, too, were God's children. No, God was so great that He didn't limit baptism to just one way. He instilled in each one the conviction of how this was to be done, and then it was important to follow what one regarded as the right way.

People were starting to get up. Mette had been so carried away by her thoughts that she had missed the end of the service.

Soon things turned lively around her. The children ran across the meadow to visit the animals. Some of the adults set up a large grill, and soon she could smell freshly grilled sausages and pork chops. Lively conversations took place while people sat down in groups to eat.

Morten and Mette sat with a group of older people. The pastor sat with them. Soon the conversation centered on the legend.

An old man knew a lot about the story. "It is said that Silja was buried by the church in our town," he said, "but since they assumed she had committed suicide, they buried her outside of the churchyard wall. In those days they were adamant that someone who had committed such a transgression not be buried in consecrated ground. Her grave was supposedly north of the church, between the churchyard and the river."

Everyone around him was quiet, listening closely to his story. The legend had always been of interest to people, and Mette realized that still was the case. Morten listened extra closely to the old man's story.

"Now it supposedly happened," the man continued with a chuckle, "that right after the funeral, they had a terrible storm. It raged throughout the town for an entire night. It rained buckets, while lightning and thunder struck continuously. It was so bad that no man dared go outside until well into the next day. Then a pale and shocked man came rushing to see the pastor. 'You have to do something … now … Silja is coming!' he screamed. The pastor got the sexton to come with him and together they ran over to the churchyard. There was Silja's coffin, sticking halfway out of the grave.

"This episode caused fear and anxiety throughout the entire town. Some thought the girl would take revenge because she wasn't buried in consecrated ground, while others thought the Devil was involved.

"Anyway, the coffin was reburied, but not long after, they had a similar storm. When the rain slowed down enough for people to get out, they saw that the same thing had happened again. The coffin was tipped halfway over, with the front end above ground.

"This caused such fear in the folks in charge of her funeral, that they immediately took the coffin and buried it on the inside of the churchyard wall. Since then, Silja has rested in peace, for nothing more happened to the coffin."

Morten shuddered. Of course, these were just old tales and superstition, but it was nevertheless eerie to hear such stories.

Another man who had followed the story with great interest asked several questions regarding the location of the first burial. The storyteller, who seemed to know a lot about it, explained exactly where it was supposed to have been. The other man sat seriously considering this.

"I have often heard the story about Silja," he said after a while, "and I have always assumed that the whole story was a tall tale from the old days. But after hearing this, I'm actually beginning to believe it might be true."

"True! What do you mean?" Morten looked at him in surprise. "Surely you can't figure out what happened so much later?"

"Well, you see," said the man, leaning closer to the group and supporting his elbows on his knees, "I've been a gravedigger in that cemetery for almost 30 years. There is not one centimeter of those grounds that I don't know. The place you described is in a pretty low spot and close to the river. The part of the churchyard that is closest to the wall is not used anymore because the river can easily run that high. The level of the ground water rises and makes it hard to dig a deep enough grave.

"On the occasions when we tried anyway, we risked the coffin's resurfacing, just like you said. The buoyancy is so persistent that the coffin will work its way out of the ground again. It is really a natural thing to happen. And the way you told the story, it was storming and rainy every time it happened. Yes, I will actually say it would be impossible to keep a coffin underground in the spot where it was buried. That was even closer to the river."

Mette let her eyes take in the dark surface of the lake. Again she felt the same unease she had experienced the first time she heard the legend. Even if everything had a natural explanation, there was still a lot of mystery to the story.

She felt a chill, even if the sun was shining. Stories related to superstition and other-wordly events seemed so strangely fascinating. It was as if unseen forces made people aware of the eeriness. It was the work of evil forces. This became clear to her in that moment. Through time, people had always assigned a supernatural significance to the legend. And then it didn't take evil forces long to join the game. The story had left a lot of fear and anxiety in its wake.

44 • *Grace and forgiveness*

Their little group was still preoccupied with the old legend. Even though most were from a neighboring congregation, these older people had heard it in one form or another. Several were able to add details that they found intriguing.

"Imagine ending your days like that," one of them said. He shook his head and sighed. "Suicide ... the last thing she did in this world was murder." His eerie words hung in the air.

"Well ... it doesn't really make a difference how you end your days," said the pastor in his good-natured way. "Unless your relationship to God is solid, it is a grim matter, regardless. And no one knows the status of the girl in regard to that."

"No, that's true," said the man, "but suicide is murder, that's my honest opinion. And how would she make up for that transgression?" With a questioning look, he examined the pastor's composed features.

Mette didn't hear the pastor's answer, for suddenly she became aware of a woman who rose hurriedly. In a glimpse, she saw a pale face with an anguished expression who now turned away from the group and started walking quickly toward the meadow. Mette rose, too. The rest of the group didn't seem to notice that the two women disappeared; they were already involved in a deep discussion on the topic.

Mette followed the woman, catching up with her by the camping area. "Is there a problem?" she asked gently, putting her hand gingerly on the woman's shoulder. A sniffle made it obvious that she was crying.

"Never mind, I'm just being stupid," she said, trying to smile. But the smile didn't quite reach her eyes. In them, Mette saw a look of great despair. Her smile disappeared again, and her tears kept running.

"Let's sit down over there," said Mette, pointing to a bench by the wall of the seter house. Without speaking, they walked over and sat down. The woman sniffled again. She pulled out a handkerchief and blew her nose before continuing.

"It just became so hard for me over there." Her voice was weak and shaky. She tilted her head to the side, as if she were unable to hold it up. "You see ... they said suicide is the worst possible offense. At least I interpreted it that way, that someone who commits suicide will not go to Heaven." Her voice was about to break, but she continued.

"My son committed suicide almost a year ago. I thought I was beginning to get back to normal, but this brought all the pain back. Oooh ..." She let out an agonized sob. "All this time, the worst part for me has been the question of where he is now."

She stopped. The pain etched on her face was overwhelming. Mette felt sorry for her. What agony she had been through. She wished she could take a big tuft of grass and stuff it in the mouth of the elderly man who had made such remarks. Imagine saying that kind of thing! The prejudices and attitudes of some people! The look on Mette's face expressed her opinion more than her words. She shuddered, but now she had to take care of this poor woman.

"How old was your son?" she asked gently.

The woman blew her nose again before she answered. "He was 19 years old."

Mette ached for her as she watched the love expressed in her suffering eyes.

"He was such a good boy," she continued. "Always helpful and kind. And he also loved Jesus." As she spoke that last word, her voice cracked completely. It took a while before she was able to say anything. Mette sat quietly stroking her hand. No one seemed to notice them sitting there. Some of the guests had gone for short walks in the area, while others went for a swim. The children scampered about, screaming ecstatically and playing with the farm animals.

When the woman continued, she was calmer. "It's just that something happened to him. Suddenly he started speaking so strangely. At first it only lasted for a short moment, but later he did it for longer periods. He seemed to see or hear strange things. Sometimes he got the idea that he had to do strange things. If he had to fix something—it might be the simplest little thing—he might destroy it. Sometimes he would take something, for example his cell phone, and smash it against the wall. Afterward, he would be really flabbergasted and ask, 'Why did I do that?'"

She stopped again. She seemed to consider something. Mette realized that she needed to talk about this, so she didn't say anything but waited for the woman to continue. It didn't take long for her to go on:

"The worst thing was that some people were convinced that religion had gone to his head. For sometimes, he imagined that God was speaking to him. Once he even thought he was St. Paul. Then he wanted to go around and preach."

"Did he see a doctor?" Mette wasn't sure if she should ask, but she did it anyway.

"Oh, yes," the woman answered eagerly. "He saw doctors several times, but they didn't seem to understood his condition, for when he was there, he seemed to be normal. He didn't remember much about how he had been during his 'spells,' either." She gave a painful sigh: "I should have gone with him, but a grown boy would rather not bring his mom along with him to the doctor.

"They noticed that he seemed depressed, but there was something else ... Oooh ... he suffered so terribly." She stopped. Her tears got the better of her again. This time it took some time for her to continue. When the woman was finally able to find the words she wanted to say, they came almost in a whisper: "There wasn't enough time to figure it out. One night ... he didn't come in ... we found him in the barn ... at the end of a rope."

Mette felt herself tremble slightly, but she tried to keep as composed as possible. How terrible.

The woman seemed to shrink. She shook with tears. Mette put her arm around her and pulled her against her. That was the only thing she was able to do for the moment.

Suddenly the woman straightened up again. She stared at Mette with intense eyes. Her agony was like a bottomless sea behind her swollen eyelids. "Where is he now?" The question erupted almost like a scream from her tense throat.

Mette looked calmly at her. She didn't reply right away. In the fraction of a moment she sent a wordless prayer to God that she would find the right answer. "Your son was ill," she said.

The woman nodded, but she continued to stare at Mette. She didn't seem to think this was much of an answer. This was something she already knew.

Mette cleared her throat before she continued: "The things he said and did were a result of his illness. I understand that people who suffer from disorders of this type often overreact to certain things. Something in the mind gets out of order, and then their behavior can become really bizarre. This is probably far from the only instance where religion is blamed for the problem. But the truth is, when people suffer from disorders like that, their sick thoughts center around the same ideas as their normal thoughts and interests do. If he had been interested in politics, he might well have been preoccupied with political affairs. Maybe then he'd have thought he was the Prime Minister, or Hitler, for that matter."

The woman nodded slightly, but she didn't answer. She just sat there waiting for Mette to continue.

"Can you wait here for a second?" said Mette suddenly. "I'm going to get my Bible. There's something in it I want to show you."

Quickly, she entered the seter house, returning right away. She looked up Paul's letter to the Romans. She started reading from Verse 33, Chapter 8: "'Who will bring any charge against those whom God has chosen? It is God who justifies. Who is he that condemns? Christ Jesus, who died—more than that, who was raised to life—is at the right hand of God and is also interceding for us. Who shall separate us from the love of Christ? Shall trouble or hardship or persecution or famine or nakedness or danger or sword?'

"And further down it says: 'For I am convinced that neither death nor life, neither angels nor demons, neither the present nor the future, nor any powers, neither height nor depth, nor anything else in all creation, will be able to separate us from the love of God that is in Christ Jesus our Lord.'"

Mette looked up at the woman, who sat there listening intently. "It is clear what this means. Nothing can separate a person from Jesus. Not even the devil. The only thing that can separate you from Jesus is you and your choice to follow the desires and temptations of the world instead of Him. You said that he loved Jesus?"

"Oh, yes." She clenched her hands in her lap while her eyes sought the mountaintops in the east. They sat in the warm sun, the children still playing around in the meadow. But the woman didn't seem to notice any of it. In her thoughts, she was back with her son. "When these ghastly spells came over him, he begged Jesus for help."

She looked directly at Mette again: "You see, he suffered from such terrible panic attacks."

Looking into her tortured face, Mette continued: "Not even his disease could separate him from Jesus and His love."

"No …" The woman looked doubtfully down at her hands, still clenched in her lap. "Maybe not the disease, but …"

Mette understood what she was thinking about. "What he did was a result of his illness. It will never be blamed on him."

"How can we be so sure about that?" Fervor came over her as she spoke the words. Her intense eyes bored into Mette. For a moment, they just sat staring at each other.

Then it was Mette's turn to let her eyes drift toward the horizon while she gave words to her thoughts: "Someone who is a child of God, and I understand that your son was that …" a quick look at the woman registered an ardent, verifying nod … "lives in the grace and mercy of God. And we are forgiven our sins, regardless of how grave they are."

"Yes, but he never had time to …" Her pained expression now was almost chiseled into her face.

Suddenly Mette took her hand in both of hers and looked directly into her eyes. "What do you think mercy is? Is it something you receive when you have managed to whisper a prayer under your covers at night after having done something you shouldn't have? No, I'll tell you what mercy is. It is something that was granted us at Golgotha that day 2,000 years ago. That's when our sins were forgiven. And not only the sins that already had been committed, but also the sins that people would commit in the future. Everything was forgiven there. A person who is a child of God lives in that mercy. We call it grace. And your son experienced that grace the very moment he committed his sin. Because of what Jesus did at Golgotha, he went directly to Jesus on that day a year ago."

The woman looked at her with her mouth half open. Her tears streamed, but her eyes had a more open look. She didn't answer right away, but sat there staring blankly. Then she started talking. Her words seemed to be more directed at herself than at Mette:

"I've never thought about it that way. But it is true. This is what the Bible says."

These new thoughts seemed to churn around in her mind for a while, but then she looked pained again. "It is just so horrible to have lost him. Why … I prayed for him so fervently during the time that he suffered so much. I asked that he be healed. Every day I asked for that, but …" She shook her head in despair.

Mette looked at her with the deepest sympathy. "It isn't always easy to understand why bad things happen," she said. "And most of them will never be explained to us here in this world. But we can try to understand some things. Let's put ourselves in God's place. You were crying about your son, who was suffering. How much more do you think God cried, He, who sees everything? He saw each indication of pain in your son's young body, and he saw every panic attack that racked him. How terrible it must have been for God to see that. This was His child, whom He loved so much.

"Parents react when their children suffer. You know a lot about that. Let's imagine a scenario. It is probably an incomplete metaphor, but I still think it says something: Imagine that your neighbor came to see you one day while your son was still small and said that he had seen him down in the road. He had fallen and hurt himself, and was in great pain. Would you then say: 'Look, here are some bandages and some ointment; take them, take good care of him, and then I'm sure he'll be all right'? No, you would never say that. You would have run out there and carried your child home in your arms.

"That's what God did to your son. He might have healed him, but that would have been the second best for him. He would still have to live in this painful world and maybe experience more suffering later in life. Now God thought this boy had suffered enough. He didn't want him to live in pain anymore. That's why he took him home. He is alright now. No more suffering. No sorrows. No want. Shouldn't we allow him to experience that joy?"

The woman looked at Mette with a strange expression in her eyes. She didn't answer right away but sat there, deep in thought.

"And then you have to keep in mind that God sees you, too," continued Mette. "He sees your tears and your pain. Maybe he cries because He sees that you suffer so much. He loves you just as much as He loves your son. Now He wants to comfort you. He will carry you in His arms, too, but you might have to stay in this world a little longer."

"Yes …" a burdened sigh sounded from the woman. "It is just so hard to understand. Of course, I have noticed His help and comfort on many occasions during this time, but then the bad thoughts return. It has been like an endless circle of pain."

She looked at Mette and smiled. This time the smile was reflected in her eyes. "Thank you. I'm sorry I bothered you with this on such a great day." Suddenly the two women became aware of the warm sun and the teeming life around them.

Mette put her arm around her and gave her a hug. "You haven't bothered me at all. It is so good that we can be of help to each other."

"You have been of real help to me," said the woman, hugging her back. "I am convinced that God Himself has spoken through you today. Anyway, that's the way I feel."

She blew her nose and rose from the bench. "Is there somewhere I can wash my face?" she asked, wiping the back of her hand across her eyes.

Mette showed her the water faucet in the dairy room before she returned to the other guests. But she wasn't quite able to follow the conversations, for her thoughts were still with the woman she just had spoken to.

Soon she saw a car going down the road, and she realized that the woman had left.

45 • Visit from the mountains

Mette sat up in bed, slightly disoriented and dazed. She rubbed her eyes while she tried to figure out what woke her up. Morten started to stir, too. "What kind of ruckus is this?" he asked, turning around to send a blurred look toward the window.

Then Mette heard it clearly. There was something going on outside. The sheep bleated and the cows bellowed. The furious ringing of the sheep's bells almost made the air vibrate. There was a great commotion out there.

Quickly, Mette jumped out of bed and looked out the window. It was gray and foggy outside. The sun hadn't yet been able to chase the fog away. A quick look at her watch told her that at this time of day she and Morten would normally be buried under their comforter. It was only 4:30 a.m.

She could see some of the sheep over by the sheep shed. They ran around in confusion while the lambs tried to locate their mothers. One of them had climbed high up on the rocky slope and tried frantically to find a safe place on the steep bedrock.

159

Morten jumped up, too, putting on some clothes. He was out the door before he had buttoned his pants. Mette didn't even bother to dress. She ran out wearing only her nightgown.

Total confusion reigned out in the meadow. Through the haze they could see sheep kicking and bouncing everywhere. Some of them had even found their way to the camping area, milling around among campers and cars. Some of the tourists were already outside, trying to chase them away.

Mette ran back in again and put on some clothes before she ran out to the meadow.

"We have to try to round them up and then chase them back into the mountains," said Morten. "This looks like the herd belonging to one of our neighbors down in town. Such big herds rarely trek down to the seter. Usually they don't like coming down here when other sheep and animals are around already."

"But how are we going to handle this?" asked Mette doubtfully. "And look at the meadow we were just about to cut." Morten, too, stared at the lovely, lush grass that now lay trampled by little hooves, their owners depositing one pile of poop after another in the grass.

"Look at our animals." Mette was getting worried. "They are scared out of their minds. I hope they won't run for the mountains."

"If you try to round up the ones over by the campers, then I will take care of the ones in the meadow," said Morten. "We have to try to chase them over to the trail by the lake. Then it will be easier to make them go back to the mountains."

There was hectic activity in the meadow. Several of the tourists came to help. Soon, they had rounded up most of the herd. Morten chased some of the animals ahead of him toward the trail, and the rest followed. Mette walked behind them to make sure all of them were there.

Suddenly one of them darted from the herd and headed for the lake. "Hurry up and get it!" yelled Morten. "It is so confused that it may go in the lake, and then it won't take long before it drowns."

Mette ran as fast as her legs would carry her. Fortunately, she was able to turn the wayward sheep around before it got to the water.

The milling throng of bleating and scampering sheep moved away from the seter area and headed up the hill toward the mountains. Morten led the way with some of the animals, and Mette made sure the rest followed. A few long-distance sprints were required before the sheep got far enough away that Morten and Mette felt they could safely leave the herd and head home. At that point, the sun was high in the eastern sky. The warm rays gave them more than they asked for, for their hike had provided them with heat aplenty.

Stripes of sweat appeared on Morten's shirt and Mette felt that she, too, was damp with perspiration. Fortunately, the early morning air was still chilly, cooling and refreshing them.

"I hope they will stay up here," said Morten, studying the white poufs of wool that soon spread out over the open landscape.

Mette and Morten sat down on a rock to catch their breath. Mette let her eyes drift across the captivating scenery. Further to the north, the mountain peaks towered majestically against the clear sky. Only a few fluffy clouds sailed lazily across the mighty firmament high above their heads.

They both sat there in silence, enjoying Nature's gigantic panorama. Suddenly,

Mette noticed an eagle sailing above them. If only it weren't looking for suitable prey in the sheep herd. The animals had calmed down and were grazing peacefully among outcroppings and underbrush. The clear tinkling of the bells created a unique mountain atmosphere, thought Mette.

The eagle sailed in wide circles over the area. It clearly had spotted some prey far down in the heather. Imagine having binoculars for eyes, Mette thought as she watched the big bird's behavior. Suddenly it dived for the ground but was back in the air again in a moment. She could see something dangling from its claws. Fortunately, it wasn't one of the poor little lambs that had been running around in the heather. It was no joke to be subject to such a stealthy attack. Soon the eagle disappeared toward the faraway mountains. It probably had its nest there and some little eaglets that were screaming for food. Naturally, the eagle had to hunt. But Nature was extraordinary. Here, the saying, "Someone's pain is another's gain," was a reality.

Mette took Morten's hand. How good it felt to sit here, next to her dear husband. He looked at her and smiled. His eyes reflected her own feelings in a deep-felt and intimate way. Her heart beat faster. The peace and quiet around them only amplified the mood and the warm feelings inside her.

Morten put his arm around her and pulled her against him. They were all alone out there in God's nature, with only the sheep as fairly disinterested spectators. Gently he held her head between his hands and kissed her. She snuggled against him and wished they could sit there forever. Her feelings swelled in her. Gentle, loving words were caresses for soul and mind for both of them.

They sat there for a long while, without minding the time. The sun warmed them more and more as it rose in the sky. The birds chirped and sang. Their tunes mixed with the sound of sheep's bells, which grew weaker and weaker as they moved further and further across the area, looking for pasture. The harmony and peace of the mountains filled them completely, a perfect setting for tenderness and love.

When they finally got up, it was with reluctance. Still, their thoughts and feelings were focused on each other. Hand in hand, they started back the same way they came. Their pace was considerably more relaxed now. They enjoyed the beautiful day and breathed in the fresh morning air.

Another commotion met them when they got back to the seter. Several of the tourists had gathered beneath the rocky slope behind the seter house. Some were attempting to climb up the steep rock. The two mountain hikers heard the yelling and commotion long before they got to the meadow.

The cause of the ruckus was a lone sheep that had climbed up there early that morning. It now stood on a narrow shelf, unable to get up or down. Children and adults tried coming to its rescue from different angles, but the bedrock was exceptionally slippery and difficult at that point. None was able to get to the animal. The sheep just stood there, shifting from one foot to another and moving back and forth. With frightened eyes, its eyes darted from one committed rescuer to another.

"What are they doing?" asked Morten worriedly as he got closer. "They are scaring the poor sheep to death with all that crying and carrying on."

Quickly he tried to calm the tourists down, but that wasn't easy. The children ran around, screaming and yelling. Everybody wanted to help, and all of them had their own opinion on how this was to be done. The adults were no better than the children.

The sheep up on the shelf was getting increasingly more frightened. One of the

161

adults was now very close. "Come here!" he yelled in a loud voice. Startled, the terrified sheep leaped right off the shelf.

A cry of terror rose from the group down on the ground as the white bundle landed on the bedrock several yards down. From there it rolled head over heels down the slope. It came to a stop between heather and moss in a small crevice not far away from the tourists. In a second, they were beside it.

A new cry sounded as they checked it out. "Dead! It's dead ..." Several children started crying. Mette wasn't able to stop her tears, either, when she saw their precious sheep lifeless on the ground.

"This is what I was afraid of," said Morten with dark eyes. "Sheep that get stuck can get so scared that they just jump without thinking about the consequences. That's why we always have to be calm and careful on rescue operations like this. These tourists obviously don't know much," he said, shaking his head.

It was a sad day, not in the least for the children, who had grown so fond of the good-natured mother sheep. Now there were two lambs that didn't have a mother to care for them. These two got extra petting and care. It was obvious they missed the mother. Bleating, they went looking for food. Aunt Anna found a bottle in which she poured some lukewarm milk. She pulled a nipple over the bottle opening, creating the perfect feeding bottle. Soon one lamb was nestled in her lap, sucking greedily. The other lamb was skeptical of its new "mother." But after some encouragement, Aunt Anna was able to make it suckle, too. Soon, all the children were busy feeding the poor, motherless lambs.

Morten brought the dead mother to town while Mette started her morning chores. It was already late in the morning, so the cows stood by the cow barn, bellowing. The wonderful feeling of peace and harmony she had up in the mountains was abruptly cut short by the chaos at the seter that morning. But as she sat with her head resting against the cow's warm belly while milking, she felt the loving feelings that still existed deep inside her. It comforted her and gave hope for a happy future.

Soon the milking was done and the cows out at pasture. Mette took the milk pails and started toward the dairy room. Then she spotted Aunt Anna over by the stream, carrying an armful of something that had been soaking in the water.

"Did you soak your firewood today?" asked Mette with a twinkle in her eye. It looked like an armful of wood.

"Wood. Honestly!" said Aunt Anna, laughing so hard that she almost lost her load. "This is fish ... It's stockfish," she said, laughing even more when she noticed Mette's puzzled expression. "It is cod that has been dried on racks up north somewhere. I've soaked it in the stream for a while, for now we're going to make lutefisk."

"Okay," said Mette, "but isn't it a little early in the year for lutefisk production? I thought that was something you made for Christmas."

The old woman's bubbly laughter sounded again. "Yes, but you know that up here at the seter we don't always follow a normal schedule. If there's something we want to prepare for the tourists, then we do it, even if it's not the right time of the year."

Mette came closer to look at the long, skinny sticks resting on her arms. "Imagine that this actually can be cooked," she said, wrinkling her nose while studying the crooked sticks.

"This is food, I tell you, and good food, too," said Aunt Anna eagerly. "When it is ready, you'll see that not much is left of the skinny sticks. First, it has to be soaked in

162

lye and then in water. When it is processed and ready, the fish will be five to seven times as big."

Mette's eyes widened. "How do you prepare it, then?"

"Look here," she said, rocking her way over to the dairy room. "First we have to cut it up into appropriately sized pieces. You can help me with that."

Mette placed the milk in the well for cooling and followed her into the room. There, she started helping with the preparations. The milk would have to wait. Several of the tourists also came to see how the fish was prepared. Many of them had heard about lutefisk. Some had even tasted it, but no one had ever taken part in preparing it.

When all the fish was cut into inch-wide pieces, Aunt Anna put all of the pieces in a big tub. Then she grabbed a bucket containing some kind of liquid. "This is potash lye," she said. "I cleaned the ashes out of the stove yesterday. I poured boiling water over it and stirred well. Then I let it sit overnight. It was just a matter of ladling off the clear lye that had formed on top of the ashes. By the way, the ashes from birch are best for this," she added, pouring the liquid over the fish. Then she poured on some more water. She tested with her fingers to see if the lye would be "slick" enough.

Mette realized that a great deal of experience was needed to get this right, and if there was anything Aunt Anna had, it was experience.

"Now it has to cure in lye for two to three days. But we have to carry it over to the pool in the stream again, for it has to be cooled," she said, explaining the process to her audience. "When it is finished soaking in the lye, then it has to be soaked in water," she continued, "and then each piece will swell up and turn almost gelatinous. It has to be soaked in water for a couple of days as well. The water should be changed several times, and it has to be kept cool at all times.

"You shouldn't really make lutefisk in warm weather like this, but I have managed to make it several times by cooling it in the pool. I hope it will come out all right this time, too," she finished.

Aunt Anna continued to talk while they carried the tub over to the pool. Several of the tourists had questions, and Aunt Anna had answers for most of them. Afterward, they sat down at the garden table by the seter house with a cup of coffee.

Morten returned in a while. He walked quickly over to the two sitting at the table. Eagerness and enthusiasm radiated from his face.

"Listen to this," he said, dropping into a garden chair. "I had an interesting phone call today. Some American tourists want to come up here in a couple of weeks. They would like to stay for a few days. They are in Norway to find their Norwegian roots. I have had visits from tourists like that several times. Usually it is people who want to see the country their family came from. But the most interesting part is that these people may be of help to us. They will visit several towns and farms that they know their relatives came from. One of them has family on a farm in the next town. I have promised to take them there and show them around in the district, so they can see a little bit of the 'Old Country' that they apparently have heard so much about.

"When I talked to them, I mentioned our problem in locating our American relatives. Right away, they were willing to help if there was anything they could do. These people aren't exactly from Minneapolis, but they are well-versed in Norwegian-American history, and they also know well the areas where it makes sense for us to look. So I thought …" He paused and smiled again as he pulled out a piece of paper on which he had written something.

"Maybe …" He looked directly at Mette. "Maybe we should take the trip we talked about this spring. What do you think?"

Mette smiled excitedly back at him, but then her doubts took over. "How do you think we can arrange it?"

Morten put the piece of paper on the garden table and pointed eagerly at something he had written. "I called a travel agency today," he said. "It turns out there are still a few seats available on the flight these tourists go back on. If we leave then, I can set it up so there isn't too much going on at the seter while we are away. I asked Ellen if she could possibly stay here and take care of the animals. And she is willing to do it."

At that moment, Aunt Anna interrupted excitedly: "You absolutely have to do this. How great it will be to get away for a while, and on such a trip. Don't even hesitate to do this. Ellen and I can handle the chores up here. You just go."

Thrilled, Mette looked from one to the other. "I must admit this sounds awfully exciting," she said.

"I had the travel agency hold a couple of tickets for us," said Morten. "So, are we going or what?"

Mette nodded at his eager eyes. "Let's go!"

All three of them started talking at the same time. Planning and preparations had to be started right away. Some parts of the seter schedule needed minor changes, but Morten didn't think it would be hard to work it out.

Mette felt herself tremble with excitement, but she still wasn't confident about locating any relatives.

"If we don't find anyone, at least we'll have a good trip," Morten comforted her when she voiced her concern. Aunt Anna agreed with him.

After making the decision, a new and suspenseful atmosphere entered their daily life. Much of the time they talked about the old letters and their American family. Would they ever find them? Was there any family left at all over there? If so, what kind of people were they?

A thousand questions churned around in Mette's mind as the days went by and their departure drew closer. Her anticipation grew, too, as she looked forward to meeting the group of American tourists. What kind of information and assistance might they be able to contribute?

Mette took out the letters, reading them again and again. The oldest ones, too, were gone through. It was not easy finding a thread going through their relatives' lives in their new country, for only a few of the letters had been saved. The only thing Mette was able to figure out was that they settled in North Dakota after having stayed briefly in a city called Beloit in Wisconsin. There, they were helped by a man called Sjur. He had emigrated from Norway almost 50 years before, and had become a man of consequence in the Norwegian-American settlement. Many of the Norwegians who emigrated at that time interacted with Sjur. Since he was from around the same district in Norway as they were, it had been natural for them to join him and his family.

Later, they left for North Dakota, where they took land. Sjur's sons followed them there to take land as well. Old Sjur came at a later date.

With time, the four siblings settled in different parts of the same district.

There was little information about their growing families in the letters. And after all, it wasn't those relatives Morten and Mette hoped to see. This was an older generation, so they would need more information if they wanted to find the younger ones.

46 • Haying in the meadow

Mette hummed to herself as she worked around the sheep over by their small shed a short distance from the cow barn. The door was left open so the animals could come and go as they pleased. Most of the time they stayed outside in the fresh mountain air, grazing in the lush pastures on the hillsides. But every day, Mette put out a treat for them in the shed to make them stay around the seter instead of straying into the mountains.

By now, the sheep were so fond of people that they came running as soon as someone came around. The lambs jumped and scampered around her. They almost snatched the food out of her hands. Mette had no problem finding someone to feed the two lambs that had lost their mother. The children were always ready and willing when they saw Mette bringing out the feeding bottles. Mette smiled at the two girls who currently sat, each with a lamb in her lap, over by the barn wall. The lambs suckled their warm drinks hungrily.

She heard Aunt Anna's voice, too. She was over by the pool, changing water on the lutefisk. Some of the lambs jumped around her, hoping that she, too, would have a treat for them. She laughed and talked to them as if they were a group of children.

A good portion of petting and hugs came with the feeding as well. Both Mette and the animals enjoyed themselves, puttering around each other. Although it took Mette's time, she allowed herself this pleasure. Nothing stressed her today.

Mette straightened her back and let her eyes dwell on the familiar scenery. This was already a lovely day, too. The sunshine was warm, even if it was not yet noon. Over on the hill she could see the cows grazing peacefully on the slope to the west. The birds were all a-twitter above her head, much more tense than she was. Every so often she saw a bird flying through the opening to the hayloft above the cow barn, followed by intense cheeping. The baby birds seemed to be arguing furiously about which one would get the first morsel of food.

She let out a contented sigh. The peace and harmony she so often felt here at the seter again gave her an intense feeling of true happiness. All the familiar sounds, the majesty of nature surrounding them, not to mention the smell of meadows and mountains, mixing with the strong odors from the animals, combined to create an earthy aura.

Over in the field, Morten was getting ready to cut the hay. A group of tourists was spread out along the trail, ready to watch what was going on. Morten had dug out an old, horse-drawn mowing machine from his barn in town. Now he was working on hitching up the horse. Mette walked closer to watch. She wondered if he would be able to make it function. He had worked on getting the old implement ready for some time. Last night he brought the sickles inside, sharpening them laboriously with a whetstone.

Carefully, he steered the horse out in the field. Morten sat down on the circular seat that Mette thought looked unstable and uncomfortable. Carefully, he released the lever that held the sickles up, and the whole, long sickle bar was lowered down on the grass. With a lurch, the horse began moving on Morten's command. With an intense rustling and swishing sound, the sickles pulled against each other as they cut the grass, which lay on the ground down where the sickles cut through.

The horse pulled the mowing machine at an even speed along the field. The skinny wheels made of steel created thin stripes in the grass.

Mette took a rake and started pulling away the freshly cut grass from the area where the next row was to be cut. She knew it wouldn't be easy to cut if there were a lot of loose grass lying there. Round after round, the horse pulled the rickety old machine while the grass fell over in long rows. Several of the tourists aimed their cameras. This was something special that they wanted to preserve for posterity.

After a while, Morten stopped to take a break.

"May I try?" Mette called eagerly. "It looks like the horse can do the job on his own anyway."

Morten looked at her, doubtful. "It really isn't that easy, and the seat is quite unsteady. I wasn't able to install a safety belt."

Mette laughed merrily at the joke. There wasn't anything to hold on to up there on the seat. But she didn't think it would be a problem. The horse was so calm and steady, and the speed was so low.

"You may try it for a while," said Morten, "but be careful with the sharp sickles."

Quickly, Mette climbed up on the circular metal seat. It was slippery to sit on, for there was no cushion. Carefully, she managed to release the sickle bar, and then she was at it. She was aware that the tourists were extra busy with their cameras.

The horse started with a jerk. Mette swayed a little at first, but soon found her balance. Steadily and surely, the machine moved forward, at speed that was much higher than she had thought.

Yard after yard of grass fell in long rows after them as they moved on. Mette had a sure grip on the reins with her left hand, while her right hand rested on the lever, ready to lift it if something should happen.

Suddenly something tugged hard at the machine, and both horse and the machinery stood stock-still.

Before Mette knew it, she was thrown in an arc, landing on the ground in front of the horse's legs. The horse was fidgety and pulled at the shafts.

"Are you okay?" Morten came running over while Mette, dazed, tried to get to her feet. "Did you hurt yourself?" He took a firm hold of her arm to help her away from the stepping legs of the horse.

"I don't think so," she said, dazed. Several of the tourists came over, too, to see if she needed help.

"I'm all right," she said, brushing grass off her clothes, "but I don't understand what happened."

Morten walked around the machine to check. "Here's why," he said. "The sickle got stuck in a piece of wood. I think it's the end pole of the *hesje*—hay-drying rack—that was never removed last year."

There was no more hay cutting for Mette that day. Morten took care of the rest. But he had to admit that he wouldn't have noticed the pole, either.

Fortunately, Mette wasn't hurt in any way, but she felt shaken. She had put on a special show for the tourists, especially for the ones who taped it.

Morten kept busy with haying all day. He staked the long poles to the ground and tied them together with steel wire. Then Mette helped hang the grass on the *hesje* to dry. Several of the tourists were eager to help, too. They worked hard while the sun beat down on their sweaty bodies.

When they were finally done, the whole group was invited for *rømmegrøt*—sour cream porridge—in the meadow. Aunt Anna had set out a huge pot for them. They all were welcome to help themselves to as much as they wanted. Food and rest felt great after working so hard all day. Mette was finally able to relax.

Suddenly a car pulling a camper came up the road and stopped close by. When Mette saw the man who jumped out of the car, she forgot both the food and the fact that she was tired. It was Arvid.

"Hello! Welcome," she called, going to meet him. "It's great to see you again."

"I missed this so much that I had to come back," he answered, laughing. Morten came over to greet him, too. Aunt Anna came chirping with a bowl of rømmegrøt even before he had time to sit down.

The mood around the table was cheerful. "You missed my show today," said Mette laughing. The others laughed, too, and told about her flight through the air.

"I would like to have seen that," said Arvid cheerfully, while looking at her with intense eyes. Mette looked quickly up at him, but soon lowered her eyes again. Something about this man made her uneasy. An inner tension built up in her that she wasn't able to define. They had had many conversations when he was there the last time. Then he had needed someone to talk to, and she had been more than willing to give him the help that he needed.

But how was it now? Was the reason for his being here still that he needed help and a break during a difficult time? Mette had conflicting feelings about it. Was it because she wanted to help him that she was so happy to see him, or was it something else? And what about Arvid? The look he sent her made her feel even more uneasy. But she didn't want to think about it now. They all were having such a good time.

After the meal, Morten helped Arvid find a good spot for his camper, and then they all went down to the lake to take a swim.

47 • Back to the Old Country

Finally the day arrived when the American tourists were expected at the seter. Morten had made arrangements for renting several campers that the Americans could use while staying at the seter. Aunt Anna was getting the lutefisk ready. It was now laid out in the dairy room, glistening and tempting. She planned to serve the visitors a real, old-fashioned lutefisk meal on their first day at the seter.

Morten left early for town to meet their guests. They were expected to arrive by train in late morning. He needed help transporting both people and campers, so he had a great deal to do.

After Mette finished her chores in the cow barn and the animals and had let them go out to pasture again, she sat down by the garden table out in the meadow. The sun wasn't as strong as it had been only a few days before, but it was still warm and comfortable. The grass was wet after a shower earlier in the morning.

While she sat there enjoying the fresh air, Arvid came strolling over to the table. "Well, I see the dairymaid is lazy today," he said cheerfully, sitting down and facing her.

Mette smiled, but then turned serious. "How are you doing?" Her voice was filled with compassion and concern. They hadn't yet had a chance to talk much in private.

167

Arvid understood what she meant right away, and he turned serious as well. A tired expression appeared on his face. "It's sort of working out in a way, but ..." He stopped and looked at her. His eyes were again filled with some of the intensity that had bothered her so much. "It isn't always easy." He didn't say any more, but just sat there looking at her.

Mette felt sorry for him. She would have liked to help him ... if only she could.

"It's so crowded here," he said after a while, a crooked smile on his lips. "It isn't easy to talk ..."

Mette understood what he meant. It was almost impossible to have the kind of conversations they had the last time he was there.

Suddenly he took her hand, which she had placed on the table, and looked eagerly into her eyes. "Couldn't we go for a hike in the mountains some day, just the two of us? Then we could talk about many things ..."

Mette felt a shiver deep inside. That would be great—just the two of them, all alone. They would be able to talk so many things over. His hand still covered hers. She allowed it to happen. He looked into her eyes, searching for an answer, full of suspense and hope. She could see that this was something he really wanted.

But what was it he was really looking for? The thought occurred to her in an instant, but she dismissed it immediately. She reminded herself that it was help that he needed, just someone to talk to. But her feelings were in turmoil and she was able neither to control nor define them. The only thing she knew at that moment was that it would be so pleasant. Just the two of them, alone ... far into the mountains.

Slowly, a smile appeared on her lips and she nodded carefully. "Yes," she said. "Let's do it."

A smile spread across his face and he squeezed her hand. Now her unease began turning into intense excitement. She looked into his eyes and put her other hand over his. They sat there for a moment while something vibrated between them.

"When will we go?" he asked, his voice ragged.

Mette cleared her throat before she answered: "Today is Tuesday," she said while thinking it over. "I don't think I can go until Thursday."

"Thursday is good," he answered and stood up. "That's a deal." He smiled at her, friendly and confidentially, while he gave her a little wink. Then he turned and walked back to his camper.

Aunt Anna came out in the same moment. She talked away without noticing the blush on Mette's cheeks. "Our guests will be here in a minute," she said. "I have churned a lot of butter for the lutefisk this afternoon. I hope Morten will remember to stop by at my house and pick up the lefses in the freezer. There's no lutefisk dinner without lefses. And I think it's about time that you started peeling the potatoes. We have to boil a lot of potatoes."

Mette rose quickly, happy for something to do. Her confused state of mind had left her off balance. Really, now she had to get her act together. She was there to work, not to sit there, lost in dreams.

Soon she was in full swing peeling the potatoes. It was a great job for sitting outside in the meadow. Soon, some of the kids came over to watch. They wondered what all those potatoes would be used for. Mette told them about the Americans they were expecting and the dinner they were to serve later. She thought there would be some lutefisk leftovers for the children, too, if they wanted a taste.

168

It was almost noon before the first cars started arriving, carrying a group of 15 people. Most were older than average. "It's mostly people of that age group who are interested in history and heritage," thought Mette as she stood watching the people as they settled into the campers.

Even if the guests were past middle age, they were still vigorous and cheerful. They checked out the area with great enthusiasm and studied everything—buildings, tools and farm animals.

"Look here," said one of the most excited ones. He pointed to the giant logs from which the seter house had been built. "It is clear that people who emigrated to America from here in the mid-1800s brought their building traditions with them. This type of house is exactly like the oldest buildings over there, too. But they did it a little differently here," he said, studying the corner of the house closely. "Here, each log ends precisely at the corner." He pointed to the neatly cut corner logs. They were stacked atop one another, precisely cut to form a neat corner. "The old houses in America have logs that stick out a little further at the corners. Just check it out the next time you see a western on TV."

He continued to study the wall. "It looks like moss was used for insulation here."

"Yes," said Morten. "Moss was shoved into all the cracks so wind and cold wouldn't creep in between the logs, and we often have to replace it here and there."

"In America," the man continued, "at least in the area I know, the Norwegian pioneers used a kind of clay for insulation between the logs."

They spent a long time looking at the old building. And they were no less excited when they entered the house and saw the old furnishings. The stove created special excitement. "They used those on the prairie in the old days, too," the same man spoke. He laughed a little as he bent over the old stove. "Now and then they even brought these out in the fields," he continued. "When they worked out in the huge fields on the prairie, it was too far to go back home to eat. So they brought the stove with them and cooked where they worked."

Mette laughed and looked out at the meadow. "We wouldn't have that kind of problem here."

After a thorough sightseeing with lots of explanations and comments, the guests went to their campers to freshen up before dinner. Mette and Aunt Anna had set a long table in the seter house. It barely seated everyone, but since they were serving the food, they omitted place settings for themselves. That way everyone fit around the table.

Aunt Anna served the butter in an exquisite, beautifully carved old *tine*—bentwood box—which she placed in the middle of the table. Deep carvings decked the inside of the lid. "It's for making a nice pattern on top of the butter," explained Aunt Anna, lifting the lid to show her work of art.

"How skilled people were in the old days, and how much care they took to make things beautiful and appealing," said Mette in admiration.

"Oh, yes," answered Aunt Anna, "everything had to be beautiful, and then it had to taste good. Party food in those days was no weight-loss diet, but then they didn't eat much fat or sweets on a daily basis, so there was no harm done."

Soon the guests started arriving. Aunt Anna seated them gracefully while Mette dished up the potatoes. A huge, wooden platter filled with steaming, boiled potatoes was placed on the table. And then Aunt Anna began dishing up the fish. There was great excitement when they realized what was on the menu. Most of them had heard about

169

lutefisk, and some had tasted it as well. This particular course was something they associated with the Old Country. But they didn't know much about how it was to be served. Aunt Anna had to give them a crash course before they could start their meal. Mette stood faithfully by her side as translator. Even if the Americans were all of Norwegian origin, they themselves didn't know much Norwegian.

"Lutefisk can be prepared and eaten in various ways," she started, "but here in this part of Vest-Agder *Fylke,* it has been customary to serve it in this particular way since olden days."

She took a piece of lefse, shaped like a triangle. The paper-thin delicacy probably looked like a pale yellow napkin to their foreign visitors. Next, she put a thick layer of butter on the lefse. Then she placed a pile of chopped potatoes and lutefisk on top of the butter and rolled it up, forming a fat sausage. They were instructed to eat it like finger food.

Following Aunt Anna's directions, the guests began their meal with enthusiasm. Few of them offered an opinion about the taste of the strong lutefisk, but in any case the food created great mirth. Both the unusual method of eating and the shivering, gelatinous fish drew amusing comments.

For dessert, they were served *multekrem*—cloudberry cream—which drew rave reviews from the guests. Aunt Anna explained that the cloudberries were picked in the mountains around the seter. "But I'm not going to tell you where," she said, laughing heartily. "The cloudberry places are always kept a secret," she continued. "If someone comes around asking if there is a lot of cloudberries in the mountains, they usually get the answer that 'this year the cloudberry harvest was really bad.' But strangely enough, when Christmas comes around, cloudberries show up on every table in town." She shook with laughter as she told them this. Her merriment spread to the guests. Her funny way of expressing herself lifted the mood in the seter house into high spirits.

"Don't you worry, we're not coming to eat your cloudberries this fall," a friendly elderly man assured her.

After the meal, they stayed at the table for some time, visiting with one another. Many of them had stories they had heard from their parents and grandparents, about the hard times in the Old Country and about their ancestors' dangerous travels into the unknown, hoping for a better existence. But they conceded that not everybody had found happiness on the other side of the ocean. Some encountered poverty and want, and some fell victim to alcohol and gambling. Weather and climate, especially in the north, were also dangerous enemies. The pioneers had to adapt to an inhospitable land. That's why some people saw it as their responsibility to greet fellow immigrants, right off the boat and ignorant about their new circumstances, and provide the assistance and information necessary for them to make it on their own.

The man who had shown such interest in their log house was named Frank. His ancestors had come from a neighboring town in Vest-Agder. He lived on a farm in North Dakota, in an area where his family had lived for over a hundred years. A diary written by the first settler in their family contained information about their family history. This man was named Sjur, and he had come from a big farm in Norway. Morten knew exactly what farm it was, so he promised to take them all over there the next day.

"This Sjur didn't really come from the farm," continued Frank. "He just worked there as a hired hand. He didn't know exactly where he came from. His mother came to the farm as a baby. Her mother was probably dead. Many women died in childbirth

170

in those days. And the father was probably dead as well. So then they needed a wet nurse. They found one among the help on that big farm. A woman there had a baby and enough breast milk to save the life of the other child. He didn't know anything more about her family.

"Sjur's mother grew up on the farm and was considered domestic help from early on. However, she was not treated well. Exploitation and abuse seemed to be common there. It almost seemed she was considered a plaything by the men on the farm." Frank shuddered before he continued. Everyone sat in anticipation, waiting for the rest of his story. For a lot of people, the past hadn't been rosy.

"Sjur was the result of their 'play,'" Frank continued thoughtfully while shaking his head. He grew up on the farm, and for all those years he was referred to as the Bastard. He had to put up with bad food, kickings and beatings. He wrote that even the horses on the farm were treated better than he was.

"This is a long time ago." Frank frowned, trying to recall something. "I believe he was born in the 1820s. In any case, he left for America in 1853, and then he was around 30. He made contact with some *Haugianers*—followers of the preacher Hans Nielsen Hauge—who emigrated at the same time. They had experienced so much hardship because of their faith that they chose to emigrate. Sjur traveled with them and arrived in New York on an emigrant ship. From there he traveled west and settled in a city called Beloit. There he married and raised a family. And it was there that he later started his transit activities."

Suddenly Mette's eyes lit up. "Did you say Beloit?" Quickly she went to the corner of the cupboard, where she had left the old letters. It didn't take her long to find what she was looking for. "Here it is, Morten," she said eagerly. "Your oldest relatives, Theodor and Vilhelm, lived in Beloit for some time, and they stayed with a man named Sjur. He was active in transit operations. Surely this has to be the same man?"

At this point Frank got excited. The rest of the group followed the conversation with great interest. They soon decided that they must be talking about the same man. Even more interesting was the fact that Morten's relatives eventually went to North Dakota and settled there along with Sjur's sons. This could mean it might be possible to find relatives through Frank.

Little by little, the guests left the table, expressing their heartfelt thanks for the food before settling into their campers. Most were tired from their long trip and jet lag, and craved a long after-dinner nap. But Frank stayed for a while, talking some more with Morten and Mette. The new information caused excitement and curiosity in all three of them.

48 • *Temptation and struggle*

Mette lay in the old double bed in the bedroom next to the dairy room, turning back and forth. She couldn't sleep. She had gone to bed almost an hour before, but sleep wouldn't come.

It had been a hectic day, so she went to bed early, making the excuse that she was sleepy and tired. And that was certainly true. But as the minutes crept along, she realized more and more that there might be something else that caused her to seek peace and quiet. For something inside her made her uneasy. She was having thoughts she didn't want to deal with, and hoped she could sleep them away. But her thoughts refused to go away.

They hadn't been that hard to deal with during the long, hectic Wednesday. She and Morten had taken off early with the American tourists to see the farm where Frank's relatives had once lived. The family now living on the farm received them with great excitement. Obviously, nothing remained of the ugly conditions that had been described in Sjur's old diary from which Frank had his information. But they were able to verify that the same family still lived there. So the visit had been an emotional experience. The farm still contained many reminders from the days when it was influential in the area. But the family presently living there didn't know that much about the older generations, so Frank's diary was studied with great interest.

It was on their way back that Mette again began feeling uneasy. First it was just excitement and anticipation over the next day's hike. But soon it developed into something that just sat there, eating away deep inside her.

She was tired … yes, that's what it was … but why couldn't she sleep?

Morten wasn't home yet. He had left for the mountains again with another group of tourists almost immediately after he returned with the first group. Come to think of it, she didn't even know if he would be back tonight. Maybe they would spend the night under some outcropping. The weather was certainly nice enough.

Mette turned over in bed again and pulled the comforter over her head, but it didn't help. Her thoughts continued churning. She had promised Arvid that they would go for a hike the next day, just the two of them, alone in the mountains. He needed to talk to her about all his problems. Of course she would try to help him in his predicament.

But thinking about that was exactly what worried her. Was it really just because she wanted to help him that she agreed to go? And was it just to get help that Arvid suggested the trip? She had felt the vibes between them at the garden table the night before, and she could still feel how her heart beat faster as she thought about it.

But they were just good friends, and that should be allowed. He needed help. And that was exactly her calling. She had seen it in that light, especially because of what she had experienced in her job with the missionary organization. That's why she had completed so many classes in ministering to the soul. Shouldn't she use her training now, when she met people who needed help?

As much as she argued with herself, the unease continued. A Bible verse came to her, but she didn't quite remember how it went. It was something about clothing that was stained. She took her Bible from the nightstand and started searching. She found it in the letter to Jude. Verse 23 read: "… snatch others from the fire and save them …" She stopped there for a while. That was just it, something about saving. Here it was clear, but there was more. She continued to read: "… to others show mercy, mixed with fear—hating even the clothing stained by corrupted flesh."

She lay completely still for a moment. What did it mean? Yes, she knew it all too well. Sensual indulgence. Sensual indulgence had no business being involved in the ministering to the soul.

How easily it got into the mix. Mette cringed. And such strong forces at work, too. How could you possibly take precautions against it? If it got hold of some poor wretch, you were completely powerless. Feelings were not easy to channel, even if it was ever so clear in the Bible that it was sinful to … she didn't complete the thought but writhed in pain. Why would she think things like that now, just a few months after her wedding to the most wonderful man in the world? The memory of their mountain hike the day they were visited by the sheep herd came back to her. How easily they got carried away by their emotions in the peace and solitude and the wonderful scenery. But at that time, her feelings had been positive and comfortable. Everything was beautiful and good.

"Oh, Morten, what's happening?" A moan escaped her.

Again her thoughts began revolving around the hike the next day. Then she and Arvid would go, alone … no one else would come. What would happen? A shiver went through her body. Again she revisited the moment when they sat at the garden table, holding hands. She could still feel how all the objections disappeared, replaced by her feeling of excitement and basic attraction. "I'll never be able to resist if …" She moaned again. Why was everything so hard? What was she going to do?

Suddenly she sat up. "What are you moaning about?" she scolded herself. "There is nothing to be worried about. Arvid is only looking for someone to talk to. That's it. Now, stop imagining things." With resolve she turned to the wall and pulled the comforter up to her chin. She wanted to sleep, and as soon as possible at that.

But regardless of her determination to push away her thoughts and worries, they were still present in full force. Her unease wouldn't go away, and sleep wouldn't come. Drops of sweat formed on her forehead. Her wide open, worried eyes stared into the dark. "Am I going crazy?"

Again she took the Bible. There was still sufficient light in the room for her to read without lighting the lamp. Wearily, she sat up and placed the Bible in her lap.

"If you, God, are the source of my worries, then tell me what to do." Her prayer came out as another moan. Clumsily, she leafed back and forth through the well-used book. Suddenly her eyes caught a verse in the letter to James. Chapter 4, Verse 8, said: "Come near to God and He will come near to you. Wash your hands, you sinners, and purify your hearts, you double-minded."

She sank back into her pillow again. Double-minded … yes, that's exactly how she felt. She had no doubt that she was a sinner, but to "wash her hands and purify her heart," no, she didn't know how to do it.

She lifted up the Bible and let her eyes scan the lines of the verse again. Maybe there was something else here that would help her in this situation. "Submit yourselves, then, to God. Resist the devil, and he will flee from you."

That it was the devil at work, she didn't doubt for a moment. But to resist him, that she wasn't able to do. This wouldn't work … "I can't do it!" A sob escaped her as the Bible fell back down on the comforter. She was lost.

Suddenly she was struck by a new thought. "You're not the one who needs to possess the strength to do this. You just keep close to God. Seek Him, like you now have sought help in His Word. And by admitting your own powerlessness, you give God the opportunity to help you."

She sat up again in wonder. She discovered yet another verse as her eyes skipped across the page of the Bible. "God opposes the proud, but gives grace to the humble."

Humility was what He asked for, nothing less. And if you were willing to be humble, you would receive His grace. Yes, grace was what she needed more than anything.

For a while she sat in deep thought. How hard this was! For did she really want to let go of this? A fierce struggle raged inside her. It was a struggle against her own passions. And how strong these forces were. Yes, she knew it. These forces were strong, for she was fighting against the devil himself.

"Oooh," she moaned, sinking back into her pillow. "I'll never be able to resist him. He is too strong for me. Lord, help me!"

At that moment she felt a wonderful peace starting to fill her. It was as if all her bad feelings were gone. Her thoughts were now much clearer.

"Come near to God and He will come near to you," the Bible had said. The meaning came to her in a flash. If you seek God with humility and reveal your problems to Him, you will also experience that God comes near you. No one can resist the devil's devious attacks with their own powers. Maybe you can do it for a while, but sooner or later you will have to concede that you have lost. The devil's power is much greater than that of people. There is only one power that is greater, and that is the power of God. It is only through His help that you can be victorious in your struggle against temptation.

People can share in the power of God through humility and honesty. By openly confessing your sins to Him, you will be victorious, for the way it works is that the devil encounters Jesus as he attacks. And he has to yield to the risen Christ. He lost his fight the moment Jesus expired on the cross. This is something the Evil One is fully aware of. There is no way he can resume that fight.

A feeling of joy filled her. There was hope. She had a savior. It was also clear to her what she must do. She jumped out of bed and began to dress. This had to be done right away. If she waited until the next day, she was afraid temptation would get the better of her, and then it might happen that she chose that instead of the help she clearly saw that God had offered her.

Quickly, she went outside and over to the camping area. The air was chilly, but clear. It would be a lovely night. Maybe the next day would be an especially fine one, she suddenly thought … an especially fine day for a hike in the mountains. But there would be no mountain hike for her.

She knocked gingerly on the door to Arvid's camper. It took a while for him to open. He had probably gone to bed.

An odd smile spread across his face when he saw her standing outside. "Well, well," he said, opening the door all the way. "Did it get too lonely in the double bed in there tonight?" The way he looked at her left no doubt as to what he thought her reason was for showing up at this time of night, and especially the night when Morten was gone.

Mette's face took on a beet red color. Stuttering, she tried to explain, but Arvid interrupted her: "Come in, come in. There's room for two in here."

Perturbed, Mette shook her head. "No, I can't."

"Can't? What kind of rubbish is that?" Arvid looked at her in surprise.

Mette took a step back and continued: "I can't go on the hike tomorrow." Her voice shook, but she continued determinedly: "I don't think it is right that we go on that trip

174

alone. I think you should rather go with Morten. You can bring your fishing poles. I'm sure that will be a much nicer trip for you."

Dark shadows appeared in Arvid's face. "A much nicer trip?" he repeated, a question in his voice as he snorted in contempt. "You realize it is you that I want to go with." He no longer tried to hide his intentions. "And if I understood you correctly the other day by the garden table, you weren't all that disinterested yourself." His statement was directed at her both as a question and an accusation.

Mette felt a rush in her inner soul. All of a sudden all the enchanted feelings and thoughts were gone. What had she been about to allow herself to get into? How could she be so naïve as to believe Arvid wanted to go hiking with her in the mountains just to talk? How close she had come to a terrible disaster. She shuddered and turned halfway around.

"Maybe it seemed that way," she said, "but my mind is made up. I can't be a part of this. So take care. I have to go now."

Before Arvid was able to say any more, she ran back through the dewy grass. She heard the door to the camper slam shut.

Another shudder went through her at the thought of how close she had been to making a grave mistake. No one would ever hear about this. She would bury it deep inside her as a bad, but educational, experience.

Sleep still eluded her for a while, but Mette had found peace and quiet. She lay thinking about what she would have encountered if she had gone on that hike. She couldn't understand how she had been able to think along those lines at all. How seductive sin could be!

When Mette came from the cow barn the next morning, she noticed that there was a camper missing in the grounds. In the seter house was an envelope with a nice good-bye for Morten and money to cover the rent for the space he had occupied. Arvid was gone. They probably wouldn't see him again.

For an instant, she felt a wistful sting deep inside, but then she reminded herself that this was probably best for all of them.

49 • At the hospital

"I wonder how they're doing at the seter?" Mette sat half asleep in the narrow airplane seat, her head resting on Morten's shoulder.

"I'm sure they're all right." Morten was almost asleep, too. He didn't sound as if he was especially worried about either people or animals back home in the Old Country. "Aunt Anna will keep track of things, and Ellen takes care of the heavy work. I'm sure of that." He shut his eyes and rested his head against the seat back. Mette felt relaxed, too, but she couldn't stop thinking about the ones back home. She didn't exactly feel homesick. Her excitement about what was ahead was too strong for that. But the seter was close to her heart, so she wasn't able to put it out of her thoughts.

The last few days had been busy. All the preparations for their trip, in addition to the hectic activity at the seter, now made it feel really good to just relax. But it wasn't

175

that easy to give her thoughts a rest.

Frank and the other Americans were a few seats ahead of them. They hadn't stayed at the seter the entire time. After four days, they had moved on. They had a lot of places to visit, so it was only on their last day that they returned. They had been on the road for more than a week.

The plan was that they would travel together to Chicago. There, their ways would part for a while. Frank and his travel companions would continue on to Bismarck, while Morten and Mette would go to Minneapolis. After a few days, they would travel to Bismarck, where they would again meet up with Frank.

Mette and Morten had prepared as much as they could for the trip. They had made notes of all the information in the old letters that pertained to their search. They had also found out which hospital Robert was affiliated with. Frank had helped them with that. He had also made reservations for them at a hotel in the city.

Mette felt her excitement grow as they got closer to their destination. She looked at her watch. Before long they would be in "the Promised Land" that their relatives had traveled to so many years ago to make a better life for themselves. There, their families might have thrived, but they were no longer in contact with their relatives back in Norway. Did Mette and Morten take on too difficult a task? Would they ever find any of their American relatives? At least they had to try.

Heavy gray clouds hung over the airport as they landed in Chicago. Now there was a frenzy of activity. The travel party was going to break up here, so they had to say proper goodbyes to everyone they had come to know so well during this time, most of whom they wouldn't see again. Frank just got a "see you later." They wrote down his phone number in case they needed help.

Now they had to board the right plane for the last leg of their trip. A bus took them to a different terminal in the huge Chicago airport.

The trip to Minneapolis didn't take long, and soon they were stretched out on their beds in the hotel room. It was good to be able to rest after the long trip.

Although they were tired when they reached the hotel, they were wide awake the next morning. Mette began tossing in bed before 5 a.m. It was impossible to sleep any longer. Quickly, she calculated the time difference in her head and had to smile to herself. No wonder she couldn't sleep any longer! At home it was almost noon, and her body was still tuned in to that time zone.

Morten woke up not much later. They decided to take an early morning walk and explore the area around the hotel.

Outside, a brisk morning breeze blew. They could see that it was going to be a nice, warm day. The traffic in the streets was heavy, but the shops still seemed to be asleep. After a long, refreshing walk, they found a place where they had an early breakfast. Then they returned to the hotel to plan the day's expedition.

Mette was excited as she hailed a taxi. Soon they were on their way to the hospital. She was glad they didn't have to locate their destination on their own. They drove up one street and down another. She lost her sense of direction before they were even halfway there. Finally, the car stopped outside a large building.

"Here we go," said Mette gravely as they stood on the street in front of the hospital.

Morten looked at her and smiled. "Are the questions you want to ask clear in your mind?" He put his arm around her and hugged her against him while looking deeply into her light blue eyes. Mette had to smile, too, at his facetious tone of voice. He knew

176

very well that she had learned all the information by heart by repeating it over and over for several days.

When they reached the main entrance, they stopped for a minute and looked around, a little confused. Where should they start?

"It's probably best that we start at the reception," said Morten, walking over to a desk. The woman on the other side of a glass screen greeted them with a friendly smile.

"Would you be able to give us some information?" asked Morten, looking at her expectantly. "We are from Norway and we're here to look for a relative. The only information we have is that he once worked at this hospital. Do you have a record of people who have worked her over the years? His name is Robert Aanensen."

The woman frowned and began looking through some papers. "I don't recognize the name," she answered, "but I will see if I can find out. Just a moment." She arose and went to another room.

After a few minutes she returned. "I'm not able to find that anyone by that name has worked here," she said with regret.

Disappointed, Mette looked up at Morten. "What do we do now?"

Morten thought for a moment. "This may be quite a few years back," he continued explaining to the woman behind the screen. "He is probably about 75 years old."

Again the woman disappeared. This time she was gone for a while. When she returned again, she shook her head. "We don't have a record of the name. I am really sorry. We don't seem to be able to help you."

Deeply disappointed, they stopped outside the hospital for a while, discussing what to do next. "Maybe it is a different hospital," suggested Mette.

Morten frowned and thought about it. "I don't think so," he said. "Frank seemed to be absolutely sure when he saw the information in the old letters. Let's go back to the hotel. There has to be an explanation for this. We'll go through the information one more time. Maybe we'll find something new."

All morning they sat in the hotel room, studying the old letters. They had brought a number of them to show to any American relatives they might find. Mette had spread them out on top of both beds. In deep silence, they both sat there, reading.

"I can't understand that there is no more information here," said Morten, tossing away a letter in exasperation.

Mette looked at him in despair. "But we can't give up just like that. There has to be something else we can do."

Morten thought. "Maybe I can call Frank. He may be able to give us some advice."

"Yes, please do that." Mette perked up again.

Morten called Frank directly from the hotel room. "We're not able to figure this out," said Morten in exasperation. "Can you help us?" He explained that the hospital seemed to be a dead end.

It was quiet at the other end. Mette sat close enough to hear everything that was said. "What was the man's name again?" asked Frank, after thinking about it for a while.

"His given name is Robert," explained Morten, "and his family name is Aanensen."

"It isn't very likely that this man kept the name Aanensen," said Frank. "It is a difficult name for Americans. And his first name may have been changed, too. Robert is often Rob or Bob or something like that."

Morten cheered up. "Yes, maybe that's why they couldn't find him. We're asking for the wrong name. But then, what might his correct last name be now?"

177

"Would they have used a place name, do you think?" continued Frank. "Or maybe he used his father's first name and added 'son.'"

"So, for instance, his name might be Bob Nelson?" Morten asked.

"Yes, that's a much more American-sounding name," said Frank. "I suggest you go there again and bring with you all the alternate names you can think of. Don't give up."

The situation looked instantly brighter to the two in the hotel room. Right away they started preparing for a new trip to the hospital.

The woman at the desk was pleasant and patient, thought Mette as they descended upon her again with all their questions. Over and over again she went through lists of names. And every so often she double-checked information with her co-workers.

"The only thing we know," she said after a long investigation, "is that a Nelson worked here some years ago. One of the older physicians here remembers him, but he has no contact with him any more. Neither has he any idea about where he lives or if he is around at all. Unfortunately it doesn't look like …" Suddenly she was interrupted by someone who came in and said something to her. Quickly she disappeared, while Mette and Morten were left waiting.

"This doesn't look very promising," said Mette, almost in tears. "Imagine traveling all this way for nothing."

Morten, too, looked disappointed. "Well, we can't really say it has been for nothing." She realized he wanted to comfort her, but she wasn't sure that it wasn't just as much to comfort himself. After all, it was his family. "We still have the trip to Bismarck to look forward to, and there at least we'll see Frank."

At that moment the woman returned. "We're expecting an older man here tomorrow. He was previously a physician at this hospital. He is taking a patient here, and he might have some information. If you get here tomorrow at noon, we'll let him know there is someone here who wants to talk to him."

Morten thanked the woman for her help and assured her that they would be back.

The rest of the day they went sightseeing around the city. Mette browsed around the stores and did some shopping. Then the two of them had dinner at a steakhouse, to try out a "real" American meal—a big piece of steak with a baked potato and salad.

"Now I don't need to eat until I'm back at the seter again," groaned Mette as they left the restaurant.

Morten laughed, assuring her that he, too, had eaten an ample amount.

The next day they arrived at the hospital at noon on the dot. They were shown to a room where they could wait. It didn't take long before the door opened and an elderly gentleman entered. He looked at them questioningly.

Morten began explaining why they were there. "We're from Norway, and we're looking for relatives that we assume are still in this country," he started. "The only information we have are some old letters, so our leads are not very specific. But we have discovered that one of our relatives once worked at this hospital."

As they talked, Morten and Mette detected a flicker of interest in his eyes.

"But we're not sure what this person's name is," continued Morten, "so we thought maybe you could help us. Maybe you worked with this man when you still practiced medicine." Morten explained the problems they had encountered regarding the name.

The older man sat thinking for a while. His face took on a cautious expression while he scrutinized them both. When he started speaking, there was something forbidding in his voice. "There are so many people of Norwegian descent here in this part of the country, and this is so long ago. It won't be easy to find people just like that."

Suddenly the door flew open. A nurse rushed in. "Please come," she called. "It is critical …"

They didn't hear any more, for she had already left. The man stood up quickly, but stopped at the door and turned to Morten: "I'll think about it. If you are here tomorrow at the same time, maybe we can talk some more." Then he, too, disappeared out the door.

With mixed feelings, they left the hospital. They had felt a strong glimmer of hope when they met the man, but as they talked to him, he didn't show much enthusiasm. Rather, he seemed reserved and hesitant.

"He seemed a little mysterious," said Mette as they stood waiting for a taxi. "I didn't see anything that leads me to believe he would do much to help us."

"We'll see tomorrow," said Morten. "Maybe everything will seem brighter then."

"Yes, let's hope so," she answered, preparing herself for disappointment.

50 • A suffering family

Mette and Morten did a lot of sightseeing during their stay in Minneapolis. They also took a trip to St. Paul, its twin city and the state's capital, just to the east. In the evening they attended a service in the Norwegian church, Mindekirken, in Minneapolis.

After the service, they visited with several people of Norwegian descent. Some of them spoke Norwegian quite fluently. Both Mette and Morten explained why they were there. Maybe someone there might be able to help? But no one seemed to know the man they were looking for.

"Many Norwegians come here," said one woman, "but we don't recognize any of those names."

They had no choice but to go back to the hospital where they had started. And it just might be that the old physician had something useful to contribute the following day.

Their wait was longer than expected when they arrived at the hospital the next day. They were shown to a waiting room, but the man they wanted to see was busy with a patient. No one knew when he would be available. "If you sit here, the doctor and the family of his patient will be here sooner or later," a nurse explained to them.

Mette sat watching the people who walked by and those who sat in the waiting room. "I wonder what brought them here?" she thought, pondering the misfortunes that might lie hidden behind their silent masks.

"I'll go see if I can get us a cup of coffee," said Morten.

While he was gone, Mette continued to study the people around her. Not many sat in the same area as they did, but people passed by frequently.

Suddenly a woman entered the room and sat down in a chair some distance from Mette. She had obviously been crying. An expression of deep suffering marked her pale face. Mette felt a deep compassion for the woman. Whatever tormented her had to be erious. The woman slunk down in her chair, her body shivering at times.

A sudden impulse made Mette get up and walk over to her. "You seem to be having a hard time," she said to the woman. "Is there anything I can do for you?"

The woman shook her head slowly as she took stock of Mette. The deep despair in her dark eyes inspired Mette to sit down next to her.

"It will take a miracle to help me," she said with a sob. "Or rather," she continued, "to help my son." Without further encouragement, she began talking. Mette thought as she listened that Americans seemed so much more open than people back home. This woman obviously had a great need to pour out her troubles to someone.

"My son is in really bad shape," she started. "He was in a car accident some months back, and since then he has been in the hospital most of the time. At times his condition worsens, like right now." She blew her nose, a new grimace of pain appearing on her face. "There is something wrong with his brain. He has had surgery several times, but this time his condition is particularly critical. My husband and father-in-law are with his physician right now. They are planning another surgery. I couldn't stand being there." A moan accompanied her last words as she receded deeper into the chair.

At this point Morten returned with their coffee. Puzzled, he glanced over at the two women who sat there talking. Without saying anything, he gave one of the coffee cups to Mette. Gratefully, she took it and handed it to the woman. "Here," she said. "Some coffee will be good for you." Appreciative, the woman took the cup and sipped the warm drink. For a while, the woman sat there, preoccupied with her worried thoughts. Mette didn't say anything, either. But then the woman started talking again:

"This has been such a difficult time for us. My husband had to take time off from work for long periods to take care of Allan."

Mette understood that she was talking about her son.

"When he is in the hospital, he needs one of us there with him almost constantly. And when he's at home, he's even more dependent on us. This has been terribly hard on us, including financially, because our health insurance doesn't cover everything."

She sat silently for a moment before she continued. "My father-in-law has been of great help to us, but there is a limit to what he can contribute in terms of money. And I suspect he took out a loan at the bank in order to help us." She moaned again.

Mette was deeply touched as she listened. If there were only some way she could help these people. But there was nothing she could do but listen. She realized the woman hadn't brought the subject up to solicit help. Rather, she had to express her despair to someone. And if all she needed was a pair of listening ears, then Mette was more than willing to provide it.

Minutes went by as the two women sat there preoccupied by the severity of the family's situation. Morten had buried himself in a newspaper.

Suddenly the woman straightened up, redirecting her focus down the corridor. Mette followed her eyes and saw two men walking toward them. To her surprise, one of the men was the elderly doctor they met the day before. The two men were engaged in intense discussion as they walked along. Mette realized there was a connection between them. Although he was retired, the old doctor had probably been called to the hospital to help out because of Allan's difficult case, thought Mette.

"How is he?" the woman asked as she went to meet the two men.

The three of them were engaged in deep conversation. Then the physician noticed Morten and acknowledged him. "Yes, it's you," he said, coming closer. "I have thought about what you asked me yesterday." He looked at both Morten and Mette searchingly. "Maybe I can provide you with some information, but that is the only thing I can do for you." He emphasized his last words, his eyes still cautious.

Mette and Morten looked at each other. There was something guarded about the doctor's manner. Morten turned to him again: "If you can provide us with pertinent information, that's all we want," he said firmly.

A tired look came over the older man's face as he sat down in a chair next to Morten. Mette noticed that the other two had disappeared down the corridor.

"So you are looking for Norwegian relatives." He stared blankly ahead. "Can you tell me a little more about those relatives?" he asked without moving his eyes.

Morten began telling him about his mother's two aunts, who had emigrated more than 80 years ago. He talked about Mina, who died not long after they came to this country, and he spoke about the family that Gunhild had joined in North Dakota.

While he spoke, the physician listened silently. Morten explained that this hospital was the only real lead they had, and that one of Gunhild's sons had once worked here.

His listener cleared his throat and looked directly at Morten. His voice changed considerably when he started talking. It was calm, but sounded tired: "My mother's name was Ginni and my father's name was Nels. They both came from Norway. My mother told me a lot about her twin sister who died of tuberculosis right after they came to America. There is no doubt that you have met the right person."

At that moment, Mette felt herself tremble. Could it be possible? Was this the Robert they were looking for? He seemed so strange.

His tired eyes swept from Mette to Morten. Suddenly he stopped, staring at his hands lying in his lap. It took him a minute for him to continue: "But there isn't much for you here."

Mette and Morten looked at each other. What was it with this man?

Morten tried another question: "What is your real name?"

"My name is Robert, but everybody calls me Bob. My last name was Aanensen, but I changed it to something less foreign. I took my father's first name, calling myself Nelson."

"That's what we thought," said Mette excitedly. "So now we have found you."

This reality dawned on Morten, too, and they both lit up. Mr. Nelson smiled as well, although he still looked sad.

Morten frowned. "You said that your mother's name was Ginni; we thought she was called Gunhild."

"It's not unheard of around here that a name is abbreviated, at least names that are foreign and difficult to pronounce," he said. "That's probably why she was called Ginni. But I can prove her name was Gunhild. I have her old passport in a drawer at home."

The man continued, his cautious look returning: "Was it just the wish to find distant relatives that brought you here all the way from Norway?"

Morten looked at Mette. The man sensed they might have an ulterior motive, since they seemed to want evidence that they had found the right person.

Mette gave a slight nod. There was no doubt that this was the right person.

"We have a very special reason for being here," Morten told the older man. Then he explained about Uncle Torkel, who had passed away. He told him about the letters they found, which led them to believe they might have relatives in America—not only relatives, but also family that was entitled to a part of the inheritance.

As he talked about the inheritance, they could see that the listener's expression changed. First he went pale, and then red spots appeared on his cheeks before his tears started running.

"Is this true? There isn't some kind of misunderstanding?" His voice was rough and unsteady. Morten assured him everything was as he had told him. He had the papers back at their hotel. They could all go there to make sure that he was correct.

"And I thought …" he cleared his throat and started over. "I thought you came here to ask me for money. I couldn't imagine what other reason you would have to look up a distant relative after such a long time. And then it is the opposite. I don't believe this."

He stood up. "Let's go somewhere where we can talk further," he said.

They found a cafe down the street. Mette didn't register what she ate; the joy of finally having found the person they were looking for overwhelmed her completely. Bob talked eagerly about his childhood and growing up in North Dakota. He also told them how hard things had been for them after his father died in an accident many years ago. And he talked about his two brothers, Willy and Mical, who both died without issue.

But he had children. He and his wife, Nancy, lived in a house in a suburb to Minneapolis. They had two children, who were both married. And they had six grandchildren. "The man you saw today is my oldest son," he ended, a sad look in his eyes.

Puzzled, Morten looked from Mette to Bob. "Your son? I thought you were here in your capacity as a doctor."

"Oh, no," the old man shook his head. "I am no longer an active member of the medical profession, but my son and his wife feel safer if I come with them whenever their son has to go to the hospital." He talked about his grandson who had been in an accident, and who had been very ill ever since. Mette had already heard the story but didn't realize until now that this man was the father-in-law referred to by the woman.

Suddenly she understood what it would mean for these people to get news about an inheritance at this time, when they were in such a dire financial situation.

Bob told them, "I have prayed and begged God for help, but I honestly didn't believe my prayers would be answered."

Mette felt that her tears were not far away. She swallowed several times before she could speak. "Yes, it is wonderful that we have such a merciful God."

"No answer to my prayers could be more direct than this," continued Bob. "And such a powerful one. I can't wait to tell Tim and Sally."

A glance at his watch made him stand up. "I have to get back to the hospital, but we have to get together later." Quickly they decided when and where to meet, before he disappeared out the door.

Morten and Mette stayed behind for a while, talking. Both were thrilled at the turn of events. That the news of the inheritance came just when it was so sorely needed made it extra special. They had no doubt there was some kind of divine intervention.

"How much money are we talking about?" asked Mette suddenly. She had never been told the exact value of Uncle Torkel's estate.

Morten thought before he answered. "You know that half of the money goes to Bob, and if the property is sold, we're talking about maybe a million Norwegian kroner on his part."

Mette gasped. "I had no idea we were talking about that kind of money."

Morten laughed at her surprised expression. "But in regard to us, the other half has to be divided by three. So we won't be rolling in money."

Mette had to laugh, too. "At least the money goes to people who really need it," she said. Morten agreed completely.

51 • On the prairie

Because of the emergency situation at the hospital, they didn't get to spend much time with their newfound relatives. But they met Bob's wife, who also kept busy doing whatever she could for the injured boy. News of the Norwegian inheritance was a shock to all of them—not in the least to the boy's mother, Sally, who was truly astonished. She beamed at Mette when they met again. "Imagine, you sitting there with the answer without our knowing it."

Mette smiled, happy she was able to help them after all.

Morten and Mette's stay in Minneapolis was nearly over. Soon they would be departing for Bismarck, where Frank awaited them. But they determined to keep in touch.

The only family member they didn't meet was Ted, Bob's second son, who lived in New York with his family.

Although they hadn't known each other long, members of the two related families who had just found one another had established a connection. They knew they would miss each other as they said goodbye. Mette and Sally had become especially close.

Bob took Morten and Mette to the airport himself. The others stayed at the hospital. Allan's surgery had gone well, but he was still in critical condition. Suspense and worry still affected the Nelsons deeply, so Morten and Mette felt they should not prolong their stay. They could come back some other time.

○ ○ ○

At the Bismarck airport, Frank stood waiting for them when their plane arrived. They greeted each other warmly.

"I have some information about your family," Frank said as they drove out of the city and began their journey along Highway 83, the long road heading north. They both listened intently to what he had to tell them.

"I know some people who live a few miles from our farm," Frank said. "After looking through some old papers, I realized they, too, are descended from the first settlers in the area. I had a talk with the 'Old Man' in the family one day, and he confirmed that he was one of the people Sjur assisted when the man first arrived from Norway. Based on the information you gave me, we figured out that this man's grandfather was the Theodor you mentioned."

"How fantastic!" Excited, Mette and Morten talked at the same time. "Then maybe we have more family in the area."

Frank shook his head. "No, I don't think so. Some moved away, and others simply died. I have been working on this for the last few days, but this is all I know."

With this information, their anticipation increased as they continued on their northward journey. A strange feeling of nostalgia filled Mette as the car sped along. Here on the Great Plains, the earliest emigrants from her country had trudged along behind prairie schooners. Horses or oxen were their only means of transportation, before the coming of the railroads.

In Norway, Mette had often heard about the flat, wide plains with long, stiff prairie grass waving in the wind. Now she saw for herself that these plains were not as flat as she had been led to believe. Rather, she would describe them as a rolling sea, for the landscape was incredibly hilly. In some places the hills were quite steep.

Mette looked toward the horizon to the west, as if she expected a band of Indians to show up over the next hill. Frank had explained to them that an Indian reservation lay to the west. "But there are no painted horsemen with feathers and arrows there any more," he said, laughing.

Mette smiled to herself. There wasn't much left of the fairy tale image many had of the Wild West. She now realized, too, that the prairie wasn't just a waving sea of grasslands. Almost everywhere lay cultivated fields where many different crops grew.

Here and there they drove past groups of houses between lines of trees. "The tree rows are called shelterbelts," explained Frank. "They have been planted to provide shelter from weather and wind."

"What kind of crops do they grow here?" asked Morten, scanning the bountiful plains extending for miles in all directions.

"Oh, a lot of different things—wheat, soybeans and corn," Frank explained. "And there's lots of grazing land on the big ranches around here."

"Ranches?" Mette puzzled. "What's the difference between a ranch and a farm?"

Frank explained obligingly: "A ranch is a place where they raise livestock. They mostly grow grass or alfalfa for hay. A farm, on the other hand, is a place where they raise various types of grain, corn or other plants."

Soon they left the main highway and turned onto a narrow gravel road leading east. Frank stopped his car in front of an enormous farm utility building. Huge tractors and other farm implements were parked outside.

"Everything seems to have its place here," said Morten, exiting from the car. Soon he sat perched high up in a huge combine. "I could use this on the seter," he called down to Mette, laughing. Mette doubled over with laughter, thinking about the tiny field at the seter. This machine couldn't even turn around there.

Frank lived with his son and his family, moving in with them when he became a widower a few years back. Morten and Mette met Frank's son and his wife. Their four children also came to take a look at the foreigners. The oldest one was already old enough to help out with the tractor in the fields, while the youngest was only 10. Morten and Mette were greeted with an openness that warmed them both. Soon, people came from all directions to meet Frank's Norwegian visitors.

Although the farm buildings were in good condition and the implements of the best quality, Frank's house and furnishings were modest. Seated around an oilcloth-covered table in Frank's kitchen, Morten and Mette were treated to their first home-cooked, American-style meal. The friendly atmosphere made them feel right at home.

After the dishes were cleared away, Frank took out Sjur's old diary. "This is where I've found most of the information about my family and Norway," he said, placing the big, worn book on the table.

Carefully, Mette turned its pages. "How in the world were you able to decipher this?" she asked, scanning the embellished Gothic letters. She had already taken a peek at it when Frank had brought it to Norway.

Frank smiled. "It was hard at first, but as I got more familiar with the letters, it became easier. My biggest problem was actually the man's language. In the beginning it is so mixed up with Norwegian that it was hard to understand what he meant. When I first started reading it, I had to look the words up in an English-Norwegian dictionary."

The next few days, Frank's Norwegian guests learned the details involving a North Dakota farm. Morten wanted to explore the workings of the machines and implements, and Frank was eager to demonstrate and explain everything.

The day after they arrived, they drove to the home of the people they now knew to be their distant relatives. They were received with teary-eyed excitement. The couple who lived there were in their 60s. Mette was taken aback. Would this be the man whom Frank called the "Old Man"? He wasn't old!

They soon learned that all the couple's children, except their oldest son, had moved away. This son was married and had a house nearby.

This farm resembled Frank's. Machinery and farm implements lined the big yard. There was no lack of food here, either, as both hosts and guests talked and ate.

As they sipped their after-dinner coffee, they recounted stories from the time the district was first settled. Martha, the woman of the house, told them her family had come from the Gudbrandsdal valley in Norway. The first emigrants from her family had arrived in America in the 1850s, settling in a town called Westby in Wisconsin.

Martha talked eagerly about shops that sold crafts and other items reflecting the town's Norwegian heritage. "You should go there," she said excitedly. "That town is still almost all Norwegian."

"Oh, if only we could," said Mette.

After some discussion, they decided that instead of going back to Chicago by air, they would make the trip by car. "We'll be spending many hours in the vehicle," said Frank, "but you will get to see a lot of America."

Both Mette and Morten assured Frank they wouldn't mind the drive. Martha and her husband, Simen, agreed to come along.

Excitement filled the old prairie home as they made plans. They would leave in two days, allowing Frank time to finish showing his guests around the district.

Suddenly, Martha jumped up from her chair. "I have something to show you," she said, disappearing out the door. Soon, she returned with a cardboard box.

"This has been sitting in the attic," she said, placing the box on the table. "I had completely forgotten about it. But after Frank gave us the information about his Norwegian relatives, I remembered. My father-in-law told me about it. His father got it from Sjur before he died. He wanted a Norwegian to have it, for he felt his own family wasn't interested in anything having to do with the Old Country. He had no family left over there, either, so he wanted our family to have it."

She took off the lid and lifted out a dark piece of cloth. It was woven from rough wool. "This was the only thing Sjur had from his mother. This is the shawl she was wrapped in as a baby when she was brought to the farm where she grew up. That's what Sjur told Grandpa."

Frank walked over to examine the shawl. With caring hands he stroked the rough cloth. "How strange," he said with reverence in his voice.

"We thought it should belong to you," Martha told him. "That is, if you want it."

"Would you really give it to me?" he said with big eyes. "I would love to have it."

"We never thought about it before, since Sjur said no one in his family was interested," she continued.

Frank shook his head. "I guess they didn't feel that way back then. But to me, this is a treasure."

That evening Morten accompanied Frank's son out to the fields, while Mette sat with Frank, studying the old shawl. The worn threads were torn in several places.

"It seems to have been worn a lot," said Mette, stroking the edge that had once been tied with fringes. A large piece was missing from one corner.

Mette took out her camera and snapped several pictures of the old garment. Frank was also photographed from all angles. "I'll send you copies when the pictures are developed, so you have proof of what a great model you are," Mette said jokingly.

They both laughed while they wrapped up the shawl to put it away.

52 • The land of the Indians

Mette and Morten spent two fantastic final days in North Dakota with Frank and his family. They went on several excursions by car to see more places where their ancestors had toiled to make a living. They also talked to Bob on the phone several times. He explained where he grew up, and where his other relatives had lived. Frank took Mette and Morten to these places, too. It was strange to think that the prairie had been cultivated by their own flesh and blood. Although the properties had changed hands over the years, they could still find reminders of the old settlers.

Frank also introduced them to the pre-settlement history of North Dakota via a visit to the site of an old Indian village. "The Mandans lived here," explained Frank as they walked around the site, exploring the large reconstructed earth lodges. "This village was abandoned long before the Europeans settled in this part of the country. A smallpox epidemic killed most of the people."

They entered one of the dwellings. Dark and cool, it featured a large, open room containing tools and artifacts. "This is so big that a lot of people could live here," said Mette, surprised.

"Yes," said Frank. "There were several dozen dwellings like this one at this location, so this was a large village at one time."

"What's that?" asked Morten as they left the dwelling. He pointed at some posts set in the ground, forming a circle. The poles were several yards tall and placed closely together. Toward the top, a braided grass rope held the stockade-like structure together.

"This was the religious center of the village," Frank answered. "This is where all important decisions were made, so it was kind of a meeting place for the 'town council,'" he said, laughing.

"The posts, what were they for?" asked Morten, studying the rough-hewn wood.

"Those posts symbolized an important event in the history of their religion," Frank replied. "According to their tradition, many years ago a terrible catastrophe struck. God had to punish the people on earth for their evil doings. He did it by sending a great flood. One man was able to save himself and his family by setting poles in the ground in this manner. He waterproofed the structure so the water wouldn't flood the interior. There they stayed until the water subsided. The grass rope shows the water level at its highest. They believed this was what saved the people from God's punishment."

Mette listened intently as Frank told the story. "But that is almost the same story as the one in the Bible," she said eagerly. "It's just that there it's about a boat—that is, Noah and his ark."

"Yes," said Frank. "There's no doubt a great flood occurred at some point in history. The Bible is not the only source for stories about the deluge; they are reflected in

186

several religious traditions around the world. But what's special about the biblical story is that it doesn't only talk about sin, punishment and judgment. It also talks about the road to salvation, and a Savior. That makes the Bible unique."

"It is obvious the flood was the reality of many people, whether or not they believe in the Bible," said Morten. "No wonder other religions recount the same story. It just confirms that what the Bible says is true."

As they walked around the Indian village, Frank told them more about the Mandans' history and traditions. And on their drive back to the farm, the two foreigners got a complete history lesson about North Dakota. They learned that the state was once part of Dakota Territory, which was split into the two states of North and South Dakota in 1889. It was after that time that most of the land was settled.

When Sjur had come to America in the mid 1800s, he first settled a short distance west of Chicago. A considerable concentration of Norwegian immigrants lived there. But as the population grew, his sons moved to North Dakota. And then he followed.

Mette felt she was getting to know this land pretty well. She looked forward to their trip. Then they would follow in the steps of their ancestors—only this time traveling from west to east!

53 • In the steps of their ancestors

The morning they were to leave, Mette peeked out the window. She groaned when she saw the clear sky and the burning sun. It would not be comfortable to drive so far in the heat, she thought. But when they started out on their trip, she was pleasantly surprised. The air-conditioned car meant they wouldn't suffer from the heat, as she had feared. The cars she was used to in Norway did not have air conditioning.

Frank drove. They picked up Martha and Simen, then headed south along Highway 83. When they reached Bismarck, they turned east onto Interstate Highway 94, which ran straight as an arrow to the North Dakota-Minnesota border. Both Martha and Simen had a lot to contribute regarding the history of the first immigrants in the district.

They spent a long day on the road, now and then stopping to check out sights of special interest or to get something to eat. Breaks were infrequent, as their goal was to get to Minneapolis. When Frank needed a break, Simen would take the wheel.

"Maybe we can stay with Bob and his wife," said Mette eagerly. Everybody thought it was a great idea.

Morten quickly dialed their number on his cell phone, but Bob was not available. His wife answered and told them he was at the hospital. Allan was worse again. He had developed an infection, and his condition was critical. Morten expressed his sympathy and didn't ask for lodging. It would be best if they stayed at a hotel.

After crossing the Red River that served as the North Dakota-Minnesota border, Interstate 94 curved to the south. Mile after mile flew by as they drove.

"What do they grow up there along those hills?" asked Morten, pointing to some steep hills. Big belts grew horizontally across the hillsides.

"Soybeans and corn," answered Frank. "Probably sunflowers in between, too."

"But why do they plant in belts?" Morten asked, eyeing the striped fields.

"It stops the dirt from running off and keeps the moisture on the hillside. That's why they plant in belts across the slope and why they vary the crop."

"The yield in these areas must be enormous, as huge as these fields are," said Morten. "It looks like they never end."

"Yes, the yield is impressive," said Simen. "You should come back here when they harvest. They bring entire trailer trucks into the fields. Then they fill up one trailer after another with whatever they grow and take it to the storage silos."

Morten's eyes shone with enthusiasm. "I would love to do that. It would be something completely different from the tractors we work with on the small farms in our mountain town."

As they neared Minneapolis, Frank told them they now had traveled close to 80 Norwegian *mil*—nearly 500 American miles. Arriving at their destination for the night, they found a decent motel and soon were able to relax, each family in a separate room.

Next morning the weather was as nice as on the previous day. Rising early, the travelers left the motel and found a restaurant that served a hearty breakfast.

After they had eaten, they were on the road again. As they approached the Wisconsin border, Frank pointed out the area where the fictional characters in *The Emigrants* book series by author Wilhelm Moberg were said to have settled.

They crossed the Mississippi at La Crosse, Wisconsin, and soon reached Westby, the small prairie town Martha had told them about. Frank stopped the car near a large poster featuring a Norwegian-like scene. Across the poster was printed in large lettering: *"Hilsen fra Westby! Kom igjen!"* (Greetings from Westby! Come again!)

The words were written in Norwegian. As they walked along the streets, they realized Martha had not been exaggerating about the town's pride in its heritage. Items in the gift shops clearly demonstrated this pride. And on the lawn in front of a cement wall, a carved wooden Viking head perched on a tree stump.

"Here Norwegians have been at work, no doubt about it," said Morten.

After driving some distance out of town, they stopped at the old home place of Martha and her family. Martha was noticeably moved. "Everything looks the same as when I was last here, except the fields. They grow different crops here now. I can remember my father telling me they grew tobacco here when he was young."

"Tobacco?!" Mette looked at Martha in surprise. "They grew tobacco?"

"Oh, yes," Martha smiled at the surprised expression on Mette's face. "It was actually an important crop for a lot of people around here."

As they strolled around the property, Martha told them about the Norwegian immigrants who had settled in the area. Mette and Morten learned that Norwegian had been the main language spoken there until well into the 20th century. "But after a while it was mixed with English," she finished.

Martha hiked to a cluster of trees some distance from the house. "An old sod house once sat here. It was the first home my family lived in after arriving from Norway. Later they built a bigger wooden house," she said. "I've been told that my grandmother was born in that sod house."

Martha turned toward the hills to the west. A sad memory seemed to sweep over her. When she started talking again, her voice was solemn.

"I remember Grandma telling me about her brother, who was some years older than she. One day in December he took off with horse and wagon to get supplies for Christmas. But he never returned. On his way back from town, he was caught in a terrible storm. Snow and wind blinded both him and the horse. They lost their way and their sense of direction.

"Some days later, they found him over there behind the hills." She pointed in the direction she had looked. "Both he and the horse froze to death. He was sitting in the wagon and the horse was still standing—as if they were moving, as if they suddenly had disappeared from this world." She shook her head sadly.

All of them listened soberly to Martha's story. Mette felt a chill as she realized the same prairie that appeared beautiful and alluring on a summer day like this had another, more vicious, side. People were so powerless against the fierce forces of Nature.

"Yes, the Norwegian immigrants experienced first hand the severity and trials of the wilderness," said Frank. "Many of them had to pay with their lives at a young age here in the New World."

After leaving Westby, they traveled south to Madison, where they spent the night.

The next day they drove west to Mt. Horeb, another small prairie town displaying its Norwegian roots. Busy streets teemed with action as they explored the town. Booths lining the sidewalks displayed everything from Norwegian sweaters and trolls to tablecloths with Hardanger embroidery. Morten and Mette stopped to watch a woodcarver demonstrating his craft at a nearby table. The carver told them he had learned his art from his Norwegian-emigrant grandparents.

They ate at a small outdoor restaurant, resting a bit before they continued on to their next destination. Martha and Simen were in charge of the travel plans now.

"Now we're going to Norway," said Simen as they crawled back into the car. The minute he turned west off the main road, it was as if they had entered another world. Tall trees and bushes marched along both sides of the road. Hills and slopes made them feel hemmed in after the many miles on the wide plains.

"You would almost think we were back home in Norway," said Mette in surprise, peering out the car window.

"Yes," said Martha. "That's probably what the first settler here thought, too."

Simen parked the car close to a dark, wooden building. "This is Little Norway," he said, stepping out of the car. The other vehicle occupants followed.

Mette gasped at the idyllic scene. It was like stepping back in time. Steep hills covered with both coniferous and deciduous trees surrounded a small, open field. At the foot of the hill, log buildings and cabins nestled among the trees—some beautifully crafted with carvings and ornamentation. Included among them were a stabbur and outbuildings, seter houses, and a stave church. A stream ran across the field. The place was landscaped with flowers and shrubs.

They bought tickets for a guided tour of the open-air museum. As they walked from house to house, the guide explained that a Norwegian immigrant had settled in this beautiful little valley. The first house there was built in 1856. With time, the place was turned into a museum. The cabins along the bottom of the hill contained artifacts that once belonged to Norwegian immigrants. Some of the objects had been brought over from the Old Country, while others were made in Wisconsin. Among the artifacts were numerous *rosemaled*—rose-painted—bowls, rockers and other types of furniture. Cookware and tools for farm work were also part of the collection.

According to the guide, the quaint stave church with its narrow, arched windows and dragon-headed gables had never been used as a church. Built in Trondheim, Norway, it had been sent aboard ship to America, where it served as an exhibit in Chicago in 1893. Later it was reassembled in this little Norwegian valley.

As they walked around the grounds, Mette noticed that the log buildings were just as Frank had described them the first day he had visited their seter. Each log extended out at the corners, not cut straight off like the logs on their seter house in Norway.

All too soon, it was time to leave. The travelers returned to Madison and continued east. "We have to visit the place where the first Norwegians settled in Wisconsin," said Simen. "Actually, this was the sixth Norwegian settlement in all of America. The first Norwegians settled there in 1838. They built a church in the area soon afterward. The old church is no longer there. The one that stands there today is a large, multi-use church. The place is called Jefferson Prairie."

"Oh, yes, Jefferson Prairie!" Frank got excited immediately. "That was the place old Sjur wrote about in his diary."

"I bet he did," said Simen. "If he lived in Beloit, then he would have been in touch with the Norwegians in that settlement."

Next, they drove to the sites where several pioneer churches had once stood. They strolled around in the graveyards, reading the inscriptions on the headstones. There were many Norwegian names on the tombstones. "Here their days ended," Mette said quietly. "They probably experienced a lot of hard work and spent many a moment yearning for their native country before they ended up here."

"Yes," said Morten. "But they also experienced progress and happiness in many ways. After all, they were the ones who built this part of the country. And even if the work was backbreaking at first, their efforts got them ahead. The later generations were able to enjoy the fruits of their labor. That is obvious today."

Mette stared blankly, dreaming. "It is strange to think that the roots of the people who live around here may be the same as ours. It makes everyone seem so connected."

Morten nodded. They stood for a while in silence, their thoughts wandering. But then Simen reminded them it was time to resume their journey to Chicago.

They continued on to Beloit. There they could find no one who had any information about where Sjur or others of their Norwegian relatives had lived. Still, it was interesting to see the town. They stopped for a proper dinner before they crossed the border to Illinois.

"Chicago is the next stop," Simen informed them. The mood turned blue at that point. The time to say goodbye was drawing near. Still, Mette and Morten had to agree that the trip had been eventful. Never would they have imagined that they would experience so much in America. Mette's mind was chock-full of impressions.

Yet it would be good to get back home. Actually, she was quite tired. But most of all, she was happy because they were now so close to their relatives on the other side of the ocean.

54 • *Uninvited guests*

"What on earth is going on here?" Mette stood in the open door to the seter house staring at the jumble of household items all over the floor. Aunt Anna was on all fours, looking through a cupboard. She jumped as she heard her voice and scrambled to her feet.

"Yes, you may ask," she said, pushing back wayward strands of hair that had fallen into her face. She looked haggard. "I don't understand this," she continued rapidly. "The door was securely closed. This girl, she absolutely wanted me to … but I wouldn't have gone … who could have …"

Her jumbled sentences added to Mette's confusion. Suddenly she felt sorry for the old woman, who had worked so hard here at the seter while she and Morten had been in America. They had gotten back home the night before, but they had gone to bed in their house in town so they could get a good night's sleep. Not until well into the day did they return to the seter.

The sight that met them there was baffling. Morten entered at the same moment. After catching his breath, he put his arm firmly around Aunt Anna's shoulders and led her over to a chair. "Sit down," he said calmly. "Then you can explain what happened."

"There has been a break-in," she said, bursting into tears. "I should have kept better watch, but Ellen absolutely insisted I go back to town for a couple of days. She felt she could manage what needed to be done up here without me. I don't think she has been in here at all the last few days, for she stays out there in Marit's camper all the time."

Finally they realized what had happened. Again, Mette felt the sting of a guilty conscience. It probably had been too much for Aunt Anna, considering everything that needed to be done while they were gone. Ellen had noticed and had wanted her to take some time off. They knew Ellen usually stayed in Marit's camper when she was at the seter. It was parked in the camping area all summer.

"When did this happen?" asked Morten, his eyes checking out everything that was dumped on the floor. "I don't know. Either last night or yesterday, I would think," she said as her tears continued to run.

Mette put her arm around her. "Don't you worry about this. It won't take me long to clear this up."

"But …" she sobbed again, "I should have looked after things better."

"You should be grateful you weren't here when it happened," said Morten. "You never know what people like that might have done to you." He started looking through the things on the floor. "Is anything gone?"

"I don't know," Aunt Anna said as she got to her feet. "That's what I was checking out when you arrived."

Morten looked over at her with a mischievous smile: "Maybe they were after your *gome*.* Did you check what's left in the fridge?"

Aunt Anna laughed through her tears. "That isn't much to break down a solid oak door for," she said as she started picking up items from the floor.

Cupboards and drawers seemed to have been searched, but they couldn't see that anything was gone. "This is strange," said Morten after a while. Obviously they were looking for something, but what would it be? There are no other valuables here but the old furniture, and that is still here."

Suddenly Mette cried out. She stood by the corner cupboard. "The box is gone!"

The other two came rushing over. "The box!" Aunt Anna put her hands together in consternation and looked at the empty spot in the cabinet where the box used to sit. "They were after the old box."

"But who knew there was a mysterious old box in the seter house?" Morten looked at her in surprise.

Suddenly she grew completely silent. Both Mette and Morten looked at her in puzzlement because it was so unusual to see her so quiet.

"It has to be they," she said quietly after a while. "I had a visit from some young people here a couple of days ago," she continued. "They were camping in the mountains with tents and fishing poles. But one day they came here and asked to buy some milk. Just then, Ellen and I sat studying the old box. The boys showed great interest in it. They tried to open it, too, but of course they couldn't do it. It has to be those boys, but I have no proof," she said, looking apologetically at Morten.

"No," he said. "There isn't much we can do about that now. We don't know if it is valuable. So there is no use to report it stolen."

The box was gone. Mette felt something start to boil inside her. She had been so excited about that box. She had been convinced it contained something interesting and that they would somehow manage to open it. And now it was gone. She understood what Morten was talking about. They might file a police report, but they couldn't expect the police to spend time and manpower tracking down a rusty old tin box that might contain only a tuft of moss.

"Do you know where in the mountains those young people camped?" asked Mette.

Aunt Anna shook her head. "The only thing I know," she answered, "is that they disappeared with their milk up the hillside over there." She pointed out the window toward the west.

Morten looked doubtfully in the direction she pointed out. Then he shook his head. "There is no use looking for them. They probably are long gone by now."

Deeply disappointed, Mette started cleaning up the mess. The box was gone and they probably wouldn't see it again … or might there still be hope? She didn't want to give up. It had to be possible to resolve this one way or another. It should be possible to figure out who those young people were. She decided to try.

Aunt Anna busied herself in helping to clean up, while Morten checked the broken lock. The door itself didn't sustain much damage, but the big latch on the inside was bent and broken away from its fasteners. They didn't always lock that door. Normally they just latched the door and left by the back door in the dairy room. The door in there had a sturdy lock.

Soon life returned to normal at the seter, but Mette had not forgotten her resolve to find the identity of the uninvited guests. Several days later they had to go to town to do some shopping. Morten had some chores that needed to be done at the farm, so Mette went to the grocery store alone. She decided to check with the people in charge of fishing licenses to find out who had bought licenses within the time frame of interest.

While she had been optimistic when she set out, her curiosity and patience were sorely tested. She learned that the man who had worked there during that time was a summer temp. He no longer worked there and would not be back. Unfortunately, that was all the help they could give her.

"Summer temp?" Mette snorted loudly to herself as she left the store. She could understand it wasn't easy to keep track of everything that went on during vacation time. But now they were well into August, and life was getting back to normal again. Still, she was gravely disappointed.

Irritated, she threw her groceries into the car and drove back to the farm.

As she neared the road by the house, she became aware of a strange car parked in the driveway. "Who might be visiting now?" she thought as she quickly headed for the kitchen. She placed her shopping bags on the counter before approaching the door to the living room. The voices in there told her that Morten was in deep conversation with another man.

Suddenly she stopped in her tracks. Rigid, she stood listening. Wasn't there something familiar about that voice? Yes, she could hear it clearly now. Shaking, she sat down on the chair next to her. There was no doubt. Tore was talking to Morten in the next room. All the bad feelings washed over her again. She wasn't able to move as she sat there, her thoughts scattered in all directions.

She thought back to the time when she worked in the office in Oslo. Tore was her co-worker there, but they didn't get along. He made snide remarks whenever she made a mistake. She always tried to do her work as competently and as close to perfection as possible, but Tore always found something to criticize. Yet he was not particular about his own work. It had irritated her beyond description. She confronted him about it more than once, but it didn't seem to help. Instead, he had become even more annoying with his arrogant taunts and comments about her. He was actually one of the reasons she had taken time off from work to seek a job at the seter last summer.

When she had discovered that Tore was one of Morten's best friends from the military, she was shocked. There had been a heated exchange between them. In his calm way, Morten had tried to explain that it was a case of wrong chemistry, and that Tore was really a great guy.

After that conversation, she had made up her mind to deal with Tore in a friendly and respectful manner. He came to their wedding, and she felt she had managed quite well. At least she didn't encounter any problems that day, so she thought perhaps the situation was resolved.

But now she sat just a few yards away from him, shaking. All the bad feelings were back. The thoughts, feelings ... and she hadn't even talked to him at all.

She could hear the voices from the next room quite clearly. What were they talking about? She remained seated, listening.

"I know this is hard for you ... yes, actually for both of you." It was Morten's voice. He sounded sincere.

When Tore spoke, he sounded desperate: "I know I'm not that good, but it should be possible to be considered a member of the human race, even if I'm not as perfect as she is. I should be entitled to some respect." The last words were pronounced with bitterness.

Mette tensed where she sat. She didn't know whom they were talking about, but she had a feeling it might be someone she knew ... yes, knew very well. A desperate need to run far away came over her, but she didn't dare move.

"You are quite different by nature, you know." Morten's voice sounded again. "I really don't think she says these things to pester you. She makes similar remarks and reminders to me all the time. I think it is just the way she is ... her way of organizing things."

Now Mette was sure. They were talking about her. This was a conversation not meant for her ears. She was filled with a feeling of deep shame, but still she wasn't able to get up from the chair. They would hear her in there for sure, and realize that she was sitting here, listening. It seemed odd that they didn't hear her come in. Sound carried very well between the living room and the kitchen, that much was clear.

There was a pause in the next room. An oppressive silence hung in the air. Mette hardly dared to breathe. What if they came out and found her here? She had never felt as wretched as she did in that moment. Her desperate impulse to flee made her entire body tremble. She wanted to get away … run … far away … But she didn't dare. She was simply unable to move.

As Tore started speaking again, his voice sounded oddly strained.

"… When she starts …" he cut himself off with a little sniffle. Then he started anew. "… it is like hearing my mother."

Again there was a pause. Morten didn't say anything. He seemed to be waiting for Tore to tell him what he wanted to say, but which was hard to get out.

Tore cleared his throat before he started again. "As long as I can remember, my mother has been harping about how useless I am. Nothing I did was good enough. Ever since I was big enough to start doing things on my own, she has criticized everything I've ever done. It got to the point that I had to go to her for even the smallest task and ask how it was to be done. I had no self-esteem whatsoever. After a while, defiance started to build in me. I didn't want to slave under her critical eye for the rest of my life. That's why I left for Oslo and got a job that involved travel. This kept me away from her long enough for me to build some kind of self-respect. But then all this happened …"

He stopped again. Everything was quiet for a long moment.

Mette felt uneasy where she sat. She felt her stomach turn, as if she were about to be sick. But it was not revulsion for the man who was talking.

Suddenly she saw this man in a totally new light. The description he gave of his mother was not that far off the description of her own behavior toward him, she could see that clearly now. It was he who was tormented … or was he? Conflicting feelings raced through her.

When Tore started speaking again, his voice was much calmer, but it still had hints of pain. "This is going to haunt me throughout my life. I don't know how to handle it."

At the same time, she heard a scraping sound, as though one of them got up from his chair. Mette took the opportunity to slip, quick as lightning, out the door. She had heard enough … Yes, she had heard more than enough.

With hurried steps, she headed for the cow barn. Now she had to be alone for a while, and the cow barn was the most obvious place to take refuge. She went straight to Caesar, who lay in his stall chewing his cud. He got up the moment she entered.

Caesar, no longer the little calf she had played with up at the seter last summer, still got excited every time she came in, either to give him a treat or just to pet him. He was the one that Mette could confide in, both in happy and sad moments. She had never had a more faithful friend.

"You have never revealed any of our secrets," she said with a wistful smile, putting both arms around the bull's thick neck. Tears running, she began pouring it all out to the calm, trusting animal. She told him everything … how she had experienced her conflict with Tore, and now the last, dramatic turn when everything was upside down. She was not the only one who had suffered. She apparently had caused him to suffer, too.

"It's one thing for you to suffer," she spoke into Caesar's ear while scratching his neck. "Another is to cause others to suffer. And that is actually much worse."

She spoke the last words in profound recognition. Her feelings still raced in her, but the bitterness and the feeling of inferiority that was responsible for her attitude toward Tore was about to be replaced by something else: a feeling of compassion and a wish to make things right and heal some of the wounds that had been sustained.

How important it was to understand the reason for other people's actions! How much harm would have been avoided if she had known about this before. And how he must have suffered. Maybe he had hurt more than she did. To have a mother like that, who didn't show her son some more understanding and respect!

No, she shouldn't blame it on Tore's mother. She didn't know his mother, at all. Maybe there was some hidden tragedy there, too.

Mette stroked Caesar several more times before going out into the fresh air. She walked across the field toward the woods with its towering, leafy canopy. The light breeze that played in her hair and tugged at her clothes would air out most of the smell from the cow barn, which she picked up when she was in there with Caesar.

Her thoughts continued to churn around in her head as she walked along. The peace and quiet there among the trees gave her the calm she needed to think everything through properly. When she later headed for the house, she determined to put this matter aside. She would do everything in her power to mend her strained relationship with Tore.

When she returned to the yard, she noticed that Tore's car was gone. She found a note on the kitchen counter. In it Morten explained that they both had left for the seter. He had seen the groceries and her car outside, so he understood that she was in the neighborhood.

55 • Showdown

Mette and Morten had a long talk up at the seter that evening. Tore had headed for the mountains with his fishing pole and wouldn't be back until late. Mette was glad to have the opportunity to talk to Morten alone first. She told him everything— that she had heard what they were talking about, and that she had taken a walk in the woods to think the matter over, and what kind of resolution she had made.

"But this won't be easy for me," she ended. "I'm going to carry those feelings for quite a while yet, so you'll have to help me."

Morten put his arms around her and held her close. "I'll do as much as I can," he promised, obviously relieved the situation seemed to have come to a positive conclusion.

Tore stayed at the seter for several days. He slept in the loft in the seter house. At first, Mette felt a certain tenseness when he was around. But after a while, things got easier. She tried to be friendly and respectful to Tore. Soon she noticed that his attitude toward her changed, too. The tension began to disappear.

One day Morten had to go to town for a meeting to settle Uncle Torkel's estate. Siri was in town from Trondheim, and they counted on spending the entire day over at Lia. Morten left right after breakfast. Mette and Tore were alone together at the breakfast table. They began talking about their strained relationship. Morten had mentioned to Tore that Mette had overheard them talking down at the farm. She realized Tore felt relieved that she knew about his problems.

They sat there for some time, talking. Both explained their feelings and what they found particularly difficult to deal with. And they both realized they had lots for which to ask each other's forgiveness. Soon Mette had to agree the description Morten gave of Tore was on the mark. He was an extraordinarily nice man. And she had worked with him for so long without realizing it. She had been preoccupied with her own hurt feelings and not recognized his positive qualities.

After this, the mood between them changed. Mette felt much lighter and freer. How great it was to clear this up. Tore seemed much more relaxed as well.

There were no longer many tourists at the seter. September was not far away, and most of the visitors they had were school groups or people from camp school. Tore helped her with some of the chores before the next group of youths arrived. Their working together was now much more positive. They talked in a relaxed and natural way.

"I'll say there's a lot of cloudberries in the mountains this year," said Tore suddenly. "I think I'll take a trip to the bogs this afternoon. It would be nice to bring some dessert back to town."

"Oh, yes, please do," said Mette. "I wish I could go with you, but unfortunately I don't have time today. And besides, Morten has promised to come with me on a berry-picking mission as soon as he has some free time. Hope it's soon."

When Tore left, Mette was alone at the seter. She stood watching him as he climbed the hill. Her thoughts centered on the young men who had camped up there and had stolen the box. She wondered if they had been able to open it, and if so, what they found. She would give anything to know. She was still upset about it. But she had no idea what to do to get it back. No, there was nothing else to do but accept that the box was gone forever, and with it, its secret contents. Mette sighed and returned to the dairy room where the cream was waiting to be churned.

When Morten returned later in the evening, Mette was curious to hear how things had turned out at Lia. He could tell her that Uncle Torkel's belongings were all distributed among them and they had decided to sell the farm. They had been in touch with Bob in America, so everything was done in cooperation with him.

"How are they doing?" asked Mette excitedly. "Is Allan still in the hospital?"

"He seems to be doing much better," answered Morten. "They were able to deal with the infection right away, so it looks like he is making progress every day. The fact they no longer have to worry about money has been of invaluable help to them."

"Oh … that's good to hear," said Mette. "I've been thinking about Allan a lot. Several times I have wanted to call them, but it somehow never happened. I'm so glad the money Uncle Torkel left will help them."

"Yes." Morten nodded in agreement. "If there hadn't been that much money to share, then I almost think I might have declined my share and given it to them."

Mette nodded her approval.

"They all send their greetings and told me to let you know that next year we have to find room for them all here at the seter. They want to come and visit us."

"How fantastic!" Mette was overjoyed. "I'm looking forward to it already."

During supper, Aunt Anna returned. She had been down in town for a few days. But since they expected a school group the next day, she had to be there at the seter. She was just as excited as Mette at the prospect of having visitors from America next summer.

56 • New demonstrations

"Look, Plum, here is a treat for you." Mette went into the old cow's stall and scratched her behind her ears while holding apple pieces up to her muzzle. The cow snapped up the goodies and chewed contentedly. Apples were something Plum liked especially well. Mette had cut the apple into pieces so it would be easier for the cow to chew. She knew apples might get caught in the cow's throat if she ate it whole, and that could be serious.

It was lovely to spend time with the animals. Even if the trip to America had been exciting and eventful, it still felt good to be back in the daily grind again.

Star stretched her head toward her, so Mette had to find some apple pieces for her, too. For a long time she puttered around, caring for the animals, before she let them out to pasture. It was so good to feel the warm bodies of the cows and enjoy the trusting attention they gave her.

She now had a new creature there in the cow barn that took a lot of her attention. A little calf came trudging along with the other animals when she went to the cow barn to do the milking in the morning. The heifer that was expected to calve soon had simply taken care of the job during the night. The nice little female calf quickly found her place among the other animals. Mette had to give her a few extra pats before she sent her out to pasture with her mother and the other cows.

It was nice and warm outside, even though fall was in the air. Up on the hillside, the leaves on the small bushy trees had started turning golden, and the heather blushed in all its glory across the uplands.

"If we only could go cloudberry picking soon," thought Mette as she stood in the door to the cow barn and watched the cows until they disappeared beyond her view. Morten had promised to show her a couple of places where they always found lots of berries. "But," she said to herself, "there is no use thinking about cloudberry picking today, for we're going to have a group of visitors."

Aunt Anna was already in full swing with preparations. She had carried her spinning wheel out to the meadow, and several baskets of wool sat on a table. A group from the high school in Kristiansand would be here to learn about carding and spinning wool. Aunt Anna could also offer a lot of stories and traditions from her omniscient memory.

Mette walked over to the table and looked at the wool in the baskets. There was wool in just about every color. She remembered well last summer when Aunt Anna demonstrated plant dyeing to a home craft organization. At that time, everybody had been active, searching for plants and helping with the dyeing process in other ways.

There wouldn't be any plant dyeing today, but she had no doubt that Aunt Anna would explain some of the processes.

"What is this?" asked Mette curiously as Aunt Anna came over to her and placed a basket of something looking like dry, thin reed or grass on the table.

"This is flax," said the older woman happily. "This is what the linen fibers look like before they are spun into threads and woven."

"Are you going to spin this?" Mette looked at her in anticipation.

A big smile spread across her round face. "Yes, I thought I would try. I haven't spun much flax before, but at least I know how it was done in the old days. So we'll see how it goes," she said. "But right now I have to go inside and check the frying

197

pan." She turned around quickly and disappeared back into the seter house.

They would be serving food to their guests as well. Aunt Anna had brought a lot of lefse from her supply down in town. Now she was laboring over the pancakes. Lefse and pancakes were on the menu. Mette had never tasted that combination, so she looked forward to the meal. Soon, she caught the delicious smell of freshly made pancakes. "Maybe I can steal a piece for a late breakfast," Mette said to herself as she entered the seter house.

Aunt Anna stood, cheeks blushing, over the hot frying pan. Sweat trickled down her brow. The temperature in the kitchen was already far above midsummer heat. A big glass containing a pale, white liquid stood next to her. She grabbed the glass and drank thirstily. Mette frowned and walked over to her. "Are you drinking dishwater?" she asked with a little laugh.

Aunt Anna laughed so hard she almost lost the glass on the floor. "No, this is no dishwater, I tell you. This is *blånna*. It is buttermilk mixed with water," she explained in answer to Mette's questioning look. "We used to drink this in the summer when I was a child. It tastes great if you're really thirsty," she said, downing what was left in the glass.

Mette wouldn't say the drink looked particularly tempting, but she didn't joke any more about it. Aunt Anna continued her frying, and before the first cars arrived, she had a big stack of thin pancakes next to her on the counter.

There was hectic activity out in the meadow as more than 20 young people poured out of the cars. Laughter and joking floated in the air. Aunt Anna was overjoyed. The youths flocked around her to observe and listen. She started by explaining how wool was prepared on the farms in the old days. Washing and dyeing were thoroughly explained. Then she took out her carding combs and placed wool on them. With practiced hands, she slid them across each other until she had a nice, plump little sausage.

Mette had seen her do this several times, so this wasn't new to her. But the students followed everything she did with great interest. Soon a whole stack of fluffy, woolen sausages piled up in the basket next to her.

Then Aunt Anna sat down at the spinning wheel. After she had the wheel turning at the right speed, she placed the sausages on a thread she had already spun. It whirled around at great speed, quickly catching up the fluffy wool. Aunt Anna pulled on the woolen sausage as it spun around, fastened to the thread. Soon the entire sausage was turned into a fine woolen thread. To this she fastened another woolen sausage. She kept the speed of the wheel even by stepping on a pedal below.

Several students wanted to try. Aunt Anna explained and assisted them, but they soon realized this work required a good deal of experience. The thread tended to tangle, and it wasn't easy to make it nice and even. Either it had big lumps or it pulled it apart. Even if they couldn't do it right, they still thought it was fun to try.

Afterward, Aunt Anna explained to them about the flax. She took the basket containing the fibers and held them up so everybody could see. "This is processed flax that has not been spun," she started. "I'll try to spin some of this, but first I want to explain how flax was grown and prepared in the old days."

Mette stood with the teen-agers and listened with great interest. She hadn't heard any of this before. Aunt Anna had so much to teach others that Mette realized she had to spend a lot of time with her in order to learn about everything.

"When I was young, I stayed for a time with my aunt in Marnardal in southern Norway," continued the excited teacher. "She grew flax, so there I learned a little about the process. I still remember her flax field. When it bloomed in the summer, it looked like a wonderful, blue carpet waving in the wind. I have never seen anything so beautiful." She motioned with her hands toward the meadow, staring absentmindedly into space. It was as if she could see it all. The students listened in silence, her vivid description captivating them.

"She grew blue flax," she said. "I know there is white flax as well, but it seems like the blue was the most common here."

Again she turned her attention to her listeners. "The field has to be harvested before the seed husks are formed. I can still remember how we labored with that."

She chuckled. The woman and her audience were entirely engrossed in her story. "Flax cannot be harvested in the same way we harvest grain. It has to be pulled up by the roots. The fibers must not be cut. We pulled up the plants in the field and then we tied them together in small bundles. After all the flax was bundled in that way, we started the next process, which was called 'retting.'

"The entire flax plant was put in a stream. It stayed there for several days. It had to go through some kind of decaying process. I still remember how my aunt would go down to the stream many times to see if the flax had finished retting. She would break a stem, checking to see how far the process had come. She knew exactly what it was supposed to look like when it was ready.

"After the retting, it was sent to a factory that did the rest for her. I remember when we got the flax back. Then it was already spun. But she also got some flax that had not been spun, and that she worked with herself. It looked like this." Again she held up the basket in front of her.

"At the factory," she continued," it went through a cleaning process. The flax stems were broken. But it was done very carefully, for only the outer layer was to be broken. The inner core had to be whole, for that is the linen fiber. In older times, this, too, was done at the farm. The flax was placed across poles, and then they beat on the flax stems with another pole. That's the way they broke down the outer layer of the stems.

"After that, the outer layer had to be rinsed away. Then it was pulled through some kind of comb. It was called 'heckling.' First it was pulled through a coarse comb and then through finer and finer combs until only the inner core was left. This was the linen that was spun into threads.

"My aunt made several beautiful damask table linens from the flax she grew herself. I have one of them here." She lifted a light gray tablecloth out of a basket. It was neatly folded. Mette gasped as she saw the gorgeous piece. Aunt Anna spread out the tablecloth so her audience could get a closer look. Admiringly, they stood for some time, studying the fine piece of home craft.

"Was this really homemade?" Mette asked Aunt Anna.

The round, cheerful woman nodded excitely. "This is as homemade as it gets," she said. "And I helped harvest the stems this tablecloth is made from." She laughed even more at the surprised looks of her audience.

Aunt Anna sat down at the spinning wheel again. She put a round, cylinder-shaped wooden implement at one end. "This is called the 'distaff,'" she explained. She wound the flax she had in her basket around the distaff. Then she began pulling out the fibers. She attached them to a thread on the spinning wheel while the wheel spun round and around. Soon a fine, thin linen thread started forming. Her experienced fingers stroked back and forth along the thread, pulling out the just the right amount of flax from the distaff.

Her audience crowded around the spinning wheel. Everybody wanted to watch. Mette was among the most interested. "I'd never be able to do that," she concluded quickly. It looked much more difficult than spinning wool.

Before long, Aunt Anna stopped the spinning wheel again. "Now you need something to eat," she said with determination, standing up quickly.

Again there was a bustle of activity. Mette brought out the food, while Aunt Anna stayed by the spinning wheel for a while, answering the students' questions. Several of them took notes on what she said.

The food was a novel experience for the students as well. They were used to pancakes, and several of them had had lefse. But no one had run into the combination of the two before. In advance, Aunt Anna had spread her lovely, home-churned butter on all the lefses. Then she folded the big lefses down the middle, cutting each of them into four triangles. Each triangle was then folded around a pancake that was also folded in half. And then it was time to dig in.

Everybody seemed to like the food. Mette enjoyed the delicious meal and decided there and then that this she would soon try again.

It didn't take long before both the pancake platter and the lefse platter were empty. Aunt Anna was worried as to whether everyone got enough to eat. But they all assured her they were more than full.

57 • See, the fields are ripe for harvest

Again it was peaceful and quiet at the seter. Mette sat in the meadow, looking around. But it was not the beautiful fall colors or the high, clear sky that she saw. Neither was it the shimmering lake that reflected the last rays of the sun.

She was gazing at another field, a waving field of flowers. Actually, it was not a field of flowers; it was a field of flax waving in the summer heat. And that flax field was not in the meadow. It was in a totally different land. She sat completely engrossed in her own thoughts, and those thoughts had wings.

As Aunt Anna had talked about the beautiful flax field, she had envisioned it in a flash. And now, after all the guests had left and she could just sit there and relax, her vision reappeared. At the same time, a Bible verse resonated inside her: "Open your eyes and look at the fields! They are ripe for harvest."

In the Bible—the 4th chapter of John—Jesus talked about a field of grain. She had always assumed it was a field of grain, but maybe it wasn't. Maybe Jesus had a flax field in mind. Fields of flax must have been a common sight for people in Biblical times, for clothes made of linen were commonplace then. Linen fabric felt cool and had great ability to absorb moisture. It was especially well suited for a sun-scorched place where people would sweat a lot.

At that moment, Aunt Anna came out in the meadow. "What are you sitting there pondering? I have never seen such a faraway look." She sat down in a chair on the other side of the garden table.

"Yes, I was really far away," Mette said, telling her what she had been thinking about. Aunt Anna listened attentively as Mette shared her thoughts.

"You may have something there. I never thought about it, but of course there could be something to it," she said. "You know, when the flax is in bloom, then you know it's going to be harvested soon."

Now Aunt Anna was engrossed in her own thoughts. But it didn't take long before her mouth started working again.

"The Bible verse you quoted is from the story about Jesus talking to a Samaritan woman. After that conversation, the woman ran back to town and told people what she had heard, and many of them started believing in God. It was what we call a revival. But before this happened, Jesus talked with his disciples. He prepared them for a time of reaping—that is, a time for reaping believers for Heaven. The field and the crops were thus a metaphor for people."

Again she stopped before continuing. "That thing about the flax, that's really a good comparison. The entire preparation process can be an allegory about what happens to people when they are saved and then continue on toward eternity."

Mette looked at her in surprise. "How do you mean?"

Aunt Anna smiled, but she had a faraway look. "Think about what I said about the stalks that must not be cut, but had to be pulled up by the roots. It is the same with a person who becomes a Christian. There has to be a fundamental change. You can't just make some changes to the exterior ... on the surface. No, you have to pull it out by the roots; the change has to go all the way to the bottom of your heart."

"Oh, yes." Mette grew eager. "And this is not something people, or the stems, can do on their own. Reapers are needed to bring in the harvest. That is something God and His angels will have to do."

"Yes, and then comes the retting. The Lord of the Harvest has to take care of that, too." The stout woman seemed to follow the story they were weaving between them with her entire body.

"If the stems immersed in the stream could talk, what do you think they would say? Maybe they had complained somewhat like this: 'What's this all about? Here I'm tossed aside in a stream, left to rot. Where is the Lord of the Harvest, and where are the reapers who spoke so loudly about making a beautiful product? Did they forget about me? Is this all I'm worth? Am I useless? Is this all? It's so dark and miserable here.'"

Mette laughed at Aunt Anna's stream of consciousness. "I know where you're going. I've heard that lecture a couple of times myself. People who have received Jesus, even those who have lived with Him for a long time, sometimes experience doubt. Everything seems dark and sad. God seems far away. They don't see anything in their life that is pleasing to God. They may experience this so strongly that they doubt whether they are children of God any more."

"Yes," said Aunt Anna. "At some point, most Christians probably experience the deep valleys and dark shadows of doubt. Often, those feelings may come right after they have decided to follow Jesus. But that particular state is a move from God. Indeed, it is the devil who shakes you up and makes you uneasy, but God allows it to happen. We have to be 'processed' and readied for the Heavenly wedding. It is a learning process."

"Retting ..." Mette looked thoughtfully at Aunt Anna. "It has to be quite humiliating..."

She nodded. "Humiliation is necessary if we're going to be refined and suitable. It is humiliating to place yourself in the hands of another, even if the other one is God."

"God has His work cut out for Him with us," Mette sighed. "Our entire life is really a refining process. I suppose that's what we call 'sanctification.'"

"Or heckling," inserted Aunt Anna with a smile. "We need to be constantly cleansed of dust and dirt that is heaped on us in life. And the cleansing will gradually go deeper and deeper. Thoughts and attitudes will have to be changed. Sins we commit will have to be dealt with, recognized and confessed. Arrogance, pride and jealousy must be faced. Our trials are designed to help us gain knowledge and experience. Through this we are strengthened in our faith and confidence in God."

"It's strange that God works in this way," said Mette.

Aunt Anna shook her head in agreement. But then she perked up. "The Bible actually says something about that in the Gospel of John, 15th chapter. It says in Verse 2: 'He cuts off every branch in me that bears no fruit, while every branch that does bear fruit he prunes so that it will yield even more fruitful.' So it's the branch that bears fruit that has to be pruned. And this is done in order for it to bear even more.

"God has a plan for each and every person. And it is a plan He follows all the time. His plan is to use some of us as reapers, and for that we need certain abilities. But the overriding goal for all of us is that we are being prepared for the Heavenly wedding. Then one day we will see the finished 'weaving' in all its glory." Again she looked dreamily into thin air.

Mette listened silently, carried away by her thoughts.

"Every linen thread woven into it," continued Aunt Anna, "is of the very best quality. Only the finest cores are included. No husks or dirt are a part of the weaving. And the linen fibers, that's us ... prepared and cleansed by the Master Himself, by His blood!"

"I wonder why God would go through so much trouble for us?" asked Mette.

"It is done with the deepest love," said Aunt Anna. "Even if we experience dark moments, He will lead us out into the light again. He is with us all the time. No one has ever experienced being left in the dark by God. Even if we don't see Him, He sees us."

She stopped for a while. Her entire face was radiant, Mette observed. The older woman seemed to reflect strength and harmony.

"The most fantastic part of being a child of God," she continued, "is that we can keep our peace with Him with a good conscience."

"That's really true," said Mette. She didn't elaborate, but she thought back to the time when she planned to go mountain hiking with Arvid. Then she had experienced that her peace was gone. She was about to do something God didn't want to go along with, and then the good peace disappeared.

"I have to keep that peace," Mette said, and then she stood up.

The sun had set and it was getting cool. Aunt Anna got up, too. Neither of them had registered that evening was about to fall on the seter area. Some sharp hoots from an owl sounded among the trees on the other side of the field. There, Nature lived its own life with many a fight to the death.

But the outcome of the fight between evil and good forces that raged in people was determined already. Jesus had won, so if we leave our life in His hands, we will be allowed to hide in Him. And then we will experience the same peace and victory that He won.

58 • Cloudberry picking

"I think we'll climb this slope." Morten pointed toward a crevice directly in front of them. It looked steep, but still seemed easy to climb. "It's pretty steep at first, but there are some great bogs up here if we only get to the top."

Morten went first, carrying his backpack, while Mette followed close behind with the berry bucket. Morten had a bucket, too, hanging from a strap on his pack.

Finally they had been able to get away on their long-awaited *multetur*—cloudberry-picking trip. The sky had been gray in the morning, but it hadn't rained, so they decided to take off as planned.

The climb was hard for a while, but their efforts were rewarded with a beautiful view when they finally reached the top. They stood on a hill with the majestic grandeur of the mountains in front of them. Low clouds sailed across the sky, allowing columns of sun rays down through the cloud cover like mighty spotlights illuminating the blushing heather. A light haze hung in the air and created an especially striking light effect in the magnificent panorama. The bogs stretched out between hills and outcroppings, while streams meandered across it all from mountain lake to mountain lake.

Mette gasped at the sight. Morten, too, stood for a while in quiet admiration. The unusual light, the silence and the vibrant colors gave them a feeling of awe. Up along a valley they could see a herd of grazing sheep.

Morten set off again. "I think we'll check out those bogs over there first," he said, pointing north toward an area where the vegetation looked particularly lush.

"Yes, let's go there," said Mette excitedly.

As they continued on, they saw more and more cloudberry plants. Morten obviously knew where to find berries. Soon they were in an area where the berries grew densely. "We're the first ones to pick here," said Mette, eagerly plucking the golden, delicious berries. Every so often one ended up in her mouth.

"Usually we're allowed to keep this area to ourselves," said Morten. "Few people are able to climb the steep crevice."

For a long while they busied themselves picking berries on the bog. Mette jumped from tuft to tuft, sweeping up all the bright yellow berries she could find. She was overjoyed. The sun gradually peeped out from behind the clouds. They could not have chosen a more beautiful day for a berry-picking expedition.

Suddenly she stopped. "What's this?" She saw something wooly under a bush. Morten came over quickly. He pulled aside some twigs and leaves, and a dead sheep appeared. His face turned dark. "This is the work of a predator." The sheep was obviously mauled to death, and some of it had been devoured. "This must have happened recently." He checked the blood that had spilled out on the ground. "It was probably killed last night."

Mette shuddered. "What kind of animal could have done this?"

"I'm not sure." He checked the sheep one more time. Then he stood up, looking searchingly into the mountains. "I just hope there aren't more cadavers like this around."

They continued across the bogs. Morten kept looking for more signs of carnage in the herds of sheep.

"How strange," said Mette pensively. "It looked like the sheep was hidden there. It was covered with twigs and dirt. You don't think people might have done this?"

Morten shook his head. "No, it is obviously the work of some predator. Some animals do that. They cover up their prey, then come back and feed some more later."

They didn't find any more sheep cadavers, but they found tons of cloudberries. As time went by, their buckets filled up.

"Let's climb up on top of that precipice," suggested Morten, pointing. "Then we can sit down to eat. We'll have a great view of the mountains."

They put down their full berry buckets before they started climbing. They had to go back down the same way.

Again they were rewarded with a view that almost took their breath away. Mette walked closer to the cliff on the opposite side. It fell steeply away down toward a lake and several bogs. Morten followed close behind her.

Suddenly they jumped. A light-colored shadow came up the cliff in front of them and disappeared, quick as lightning, down the opposite side of where they came from.

"What was that?" Puzzled, Mette looked in the direction where the shadow had disappeared. Morten ran over to the slope, but it had already vanished between outcroppings and underbrush.

"At least it wasn't a fox," he answered. "It wouldn't dare rush down these steep slopes at such speed, and there is no way it could be a hare."

For a while they both studied the ground where the animal rushed by them.

"Look!" Morten called out. He pointed to a muddy spot where previously there had been a puddle. Morten shook his head as he examined the tracks. "This is no dog. Dog tracks have a distinct claw mark here in front." He pointed down in the mud. "There is no claw mark here. These look like cat tracks, only bigger."

He straightened up and looked out over the mountains with searching eyes. "There is no doubt as to what animal this is. And it explains, too, what has been in the sheep herd. This has to be a lynx."

Mette gasped. "Lynx? But aren't they dangerous?" She gaped at Morten with concern in her eyes.

Morten smiled. "It is no threat to us. You saw it was much more afraid of us than we were of it. We probably happened upon it as it was basking in the sun over there on the slope. Lynx like to stay high up on a slope, where they have a good view during the day. And they usually hide their prey, too, when they want to save some of their food for later," he said as his eyes darkened. "No, there is no doubt what the culprit is here."

While they ate their lunch, they sat talking about what they had seen. Morten worried about the sheep grazing in the area. "It won't be long before they are brought down from the mountains now," he said. "I just hope this lynx won't be able to kill too many of them before that time."

They took their time eating. No chores awaited them at the seter before milking time, so they could relax. Mette enjoyed the peace and quiet to the utmost.

They stretched out on the bedrock and allowed themselves a short nap before they started their descent.

When they got down, they quickly found their buckets, nearly full of delicious cloudberries. Fortunately, Morten had brought his backpack. In it they had two plastic bags, so they could empty their buckets into the bags and pick more berries before they started back home again.

"I think we'll take a route to the west," Morten said after a while. "Then we'll come

204

down in a different area and end up on the hill to the west of the seter."

It was a long hike, but Mette enjoyed the great trip all the way. Along the way, they stopped at a little mountain lake to catch their breath. Mette sat down on a rock by the water. "Look here," she said, pointing at something between the rocks by the bank. "There were people here not too long ago."

Morten came over to her. "Yes, someone had a fire here. And over there, they must have pitched a tent," he said, gesturing toward the bank. They saw clear signs of people, for the grass was pushed down and trampled flat. Here and there, garbage littered the ground.

"People should pick up their trash," said Mette, irritated. She began to collect the litter that lay on the ground.

Suddenly she stopped, peering down into the heather. "Look!"

Morten came running when he heard her cry, for it came out almost like a scream. "What is it?"

Mette didn't answer, but lifted something from the ground. It was an old, rusty tin box.

"The box!" Morten stood gaping. Then he checked it more closely. "It has not been opened," he stated.

"No," said Mette, sighing in relief. "But they worked hard on it." Scrape marks in the rust, along with some dents, indicated someone had hit it with something hard.

"They probably weren't able to open it, so they just threw it away here," said Morten. "But now it's going to be opened!"

Mette looked quickly at him. There was a tiny smile on his lips, but the remark was made with a resolve that told her this wasn't going to cause him any more trouble.

They didn't rest for long at the lake. Both were preoccupied with the box. Now they had to find out what was hiding inside.

59 • Great expectations

Even though Mette was tired after the long mountain hike, she finished the barn chores in record time. The animals didn't get any extra attention that day, and the milk was just poured into a container she placed in the pool for cooling. All her thoughts centered on the old box. Morten had placed it on the garden table. He had brought out some tools, and while she milked, he worked on the box. Mette was so curious that she wasn't able to concentrate properly on her work. Fortunately, this was a routine job for her now, so she could do most of it without thinking about what she was doing.

There were no tourists at the seter at the moment. This late in the year, their visitors were mostly students. So Mette was alone in the barn doing her evening chores.

Soon the cows were outside grazing again. The little calf jumped and kicked around her. Pia came over, too, hoping to get some attention, but Mette just stroked her a couple of times. Pia wasn't allowed to suck on her fingers tonight.

As soon as she was finished with her chores, Mette ran over to Morten to see how the "break-in" was going.

"Do you think you'll be able to get it open?" she asked excitedly, sitting down next to him on a chair. "I think I'll manage," he answered, "but it takes time. This is difficult material to get through." He was working on it with a hacksaw. She could see that he took great care not to damage the contents. The saw blade ate through the sturdy metal, fractions of an inch at a time.

The sun was sinking behind the mountains to the west, but neither of them paid any attention to the beautiful, reddening sky. Nor did they notice the fresh breeze that kicked up and grew stronger and stronger. Their full attention was on the little saw that steadily fought its way through the metal. Mette craned her neck to see how far the work had progressed. Morten had begun sawing right below the edge of the lid. Systematically, he worked his way around the sides of the box. Now and then he had to take a break to give his fingers some rest.

"Now just this corner is left," he said in a while, "and then maybe we can bend the lid open." Mette was so excited she was almost trembling. What might it be that had been hidden in the cave? In Aunt Anna's opinion, it had to have been there for a very long time. It didn't seem logical that it had just been tossed aside; it was far too well hidden for that.

"There," said Morten, putting down his tools. "Now we have to try to bend the lid open." He took a firm hold of the box and tugged at the lid, but it didn't budge. "I have to find some stronger remedy," he said, walking over to the car. After rummaging around, he brought several tools back to the table. He placed a long, sturdy screwdriver in the narrow slit, and soon the gap started to widen. Soon it was large enough for a slim hand to get through. It didn't take Mette long to try. Carefully, she squeezed her hand into the box. She fumbled around inside until she got hold of something at the bottom. Gently, she pulled it out. She sat there frowning, looking at an old piece of fabric.

"Did we just about risk life and limb for this old rag?" she asked, looking at Morten's red fingers. "And the break-in. I wish those boys who camped in the mountains knew for what they risked their freedom and a clean record." Disappointed, she threw the piece of fabric on the table.

Morten started laughing. "It's incredible how inquisitive people are. How much have we risked to find out what this box contained?"

Mette had to laugh, too. She picked up the fabric, scrutinizing it.

Slowly her smile vanished, and an expression of wonderment appeared on her face. "Haven't I seen this before?"

It was a rough, woolen piece of material. At one end, some long threads hung from it, tied on as a fringe.

Morten didn't look at Mette; he was consumed by the box. He had turned it upside down. Then a yellow, brittle piece of paper fell out. Before he had time to show it to Mette, she was already in the seter house. A moment later, she was back with a stack of photos.

"Look," said Morten when she returned. "Look what I found."

Mette stared at the piece of paper. "Does it say anything?"

"Yes, I think so, but it is very faint."

Mette stretched her head over his shoulder while he studied the few letters that were written there. *"Farvel mit baan,"* he spelled out.

"What would that mean?" asked Mette, puzzled.

Morten shook his head. "I have no idea. But what did you bring?" He became aware that she held something in her hand.

"Look," said Mette eagerly, placing the entire stack on the table. It was the pictures they took during their trip to America. Quickly, she thumbed through until she found the one she was looking for.

"Look here." She held up a picture of Frank. He sat with the old shawl in front of him. "This little piece of fabric looks very similar to the old shawl we saw in America."

Now Morten got excited, too. He took the picture and placed it on the table. Then he put the rough little piece of fabric right next to it.

"Do you see?" Excitement lit his eyes. "This little piece of fabric matches exactly the part of the shawl that was torn off. There is no doubt about it. This is the missing piece."

For a moment they sat there gaping. "What might this mean?" Mette asked.

Morten looked at the little piece of paper again. "This seems to be a farewell, for the first word is clearly 'goodbye.' But the last word seems more unusual."

Suddenly he grabbed his cell phone and dialed a number. Mette could hear that he was talking to Aunt Anna. A bit later he put down the phone. "Aunt Anna told me that the last word here is *'baan,'* which means 'child.' That's the way they said it here in the old days."

"Farvel mitt barn!" (Goodbye, my child). Mette tried out the words.

Suddenly Morten slapped the table. "That's it. Yes, that's the way it has to be. Frank told us about Sjur, who came from a farm in this area. His mother came to that farm when she was a baby. Do you think Silja was Sjur's grandmother?"

They both sat there silently again. But then Mette burst out, "Of course! It had to be that way. The child was taken from her after birth. It was probably the child's father who arranged it. Maybe there was a fight between them when this happened, so this piece of the shawl was ripped off in the fray. And then the poor mother 'buried' in this box what she had left of her little one before she jumped into the lake."

Deep reverence came over them both as they contemplated this. The legend had suddenly come back to life. Might it be possible it was not just a legend?

Yes, there was no doubt about it. Mette remembered what the old gravedigger had talked about the Sunday they held the church service over by the lake. What he said about Silja's coffin was also something that confirmed such a notion.

Morten was the one to break the silence first. Absentmindedly, he stroked the dark woolen fabric with his hand. "What a tragedy …" It was as if the seriousness of the situation suddenly hit him. That poor girl, who didn't see another way out but to end her life. Maybe something traumatic had happened before she took the drastic step.

Mette looked at the piece of fabric again. It would take a lot of strength to tear it off. "How different things must have been in those days," she said, sighing heavily. Morten nodded.

The sun was now behind the mountains as dusk fell. The cool breeze in the meadow penetrated their clothes and chilled their skin. This evening had made an indelible impression on them, for now they knew exactly what the rocky slope over there had been hiding for so many years.

As if on command, they both got up and walked to the snug, cozy seter house. •

RECIPES

• Dravle •

This is Dravle like they make it in Sirdal in Vest-Agder Fylke. In the old days, Dravle was a staple on festive occasions, whether a wedding or a funeral. Today, this is still party food, and that explains the big recipe.

1 quart first milk
6 quarts whole milk
10-11 eggs

1 quart sour milk (cultured milk)
3 to 3½ cups sugar

In a large pot, bring the whole milk to a boil. In a bowl, mix the whole milk, the cultured milk, eggs and sugar. Pour the mixture into the boiling milk. Stir to mix, then do not stir the pot again. Simmer at low heat for 7 hours. Keep the lid on, although it may be pulled just a little aside to vent. When the Dravle is done, it should be left in the pot until it has cooled completely, for that makes it easier to handle. The cheese curd is now a thick and firm "cake" on top of the whey. Pour the whey off carefully. Then invert the cheese "cake" onto a platter and it is ready to be served. For lefse, it is cut into ¼-inch slices. Usually, the lefse is then spread with butter and sprinkled with sugar and then folded and cut into smaller pieces. Dravle can also be served on lefse and eaten in the same way as the Eggost.

• Pancakes •

This, too, was food for special occasions in older times. Back then, they were often served with lefse. A piece of lefse and a piece of pancake were buttered and folded in a special way. I haven't heard that this recipe was widely used. But in any case, it was used in Mandalen, Vest-Agder. These days, pancakes are mostly a dish for children. They are eaten with butter and sugar or butter and jam, preferably blueberry jam. Pancakes served with pea soup is a good everyday dinner.

1 quart milk (may be mixed with
  some cream)
3 eggs
½ teaspoon salt

¼ to ½ cup sugar
1 teaspoon vanilla sugar
4 tablespoons melted butter
Wheat flour

Mix everything well in a bowl. Add enough wheat flour to make a relatively thin mixture. Allow the mixture to rest before frying. Heat a round frying pan, and add some butter so the pancakes don't stick. Pour about 3 ounces of the mixture into the pan. Rotate the pan so that the mixture covers the pan completely. The pancake is supposed to be thin, but still thick enough not to break apart when turned over. Fry until light brown on both sides. As the pancakes are done, stack them on a platter or fold them into quarters and place them on a platter. Serve warm or cold.

• *Eggost (Søtost)* •

There are several recipes for Eggost. This recipe is from my mother-in-law, who came from Hægebostad in Vest-Agder Fylke. My father-in-law, who is from Eiken in the northern part of Hægebostad, also had this type of Eggost in his childhood home. But there they call it Søtost (Sweet Cheese). That's because they also use something called Saltost (Salt Cheese) or Dravlost. It is the same cheese, but with a little salt instead of sugar. The salt is added to the cheese curd after it has been removed from the whey.

1 quart milk (maybe a little more)	½ quart sour milk (cultured milk)
¾ cup sugar	4 eggs

Bring the milk to a boil. In a bowl, mix sour milk, eggs and sugar. Pour the mixture into the simmering milk. Stir carefully a couple of times with a spoon. Allow it to simmer for about 15-20 minutes, until the cheese curd has formed and the whey is almost clear around and under it. Do not stir the cheese curd. Remove the cheese carefully with a slotted spoon and put it on a platter. Allow the liquid to run off. More liquid will run off as it rests on the platter. Pour it off or soak it up with a paper towel. When the cheese has cooled, sprinkle the Eggost with cinnamon and serve. Eggost is used on lefse, potato lefse or bread (preferably white bread).

• *Gome* •

Gome recipes vary from district to district. This is the recipe I use, and that my mother and grandmother used before me.

4 quarts whole milk	Raisins (a fistful)
1 quart sour milk (cultured milk)	1 teaspoon salt
1 cup sugar	1 tablespoon flour (mixed with the
1 teaspoon cardamom	sour milk until no lumps are left)
Cinnamon sticks, small (a couple)	Flour for thickening

In a large pot, bring the whole milk to a boil. Then add the sour milk and flour mixture. Heat the sugar in a large pan until dissolved and cook until brown, stirring continuously so the sugar doesn't burn. Then add the boiling milk. Stir carefully until the sugar is completely dissolved, but make sure that the cheese curd, that soon will form, is not broken up. The browned sugar will give the gome a nice, brown color. Allow the gome to simmer for a couple of hours until the cheese curd has been reduced to the desired thickness. After about 1½ hours, stir in the raisins and the cinnamon. When the Gome has been reduced to the desired thickness, spoon up some of the whey (the runny part) and cool. Add salt and cardamom and flour to the cooled whey. If you think the Gome needs more sugar, add it to the whey mixture as well. Combine it with flour to make a thickening mixture. Stir in the whey-flour mixture and cook to desired consistency, like porridge. Remember that the Gome will thicken more as it simmers. Stir the Gome carefully, so the cheese curds are not broken up, but still well enough to avoid lumps in the thickener. Let simmer for about 10 minutes. Remove the Gome from the pot and place it in a bowl for cooling. It is served cold on lefse, flatbread, potato lefse or bread. It can also be frozen, but then it has to be brought to a boil again after defrosting and then cooled before serving.

• *Lefse and Flatbread* •

In the old days it was important to create variations in the food, using what was available around on the farms. Milk and eggs were the most common ingredients available to them. Regular bread wasn't used that much for every day. Instead, the Norwegians used flatbread. And then it was important to make something to accompany it. This was the basis for the food for festive occasions that emerged over time. And they knew how to make it taste good.

When baking lefse and flatbread, the cooking methods vary somewhat, depending on the exact tools used, so it is hard to give an exact recipe. But I would like to say something about the way potato lefse and potato flatbread is made here in Vest-Agder. First, potatoes are boiled and peeled. They have to be cooled a little before used in the dough. Sometimes they need to be completely cooled, depending on the potato variety and the time of the year. And even if the same variety of potatoes is used, there still may be a difference in the consistency of the potatoes from field to field. Also potatoes dry out when stored, and this can also influence the consitency of the dough. The potatoes are then ground in a meat grinder. (Do not use a food processor, as this will alter the consistency of the pototes.) Do not make a big batch at a time, for the lefse mixture may soften while it rests.

Knead in wheat flour until the dough is easy to knead or roll out. For flatbread, some whole wheat flour can be added to the wheat flour. It is a matter of expeience to know how much flour to add to the dough.Too little flour makes the dough sticky and hard to roll out. Too much flour makes the lefses hard, stiff and inflexible. More flour can be added to the flatbread dough, for the flatbread is supposed to be hard and crispy.

Tear off a piece from the dough (about the size of a tennis ball), shape it into a round, and flatten it into a disk. Roll the dough disk into a thin piece. After rolling it out to about half size, sprinkle flour on it and turn it over. With the other side up, continue rolling it out. Be careful that it doesn't stick to the baking surface, as it tears easily.

Sprinkle flour on the baking surface as needed. The baking surface may vary. We normally use a thick piece of cardboard that has been cut to the size of the griddle. Then it is easy to turn the dough without tearing it. You'll have to use a rolling pin with grooves. The shape of the grooves influences the result. Some use rolling pins with checkers on them.

Then the lefse has to be baked. It is rolled around a "fløy"—a long, flat stick. It is a matter of experience to easily transfer the lefse from the baking table to the griddle. The griddle is a large, round and flat baking implement. Now, only electrical griddles are used, but in the past they used a round, flat iron sheet that was placed over the wood stove, the wash boiler or in the fireplace. I remember my grandmother baking lefse in the fireplace on a sheet of iron.

When the lefse is placed on the griddle, it is moistened. We normally use a rag that is tied to the end of a stick. It is dipped into a bowl of water that has been lightly salted. Then the rag is brushed carefully over the lefse. The baking time is relatively short, for the lefses require high heat. When done on one side, it has to be turned over and baked on the other side.

Flatbread is made the same way, but it is not moistened on the griddle. Also, it is baked at lower heat, so it becomes nice and crispy. Lefses may also be baked at lower heat and without being moistened. Then they come out hard, and have to be soaked in water before serving. That kind of lefse may be stored over long periods of time in a dry place, the same way that flatbread is stored. But now that people have freezers, soft lefse is most common.

The lefse may be spread with butter and cut into appropriate serving pieces before they are frozen. Then they are ready to be served when they come out of the freezer. They thaw quickly. When preparing the lefse for freezing, butter is spread on the entire surface. Then the sides are folded in to make a rectangular piece. This is then folded again to make an approximately 6-inch by 16-inch rectangle. This piece is then cut into 2-by-3-inch wide servings.

We use lefse as an accompaniment to various dinner dishes. It is good served with cod or lutefisk. Then the lefses are cut into eight triangles, like cutting up a pizza, and stacked (or wrapped and placed in the freezer ready to be served). Then the triangles are buttered, and potatoes and fish placed on top. This is rolled up like a sausage and eaten as finger food.

When serving cured lamb, the lefse is used in the same way, especially for ribs. Then the lefse is not buttered, but dipped into the rib drippings. The meat can also be grilled in the fireplace or over an outdoor fire pit. Then the meat is wrapped in the lefse along with boiled potatoes. This is called *glosteik*. This used to be served for Christmas Eve dinner in the inland districts in Sørlandet in southern Norway.

• *Prim* •

Prim is made from whey. When making one of the dishes where the whey is poured off after the cheese had curdled, leftover whey was used for Prim. It was important to remove as much of the cheese curds as possible, otherwise the Prim would be lumpy. The whey was then reduced to Prim. It might take several hours, depending on the amount of whey. At the end of the cooking process, the Prim has to be stirred so it doesn't burn. Then it has a sticky, brown consistency. Sometimes it is thickened to make a bigger batch and to make it thicken faster. Prim is served as a spread for lefse, flatbread and bread.

• *Kalvedans (Råmelkspudding, Kyrost)* •

This is a cheese made from first milk (colostrum). First milk is the milk from a cow that has recently calved. Then its milk is thick, fat and yellow. Usually, the three first milkings after the calf has had its fill is used for kalvedans. The thickness of the milk varies from cow to cow. If the milk is too thick, it has to be mixed with some whole milk before cooking, so the cheese won't be too firm. Is it too thin, it may be difficult to have it thicken at all. This is something you have to experiment with.

For each quart of first milk, add about 3½ ounces of sugar. Pour the milk into a jar and place the jar in a pot filled with water. The water level has to go as far up on the outside of the jar as the milk inside. Cover the jar and bring it to a simmer. Make sure that the water doesn't boil too hard; it is supposed to stay at a simmer. Allow the milk to cook until all the first milk has thickened. Test with a spoon in the middle of the pudding. It will probably be done in less than an hour. Kalvedans can be served lukewarm or cold. It can be served as a dessert with a red fruit sauce or as a spread with cinnamon and maybe some sugar sprinkled over it.

• *Lappekaker* •

*Lappekaker are quite like American pancakes. In older times, the Lappekaker were served at special occasions as well. For weddings, funerals and other festivities, Lappekaker was always on the menu. While it is still used as party food in some places, today it is considered an everyday food, or a little something for coffee. Lappekaker have different names, depending on the area of the country. In the northern part of Vestlandet in western Norway, it is called **Svele**, and in Hallingdal it is called **Kvikaku**. I'm sure there are a lot of other names as well, but the following is a Kvikaku recipe from Hallingdal.*

3 cups sour milk (can be mixed with sour cream)	3 eggs
1¼ cups sour or sweet cream (or a mixture of the two)	6 tablespoons sugar
	1 teaspoon baking soda
	½ teaspoon salt

Mix everything thoroughly in a bowl. Add enough wheat flour to make a thick mixture. Allow to rest for about ½ hour before baking. Bake until light brown on both sides in a frying pan or on a griddle. They are supposed to be almost the same size as an American pancake.

• *Pea Soup/Meat Soup* •

4 pounds salt-cured dried lamb or sheep (including bones)	1 pound carrots, sliced
2 quarts water	1 pound rutabaga, chopped
½ leak, sliced	½ pound celery root, chopped
Celery (leaves, cut up)	2 ounces onion, finely chopped
	Salt, to taste

Soak the peas overnight in a large bowl with plenty of water. Let the meat, leek and leaves of celery simmer for 1 hour. Then add the peas. Cook for another hour, until the peas are slightly tender. Then add carrots, rutabaga, celery root and onion. Let the soup simmer 20 to 25 minutes. Add salt to taste. Serve with boiled potatoes.

• *Onion Gravy* •

2 ounces butter	1 onion, finely chopped
2 ounces wheat flour	1 tbsp. sugar
2 quarts stock (from soup)	1 tbsp. vinegar (7%)

Melt the butter in a casserole, adding the flour when the butter is completely melted. Mix well. Add the stock, stir and bring to boil. Then add onion, sugar and vinegar. Let the gravy simmer for 5-10 minutes.

• *Lapskaus* •

Lapskaus was probably one of the most common dinner dishes in Norway some years back. It also seemed to be a very common dish among the Norwegians who emigrated to America some generations back.

For every pound of meat add:	**2 pounds potatoes**
1 pound carrots	**$^1/_2$ leak**
$2^1/_2$ ounces celeriac	**$^3/_4$ quart broth**
$5^1/_2$ ounces rutabaga	**Salt and pepper to taste**

Dried sheep meat can be used for Lapskaus, but leftover meat from a soup, for example, may also be used. The most common meat for Lapskaus is probably lightly salted pork. The meat is cut into small pieces and boiled in a broth with vegetables and potatoes that also are cut into small pieces. Simmer all the ingredients until tender. Stir the pot now and then so that the Lapskaus doesn't burn. Serve warm with flatbread.

• *Salt curing and drying of sheep's meat* •

This recipe explains how salt curing is done, using a whole sheep or lamb. Both lamb and sheep's meat can be salt cured and dried, but the meat should not be too lean. The meat is cut into large pieces. Legs, shoulder and ribs are the most common cuts to be used for curing and should be prepared whole.

Salt curing: The freshly cut meat is placed in a large tub for salting. Rub each piece of meat with rough salt. (Fine salt may be used, too, but a lot of salt is needed; the fine salt is more expensive than the rough, so most people use the rough salt.) Stack the pieces of meat, skin side up, as tightly together as possible and place a thick layer of salt between each layer. Cover the vat with plastic or other suitable material. Lightly weight the meat. Place in a cool place.

The top piece of meat should be rubbed with salt several times during the first days of curing. The salt between the layers of meat or at the bottom of the vat may be used. After a couple of days, a salt brine may be prepared and poured over the meat to ensure that the salting process is successful. Salt brine: $4^1/_2$ to $5^1/_2$ pounds rough salt is brought to a boil in 6 quarts of water. Cool completely. (Allow it to stand overnight.) The brine is then poured over the meat. Even if not adding salt brine, there still will be a relatively large amount of brine in the vat as liquid is extracted from the meat. This brine may be poured over the meat on a regular basis.

Soaking: After about 2 weeks, the ribs and shoulder are removed from the salt brine and placed in a large tub filled with clean, cold water. (The legs, which are the thickest pieces, are left in the salt brine for one more week.) After a day soaking in water, the meat is removed. Dip it in the salt brine to give it a salt coating, and then hang it to dry. The legs should be removed from the brine a week later and then soaked in the same manner, but the soaking time is then $1^1/_2$. days. Then dip them in the salt brine and hang to dry.

Drying: The meat is hung to dry in a warm, airy place. In older times, the meat was often hung from hooks in the ceiling by the stove in the kitchen or by the wood stove in the living room. Some people still do that today. It is important to keep the heat high until a crust has formed on the surface of the meat. After a while, the heat can be reduced, but it is important that the temperature stays even and warm. After a couple of weeks, the drying process is finished. The legs need more time for the drying process, too. A rule of thumb is that the meat needs as much drying time as curing time in the salt brine. So the pieces that stay in the brine for two weeks need two weeks of drying, while the pieces that stay three weeks in the salt brine need three weeks of drying. Now the meat is ready for use.

Following is the way lamb and sheep's meat were prepared at the farms of Eiken and Hægebostad in Vest-Agder (and other locations in the area):

• Pinnekjøtt •

The ribs can be cut apart and used for Pinnekjøtt. It is then steamed in a large pot on top of a thick layer of birch twigs. Water is poured on to cover the twigs, and more water has to be added several times during cooking time. It is traditionally served with creamed rutabaga and boiled potatoes. The cooking time for Pinnekjøtt is 3 to 4 hours. The ribs may also be placed in a pan and heated in the oven. They are done in about an hour. Then they are served with lefse and boiled potatoes. Salt cured, dried lamb or sheep's meat is excellent for both meat-based soups and pea soup. The meat from the leg or shoulder is most often used, cut into small pieces and boiled. The cooking time of the meat for meat-based soups or pea soup is 2 to 3 hours. Cured lamb or sheep's meat may also be eaten without any further preparations. It is great as a cold cut. The leg is also called *Fenalår*. Then the cold meat is cut into thin slices and served on flatbread or lefse. Just remember to cut across the fibers.

• Glosteik •

In some places they held off soaking the meat until the meat was to be cooked—that is, after the drying. But that wasn't always practical. By soaking it in water before drying it, the meat was ready to be used when it had finished drying. Afterward, the meat was hung in an airy attic or a storehouse, and when a piece was needed, it could just be cut off and fried in a pan or in the fireplace for Glosteik. It might be stored for several weeks, but the taste would deteriorate somewhat over time. Nowadays, the meat is usually frozen after it has been dried. But the quality of dried meat deteriorates even when the meat is frozen, so it shouldn't be kept for more than 4 to 5 months.

• Kvit Steik •

Cured sheep's meat was used for a lot of different courses. At Eiken they made something they called Kvit Steik (white meat). The dried meat was then cut into small pieces. Then it was fried in a frying pan and then added to a thick, white gravy. This dish was served with boiled potatoes. •

217

218

· DEL 1 ·
SETRA

1 • Et overraskende møte

Sola steikte ubarmhjertig på skikkelsen som trasket oppover den smale grusveien. Ryggsekken var stor og veide mer enn hun likte. Men hun hadde ikke lyst til å sette seg for å hvile riktig ennå. Hun hadde langt igjen å gå, så det var best å henge i. Egentlig hadde hun bare godt av å svette litt etter alle timene hun hadde tilbrakt ved skrivepulten der inne i byen, tenkte hun. Ja, faktisk var det en deilig dag. Fuglene kvitret over hodet på henne. Og myrene langs veien, omkranset av de kronglete bjørketrærne, gav henne virkelig følelsen av å være i høyereliggende trakter av landet.

Den friske luften spredte glede i hele kroppen. Ja, Mette var i det hele tatt i et strålende humør. Ikke engang den tunge sekken greide å ta knekken på det. I det fjerne kunne hun skimte høye, nakne fjelltopper med noen hvite flekker øverst oppe. Hun funderte litt på om snøen ville forsvinne helt der oppe i løpet av sommeren.

Når hun betraktet dette eventyrlige landskapet, gav det henne ilinger nedover ryggen ved tanken på alle ukene hun skulle tilbringe i disse traktene. Men at det kunne være så varmt her oppe, hadde hun ikke forestilt seg. Hun hadde feiret sankthans i byen for to dager siden. Der hadde hun jammen hutret, og hun hadde trukket nærmere bålet utpå kvelden.

Veien snodde seg mellom knauser, myrer og tjern. Den så egentlig nokså skrøpelig ut, men det gikk nok fint an å kjøre der med bil. Av og til kom hun forbi bredere partier som var laget for at det skulle gå an å passere møtende trafikk.

Etter å ha passert en ganske stor fjellknaus fikk hun se et idyllisk tjern som lå like ved veien. En stor, flat stein strakte seg ganske langt ut i vannet.

Dette må være et ideelt hvilested, tenkte Mette og gikk ned til vannkanten. Lenger borte sto noen forholdsvis store bjørketrær. Hun tok av seg sekken og satte seg i skyggen under trærne. Det var deilig å få av den tunge byrden fra ryggen. Hun angret litt på at hun hadde stappet så mye i den da hun dro fra jernbanestasjonen nede i bygda. Mye av det kunne hun jo bare ha latt ligge der i oppbevaringen sammen med kofferten.

Hun var kommet med toget mye tidligere enn beregnet. Toget hun skulle ha tatt, var ventet til stasjonen klokka fem om ettermiddagen. Men av en eller annen grunn var det blitt innstilt, så hun måtte ta et tidligere tog. Derfor hadde hun vært framme allerede klokka tolv.

Mette så på klokka. Den var nesten halv to. Hun visste ikke riktig hvor langt hun hadde igjen å gå. Kanskje hun kunne være omtrent halvveis. Men nå ville hun i hvert fall ta seg en god hvil. I sekken fant hun nista hun ikke hadde spist på toget, og ei halv flaske lunken brus. Det skulle virkelig smake med en matbit.

Mens hun spiste nøt hun synet av det speilblanke vannet. Av og til ble det kruset opp litt av en svak bris som feide over. Tanken på dette eventyret hun hadde lagt ut på, gav henne nye ilinger i kroppen.

Det var faktisk allerede rett etter jul at hun hadde begynt å tenke på at hun trengte litt forandringer i tilværelsen. Hun jobbet på et kontor i Oslo, for en misjonsorganisasjon. I åtte år hadde hun jobbet der. Hun drev med organisering av arrangementer og annen misjonsvirksomhet i inn- og utland. Ut på reise måtte hun rett som det var. Nesten hver sommer hadde hun besøkt misjonsstasjoner rundt om i verden. Dette arbeidet hadde hun alltid opplevd som rikt og givende. Og mulighetene hun hadde fått til å se så mange eksotiske steder, var hun svært takknemlig for. Men etter hvert hadde hun begynt å føle seg sliten. Travelheten, som hun tidligere bare hadde likt, begynte å tappe henne mer og mer for krefter. Mange skremmende eksempler hadde hun sett på forkynnere og misjonærer som ble utbrente og trengte lang rekonvalesenttid for å komme tilbake igjen i tjenesten. Hun skjønte at hun var i ferd med å havne i samme situasjon.

En annen ting som også hadde blitt problematisk den siste tiden, var forholdet til Tore, en av kollegene. De gikk ikke så godt sammen. Flere episoder hadde gått sterkt inn på henne. Også det hadde vært med på å tappe henne for krefter. Derfor hadde hun valgt å gjøre noe med dette før det kom for langt. Hun ville hoppe av for en tid, og gjøre noe helt annet.

Da kom hun over en annonse i en lokalavis et sted hun var på møte. En bonde søkte etter hjelp på gården sin. Det var seterdrift han trengte hjelp til. Han trengte rett og slett ei budeie. Mette hadde ledd litt med det samme hun leste den. Der var altså fremdeles noen som søkte etter budeier her i landet. Det visste hun ikke. Men hun var jo oppvokst på gård, så dette arbeidet var kjent for henne. Ja, etter hvert som hun tenkte over det, følte hun seg mer og mer tiltrukket av tanken om å søke på jobben. Det var jo bare for noen måneder. Og dette måtte da være den perfekte avvekslingen fra det stresset som hun nå følte som en stadig sterkere belastning.

Slik ble det altså til at hun søkte. Men først hadde hun ringt til bonden for å forhøre seg litt nærmere om hva jobben besto i. Hun fikk inntrykk av at det måtte være et eldre ektepar som drev denne setra*. Det var forresten ikke vanlig seterdrift. De drev mer for turistnæringen. Vår og høst kom også grupper fra leirskoler for å se hvordan seterdriften var i eldre tider.

Bonden, som hun fikk greie på het Morten, snakket om Anna som kunne fortelle om dette fra sin tid som budeie i yngre år. Mette gikk ut fra at Anna var kona hans. Arbeidet som kom til å falle på Mette, var enkelt nok. Det vanlige gårdsarbeidet var hun sikkert vant med. Bare tre–fire kuer å melke, noen ungdyr og sauer som måtte sees etter, og litt høy som skulle tørkes. Så måtte hun nok hjelpe Anna en del innimellom når hun skulle ha demonstrasjoner.

Da beskjeden kom om at hun hadde fått jobben, ble hun vilt begeistret. Hun søkte permisjon fra kontorjobben i byen, noe som heller ikke bød på særlige problemer.

Nå satt hun altså her, på vei mot den nye arbeidsplassen sin. Ingen hadde møtt henne på stasjonen, noe hun var fullstendig forberedt på. Flere ganger hadde hun forsøkt å ringe Morten, men hun fikk ikke svar. Derfor fikk hun heller ikke gitt beskjed om at hun kom tidligere enn avtalt. På stasjonen var det imidlertid en som kunne fortelle henne hvor denne setra lå. Hun kunne ikke gå feil, påsto han. Og han skulle si fra til Morten hvis han dukket opp der for å hente henne. Bagasjen kunne hun bare sette i oppbevaringen, så kunne de hente den senere. Så enkelt var det. Derfor hadde hun lagt i vei alene.

Mette var ferdig med å spise. Hun burde nok se til å komme seg videre. Men vannet som lå der så speilblankt og fristende, fikk henne til å føle en intens trang til å få vasket av seg noe av svetten. Så deilig det ville være med et aldri så lite bad. Det måtte hun da kunne ta seg tid til. Raskt fikk hun fisket opp en badedrakt fra sekken. Skiftingen gikk også raskt. Her var det jo ingen hun trengte å gjemme seg for, øde og forlatt som det så ut til å være milevis omkring.

Da hun hoppet uti, gikk det som sjokkbølger gjennom kroppen. Vannet var mye kaldere enn hun hadde trodd. Det ble bare noen raske svømmetak, så krabbet hun opp igjen på den fine flate steinen. Men avkjølingen gjorde henne godt. Hun satte seg litt for å la sola gi henne varmen tilbake igjen i kroppen.

Så spratt hun opp. Det var best å komme videre. Hun ville helst være framme før gubben der oppe dro for å hente henne på stasjonen. Raskt vrengte hun av seg badedrakta og strakte seg etter håndkleet. I det samme hørte hun en lyd bak noen busker i nærheten. Forundret snudde hun seg for å se hva slags dyr det kunne være som var der. Men det var ikke noe dyr. Hun ble stående som lammet og stirret inn i de vidunderligste dype, mørke øyne hun noen gang hadde sett. Et eiendommelig vakkert ansikt med et veltrimmet skjegg og ei mørkebrun, særdeles velstelt hårmanke, sto der og betraktet henne. Plutselig snudde han seg og forsvant bak kratt og knauser igjen.

I det samme ble Mette oppmerksom på sin egen tilstand. Lynraskt trev hun håndkleet og dekket kroppen med det. Hva måtte vel denne mannen tro om henne? Aldri i sitt liv hadde hun vært så flau. Han måtte vel tro at hun sto der for å vise seg fram. Noe så pinlig. Klærne kom på i en fart, men nå var det ikke snakk om at det kunne gjøres uten å dekke seg til.

På veien videre oppover tenkte Mette mye på denne mannen. At hun kunne ha opptrådt så lettsindig. Hennes eneste trøst var at hun ganske sikkert aldri kom til å møte ham igjen. Likevel var skamfølelsen som en verkende byll i hennes indre. Hun burde jo ha tenkt på at det kunne være folk i fjellet. Morten hadde jo fortalt om alle turistene som vandret der.

Etter dette ville hun være nøye med hvordan hun opptrådte, selv om hun trodde at hun var helt alene, det var i hvert fall helt sikkert.

2 • Setra *

Mette var egentlig overrasket over hvor mye skog det var så pass høyt til fjells. Hun var kommet inn i et område hvor det var ganske mye furu. Noen av dem var temmelig store også.

Hun fulgte en dal oppover, kunne hun se. Etter sola å dømme gikk hun i nordlig retning. Langt der framme, og på begge sider kneiste fjelltoppene høyt til værs. Terrenget var temmelig kupert, så hun kunne ikke akkurat kalle dette noen fjellvidde. Men dit ville hun vel komme om hun bare gikk langt nok.

Med ett var hun ute av skogen. Veien gjorde en sving rundt noen knauser, og der videt terrenget seg ut i en stor slette. Mette ble bare stående og se. Veien fortsatte rett over sletten som skrånet svakt oppover og endte ved noen små bygninger. Disse lå lunt plassert ved foten av en liten fjellskrent. Bak skrånet terrenget ganske bratt oppover. På høyre side var det et stort jorde. Det var nokså smalt, men strakte seg temmelig langt bortover mot øst, og endte ved et stort tjern. Jordet var oppdyrket, og graset sto alt langt og frodig. På venstre side av veien var det satt opp et gjerde, og noen kuer gikk og beitet i ei kupert skråning litt lenger borte.

Et mer idyllisk sted hadde Mette aldri sett. Hun skjønte at hun nå var kommet fram. Dette var altså setra der hun skulle jobbe i nesten tre måneder. Synet fylte henne med en ubeskrivelig fryd. Dette vakre lille stedet omkranset av fjellene i nord, skogen i sør og det forlokkende tjernet mot øst, var mer enn hun hadde våget å drømme om. Mot vest skrånet beitemarka oppover, og endte nok i fjell og vidder.

Her kommer jeg til å trives, tenkte hun mens hun fortsatte å gå bortover mot seterbua. Det sto en bil utenfor, så hun skjønte at der var folk.

Fra seterbua gikk det en sti langs det langstrakte jordet ned mot tjernet. På øvresiden, mellom stien og fjellet, var en ganske stor, åpen plass. Gresset var kortklippet, og det sto et par campingvogner der.

Til venstre for seterbua, på den andre siden av gjerdet, var en annen bygning som hun skjønte måtte være fjøset. Og bak den igjen, helt innved fjellet, sto et lite skur. Kanskje det var et lite sauefjøs. Alt bar tydelig preg av å være i bruk.

Da Mette kom helt fram, så hun at døra sto halvt åpen, men hun så ingen folk noen steder. Forsiktig banket hun på, men ingen reaksjon var å høre. Hun tok av seg ryggsekken og satte den inntil veggen. Så tok hun seg en tur bort til fjøset og tittet inn. Der sto det en del redskaper og bøtter. I en krok sto noen sekker med fôr. Men ingen levende skapning var å se.

Nei vel, tenkte hun. Her fikk hun bare slå seg til ro og vente. Det måtte jo før eller

---

Ei seter* er en sesongdrevet gård i de norske fjellområder. Den blir bare brukt om sommeren for å utnytte resursene i fjellet. Det er en gammel landbrukstradisjon. Det primære formål er beiting. Med melkeproduksjon på et avsidesliggende sted blir den lite holdbare melken omdannet til mer holdbare produkter som smør og ost. I moderne tid blir det meste av melken sendt til et lokalt meieri. En lang rekke melkeprodukter stammer fra setertradisjon. Et annet formål med setra er produksjon av høy som blir brakt ned til hovedgården og brukt som vinterfôr. En verneverdig kulturskatt av legender, musikk og lyrikk har grodd frem fra setertradisjonen, og livet på setra er rikelig avbildet i norsk literatur.

siden komme folk på grunn av dyra som gikk der borte. Hun gikk tilbake til seterbua og listet seg inn den åpne døra.

Innenfor ble hun bare stående og se. Det var tydelig at årene måtte ha stått stille der en stund. Alt var ordentlig, rent og ryddig. Men det var ikke mange moderne hjelpemidler. En stor vedovn sto langs den ene veggen. Det var en ovn, maken til en som hun hadde sett i det gamle huset til besteforeldrene sine da hun var liten. Den ble ikke bare brukt til oppvarming, men kanskje helst til matlaging. På toppen var en stor flate med mange ringer. Der ble det fjernet ringer i forhold til det kokekaret man skulle sette på. Mette smilte for seg selv. Det skulle bli moro å prøve seg på disse gamle tingene.

Men litt lenger borte så hun en mer moderne gasskokeplate. Så var man altså ikke helt avhengige av de gamle metodene.

Enda lenger borte, langs samme vegg, gikk en bratt trapp, eller stige, opp mot en hems under mønet. Lengst inne i rommet var det plassert en sofalignende benk. I hjørnet rett ved siden av sto et vakkert utskåret skap.

Til venstre for der hun sto så hun et stort trebord. Det var trukket helt bort til veggen under et vindu. På hver side av bordet var det plassert trebenker til å sitte på. Over bordet hang en vakker parafinlampe. Det var tydelig at det ikke var strøm der inne i det hele tatt.

Plutselig fikk hun en følelse av uro. Hva var det egentlig hun hadde gitt seg ut på? Når hun tenkte seg om, visste hun nesten ingenting om den virksomheten som hun nå skulle ta til med. De korte samtalene hun hadde hatt med bonden, hadde ikke gitt henne så mange slike opplysninger. Hun hadde i det hele tatt ikke tenkt på å spørre om så mye. Hele greia hadde bare virket så eventyrlig. Var dette kan hende noe som ville bli mer en vond drøm enn et vakkert eventyr? Nei ... hun ville ikke tenke slik. Nå var hun her, og dette ville hun gjøre det beste ut av.

En lyd fra et sted bak en av dørene der inne i rommet fikk henne til å skvette. Kunne det være folk i huset likevel? «Hallo, er det noen her?» ropte hun. I det samme gikk ei dør opp, og ei rund lita kone kom til syne.

«Nei men i all verden, er det folk her?» sa hun forskrekket. «Jeg holdt bare på å gjøre i stand rommet til ei som skal komme og hjelpe oss litt her på setra i sommer, så jeg hørte ikke at det kom noen.» Hun pratet i vei, så det tok en stund før Mette fikk anledning til å presentere seg. Og enda mer forskrekket og ivrig ble kona da hun fikk greie på hvem det var som sto der i seterbua med den store ryggsekken, og hvorfor hun var der og ikke på stasjonen.

«Nå har jeg aldri hørt på maken. Har du virkelig spasert hele den lange veien? Og Morten som skulle hente deg på stasjonen! Han kommer til å bli overrasket, kan jeg tenke. Det varer nok ikke så lenge før han er her.» Hun tittet fort på klokka. «Bilen hans står her utenfor, så han må jo innom her først. Han er bare ute for å se til noen av de dyra som beiter i området her. Det var visst noen gjerder som måtte repareres.» Hun så litt undersøkende på Mette, og så lo hun igjen. «Og vi som trodde det var en eldre dame vi kunne vente oss, og så dukker denne ungdommelige skjønnheten opp. Ja, ja, alder har vel ikke så mye å bety. Du skal i hvert fall være velkommen. Nei, nå står jeg her og skravler uten i det hele tatt å presentere meg selv. Jeg er altså tante Anna. Alle kaller meg tante, enten jeg er tante til dem eller ikke. Jeg liker faktisk best det navnet. Bare Anna blir liksom så høytidelig og stivt. Nei, kall meg tante Anna du også. Det vil jeg sette mest pris på.»

Mette måtte smile. Hun likte allerede denne snakkesalige, eldre damen. Det var forunderlig slik som hele den runde kroppen hennes levde med i det hun sa. Og øynene forsvant nesten helt bak de digre bollekinnene når hun lo. Merkelig at hun kunne se noe i det hele tatt, for hun lo jo nesten hele tiden.

Den smittende latteren virket på Mette slik at uroen hun hadde følt for et øyeblikk siden, forsvant som dugg for sola. Denne kvinnen ville hun ikke få noen problemer med å trives sammen med. Det var hun sikker på. Og hvis mannen hennes var like hyggelig som hun, ville dette komme til å bli en riktig trivelig tid.

Like snakkesalig som tante Anna visste hun at Morten ikke var. Hun syntes heller han hadde vært litt fåmælt og taus i telefonen, men han hadde absolutt virket hyggelig.

«Nå må du komme her og se rommet ditt,» sa tante Anna og vagget den tunge kroppen sin tilbake over gulvet.

Mette ble begeistret med en gang da hun fikk se det lille, smale rommet som skulle være hennes. Utsikten fra vinduet var ikke akkurat den beste. Hun så bare rett inn i fjellet på baksiden av huset. Det var helst de stokkbygde veggene og de gammeldagse møblene som gav rommet et spesielt romantisk preg. Taket skrånet ned mot ytterveggen, så vinduet ble ikke så veldig stort. Kanskje var dette et påbygg som var gjort en tid senere enn hovedhuset.

Det sto to senger i rommet, en i hver ende. De var laget av solid tre og var av den typen som kunne trekkes ut. Den ene kunne trekkes ut i lengden, mens den andre var uttrekkbar i bredden. Det kunne altså bli ei dobbeltseng og ei barneseng. Mellom sengene, langs ytterveggen, sto en stor kommode. Den var et praktfullt stykke håndverk med vakre utskjæringer. På veggen over den, ved siden av vinduet, hang et nydelig speil. Rammen var også i utskåret treverk.

Det fantes ingen klesskap i rommet. Hvis hun ville henge opp noe av tøyet sitt, måtte hun henge det på noen treknagger som var satt inn i stokkene i veggen. Foruten to små nattbord og noen ryer på gulvet var det ikke noe mer i rommet.

«Tror du at du kan være her?» spurte tante Anna. «Det er ikke så stort et rom, men jeg har vasket alt, og lagt rent sengetøy i senga.»

«Dette er helt flott,» svarte Mette begeistret. Hun dro ut en av de tunge skuffene i kommoden. Der var det god plass, så hun. «Ja, her vil jeg komme til å trives,» sa hun. Tante Anna smilte om mulig enda bredere. «Men nå må du ha mat,» sa hun. «Du må da være skrubbsulten etter denne lange marsjen.»

Plutselig kjente Mette at det var akkurat det hun var. Det skulle virkelig bli godt med mat. Tørst var hun også. Tante Anna kommanderte henne ned i en stol. Der satt hun og betraktet den trivelige damen som hun allerede hadde begynt å like så godt. Munnen hennes gikk i ett mens hun arbeidet. På den korte tiden hun brukte på å stelle til måltidet, rakk hun å fortelle en hel masse om det arbeidet som nå lå foran den nye budeia. Hun fortalte om kyrne som skulle melkes. De hadde ikke så mange dyr, bare tre–fire kyr og noen sauer. Og så gikk det noen kviger lenger inne på fjellet som skulle kalve litt senere.

Det var gårdsturisme de drev med på denne setra, så melka ble ikke sendt til meieriet. Det de ikke brukte for å vise turister og skolebarn hvordan de laget ost og smør i gamle dager, det gav de til dyra.

De hadde bare to kyr som melket for øyeblikket, de andre to var «gjellkyr», sa tante Anna og tok det som en selvfølge at Mette forsto hva det betydde, nemlig at de ventet kalv og hadde derfor sluttet å melke for en tid. Så melkejobben ville ikke bli altfor tung for henne foreløpig.

Morten hadde begynt med denne driftsformen da han fikk seg fast jobb i bygdas bank. Det var forresten bare om sommeren og høsten han drev med dette. Han hadde fått en ordning med banken slik at han hadde fri fire måneder på denne årstiden.

Mette stusset litt. Da var nok Morten en del yngre enn tante Anna, tenkte hun. For den aldrende kvinnen måtte da være langt over de sytti.

Plutselig gikk døra opp. En mann kom inn og gikk raskt bort til en benk hvor han helte vann i et fat og begynte å vaske hendene. Mette kjente i det samme at hun stivnet til der hun satt. Så følte hun at hun ble blussende rød helt ut i hårroten. Mannen snudde seg, og et øyeblikk var det som alt sto stille. Til og med tante Anna var taus. Eller kanskje det bare var Mette som ikke hørte henne. For der stirret hun rett inn i et par dype, mørke øyne … de vakreste øyne hun noen gang hadde sett. Jo forresten … en gang før hadde hun sett dem. Det var der nede ved vannet. Der sto altså den mannen som hun hadde sett da hun badet … Ja, den mannen som hadde sett henne da hun badet …

Skamfølelsen vellet innover henne igjen med full styrke.

3 • Bonden

For Mette føltes det som en evighet, men sannsynligvis varte det bare et øyeblikk. Stemmen til tante Anna brøt gjennom, og så virket alt normalt igjen. Kanskje hadde det virket normalt for de andre hele tiden. Kanskje det bare var Mette som hadde følt dette intense øyeblikket. Det virket ikke som om mannen i det hele tatt dro noen slags kjensel på henne.

For Mette ble den intense spenningen avløst av en smule forvirring. En forvirring som på ingen måte ble mindre da tante Anna igjen satte i gang sin ordstrøm:

«Der er du jo, Morten. Ja nå kan du spare deg den turen ned til bygda i ettermiddag, for her sitter damen vi har ventet på. Slett ingen gammel kone, slik som vi trodde. Kan du tenke deg! Hun har spasert den lange veien, helt fra stasjonen og opp hit.»

Hele historien var fortalt før noen av de to andre rakk å si et ord.

Mette kikket fra tante Anna til mannen, og tilbake på tante Anna igjen. Hva var dette? Hun hadde kalt denne mannen for Morten. Var dette bonden? Mettes forvirring var total. Men han kunne da ikke være mer enn i trettiårene. Slett ikke særlig eldre enn henne selv. Og hva med at de hadde trodd at hun var en gammel kone? Hun hadde da skrevet fødselsdato og år i søknaden. Og tante Anna … Mette gikk helt i surr.

Som vanlig trengte hun ikke vente lenge på forklaringer når tante Anna hadde ordet:

«Da vil jeg bare få presentere min nevø for deg.» Tilgjort høytidelig henvendte hun seg til Mette. Morten kom bort og hilste som om han aldri skulle ha sett henne før. Dette gjorde at Mette slappet litt mer av. Han kjente henne altså ikke igjen. Det var nok forklaringen. Hun presset fram et forsiktig smil da han tok hånden hennes. Enda en gang så hun ham granskende inn i øynene, men der fantes ingen tegn til gjenkjennelse som hun kunne se.

Dette var altså bonden og arbeidsgiveren hennes. Det var altså denne mannen hun skulle arbeide for denne sommeren. Hun følte en svak skjelving gå gjennom kroppen mens hun betraktet den spenstige skikkelsen foran seg. Det brune fjeset fortalte at han hadde tilbrakt mye tid ute i sola.

Plutselig rettet hun seg opp. Hva var det hun sto der og dirret for? Hun pleide da slett ikke å reagere slik om hun hilste på en fremmed mann. Ikke skulle vel han heller få vippet henne av pinnen. Fast bestemt på å gå inn i tjenesten som budeie, og ikke noe annet, gjengjeldte hun håndtrykket og presenterte seg.

Etter at Mette hadde kommet seg av den første forskrekkelsen, gikk hun for fullt inn for å sette seg inn i arbeidsoppgavene sine. De ble sittende en lang stund rundt det store spisebordet og snakket om arbeidet.

Morten fortalte om turistene de ventet den første uka. Han hadde opplegg og planer klare. Tante Anna spilte en viktig rolle i det hele. Hun skulle demonstrere separering av melk og kjerning av fløte. Så var det ostekoking og laging av en rekke gamle, tradisjonelle matretter. Mette skulle hjelpe til med det som trengtes.

I tillegg skulle Mette ha ansvaret for de dyra som måtte ha daglig stell der på setra. Antagelig ville det være både barn og voksne rundt henne mens hun arbeidet og turistgruppene var der.

Mette satt og frydet seg. Dette hørtes virkelig spennende ut.

«La oss ta en tur for å se oss omkring,» sa plutselig Morten. Mette spratt opp. «Ja, la oss gjøre det,» svarte hun kjapt. Hun gledet seg virkelig til å komme ut og kunne ta hele denne herligheten i nærmere øyesyn.

Det ble virkelig en interessant omvisningstur for den nye budeia. Morten fortalte ivrig og engasjert om alt de så og alt som skulle gjøres. Fra fjøset gikk de bort til noen sauer som gikk og beitet. Lammene kom løpende mot dem og strakte snutene opp mot hånden til Morten. Han lo og klødde dem bak ørene. «De venter nok å få noe godt,» sa han. «Vi pleier å gi dem noe her så de skal holde seg rundt setra. Det er jo for at turistene skal få se dem at de er her. Så da bør de jo ikke dra for langt til fjells.»

Bak seterbua så Mette at det var laget til et ildsted av noen steiner. Morten fortalte at de brukte det når det var for tørt og utrygt å brenne andre steder. Det var helst når det var leirskoleklasser der at det ble brukt. Og så brukte også tante Anna det til noen av demonstrasjonene sine.

Morten viste henne også stedet der telt og campingvogner ble plassert. De sto i området ved enden av seterbua hvor gresset var kortklipt. Enda var det ikke kommet særlig mange vogner, men snart ville det bli fullt der, sa han. Han fortalte også at ei av de vognene som sto der nå, tilhørte søsteren hans. Hun og familien pleide å være der så ofte de hadde anledning.

De fortsatte stien nedover mot tjernet. «Dere har virkelig et idyllisk tjern her,» sa Mette. Fra stedet der de gikk, kunne de se en dal som strakte seg østover på den andre siden. Det var også mulig å skimte noen bygninger i lia langt der borte. «Hva slags bygninger er det vi kan se der?» spurte hun og pekte. «Det er Fjellbu-setra,» svarte Morten. «Det er ingen drift på den lenger, men den blir brukt som feriested både sommer og vinter.»

Snart var de helt nede ved vannkanten. Der var det ryddet til et fint badested. De satte seg på en stein som lå naturlig til som en benk på stranden.

«Her kommer jeg nok til å tilbringe en god del tid, vil jeg tro,» sa Mette og lo. Morten lo også. «Du blir nok ikke alene om det, kjenner jeg meg selv og andre her rett.»

En stund ble de bare sittende og betrakte det vakre landskapet. I enden av vannet mot nord kunne de se en smal dal som strakte seg innover fjellet. Midt uti vannet var en liten holme, hvor noen små kronglete busker klorte seg fast. Vannet lå nesten speilblankt i solskinnet. Bare noen svake krusninger fra en lett, mild fjellbris brøt det idylliske vannspeilet. Sola var fremdeles sterk og steikende. Mette kjente at hun hadde fått bortimot det hun kunne tåle av den på de nakne armene og fjeset denne dagen. Det kortklipte håret hennes gav ingen beskyttelse for nakken, som nå lå bar og åpen for de sviende strålene. Det lyse, blonde håret viste tydelig at huden hennes ikke var av den mest robuste under slike forhold. Men den vakre utsikten og den fredfulle atmosfæren gjorde at hun ikke hadde lyst til å bryte opp ennå.

«Er det du som eier alt dette?» Mette var helt oppslukt av inntrykkene.

«Tjernet her og områdene vi kan se på denne siden, er det jeg som eier,» svarte Morten. «Men lia og dalen der borte på den andre siden tilhører dem som eier Fjellbu-setra.»

«Har tjernet et navn? Og setra di, hva heter den?» Mette slo ut med armen mot vollen og bygningene de nettopp var kommet fra.

Morten lo litt. «Tenk at vi ikke har kommet på å fortelle deg det. Tjernet her heter Siljatjernet. Og da er det jo forståelig at setra heter Siljatjernsetra.»

«Siljatjernet … » Mette tygde litt på ordet. «Det høres liksom så svensk eller finsk ut.»

«Ja, kanskje det kan virke slik. Men opprinnelsen til navnet er nok så norsk som det kan bli,» svarte Morten. «Navnet kommer fra et sagn som har gått her i traktene i årevis.»

«Et sagn? Så spennende. Hva forteller det sagnet?» Mette kikket spent bort på ham.

Han satt med albuene på knærne og støttet hodet i hendene mens blikket gled over den blanke, mørke vannflaten. Et øyeblikk var det som om han var fordypet helt i en fjern fortid. Men så begynte han å fortelle. «For mange år siden, sikkert to–tre hundre, sies det at her var ei budeie på denne setra som kom opp i store vanskeligheter. Hun kom fra en husmannsplass i bygda og hadde tjeneste på gården vår. Så viste det seg at hun var blitt med barn. Det sies at det var sønn til en storbonde i en av nabobygdene som var faren. Men han ville ikke vedkjenne seg dette forholdet. En nokså klassisk historie, som du forstår. Jentas foreldre fryktet skandale. Og aller mest fryktet de storbonden, som hadde stor makt i vide kretser. Derfor ble jenta sendt til fjells som budeie. På den måten ble hun jo gjemt bort for en tid. En morgen kom den lille fårehunden hennes ned til bygda. Den var helt ustyrlig, så de skjønte at noe galt var fatt oppe på setra. Da de kom opp hit, fant de kyrne utenfor fjøsdøra. De rautet og var svært urolige. Det var ikke vanskelig å se at de ikke hadde blitt melket. Men budeia kunne de ikke finne noen steder. Etter en tid fant de henne druknet her i vannet. Det underlige var at liket ikke bar noe barn. Etter det begynte rykter og spekulasjoner å svirre. Noen mente hun hadde født barnet og drept det. Så hadde hun gravd det ned og druknet seg selv. Andre mente at barnefaren hadde hatt kontakt med jenta her oppe. Og da barnet var født, tok han det med seg og satte det vekk til folk utenfor bygda. Dette skulle ha blitt for tøft for den stakkars jenta, så hun hoppet i vannet og druknet. Denne historien, i mange forskjellige versjoner, har versert her siden. Jenta het Silja, derfor har tjernet og setra fått dette navnet.»

Mette grøsset litt. Plutselig fikk hele idyllen foran henne noe uhyggelig over seg. «Tror du dette er en sann historie?» Blikket hennes gled også over den mørke vannflaten nå.

Morten lo. «Jeg vet ikke. Men om så skal være, så har nok ikke dette vært den eneste uhyggelige hendelsen her omkring i hundreårenes løp. Vi har bare ikke bevart alle historiene slik som denne. Og godt er vel det.»

Mette måtte også smile. Selvfølgelig var det ingen grunn til å la denne uhyggen fra fortiden få prege denne vakre dagen. Sagn fantes jo alle steder. De var egentlig bare med på å krydre historiens gang litt ekstra.

Morten reiste seg. «Det er vel best vi kommer i gang med kveldsmelkingen. Jeg blir med deg til du får gjort deg kjent med dyra og arbeidet.»

Mette reiste seg også. Så gikk de begge tilbake til fjøset igjen.

4 • «Byjente»

Sola var ikke kommet særlig langt opp på himmelen da Mette våknet den første morgenen i den nye jobben. Hun tittet ut av det lille vinduet. Denne dagen så også ut til å bli en varm og fin dag. To små lam svinset rundt en av sauene der ute. De lette tydeligvis etter frokosten. Der fant de hver sin spene og satte i gang med måltidet. De små halene svirret ivrig rundt i luften. Mette måtte smile. Hvilken bekymringsløs verden de levde i.

Hun kledde på seg og gikk ut til tante Anna, som var i full sving med å koke kaffe til frokosten.

«God morgen. Har du sovet godt? Se så fin en dag vi får i dag også. Det er jo godt når vi skal til med slåttarbeid …» Ordene fosset ut av henne som vanlig. Om hun kom med et spørsmål, var det ikke alltid at hun ventet på svar.

Mette forsøkte å svare når det bød seg en anledning, ellers lot hun henne bare snakke uten å la seg stresse av det. Men hun hadde faktisk oppdaget at den gamle, trivelige kona kunne være taus og lytte også. De hadde sittet sammen kvelden før og snakket en del alle tre. Da hadde Mette fortalt fra sin barndom hjemme på det lille småbruket hvor hun hadde vokst opp. Hun hadde også fortalt om jobben sin og de mange reisene hun hadde vært på. Da hadde tante Anna lyttet i taushet i lange perioder. Det var bare da Mette fortalte om sin kristne tro, at iveren til den gamle hadde sprudlet over igjen. Også Morten hadde vist begeistring for akkurat det. Det at de alle tre delte en slik viktig interesse, gjorde at de med ett følte seg mer sammensveiset.

Frokosten kom på bordet, og Mette lærte hvor de forskjellige tingene var å finne. Ved siden av soveværelset hennes var det en ganske stor melkebod. Der var det meste av maten å finne. Da hun kom inn der, ble hun stående og se seg om litt forundret. Borte i et hjørne sto et stort kjøleskap. I taket var det en lyspære, og på veggen over en benk kunne hun se en stikkontakt. Dette stemte da ikke med resten av huset. Her var det tydeligvis strøm, men hvor kom den fra? Hun måtte spørre tante Anna.

«Morten har skaffet et solcellepanel slik at vi kan ha litt strøm her inne,» forklarte hun. «Det ble etter hvert vanskelig å oppbevare all melkematen uten muligheter til å få kjølt den ned. Det hender jo også at vi har bruk for noe som det trenges strøm til. Men Morten er nøye på at det bare skal være dette rommet vi har strøm i. Resten av setra skal være som i gamle dager.»

Snart sto også Morten opp. Han hadde rommet sitt oppe på hemsen.

«I dag får vi besøk av en gruppe amerikanske turister,» sa han mens de spiste. «De skal være her i tre dager. Disse dagene skal vi for det meste bare drive vanlig, gammeldags seterdrift. Turistene kommer til å gå rundt og se på det som foregår.»

«Når kommer de?» Mette var ivrig etter å komme i gang for alvor.

«Jeg skal kjøre ned til bygda for å hjelpe med transporten av vognene,» svarte Morten. «De har leid en del campingvogner som de skal bruke som losji. Avtalen er at vi skal møtes der nede klokka elleve nå i formiddag. Da kan jeg forresten hente kofferten din fra stasjonen. Du savner vel den, kan jeg tenke.»

Etter frokost gikk de ut for å stelle dyra. Morten ropte på kyrne. De gikk og beitet borte i lia. Da de hørte stemmen hans, begynte de å gå bortover mot fjøset.

«De kjenner stemmen din, ser jeg,» sa Mette.

«Du bør rope litt du også,» sa han. «De må jo bli kjent med din stemme også.»

«Ja, jeg må vel øve inn noen finurlige kulokker,» sa hun og lo.

Da de to melkekyrne var bundet i hver sin bås, satte hun seg på en liten krakk med bøtta mellom knærne. Kua trippet litt urolig. Den merket godt at det var et fremmed menneske i fjøset. Men da Morten klødde den bak øret og snakket beroligende til den, ble den straks roligere.

Melkingen gikk ganske greit. Hun oppdaget at hun ikke helt hadde glemt kunstene fra sin barndom. I jevne, taktfaste tak presset hun melka ut av spenene. Den strømmet ned i bøtta i lange, tykke stråler. Det var første gang hun prøvde denne melkemetoden her. Kvelden før hadde Morten vist henne hvordan hun skulle bruke den bensindrevne melkemaskinen, så da hadde de melket maskinelt. De brukte begge melkemetodene der på setra, men når det var turister der, brukte de nesten alltid den gamle håndmetoden.

Snart var bøtta full. Men da var det heller ikke mer å få ut av kua. To bøtter med melk kunne hun bære inn i melkeboden en stund senere. Tante Anna sto klar med separatoren. «Det er best vi får separert den med det samme,» sa hun. «Skal vi få ut fløten skikkelig, bør melka helst være litt varm.»

Mette helte den ene bøtta med melk opp i den store beholderen på toppen av separatoren. Så begynte tante Anna å dra sveiven sakte rundt. Det tok litt tid før hun fikk opp den rette farten, men snart rant det ut to fine stråler. En blekhvit kraftig stråle rant ned i bøtta igjen. Det var skummet melk. Lenger borte rant en mindre stråle ned i ei skål. Den var mye hvitere på fargen, og det som rant ut, så nokså tykt ut. Det var fløten.

«Det er viktig at vi drar i riktig tempo her, så fløten får den rette tykkelsen,» sa tante Anna. «Du må gjerne prøve deg på den andre bøtta.»

Med god veiledning fra tante Anna greide Mette å separere hele bøtta. Etterpå bar de den skummede melken ut igjen til dyra.

På baksiden av seterbua var det en dør rett inn til melkeboden. Det var den de brukte når de bar melken inn og ut. En praktisk og god løsning, syntes Mette, så slapp de å gå gjennom hele huset med bøttene.

Det var også en vannpumpe og en stor vaskekum der i boden. «All oppvask gjør vi her,» sa tante Anna. «Det er så greit å kunne holde alt sølet vekk fra hovedrommet der inne, for det må vi ofte bruke til demonstrasjoner når vi har besøk her.»

Etter hvert kom Morten sammen med turistgruppen. Den besto av fire familier med barn i forskjellig alder. Og så var det noen ektepar og enkeltpersoner i tillegg, til sammen tjuefem personer. Mette undret seg litt over hvordan de kunne greie å kjøre de store campingvognene på den smale veien.

Snart var vognene plassert på campingområdet, og barna løp rundt på oppdagelsesferd. Lammene var de første som fikk besøk. I viltre sprett tumlet de rundt på vollen. Mette måtte le der hun sto og betraktet dem. Hun husket sin egen barndom. På samme måte hadde hun lekt med dyra hjemme på gården. Hun kunne godt huske når de skulle slippes ut for første gang om våren. Kuer og kalver løp rundt på jordet i vill galopp mens halene sto rett til værs. Og de hadde fulgt med i dansen. Ofte hadde de lekt at de var i den ville vesten.

Det var ikke lenge hun kunne stå der og se på dem. Hun måtte inn igjen for å hjelpe tante Anna. Som velkomst skulle gjestene få servert god, gammeldags setermat. Egentlig skulle turistene selv ha ansvaret for sin egen bevertning. Dette var bare en liten anledning til å få vist litt av den tradisjonsrike maten.

Et stort bord var plassert foran huset. Mette og tante Anna begynte å bære ut *flatbrød**, *lefser** og vanlig, hjemmelaget grovbrød. Der var *eggost**, *gome**, *dravle**, *prim** og annen ost. Og så var det et stort fat med hjemmekjernet smør. Alt laget av melka på setra. Tante Anna hadde forberedt dette i god tid. Der var også fenalår og spekeskinke.

Maten ble mottatt med jubel og begeistring. Det ene fatet etter det andre ble bunnskrapt.

Mette og tante Anna sto og betraktet gjestene som satt rundt på vollen og spiste. «Er alt dette mat som har sin tradisjon her i distriktet,» spurte Mette.

«Å nei.» Tante Anna vagget på den store kroppen. «Jeg har plukket opp ting rundt om fra hele landet. Kommer jeg over noe nytt, så får jeg ikke fred før jeg har prøvd det.»

Igjen ble de sittende og se på gjestene.

«Det er dette som gir meg inspirasjon til å holde på,» sa hun da de så på de tomme fatene etterpå. «Den takknemligheten og begeistringen som disse viser, gir meg slik lyst til å gjøre mye mer.» Hun smilte så øynene var aldeles forsvunnet i ansiktet. Men de røde flekkene i kinnene fortalte at hun, i hvert fall for denne dagen, hadde gjort nok. Mette bad henne gå inn til seg selv for å hvile litt. Hun kunne greie oppvasken uten hjelp. Motvillig ble oppfordringen etterkommet. Det var tydelig at hun følte seg sliten.

Tante Anna hadde et stort rom under hemsen. Det hadde hun også til lager for ull og garn og andre ting som hun brukte til demonstrasjonene sine. En gammel rokk sto også der inne, hadde Mette sett. Hun gledet seg virkelig til å se alt dette i bruk.

Senere på ettermiddagen tok Morten ljåen og gikk bortover mot den delen av jordet som lå nærmest tjernet. Mette fulgte etter med ei rive. Gresset var egentlig ikke langt nok til å bli slått ennå, men han ville ha litt mykt, godt høy til sauene. Og det burde slås ganske tidlig, sa han.

Med lange, sikre drag begynte Morten å slå enga. Mette fulgte etter og raket vekk det nyslåtte gresset litt etter ham, slik at det ikke ble liggende i veien når han skulle begynne på neste rad. Slik gikk de og slo og rakte rad etter rad.

Snart var der en flokk av turister rundt dem. Fotoapparater og filmkameraer summet og gikk. Dette var visst et arbeid de virkelig forbandt med gammeldags gårdsdrift.

Barna fikk beskjed om å holde seg litt unna så de ikke kom borti ljåen.

«Når disse reiser, kommer det en ny slik gruppe da?» spurte Mette da de gikk tilbake igjen mot fjøset med redskapene.

«Nei,» sa Morten. «Til helga vil jeg ha minst mulig telt og vogner på campingområdet. Da skal vi ha misjonsstevne her oppe.»

«Misjonsstevne?» Mette så overrasket bort på ham.

«Ja, vi pleier hvert år å arrangere et slikt stevne her. Det har vært en tradisjon i mange år.»

«Kommer det mye folk på disse stevnene?» spurte Mette ivrig.

«Å ja, dette er et svært populært arrangement. Du må regne med å stelle til en masse mat.»

«Mat! Skal vi servere dem alle sammen?» Mette så sjokkert på ham.

Morten måtte le. «Tante Anna pleier alltid å koke rømmegrøt til dette stevnet. Og så steker hun *lappekaker** i pausen, så folk kan få dem rykende varme.»

Mette pustet ut litt. Det hørtes jo ikke så avskrekkende ut. «Det skal bli moro,» sa hun. «Skal si setra her blir utnyttet på en variert måte. Vi skulle bare hatt litt flere dyr. Jeg tror helst det er dem de yngste blant turistene liker å stelle med.»

Norske oppskrifter på mat i dette og følgende kapitler, som er merket med stjerne, kan finnes på side 435.

«Dyra kommer etter hvert,» sa Morten. «Over helga får jeg opp noen geiter, men dem vil jeg ikke ha her før etter at stevnet er gått av stabelen. Da kommer det så mange biler hit, og jeg vil helst ikke ha geitene til å skubbe for mye borti dem. De dyra er det jo ikke så lett å gjerde inne. Og så kommer det også snart noen kalver. Den ene av de kyrne som går her, venter jeg skal kalve når som helst. Og flere kalvinger blir det utover sommeren. Jeg passer alltid på å ha noen som skal kalve mens de er her på setra. Det er jo en ekstra opplevelse hvis noen av turistene får være med på en kalving.»

Da de kom bort mot seterbua, stoppet Mette for å snakke med noen barn som lekte på vollen. Morten fortsatte mot fjøset med redskapene. Da la hun plutselig merke til noen menn som kom gående over beitemarka. De bar ryggsekker, så det var tydelig at det var noen som hadde vært på vandretur i fjellet. Mette gikk bort for å åpne grinda for dem.

En av mennene stoppet og kikket på henne. «Ser man det …» sa han mens et underlig smil lekte om munnen. Så fortsatte han i det samme tonefallet: «Skal si Morten vet å innrette seg … her oppe i ensomheten … langt fra folk …» En liten latter unnslapp ham med det samme.

De andre snudde seg og lo da de hørte hva han sa. Det virket som de forsto en dypere betydning av bemerkningen.

Mette kjente at hun ble varm i hodet. Hva var det disse mennene antydet? Forvirringen hun et øyeblikk hadde følt, begynte å vike plassen for noe dirrende nede i magen. Hun svarte ikke noe, men sto bare og stirret på ham med et intenst og utfordrende blikk.

Mannen så ikke ut til å la seg skremme av de lynende øynene. Han fortsatte bare like ufortrødent. «Ja dette var virkelig litt av et prakteksemplar av ei budeie.» Latteren rungt igjen fra kameratene. «Og så ei fra byen, fikk jeg høre. Visste ikke at byjenter kunne finne pattene på ei ku. Men … det kan jo være andre kvalifikasjoner som teller tyngre … ja, Morten vet nok …»

Han kom ikke lenger, for Mette følte at noe var i ferd med å eksplodere inni henne. En mer ufyselig og ekkel fyr hadde hun aldri i sitt liv møtt. Hun tok seg ikke tid til å analysere bemerkningene hans, men avbrøt med en kraft og intensitet så han forskrekket rygget et par skritt tilbake. «Jeg akter ikke å stå her og høre på slik råttenskap fra et dyr som tydeligvis kun tenker på og følger sitt primitive instinkt,» freste hun. «Slike har vi ikke bruk for her på setra. Veien til bygda er i den retningen.» Hun rettet en dirrende pekefinger mot veien. Dermed snudde hun og marsjerte mot seterbua. Om det var noen som fortsatt lo, så fikk hun ikke greie på det, for hun var altfor sint til å ofre dem et eneste blikk.

Tante Anna så forskrekket opp da hun kom brasende inn. Men hun stoppet ikke for å gi noen forklaring, gikk bare rett inn på rommet sitt. Der ble hun sittende en lang stund. Hjertet dunket hardt og fort mens hun knyttet hendene krampaktig i fanget. At det gikk an å snakke på en slik måte! Hun var så rasende at hun nær kunne ha revet ham i filler. Byjente … var det betegnelsen hun gikk under! Og da i en så negativ betydning som det gikk an å få det.

Men hun skulle vise dem. De skulle få se at hun ikke var noen analfabet på dette området. Ingen skulle få grunn til å si at hun vek tilbake for gårdslivets harde strabaser. Det skulle hun i hvert fall sette alt inn på. Ikke skulle hun bli for avhengig av denne bonden heller. Nei, en jobb var det hun hadde fått her, og den skulle hun utføre så godt hun kunne. Noe mer var det ikke.

Det tok tid før hun var så rolig at hun kunne gå ut for å møte de andre igjen. Men omsider kjente hun at den voldsomme spenningen la seg. Hun bestemte seg for ikke å nevne noe om episoden. Det var nok best å ikke lage noe oppstyr rundt dette.

5 • Spenning i fjøset

Da Morten begynte å rope på kyrne for å få dem hjem til melketid, ble det virkelig liv i barna. De voksne kom også for å se på melkingen. Kyrne gikk og beitet nokså høyt oppe i lia, så det tok en stund før de kom. Men de to som skulle melkes, reagerte raskt da de hørte Morten sin stemme. Mette ropte også noen ganger. Det var jo best at de ble vant til at det var henne som skulle gjøre dette arbeidet nå.

«Vi er nok litt for tidlig ute i kveld,» sa Morten. Han så på klokka. «De pleier alltid å trekke nedover mot fjøset når det nærmer seg melketid. Det virker faktisk som om de kan klokka.» Morten lo litt mens han så på de to kyrne som kom traskende mot dem. Litt lenger borte kom også den tredje kua gående. Selv om den ikke skulle melkes, visste den at det nå vanket noe ekstra godt i fjøset. Men den hadde god tid. Ingen av dyra lot seg stresse av alle folkene som var der. De var jo vant til mange slags besøk.

«Dette var da rart.» Morten skygget med hånden for øynene og kikket oppover lia. Ku nummer fire var ikke å se noen steder. «Det er den kua som snart skal kalve,» sa han. «Bare den ikke har stukket seg vekk der oppe et sted med det arbeidet. Det er best jeg går for å se etter den.»

Morten dro straks av sted. Noen av de største barna fulgte ham hakk i hel.

Da Mette hadde gitt litt kraftfôr til de kyrne som nå hadde funnet båsene sine, tok hun bøtta og melkekrakken og satte seg til å melke. Igjen var det filming og blinking av blitslamper. Turistene sto rundt henne i en tett ring. Spørsmål om både det ene og det andre måtte hun svare på. Nå var hun glad for at hun hadde vært bondejente som barn. Det gjorde at hun var i stand til å svare på de fleste spørsmålene. Hun skjønte også hvorfor Morten hadde lagt så stor vekt på at hun måtte være språkkyndig for å få denne jobben. Han hadde sagt at hun burde mestre engelsk og tysk rimelig bra. Og nettopp disse språkene var Mettes sterke sider. På grunn av sitt arbeid, og all reisingen i forbindelse med det, hadde hun lagt stor vekt på å lære seg i hvert fall engelsk skikkelig. Men tysk kunne hun også ganske bra. Og fransk og spansk kunne hun gjøre seg forstått på.

Noen av dem som sto rundt henne, vred litt på nesene og gikk ganske raskt ut av fjøset igjen. De syntes nok at lukten fra dyra ble litt for sterk. En av de minste guttene kom seg også fort ut. Han sto ganske nær bak ei av kuene. Plutselig løftet den på halen, og det kom en kraftig stråle ut bak. Den lille gutten ble truffet rett i siden. Med hyling og rop på mamma styrtet han ut, mens resten av flokken sto tvikroket av latter.

Etter at den verste latterbølgen hadde gitt seg, bad Mette barna om å hente hver sin kopp, så skulle de få smake på melken. Flere av dem lystret med det samme. Snart var de tilbake igjen. Med ivrige øyne fulgte de Mette som tok kopp etter kopp og fylte dem med melk rett fra spenene.

Overraskelsen var stor hos de fleste da de kjente smaken på den varme melka. «Dette var jo godt,» sa ei lita jente. Hun hadde drukket opp hele koppen og bad om å få mer. Mette lo og fylte opp på nytt. «Ferskere enn dette går det ikke an å få melka,» sa hun.

Det var likevel ikke alle som var like begeistret. Noen syntes den varme væsken bare var ekkel og spyttet den ut igjen.

Idet Mette var på vei inn mot boden med melkebøttene, fikk hun se Morten komme nedover lia med den savnede kua. Hun pustet lettet ut. Da hadde den altså ikke gått så altfor langt av sted. Og det så heller ikke ut til at den hadde kalvet.

Hun kom fort tilbake og slapp ut igjen de kyrne som var i fjøset. Kua Morten kom med, så stor og rund ut på grunn av den ventede kalven. Juret var ekstra stort og hovent.

«Se der,» sa en av guttene og pekte på de sprikende spenene. «Det ser ut som en oppblåst gummihanske.» Alle lo av den slående beskrivelsen.

«Det er nok ikke så lenge før den kalver,» sa Morten. «Den er allerede kalvsyk. Det var nok derfor den ikke kom sammen med de andre nå i kveld. Den ville nok prøve å finne seg et sted i ro og fred hvor den kunne kalve.»

Han bandt kua i en av båsene i fjøset. Så gav han den litt mat. Han fant også et fang med gammelt høy på høyloftet over fjøset. Det spredte han utover i båsen så den skulle ha det rent og tørt der. «Nå må vi bare la den få så mye ro som mulig, så kommer nok kalven om ikke altfor lenge.»

«Kommer kalven nå?» En av guttene sto og stirret på Morten med store øyne. Så stirret han bort på kua. Morten lo litt da han så alle de spente øynene som fulgte med på det han sa og gjorde. «Vi må nok regne med at det kommer en liten en til her i fjøset i natt,» svarte han.

«Kan vi få være her og se på?» Det var en av dem som hadde vært med på å hente hjem kua, som spurte.

«Jeg vet ikke når den kommer til å kalve,» svarte Morten. «Det kan bli midt på natta.»

«Det gjør ingen ting,» ropte flere av dem i kor. «Vi skal nok greie å holde oss våkne.»

Morten så litt betenkt ut. Han kikket fra den ene til den andre av dem. De ivrige, oppspilte barneøynene gjorde det umulig for ham å nekte dem dette. «Da må dere love meg en ting,» sa han alvorlig. «Kua trenger ro og fred. Dere må love at dere er stille og rolige når dere er inne hos henne i fjøset.» Ivrig nikking gav til kjenne at de forsto det. «Og hvis dere ser noe uvanlig med den,» fortsatte han, «så må dere komme og si ifra til meg.»

Barna tok oppgaven svært alvorlig. Det var som om de hadde fått et stort ansvar. De eldste passet etter hvert nøye på at de små var stille når de listet seg inn i fjøset.

Utover kvelden la Mette merke til at barna stadig smatt inn fjøsdøra. Noen ganger ble et par av dem værende en lang stund før de gikk tilbake igjen til familien i campingvogna. Mette tok seg også en tur ut for å se til kua. Den lå på det tørre høyet i båsen. Juret var så sprengt at det så vondt ut å ligge. Det kan ikke vare lenge før kalven kommer nå, tenkte hun. Senene ved haleroten var helt slappe og nedsunket, kunne hun kjenne. Det var et sikkert tegn på at kalvingen ikke var langt unna.

Plutselig sluttet den å jorte. Det kom noen halvkvalte raut mens det gikk trekninger gjennom den store kroppen. «Nå er riene i gang,» sa Mette til de to barna som for øyeblikket delte melkekrakken for å våke over den fødende.

De spratt opp som på kommando. «Kommer den nå?»

«Nei, nei.» Mette måtte le. «Det kan ennå ta en lang stund før noe skjer. Men nå er i hvert fall fødselen i gang.» Hun kunne se hvordan spenningen økte hos de to. «Men dere må huske at den trenger ro,» fortsatte hun.

De to nikket bare til svar. De var så preget av stundens alvor at de ikke våget å bruke stemmen for å gi henne svar.

Mette gikk inn igjen og overlot våkingen til de ivrige barna. Hun fant Morten fordypet i noe borte ved spisebordet.

Han kikket opp da hun kom inn. «Hvordan går det i fjøset?» spurte han.

«Fødselen er nok i gang,» svarte hun, «men der er ingenting å se til kalven enda.» Hun gikk bort til kokeplaten og skjenket seg en kopp kaffe av kjelen som sto der. «Nå har vi jo så bra med folk til å våke at vi ikke behøver å være redde for at noe skal skje uten at vi får greie på det,» lo Mette.

Morten lo også. «Skal si det ble fart i disse barna da de fikk greie på at det var fødsel i vente i fjøset,» sa han.

Med den fulle kaffekoppen satte Mette seg ved bordet rett overfor Morten. Da så hun at det var Bibelen han satt og leste i.

Som svar på det spørrende blikket hennes sa han: «Jeg tenkte at jeg måtte forberede meg litt til stevnet på søndag. Så kom jeg over noe her som jeg synes ble så alvorlig. Det er hos profeten Jesaja, kapittel femtiseks og fra vers ni. Hør hva som står der:

Kom, alle dyr i marken, kom og et, alle dyr i skogen! Israels vaktmenn er blinde, ingen av dem merker noe. Alle er lik målløse hunder, som ikke er i stand til å gjø. De ligger der og drømmer, liker best å sove. Men grådige hunder er de, aldri blir de mette. Og de skal være gjetere, de som ikke forstår å passe på! De vender seg alle hver sin vei til sin egen vinning.

Mette satt og lyttet mens han leste. Men hun skjønte ikke hva som var så alvorlig med dette. At noen grådige hunder som helst ville sove hadde noe alvorlig å si, kunne hun ikke forstå.

Da Morten var ferdig med å lese, kikket han opp på henne. Han smilte da han så de forvirrede øynene. «Jeg har nok lest dette før,» sa han, «men nå var det som om noe av betydningen her gikk opp for meg for første gang. Jeg ser det i lys av mange situasjoner som nok også vi har her i vårt land. Her står at Israels vaktmenn er blinde. Og så blir de sammenlignet med vakthunder som ikke gjør jobben sin. Vakthunder som bare er opptatt av egen nytelse og vinning. Hundene her er tydeligvis et bilde på de åndelige lederne. Og de er vel et bilde på våre åndelige ledere også?»

Han var ivrig nå. «Disse lederne som her blir beskrevet, har en viktig jobb å gjøre. De skal varsle hvis farer eller fiender dukker opp. Men de gjør ikke jobben sin, og grunnen til det er at de ikke ser noen farer, fordi de sover.»

Nå begynte det å demre for Mette. «Hvor var det du sa at dette sto?» Hun strakte seg over bordet for å se hva det var han hadde lest.

Han pekte på versene og skjøv Bibelen over til henne. «Kom, alle dyr i marken,» leste hun. «Det må jo bety at fienden har lagt merke til at vaktholdet er dårlig. Og så blir det oppfordret til angrep.»

«Nettopp!» Morten holdt en pekefinger i været. Iveren hans var i ferd med å smitte over på henne nå, for hun begynte å forstå hva han mente. «Du mener altså at denne situasjonen også kan finnes blant noen av de åndelige lederne i vår tid, og i vårt land?»

«Ja, og ikke bare det,» sa han. «Her tror jeg vi har en alvorlig advarsel til alle kristne. Vi har alle et ansvar for å reagere hvis ting som kan være med på å føre oss bort fra Gud, vil snike seg inn mellom oss.»

Mette så plutselig litt betenkt ut. «Det står her at vaktmennene er blinde, og at de sover. Vi har jo mange oppfordringer i Bibelen om å våke, men hvordan tror du det menes at vi må gjøre dette?»

Morten tenkte seg litt om før han svarte. «Jeg tror egentlig ikke vi mennesker har så mange forutsetninger for å greie dette vaktholdet. Men jeg tror at Guds ord kan gi oss de rette kvalifikasjonene hvis vi ønsker å la oss prege av Ordet. Jeg tror faktisk at dette er noe vi må ha hjelp til fra Gud selv. Hvis vi leser Bibelen, vil vi nok finne den veiledningen vi trenger.»

«Ja, du har nok rett i det.» Mette satt fremdeles og studerte versene. «Det er litt skremmende det som står i vers ni og ti her. Det er nok fristeren som roper på sin hær, den som her er beskrevet som dyr i marken. Disse sover ikke. De ser situasjonen akkurat slik som den er. Og de er parat til å utnytte den. Men det må jo også bety at de ser når vaktholdet er i orden. Når de ser det, blir vel ikke angrepene satt i verk?»

«Du er inne på noe vesentlig der,» sa Morten. «Men det er nok en illusjon å tro at de som er våkne, ikke blir angrepet. Eller rettere sagt: Det er nok ikke lett å holde seg våken på alle punkter til enhver tid. Jeg tror at dette vaktholdet helst blir gjort i bønn. Det kan godt hende at svikten først og fremst ligger hos forbederne når vi ser en leder som klart handler og lærer i strid med Guds ord.»

En lang stund ble de sittende og snakke om dette. Grunnen til at Morten hadde sett dette så alvorlig, var at han opplevde seg selv som en åndelig leder i bygda. Han satt både i menighetsrådet og i bedehusstyret. I tillegg til det hadde han i årenes løp vært med i utallige styrer og råd med viktige lederfunksjoner.

«Jeg vet i hvert fall en ting,» sa han etter en stund. «Jeg kan ikke gå fram med en løftet pekefinger og advare i øst og vest. Jeg tror det viktigste er å arbeide i bønn, og så ta de sakene som dukker opp etter hvert. Når man ber om visdom, så tror jeg Gud vil gi veiledning i den enkelte saken vi kommer opp i.»

Det var tydelig at dette var noe som hadde grepet ham. Men Mette kunne ikke lese ut av det han sa, om det var noen spesielle saker han tenkte på.

Plutselig ble døra revet opp, og en gutt kom styrtende inn. «Nå skjer det noe i fjøset!» ropte han. Øynene trillet nesten rundt i hodet på ham av iver.

Morten kom seg på beina og var ute på et øyeblikk. Mette fant fotoapparatet sitt og fulgte etter. Dette ville hun passe på å få foreviget. En slik begivenhet var det ikke sikkert hun ville få oppleve igjen.

Det så ut til at alle barna hadde fått beskjed, for nå kom de løpende. I hvert fall kom de største som ikke hadde sovnet.

Noen røde stråler tegnet seg på himmelen i vest som den siste hilsen fra en dag som gikk mot natt. Skumringen begynte å senke seg over fjellene. Men ingen hadde tid til å se på det vakre landskapet. Ei rekke av spente barn, og noen voksne også, styrte sine raske skritt mot fjøsdøra.

Inne i fjøset var det tydelig at der var ei som kjempet en hard kamp. Kraftige stønn og hese raut kunne høres i den stille natta. Så lydløst som mulig smatt den ene etter den andre inn gjennom døra. Det ble likevel litt uro da det begynte å fylles opp med folk rundt kua.

«Nå må dere prøve å være helt rolige,» hvisket Morten. «Den ligger greit nå, men det skal ikke mye til før den blir skremt, slik at den reiser seg opp, og det bør den ikke gjøre, for da vil fødselen bli så mye tyngre.»

Han snakket beroligende til kua og klappet den forsiktig på ryggen. Bak, under halen hennes, viste det seg noen små, hvite klauver. Kua lå nokså rolig en stund mens pusten gikk i lange kast.

Men plutselig begynte det å arbeide i den store kroppen igjen. Ei ny ri satte inn. Et langt ul unnslapp den frådende kjeften. De små klauvene kom lenger fram og viste begynnelsen på et par tynne kalvebein. Det hang ei tykk hinne utenpå dem. Gang på

239

gang raste de harde fødselsriene gjennom det kjempende dyret. Minuttene gikk, men ingen tenkte på å se på klokka. Alle stirret som hypnotiserte på det som foregikk der på fjøsgulvet.

«Må vi ikke hente dyrlege?» spurte en liten, skjelvende stemme. Smertene som tegnet seg over den frådende kjeften til kua, fikk tårene til å sprette i barneøynene.

Morten så bort på ham og smilte. «Dette går nok bra,» sa han beroligende. Den har det ganske hardt nå, men det går over så snart kalven er født. Dette er helt naturlig. Vi må bare ta det med ro og vente.»

Plutselig kom det ut en stor pose full av vann. I det samme satte kua i et brøl, og vannet skvatt utover gulvet. Det hørtes et skrik fra tilskuerflokken. Ei jente forsvant ut døra. Flere andre fulgte etter. Dette ble litt for sterk kost for noen av dem, mens andre ble enda mer interessert i det som foregikk.

Da kua igjen roet seg litt, henvendte Morten seg til en av de guttene som hadde fulgt ivrig med hele tiden. «Kan du hjelpe meg litt?» spurte han. Gutten var straks parat. «Ta et godt tak rundt denne lille kalvefoten her. Jeg skal holde rundt den andre. Når kua igjen begynner å trykke, må du trekke forsiktig bakover. Vi må hjelpe henne litt på slutten. Kalven kommer snart nå.»

Med skjelvende, men besluttsomme hender grep gutten et godt tak rundt den våte og slimete foten. De ventet i taushet noen minutter. Nå kunne de også tydelig se at en liten snute var i ferd med å sprenge seg vei ut i dagen.

Snart ble det uro i kua igjen. Sakte, men sikkert kom mer av det lille hodet til syne. Morten og gutten trakk forsiktig i kalven. Med ett sa det svupp, og hele hodet var framme. Gutten falt nesten bakover i forskrekkelsen. Morten måtte le.

Det var ikke så mange tilskuere igjen der inne, men de som var der, sto som trollbundet av den sterke opplevelsen. Et filmkamera surret og gikk hele tiden. Og rett som det var kom det blink fra fotoapparater. Dette var en opplevelse de kanskje aldri ville få oppleve maken til. Mette sparte heller ikke på filmen.

Morten renset den lille kalvemunnen for slim og hinner. Mette fant også et håndkle som han kunne tørke den litt med.

Kua var rolig igjen. Den hadde lagt hodet ned på gulvet og peste i utmattelse.

«Stakkars ku,» kom det skjelvende fra den lille gutten igjen. Tårene sto fremdeles i øynene hans. Men han holdt tappert ut. Dette ville han tydeligvis ha med seg slutten på.

Det var ikke lenge kua fikk fred. Snart begynte riene å arbeide igjen. Morten og gutten tok et nytt tak i kalveføttene. Et kraftig, langstrakt brøl presset seg ut av den idet resten av kalven seg ut. Den landet i høyet med et klask. Det hele skjedde så fort at gutten falt helt over ende på gulvet. Han peste som om han skulle ha holdt pusten en lang stund. Vann og blod skvatt rundt dem. Tilskuerne måtte hoppe til side for ikke å bli tilgriset. Mette fikk en kraftig sprut oppover beinet, for hun var mer opptatt av å fotografere enn å komme seg unna. De to fødselshjelperne greide heller ikke å unngå sølet. De hadde slim og blodflekker over hele seg. Gutten så ikke ut til å bry seg om det, men spenningen og reaksjonene på den sterke opplevelsen han hadde vært med på, gjorde at han skalv over hele kroppen.

Morten begynte å gni kalven med litt høy. Snart lød det et spedt raut fra den pjuskete skapningen på gulvet. Den løftet sjanglende opp det lille hodet, og ristet det litt ukontrollert. Morten lo. «Det er i hvert fall liv i den nyfødte,» sa han. «Stor er den også, så det var ikke rart at fødselen var litt hard.»

Forsiktig løftet han kalven fram til kua så hun kunne slikke den ren. Han løsnet tauet den var bundet til båsen med så den kunne komme skikkelig til. Mette skrapte vekk hinner og vann fra gulvet, og la på nytt høy.

«Nå kan disse to kose seg her i fjøset i natt,» sa Morten. Kua hadde reist seg og var i full gang med å rengjøre kalven sin.

«Skal vi melke den nå?» spurte Mette.

«Nei,» svarte Morten. «Jeg lar kalven gjøre den jobben i kveld. Så får vi se i morgen om det er noe å melke ut av den. Det kan godt hende jeg bare lar kalven gå ute sammen med den og die. Det er jo det enkleste. Og så er det jo litt koselig for turistene å se på også.»

Alle forlot fjøset, men det var tydelig at denne opplevelsen hadde gjort sterkt inntrykk på dem som hadde vært til stede.

Da de kom ut, var det mørkt, men borte over fjellene i øst bar himmelen bud om en ny dag. Den korte natta ville snart være over.

Mette kjente at trettheten begynte å melde seg. Det skulle bli godt å komme i seng. Så altfor fort ville det være morgen igjen–og en ny arbeidsdag.

6 • «Kalvedans» og lakrispastiller

Neste morgen var flere av barna tidlig oppe, til tross for at de kom sent i seng kvelden før. Alle var spente på hvordan det sto til med den nyfødte i fjøset. Da Mette kom ut dit, satt fire gutter og ei jente på noe høy borte i et hjørne og betraktet den lille kalven. Han balanserte rundt på de lange, tynne beina sine og lette etter spenene til mora. Det var en kvigekalv, altså ei lita jente, hadde Morten fortalt dem kvelden før. Derfor hadde de gitt den navnet «Missi». Noen av de modigste var borte av og til og klappet den litt på halsen. Men så lenge den var så nær den store kua, lot de den helst være i fred, for hun virket litt skremmende, syntes de.

De andre kyrne sto utenfor og ventet på å komme inn i fjøset. Mette slapp inn de to som skulle melkes, og bandt dem i hver sin bås.

Det ble igjen folksomt i fjøset. Mange hadde lyst til å se på. Morten kom også ut. Han melket det som var igjen i juret til den nye moren etter at kalven hadde forsynt seg. «Den greier visst ikke å drikke opp alt,» sa han, «så vi får litt til råmelkspudding også.»

Mette smilte begeistret. «Det skal bli deilig,» sa hun. «Jeg kan huske at min mor kokte pudding av råmelk. Hun kalte den for Kalvedans. Vi barna var vilt begeistret for den. Nå er det mange år siden jeg har smakt slik pudding.»

Morten lo litt. «Jeg skal spørre tante Anna om hun kan koke litt i dag. Så kan vi servere en smak til alle disse interesserte barna her.»

Tante Anna ville mer enn gjerne lage Kalvedans. Hun fylte en krukke med den tykke, gule råmelken og satte den i en stor gryte som hun helte litt vann i. Gryta satte hun på komfyren. «Nå må den stå og koke i dette vannbadet til melka er helt stiv,» sa hun. «Det kommer nok til å ta en stund. Denne melka er så «rå» at den sikkert kommer til å bli stiv og fin. Men det skal ikke gå mange dagene før melka til den nye moren blir mye tynnere og mer normal. Da går det ikke an å få den stiv på denne måten.»

Mens melka kokte, demonstrerte hun både separering av den andre melken og kinning av smør for turistene. Hun pratet og forklarte i ett sett. Mette hadde sin fulle hyre med å rekke å oversette det alt sammen, for hun snakket jo på norsk hele tiden.

Det var helst de voksne som viste interesse for dette. Barna så på en stund, men så løp de ut for å leke med lammene og Missi.

Utover dagen fikk Mette mye tid til å prate med turistene. Hun hadde det ikke så travelt. Varmen var også så intens at det føltes ubehagelig å stresse for hardt.

Mange likte å kunne slå av en prat med henne. Barna kom også med ivrige spørsmål om både det ene og det andre.

«Nå vil jeg ned til tjernet for å bade,» ropte hun etter en stund da hun fikk se den ene etter den andre trekke inn i skyggen bak seterbua. «Hvem vil være med?» Et hyl fortalte at hun ikke ville bli alene på badeplassen.

Snart samlet det seg en hel flokk av voksne og barn nede ved tjernet. Mette var en av de første som hoppet uti. Iskaldt, tenkte hun i det samme hun dukket under. Men det varte ikke lenge før hun hadde vent seg til temperaturforskjellen. Da føltes det bare kjølig og deilig.

Lek med spruting og begeistrede hyl ble mer og mer øredøvende etter hvert som flere kom ut i vannet. Mette gikk opp på land igjen. Hun satte seg på steinbenken og så på de elleville barna. Noen av de voksne var også med på leken. En mann dukket under vann mens et av barna sto på skuldrene hans. Så rettet han seg fort opp igjen. Gutten ble kastet høyt opp i luften, og falt i vannet igjen med et plask. Flere kom til og ville ha samme behandling.

Plutselig kom Morten bort og satte seg ved siden av henne. «Sitter du her,» spurte han. «Skal du ikke ut og være med i leken?» Mette ristet på hodet. «Jeg …» hun nølte litt. «Jeg er nokså pysete i vann,» sa hun og lo litt sjenert. «Er du pysete?» Morten lo også. «Jeg synes da slett ikke du virker slik. Du hamler jo opp med det meste her på setra. Jeg trodde ikke det var den ting som du ikke mestret?»

Mette lo litt av den vennskapelige ertingen. Men så ble hun alvorlig igjen.

«Du skjønner det,» sa hun. «Jeg hadde en vond opplevelse da jeg var barn, og den vil liksom ikke slippe taket i meg. Jeg var med far en gang for å fiske. Vi hadde en liten båt. Sjøen var urolig, men ikke verre enn at far mente det var trygt å legge ut. Plutselig kom det et vindkast, og båten gjorde en brå bevegelse. Jeg var helt uforberedt, så jeg falt bakover mot ripa. Og før noen visste ordet av det, lå jeg i sjøen. Far var rask til å få dratt meg opp igjen, men de øyeblikkene jeg lå der blant de skvulpende bølgene trodde jeg at jeg skulle dø. Jeg husker det som om det var i går. Siden har det vært slik for meg at med en gang det blir litt bølger og kav rundt meg når jeg bader, så kommer panikken fra den gangen tilbake igjen. Jeg blir helt stiv i kroppen, og føler at jeg er i ferd med å drukne igjen. Dette trodde jeg at jeg skulle greie å vokse av meg, men til nå har jeg ikke greid det.»

Morten var også alvorlig nå. «Du er nok ikke den eneste som har det på den måten,» sa han. «Selv har jeg ikke opplevd noe slikt, men jeg har hørt om mange andre som har det likedan. Vannskrekk er ikke noe å spøke med. Beklager det jeg sa, det var ubetenksomt.»

«Det gjør ikke noe,» smilte Mette. «Men nå må du komme deg i vannet så du kan bli med på leken.»

Han reiste seg og gikk bort til en stein litt lenger unna. Fra den stupte han elegant uti. Vannet var mye dypere der. Med lange, kraftige tak svømte han utover mot holmen som lå der midt ute i tjernet. Flere av turistene fulgte etter. Mette betraktet ham der han svømte. Det mørke håret lå nå klistret bakover hodet. Men selv da så det pent og velstelt ut. Hun kjente noen ilinger gå gjennom kroppen mens øynene hvilte på den svømmende skikkelsen.

Plutselig satte hun seg mer opp. Hun skjente på seg selv. Hva var det hun satt der og fantaserte om? Nei, her var hun på jobb, ikke noe annet. Det måtte hun ikke glemme.

Enda en stund satt hun og så på dem som badet. Alle så ut til å stortrives i det friske fjellvannet. Hun var jammen glad for denne badeplassen. Når det ikke fantes dusj eller badekar på setra, var dette en alle tiders erstatning. Hun måtte igjen tenke på den store forskjellen mellom det livet hun pleide å leve i byen, og så dette. Der hadde hun alt hun kunne ønske seg av hjelpemidler og bekvemmeligheter. Her måtte hun greie seg med tjernet som badekar, og en gammeldags utedo borte ved fjøset i stedet for vannklosett. Hver dag kom hun nok til å ta seg en dukkert i dette kjølige vannet, for alt arbeidet med dyra krevde jo litt ekstra hygiene.

Etter hvert begynte den ene etter den andre å trekke oppover mot setervollen igjen. Mette fulgte også med.

Da alle var tilbake igjen, trakk tante Anna fram rokken for å demonstrerte karding og spinning for turistene. Hun satt ute på vollen med store kurver fulle av ull og garn rundt seg.

Først kardet hun opp ulla slik at den ble fin og luftig, uten noen knuter eller klumper. Med øvet hånd greide hun i en fart å lage en fin liten «pølse», som hun la i ei kurv. Så la hun ny ull på kardene, og vips, så hadde hun en ny pølse. Snart hadde hun en hel stabel med ullpølser i kurven.

Så satte hun seg til rokken. Hun hjalp til med hånden for å få sving på det store hjulet. Så tråkket hun i vei på pedalen, og hjulet sveiv så det suste. Det så nesten ut som en tryllekunst, syntes noen av barna da de så på hvordan ullpølsene ble forvandlet til en lang, tynn tråd. Den ene pølsen etter den andre ble festet til tråden som tvinnet seg lynraskt rundt og rundt.

Tante Anna arbeidet jevnt og trutt. Føttene, fingrene og munnen gikk i ett. Det var helt utrolig at hun, i et slikt tempo, kunne konsentrere seg om alt dette på en gang. Mette hadde igjen et krevende arbeid bare med å være tolk. Tilskuerne fikk informasjon om alt som hadde med behandling av ull å gjøre. I tillegg fikk de den ene historien etter den andre fra livet på setra i gamle dager. Etterpå fikk alle hvert sitt lille garnnøste som suvenir.

Mette hjalp henne med å bære inn alle kurvene igjen. Hun betraktet de fine fargene på ulla og garnet. Noe var gult, og noe var grønt. Der var blått og brunt garn også. «Er dette ull du har kjøpt?» spurte hun.

«Å nei.» Tante Anna humret der hun gikk med rokken mot seterbua. «Dette er ull fra sauene våre her på setra.»

Mette så forbauset på henne. «Men alle disse fine fargene, hvordan får du det til?»

«Det er plantefarging,» svarte hun. Tante Anna fortsatte før Mette rakk å spørre mer: «Jeg skal demonstrere det senere, men ikke for denne gruppen. I neste uke kommer det et husflidlag som skal lære om plantefarging. De skal være med på hele prosessen, så vi kommer til å bruke en hel dag.»

«Det gleder jeg meg virkelig til,» sa Mette begeistret. Hun studerte nøye garnnøstene med de klare, skarpe fargene.

«Du må gjerne ta noe av garnet hvis du vil bruke det til noe,» sa tante Anna da hun

243

så Mettes interesse.

«Kan jeg det?» Mette så ivrig fra tante Anna til de fine nøstene. «Kan jeg ta litt og strikke noe som jeg kan ha som et minne fra denne sommeren?»

«Ja, bare forsyn deg,» svarte den blide damen. «Jeg greier ikke å bruke opp alt jeg lager. Det meste må jeg gi bort likevel.»

Ivrig plukket Mette ut noen nøster før hun satte kurvene inn på rommet til tante Anna igjen. Det var nøster med farger som hun syntes passet fint sammen. Strikkepinner fikk hun også låne av henne. Hun kunne nesten ikke vente til hun fikk anledning til å sette seg ned med strikketøyet.

En stund senere sa tante Anna at Mette kunne gå ut og invitere gjestene på Kalvedansen. Puddingen sto ferdig, rykende varm, på et bord på vollen.

Snart samlet en stor flokk seg med tallerken og skje rundt krukken. Tante Anna begynte ivrig å dele ut.

Plutselig kom en liten gutt løpende gjennom grinden borte ved fjøset. «Se her,» ropte han. «Noen har gitt lakrispastiller til sauene. Jeg fant en masse av dem borte hos lammene.» Han viste noe han hadde i hånden. «Se, og der er masse igjen der borte.»

Mette tittet ned i den lille hånden. «Nei, men kjære lille venn, dette er ikke lakrispastiller. Har du prøvd å smake på dem?» Hun så urolig ned på den ivrige gutten.

«Nei, jeg gav bare til lammene, men de ville ikke ha dem.»

«Det ville de nok ikke,» sa Mette og lo godt, «for dette er sauebæsj. Bare legg merke til det når de må på do.»

Lynraskt slengte han alle de små, svarte kulene på marka, og tørket hånden febrilsk på buksebaken. To digre øyne stirret skrekkslagent opp på henne. Latterbrølene rundt dem fikk den lille til å føle seg litt flau og sjenert.

«Det var slett ikke rart at du tok feil.» Mette syntes at hun måtte trøste ham litt. «Det ser jo helt likt ut. Hvem som helst kunne ha gjort den tabben. Kom heller bort hit, så skal du få smake på Kalvedansen.»

Råmelkspuddingen ble en ny smaksopplevelse for gjestene. Tante Anna strødde sukker og kanel på porsjonene etter hvert som hun delte dem ut. Den lyse, gule puddingen forsvant raskt fra skålene. Noen bad også om å få påfyll. «Dette smaker nesten som karamellpudding,» sa ei jente som hadde spist sin andre porsjon.

Snart var krukka til tante Anna tom. Mette var slett ikke sikker på om Anna selv hadde fått noe, men det så ikke ut til å bekymre henne det minste. Hun smilte fornøyd. For henne var det alltid tilfredsstillelse nok å se de begeistrede fjesene når gjestene fikk smake noe av det hun hadde laget, og som de så tydelig likte.

7 • Stevne

Mette sto og betraktet landskapet rundt seterbua. Sola var i ferd med å bryte helt gjennom skydekket. Det så faktisk ut til å bli en fin dag, til tross for den dystre morgenen. Stevnet kunne gå av stabelen uten nevneverdige værproblemer, så det ut til.

Hun hadde våknet tidlig og hørt regnet tromme på taket. Og da hun kom ut, ble hun møtt av ei tung, grå tåke som hang over vannet. Tanken på arrangementet de hadde planlagt der ute på vollen, hadde bekymret henne ganske mye. Riktignok hadde Morten satt opp noen plastpaviljonger på campingområdet, men det ville likevel bli en fuktig fornøyelse hvis regnet skulle vedvare.

Men nå så det altså ut til at sola hadde fått overtaket. Regnet hadde sluttet for en god stund siden, og store sprekker i skylaget slapp de varme strålene gjennom. Tåka og den rå lufta måtte mer og mer slippe taket.

Mette merket at skuffelsen og tungsinnet fra morgenen var i ferd med å vike plassen for den forventning og spenning som hun hadde hatt dagen før. Hun hadde virkelig gledet seg til dette misjonsstevnet. Ikke minst hadde hun gledet seg til å skulle være med på å servere den gode setermaten som tante Anna hadde laget. Og så hadde hun gledet seg til å treffe folk fra bygda. Det var ikke så mange derfra hun hadde fått anledning til å hilse på.

Men forkynnelsen var vel det hun hadde gledet seg mest til. Hun hadde ikke vært til kirke eller på møte på ganske lang tid. Den åndelige hungeren hun kjente i sitt indre, gav henne en sterk forventning til denne dagen.

Tante Anna var i full gang med *rømmegrøten*. Den skulle lages skikkelig, helt fra grunnen av. Ingen halvfabrikata fra kjøpesenteret ble godtatt av henne. Og hun var flink. Grøten kom til å bli perfekt, det var Mette sikker på.

Hun gikk inn igjen for å lage røra til lappekakene. De skulle steke dem i matpausen på den store hella der inne. Folk skulle få dem servert rykende varme.

I det samme kom Morten kjørende. Han hadde vært nede i bygda for å låne høyttaleranlegg og noen stoler fra bedehuset.

Mens Mette og tante Anna gjorde klar maten, rigget Morten til utstyret ute på campingområdet. Han hadde en liten lastebil som han koblet høyttaleranlegget til. Stolene ble satt ut, og talerstol hadde han også skaffet.

Snart var alt klart til innrykk. Det varte heller ikke lenge før de første bilene begynte å komme. Denne stevnedagen på Siljatjernsetra var for mange en tradisjon som de nødig ville gå glipp av. De tok med det de trengte for å tilbringe hele dagen der. Noen kom ganske tidlig for å kunne rigge seg til på en grei plass. De som hadde vært der mange ganger, visste at det etter hvert kunne bli ganske trangt på området. Det var et populært arrangement, ikke minst på grunn av den gode setermaten til tante Anna.

Varmen der inne i seterbua ble ganske intens etter hvert, så Mette var glad da de var ferdige med det som skulle gjøres der, og kunne gå ut. Et par bord ble plassert langs seterveggen. Der skulle maten settes fram når første møte var ferdig.

Mette satte seg på en ledig stol i skyggen under en av paviljongene. Morten hadde bedt henne om å lese et ord til åpning. Det hadde hun forberedt, men hun følte at hun trengte å roe seg ned litt før det hele ble satt i gang.

Fra plassen sin kunne Mette se det meste av forsamlingen. Der var ikke mange kjente fjes. Men hun følte likevel en spesielt god fred. Sangen fra koret, som var kommet for å delta, tonet vakkert utover fjellet fra de sterke høyttalerne. De som satt nærmest, følte nok kanskje at lyden ble i kraftigste laget.

Ikke lenge etter gikk Morten fram og ønsket forsamlingen velkommen til et nytt stevne på Siljatjernsetra. Så ble Mette presentert, og ordet ble hennes.

Hun brukte ikke mye tid på det hun skulle si. Men hun bad en inderlig bønn. Hun takket Gud for den fine dagen, og for alle dem som var kommet til stevnet.

Det første møtet forløp etter planen. Predikanten som talte, var en ung og livlig kar. Mette kjente ham litt fra sin tid i misjonsarbeidet.

Sola steg stadig høyere på himmelen. Det var godt at de hadde paviljongene å sitte under, tenkte hun, ellers ville det fort ha blitt uutholdelig der i solsteiken.

Egentlig fikk hun ikke konsentrert seg skikkelig om talen, for etter en stund syntes hun at hun måtte gå inn for å hjelpe tante Anna med maten.

Da koret sang den siste sangen, begynte Mette å bære ut rømmegrøtgryta og flatbrødleivene. Tante Anna var i full gang med å steke lappene. Snart sto folk i kø for å forsyne seg. Til lappene hadde hun gjort klart hjemmelaget smør i et fat, og to store krukker med syltetøy. Det var blåbærsyltetøy og bringebærsyltetøy, også noe hun selv hadde laget. I et stativ sto et fenalår som folk kunne skjære av til grøten og flatbrødet.

Alle så ut til å stortrives. Barna lekte rundt på vollen. Noen hadde tatt seg en tur bort i lia for å se på dyra som gikk der og beitet.

Plutselig ble Mette oppmerksom på ei grind som sto åpen. Der ville nok dyra raskt kunne smette ut og skubbe borti bilene som sto tett i tett bortover veien. Barna tenkte nok ikke på hvor viktig det var at grindene var lukket på en dag som dette. Hun løp bort og lukket den forsvarlig. Det var nok best at hun holdt et lite øye med den, i hvert fall i matpausen mens folk flakket rundt på hele området, tenkte hun.

Da hun snudde seg for å gå tilbake igjen, kom det en mann sakte gående mot henne. Hun kjente ham ikke, men hun hadde sett ham sammen med noen andre fra bygda, så hun gikk ut fra at også han var fra distriktet. Han stoppet foran henne. Det så ut som om han ville si noe, men han så bare på henne. Øynene bar preg av et dypt alvor. Mette kjente at hun ble urolig. Det var noe ved ham som hun ikke kunne tolke. Hennes første tanke var: nå igjen!

De intense øynene hans fikk det til å gå kaldt nedover ryggen på henne. Hva var det denne mannen ville? Plutselig begynte han å snakke. Stemmen var anspent.

«Du må passe deg.» Han bøyde seg litt nærmere og senket stemmen: «Du bør være klar over at slik som Morten driver det …»

Han stoppet brått da han ble oppmerksom på at Morten sto og snakket med et eldre ektepar ikke lenger unna enn at han godt kunne høre hva de sa. Forvirringen som de flakkende øynene med ett gjenspeilte, gav henne en enda sterkere følelse av uhygge.

Brått snudde han seg og gikk tilbake til de andre.

Mette ble stående og stirre etter ham. Denne gangen var det ikke sinnet som overmannet henne, men heller en uro og nysgjerrighet. Hva var det som foregikk her? Hva var det disse mennene antydet, var det noe mystisk med Morten? Hva var det denne mannen mente at Morten drev med?

Sakte gikk hun tilbake til forsamlingen mens tankene tumlet rundt i hodet hennes. Hun trampet ergerlig i bakken. Hvorfor skulle slike uromomenter dukke opp når det var fred og velsignelse hun ønsket å oppleve? Nei, hun ville ikke la dette ødelegge denne fine dagen. Hun ba en stille bønn om hjelp til å konsentrere seg om det gode, og ikke om den uroen og uhyggen som nå var i ferd med å legge seg inn over sinnet hennes.

Etter hvert som hun ble opptatt med arbeidet og praten med gjestene, kom episoden mer og mer på avstand. Freden fikk igjen fylle hennes indre.

8 • Kom til Meg, alle dere som strever...

Morten kalte folk til samling igjen. Det var blitt enda trangere på campingområdet, for flere hadde kommet til under pausen. Praten summet og gikk, så det tok litt tid å få så pass ro at møtet kunne begynne.

Da koret hadde sunget noen sanger igjen, gikk den neste predikanten fram. Han var en liten, spedlemmet mann, litt oppe i årene. Men da han begynte å tale, ble forsamlingen slått av den kraft og intensitet som preget røsten hans. Han begynte talen uten noen slags form for innledning. Rett på sak gikk han.

«Kom til meg, alle dere som strever og bærer tunge byrder ...»

Ordene runget innover fjellet. Så ble det helt stille. Han sto noen lange sekunder og så utover forsamlingen. Da han begynte å snakke igjen, var stemmen mye svakere, men om mulig enda mer intens: «Har du noe du bærer på—noe tungt—noe du er alene om – noe du ikke kan be naboen eller familien om hjelp med? Hvordan har du det egentlig—i dag?»

Forsamlingens oppmerksomhet var fanget fra første øyeblikk. Alle satt i åndeløs taushet med blikket rettet mot talerstolen.

«Kom til meg ...» fortsatte han. «Det er ikke predikanten som ber deg om dette.» Røsten runget igjen med full styrke. «Nei, det er ikke predikanten, men den allmektige Gud. Han som har all makt i himmel og på jord. Det er Han som sier dette—gjennom sin sønn, Jesus Kristus.»

Det ble et øyeblikks taushet igjen. Han lente seg framover og støttet den ene albuen på talerstolen. Med en pekefinger litt opp i været var det som om han skulle komme med en viktig betroelse. «Vet du egentlig hva «all makt i himmel og på jord» betyr? Tenk litt på det.» Stillhet igjen.

«All makt,» fortsatte han, «det er noe ubegrenset det. Så jeg ikke bare tror, men jeg er overbevist om at det ikke sitter noen her i denne forsamling som bærer på noe som er for komplisert, stort eller vanskelig til at Gud kan ta seg av det. Heller ikke finnes det noe problem som er for lite eller bagatellmessig til at Han bryr seg om det. Og det underlige er,» sa han og rettet seg opp mens han begynte å bla i den store Bibelen sin, «at dette er heller ingen for lite begavet, eller for lite bevandret i Skriften, til å kunne forstå. La oss lese det som står om dette i Matteus' evangelium. Vi leser fra ellevte kapittel og femogtjuende vers.

På den tid tok Jesus til orde og sa: Jeg priser deg, Far, himmelens og jordens Herre, fordi du har skjult dette for kloke og forstandige, men åpenbart det for enfoldige.

Hørte dere det!» Røsten tiltok i styrke igjen. «Han har åpenbart disse mektige sannheter også for dem som ut ifra menneskelig bedømmelse ikke skulle ha forutsetning for å forstå det. Men det at det er skjult for kloke og forstandige, betyr ikke at slike ikke har muligheter for å kunne forstå det. Nei, det betyr nok heller at mange med fremragende evner og utdannelser likevel må stille bakerst i rekka når det gjelder de åndelige åpenbaringene. For der hjelper det ikke med alt det menneskelige vett og forstand vi kan stille opp med. Der gjelder kun det åndelig lys som Gud gir. Eller for å si det med ordene videre her i teksten: De som Jesus åpenbarer Faderen for.»

Mette hadde Bibelen sin oppslått i fanget. Hun fulgte nøye med da predikanten fortsatte å lese.

«Alt har min Far overgitt til meg. Ingen kjenner Sønnen uten Faderen; heller ikke kjenner noen Faderen uten Sønnen og den som Sønnen vil åpenbare det for.» Han la ekstra trykk på de siste ordene.

«Dette er altså grunnlaget for det jeg begynte denne talen med i dag. For i neste vers kommer akkurat det jeg da sa. Kom til meg, alle dere som strever og bærer tunge byrder, og så står det så fint videre – et løfte som vi alle kan stole på – så vil jeg gi dere hvile.

I versene videre er det gjemt noen meget dype sannheter. Noen vil nok si at de er for vanskelige å forstå, mens andre kan vitne om at de har fått et glimt inn i disse dybdene: Ta mitt åk på dere og lær av meg, for jeg er tålsom og ydmyk av hjertet, og dere skal finne hvile for deres sjeler. For mitt åk er godt, og min byrde lett.

Et åk har jo til alle tider vært forbundet med noe tungt. Gud ber oss altså om å ta på oss en byrde – en byrde som er fra Ham. Dette skal gi oss nødvendig lærdom. Jeg er redd for at mange i dag oftere ber Gud om å fjerne de byrdene som kommer på, i stedet for å gå inn under åket, og derved tilegne seg den kunnskap som dette gir. – Men hvordan henger nå dette sammen?»

Det ble liv i den lille mannen der framme på talerstolen. Han fikk problemer med å konsentrere seg om å tale inn i mikrofonen. Men stemmen bar visst nesten like godt enten han talte inn i den, eller svinset rundt omkring den.

«Ja, hvordan kan dette henge sammen? Var det ikke nettopp det vi ble oppfordret til – altså å komme til Ham med vår byrde? Var det ikke det som sto her?

Jo, det sto at vi skulle komme til Ham med byrdene våre. Men legg merke til hva løftet gjelder: – så vil jeg gi dere hvile.»

Det ble en lengre pause etter det siste ordet. Det var som om han ønsket at akkurat det ordet riktig skulle synke ned i forsamlingen.

«Hvile,» fortsatte han. «Det er hvile han lover oss her. Og hvile er nok det vi mennesker trenger mer enn noe annet. Det er nettopp det Gud ser. Det er tyngden av byrden Han vil hjelpe oss med. I vers tretti står det også: For mitt åk er godt, og min byrde lett.

Hvordan kan Gud si at byrden er lett? Jeg tror mange som har opplevd tunge ting, kan bli provosert av en slik uttalelse.

Eller – kanskje de heller opplever den som befriende og trøstende fordi de skjønner hva det betyr. Nemlig at denne byrden skal vi få komme til Gud med, og så vil Han hjelpe oss å bære den. Det er jo klart at når en som har all makt i himmel og på jord, bærer byrden sammen med oss, da blir ikke den biten vi må bære nødvendigvis så tung. I hvert fall blir den ikke tyngre enn at vi kan greie det. Men for at vi skal få den lærdom som Han ønsker, eller at andre skal få lærdom ved det vi må bære, så lar Han oss få noen byrder og åk gjennom livet.

Det Han kanskje aller helst vil lære oss, er nok nettopp dette at vi skal komme til Ham. Vi mennesker er jo engang slik at når vi har det godt, så føler vi at vi greier oss så utmerket på egen hånd. Men når motgangene kommer, da blir også bønnen tatt i bruk.

Gud vil ha oss på bønneplassen. For å få oss dit tar han ofte i bruk noen – for oss – uforståelige midler.»

Det ble stille igjen et øyeblikk. Predikanten der framme på talerstolen så litt fjernt ut i luften. Det kom et drag av smerte over ansiktet hans. Da han fortsatte, var stemmen på en måte svak og helt annerledes. Men likevel kom ordene med en intensitet, liksom fra det innerste av hans sjel:

«Det ligger så på meg dette. Her i denne verden må vi nok regne med mange slags vanskeligheter og lidelser. Men der er et sted å gå for å få hjelp. Og det er dette stedet jeg i dag ønsker å peke på for dere. Dette stedet er Jesus. Bruk dette stedet. Dere finner det her.» Han løftet den store Bibelen sin høyt over hodet. «Her i Ordet er det hvile å hente, for her er Jesus å finne.

Nå vil jeg også si at vi må selvfølgelig ikke tro at alle lidelser er gitt oss fra Gud for at vi skal bære på dem. Nei, dette vi har lest i dag, er et ord om å overlate vår sak helt og fullt til Herren. Og så vil Han ta seg av den slik som Han ser at det er rett. Mange lidelser tar Han fra oss når vi kommer til Ham med dem, for Han ser at disse vil hindre oss i å være det redskap for Ham som Han ønsker. Ja, noen ganger tar Han det bort uten at vi forstår hvorfor. Og likedan, andre ganger må vi bære noe uten at vi forstår grunnen til det. Sykdommer, for eksempel ...»

Han stoppet litt. Det så ut som han tenkte seg litt om før han fortsatte. «Når det gjelder sykdommer, så vil jeg gjerne ha sagt at vi skal være frimodige og bruke Bibelens ord og løfter. I Jakobs brev kapittel fem står en beskrivelse av hvordan vi skal gå fram når det gjelder akkurat dette. Helbredelse kan vi få oppleve i dag like så vel som folk på Bibelens tid fikk oppleve det. Men noen ganger må vi nok regne med å bære også sykdommen.»

Mette satt og lyttet med stigende interesse. Det var en ånds-atmosfære som fikk henne til å tenke på at nå satt de under Mesterens talerstol. Den lille mannen der framme var bare et redskap i Hans hånd – på samme måte som mikrofonen og høyttalerne var viktige redskaper for å få dette budskapet ut til folket.

Han holdt ingen lang tale, men mot slutten la han ut om Guds omsorg og kjærlighet til enkeltmennesket. Hver enkelt av dem som satt der og lyttet, var helt unike personer i Guds øyne, sa han. Det var bare gode tanker Gud hadde for dem. Og han brydde seg om den enkelte som om der ingen andre skulle være i hele verden. Ingen måtte la seg lure til å tro noe annet.

Idet han avsluttet og gikk ned for å sette seg, stilte koret opp igjen for å synge. Første sang ble introdusert som en tekst inspirert av versene i Jobs bok, kapittel trettiseks. Det var visst helst vers femten og seksten.

Da sangen begynte å tone utover forsamlingen, følte Mette igjen en vidunderlig fred ved den hellige atmosfæren. Ordene i sangen føyde seg helt inn i det taleren hadde sagt.

Er det mørkt på din himmel?
Er det mørkt i ditt hjem?
Er det mørkt i ditt innerste sinn?
Har du opplevd at livet har vist seg fra vrangen,
så tankene helt går i spinn?
Har du stilt deg et spørsmål og krevet et svar,
og følt taushet fra Himmelens Far?

Dine spørsmål er mange.
Dine krefter er små.
Dine hender er knyttet i bønn.
Og de hender er rettet mot Ham som har lovet
å hjelpe sin datter og sønn.
«Bare vent nå, mitt barn, jeg har noe å si.
Snart din prøvelsestid er forbi.»

Se, det lysner bak skyen.
Se, det lysner i øst.
Endt er natten som føltes så lang.
For fra Ordet det lyser et løfte til deg, som til Job
det ble kunngjort en gang.
Gjennom trengsel blir øret ditt åpent for Ham.
Bare lytt, for Han er der – Guds Lam.

Snart vil øyet ditt våkne.
Snart det lysner av dag.
Snart en stråle fra sola deg når.
Du vil se at de løfter som Bibelen gir,
de er sannhet som aldri forgår.
Han vil lede deg ut av den trengsel du har.
Takk din Frelser, din Gud, ja, din Far.

Denne sangen, og talen til den aldrende mannen, hadde virkelig truffet folk hjemme. Mange bad om å få ordet etterpå. Det ene gripende vitnesbyrdet etter det andre ble avlagt. Morten var tydelig litt i villrede om når han kunne avbryte. Klokka var alt blitt mye, og spesielt predikantene hadde lang vei å kjøre for å komme hjem.

Til slutt måtte han bare skjære gjennom og avslutte det hele.

9 • *Samtale under seks øyner*

Plutselig ble det uro i flokken. Noen reiste seg og begynte å rydde sammen tingene sine. Andre fortsatte en samtale de hadde begynt på i matpausen. Og noen benyttet anledningen til å hilse på kjente som de ikke hadde truffet på en stund. Men mange var nok preget av alvoret i møtet og hadde tanker de ønsket å dele med hverandre.

Etter en stund ble Mette oppmerksom på ei kvinne som gikk bort til Morten. Han hilste hjertelig på henne. Mette sto og ryddet av et bord i nærheten, så hun hørte godt det som ble sagt. Det var tydelig at disse to kjente hverandre.

«Nå er det jammen lenge siden jeg har sett deg,» sa Morten. «Bor du inne i byen ennå?»

«Nei,» svarte kvinnen. «Jeg har bodd i Oslo i flere år. Men nå har jeg flyttet til min søster. Hun bor jo i barndomshjemmet vårt her i bygda.»

«Så du har det,» sa Morten. «Da kommer vi vel til å se mer til hverandre i tiden som kommer. Det blir jo hyggelig.»

Kvinnen svarte ikke. Hun vred litt på seg og så ned i gresset. Morten betraktet henne et øyeblikk i taushet.

Mette kikket også bort på de to som sto der og pratet. Det var noe eiendommelig ved denne kvinnen. Hun var svært tynn. Det at hun var så liten av vekst, gjorde vel at hun så ekstra spinkel ut. Men det som var mest iøynefallende, var ansiktsuttrykket. Øynene virket nesten enorme i det bleke ansiktet. Der var også noe vaktsomt over blikket som gav et litt nervøst preg. Hun virket dradd – som om hun var trett og sliten. Det var også tydelig at hun ikke sto der og pratet for å friske opp gamle barndomsminner. Nei, det måtte være noe spesielt denne kvinnen ville. Morten hadde nok også lagt merke til det, for han sto som om han ventet på at hun skulle komme med det som lå henne på hjertet.

Hun rettet seg opp og tok liksom sats før hun sa: «Det var noe spesielt jeg ville snakke med deg om …» Hun nølte litt. «… på tomannshånd. Jeg våget ikke å ta kontakt med predikantene, og dessuten så er jo de reist nå. Men det må da være det samme hvem det er …»

Hun stoppet opp og fullførte ikke setningen. «Jeg kjenner jo deg fra før,» fortsatte hun litt skjelvende, «så jeg tenkte at kanskje jeg kunne få en prat med deg.»

Morten betraktet henne oppmerksomt. Han ante visst at det måtte være noe helt spesielt hun ønsket å snakke om.

«Ja, selvfølgelig kan vi ta en prat. Det er bare hyggelig det,» sa han. «Vi kan gå inn i seterbua. Der er vi for oss selv. Men vi har et prinsipp som jeg helst vil følge. Ved slike samtaler pleier vi alltid å være tre til stede. Har du noe imot at medhjelperen min, Mette, også blir med?»

«Nei, det er helt i orden det,» svarte kvinnen litt åndsfraværende.

Morten gav tegn til Mette at hun skulle følge med, og så gikk de inn alle tre. Han satte kroken på innsiden av døren slik at de ikke skulle risikere å bli forstyrret mens samtalen pågikk.

Kvinnen ble vist til rette i en stol ved bordet. Selv satte han seg på benken, rett overfor henne. Mette tok strikketøyet og satte seg litt unna. Hun forsøkte å være opptatt med det hun strikket, slik at ikke hennes nærvær skulle virke sjenerende. Det var jo Morten denne kvinnen ønsket å snakke med, og ikke henne.

Kvinnen vred seg litt i stolen der hun satt. «Det er så godt å komme på slike steder der Guds ord blir forkynt,» begynte hun. «Det er så godt å høre om at vi har en Gud som hører oss når vi ber, og bryr seg om oss samme hvordan vi har det.»

«Ja,» sa Morten. «Det er det virkelig godt å høre om. Og det er godt å vite.»

«Ja,» svarte kvinnen litt nølende. Et nervøst drag lå over hele ansiktet. Hun vred hendene i fanget. De store øynene stirret rett framfor seg uten å feste blikket på noe spesielt.

Mette gløttet bort på henne. Hva var det som plaget denne spinkle kvinnen? Aldri hadde hun sett noe så forknytt. Hun snakket om at det var godt å høre om en Gud som hørte bønn, men det virket slett ikke som hun hadde trygghet på at det virkelig var tilfelle.

Nesten som et svar på Mettes tanker sa kvinnen plutselig: «Tror du Gud hører alle våre bønner – samme hva vi ber om?»

Morten nølte litt. Han skjønte visst at det lå mer bak spørsmålet enn det hun sa. «Det er kanskje en spesiell bønn du har bedt som du ikke synes du har fått svar på?»

Kvinnen så ned på hendene sine og vred dem enda hardere. «Ja … nei … jeg vet ikke,» hvisket hun.

Morten lente seg lenger fram over bordet og så henne direkte inn i øynene. «Kjære deg, Solfrid,» sa han vennlig, «hva er det som plager deg?»

Hun så på ham et øyeblikk før hun senket blikket igjen. Noen rykninger rundt munnen fortalte at gråten ikke var langt unna. «Det er bare det,» hvisket hun. «Jeg er så redd.»

Og så var det som om en demning brast. Mens tårene rant nedover kinnene, begynte hun å fortelle: «Jeg har fått kreft. Det ble oppdaget for noen uker siden. Jeg hadde lenge gått og følt meg litt slapp og trett. Tynnere var jeg også blitt. Men jeg hadde ikke så mye vondt. Legen trodde det hele skyldtes et virus eller litt blodmangel, men han tok en del prøver for sikkerhets skyld. Og da var det altså at dette viste seg. Jeg ble operert for en svulst i magen, men det viste seg at det er spredning til hele kroppen. Det er ikke noe håp om at jeg kan bli frisk igjen. Jeg får bare en del behandlinger som forhåpentligvis skal hindre at sykdommen utvikler seg så raskt.»

Stemmen skalv, og rett som det var gikk der skjelvinger gjennom hele kroppen hennes. Tårene rant hele tiden.

«Og så er det disse behandlingene,» fortsatte hun. «De blir til tider som et mareritt for meg. Av og til kaller jeg dem halmstrået. Du vet det kan jo hende at de kan hjelpe så godt at jeg enda kan få mange gode år. Men så kommer de tidene igjen da jeg kaller dem langpining. Hvis jeg ikke kan bli frisk, og sykdommen bare skal fortsette å utvikle seg, så er det jo mye bedre at det går fort, slik at lidelsene ikke varer for lenge.»

Strikkepinnene til Mette hadde sluttet å arbeide. Hele ideen sin om å være diskré i bakgrunnen hadde hun glemt. Hun satt og stirret på Solfrid, som hun skjønte kvinnen het. Men det var visst ingen av dem der borte som la merke til henne. Morten hadde lagt hånden sin over Solfrids på bordet. Og dyp medfølelse tegnet seg klart i de mørke øynene hans.

«Dette var virkelig vondt å høre,» sa han. Det kom et hikst fra Solfrid idet hun fortsatte: «Jeg er så redd.» Ordene kom fra en strupe som var presset til det ytterste.

Plutselig var det som om det glimtet til i øynene hennes. «Gud,» sa hun. «Gud, Han har all makt – ikke sant?»

«Jo.» Morten nikket litt nølende. Han så ut til å tenke at nå var de inne på noe som lett kunne bli mennesketanker også.

«Ja,» fortsatte hun med anstrengt iver. «Det er egentlig derfor jeg er kommet hit nå. Gud kan helbrede, jeg vet det. Kan ikke du be for meg. Kanskje du kan salve meg med olje slik som predikanten snakket om. For Gud kan helbrede,» gjentok hun. «Tror ikke du også på det? Det er mitt eneste håp!»

Hun virket et øyeblikk nesten desperat. Morten ventet litt før han svarte. Det var tydelig å se at hele hans indre verket for denne kvinnen. Hele den anspente kroppen til Solfrid vitnet om behovet for et bekreftende svar.

«Har du tro for å bli helbredet da?» spurte Morten mildt.

«Tro!» Det var som en eksplosjon ut av munnen hennes. Hun spratt opp av stolen. «Så du er også av disse som mener man ikke kan bli helbredet uten at man greier å tro nok. Skjønner du ikke …» Et vilt blikk flakket rundt Morten uten å feste seg direkte på ham. «Skjønner du ikke … jeg greier ikke dette … dette med tro … jeg er så syk … jeg orker ikke mer.» Den desperate stemmen hennes gikk mer og mer over fra raseri til gråt mens hun snakket.

Morten hadde også reist seg nå. Han tok henne varsomt i armen og førte henne forsiktig ned i stolen igjen. «Nei, kjære deg, Solfrid,» sa han. «Nå misforstår du meg.» Det fortvilte blikket hennes møtte hans rolige, omsorgsfulle øyne. «La meg forklare dette litt for deg. Tro er ikke noe man må streve for å greie å få til. Tro er en gave som blir gitt oss fra Gud selv. Gud, Han ser din situasjon, og Han ser dine behov. Men Han ser også sin egen situasjon, og sitt behov. Disse to tingene, altså vår situasjon og Guds situasjon, kan ofte se ut som om de kommer i konflikt med hverandre. Men saken er bare den at Gud ser hele situasjonen i et annet lys enn vi kan. Dette lyset tilhører en annen dimensjon, en annen verden. Vi mennesker er ikke i stand til å se eller forstå dette. Vi har ikke de mekanismene som skal til for å fange inn dette lyset helt klart. Vi må leve her i verden som i en slags skodde. Men vi har Guds ord. Og i Guds ord finnes det som kan hjelpe oss til å leve i denne skodden. Gud ser altså på vår situasjon på en helt annen måte enn vi gjør. Det som forsvinner ut av vår verden, forsvinner ikke ut av Hans.

Vi klamrer oss til livet, og det er ikke så rart, for det er en del av skaperverket. Det er helt naturlig. Alle mennesker gjør det. Men Gud er Herre over liv og død. Når et menneske som har tatt imot frelsen i Jesus Kristus, dør, da er det ikke en ulykke som skjer. Det er bare en forflytting i Hans øyne. Forfremmet til Herligheten hører vi sagt enkelte ganger i begravelser.

Men så er det også slik at Gud har gitt oss en vei å gå med dem som er syke. Det var det predikanten snakket om der ute i dag. I Jakobs brev kapittel fem står det at man skal salve og be for dem. Og så står det at troens bønn skal hjelpe den syke. I hvert fall er det ordlyden i den bibeloversettelsen som jeg har her.»

Morten fant Bibelen sin og slo opp det skriftstedet han nevnte. «Se her,» sa han. «Det står hjelpe den syke, ikke helbrede den syke.»

Solfrid bøyde seg ivrig over Bibelen og leste hele verset for seg selv. Hun var litt roligere, men fremdeles virket hun anspent og trykket. «Men Gud helbreder da, gjør han ikke det, mener du?»

«Jo, selvfølgelig,» svarte Morten. «Det er det som er så ufattelig for oss. Gud helbreder, ja, Han helbreder svært mange også i vår tid. Men hvem – og hvorfor – gir Han oss ikke alltid lys over. Men dem Han gjør dette med, og det var det jeg ville fram til, dem gir Han også en spesiell tro for dette. Noen får det som en indre visshet, kanskje gjennom et ord de har lest i Bibelen. Eller de får det ved forkynnelse av Ordet. Andre kan få det som en mer ubevisst innskytelse. Ja, det er så mange måter dette kan skje på. Poenget er at de gjør det Bibelen sier og søker forbønn for problemet.»

«Men det er jo akkurat det jeg gjør nå,» sa Solfrid. Igjen virket hun nesten desperat.

«Ja,» sa Morten. «Og du gjør helt rett i det. Jeg ville bare snakke med deg om dette først, for det er så lett å forveksle denne troen med vårt eget inderlige ønske.»

Solfrid sank litt sammen der i stolen igjen. Tårene begynte å renne på nytt. «Men hvordan i all verden skal jeg kunne vite forskjellen på det da?» sa hun helt oppgitt.

Mette fulgte samtalen med stor interesse. Hun var igjen tilsynelatende mest opptatt av strikketøyet. Strikkepinnene gikk iherdig, men hun måtte nok rekke opp en del etterpå, for hun greide ikke å konsentrere seg om mønsteret.

«Kjære deg,» sa Morten. «Jeg håper ikke jeg har forvirret deg aldeles med det jeg har sagt. Selvfølgelig er det umulig i mange situasjoner å forstå den forskjellen. Men det har ikke så mye å si. For Gud er ikke avhengig av at du forstår det for å kunne helbrede deg. Han er i det hele tatt ikke avhengig av noen prestasjon fra din side. Alt som skal gjøres, er gjort. Det gjorde Jesus på korset en gang. Det eneste han ber deg om, er at du går og søker forbønn. Og er du i tvil om det er den ene eller den andre kategorien du tilhører, så er det bare å gjøre dette. Vær aldri redd for å be om forbønn, for løftet her gjelder alle. Bønnen skal hjelpe den syke. Og har Gud gitt deg tro for å bli helbredet, så blir du det, enten du skjønner det eller ikke. Men grunnen til at jeg har sagt alt dette, er at enkelte kan bli så skuffet etter at de er blitt bedt for, hvis ikke noe skjer. Ja, faktisk kan det gå på sjelefreden løs. Jeg vil så nødig at det skal skje med deg. Jeg vil salve og be for deg nå. Men jeg vil at du skal være trygg på at du er i Guds hender –

samme hva som skjer. Jeg vil at du skal forstå at Guds veier av og til ikke er våre veier. Ja, at av og til må vi bare akseptere det uten at vi noen gang vil kunne forstå det. Men helbredelse er en fantastisk ting som Gud kan la skje. Og det vil vi nå be Ham om å gjøre.»

Morten så litt på henne der hun satt i stolen. Hun var svært blek, men den anspente kroppen virket litt mer avslappet.

«Ja,» sa hun rolig. «La oss gjøre det. Og når det gjelder det med å akseptere, så må du be om et under der også.»

«Ja,» sa Morten. «Vi trenger mange under fra Gud. Og jeg er overbevist om at Han ikke vil spare på dem når det gjelder deg.»

Morten reiste seg. Han tok den lille oljeflasken som lå i bibelomslaget. «Kanskje du også vil være med på dette?» sa han henvendt til Mette.

Raskt la hun strikketøyet fra seg og gikk bort til Solfrid. De stilte seg på hver sin side av henne.

«Kan vi få lov til å legge hendene på deg?» spurte Morten. Solfrid nikket. Han helte en dråpe olje på en finger og strøk den over Solfrids panne. Så bad han en inderlig bønn om hjelp og trøst for den syke. Ham bad om at hvis det var Guds vilje at hun skulle bli frisk, så måtte Gud gjøre det etter det ord og løfte som står i Hans ord. Var det derimot slik at Gud ville ta henne hjem, så måtte Han gi henne kraft til å akseptere det. Han bad inderlig om at hun måtte få merke Guds omsorg og kjærlighet.

Mette bad også. Hun bad om at Solfrid måtte få være et lys for Ham, enten ved en helbredelse, eller gjennom sin sykdom. Til slutt bad hun om at Guds navn måtte bli herliggjort gjennom denne kvinnen.

Solfrid hadde gjemt ansiktet i hendene. Skuldrene hennes skalv lett i stille gråt.

Etter at de hadde bedt, ble det helt stille. Ingen ville bryte den hellige atmosfæren som fylte rommet. Til slutt reiste Solfrid seg og gikk stille mot døra. «Takk,» sa hun enkelt. Så gikk hun ut.

De visste ikke helt hva som rørte seg inni henne, men de lot henne gå. Nå måtte Gud få lov til å bearbeide henne etter Hans plan og vilje.

Da Solfrid hadde lukket døren etter seg, satte Morten seg ned på benken og gjemte ansiktet i hendene. Mette satte seg også ned. Ingen sa noe på en stund.

Plutselig så Morten opp på henne. Han virket dradd i ansiktet. Dype rynker lå over pannen. Det var tydelig at episoden hadde gjort sterkt inntrykk på ham. «Jeg pratet visst altfor mye for henne.» En sterk uro preget hele mannen.

«Det tror jeg ikke du gjorde,» sa Mette. «Det er jo klart at en lang tale til et så sykt menneske ikke alltid er på sin plass, men jeg tror at det du sa, var nødvendig i akkurat denne situasjonen.»

Morten fortsatte, mer til seg selv enn til henne: «Jeg fikk bare en slags fornemmelse av at det sterke ønsket hennes om å bli helbredet var et utslag av sykdomsangsten, og ikke noen slags minnelse fra Gud. Men jeg kan selvfølgelig ta feil. Det skal jo ikke alltid så sterke minnelser til for at Gud helbreder.»

«Det er ikke lett å skulle hjelpe mennesker i så dype kriser som Solfrid var i her,» sa Mette. «Jeg tror bare vi må stole på at Gud tar seg av henne. Vi har jo lagt henne i Hans hender. Jeg tror ikke vi kan gjøre mer enn det akkurat nå.»

«Ja.» Morten nikket og reiste seg. «Dette får være Hans sak nå.» Så gikk han ut igjen for å begynne oppryddingen etter stevnet.

10 • Fjelltur

M orten sto i fjøsdøra og speidet oppover lia i vest. En frisk bris lekte i det mørke
håret. I øst strevde sola med å få bukt med den kjølige disen som natta hadde
lagt etter seg. Noen skyer hindret den i få den makta den gjerne ville ha. Stillheten ble
bare brutt av den sprø klangen til sauebjellene og de vanlige lydene fra melkespannet
som Mette holdt på å løfte vekk fra den siste kua hun hadde melket. Noen klare fløyte-
toner fra en fugl oppe i skråningen fylte også luften fra tid til annen.

Mette gikk også bort til døra. En stund ble de stående der i taushet begge to. Hun
opplevde en vidunderlig fred og ro senke seg innover sjel og sinn ved stillheten og harmonien, dyra og naturen der på setra. Hun følte at hun var i ferd med å bli ett med det
alt sammen. Det fylte henne med en indre fryd og glede som hun vanskelig kunne
beskrive.

Morten snudde seg plutselig og så på henne. «Jeg undres på …» Han stoppet og lot
igjen blikket gli granskende oppover lia. «… Jeg skjønner ikke hvor de kan ha blitt av.»

Mette så på ham og la merke til et bekymret drag over ansiktet. Hun lurte på om
det han sa, var ment til henne, eller det bare var noe han sa til seg selv. «Hvem er det
du venter at skal dukke opp der oppe?» spurte hun.

Morten så på henne igjen og smilte. Han oppfattet spøken i spørsmålet og svarte i
en tilgjort alvorlig tone: «Jeg syntes jeg så Trylska sette grautgryta over grua der hvor
du ser røyken stige opp fra fjellet. Men så ble hun liksom borte for meg.»

«Trylska?» Mette så forvirret på ham. Hun skjønte at han spøkte, men hun forsto
likevel ikke riktig hva han sa.

«Ja,» lo han. «Som barn pleide vi alltid å si at det var trollene som kokte middag
over grua når vi så tåka ligge i slike små dotter oppover fjellsidene. Og Trylska, det er
jo kona til trollet.»

Mette måtte også le. «Jeg kan godt forstå at disse fjellene kan sette fantasien i sving
hos noen hver.»

«Men …» hun ble mer alvorlig igjen, «jeg tviler på at det var Trylska du kikket så
granskende etter for et øyeblikk siden.»

«Nei, det var nok ikke det.» Morten ble også alvorlig. «Jeg skjønner ikke hvor de
to kvigene kan ha blitt av. De pleier som regel å komme ned hit til de andre dyra fra tid
til annen, men nå har jeg ikke sett dem på flere dager. Et par ganger har jeg tatt noen
små turer innover fjellet, men jeg har ikke sett noe til dem der heller. Riktignok har
gresset vokst godt disse varme dagene, så de finner nok mye mat å spise. Men det er
den ene kvigen jeg er bekymret for. Den skal snart kalve, og jeg vil helst ha den her i
fjøset når det skjer.»

Igjen ble han stående og speide utover. «De er i hvert fall ikke å se noen steder her
omkring,» sa han etter en stund. Så tok han melkebøttene for å bære dem inn i melkeboden. Mette slapp ut kyrne på beitet igjen før også hun gikk inn.

Morten tømte melka i et stort spann og bar det til en kulp i en bekk borte ved fjellet. Der kunne den stå og holde seg kjølig i det kalde kildevannet.

«I dag og i morgen kan du ta deg fri,» sa Morten da de kom inn i seterbua igjen.
«Det er ikke så mye som skal skje her oppe disse dagene, og du må jo få tatt ut fritiden
din litt skikkelig av og til. Du kan bare bruke bilen hvis du vil. Jeg trenger den ikke, for
jeg må innover i fjellet for å se til de to kvigene. Det kan godt hende jeg blir der til i

255

morgen. Været er jo så fint at det sikkert vil gå bra å overnatte under åpen himmel. Det pleier jeg ofte å gjøre om sommeren.»

Mette så interessert på ham. «Det må være fantastisk å kunne vandre rundt slik i fjellet.»

Et øyeblikk møtte han øynene hennes. Et lite smil lekte om munnen. «Vil du bli med?» Et glimt av iver lyste opp i øynene hans.

«Kan jeg det?» En plutselig begeistring sto skrevet over hele ansiktet hennes.

«Det må du gjerne, men utstyr deg godt. Hvis vi må overnatte, kan det bli kjølig utover natta.»

Det ble med ett en hektisk aktivitet med raske forberedelser. På mobiltelefonen fikk Morten tak i Petter, naboen nede i bygda. Han hadde en avtale med ham om at de kunne spørre ham hvis de trengte ekstra hjelp. Det var også han som tok seg av dyra til Morten om vinteren. Nå lovet han å komme opp på setra for å ta dyrestellet til de kom tilbake igjen. Tante Anna var også nede i bygda. Hun kom ikke opp igjen før hun skulle demonstrere for husflidlaget i slutten av uka.

Mette pakket ryggsekken med ekstra klær, mat og noe utstyr som Morten sa de burde ta med. «Soveposer blir for mye å dra på,» sa han. «Jeg pleier å greie meg bra med bare et teppe.»

Mette var glad for det. Hun syntes sekken ble full nok som det var. Morten hadde i tillegg en stor taukveil som han la over skulderen. «Når man skal ut og lete etter dyr på denne måten, blir det som regel alltid bruk for masse tau,» sa han da han så at Mette stirret forundret på oppakningen hans.

Snart dro de i rask marsj oppover lia. Det var blitt ganske varmt i luften, så det meste av klærne hadde Mette lagt i sekken. T-skjorte og kortbukse greide seg fint for dem som skulle ut og vandre i slik en sommervarme. Men gode sko hadde hun i hvert fall tatt på seg.

Det første stykket skrånet ganske bratt oppover. Mette var glad for at hun var så pass veltrent som hun var. Noen muskelbunt var hun riktignok ikke, hun var heller ganske slank. Men spinkel var hun heller ikke. Hun hadde vært glad i trening og turgåing. Oslo var jo en by med rike muligheter til slikt, så det bød ikke på særlige problemer å holde tritt med Morten nå.

Før de nådde toppen av lia, kjente Mette at svetten rant nedover ryggen. Egentlig var det bare deilig å kunne få bruke kreftene på denne måten. Tappert fortsatte hun i samme tempo. Det var ikke så mye de kunne få prate sammen mens de gikk. Terrenget var så pass ulendt at de ofte måtte gå i gåsegang.

Da de nådde toppen, fikk Mette se et landskap som strakte seg vidt utover. Langt der framme kneiste noen fjelltopper. Rundt omkring var det høydedrag med vide myrer innimellom.

«Det må da gå an å plukke masse multer her om høsten,» sa Mette da de stoppet et øyeblikk for å puste ut litt.

«Å ja,» sa Morten og pekte mot et myrområde i sørvestlig retning. «Der borte er de beste multemyrene våre. Hvis det bare ikke blir frostnetter sent på våren, så bugner det av bær der når høsten kommer.»

«Tror du de blir modne før jeg reiser?» spurte Mette ivrig.

«Ja, det skulle jeg tro,» svarte han. «Men vi må være nøye på at vi ikke plukker dem for tidlig. Hvis vi plukker kart, vil ikke de plantene vi har plukket fra bære igjen før det er gått fra fem til sju år.»

Mette så overrasket på ham. «Det visste jeg ikke. Er det derfor det snakkes så mye om at man ikke må plukke multekart?»

«Ja.» Morten var alvorlig. «Det er mange som ikke skjønner det. Rett som det er kan vi oppleve rene kappløpet her for å komme først til de beste bærområdene. Multene er gjerne bare røde når de begynner plukkingen.»

«Hvordan må de være for at man trygt kan ta dem da?» spurte Mette.

«De må ikke taes før de slipper hamsen. Da er de saftige og gule. Det er de bærene som også gir det beste syltetøyet og den beste desserten,» svarte Morten.

De fortsatte vandringen langs en liten bekk som gikk i nordvestlig retning. Noen steder kunne Mette se at det var satt opp gjerder i lange strekninger. Morten forklarte at det var han og noen av dem som eide de tilstøtende områdene som hadde vært sammen om det arbeidet. På den måten kunne de la dyra gå tryggere innover fjellet. Men det var jo umulig å gjerde av alt, så de hadde utnyttet naturlige stengsler så godt de kunne. Fjell og bekker var fine gjerder, i hvert fall for kvigene.

De nærmet seg en liten høyde, og Morten sa at han gjerne ville opp der. Kanskje de kunne få øye på dyra de lette etter der oppe fra.

Igjen ble det tung klatring. Noen steder var det ganske bratt. Morten måtte hjelpe Mette et par ganger for at hun skulle greie de hardeste kneikene. Det tok en stund før de var oppe. Men endelig kunne de slappe av litt og beundre det mektige skuet som møtte dem på toppen.

Utsikten der oppe fra var fantastisk. Mette ble bare stående og stirre i taus hengivenhet. Den nakne fjellvidden strakte seg milevis i alle retninger. Lengst borte i horisonten forsvant de høye tindene nesten i en svak, blå dis. Noen steder, der fjelltopper lå litt nærmere, kunne hun se hvite flekker på toppene. Noen seiglivede snøflekker hadde kloret seg fast i de dypeste nordvendte kløftene. Den friske brisen som feide over fjellet, gjorde nok sitt til at de fikk sterkere fotfeste.

Nede i dalene vokste kratt og fjellgress frodig. Små bekker rant i snirklete krumspring langs dalbunnen. Innimellom blinket små, blå fjellvann i solskinnet.

Mette trakk pusten i lange drag. Den friske luften og det mektige panoramaet gav henne nesten en berusende følelse. Så glad hun var for at hun fikk være med på denne turen. Hun fant fotoapparatet og knipset flere bilder.

Morten hadde tatt fram kikkerten som han hadde i ei snor rundt halsen. Gjennom den gransket han nøye viddene omkring. Men samme hvor nøye han saumfarte området, kunne han ikke få øye på dyra noen steder. «Vi må nok bare fortsette letingen,» sa han og senket kikkerten. Her er det ikke antydning til noen kviger.»

Morten var godt kjent i fjellet, så det var tydelig at ruten han hadde valgt, ikke var tilfeldig. Målbevisst fortsatt han mot de høye fjellene i horisonten. Og rett som det var klatret de opp på nye høyder for å speide utover. Men like negativt var resultatet hver gang. Ingen kviger fikk de øye på. De kom over både sauer og geiter som gikk og beitet i dalsidene. Men dyra de selv var på utkikk etter, var ikke å se.

Utpå dagen bestemte de seg for å ta en hvilepause ved et vann. Morten tente opp et bål mellom noen steiner i vannkanten. Mette tok fram maten hun hadde pakket. Et stort stykke tørket fårekjøtt ble skåret opp i strimler. Morten spikket noen pinner som han spiddet kjøttet på. Så begynte han å steke det over bålet. De hadde også tatt med noen potetlefser. Etter hvert som kjøttstrimlene ble ferdig stekt, pakket han dem inn i lefsebitene, og så kunne de spise det nystekte kjøttet. Aldri hadde Mette smakt noe så deilig.

«Slik pleide mine foreldre å steke tørket fåreribbe i peisen på julaften da de var barn,» sa Morten. «Min far pleide også å gjøre det enkelte vinterkvelder da jeg var liten. Minnene om disse kveldene rundt peisen er vel noe av det kjæreste jeg har,» sa han og så drømmende ut i luften. Et svakt smil lå rundt munnen hans.

For Mette var smaken og tradisjonen helt ny, men hun skulle gjerne spise dette igjen. Den sterke, salte fåresmaken satt igjen i halsen lenge etterpå.

Etter at de hadde spist, ble de sittende og se utover vannet. De fant en skyggefull plass bak noen steiner. Sola stekte ganske sterkt, så det var godt med den skyggen de kunne finne.

Plutselig snudde Morten seg mot Mette og så henne granskende inn i øynene. Et muntert uttrykk glimtet i de mørkebrune øynene hans. Mette ble litt forlegen over det intense blikket.

«Aldri har jeg sett så blå øyne noen gang,» sa han omsider.

Mette ble aldeles overrumplet over den nærgående bemerkningen.

Han begynte å le. «Jeg har bare lagt merke til det. Beklager hvis jeg var for nærgående.» Han flyttet blikket, og så utover vannet igjen.

Det tok noen sekunder før Mette greide å si noe. «Ja, jeg er visst nokså blåøyd, det har jeg ofte fått kommentert, sa hun omsider.» De lo begge to. «Det er noe jeg har arvet etter min far,» fortsatte hun. «Han har også svært blå øyne. Faktisk mye lysere enn mine. Det har ført til at folk som ikke kjenner ham, tror at han er full. Han ser nemlig så sløv ut i blikket.»

«Nå var det ikke slik jeg mente det,» sa Morten fort. «Øynene dine er vakre som bare det. Kan du ikke fortelle litt om deg selv?» fortsatte han. «Hvor gammel er du for eksempel? Man skal visst ikke spørre en kvinne om alderen, men jeg trodde ...» Han stoppet og så på nytt granskende på henne.

Igjen følte Mette at rødmen spredte seg over ansiktet hennes. Men hun svarte så naturlig hun kunne. «Jeg blir trettito til høsten.» Plutselig snudde hun seg og så utfordrende på ham. «Hvis du leste søknaden min, så sto fødselsdatoen der.»

«Det var nettopp det,» svarte han og rynket brynene. «Jeg syntes så tydelig det sto at du var født i førtito. Men det var altså syttito?»

Enda en gang kjente Mette at rødmen steg, denne gangen helt ut i hårrota. «Beklager,» sa hun stille mens hun stirret ned i marka. «Jeg var på reise da jeg skrev den søknaden, og der hadde jeg ikke adgang til PC. Jeg vet at jeg har ei fryktelig stygg håndskrift. De sjutallene kan lett se ut som firetall når jeg må skrive dem for hånd.»

«Det er altså der forklaringen ligger,» lo Morten. «Jeg har virkelig undret meg over dette. Men det har da ingen ting å bety. Da er du altså ett år yngre enn meg.»

Mette lot seg ikke merke med at hun likte å få den opplysningen. Men hun hadde gjettet at han måtte være omtrent på den alderen.

«Du har kanskje noen søsken også?» fortsatte han.

Mette begynte å fortelle om familien sin. Hun fortalte om foreldrene som bodde i en av de små sørlandsbyene—Grimstad i Aust-Agder fylke—og om søstera som var gift og bodde i samme by. Hun fortalte om tre små nevøer som hun forsøkte å besøke så ofte hun kunne. Så fortalte hun om gården hvor hun vokste opp. Den var nå solgt til en av fars yngre brødre. Sin barndomstid der hadde hun fortalt om den første kvelden hun var på setra, så det sa hun ikke så mye om.

Morten lyttet oppmerksomt. Av og til kom han med et spørsmål, og Mette fortsatte å fortelle. Snart syntes hun at han måtte ha fått greie på alt om henne og familien hennes, den kristne oppdragelsen hun hadde fått, og det trygge hjemmet hun hadde vokst opp

i. Tilværelsen hennes hadde vært nokså uproblematisk i oppveksten. «Kanskje det kan føre til problemer senere?» avsluttet hun. «Man trenger jo litt motganger for å herdes i livet.»

Morten smilte et litt vemodig smil. «Jeg tror du skal takke for alt det gode, og så får man ta det tunge når det kommer.» En skygge gled over ansiktet. En stund satt han stille som om han var fortapt i gamle minner.

Plutselig begynte han å fortelle om sin egen familie. Han fortalte litt om faren som så brått døde av hjerteinfarkt for åtte år siden. Han nevnte også moren som hadde vært svakelig over lengre tid før også hun døde. Det var et par år siden nå.

Så fortalte han om de to søstrene han hadde. Marit var gift og bodde nede i bygda, og så var det Siri som bodde i Trondheim med sin familie.

Mette lyttet interessert. Tante Anna hadde også fortalt en del om familien, men det var litt fint, syntes hun, at Morten sa det selv. Han var som regel ikke så meddelsom når det gjaldt personlige ting.

Det var likevel ikke lang tid han brukte på disse familieredegjørelsene før han så på klokka. «Jeg tror vi må komme oss videre hvis vi skal ha håp om å finne rømlingene i dag,» sa han og reiste seg. Raskt pakket de sammen sakene sine. Så bar det av sted igjen.

11 • Stokken i vannet

Igjen strevde de seg oppover mot en ny høyde. De hadde funnet ut at det var lettest å lete når de sto så høyt at de hadde vid utsikt over fjellet og viddene.

Vel oppe tok Morten fram kikkerten på nytt og lot blikket gli rundt hver knaus og dal. Mette satte seg rett ned på det flate fjellet. Hun var sliten etter alle de fjellskrentene de hadde klatret opp på. Det var virkelig godt med en hvil der på toppen.

«Jeg begriper ikke dette.» Morten speidet igjen og igjen utover. «Hvor kan de ha blitt av?» Han senket kikkerten og så betenkt ut i luften. «Hvor skal vi ta veien nå tro? Vi har gått i en bue rundt disse viddene. Fortsetter vi mot sør nå, så er det ikke mer enn en time eller to, så er vi på setra igjen.» Han så på klokka. Den var nesten fem. «Hva tror du?» Han så direkte på Mette. «Skal vi gå tilbake? Da er vi på setra i god tid før det blir skikkelig kveld. Eller skal vi ta turen lenger østover? Kanskje de har greid å krysse bekken der borte i den dalen der.» Han pekte mot et dalføre øst for der de sto. Mette så i den retningen han pekte. Hun kunne ikke se bekken, men hun så fjell og vidder på den andre siden av dalen. Det ville bli en hard tørn å komme opp de dalsidene der borte.

«Tror du kvigene ville greie å komme opp der om de kom over bekken?»

Mette så tvilende ut. Morten så også betenkt ut.

De diskuterte forskjellige muligheter en stund. Det var jo aldeles umulig å vite hvor de skulle lete. Selv om Mette følte seg litt sliten etter dagens vandring, så hadde hun slett ikke lyst til å gå tilbake til setra igjen ennå. Været var fint. De skyene som var å se på himmelen, greide ikke å holde solsteiken borte særlig lenge av gangen. Men varmen var heller ikke for plagsom, for en frisk bris feide over viddene og gav kjøling til de svette kroppene deres. I hvert fall kjentes den godt der oppe i høyden hvor de var.

Etter å ha hvilt en stund tok Morten kikkerten og gikk litt bortover det flate fjellet.

Mette reiste seg også og fulgte etter.

Plutselig stoppet han med et rykk. «Hva var det?» Han sto stille og lyttet. Der hørte også Mette en lyd. Den kom fra et sted langt der nede. Raskt fikk de på seg ryggsekkene og gikk i den retning lyden var kommet fra. Snart var de framme ved et sted hvor fjellet stupte bratt ned mot en dal. De sto på fjellskrenten og speidet utover. Under dem så de et blankt lite fjellvann som lå nesten helt inn til fjellsiden.

Igjen kom den rare lyden. Nå kunne de høre at det var en kort rautelyd fra ei ku. «Se der!» Morten ropte forskrekket og pekte mot noe kratt inne ved bredden. Der sto det ei ku og stirret urolig utover vannet. Snart beveget den seg til den ene, og snart til den andre siden. Det så ut som om den hvert øyeblikk kunne hoppe ut i vannet.

«Er det ei av kvigene dine?» Mette betraktet den rare oppførselen med stigende undring.

«Jeg vet ikke.» Morten gransket den gjennom kikkerten. «Men det er jo svært sannsynlig.»

«Det ser ut som at det er den stokken der ute i vannet den er interessert i,» sa Mette og pekte mot noe som lå og duvet dypt i vannskorpen.

Morten lot kikkerten sveipe over vannflaten. Plutselig satte han i et nytt rop. «Stokken! Var det stokken du sa?»

Mette så forskrekket på ham. Han var jo aldeles på styr.

«Det der er ingen stokk, kan jeg fortelle deg!» ropte han opprørt. «Det er den andre kvigen. Den ligger nesten helt nedsunket i vannet der. Jeg er faktisk nokså sikker på at dette er mine kviger.»

Med ett ble det fart på dem begge. Litt lenger borte var det en kløft hvor fjellet skrånet litt slakere nedover. «Her tror jeg vi kan greie å komme ned,» sa Morten. De var rett over det stedet hvor kvigen var.

«Se her!» Forundret pekte han nedover skråningen. Mette kom nærmere. Der kunne hun se at mose og lyng var revet bort i store flak. De fortsatte nedover. Og hele veien var det tydelige spor etter noen som hadde vært der før dem.

«Kvigen må ha falt ned her,» sa Morten. «Men hvordan i all verden har den klart å komme helt opp hit?» Mette så forvirret oppover de bratte fjellsidene. Morten stoppet og pekte mot sør. «Der borte stiger det ikke så bratt oppover. Den har nok kommet opp den veien.»

Rett som det var måtte Mette ned på baken for ikke å gli for fort nedover. Sekken var det også vanskelig ha kontrollen på.

Det kom stadig nervøse raut fra den urolig kvigen inne på land. Fra «stokken» i vannet kom det også noen anstrengte tryt.

Da de kom ned til vannkanten, gikk plutselig den alvorlige situasjonen opp for Mette i hele sin gru. Hun kjente at hun skalv der hun sto og så på dyret som lå nesten under i vann. Det var bare hodet og litt av ryggen som var synlig. «Hvordan har den kommet så langt ut?» undret hun.

«Den har nok kavet for å komme opp,» mente Morten. «Så har den bare beveget seg lenger utover. Vannet er jo ganske grunt her, men på bunnen er det tykk gjørme. Den sitter nok fast i denne gjørmen.»

Han vrengte av seg ryggsekken og begynte å rote fram noe av det utstyret han hadde der. «Heldigvis har jeg godt med tau med. Det kommer vi til å få god bruk for nå, vil jeg tro.»

Da den andre kvigen fikk øye på dem, satte den i med noen lange raut. Så kom den byksende og holdt på å rive Morten over ende. Mette måtte le. «Det er i hvert fall ingen tvil om at det er dine kviger,» sa hun. «Denne kjenner deg tydeligvis godt igjen.»

Morten så på det ivrige dyret. Så rettet han blikket mot vannet igjen. «Det er den som snart skal kalve, som ligger der ute,» sa han med bekymring i stemmen.

«Hvordan skal vi få den inn til land?» spurte Mette. Hun sto helt tafatt og stirret på det stakkars dyret.

Etter en del rådslagning ble de enige om å prøve og trekke den inn mot land med et tau. Hvis de begge svømte ut, så kunne de se hva de måtte gjøre.

Fort fikk de på seg badetøy. For Mette gikk det ganske fort, for hun hadde sitt på seg under de andre klærne. Hun hadde håpet på å kunne få en dukkert i et vann et eller annet sted på turen. At det skulle bli under slike dramatiske omstendigheter, hadde hun ikke drømt om.

Med taukveilen over skulderen begynte Morten å svømme ut mot kvigen. Mette trengte litt lenger tid for å komme uti. Vannet var ganske kaldt, syntes hun. Men snart var også hun på vei ut. Det var ikke så lett å svømme i dette vannet. Stadig kom hun ned i gjørmebunnen med beina. Svarte skyer av grums steg mot overflaten.

Morten festet tauet rundt halsen på kvigen da han kom bort til den. «Kan du holde dette?» spurte han da Mette kom nær nok. Han rakte henne kveilen med tau. Hun tok det mens hun strevde med å holde beina unna den verste gjørmen.

Plutselig begynte kvigen å bykse med kroppen. Den slo med hodet så vannet skvatt rundt dem. Morten var uforberedt, så han falt bakover og dukket under vann. Han veivet med armene så spruten sto. Et kaotisk øyeblikk var hele vannet rundt dem i et eneste kok. Bølgeskvulp slo opp i ansiktet på Mette. Hun trakk fort pusten og slukte en stor slurk med vann.

Med ett følte hun det som en klam, kald klo grep om henne. Panikken kom veltende for fullt. Opplevelsen fra barndommen sto igjen levende for henne. Hun ble stiv i hele kroppen, og greide ikke å tenke klart. Et nytt hikst førte enda en munnfull vann ned i halsen. Armene slo febrilsk mot vannflaten. Gjørmen virvlet rundt henne, og sprutet opp i luften. Nå dør jeg! Tanken var der med det samme.

Da kjente hun en arm som la seg rundt skulderen hennes. Varsomt, men bestemt, ble hun trukket inn mot en sterk skulder. Den rolige stemmen til Morten hvisket inn mot håret hennes: «Dette går bra. Ta det bare helt med ro.»

Sakte kjente hun at skrekken begynte å slippe taket. Musklene slappet gradvis av, og hun lot hodet falle inn mot den trygge skikkelsen. Et hikst unnslapp henne mens en skjelving gikk gjennom hele kroppen.

Det hele varte bare noen øyeblikk. Så løsnet Morten forsiktig grepet, og alt var som før igjen. «Kan du ta denne tauenden og svømme inn mot land?» Morten rakte henne tauet som om ingen ting var hendt. «Hvis du svømmer inn dit,» sa han og pekte mot et sted hvor en landtunge strakte seg litt lenger ut i vannet, «så kan vi forsøke å dra henne inn der. Vannet er litt dypere ved de steinene, og bunnen ved bredden er fastere.»

Mette tok tauet og svømte mot land. Morten hadde knyttet sammen to av dem, så det var ganske langt.

«Når jeg sier fra, må du trekke forsiktig i tauet,» ropte han da han så at hun var kommet vel i land. Mette hentet et håndkle som hun la over skuldrene, og så satte hun seg for å vente på beskjed. Hun så seg litt rundt. Det var litt bedre plass på land der hun nå satt. Men det var likevel ikke langt bort til stedet der fjellveggen reiste seg nesten loddrett opp, kanskje sju-åtte meter. Bredden var gresskledd med noen steiner innimellom. Hun kikket oppover kløften hvor de kom ned. Kvigen hadde nok blitt fristet av det frodige gresset som vokste der, og så hadde den glidd utfor.

Det var et vakkert sted. Vannet lå så idyllisk mellom fjellene. Det vokste noen små, kronglete bjørker langs bredden. Hun la også merke til at det så ut til å være mulig å ta seg fram rundt hele vannet, så de kom nok ikke til å få problemer med å komme seg videre med dyra. Hadde ikke omstendighetene vært så dramatiske, så hadde hun virkelig nytt den vakre naturen der ved vannet. Men nå kunne hun ikke konsentrere seg om noe annet enn det som foregikk i den andre enden av tauet. Det så ut til at Morten hadde en stri tørn der ute hos kvigen. Gang på gang dukket han under vann. Han dyttet og løftet, men like dypt så det ut til at det stakkars dyret lå. Snart var han på den ene siden av kvigen, og snart på den andre.

«Nå må du prøve å dra,» ropte han plutselig. Mette reiste seg raskt og strammet inn tauet. Men det så ikke ut til at det var noen bevegelse i den tunge kroppen. Det virket heller bare som om hun dro hodet ned under vann.

Igjen forsvant Morten. Mette syntes det var en evighet før han dukket opp igjen. Men endelig kom hodet hans til syne over vannskorpen.

«Jeg ser ingenting i denne gjørma,» ropte han. «Men det kan virke som den er skadet i et av beina. Det sitter helt fast i gjørma. Den har tydeligvis ikke kunnet bevege det. Jeg tror jeg fikk løsnet det litt. Prøv å dra igjen nå.»

Igjen strammet hun tauet. Først så det ikke ut til at det skjedde noe som helst. Men så kom det et rykk i tauet, og sakte, men sikkert begynte den tunge dyrekroppen å bevege seg nærmere land. Morten dyttet så godt han kunne der ute. Litt etter litt kom de ut på dypere vann, og der gled det litt lettere.

Det var ikke mange sprellene kvigen greide å gjøre. Ikke kom det særlig mange lyder fra den heller. Den så helt utslitt ut. Kanskje hadde den ligget der og kavet lenge.

Da de kom inn mot land, der bunnen var fastere, merket de helt tydelig at det ene beinet var skadet. Den greide ikke å sette det under seg i det hele tatt. Utmattelsen var nok også litt av grunnen. Den prøvde å sette frambeina på den faste grunnen, men falt framover i vannet. Det friske bakbeinet kavet febrilsk et øyeblikk for å få feste.

Det ble en kamp både for kvigen og de to som skulle hjelpe, for å få den på land. Men etter mye strev lyktes det likevel. Utmattelsen hos det skadede dyret så ut til å være total. Den lå nesten livløs med beinet rett utstrakt. Hodet lå på bakken, og tunga hang ut av kjeften.

«Stakkars dyr.» Mette bøyde seg ned og strøk den over hodet og halsen. Den enset henne ikke i det hele tatt.

Morten fant teppet sitt og la det over den våte dyrekroppen før han selv fikk på seg tørre og varme klær.

Mette kledde også på seg. Hun så at Morten hutret etter det lange oppholdet i det kalde vannet. Det var tydelig at strabasene også hadde tatt på kreftene hans. Hun skjenket i en kopp kaffe fra termosen og rakte den over til ham. «Hvordan går det med deg?» spurte hun og satte seg ved siden av ham i gresset.

«Takk skal du ha,» sa han og tok imot den varme kaffekoppen. «Det går fint med meg.» Han smilte litt matt. «Jeg må bare puste ut litt. Det var en skikkelig tørn, dette her.»

De satt i taushet en stund. Den andre kvigen hadde roet seg og gikk og beitet lenger borte på bredden. Vannet lå igjen stille og blankt. Bare noen gjørmespor borte i vannkanten fortalte om den harde kampen de nettopp hadde gjennomkjempet sammen.

12 • «Keiseren»

Morten drakk kaffen mens han hele tiden betraktet dyret som lå der på bakken. Han var fortsatt taus, men Mette kunne se at det foregikk en hektisk aktivitet oppe i hodet hans. De dype rynkene mellom øynene fortalte at han sto foran en vanskelig beslutning som måtte taes.

Mette sa heller ingenting. Det var på en måte ikke rom for ord i den situasjonen de var havnet i. Ikke visste hun hva hun skulle si heller. En mer fortvilet situasjon hadde hun ikke opplevd.

Der satt de altså. I mer enn en time hadde de arbeidet med kvigen. De hadde fått den på land, men tilstanden var vel så kritisk som den kunne bli. Det var i hvert fall helt umulig å få den med hjem slik tilstanden i øyeblikket var. Klokka var over seks. Det begynte å bli kveld. Nei ... Hun sukket for seg selv. Situasjonen var absolutt fortvilet. Hun visste virkelig ikke hva hun skulle si.

Plutselig reiste Morten seg. Han brettet teppet til side og begynte å undersøke den tilsynelatende livløse dyrekroppen. En liten bevegelse med hodet viste at det tross alt ennå var liv i dyret. Det gikk også fra tid til annen noen rykninger gjennom den store kroppen. Morten la øret ned mot brystet på den for å lytte etter hjerteslagene. Så strøk han over det store midtpartiet med begge hendene. Igjen og igjen lot han hendene gli over magen på kvigen.

Da han igjen satte seg ned, var rynken mellom øynene om mulig enda dypere. «Den lever,» sa han, «men det varer nok ikke så lenge. Der er antakelig flere skader enn de i foten. Den må nok bare avlives. Det som bekymrer meg, er imidlertid at vi med det også avliver kalven inni henne. Jeg kunne tydelig kjenne at det var liv i den, og den er jo faktisk fullbåren.»

Han satt og så ut i luften mens han snakket. Mette kjente at noe snørte seg til inni henne. At et dyr måtte avlives var ikke fremmed for henne. Det hadde hun opplevd mange ganger i sin barndom hjemme på gården. Men dette var litt spesielt. Kvigen ville bare lide ved å bli liggende slik. Det beste de kunne gjøre for den var å ta livet av den. Men kalven ... Det virket liksom så meningsløst.

Hun reiste seg og gikk bort for å se nærmere på den. «Når skulle den ha kalvet?» spurte hun.

Morten kom også bort til henne. «Den har ikke mer enn en ukes tid igjen,» svarte han.

Forsiktig la Mette en hånd ned på den store magen.

«Kjenn her,» sa Morten.

Mette lot hånden gli ned mot det stedet som han viste henne. Der kunne hun tydelig kjenne noen bevegelser. En inderlig medlidenhet med denne lille skapningen fylte hele hennes indre. «Er det noe vi kan gjøre?» Gråten var ikke langt unna. Hun måtte svelge noen ganger for at stemmen skulle virke normal.

Morten så heller ikke ut til å være uberørt. Han svarte ikke med det samme, men undersøkte området grundig en stund.

Endelig rettet han seg opp og så rett på Mette. «Hvis du vil hjelpe meg, så kan vi gjøre et forsøk.»

«Ja ...» Hun dro litt på det. «Hva vil du jeg skal gjøre?» Stemme hennes var nesten bare en hvisking. Hun skalv lett. Hva var det han ville ha henne til å gjøre?

Morten gikk rundt kvigen et par ganger, for å studere den fra alle sider, før han fortsatte. «Vi må prøve å ta ut kalven.»

Det kom et hikst fra Mette.

Morten så igjen rett på henne. «Tror du at du kan hjelpe med det?»

To skrekkslagne øyne møtte hans. Hun greide ikke å svare. Skjelvingen hennes økte i styrke.

Morten senket blikket igjen. Det så ut som om all styrke og pågangsmot rant ut av ham. Stemmen hans var også bare en hvisking da han fortsatte. «Selvsagt er dette for mye forlangt. Beklager. Det er nok ikke mye vi kan gjøre her.»

Da var det som om Mette kjente at hun fikk mot, og noen krefter som hun aldri siden fant ut hvor kom fra. Hun rettet seg opp. Med klar, fast stemme sa hun: «Det er klart jeg skal hjelpe deg. Hvis det er noe vi kan gjøre for å redde kalven, så må vi selvsagt prøve det.»

Morten så forundret opp på henne. En gnist av håp tentes igjen i øynene hans med det samme. «Tror du vi kan greie det?» Stemmen hans var fremdeles bare en hvisking.

«Bare si hva jeg skal gjøre, så gjør vi et forsøk.» Skjelvingen i kroppen ville ikke helt slippe taket, men hun var fast bestemt på å gjøre sitt beste.

Morten reiste seg raskt. På nytt begynte han å undersøke kvigen. «Pulsen er svak, men hun lever ennå,» sa han. «Har du kniv med deg i sekken?»

Mette tenkte seg om et øyeblikk. «Jeg har den kniven som vi skar opp maten med. Det er nok bare en brødkniv.»

«Det får greie seg,» sa Morten. Han var i full gang med å undersøke magen til kvigen nøye. «Jeg har en tollekniv i min sekk. Vi får prøve å bli hjulpet med det.»

Mette fant knivene, og Morten strøk dem en stund mot hverandre for å gjøre dem så skarpe som mulig. Mette sto stiv av spenning. Enda visste hun ikke hva det var hun måtte gjøre. Hun ville helst ikke tenke på det. Bare få det hele unnagjort.

Morten gav henne brødkniven og satte seg på huk ved hodet til kvigen. «Når jeg sier fra, kan du da stikke kniven dypt inn der?» Han pekte på et punkt på halsen til dyret.

Mette kjente at noe veltet seg langt der nede i magen et sted. Men hun svelget hardt og satte seg besluttsomt ned ved siden av ham. «Var det der?» hun pekte for å forsikre seg om at hun hadde oppfattet beskjeden rett. Morten nikket og snudde seg mot den midtre delen av dyret. Igjen lot han hånden gli undersøkende rundt den store vomma. Mette var så opptatt av punktet på halsen hvor hun skulle stikke at hun ikke så nøye la merke til hva Morten foretok seg.

«Er du klar?» Mortens stemme var anstrengt til det ytterste.

«Ja, jeg er klar.» Hele kroppen til Mette var i helspenn. Hver fiber var konsentrert om det lille punktet der på halsen.

«Stikk nå!»

I det samme ordene lød, sank det lange knivbladet dypt inn i halsen. Det som så skjedde, var hun på ingen måte forberedt på. En skjelvende rykning gikk gjennom kvigen mens blodspruten sto rett til værs. Et halvkvalt skrik unnslapp henne da hele armen, fjeset og en del av brystet ble farget rødt av den tykke, varme væsken. Raskt reiste hun seg og strøk seg over øynene med hånden for å fjerne så pass mye blod at hun kunne se klart igjen. Et øyeblikk ble hun stående og svaie. Det der nede i magen hadde visst ikke til hensikt å forbli der. Men etter noen kraftige innåndinger av den friske fjellufta så det likevel ut til å falle litt mer til ro.

Endelig greide hun å vende oppmerksomheten mot det som foregikk ved siden av henne. Hun så på Morten. Han sto på kne med begge armene dypt inne i magen på det døde dyret. Raskt dro han ut en stor pose av blodige hinner. Med et snitt åpnet han hinneposen, og en pjusket, våt kalv kom til syne.

Han arbeidet raskt og konsentrert. Snart var kalven befridd fra alle spor av sin til nå beskyttede tilværelse. Mette gikk nærmere og betraktet den lille som lå der i gresset. Den lå helt livløs. Morten dasket den litt og prøvde å rense ut mer slim og hinner fra munn og nese. Det så ikke ut til å hjelpe stort. Like livløs lå den der.

Mette kjente at klumpen i halsen var i ferd med å briste. Var det forgjeves? Den hadde jo vært i live for et øyeblikk siden, det hadde hun selv registrert.

Der bøyde Morten seg ned og la munnen inn til nesen på kalven. I lange drag blåste han luft inn i de slimete neseborene. Mette tok håndkleet sitt, og med skjelvende hender begynte hun å gni den våte kroppen. De arbeidet i taushet en god stund, hver konsentrert om sitt.

Plutselig kom det en surklelyd fra kalven, og så hørte de en spe lyd slippe ut av den lille kjeften. Begge stirret ned på den i åndeløs spenning. Et nytt lite raut lød mens den ristet svakt på hodet.

«Den lever!» jublet Mette.

I det samme kom den andre kvigen bort til dem. Den hadde visst forstått at det foregikk noe der ved vannkanten som også den hadde lyst til å være med på. Det så ikke ut til at den enset den døde venninnen sin i det hele tatt. Men den nyfødte kalven viste den større interesse for. Den snuste litt på den. Så med ett ble det liv over bevegelsene. Med raske nikk dunket den borti den våte bylten. Den lange, ru tunga satte raskt i gang med en effektiv rengjøringsprosess.

«Den er visst ikke riktig fornøyd med arbeidet mitt,» sa Mette med en skjelvende latter.

Morten trakk seg også litt tilbake. «Jeg tror dette er et arbeid den greier bedre enn oss,» sa han.

Der løftet kalven litt på hodet og ristet det så ørene flagret. Mette lo. Nå kjente hun at hun var helt våt i ansiktet. Hun skjønte også at det ikke skyldtes verken blodet fra den døde kvigen, svette eller vannet hun hadde svømt i. Det var rett og slett klumpen i halsen som hadde bristet uten at hun hadde merket det. Hele ansiktet hennes var vått av tårer.

«Den lever!» Gleden fikk tårene til å renne enda mer. Morten smilte også. De så på hverandre …

Et øyeblikk sto de bare og måpte i forbauselse. Så brast de i latter begge to. Hvilket syn de var. Mette med blodflekker overalt. I fjeset hadde tårene laget striper i det størknede blodet. Klær og hår så ut som om hun hadde badet i en blodpøl.

Morten så ikke så mye bedre ut. Armene og brystet var dekket av slim og blod. Det hele hadde rent ned i fanget hans. Mette tenkte at de buksene kom han nok aldri til å få rene igjen.

«Jeg rakk akkurat å få på meg det jeg hadde med av klær før jeg begynte på denne jobben,» sa Morten. «Ikke fikk jeg med meg vaskebrettet heller.» Igjen overmannet latteren dem.

De gikk bort til vannkanten og vasket av det verste fra fjes og armer. Så satte de seg i gresset. De betraktet kvigen som møysommelig slikket kalven over hele kroppen. Etter en stund så det ut til at den mente det fikk være nok, for den gikk ned til vannkanten for å drikke. Kalven lå stille på bakken. Den lettet litt på hodet, så de så det var liv i den. Men ellers så den nokså svak ut. Morten hentet teppet som han hadde brukt på moren. Det pakket han godt rundt den nyfødte.

«Tror du den greier seg?» Mette så bekymret på den lille bylten.

«Jeg vet ikke.» Morten så også bekymret ut. «Det kommer an på om vi kan greie å få i den mat.»

«Mat!» Mette stirret forbauset på ham. «Hva slags mat skal vi gi den her?»

«Slik den ser ut nå, så greier vi nok ikke å få i den noe som helst,» mente Morten. «Den ser også for svak ut til å flyttes. Jeg tror bare vi må sitte her en stund og se hvordan det går med den. Så må vi prøve å bære den ned til setra etter hvert. Der er det nok av melk den kan få.»

Igjen ble de sittende og se på den lille som i taushet kjempet en kamp om liv eller død der under teppet.

«Så nydelig den er,» sa Mette etter en stund. «Er det gutt eller jente?»

Morten smilte. «Det ble en gutt. Det fikk jeg da med meg. Men den er jo veldig liten. Det kan forresten være en fordel med tanke på hjemveien. Hvis vi må bære den helt hjem, blir den sikkert tung nok.»

Han snudde seg mot Mette. Nå var han alvorlig igjen. «Du har gjort en kjempejobb i dag. Hjertelig takk skal du ha!»

Mette smilte. Nå kjente hun hvordan gleden begynte å fylle henne. De hadde greid det. Og om nå ikke kalven skulle greie seg, så hadde de i hvert fall gjort det de kunne.

«Du var også en ypperlig kirurg,» lo hun. «Tenk, keisersnitt ute i villmarka!» Plutselig stoppet hun opp og så begeistret på ham. «Vet du hva jeg synes? Hvis denne lille krabaten overlever, bør den få navnet Keiseren.»

Morten lo. «Det var virkelig et passende navn. La oss kalle den det.»

13 • *Soloppgang*

Mette vred på seg. Aldri hadde hun kjent en verre madrass. Det var aldeles umulig å få sove. Mørket hadde senket seg over fjellet og viddene for en god stund siden. Fra et sted like i nærheten hørte hun de lette skvulpene av små bølger som slo mot steinene på stranden. Hun hørte også det jevne åndedrettet til Morten. Han sov, det var ingen tvil om det. Var det noe han trengte nå, så var det søvn. Dagens begivenheter hadde vært en stor påkjenning for ham, det visste hun.

Hun snudde seg på nytt. De greinene hun hadde brukt for å lage seg en seng av, kjentes ut som kniver mot den ømme ryggen. Det ville sikkert vært bedre å ligge rett på bakken slik som Morten hadde lagt seg. Hun skimtet konturene av ham der borte i mørket. Han hadde lagt seg tett inntil kalven. På den måten kunne han gi litt varme til den nyfødte, og så kunne han få litt av teppet som lå rundt den.

Mette hadde lagt seg inntil fjellveggen for på den måten å skjermes for vinden, om den skulle øke på i løpet av natta. Men det hadde hun ikke behøvd å bekymre seg over, så det ut til. Natta var forbausende varm og stille til å være så høyt til fjells. Morten hadde sagt at de hadde opplevd en overraskende varm periode denne tiden hun hadde vært på setra. Det pleide visst ikke alltid å være så bra. Hun var i hvert fall glad for at de ikke i tillegg skulle ha værproblemer på denne turen. De hadde da møtt problemer nok som det var.

Der lå hun altså, midt på natta, under en fjellvegg. På den ene siden lå ei død kvige og en nyfødt kalv. Og på den andre hadde den levende kvigen lagt seg til ro. Alle levende vesener her i dette fjellødet så ut til å sove … bare ikke hun.

Etter å ha flyttet litt på bjørkeriset under seg lukket hun øynene på nytt i et tappert forsøk på å få seg litt søvn. Men så kom alle tankene. Kveldens hendelser kvernet rundt i hodet. Kvigen der ute i vannet. Den forferdelige opplevelsen da vannskrekken plutselig holdt på å overmanne henne. Og så den vidunderlige følelsen som skrekken hadde blitt avløst av. Det øyeblikket da hun lå mot den trygge skulderen til Morten. Enda kunne hun kjenne varmen langt der inne i seg når hun tenkte på det.

Så var det kvigen … blodet … kalven … En ting var hun helt bestemt på. Dette måtte hun skrive ned i dagboka si så fort hun kom tilbake til setra. Hver kveld hadde hun skrevet de begivenhetene hun hadde vært med på, ned i den boken. Opplevelsene på denne turen ville bli stoff til mange sider.

Sakte, men sikkert ble minuttene til timer mens kroppen til Mette bare ble stivere og ømmere.

Plutselig satte hun seg opp. Det med å sove kunne hun like godt bare gi opp. Hvis ikke søvnen kom til henne, så kunne det ikke nytte for henne å hente den inn. Borte i øst kunne hun se at himmelen begynte å bli atskillig lysere. Mørket rundt henne var heller ikke så tett lenger. Møysommelig reiste hun seg. Det var nok ikke bare det ubehagelige underlaget som hadde gjort henne så stiv. Det var nok like mye lemsterhet etter strabasene dagen i forveien.

Forsiktig begynte hun å klatre opp den kløften hvor de var kommet ned. Himmelen så helt klar ut, så hun tenkte at en soloppgang over disse fjellene sikkert ville bli en fantastisk opplevelse. Der oppe på fjellet var det jo en fabelaktig utsikt.

Det tok tid å komme opp, for hun måtte være forsiktig med hvor hun satte føttene i det svake lyset. Der var også lite å holde seg i om hun skulle gli.

Da hun endelig kom opp, ble strevet belønnet med et panorama som fikk henne til å gispe. Sola var ikke kommet til syne over fjellene i øst, men de lange strålene fra den gryende morgenen skapte en eiendommelig skyggevirkning innover fjellheimen.

Lenge ble hun stående og betrakte det overveldende skuet. Sakte, men sikkert ble toppene farget gylne i det sterke skinnet fra horisonten. Fjellsidene og dalene lå ennå i duse skygger. Flere steder var bekker og tjern dekket av en ullen tåke. Søyler av tåke steg også opp flere steder langs fjellsidene. Hun måtte smile da hun husket Mortens forklaring på dette fenomenet morgenen før. Det var sannelig ikke rart at fortidens mennesker hadde blitt bundet i slik en fantasiverden. De som levde så nær naturen, hadde nok stadig slike synsopplevelser. Og sannelig kunne fantasien spille noen hver et puss under disse forholdene.

Hun satte seg på en flat stein som lå der på fjellplatået, mens en underlig stemning fylte henne. Lufta var kjøligere der oppe enn den hadde vært nede ved vannet hvor hun hadde ligget. Det blåste også mer, så hun måtte trekke jakken bedre om seg. Men følelsen av å være en ørliten brikke i det enorme … gav tankene hennes frie vinger.

Skyggene skiftet etter som lyset fikk mer og mer tak. De gylne toppene skapte ekstra klare kontraster til de mørke fjellsidene og dalene. Der hun satt og betraktet den stadig skiftende lysvirkningen, forsto hun hvilken redsel dette måtte skape hos de menneskene som trodde på de underjordiske og overnaturlige fenomener. Så levende det

267

måtte fortone seg for den som trodde på at ei hulder kunne dukke opp i dette landskapet og lokke en stakkar inn i fjellet. Det kunne ikke være vanskelig å overbevise den som ikke visste om noe annet, at dette var livets sannheter.

Et fredfullt smil gled over ansiktet hennes der hun satt. Så glad hun var for at hun visste om en annen sannhet. Hun visste om en som hadde seiret over alle disse onde krefter og redsler. Det var en som hadde stått fram en skinnende lys morgen etter at han en mørk dag og natt ble lagt død i en grav. Denne mannen var Jesus Kristus. På grunn av Hans seier over de mørke maktene hadde hun ingenting å frykte der hun satt.

Selvfølgelig kunne hun bare ha trøstet seg med at de gamles tro kun var fantasi og oppspinn. Men hun visste at de redslene de den gang opplevde, bunnet i de onde krefters innvirkning på deres liv. Og de kreftene var reelle nok. De hadde virkelig grunn til å frykte. Det var sterke krefter det var snakk om. Men disse kreftene fikk oppleve sin overmann den gangen da graven brast den skinnende påskemorgenen for snart to tusen år siden.

En ubeskrivelig fryd fylte hennes indre. Uten at hun helt var klar over det selv stemte hun i en sang: «Jesus lever, graven brast. Han sto opp med guddoms velde …»

I det samme brøt solas første stråler fram over fjelltoppene. På et øyeblikk var hun innhyllet i et flammende lys. Og mens dette lyset stadig fikk mer og mer tak, tonet strofene fra den friske påskesalmen ut over viddene.

Da hun kom til strofen Jesus mørkets fyrste bandt, stoppet hun. Ordene ble så forunderlig levende. Det var som om hun i dette øyeblikket opplevde akkurat det konkret. De klare solstrålene der borte i øst var som et mektig symbol på Jesu guddommelige makt over mørket og de onde kreftene, her symbolisert ved tåken og de mørke skyggene mellom fjellene.

Lyset fikk etter hvert mer og mer overtaket. Tiden gikk, men hun satt bare der og betraktet forvandlingen uten å ense klokken. Hun ville fange inn hver stråle og la dem få lov til å gi liv og varme til den kalde kroppen.

Tankene fortsatte å arbeide. Selvfølgelig kunne hun ha lagt seg til der nede i skyggen under fjellet. Kanskje ville hun ha følt at hun hadde det bra nok om hun hadde fått seg en blund der. Men dette fantastiske synet, og opplevelsen, hadde hun gått glipp av. Også det talte til henne. Hvor mange var det ikke som gikk omkring i mørket, åndelig talt. De mener de har det bra nok. Trenger ingen forandring. Grunnen var nok at de ikke forsto hva det var de gikk glipp av. De forsto heller ikke hva som var gjort i stand for dem av herligheter i «det guddomlige lys». Jesus vant en seier over ondskapen og mørket. Denne seieren skulle også bli menneskene til del. Den åpnet Himmelveien for alle. Den ble gitt som en gave til hvert menneske på jorden. Det er bare for dem å ta imot den, og la seg prege av dette himmelske lyset.

På nytt stemte hun i den lyse påskesalmen.

Jesus lever, graven brast!
Han sto opp med guddoms velde.
Trøsten står som klippen fast
at Hans død og blod skal gjelde.
Lynet blinker. Jorden bever.
Graven brast, og Jesus lever!
Jeg har vunnet, Jesus vant,
døden oppslukt er til seier.
Jesus mørkets fyrste bandt,

jeg den kjøpte frihet eier.
Åpen har jeg Himlen funnet.
Jesus vant, og jeg har vunnet!

Hun satt der i stillheten og nøt opplevelsen. Dette øyeblikket ville hun gjemme i sitt indre for all framtid. Det var som om Jesus var der sammen med henne i lyset og gav henne et glimt inn i de evige sannheter. Freden hun kjente fylte henne med en ubeskrivelig glede.

Plutselig steg en lyd opp til henne. Det var et langt raut fra ei ku. Mette reiste seg raskt. Det føltes nesten som å våknet av en drøm, bare med den forskjell at freden og de sannhetene hun hadde fått så klart åpenbart, fortsatt var like virkelige for henne.

Da hun kom bort til fjellskrenten, så hun kvigen som gikk der og beitet langs vannkanten. Morten satt oppe, men hun kunne ikke så tydelig se hva han holdt på med. Raskt begynte hun nedstigningen igjen. Flere ganger undret hun seg over hvordan hun hadde greid å komme opp denne veien i mørket. En gang holdt hun på å falle. Hun måtte klore seg fast i noe lyng for ikke å rase nedover.

Da hun var vel nede ved vannet igjen, så hun at det var kalven Morten stelte med. Den lå i fanget hans mens han strøk den over hodet og halsen. Tre av fingrene sine hadde han stukket inn i munnen på den, og den sugde begjærlig.

Han så opp på henne og smilte da hun kom nærmere. «Har du sett så kvikk den nå ser ut?» sa han.

Mette stirret forundret. Så falt hun ned ved siden av dem og la hodet helt inntil halsen på det lille dyret. «Så nydelig du er, Keiseren,» hvisket hun inn i det lille øret.

Morten lo. «Det ser virkelig ut til at den kommer til å greie seg,» sa han. «Nå må vi bare få den ned til setra så den kan få seg noen livgivende melkedråper. Moren til Missi kan sikkert avse litt.»

Mette så på klokka. Den var litt over seks. «Når tror du vi er nede?» spurte hun.

«Jeg vet ikke riktig.» Morten så litt betenkt ut i lufta. «Det kommer an på hvor ofte vi må stoppe. Men jeg håper vi greier det på et par timer.»

De begynte å gjøre seg klar for hjemtur. «Vi tar bare med oss det aller nødvendigste av utstyret,» sa han. «Jeg må jo opp igjen hit snart for å grave ned den døde kvigen. Da kan jeg hente det vi ikke får med oss nå.»

Det de syntes de måtte ha med, la de i sekken til Mette. Morten tømte sin helt. «Vi må se om vi kan få kalven til å sitte i denne,» sa han.

Det ble en møysommelig jobb å få den ned i ryggsekken, men etter en stund så det ut til at det skulle gå bra. Mette hjalp med å få den opp på ryggen til Morten. Framparten av kalven stakk opp over kanten. Frambeina la de over skuldrene hans slik at han kunne holde dem fast framme på brystet. De bandt også et tau rundt så den ikke skulle falle ut hvis den begynte å sprelle for mye.

Dermed la de i vei. De gikk langs vannkanten mot øst. «Der borte i enden av vannet går det en dal nedover, sa Morten. Det er den som kommer igjen nede ved Silja-tjernet. Vi kan bare følge den. Det er ganske greit å gå der.»

Morten gikk først med kalven på ryggen. Så fulgte kvigen etter ham. Sist i følget gikk Mette. Hun måtte se etter at kvigen fulgte med, og gikk rett vei.

Turen nedover gikk ganske greit. Kalven lå rolig og betraktet de nye omgivelsene rundt seg. Av og til kom det noen sprell, men den greide ikke å komme opp, så den la seg fort til ro igjen.

En gang stoppet Morten med et forskrekket utrop. Så begynte han å le. En våt stripe kom til syne nedover baken og buksebena hans. «Jeg visste ikke at det var noe vått som kunne komme ut av denne lille stakkaren. Den har jo enda ikke fått inn noe.»

Mette måtte også le. «Naturen må gå sin gang, vet du,» sa hun.

Det var ikke mange pausene de tok. De ville helst være nede ved setra så fort som mulig. Det var også lettest å styre kvigen når de var i bevegelse. De fulgte en gammel sti. Morten fortalte at den ble flittig brukt før i tiden da de hadde mange dyr rundt omkring på setrene i området. Gjetere fra forskjellige steder brukte den når de skulle føre buskapen til beitemarker inne i fjellet. I de senere årene var det mest i jakttiden at den var i bruk.

Mette fikk ikke så mye anledning til å nyte naturen omkring seg. Hun var mest opptatt av at kvigen skulle gå rett vei. Et par ganger ville den stikke ut fra stien, så hun måtte løpe rundt for å snu den.

Da de endelig skimtet Siljatjernet mellom noen busker og trær, pustet hun lettet ut. Hun kjente godt at hun hadde en søvnløs natt bak seg. Det skulle virkelig bli godt å krølle seg sammen under den myke dyna. Det var jo fridagen hennes, så hun behøvde ikke å tenke på noen slags plikter.

Kvigen satte i noen lange raut da de nærmet seg fjøset. Den kunne visst merke at den nå var i nærheten av noen flere eksemplarer av sin egen rase. I det samme kom Petter til syne i fjøsdøra. Han bar ei melkebøtte i hver hånd. Da han fikk se følget som kom gående mot ham, stoppet han så brått at melka skvatt ut av bøttene. To skrekkslagne øyne stirret på dem. Mette tittet litt nedover klærne sine og skjønte fort hva som hadde forårsaket sjokket. Et mer skremmende syn kunne visst ikke en stakkar bli møtt av en tidlig morgen. De måtte le.

«Hva i all verden har hendt med dere?» ropte han da de kom nærmere. Morten gikk bort til fjøset for å sette fra seg børen mens han begynte å fortelle hva de hadde opplevd. Mette skjønte at hun var overflødig. Lettet gikk hun inn i seterbua. Etter en rask vask stupte hun i seng. At hun ikke hadde spist siden kvelden før, hadde hun helt glemt. Søvnen overmannet henne før hun rakk å snu seg mot veggen.

14 • «Potteblått»

Tidlig fredag morgen var tante Anna på plass i seterbua igjen. Hun hadde hørt om opplevelsen deres inne i fjellet, så munnen gikk enda mer iherdig enn før. Mette var oppriktig glad for at den eldre kvinnen var så flink til å kombinere pratingen med arbeidet hun skulle gjøre. Hadde hun ikke vært det, ville de ikke få gjort stort den dagen, var Mette redd for. Det var likevel trivelig å ha henne tilbake igjen. Hun hadde savnet den muntre latteren og de friske replikkene disse dagene.

Det var bearbeidelse av ull, og da helst fargingsprosessen, de skulle vise gjestene denne dagen. Tante Anna hadde gjort klar en stor haug med ull. Den lå midt på gulvet. Flere store gryter ble satt bort til ildstedet ved fjellet bak seterbua. Mette bar bort mange fang med ved. Over ildstedet lå det en rist. Den var stor nok til at de kunne sette tre-fire gryter oppå samtidig. Tante Anna hang opp en snor mellom seterbua og et tre borte ved fjellet. «Her kan vi henge opp ulla til tørk etter at den er farget,» sa hun. «Det vil bli skyggefullt og fint her utpå ettermiddagen.»

De varmet opp noe vann som de helte over i ei stor balje. Oppi det la tante Anna et fang med ull.

«Er det folk her fra bygda som kommer?» spurte Mette da de satt og drakk en kopp kaffe etter at alle forberedelsene var unnagjort.

«Nei,» sa tante Anna. «De kommer fra en annen bygd, men det er ikke så fælt langt unna. Vi kan nok vente dem når som helst nå. Der har vi visst de første allerede.» Hun reiste seg fort og gikk for å ta imot bilen som i det samme svingte opp til huset. Mette gikk etter. En hjertelig hilsen ble utvekslet mellom tante Anna og de to damene som kom ut av bilen. Det var tydelig at de kjente hverandre godt fra før. «Kom og hils på budeia vår,» sa hun.

Da Mette ble presentert for de to nyankomne, forsto hun at dette ikke var folk fra husflidslaget. Den ene het Marit. Det var søster til Morten. Den andre var venninnen hennes. Hun het Ellen. Det var Marit som eide den ene av campingvognene som sto borte på campingområdet. Nå hadde disse to tenkt å være på ferie der en stund.

Mette fikk fort kontakt med de to damene. Snart satt de i ivrig samtale alle fire.

Det varte heller ikke lenge før gjestene fra nabobygda kom. Fjorten damer og noen barn veltet ut av bilene som ble parkert på campingområdet. Mette hadde satt ut noen bord og stoler på vollen. Der ble alle plassert til en kopp kaffe og grundig orientering før arbeidet skulle settes i gang.

Tante Anna frydet seg tydeligvis stort over muligheten til å kunne prate uhindret til så mange interesserte mennesker. Først fortalte hun om sin barndom på gården. Moren hennes hadde vært spesielt interessert i dette arbeidet. Det var av henne hun hadde lært alt det hun nå skulle vise dem.

Så snakket hun litt om stell og klipping av sauene. Når ulla skulle spinnes, var det alltid best å spinne den uvasket. Det fettstoffet, lanolinen, som fantes i ulla, virket slik at spinningen gikk mye lettere, sa hun. Derfor pleide alltid moren hennes å spinne ulla før hun farget den. Nå hadde ikke tante Anna orket å spinne så mye ull som de kom til å trenge til fargingen, derfor ble det bare selve ulla de kom til å farge denne dagen. Og hvis de ønsket å bruke ulla til toving, så kunne den jo heller ikke være spunnet.

Denne ulla hadde hun vasket nøye. Det var svært viktig før all farging. Hun forklarte hvilke vaskemidler som måtte brukes til det, og hvordan vannet måtte være både med temperatur og kalkinnhold.

Alle lyttet oppmerksomt. Av og til ble det skutt inn et spørsmål, og tante Anna forklarte villig alt de ønsket å vite. Det var ikke den ting hun ikke hadde greie på.

«Før vi går i gang med arbeidet, vil jeg forklare litt om selve prosessen,» fortsatte hun. «Det er alltid viktig at vi bruker unge planter. Nede på gården pleide vi å si at dette arbeidet måtte gjøres unna før sankthans. Fargestoffet er friskest og finest i de nye skuddene. Her oppe kan vi nok drøye det litt utover sommeren, for her kommer våren atskillig senere. Det går selvsagt an å plukke plantene om våren, og så tørke dem for å bruke dem senere på året, men fargene blir ikke helt de samme da. De fleste plantene skal plukkes i tørt vær, så slik har vi ideelle forhold nå.

Det første vi må gjøre, er å beise ulla. Jeg har kjøpt noe som heter alunbeis. Det må koke forsiktig sammen med ulla i en time. Denne beisen virker slik at fargen fester seg til ullfibrene. Mens det koker, kan dere dra ut for å finne planter til fargingen. Egentlig skal ulla ligge ganske lenge i beisen. Den må kjøles ned mens den ligger i vannet. Vi får se hvor lenge vi får tid til å la det ligge i dag. Vi har jo bare denne dagen til rådighet.»

271

Det ble mange opplysninger på en gang. Noen satt og noterte for å få med seg alt. Tante Anna delte dem inn i fire mindre grupper. Hver av gruppene fikk beskjed om hva slags plantesort de skulle lete etter. Ei gruppe skulle plukke bjørkeløv, og ei skulle finne einer. Da sa hun at det var viktig at de bare tok de nye skuddene på einerbuskene. Så skulle ei gruppe finne mose. Hun hadde en liten dusk av mose liggende på bordet for å vise hvilken sort de skulle lete etter. Den fjerde gruppen skulle plukke lyng.

Dermed dro hele flokken bort til grytene for å se hvordan beisingen skulle gjøres. Tante Anna målte opp beis og rørte det ut i den ene gryta med vann. Så la hun den ulla som de hadde lagt i bløt, over i vannet som hun hadde hatt beis i. Hun var nøye med at det nye vannet hadde samme temperatur som det vannet ulla nettopp hadde ligget i. Hun var også nøye med at hun ikke la mer ull i gryta enn at det lå romslig. «Vi må ikke stue det nedi,» sa hun. «Da kan det lett bli skjoldete. Nå må dette koke langsomt opp.»

Etter at de hadde gjort ulla klar til beising, dro alle av sted for å finne de rette plantesortene. Noen tok veien mot tjernet, mens andre dro oppover lia. Mette ble igjen for å hjelpe tante Anna. Hun fulgte med på alt med stigende interesse. Rett som det var måtte hun fram med penn og papir. Dette ville hun ha med seg gangen i. Tante Anna kvitret i vei hele tiden. Der var så mange detaljer å ta hensyn til at Mette nesten gikk litt i surr av og til. Hun måtte rett som det var spørre om igjen.

«Du snakker hele tiden om at vi må koke denne ulla.» Hun sto og så litt undrende på de store grytene ved ildstedet. «Jeg trodde ikke det gikk an å koke ull i det hele tatt?»

Tante Anna lo mens hun rørte rundt i gryta. «Hvis du koker ullgenseren din, så vil du nok få deg en ubehagelig overraskelse,» sa hun. «Men ulla her skal jo kardes opp igjen etterpå. Da blir den like fin. Og om vi koker garn som er spunnet, så går også det bra, vi må bare være forsiktige med oppvarming og avkjøling. Det må gå sakte. Vi må heller ikke arbeide for mye med det som ligger i gryta. Tørkingen må også gå langsomt. Det er derfor vi må henge det til tørk i skyggen. Spesielt den siste delen av tørketiden må gå sent.»

Mens de ventet på at planteplukkerne skulle komme tilbake, gikk Mette en tur rundt på vollen. Et av lammene kom løpende bort til gjerdet da det fikk øye på henne. Det håpet visst på å få noe godt fra hånden hennes. Hun hadde ikke med seg noe, men hun gikk inn til det og tok det myke dyret inn til seg i fanget. Med den ene hånden strøk hun over den krøllete ulla, mens hun med den andre klødde det bak ørene. Dette var en behandling det virkelig likte. Lenge ble de sittende der i gresset og kose seg sammen. Om det var Mette eller lammet som koste seg mest, var ikke lett å si. Hun følte igjen at hun var i en atmosfære av harmoni som gav en vidunderlig tilfredsstillelse. Sjelden hadde hun opplevd en slik fred.

Borte ved et av bordene så hun at Morten satt og pratet med Ellen. Det var tydelig at de kjente hverandre godt. De lo og så ut til å stortrives i hverandres selskap. En skygge gled over ansiktet til Mette. Hvem var egentlig denne Ellen? En venninne til Marit, hadde de sagt. Men hva med Morten? Kunne det kanskje tenkes …

Nei, han hadde da aldri gitt utrykk for at han hadde noen spesiell venninne.

Mette tenkte litt nøyere på det. Hva visste hun egentlig om Morten? Han hadde fortalt en god del om familien, setra og dyra, men om seg selv hadde han ikke sagt stort. Hun visste en del om de kristne interessene hans, men lite om ham personlig. Hva han følte og tenkte holdt han ganske godt for seg selv. Den dagen de var på fjelltur hadde de snakket ganske fortrolig sammen da de hadde matpause, men det var mest hun som hadde pratet. Morten hadde lyttet interessert til alt hun sa. Det lille han selv hadde fortalt, var jo mest om foreldrene og familien. Og slike nære, personlige ting hadde hun dessuten ikke frimodighet til å spørre om hvis han ikke selv brakte det på bane. Han var på ingen måte som tante Anna. Henne skulle man ikke være lenge sammen med før man visste det meste av det som rørte seg innenfor skautet. Nei … Morten var helt annerledes.

Mette betraktet dem der de satt. De brydde seg visst ikke om noen andre omkring seg. Begge viste en glødende iver og interesse for det den andre sa. Det var visst noe helt spesielt de diskuterte. «Slik intens fortrolighet har aldri Morten vist meg,» tenkte hun plutselig, men skammet seg med det samme. Hvorfor i all verden skulle han det? Hun var jo bare budeia på setra. Det var kun arbeidet som bandt dem sammen.

Sakte reiste hun seg og gikk inn i seterbua til tante Anna. Hun hadde lyst til å spørre henne litt om denne Ellen, men hun våget ikke å si noe. Dessuten snakket tante Anna i ett sett om maten de måtte forberede til gjestene kom tilbake. De skulle servere den vanlige rømmegrøten. Mette fant fort ut at det var best hun også konsentrerte seg om den. Hun fant nok ut av tingene etter hvert.

Snart kom den ene etter den andre tilbake med bæreposer fulle av planter. Bjørkelauvet og opphakket lyng ble lagt i hver sin gryte og satt til koking. Tante Anna hadde også lagt noe ull i vann som hun hadde beiset tidligere. «Denne ulla kan vi begynne å farge med den gang,» sa hun. «Den ulla som skal farges med einer, trenger forresten ikke beis. Einerfargen fester seg godt nok til fibrene som det er, så den kan vi også begynne å farge med det samme.»

Eineren ble hakket opp og lagt lagvis med ulla i ei stor koppergryte. Den ble også straks satt over varmen. «Nå kan dette stå her og koke mens vi spiser,» sa tante Anna.

Under måltidet måtte Mette stadig bort for å passe på at det kokte jevnt og fint i grytene. Vedhaugen hun hadde båret bort om morgenen, minket jevnt og trutt. Snart måtte hun hente noen fang til.

Alle koste seg ute på vollen. Barna måtte rett som det var bort til lammene. Kalvene fikk også besøk. Keiseren var kommet seg forbløffende på de dagene den hadde vært på setra. Han og Missi kom godt ut av det med hverandre, og moren til Missi tok seg helt naturlig av den nye kalven. Begge fikk lov til å die den gamle kua. Barna frydet seg med dyra.

Etter måltidet viste tante Anna prøver av ting hun hadde farget tidligere. Det meste var nøster med garn, men hun hadde også en del ull. Alle var overrasket over de fine, klare fargene hun hadde fått.

«Dette er farget av orebark,» sa hun og holdt opp et nøste med en sterkt grønnaktig farge. «Til denne,» sa hun og holdt opp et lysegult nøste, «har jeg brukt granlav.»

Ei jente i tiårsalderen sto på hodet i kurven og rotet i nøstene med alle de fine fargene. Hun tok opp et med en klar, blå farge. «Har du brukt blåbær for å få farge på dette?» spurte hun. Tante Anna lo. «Nei, jeg har nok ikke brukt blåbær,» svarte hun. «Den fargen finner vi ikke her i naturen. Det er en farge jeg har kjøpt. For å få til den blåfargen må jeg bruke en stein som kalles indigostein. Den må løses opp i noen kjemikalier før den kan tilsettes ulla. Men før i tiden brukte de en annen metode.» Hun rugget på seg og lo. «Dere kan jo prøve den hvis dere vil. Steinen måtte de kjøpe. Men for å få løst den opp brukte de helt alminnelig urin. Derfor kalles denne fargen fremdeles for «potteblått».»

Jenta stirret skrekkslagen på den gamle damen. «Har du gjort det?»

«Å ja. Du kan da skjønne at jeg måtte jo prøve.»

Det blå nøstet falt øyeblikkelig ned på marka. «Æsj,» sa hun og gren på nesa. Hånden ble tørket intenst mot bukselåret.

Tante Anna satte igjen i gang sin trillende latter. «Du kan slappe helt av. Jeg har ikke tisset på det garnet der.» Alle lo. Jenta pustet lettet ut, men hun ville ikke plukke opp nøstet igjen.

Det ble en usedvanlig hyggelig ettermiddag. Ingen hadde problemer med å få tiden til å gå de lange timene mens ull og farge måtte koke. Praten gikk i ett hele tiden. Mette hjalp med å passe tiden til de forskjellige grytene. Etter at bjørkeløv og lyng var ferdig kokt, ble det silt av. Nedi den suppa som de da fikk, ble den beisede ulla lagt. Så skulle det hele koke igjen en time.

Etter at alt var kokt, måtte ulla skylles grundig. Alle jobbet iherdig. Tante Anna fortalte om variasjonene de kunne gjøre for å få fram forskjellige fargenyanser. Det ble for eksempel forskjellige fargetoner etter om de kokte i jerngryte, aluminiumsgryte eller koppergryte. De kunne også få andre farger ved å dyppe ulla over i ei anna «suppe» når den var ferdig kokt i en. Både Mette og de andre noterte iherdig. Spørsmålene ble etter hvert mange og mer inngående. Flere gav utrykk for at de hadde lyst til å prøve dette igjen når de kom hjem. De ba om å få tante Annas telefonnummer slik at de kunne ringe henne hvis de skulle bli stående fast i noe.

Da kvelden kom, hang det flere ulltuster på snoren bak seterbua. Tante Anna sa at de kunne ta hele ulla med seg hjem. De kunne dele den mellom seg og tørke den ferdig hjemme.

Det ble sen kveld før de siste forlot setra. Mette kunne se at tante Anna var sliten, så hun sa at hun bare måtte gå til sengs. Resten av ryddingen kunne Mette ta alene.

15 • Kjemien stemmer ikke

Morten stakk hodet inn av fjøsdøra. «Kan du greie det som skal gjøres her på setra i dag?» spurte han. «Jeg har fått besøk av en kamerat. Vi tenker å ta en tur inn på fjellet for å fiske.»

«Ja da,» svarte Mette. Hun sto og klappet Keiseren med den ene hånden mens den ivrig sugde på fingrene på den andre. «Det er jo ikke så mye som skal foregå i dag, så det skal nok gå bra. Bare dra dere.»

Hun fortsatte å pusle rundt dyra en stund før hun slapp dem ut. Det var alltid så trivelig å høre de fornøyde bevegelsene og sukkene fra dem når de hadde fått sitt stell.

Da arbeidet var unnagjort og dyra ute igjen på beitet, gikk Mette bort og satte seg i en hagestol på vollen for å slappe litt av i den varme sola. Aldri ble hun mett av å betrakte det vakre landskapet rundt setra. Tjernet lå der og blinket like innbydende som første gang hun så det.

Oppe i skråningen bak seterbua satt det noen ryper. De flakset opp da de så henne, og fløy innover mot fjellet og viddene. På den blå himmelen var det bare noen få ulne skyer å se. Blikket hennes fulgte en ørn som seilte på strake vinger mot fjellene på den andre siden av tjernet. Kanskje den hadde et rede der? Hun hadde sett den flere ganger kretse rundt i området på jakt etter mat.

Med et tilfreds sukk lente hun seg tilbake i stolen. En behagelig døsighet kom over henne. Bjelleklangen og brekingen fra sauene som gikk og beitet fredelig borte i lia, fikk henne igjen til å føle den fullkomne freden og harmonien som hun så ofte hadde opplevd her i fjellet.

Plutselig satte hun seg opp med en brå bevegelse. Hun hadde fått øye på to menn som gikk nedover stien. Den ene var Morten, det så hun godt. Men den andre var det også noe kjent ved. Med ett stoppet de. Morten pekte mot dalen i enden av tjernet. Han forklarte sikkert veien de måtte gå. Dette var altså kameraten hans, men det var da virkelig noe kjent ved ham.

Der snudde de seg mens Morten fortsatte å peke langs fjellet i nord. Mette kjente at hun stivnet der hun satt. Nå så hun ansiktet, og det var ingen tvil. Det var Tore. Morten og Tore var altså kamerater ...

Et øyeblikk senere fortsatte de to mennene sin vandring og forsvant bak busker og kratt ved vannkanten.

Tanker og følelser raste inne i hodet på Mette. Mye av grunnen til at hun hadde søkt seg bort fra kontoret for en stund, var jo nettopp Tore ... kollegaen hennes. Det anspente forholdet som hadde oppstått mellom dem hadde etter hvert slitt litt for mye på henne. Hun greide rett og slett ikke å takle den overlegne måten han behandlet henne på. Og fant han en feil ved det hun gjorde, så unnlot han aldri å bemerke det. Nå var altså denne mannen her.

Raskt reiste hun seg og gikk inn i seterbua. Hun var alene, så hun kunne styre dagen og arbeidet som hun ville. Noen turister var det riktignok på campingområdet, men de skulle ikke ha noen demonstrasjoner eller tjenester denne dagen. Det var kun en del forberedelser for neste dag som måtte gjøres.

Med besluttsomme bevegelser satte hun i gang med arbeidet. Hun ville ha det unnagjort så fort som mulig. Så ville hun ta bilen og dra ned til bygda. Aldri i livet om hun ville være der når de kom tilbake igjen. Hun orket simpelthen ikke å treffe Tore her oppe.

o   o   o

Det var allerede blitt senere enn vanlig melketid da hun igjen svingte bilen opp foran seterbua. Lettet registrerte hun at gjesten var reist, for der sto ingen bil utenfor. Morten fant hun inne, bak en avis. Han kikket opp i det samme hun kom inn. Mette sa ikke noe med det samme. Men nysgjerrigheten på hvordan det kunne henge sammen at de to var venner, gjorde at hun snart kom med et spørsmål. «Du kjenner altså Tore, skjønner jeg?»

Morten smilte forbauset. «Så han er en kjenning av deg også?»

Hun gjengjeldte ikke smilet. I stedet satte hun opp en litt trassig mine. «Ja, og han er den mest motbydelige mannen jeg kan tenke meg.» En heftig bevegelse med foten fastslo bemerkningen som et faktum.

Smilet til Morten forsvant sakte mens han hevet øyebrynene. Avisen sank ned i fanget. «Det var da veldig,» sa han på sin rolige og overveiende måte. «Han er faktisk en av de beste kameratene mine. Vi ble kjent i militæret, og siden har vi holdt kontakten. Hva slags sammenheng er det du kjenner ham fra, siden du har opplevd ham slik?»

«Vi arbeider faktisk sammen på kontoret,» svarte hun. Og så rant det ut av henne alt det hun hadde opplevd og følt. Hvordan han hadde hakket på henne ved den minste gale ting hun gjorde, og den overlegne måten han behandlet henne på. Hun fortalte hvordan dette hadde slitt på henne i den ellers så travle arbeidssituasjonen de hadde hatt. Til slutt hadde hun følt at hun ikke orket mer.

275

Morten satt og lyttet i taushet. Da hun hadde fått utøst seg, ble det stille mellom dem et øyeblikk. Morten kremtet litt før han begynte å snakke igjen. «Jeg tror nok du må ha misforstått ham litt. Han er godheten selv. Det er nok rett som du sier at han kan virke litt overlegen, men det er ingenting å bry seg om. Det er bare hans måte å være på. Ja, det er rett og slett hans natur.»

Mette kjente at noe inni henne begynte å koke. Hun gikk et skritt nærmere mens hun bøyde seg litt fremover. De lyseblå øynene lynte, og de ellers så fyldige leppene var presset sammen til en hvit strek.

«Bare hans natur?» Ordene kom i en illevarslende lav tone. «Det skal jeg si deg,» fortsatte hun med atskillig mer intensitet. «Hvis du visste hvordan det føltes til stadighet å bli minnet på sin udugelighet, så tror jeg du hadde sagt noe annet. At et menneske skal kunne unnskyldes med at de bare er slik, når de er i ferd med å ødelegge et annet menneske, det går bare ikke an!»

Hun stoppet litt. Morten satt igjen taus, men et bekymret uttrykk hadde lagt seg over ansiktet hans. Et øyeblikk stirret hun bare på ham med et vilt blikk. Så fortsatte hun: «Jeg begriper virkelig ikke hvordan du kan være venn med en slik fyr.» Så snudde hun seg brått om og styrtet ut av døra.

På et øyeblikk fikk hun kyrne inn i fjøset. Raseriet hun følte inni seg gjorde at hun arbeidet med en intens heftighet. Hun satte seg på krakken og begynte å melke. Heldigvis var det ingen turister der for å se på. Hun følte slett ikke behov for selskap akkurat der og da.

Plutselig begynte tårene å renne. En heftig gråt overmannet henne nesten helt. Alle de vonde følelsene kom tilbake igjen. Følelsen av utilstrekkelighet. Sårheten ved stadig å bli pirket på de mest ømme punktene. Ydmykelsen ved å bli gjenstand for spydigheter og nedlatenhet. Og nå følelsen av å ikke bli forstått av en som hele tiden hadde vist henne forståelse, varme og respekt.

En annen følelse som også plaget henne sterkt, var at hun hadde vist slik kraftig reaksjon på dette. Hvorfor måtte hun alltid bli så sint? Det skapte jo bare ubehageligheter for henne selv. Hvor mange ganger hadde hun ikke måttet gå og be noen om tilgivelse nettopp på grunn av dette heftige temperamentet sitt. Og nå var det Morten …

Hun lente hodet inn mot kua og lot tårene renne nedover den varme kumagen. Hendene la seg slapt ned i fanget. Bøtta var bare halvfull, men konsentrasjonen om arbeidet var borte.

Med ett ble hun oppmerksom på en bevegelse borte ved døra. Det var Morten som kom stille inn i fjøset. Hun kikket forsiktig opp, men sank bare inn mot kua igjen.

«Jeg må bare be om tilgivelse for at jeg uttrykte meg så klossete,» sa han stille. Mette så forundret opp på ham. «Det er da ikke du som skal be om tilgivelse. Det var jo jeg som overreagerte,» sa hun litt forvirret.

«Nei,» sa Morten. «Jeg forsto bare ikke hvor dypt dette hadde gått inn på deg. Dere har nok svært forskjellig natur, og da er det ikke så sjelden at ting kan skjære seg. Det er noe som det slett ikke må taes for lettvint på.»

Mette kjente at ordene hans gjorde henne godt. Det fantes altså forståelse hos ham likevel.

Kua flyttet litt urolig på seg. Den merket godt at melkingen ikke gikk som den pleide. Uten nærmere forvarsel langet den ut et bein og traff bøtta så den trillet bortover gulvet, mens melka skvatt til alle kanter. Mette for opp i forskrekkelsen. Spenningen i hennes indre fikk det til å koke over igjen. «Kan du ikke stå stille, ditt krek av ei ku!» skrek hun og deljet hånden mot baken på den. «Den melka skulle tante Anna koke gome av.»

«Ja, bare la det gå ut over kua,» sa Morten. Mette la merke til at han nesten krøket seg av latter. Men det var ingen ironi eller spydighet i stemmen hans. Tvert imot virket det mer som vennlighet og omsorg.

Mette sank ned på melkekrakken igjen. «Hvorfor kan jeg aldri greie å styre sinnet mitt?» sukket hun. «Nå må jeg vel be kua også om tilgivelse.»

På ny lød latteren fra Morten. Hun måtte også smile litt. Så trygg og befriende den latteren var.

Morten hjalp henne med å få ferdig kveldsmelkingen. Etterpå satte de seg ute på vollen. Mette kjente fremdeles på en sår følelse inni seg. Det var så vondt å bli minnet på dette igjen. Disse dagene hun hadde tilbrakt her oppe på setra, hadde hjulpet henne til å få det hele litt på avstand, men nå vellet alt sammen fram igjen med full styrke.

Det var Morten som først brøt tausheten. Han begynte å snakke om Tore, hvordan de var blitt kjent, og hvordan de hadde opprettholdt vennskapet etterpå.

Mette lyttet forbauset mens han beskrev Tore som en litt svak og sårbar person. Dette kompenserte han gjerne ved en overlegen og tøff framferd. Han var dyktig til å administrere og ordne opp i kompliserte saker. Men når det gjaldt pertentlighet og nøyaktighet i mindre saker, så følte han seg nok mer usikker.

Han stoppet et øyeblikk mens han så granskende på Mette. Hun satt der bare taus. Det var vanskelig for henne å få denne beskrivelsen til å stemme med Tore.

«Du er nok Tores rake motsetning,» fortsatte Morten. «Jeg kan tenke meg at han har følt seg nokså liten og klossete i møte med din dyktighet og pertentlighet. Kan tenke meg at han har følt at alle hans svake sider ble åpenbart i samarbeid med deg. Dette kan jeg så gjerne tro har ført til at han har behandlet deg på denne måten.»

«Men jeg er da slett ikke verken pertentlig eller særlig dyktig,» sa Mette og så sjokkert bort på ham. «Det er jo nettopp det som er problemet. Han pirker jo på alle feilene mine. Jeg føler rett og slett at jeg ikke er i stand til å gjøre noe riktig når jeg er sammen med ham. Ja, det virker faktisk som han fryder seg hver gang han greier å ta meg i å gjøre en feil.»

«Jeg tror faktisk han ser at du er mye dyktigere enn han er selv. Det har han sikkert vanskelig for å takle. Derfor blir det kan hende en tilfredsstillelse for ham når han ser deg gjøre en feil.»

De satt stille en stund begge to. Mette forsto egentlig hva Morten mente. Når hun tenkte seg om, måtte hun nok gi ham rett. Men det var bare så fortærende ergerlig å skulle unnskylde denne mannen som hun så ofte hadde blitt så ergerlig på. Hun hadde ikke tall på alle de gangene hun hadde blitt såret.

«Hvis han er slik som du beskriver ham, hvorfor oppfører han seg slik da?» sukket Mette litt oppgitt.

Morten smilte. «Det er vel dette man kaller at kjemien ikke stemmer,» sa han. «Noen ganger kan det oppstå store konflikter på grunn av det. Og det er ikke alltid så lett å gjøre så mye annet med det enn å akseptere hverandre slik vi er. Det er slett ikke sikkert at han aner noe om at du har tatt deg nær av dette. Eller har du kanskje snakket med ham om det?»

«Nei.» Mette ristet svakt på hodet. Bare tanken på å skulle gjøre noe slikt fylte henne med skrekk.

«Det kan godt hende at det er lurt å ikke ha for mye med hverandre å gjøre,» fortsatte Morten. «Jeg tror ikke det er galt å prøve å unngå konflikter og sårede følelser ved

å holde seg på en viss avstand. Men hvis du kunne greie å ikke ta deg nær av det han
sa, så er jeg sikker på at dette problemet ville bli atskillig mindre. Det er ikke alltid så
lett å skulle forsøke å forandre et annet menneske, vet du. Da er det gjerne enklere å
gjøre noe med seg selv.»

Igjen ble de sittende i taushet.

Snart reiste Mette seg. «Du må ha takk for din tålmodighet,» sa hun litt sjenert.
«Jeg skal tenke på det du har sagt, men jeg trenger nok litt tid …» Hun stoppet brått.
Så snudde hun seg og gikk raskt inn i seterbua.

16 • Bedehusformannen

Morten kom inn og sparket av seg skoene ved døra. Han virket trett der han slengte
seg ned på benken ved bordet. Et dypt alvor preget hele mannen. Mette skjenket
i en kopp kaffe til ham, men sa ikke noe. Tausheten hans inviterte absolutt ikke til noen
samtale, så hun fortsatte bare med det hun holdt på med borte ved benken. Men det var
likevel ingen trykkende taushet. Atmosfæren var trygg. De kunne godt være i samme
rom uten at de nødvendigvis måtte prate så mye.

Etter en stund snudde Mette seg og så på Morten. Det så ut som han hadde oppdaget
noe forunderlig der nede i kaffekoppen. Tankene hans måtte i hvert fall være langt borte
fra det som foregikk rundt ham. Mette hadde lyst til å spørre hva det var han tenkte så
på, men hun våget ikke. Hvis ikke han ville dele tankene sine med henne, så skulle han
få slippe det. Hun ville ikke trenge inn i noe som hun kanskje ikke hadde noe med.
Men så tankefull som dette hadde hun nesten aldri sett ham. Og det skapte uten tvil
ganske sterk nysgjerrighet hos henne.

Hun tok fram brød, smør og noe pålegg og satte det på bordet. Så skjenket hun i en
kopp kaffe til seg selv, og satte seg til bords hun også. Plutselig var det som om Morten
våknet. «Å, det skal virkelig bli godt med noe mat nå,» sa han. «Jeg er skrubbsulten.»

De spiste sammen i taushet en stund. Mette kikket ut av vinduet, og snart var hennes
tanker også langt borte.

Da Morten begynte å snakke, kvakk hun til. Han lo. «Du var langt borte nå,» sa han.

«Ja, kanskje like langt borte som du har vært siden du kom inn,» svarte hun og
smilte tilbake.

«Uff, ja,» sa han, og smilet var borte med ett. «Det er så mange problemer man
kan komme borti. Og det ser ut som om jeg roter meg oppi de fleste.» Han sukket og
tok en stor slurk av kaffen.

«Vet du hva? Noen ganger blir jeg så frustrert at jeg får lyst til å stenge meg inne
her oppe på setra og aldri vise meg for folk mer.»

Mette sperret opp øynene over det voldsomme utbruddet til den ellers så rolige og
avbalanserte mannen.

«Men hva er det som har skremt deg så vanvittig da?» spurte hun forbauset.

Han lo litt og ristet oppgitt på hodet. «Det er disse holdningene og meningene som
krasjer så totalt mellom generasjonene,» svarte han.

«Å?» Mette hevet øyenbrynene igjen og stirret forvirret på ham.

278

«Jeg var jo nede i bygda en tur i dag,» fortsatte han. «På butikken fikk jeg se en ny plakat som var blitt hengt opp siden sist jeg var der. Eller rettere sagt, jeg ble gjort oppmerksom på den av en nokså opprørt eldre herre. Der fikk jeg virkelig høre hva slags utglidninger som bedehuset nå sto i fare for å innlate seg på. Plakaten gjaldt nemlig invitasjon til å bli med i en dansegruppe på bedehuset.»

«Dansegruppe?» Mette så forbauset på ham. «Skal de starte ei dansegruppe på bedehuset her?»

«Ja,» lo Morten. «Ifølge denne mannen, som tydeligvis bare hadde lest to av ordene på plakaten, nemlig dans og bedehuset, så er det visst slik. Og så later det til at det er jeg som står med det fulle og hele ansvaret for denne «styggedommen», siden jeg er formann i bedehusstyret.»

Mette fortsatte bare å stirre forvirret på ham. «Men hva sto det da på denne plakaten?» spurte hun.

«Ja … det var nettopp det. Før jeg kunne enten forsvare eller forklare, så måtte jeg bort og se hva det var som sto der. Og da gikk det jo opp for meg hva det hele dreide seg om. Vi hadde det oppe i styret tidlig i vår. Det var noen jenter som hadde lyst til å starte med triadans. De demonstrerte litt for oss, og vi syntes dette var greit nok. Det var jo bare noen bevegelser de laget til musikk. Jentene kunne vel være i titol-vårs alderen. Jeg syntes det hele minnet mest om de bevegelsessangene vi er vant til fra søndagsskolen. Litt mer avansert var det nok, og musikken var det nok også litt mer futt i. Men det som tiltalte meg mest ved dette, var den iveren de la for dagen. For dem var det ikke bare bevegelser til noen rytmer. Det var noe de ville med det … noe de ville formidle. De ville understreke budskapet i sangene med bevegelser. Det var faktisk evangeliet de ønsket å formidle.

Nå vet ikke jeg hvor bevisste de var alle sammen, men det er noe som ikke jeg syns at jeg kan dømme om. Denne formen for dans var heller ikke noe jeg kunne greie å forbinde med den dansen vi er vant til fra diskotek eller andre liknende fester. Dette var noe helt annet. Det er bare dette ordet dans som får enkelte til å trekke en forbindelse.»

Mette smilte litt. «Dette er nok ikke det eneste stedet hvor dette emnet har skapt høye bølger,» sa hun. «Vi har vært borti det flere ganger i vår virksomhet også. Men hva tror du?» Hun rynket brynene og ble alvorlig igjen. «Jeg tenker på det du leste fra Jesaja den kvelden før stevnet. Husker du det om vaktmennene som sov, og så kom fienden seg inn i flokken?»

Morten nikket. «Ja, jeg har tenkt mye på det. Lurer du på om dette kan være noe som sniker seg inn i vår flokk, og så er det ingen som er våkne nok til å advare mot det?» spurte han.

«Jeg vet ikke.» Mette så litt tvilende ut. «Men jeg vet at enkelte steder er det et sterkt ønske om å lage virksomheten på bedehuset så lik diskoteket som mulig – for å få flere inn. De ønsker å viske skillelinjene mest mulig vekk, og det som det ofte går ut over da, det er forkynnelsen av Guds ord.»

«Jeg er klar over det,» svarte Morten. «I de tilfellene er det helt klart at versene i Jesaja femtiseks er av betydning. Men det jeg snakker om her, synes jeg ikke har noen sammenheng med det i det hele tatt. Tvert imot. Her brukes dansen for å fremheve budskapet. Det er en stor forskjell på det.»

«Jeg forstår hva du mener,» sa Mette. «Men jeg tror det ligger mange følelser her. Ofte har jeg hørt vitnesbyrd der folk har fortalt om hvordan de ble frelst. De måtte bryte over tvert med det verdslige livet. Dansen var en del av det livet som de ble frelst fra.

Den er for mange også svært besnærende. De føler det nesten som de blir lokket tilbake til verden igjen når det blir snakk om dans.»

«Ja, jeg forstår veldig godt de tankene,» sa Morten. «Jeg tror bare at vi må bli flinkere i dag til å forklare forskjellen på dette. Og så tror jeg folk må bli flinkere til å lytte. De som lukker ørene med en gang ordet dans blir nevnt, får jo aldri muligheten til å lære noe om denne forskjellen. Etter hvert som de blir kjent med den kristne formen for dans, vil de skjønne at dette ikke er noe de kan forbinde med sitt tidligere liv. Det de da vil merke det på, er ånden. Det er i det hele tatt den som er den store forskjellen. Vi kan egentlig ikke dømme mellom kristne og ikke kristne tiltak på noen annen måte. Det er Ånden som viser hva som er av Gud, og hva som ikke er av Ham. Men vi kan med våre negative holdninger stenge slik at vi ikke merker den åndelige kraften i dette.

Selvsagt kan det gjøres mye galt på dette området også. Men det jeg kjempet for, er at vi ikke avviser noe som er fra Gud. Det er et ordtak som sier: Kjærlighet oppfinnsom gjør. Jeg tror at det er en passende beskrivelse av Gud. Han ønsker å få alle med seg til himmelen. Og kan Han oppnå det, så skyr Han ingen midler. Hans kjærlighet til oss er så stor. Nå ser Han at en del unge mennesker har sansen for denne måten å forkynne Ordet på, og da nøler Han ikke med å bruke den. Jeg har sett en del av denne forkynningsformen. Det har vært utrolig gripende. Der hvor midlene fremhever budskapet, kan det oppnåes en enestående kontakt. Men selvsagt er det tilfeller der midlet blir sentrum og hovedsak, og da blir det noe helt annet. Dansen og musikken må ikke overdøve budskapet.»

Mette tenkte litt på det han hadde sagt. Så sa hun: «Du tror ikke at dette kan være med på å skyve vekk noen, jeg tenker da på de eldre?»

«Morten måtte også tenke seg litt om før han svarte. «Jeg vil vel kanskje heller snu spørsmålet slik: Kan det tenkes at vi skyver noen ut med de vanlige formene vi driver etter i dag? Jeg tenker da på de unge.»

Mette måtte le. Morten lo også.

«Hvordan har det blitt slik, tror du?» spurte Mette. «Jeg mener: Hvorfor er det blitt slik at dansen er regnet for å være så syndig her i landet. Kommer vi til andre land, så er det helt annerledes. Til og med i Bibelen blir jo dansen regnet for å være et middel til å ære Gud med.»

Morten ble ivrig med det samme. «Det tror jeg har en sammenheng med vår historie,» svarte han. «Jeg vet ikke om jeg har rett, men jeg tror det kommer av at dansen en gang i tiden hørte til den hedenske gudsdyrkelsen her i landet. Da kristendommen ble innført, måtte de som tok imot den, bryte med alt det hedenske, deriblant dansen. Men så gikk århundrene. De kristne var hele tiden nøye med at dansen var synd. Den måtte de ta avstand fra. Men de glemte hvorfor den var synd. De glemte at de hadde brutt med dansen på grunn av at den ble brukt som et innviet middel i et hedensk ritual. Så lenge den var et innviet middel, hadde djevelen makt over dem som utøvde den. Det de ikke tenkte på, var at djevelen ville miste makten over dette middelet hvis det ble brukt for et annet formål.»

«Det kan godt hende at du har rett i dette,» sa Mette. «Men i de verdslige kretser har jo dansen florert hele tiden. Og det er jo det miljøet de viser til, de som har blitt kristne i vår og våre foreldres generasjon. Altså de som i vår tid forbinder dansen med synd.»

«Dette kan nok virke ganske forvirrende,» svarte Morten. «Det som er viktig, er at vi nettopp ser hvordan dette er i andre land. Der fungerer dansen både som en del av det verdslige miljøet og et middel til å dyrke Gud med. Det er faktisk på samme måte som sang og musikk. Her finnes jo mye verdslig musikk, og ikke minst sangtekster. Men vi kan da ikke si at vi ikke vil bruke sang og musikk på bedehuset for det. Vi bruker da sangen til å prise Gud med, selv om det synges aldri så mange verdslige sanger andre steder.

En ting som vi i denne forbindelse hele tiden må ha klart for oss, er det jeg sa til å begynne med. Dans er så mye forskjellig. Det er jo himmelvid forskjell på for eksempel denne triadansen og den pardansen som mest blir brukt på diskotekene.»

Det ble en liten pause. Begge satt og tenkte på det de hadde snakket om. Plutselig smilte Mette igjen. «Det var da svært så alvorlige vi ble i dag. Jeg tror ikke du skal ta denne kritikken så hardt innover deg. Slike kollisjoner mellom generasjonene vil vi nok møte til alle tider. Jeg tror vi skal være mest opptatt av å forkynne det Gud gir oss å gå med, og på den måten han viser oss at vi best vil nå fram. Da tror jeg at Hans ord vil seire til sist, uansett uenigheter.»

Morten så på henne, og smilet han sendte var fylt av varme og takknemlighet. «Det tror jeg virkelig du har rett i. Nå glemmer vi hele denne episoden, og så må du være med og be for meg at jeg ikke må gjøre noe galt med det jeg sier. Vil du det? Det kan jo hende at jeg tar feil i et og annet.»

Det humoristiske glimtet i øyet hans fikk henne til å le høyt. Men løftet hun gav om å be for ham, visste hun at hun ville komme til å holde.

Ikke lenge etter gikk Morten ut igjen, men Mette ble sittende en stund til med kaffen. Det var virkelig en dyp samtale de hadde hatt. Egentlig likte hun ikke å diskutere slike vanskelige stridsspørsmål. Hun ble så lett engasjert, og da kunne hun ofte komme til å si ting som hun angret på etterpå. Men her var det helt annerledes. Sammen med Morten følte hun seg så avslappet og fri. Hun kunne si akkurat det hun mente uten at han tok det ille opp. Og det han sa, opplevde hun aldri som harde eller kritiske ord mot henne.

Ofte hadde de hatt slike samtaler og diskusjoner. Særlig om kvelden når alt arbeidet var unnagjort. Av og til kunne det bli sent før de gikk til ro. Disse samtalene kom helt sikkert til å bli noe av det hun ville savne mest når hun skulle reise fra setra.

17 • Besøk fra Russland

Dagene gikk og ble til uker. På campingområdet kom det stadig nye vogner og telt, mens andre brøt opp og reiste. Morten tok rett som det var grupper med turister med seg innover i fjellet. Mette hadde nesten alltid en flokk av barn og voksne rundt seg mens hun stelte dyra. Rett som det var måtte hun demonstrere både det ene og det andre. Tante Anna var også stadig i virksomhet, men hun var der ikke så lenge av gangen. De forsøkte å avlaste henne så godt de kunne. Hun ville helst ikke være ved det, men de merket godt at hun fort ble trett og sliten. Hun var jo slett ingen ungdom. Men Mette hadde lært utrolig mye av den aldrende kvinnen, så hun kunne greie seg godt på egen hånd etter hvert.

Av og til tok hun en tur ned til bygda. Det hendte jo at hun måtte handle litt, men mesteparten av tiden var hun der oppe på den avsidesliggende setra. Hun måtte smile når hun tenkte på det. Ikke hadde hun fjernsyn eller internett. En radio var det i seterbua, men den gikk på batteri, så de hadde den ikke så mye på. Det var mest nyheter og værmeldinger som ble prioritert. Det kom til å bli rart å komme tilbake til sivilisasjonen igjen, tenkte hun. Riktignok hadde hun mobiltelefon, så hun kunne holde kontakten med familie og venner, men det var ikke så mye hun hadde brukt den heller.

Ensomt var det likevel ikke. Hun var blitt kjent med mange av turistene. Noen kom hun til å holde kontakten med videre. Og så var jo Marit og Ellen der fremdeles. Hun kom godt ut av det med dem, selv om hun fremdeles undret seg over Ellens fortrolighet med familien.

Været hadde for det meste holdt seg varmt og fint. Den lange tørkeperioden begynte å sette sine spor. Morten var litt bekymret. «Nå trenger vi regn,» sa han en morgen da han sto i døra og så på de brune flekkene som var begynt å vise seg på vollen.

Mette syntes det hadde vært godt med det fine været, men hun forsto jo selvsagt problemet. Bøndene nede i bygda trengte regn til neste avling. Gresset der på setra ble kun slått en gang, så det betydde ikke så mye for det, men de trengte beite til dyra.

Enga ute på vollen hadde de slått for en stund siden. Mette hadde frydet seg over å kunne være med på det kjente og kjære arbeidet som hesjingen var. Hesjing var vel noe av det hun forbandt mest med sin barndoms sommer. Riktignok hadde hun ikke frydet seg like mye over det den gangen hun var barn. Da syntes hun ofte det kunne bli vel langtekkelig og kjedelig å gå der dag etter dag og henge gress opp på de ståltrådene. Men nå var det annerledes. Det var jo kun dette ene jordet som skulle hesjes, og det greide de lett på en dag. En del av turistene hadde også vært med og hjulpet til. Det barna hadde likt best, var når de skulle kjøre høyet inn på høyloftet. Morten hadde lånt en hest og ei høyvogn nede i bygda. Det var en rolig og snill gamp. Den gjorde seg ikke det minste av at barna løp og spratt rundt den. Av og til lot Morten et av dem sitte på ryggen til hesten når de skulle kjøre inn et lass.

Inne i høyet på låven fikk barna nå en ny lekeplass. De stortrivdes med å kunne boltre seg der.

Ute på vollen gikk dyra mer fritt. Etter hvert var det faktisk blitt ganske mange av dem der. Petter hadde vært oppe med et par kuer og noen geiter til, så nå hadde hun flere dyr som måtte melkes. Missi og Keiseren diet fortsatt si ku, og det gjorde de ganske effektivt, så hun slapp å melke den. Men hun frydet seg over arbeidet, så om hun hadde fått det mer travelt i fjøset, så syntes hun bare det var trivelig.

«I morgen får vi et spesielt besøk,» sa Morten da de satte seg til frokostbordet. Det var bare de to som var der. Tante Anna hadde reist ned til bygda dagen før, og Marit og Ellen var ute i campingvogna. «Det er noen russiske turister som kommer,» fortsatte han begeistret. «En gruppe fra bygda her var på besøk der borte for et par år siden. Ellen og jeg var med den gangen. Vi besøkte en menighet der. Det var utrolig interessant å bli kjent med disse menneskene. I fjor var en gruppe derfra på besøk her i bygda, og en del av tiden tilbrakte de her på setra. Mange interessante kontakter ble etablert da, derfor ville de komme tilbake i år. Reisen blir visst sponset en del av noen foreninger her. Ellen har stått i bresjen for dette. Det var hun som spurte om vi også i år kunne ta imot disse gjestene noen dager.»

Mette lyttet interessert mens Morten fortsatte å fortelle fra turen de hadde hatt til Russland. Ellen ble nevnt som en naturlig del av det hele. Igjen ble hun sittende med den stigende undringen. Kunne det være mer enn bare vennskap mellom dem? Nei huff – nå var hun inne på de tankene igjen. Hvorfor hang hun seg så opp i det? Morten måtte da kunne leve sitt liv som han ville uten at hun hadde noe med det.

Hun konsentrerte seg om å delta i det han sa. De la noen planer for besøket, men mest skulle gjestene bare være der og ta del i seterlivets daglige rutiner. Folk fra bygda ville komme opp for å besøke dem. De kom visst til å ha noen arrangementer i anledning besøket.

○ ○ ○

Neste dag opprant, som første dag på lenge, med gråvær og litt regn. Gjestene ble installert i innleide campingvogner. Det var nitten voksne mennesker med i følget. De fleste var kvinner. Gjensynsgleden med dem de hadde møtt før, var stor. Ellen var spesielt opprømt over besøket. Det så ikke ut til at været la noen nevneverdig demper på deres begeistring. Disse folkene var visst ikke vant til verken fjell og vidder eller dyr. Mette fikk også fort kontakt.

Språket kunne til tider by på litt problemer, men de fleste kunne litt engelsk, så de greide seg likevel ganske bra.

Utpå kvelden kom det opp noen fra bygda. Det ble ganske trangt inne i seterbua. Morten mente at de måtte være der inne, for det var det eneste stedet hvor de kunne være samlet alle sammen under tak.

Det ble en uforglemmelig kveld. En i følget fra Russland var tolk for dem som ikke kunne så mye engelsk, og Morten tolket fra engelsk til norsk for dem av de norske som ikke kunne forstå nok engelsk. Den ene historien etter den andre ble fortalt.

Russerne ble på setra i nesten en uke. Stadig fikk de besøk fra bygda. Noen kom også fra andre bygder. Rett som det var ble de hentet til arrangementer rundt om i distriktet. Morten var med på det meste. Mette var også av og til med, men som oftest ble hun igjen på setra. Hun hadde jo ansvaret for dyra, og dem kunne de ikke være borte fra så lenge av gangen.

Da uka var omme, ble det tatt en rørende avskjed med gjestene. Mette og Morten sto og vinket da bilene svingte ned veien. Ellen ble med dem ned til bygda. Hun ville se dem skikkelig av gårde, sa hun. De hadde buss som sto og ventet på dem der nede.

Senere på dagen kom Ellen opp igjen. Hun virket alvorlig og urolig da hun kom inn i seterbua. «Hvor er Morten?» spurte hun.

Mette sto klar med melkebøttene. Hun skulle ut i fjøset for å melke. «Han gikk bort til Marit i campingvogna,» svarte hun. «Du finner ham sikkert der.»

Mette gikk mot fjøset mens Ellen løp bortover vollen. Mette stoppet litt og kikket etter den opprørte damen. Hva var det som sto på nå tro?

Etter at Mette hadde gjort seg ferdig med dyrestellet og satt all melka til kjøling i kulpen, gikk hun inn i seterbua igjen. Det var ingen der inne. Hun kokte kaffe og satte fram kveldsmat, men det kom ingen inn for å spise. Undrende kikket hun ut av vinduet. Da oppdaget hun at Morten sin bil var borte. Enda mer forundret gikk hun tilbake til bordet. Det var visst ikke annet å gjøre enn å spise alene.

○ ○ ○

Da Mette gikk til fjøset neste morgen, var Morten ennå ikke kommet. Hun gjorde seg raskt ferdig og gikk bort til Marits campingvogn for å høre om hun kunne få en forklaring der. Enda større ble hennes undring da hun fant den låst og forlatt. De hadde altså reist ned til bygda alle tre. Hva kunne det være som hadde hendt? Hvorfor hadde de dratt så raskt uten å si noe til henne? Mette kjente at hun ble urolig. Hun visste at Morten ventet en turistgruppe utpå ettermiddagen. Da måtte han i hvert fall være tilbake … hvis det da ikke var en ulykke som hadde hendt. Hun merket at hun begynte å tenke det verste.

Det var en god del som skulle forberedes til det ventede besøket. Hun begynte å arbeide automatisk, men tankene var langt unna. Alle de tankene hun ikke hadde tillatt seg å tenke, kom med ett fram. Morten … Ellen … Ellen og Morten …

Grøten hun arbeidet med, holdt på å bli svidd. I siste liten fikk hun berget den fra varmen. Tankene ville ikke gi henne fred, og så gikk det fullstendig ut over konsentrasjonen.

Plutselig hørte hun bildur fra veien. Hun styrtet til vinduet. Det var turistene som begynte å komme.

Snart var vollen full av biler og folk igjen. Hun gikk ut for å ta imot dem. Der fikk hun øye på Morten midt i en klynge. Hun hadde lyst til å løpe bort for å spørre ham om hva som hadde hendt, men hun besinnet seg. Han sto i ivrig samtale, så hun fant ut at det nok ikke var det rette øyeblikket for forklaringer.

Hele ettermiddagen var de hektisk opptatt hver med sitt. Ikke et øyeblikk fikk de anledning til å snakke alene sammen. Mette la forresten merke til at Morten virket helt normal. Han spøkte og lo innimellom, så det kunne nok ikke være så alvorlig det som hadde hendt.

Det var ikke før sent på kvelden at hun fikk et par ord med ham alene. Han kom inn for å hente noe utstyr han hadde liggende på benken. «Jeg må ned til bygda igjen,» sa han.

«Har det hendt noe?» Mette så spent på ham.

Han ristet litt på hodet og lo.

I det samme kom en gutt stormende inn døra. «Dere må komme!» ropte han. Ei av geitene har kommet seg inn i campingvogna vår. Mamma er helt vill!»

Morten løp ut. Mette fikk på seg et par sko og fulgte etter. Borte ved vogna sto ei dame og hylte. Hun løp fram og tilbake foran døren. En liten flokk forskrekkede turister hadde samlet seg ved vogna. Der inne fikk de se ei av geitene stå på hodet i en kjølebag og forsyne seg. Et brød lå på gulvet. Det var revet ut et stort stykke av det. En mann forsøkte å skyve det frekke dyret mot døra, men geitebukken ville ikke gi slipp på godsakene den hadde funnet.

Morten hopper fort inn, og med felles anstrengelser fikk de to mennene ut den gjenstridige geita.

«Jeg vet ikke riktig hva vi skal gjøre med den,» sa han til Mette. «Jeg tror bare vi må stenge den inne i fjøset i natt. Så får vi se hvordan den oppfører seg i morgen.»

«Jeg kan ta den med bort dit,» sa Mette. Hun tok et godt tak i ragget og dro den med seg. Den gutten som hadde kommet med beskjeden, fulgte med.

«Den er egentlig snill,» sa gutten da de gikk mot fjøset. «Jeg hadde sikkert greid å få den ut alene hvis ikke mamma hadde blitt så hysterisk.»

Mette måtte le. «Hvis hun ikke er vant til dyr, så var sikkert dette litt skremmende.» Mette syntes hun måtte ta den stakkars moren litt i forsvar.

«Hun behøvde i hvert fall ikke ha hylt slik,» sa gutten. «Hun vekket jo opp hele campingplassen.»

«Nå må du lukke døra etter oss så den ikke smetter ut igjen,» sa Mette til gutten da de gikk inn i fjøset. Hun fant et fang høy og noe kraftfôr som hun gav den for å få den til å roe seg der inne.

Da de kom ut av fjøset igjen, var Morten allerede reist. Gutten løp tilbake til campingvogna, mens Mette gikk inn igjen i seterbua.

Den kvelden ble Mette sittende lenge i senga med dagboka i fanget. Parafinlampa, som hun hadde plassert på nattbordet, gav et trolsk skinn over de gamle veggene. Ute var det helt mørkt. Det hun skrev i boka, ville hun aldri la noen få lese. Kanskje hun ikke ville våge å lese det selv heller noen gang. En underlig uro begynte å ta form i hennes indre. Hvordan ville dette gå …

Plutselig kom hun på det den mannen hadde sagt den dagen de hadde stevnet. Hun måtte passe seg, hadde han sagt. Kunne det være noe med Morten som det var grunn til å være på vakt overfor? Men hva i all verden skulle det være? Han virket da som godheten selv til daglig.

Med ett la hun dagboka fra seg og blåste ut lampen. Nå ville hun ikke tenke mer. Nå ville hun sove.

18 • Samtale ved bålet

Møysommelig strevde Mette med å få bålet til å flamme skikkelig opp. Skulle de greie å steke pølser der snart, måtte det bli kraftigere fyr i det. Hun la på mer tørr ved som hun hadde tatt med seg fra setra.

De hadde besøk av en leirskoleklasse. Nå satt hele klassen ved kanten av tjernet mens Morten fortalte om sagnet og livet der på setra i gamle dager. Pølsene lå klar til steking. Morten hadde spikket en masse pinner som de skulle bruke som grillspyd. To leirskolelærere var også med. Alle satt og lyttet oppmerksomt til det Morten fortalte.

Snart flammet bålet mer opp, og glørne begynte å dannes mellom vedskiene. Morten avsluttet fortellingen sin og inviterte til pølsegrilling. Med ett ble det livlig rundt bålet. Mette skjenket saft i pappbeger som hun delte ut til elevene. Snart sto en hel ring av skoleungdom rundt bålet med pølser på hver sin pinne. Prat og latter runget utover.

Etter hvert trakk Mette seg litt unna flokken. De fleste hadde satt seg på marka langs bredden for å spise pølsene. Hun lot blikket gli over flokken med livlige gutter og jenter. Det stoppet ved Morten. Han sto og pratet med en av lærerne. De lo og hadde det visst like hyggelig som ungdommene. Det så slett ikke ut til at han slet med noen slags problemer.

Etter den dagen de måtte hente ut geitebukken fra campingvogna, hadde de ikke fått mange anledningene til å snakke sammen. Det så heller ikke ut til at Morten hadde behov for å fortelle noe til henne. Mette våget ikke å spørre mer om det. Hvis ikke han ville si noe, så var det nok ikke noe hun hadde noe med. Det var gått over en uke siden det hendte. Den åpne, fortrolige tonen hadde de nok på en måte ennå, men likevel var det kommet noe stengt mellom dem, syntes Mette. I hvert fall greide ikke hun å dele denne uroen som hadde kommet over henne, med ham.

Ellen hadde hun heller ikke sett noe mer til. Morten hadde flere ganger vært nede i bygda, men hun visste lite om hva det var han foretok seg der.

Hun kikket opp på skyene. Bare det ville holde tett til de var ferdige med denne dagen. Himmelen var blitt ganske grå, og det var mye kjøligere i lufta. De var allerede kommet langt uti august. Litt vemodig tenkte hun at nå hadde hun bare vel tre uker igjen av jobben sin. Men kanskje det var best at hun kom seg tilbake til byen igjen. Her hadde hun begynt å få så mange underlige tanker.

Rutinene var blitt en del endret etter at leirskoleklassene begynt å komme. Det ble mer undervisning og mindre demonstrasjoner av det daglige seterlivet. Egentlig hadde hun gledet seg til høsten. Det ville bli en ny utfordring med alle skoleungdommene.

Plutselig kom en gutt bort til henne. Han satte seg ved siden av henne og bet et stort stykke av ei nokså svartbrent pølse. I taushet betraktet han et lite gullkors som hun hadde i et kjede rundt halsen.

«Så fint smykke du har,» sa han omsider.

Mette smilte. «Liker du det? For meg er det i hvert fall veldig kjært,» svarte hun. «Er du sånn kristelig?»

Spørsmålet kom helt naturlig, og Mette måtte smile igjen. «Ja jeg er en kristen.»

Gutten fortsatte å se på smykket mens han tygde iherdig på pølsen. De satt i taushet en stund igjen. Men så festet han blikket rett på henne og sa: «Jeg skal sånn konfirmeres til neste vår. Men jeg vet ikke om jeg vil.»

Mette ble alvorlig. Gutten senket blikket som om han hadde sagt noe galt.

«Hvorfor tror du at du ikke vil?» spurte hun vennlig.

Han svarte ikke med det samme. Blikket var festet på en mosedott på bakken mens han med skoen sparket åndsfravær-ende i marka. Han virket litt mutt, men Mette tenkte at det like gjerne kunne være sjenanse. Kanskje dette var noe han trengte å prate om.

«Er det en spesiell grunn til det?» fortsatte hun.

«Jeg vil konfirmeres, men jeg vet ikke om jeg vil gjøre det i kirken,» svarte han omsider.

Mette la merke til en bekymret rynke mellom øynene. Dette var tydeligvis noe som virkelig opptok ham.

«Er du døpt?» Mette syntes hun måtte spørre om det før hun kunne si noe mer til ham om emnet.

Gutten stirret forskrekket opp på henne. «Ja selvfølgelig,» svarte han. «Man kan ikke bli annet enn døpt med slike foreldre som jeg har. De er litt teite.»

Mette måtte smile igjen. Så godt som hun kjente seg selv igjen i denne gutten. Hvor teite hadde ikke hennes foreldre også fortonet seg for henne da hun var i den alderen.

«Vet du hva?» Mette så rett på ham, og smilet blinket fortsatt i øynene hennes. «Jeg hadde også noen forferdelig teite foreldre da jeg var på din alder. Men nå er de faktisk blitt ganske fornuftige.»

Gutten måtte også smile. Han skjønte visst poenget hennes. «Du mener altså at det kan være håp for mine også?» De lo begge to. Men snart ble han alvorlig igjen. «Det er bare det,» fortsatte han. «De vil så gjerne at jeg skal konfirmeres i kirken, men jeg vet ikke om det er rett. Jeg har nemlig en kamerat som tilhører «De frie». Vi har pratet mye sammen om dette med Gud og Jesus og sånn. Det han sier høres så rett ut, og han skal konfirmeres på en annen måte.»

Mette tenkte seg litt om før hun sa noe. Hun skjønte at det var viktig at hun ikke sa noe galt til ham.

«Jeg vet at de praktiserer både dåp og konfirmasjon på en annen måte,» begynte hun. «Jeg tror ikke vi skal fundere så mye på om det ene er rett og det andre kanskje galt. Det jeg tror vi må tenke over, er hva som er rett for meg. Hvordan skal jeg forstå Bibelen i disse spørsmålene.»

Gutten ble med ett litt aggressiv. «Hvordan i all verden skal jeg kunne forstå dette? Det er jo så vanskelig. Det er jo så mange forskjellige meninger om det.»

«Du har helt rett i det,» fortsatte Mette. «Dette er slett ikke så lett å forstå. Du sa at du var døpt. Kanskje du også har gått på søndagsskolen eller på annen måte lært om Bibelen?»

«Å, ja da. Jeg har lært det som er å lære i Bibelen, tror jeg. Men alle snakker jo bare om sin egen måte å forstå dette på. Det er det som er så forvirrende.»

Mette tenkte seg om litt igjen. «Er det noe spesielt du synes er vanskelig å forstå?» spurte hun.

«Det er jo dette med om vi vil høre Jesus til, og om hvordan vi blir kristne,» svarte han raskt.

«Vil du høre Jesus til da?» Mette så granskende på ham.

«Ja, selvsagt vil jeg det. Men jeg vil at det skal være ordentlig. I kirka sier de at vi blir Guds barn når vi blir døpt, men hvordan i all verden kan vi bli det når vi er så små at vi ikke er i stand til å bestemme oss for noe som helst?»

«Kan jeg få lov til å prøve å forklare dette for deg?» Hun så alvorlig, men vennlig på ham. De var så konsentrert om samtalen at de ikke la merke til de andre som lo og pratet rundt bålet. Begge forsto at dette var et viktig øyeblikk som de måtte utnytte.

«Frelsen,» begynte Mette, «den består av to ting. Det er dåpen, og så er det troen. Som jeg forstår så er det dette med troen du har problemer med. Du kan ikke forstå at et lite spedbarn kan tro.»

«Ja nettopp,» svarte han ivrig. «Akkurat det er det.»

«Nå skal du høre,» sa Mette og fortsatte. «Dåpen er som en pakt som blir inngått mellom Gud og mennesket. Det er en pakt om å høre sammen. Da blir også troen lagt ned i barnet. Troen er en gave som Gud gir. Det eneste vi mennesker må gjøre for å få denne gaven, er å ta imot den. Et lite spedbarn har ingen problemer med dette. Det tar imot alt det får, også denne troen. Da er det mye vanskeligere med oss voksne. Vi tar ikke imot hva som helst uten videre.

Men denne troen trenger næring for å vokse og utvikle seg. Når et lite barn blir båret til dåpen, lover foreldre og faddere at de skal sørge for at barnet blir opplært i Guds ord. Det er for at troen skal vokse.»

Nå ble det liv over gutten igjen. Det var som om han protesterte med hele seg. «Det der virker bare ikke,» sa han heftig. «Bare se så mange det er som er blitt døpt, men hvor mange er det som er kristne når de blir større?»

Mette måtte smile litt over iveren hans. «Jeg skjønner godt at dette kan virke litt frustrerende. Selvsagt ser vi mange som bærer barna sine til dåpen uten å mene stort med det de gjør. I hvert fall er det så altfor ofte at løftet om å lære barna opp i den kristne tro ikke blir holdt. Og like ofte ser vi nok at mange velger å gå bort fra Gud, selv om de er blitt opplært i troen som barn. Dette er nok de kristnes største sorg. Men like fult så står dåpen ved lag gjennom hele livet.

Troen, den kan vi miste hvis vi velger å leve et liv borte fra Jesus og hans frelse. Og da mister også dåpens kraft makten i vårt liv. Men hvis dette mennesket senere blir frelst, da får det troen tilbake igjen. Og da er det at det underlige skjer. Dåpen får igjen sin makt i livet. Den pakten som ble opprettet med Gud den gang vi var et lite spedbarn, får igjen sin fulle makt. Den behøver vi ikke å opprette på nytt.»

Mette stoppet opp litt i sin enetale. Hun var litt i tvil om hvordan hun skulle fortsette, eller om gutten i det hele tatt forsto noe av det hun sa. Han satt litt i taushet. Men så sa han mens han så litt grublende ned i marka: «Hvordan kan man vite det? Jeg mener, hvordan kan man være sikker på at dåpens pakt virkelig er i orden når vi igjen velger å bli kristne etter kanskje å ha vært borte fra Jesus i mange år? Hvordan kan jeg være sikker på at min dåp fremdeles virker nå når jeg begynner å bli voksen?»

Spørsmålet viste klart for Mette at han hadde forstått det hun sa. Nå gjaldt det bare at hun fikk forklart dette slik at han også forsto den fulle meningen.

«I det gamle testamentet i Bibelen finner vi mange underlige beretninger,» fortsatte hun. «Der står det om konger og profeter, og mange merkelige hendelser. Der står også mye om Israelsfolkets historie. Jeg går ut fra at du har hørt en del om det?»

Gutten så på henne og nikket forsiktig. «Jeg har jo hørt om Abraham og Moses og dem. Men når jeg leser i den delen av Bibelen, så forstår jeg ikke så mye.»

Mette smilte og gledet seg over denne ungdommen som så tillitsfullt åpnet seg for henne. «Du har hørt om Abraham,» fortsatte hun. «Kan du huske om du har hørt den beretningen da Abraham måtte ut og telle stjernene? Da Gud talte til ham og sa at ætten hans skulle bli så tallrik som stjernene på himmelen?»

Gutten nikket. «Den fortellingen husker jeg,» svarte han ivrig.

«Da gjorde Gud en pakt med ham og ætten hans,» fortsatte hun. «Den pakten Gud gjorde med Abraham, den gjaldt for hele folket så lenge de skulle være her på jorden. Det var en pakt mellom Gud og menneskene om å høre sammen. Den gjelder også for dem som tar imot Jesus og lever som Hans barn i dag. Den pakten kan vi regne som et bilde på dåpen. Guds folk ble liksom skapt ved Abraham. Helt i begynnelsen av dette folkets liv inngikk Gud en pakt med dem. Men så vet vi hva som skjedde med dette folket. Det var slett ikke alltid de levde slik som Gud ville de skulle leve. Det ser vi spesielt i historien om Moses og vandringen i ørkenen. Du husker den, gjør du ikke?»

Gutten nikket ivrig.

«Du husker kanskje at de rett som det var satte seg opp mot Gud,» fortsatte hun, «og han måtte straffe dem. Når de så angret, og kom tilbake til Gud igjen, fikk de oppleve tilgivelsen. De ble innlemmet i folket igjen. Men pakten behøvde de ikke å fornye. Den sto ved lag. Den hjalp riktignok ikke noe mens de var ulydige og gikk borte fra Guds veier. Men med en gang de kom tilbake igjen, var den der, og de fikk erfare velsignelsen ved den. Slik er det med dåpens pakt også. Med en gang vi kommer tilbake til Jesus igjen og blir frelst, så står pakten der og gjelder like fullt som den gangen den ble gitt da du var et lite barn.»

«Åååå …» Det kom et undrende lys over ansiktet til den oppmerksomme tilhøreren. Men så mørknet det til litt igjen. «Men …» Gutten dro litt på det. «Disse folkene som gjorde opprør mot Gud i det gamle testamentet … Du sa at Gud måtte straffe dem for det gale de gjorde. Må han ikke straffe oss også når vi gjør noe galt, for eksempel dette med å gå bort fra hans vei?»

«Jo,» svarte Mette ivrig. «Det må han virkelig. Men vet du hva? Den straffen slipper vi å lide. For den straffen var det Jesus tok da han døde på korset.»

Plutselig lyste det opp i ansiktet igjen til den friske ungdommen som satt ved siden av henne. «Det er jo sant! Nå skjønner jeg det.» Et smil bredte seg utover hele ansiktet hans. «Da er dåpen min like bra som dåpen til dem som døper seg som voksne?» Påstanden lyste som et spørsmål mot Mette. Det var en påstand han tydeligvis ville ha en bekreftelse på.

«Ja, det kan du være helt sikker på.» Mette gjengjeldte det lyse smilet. Og så fortsatte hun: «Nå har jo du erfart at det finnes forskjellige syn på dette. Det jeg har forklart deg her, er det lutherske synet. Det er jo det du er blitt opplært i. Jeg tror det er viktig at vi er klar over vårt eget syn, og så må vi respektere andres, selv om vi ikke helt kan forstå dem alltid.»

Han nikket iherdig. Plutselig snudde han seg mot henne. «Takk skal du ha. Det var en fin prat vi fikk.»

Mette smilte av den veslevoksne måten å uttrykke seg på. Men hun var glad for at det tydeligvis hadde blitt til hjelp for ham, det hun hadde sagt.

Idet han reiste seg fra stedet han hadde sittet, tok Mette opp en penn fra lomma. Hun fant også en papirbit. På den skrev hun et skriftsted. «Les dette når du kommer hjem,» sa hun.

Gutten tok ivrig lappen og kikket på den. «Ja, det skal jeg gjøre,» sa han. Dermed stappet han papirbiten i lomma og gikk tilbake til de andre.

Mette så etter ham. Det skriftstedet hun hadde skrevet til ham, hadde også for henne en gang blitt til stor hjelp når det gjaldt disse spørsmålene. Det var hentet fra Paulus sitt andre brev til Timoteus. Det var det tredje kapittel, vers fjorten og femten. Hun siterte versene for seg selv etter hukommelsen: «Men du skal holde fast på det du har lært og er blitt overbevist om; du vet jo hvem du har lært det av. Helt fra barndommen har du kjent de hellige skrifter, de som kan gi deg visdom som leder til frelse ved troen på Kristus Jesus.»

Plutselig begynte flokken å bevege seg oppover mot setervollen. Mette hadde vært så opptatt av egne tanker at hun ikke hadde registrert beskjedene som ble gitt. Hun reiste seg raskt og begynte å rydde sammen restene etter maten. En stund sto hun bøyd og plukket opp pappbeger og annen søppel som var slengt rundt på marka. Da hun reiste seg opp igjen, ble hun helt overrumplet over å møte det intense blikket til Morten. Han hadde blitt stående igjen da de andre gikk. Plutselig snudde han seg og gikk raskt etter ungdommene.

Mette så undrende etter ham. Han hadde stått og stirret på henne … Igjen begynte det å arbeide i hennes innerste. Hvorfor hadde han gjort det?

19 • Guds vesen

Det var lørdag, og Mette hadde fri. En hektisk uke lå bak, så hun gledet seg til å kunne ta det litt med ro igjen. Denne dagen ville hun bruke til litt handling, og kanskje en kjøretur rundt i bygda. Morten hadde sagt at hun kunne bruke bilen hele dagen om hun ville. Han var også i bygda. Hun skulle plukke ham opp når hun kjørte oppover igjen.

Aller først dro hun til handlesenteret. Det var ikke akkurat så stort et senter, men så var heller ikke bygda så stor. Hun begynte å bli litt kjent etter å ha vært der en del ganger i løpet av sommeren. Noen hilste på henne da hun kom. De fleste visste at det var hun som jobbet oppe på Siljatjernsetra.

Litt lenger inne i butikken gikk hun forbi to menn som sto og pratet. I det samme hun passerte dem, ble de så underlige i ansiktet. Praten stoppet helt opp, og de stirret litt rart på henne. Hun svingte rundt en reol og begynte å se etter noe i en hylle. Fra der hun sto kunne hun ikke se mennene, men hun hørte dem ganske bra. De lo litt. «Det var dama fra setra,» hørte hun den ene si. «Skal si hun holder det gående.» Begge brast i latter igjen.

Mette følte seg uvel. Det var tydelig at disse ordene ikke var beregnet for hennes ører. Det var også klart at betydningen av det de sa, var av det grove slaget.

Hun hadde ikke lyst til å høre mer, så hun skyndte seg vekk. Men hvorfor snakket de om henne på den måten? En stund ble hun gående og tenke på det. Igjen ble hun minnet på møtet hun hadde hatt med de mennene oppe på setra tidligere på sommeren. Da hadde hun blitt fykende sint. Nå ble hun bare urolig og usikker. Hun husket også mannen som hadde forsøkt å komme med en advarsel til henne på stevnet. Hva kunne dette bety? Samme hvor mye hun vred hjernen sin kunne hun ikke begripe hva det var de mente. At det var noen som hadde en temmelig skitten fantasi, skjønte hun i hvert fall. Det var nok best å bare glemme det hele.

Mennene var forsvunnet da hun skulle gå ut igjen, og det var hun glad for. Det var en fin dag. Hun ble stående litt utenfor butikken og betraktet de vakre omgivelsene. Gårdene lå utstrakt på begge sider av hovedveien. Butikken hun sto ved, lå også nær veien. Den var en del av et større kompleks med bank, postkontor, legekontor og en del andre offentlige kontorer.

Veien skar gjennom bygda fra øst mot vest. Det var på sørsiden av veien hun sto. Bedehuset lå også på den siden, bare litt lenger i østlig retning. Kirken lå i nærheten av det, men på den andre siden av veien. Fra der hun sto kunne hun se veien som gikk oppover mot setra. Den gikk rett nordover. Det var bare et lite stykke bortenfor butikken at man måtte ta av for å komme inn på den. Der lå også gården til Morten.

I nord og vest var bygda omkranset av vidstrakte heier og fjell. Mot øst gikk en dal nedover, og i sør var det mest skog å se. Jernbanen gikk også der på sørsiden av bygda et sted.

Hvilken vakker bygd, tenkte Mette. Gårder og hus lå badet i solskinn under de majestetiske fjellene og heiene. Blikket hennes søkte mot gården til Morten. Hun kunne ikke se den skikkelig, men det store, vakre våningshuset stakk seg fram bak noen trær. Uthuset visste hun lå like bak. Mette smilte litt for seg selv. Tenk å bo alene med så mye plass.

«Hallo, er det ikke Mette.»

Den plutselige avbrytelsen fikk henne til å skvette. Hun snudde seg og fikk se ei dame som kom ut av butikken. Mette ble litt forvirret, for hun kunne ikke huske at hun hadde sett dette mennesket før.

Damen så forvirringen og lo. «Jeg husker deg igjen fra stevnet dere hadde på setra i sommer,» sa hun forklarende mens hun kom nærmere. «Jeg er forresten søster til Solfrid. Jeg vet at du snakket med henne da.»

Mette hilste hjertelig på henne. Det var helt umulig å se at denne kraftige kvinnen kunne være søster til den spede lille Solfrid. Hun ble alvorlig igjen. «Hvordan går det med din søster?» spurte Mette. «Jeg har så ofte tenkt på henne.»

Det kom et lidende drag over ansiktet til kvinnen. «Det går nok ikke så bra. Hun har mye vondt, og behandlingene tar svært på henne. Akkurat nå ligger hun på sykehuset. Jeg tror egentlig ikke det er så mye hjelp i de behandlingene heller. Kreften er kommet for langt. Men de må jo gjøre det de kan,» sa hun og sukket. «Det er slett ikke sikkert at hun noen gang vil komme ut av sykehuset igjen,» fortsatte hun med en stemme som så vidt bar.

Mette så for seg det forpinte ansiktet til den lidende skikkelsen den dagen de hadde hatt stevne. Det krympet seg inni henne av medlidenhet. De ble begge stående i taushet et øyeblikk. Mette visste ikke riktig hva hun skulle si. Den andre så ut i lufta. Søsterens sykdom hadde satt sine dype spor i henne, det var lett å merke.

Med ett så hun på Mette igjen. «Det er så vondt ...» Hun stoppet og så ned i bakken. Det ble en liten pause igjen. Så fortsatte hun: «Jeg vet ikke hvordan jeg skal greie dette.»

Mette ønsket at hun kunne ha gjort noe for å hjelpe i denne lidelsen, men hun visste ikke hva det skulle være. «Jeg skjønner godt at det må være forferdelig vondt for deg å se din søster lide på denne måten,» sa hun.

Kvinnen så fortsatt ned i bakken. De dype rynkene i pannen så ut som om de hadde grodd fast. Stemmen var svak og skjelvende da hun snakket igjen. «Det er så vondt ... det er så vanskelig å tenke på ...» Det hun ville si var tydeligvis noe som det var vanskelig for henne å snakke om.

Plutselig så hun opp på Mette igjen, og stemmen ble mer intens. «Kan du begripe dette? Der gikk hun i uke etter uke, ja, måned etter måned, mens svulstene bare vokste og spredte seg inni kroppen hennes. Og så merket hun ingenting. Hun hadde ikke mer plager enn jeg har når jeg er trett etter en arbeidsdag. Da sykdommen endelig ble oppdaget, var den kommet altfor langt til at de kunne gjøre noe med den.»

Tårene begynte å renne nedover ansiktet hennes. «Det som plager meg er at det kan like godt være meg som går med dette.» Stemmen hevet seg gradvis mens hun snakket, og øynene fikk noe febrilsk over seg. «Hvordan kan jeg være sikker på at dette ikke vil komme til å ramme meg også?»

Mette forsto at denne kvinnen var alvorlig redd. Det hun trengte, var trøst og hjelp. Hun hadde virkelig angst for denne sykdommen. Forsiktig la hun hånden på skulderen til den forpinte kvinnen. «Jeg har forstått det slik at du er en kristen?» sa hun mildt spørrende.

Kvinnen nikket.

«I slike krisesituasjoner,» fortsatte Mette, «kan det ofte være vanskelig å tro at vi har en Gud som virkelig er der ... hos oss. Men jeg er sikker på at du kjenner litt til Guds vesen.»

Kvinnen så litt spørrende på henne. «Ja?» Hun dro litt på det. Hun skjønte visst ikke riktig hvor Mette ville hen.

Mette smilte av det forvirrede blikket. «Jo ... jeg tror du kjenner Guds vesen, derfor vil jeg spørre deg: Er det Guds vesen å tenke slik: Nå vil jeg la denne kvinnen her få oppleve alle detaljer ved denne sykdommens grusomhet for å vise henne hvilken sykdom også hun skal dø av en gang! Jeg vil plassere henne der ved søsterens sykeseng og vise henne hvert smertedrag, og hver angstbølge i den forpinte kroppen, slik at også hennes angst kan bli fullkommen.»

Mette kjente at det ble en intensitet i ordene. Egentlig hadde hun aldri tenkt disse tankene før. De kom bare for henne der og da. Overfor denne angsten og smerten så hun dette som den mest naturlige ting av verden.

Kvinnen stirret på henne med åpen munn. Hun svarte ikke.

Mette fortsatte enda mer inntrengende: «Er det Guds vesen, tror du?»

Kvinnen ristet sakte på hodet. «Nei ,» sa hun. Så ble det mer tyngde i ordene. «Nei, det er det så sannelig ikke. Men ...»

Et nytt smertedrag skyllet over henne. «Det er jo mange av dem som får denne sykdommen, og som absolutt vet hva den innebærer. Sykepleiere og andre som kjenner godt til dette, får jo også kreft?»

«Ja da,» sa Mette, «men ditt problem er angsten for sykdommen. Det er da ingenting som tilsier at også du skal få det samme som din søster. Så håpløst å gå rundt med en angst for noe som du sannsynligvis aldri vil oppleve. Det tror jeg slett ikke Gud vil at du skal slite med. Nå vil han at du skal være en støtte og hjelp for Solfrid, og så må du se på dette som hennes sykdom. Angsten din er en realitet, det skjønner jeg. Og det ser Gud også, derfor tror jeg at han vil si akkurat dette til deg nå.»

291

Et smil gled over ansiktet til den kraftige kvinnen. Mette kunne se at kroppen gradvis slappet av. Enda en stund sto hun og «tygget» på det hun hadde hørt.

Plutselig la hun begge armene rundt halsen til Mette og gav henne en klem. «Takk skal du ha,» hvisket hun inn i øret hennes. «Dette har jeg aldri tenkt på før. Du har helt rett. Gud vil nok ikke at jeg skal lammes av denne redselen nå.» Hun slapp henne og gikk et skritt tilbake. «Vet du hva?» Hun så alvorlig på Mette. «Dette holdt faktisk på å ødelegge meg helt. Jeg har ikke greid å besøke min søster på flere dager. Men nå kjenner jeg at denne forferdelige angsten er i ferd med å slippe taket.» Smilet lå over ansiktet igjen.

«Forresten,» fortsatte hun, «så ba Solfrid meg om å spørre Morten, hvis jeg traff ham, om du og han kunne komme og se til henne en dag. Hun er så takknemlig for den forbønnen hun fikk hos dere.»

Mette ble litt forvirret med det samme. Hun kjente jo egentlig ikke damen. Men de strålende øynene til søsteren gjorde at hun ikke kunne nekte dette. «Jeg skal snakke med Morten om det,» svarte hun.

Dermed snudde kvinnen seg og gikk mot en av de parkerte bilene.

Mette la varene inn i bilen sin og satte seg bak rattet. En stund ble hun sittende der i dype tanker. Så startet hun besluttsomt bilen og kjørte bort til gården til Morten.

Hun fant ham ute på gårdsplassen. Litt forundret så han bort på henne da hun kom ut. «Skal du alt tilbake igjen? Jeg trodde du virkelig ville utnytte denne dagen og komme deg litt vekk fra slaveriet der oppe.» Et skøyeraktig glimt lekte i øynene.

Mette smilte. Men så ble hun alvorlig igjen. Hun fortalte om møtet ved butikken.

Morten ble også alvorlig. «Det er ikke sikkert hun lever så lenge,» sa han stille. «Kanskje det er best vi drar til sykehuset så fort som mulig.»

«Det var det jeg også tenkte,» sa Mette.

«Hvis du kan vente et par minutter til jeg har fått på meg noen andre klær, så kan vi dra med det samme,» sa han.

Mette smilte. «Få på deg fillene, du, så drar vi!»

Morten forsvant raskt inn i huset mens han lo av den kvikke replikken hennes.

20 • Sykebesøk

Sykehuset lå i en by et stykke unna. Det tok nesten to timer før de var framme. Morten kjørte. Mette var glad for å slippe, for hun var ikke så kjent på denne veien. Ikke visste hun hvor sykehuset lå heller. Mens de kjørte, fortalte Morten fra sin barndom, da de lekte sammen på skolen. Solfrid var ei av de muntre, glade jentene han husket fra den gangen. Det var ikke til å tro at hun nå lå der for døden.

Da de gikk ut av bilen på parkeringsplassen, ble de stående et øyeblikk. Ingen av dem følte seg særlig høye i hatten. Hvordan skulle de takle dette alvoret som de nå ble stilt overfor? Hvordan var tilstanden hennes denne dagen? Mange spørsmål gjorde dem usikre.

Plutselig begynte Morten å gå mot inngangsdøra med besluttsomme skritt. «Nå er vi her, så nå er det ikke noe annet å gjøre enn å gå inn,» sa han. Mette fulgte tett etter.

En av sykepleierne viste dem til det rette rommet. «Det kan nok hende at hun ligger og sover,» sa hun før de gikk inn, «men hun våkner sikkert fort. Hun har fått ganske mye medisiner, så hun er litt omtåket av og til. Men jeg tror ikke det skal by på altfor store problemer å snakke med henne. Bare ikke bli altfor lenge. Hun blir fort sliten.»

Mette og Morten gikk stille inn gjennom døra. Ved første øyekast så det ikke ut til at det lå noen under den store dyna. Men så fikk de øye på et blekt lite ansikt på puta. Hun lå med lukkede øyne. Det så ut som hun sov. Ved siden av senga sto et stativ hvor det hang noen poser. Slanger gikk ned til nåler som var satt fast i de tynne armene og hendene. Alt som lå på nattbordet, tydet på at det var en meget syk pasient som lå der.

En stund ble de bare stående og se på henne. Ingen av dem sa noe. De ville ikke vekke henne hvis hun sov.

Mette husket henne godt igjen fra stevnet, men om hun var liten og tynn den gangen, så var hun enda magrere nå. Kinnene var helt innhulte, og skuldrene så bare ut som skinn som var trukket utenpå knoklene. Håret var også nesten borte. Mette kjente at klumpen i halsen vokste. Stakkars lille menneske, tenkte hun.

Sakte gled øyelokkene opp på den syke i senga. Et øyeblikk ble hun liggende og stirre på de to som sto der.

Morten tok hånden hennes og trykket den forsiktig. «Hallo Solfrid,» sa han. «Vi ville bare se hvordan det sto til med deg. Søsteren din sa at du var her.»

Et smil bredte seg over det lille ansiktet. Stemmen hennes var sped, men forbløffende klar da hun svarte: «Så fint at dere kunne komme. Jeg ville så gjerne få takket dere for det dere gjorde for meg den dagen oppe på setra.» Hun flyttet blikket over til Mette. «Jeg var så redd for at jeg skulle dø før jeg fikk snakket med dere, derfor ba jeg henne gi dere beskjed. Hjertelig takk for at dere kunne komme.»

Begge så litt forvirret på henne. Hva var det egentlig hun takket dem så for? Hva i all verden var det de hadde hjulpet henne med? Mette skjønte ingen ting. Hun hadde jo den gangen bedt om forbønn fordi hun ønsket å bli helbredet, men hun hadde jo ikke blitt det. Hva var det da hun var så takknemlig for?

Solfrid la visst merke til forvirringen. Hun smilte et rolig smil, og så lukket hun øynene. Smilet lå hele tiden over munnen hennes, så de skjønte at hun ikke sov. «Dere er visst forbauset over at jeg vil takke dere,» fortsatte hun mens hun lå der med lukkede øyne. Så åpnet hun dem igjen og så rett på Morten. «Da jeg var der oppe hos dere, var jeg inne i en forferdelig krise. Jeg skjønte at denne sykdommen kom til å ta livet av meg. Selv om jeg var trygg på at jeg var et Guds barn, så var jeg likevel livredd. Jeg ville ikke miste livet. Akkurat da var det ikke noe annet jeg heller ville enn å leve. Og jeg visste at den eneste muligheten jeg hadde til å bli frisk, var helbredelse. Jeg var faktisk desperat. Jeg ville bli helbredet. Det var slik for meg da at jeg forsøkte å tvinge Gud til det. Da jeg søkte forbønn, var det faktisk det jeg forsøkte å gjøre. Men du, Morten, du forsto visst litt av det?»

Et spørrende blikk var rettet mot ham. Han hadde satt seg på en stol like ved senga.

«Jeg vet ikke,» svarte han. «Men jeg var redd for at du skulle komme til å bli skuffet hvis ikke det du ønsket, kom til å skje. Derfor holdt jeg visst en lang tale for deg. Etterpå tenkte jeg at det nok var altfor mye prat for et sykt menneske.»

Solfrid smilte mens øynene lukket seg igjen. «Akkurat der og da greide jeg nok ikke å ta til meg alt, men senere kom det du sa tilbake til meg og gav meg ro.» Hun så på ham igjen. «Hele talen til den predikanten …» Hun stoppet litt for å komme på navnet, men så gav hun det visst opp og fortsatte: «… og det du sa, har blitt til ufattelig

293

hjelp for meg.»

Nå var stemmen svakere, og Mette var redd for at dette ble en litt for hard påkjenning for henne. Kanskje hun ikke orket å prate så mye. Urolig sto hun og fulgte med i det som ble sagt. En stund lå den syke helt stille i senga med lukkede øyne. Kanskje hun hadde sovnet? Mette satte seg stille ned i en stol ved enden av senga. Morten satt også stille og holdt Solfrid i hånden.

Det varte ikke lenge før hun åpnet øynene igjen. Hun fortsatte som om det ikke hadde vært noen pause. «Dere siterte jo begge fra versene i femte kapittel av Jakobs brev i Bibelen. Du sa at det sto der at man skulle salve og be for den syke, og så skulle troens bønn hjelpe den syke.» Hun la ekstra trykk på den siste delen av det hun sa.

«Vet dere! Det var akkurat det jeg fikk oppleve.» Et fredfullt drag lå over hele skikkelsen. «Jeg fikk oppleve det!» Stemmen var klar og intens. «Gang på gang fikk jeg oppleve at angsten bare forsvant når jeg tenkte på dette verset. Andre vers i Bibelen kom også for meg. Slike som det predikanten siterte … det med å komme til Ham med alt det vi strever og bærer på … så vil Han gi også oss hvile. Ja, denne hvilen fikk jeg oppleve. Det er helt ufattelig at det går an. Jeg ville aldri ha forstått det hvis ikke det var for at jeg opplevde det.»

Igjen ble det en pause. Mette kjente at hun var beveget helt inne i sitt innerste. Morten var heller ikke uberørt, det kunne hun se. Men de sa ikke noe. Denne gangen var det Solfrid sin tur til å snakke. Det var som om akkurat det lå klart i lufta.

Snart begynte hun å snakke igjen. «Hvor mange ganger har jeg ikke ligget her og gruet for en undersøkelse jeg skulle igjennom …» Stemmen var svakere nå. Hun så heller ikke på noen av dem, men øynene var åpne. «… så har jeg minnet Ham om disse versene. Det er ikke alltid jeg orker å be, men det ser det ikke ut som om Gud er avhengig av. Det er nok at jeg bare minner Ham på disse versene, så kommer freden tilbake igjen. Ofte har jeg opplevd at jeg kunne sove helt til jeg ble fraktet ned til undersøkelsesrommet. Ja … troens bønn hjelper den syke …!»

Det siste ble sagt som en konklusjon som var ufravikelig. Hun sank litt sammen på puta. De kunne godt se at denne samtalen hadde tatt på henne. Mette og Morten vekslet blikk. Hadde de sittet for lenge hos henne, tro? Hadde de trettet henne ut for mye? Men de greide ikke å bryte opp ennå. Det virket som om dette var noe som det var viktig for henne å få sagt.

En lang stund lå hun bare stille på puta. Ingen sa noe. Så åpnet hun øynene igjen. Smilet var tilbake. «Det var godt å se dere,» sa hun.

De skjønte at besøket var over. Morten reiste seg forsiktig.

Med ett grep hun fastere om hånden hans. «Nå må dere ikke tro at jeg hele tiden ligger her i denne vidunderlige freden,» sa hun. «Angsten kommer stadig tilbake. Av og til må jeg be sykepleierne om å få valium også. Men en ting vet jeg: Gud er her hele tiden, enten jeg har det fredelig eller er urolig. Jeg er i Herrens hender, det vet jeg. Og så er det jo velsignet at det finnes så mye medisiner og behandlinger. Jeg har ofte takket Gud for valiumet.»

Blikket hennes boret seg inn i øynene til Morten. «Dere må fortsatt be for meg. Jeg vet at jeg fremdeles trenger det mer enn noe annet.»

Morten nikket. «Det kan vi i hvert fall love deg,» sa han.

«Ja … angsten kommer,» sa hun mens hun sank tilbake i putene. «Du vet … hvis jeg ikke hadde fått uro og angst, så hadde jeg heller ikke opplevd hvor vidunderlig hans fred virkelig er,» avsluttet hun med et blekt smil.

Mette tørket bort en tåre som hadde funnet veien helt ned på haken hennes. Morten strøk den svake kvinnen over kinnet da han sa farvel.

Solfrid snudde seg mot Mette. «Takk for at dere kom. Så møtes vi igjen.» Hun pekte med en slapp hånd oppover mens et lite glimt av humor blinket i de matte øynene.

«Ja, vi møtes igjen,» sa Morten med sterkt beveget stemme. Mette bare nikket. Så forlot de rommet.

De sa ikke så mye til hverandre før de var ute i bilen igjen. Besøket hadde gjort et sterkt inntrykk på dem begge. Men da de svingte ut fra parkeringsplassen, sa Morten: «Dette gir meg i hvert fall større frimodighet til å be for syke. Uansett så blir det til hjelp for dem, ser det ut til. Men så ubegripelig Hans veier er. Jeg er glad for at Han ikke krever at jeg må forstå alt Han gjør, eller hvorfor Han handler som Han gjør.»

Mette svarte ikke med det samme. Tankene hennes arbeidet hektisk. «Jeg som trodde at vi skulle til et døende menneske for å gi trøst,» sa hun etter en stund. «Det var i hvert fall ikke mye jeg fikk sagt.»

Morten smilte. «Det hadde vært en før oss med den trøsten. Vi hadde nok aldri greid å gi slik trøst.»

«Nei,» sa Mette. «Det er jo godt å merke at vi har en Gud som er mektig til å hjelpe helt inn i døden.»

De snakket en stund om det de hadde opplevd der ved Solfrids sykeseng. Begge følte det som om de hadde vært på hellig grunn. Hele atmosfæren der inne hadde åndet av en vidunderlig fred, samtidig som tragedien absolutt var et faktum. Skillet mellom liv og død ble plutselig så lite. Himmelen kom dem så nær.

Selv om opplevelsen hadde preget dem sterkt, måtte de jo fortsette sitt daglige virke. Morten hadde en del ting han ville ordne med når han først var i byen, og Mette hadde lyst til å ta en titt i noen butikker. De skilte lag og avtalte at de skulle møtes et par timer senere.

21 • Nattlig besøk

Søndagen ble en stille dag på setra. Morten dro tidlig, sammen med noen andre menn, innover i fjellet. Mette tok bilen og reiste til kirke om formiddagen. Etterpå ble hun med tante Anna hjem til middag. Utpå ettermiddagen dro de begge opp igjen til setra.

Tante Anna pratet i vei hele tiden som hun pleide. Mette undret seg over seg selv, at hun ikke ble mer lei av den stadige ordflommen. Alltid hadde hun noe å snakke om. Men det var aldri sladder eller negativ omtale av andre. Forunderlig nok greide hun hele tiden å snakke om noe positivt og interessant. Man ble rett og slett oppløftet i sjel og sinn av å være sammen med den frodige damen.

Denne søndagen ble en ekstra koselig dag. Bare de to, alene sammen, hele dagen. Mette frydet seg. Det var så godt å kunne slappe av uten alle disse forvirrende tankene som hun hadde vært så plaget av i det siste. Hint og reaksjoner som hun ikke greide å tolke. Ingenting var så frustrerende som det.

Neste dag ventet de en ny skoleklasse. Tante Anna måtte gjøre noen forberedelser til det besøket, og Mette hadde jo dyra som skulle ha sitt stell. Hver puslet med sitt i fred og ro. Etterpå dekket de et kveldsbord rikt på godsaker fra tante Annas kjøleskap. De satt lenge og koste seg med maten og hverandres selskap.

«Det er fantastisk å se hvordan Morten har greid seg,» sa plutselig tante Anna mens hun tygget på en tykk grovbrødskive med gome på. Den brune ostemassen lå i en stor topp oppå brødskiva. Det var helt utrolig at hun greide å bite over alt sammen. Mette dvelte likevel ikke så lenge ved det bugnende brødstykket, for den bemerkningen hun nettopp var kommet med, interesserte henne enda mer. Før Mette rakk å spørre noe mer, fortsatte hun å snakke.

«Det var slett ikke så lett for ham da han ble alene. Han fikk jo eneansvaret for gården og alle dyra. Men Marit har jo vært til utrolig hjelp for ham. Hun følte nok et visst ansvar for lillebroren sin. Og så har han jo hatt Ellen ...»

Mette kjente at noe stakk inni henne med det samme det navnet ble nevnt. Tante Anna kjente visst til det meste der i familien, og det virket som om Ellen var en ganske naturlig del av den.

Mette sukket litt. Et alvorlig drag gled over ansiktet hennes. Kunne det kanskje også tenkes at tante Anna hadde kjennskap til de forholdene som hun hadde fått slike underlige antyd-ninger om? Nei. Hun slo tanken fra seg med det samme. Denne snakke-salige damen hadde aldri greid å holde på slike hemmeligheter. Var der noe «grums» her, så måtte det helt klart være noe som ikke hun hadde kjennskap til. Det var Mette sikker på.

Da tante Anna sa at hun ville trekke seg tilbake til sitt eget værelse, gikk også Mette for å legge seg. Det gylne lampelyset gav en koselig atmosfære i rommet der hun satt i senga med dagboka, men hun greide ikke helt å nyte den. Hun tenkte på Ellen og resten av familien til Morten. Alle disse uklarhetene og anelsene syntes hun nesten begynte å slite på henne.

Nei, hun ville ikke tenke på det. Søvnen begynte også å gjøre seg gjeldende, så hun la dagboka fra seg på nattbordet og slukket lampen. Ikke lenge etter lå hun i dyp søvn.

Plutselig våknet hun og satte seg opp i senga. En isnende frykt krøp nedover ryggraden hennes. Det var noen ute i seterbua. Hun hadde hørt en lyd. Forundret tente hun lommelykta som lå på nattbordet og så på klokka. Den var halv to. Mørket lå tett utenfor vinduet. I åndeløs spenning satt hun og lyttet. Hvem var det som snakket der ute, tro? Der hørte hun det igjen. En kraftig mannsrøst tordnet i vei: «Du må forstå at slik det hele har utviklet seg ...» Resten av setningen forsvant i lyden av noe som ble skjøvet over gulvet.

Svaret som ble gitt, kunne hun ikke oppfatte, men hun hørte at det var Mortens stemme. Det var altså Morten som fikk denne kraftige tiltalen. Igjen lød den opphissede mannsrøsten: «Disse konsekvensene burde du ha forutsett.» Resten av utbruddet hørte hun bare bruddstykker av: «... ingen kan vite ... løgn eller sannhet ...»

Morten sin stemme var fortsatt svært svak. Det var som om han krympet seg under en berettiget overhøvling.

Plutselig blandet en tredje stemme seg inn i samtalen. Den var ikke fullt så opp - hisset, men den var alvorlig. Tydelig kunne hun høre den klare stemmen: «Man må nok regne med at det kan bli snakk om politianmeldelser.»

Deretter ble det en del snakk som hun ikke kunne oppfatte noe av. Stemmene var svakere en stund, helt til den første skar gjennom igjen. «Dette burde du ha tenkt på før du ansatte henne!»

Mette kjente at redselen var i ferd med å lamme henne helt. Det var jo henne de snakket om. Hva kunne dette være for noe? Hun hadde lyst til å gå opp og lytte nærmere døren, men hun våget ikke å røre seg. Hva ville skje hvis de fikk greie på at hun var våken og hørte det som ble sagt?

Der hørte hun at ytterdøren ble åpnet og lukket igjen. En bildur fortalte snart at noen forlot setra. Mette slappet av litt igjen. Men uhyggen og frykten ville ikke slippe taket. Hun kunne ikke begripe dette. Nå hadde hun klare bevis for at Morten var innblandet i noe. Men hun skjønte ikke hvordan det kunne henge sammen. Han var jo så hjelpsom på alle måter. Aldri hadde hun følelsen av at han hadde noe uoppgjort, verken med mennesker eller Gud. Den indre styrken hans hadde hun følt, og selv blitt styrket av, mer enn en gang. Roen og harmonien ved hans vesen gav alltid en trygg atmosfære for dem som var i hans omgivelser.

Mette var fullstendig forvirret. Og så den bemerkningen som helt klart måtte ha noe med henne å gjøre.

Denne usikkerheten gav en uro som fullstendig feide alle tanker på søvn unna. Hun kjente at hun skalv der hun lå. Krampaktig trakk hun dyna tettere opp mot halsen, men redselen fikk bare den anspente kroppen til å skjelve enda mer.

Plutselig satte hun seg opp og tente lampa. «Kjære Gud,» ba hun idet hun strakte seg etter Bibelen som lå på nattbordet. «Hjelp meg. Jeg er så redd!»

Hun åpnet Bibelen for å finne noe som kunne gi henne ro og trøst. I det flakkende lampelyset festet hun blikket på den siden hun vilkårlig hadde slått opp, og begynte å lese. Det tok litt tid før hun greide å konsentrere seg om ordene som sto der. Men så ble hun sittende og stirre. Hva var det hun leste? «Du skal ikke frykte for nattens redsler, for piler som flyr om dagen.» Hun flyttet blikket opp til toppen av siden. «Salmene,» sto det. Det var altså i Salmene hun leste. Salme nittien, sto det.

Aldri før hadde hun blitt så forundret over noe hun hadde lest i Bibelen. Det var som om Gud hadde svart henne øyeblikkelig da hun i sin redsel ropte til Ham. Ja, hun var overbevist om at det var det Han hadde gjort. Hun kjente at hennes indre ble fylt av en vidunderlig fred. Redselen var helt borte.

Det var i vers fem disse ordene sto. Nysgjerrig flyttet hun blikket til vers fire. For å få med seg hele verset måtte hun bla om en side.

«Han dekker deg med sine fjær. Under Hans vinger finner du ly. Hans trofasthet er skjold og vern».

Et fredfullt smil gled over ansiktet hennes. Hun var trygg, for hun hvilte under Guds beskyttende vinger. Hun la seg ned på puta igjen og sendte en inderlig takk opp til sin Himmelske Far. Han så henne. Han så redselen hennes. Og Han brydde seg om henne. Hvilken trygghet hun eide!

Undringen var der fremdeles. Undringen over det hun hadde hørt. Det var noe hun ikke forsto … noe som ikke stemte. Men dette var tydeligvis ikke noe hun behøvde å frykte for. Hun kunne bare slappe helt av.

Raskt slukket hun lyset. Nå kunne hun legge seg trygt. Og snart sov hun fast igjen.

Selv om nattesøvnen hadde blitt en del forstyrret, våknet Mette tidlig neste morgen. Tante Anna var ennå ikke stått opp da hun gikk ut i seterbua. Morten var heller ikke å se. Nattas hendelse sto fortsatt klart for henne. Redselen var hun kvitt, men nysgjerrigheten hennes var blitt satt på en hard prøve.

Så raskt hun kunne gjorde hun unna fjøsstellet. Dyra var nok litt forundret over at hun kom så tidlig. De var flinke til å holde rede på klokka. Det at Mette i dag var nesten en time tidligere enn hun pleide, merket de godt.

Hun visste at Tante Anna skulle bruke ganske mye melk denne dagen, så hun satte inn et stort spann i melkeboden. Geitene trasket i hælene på henne som de pleide. Hvor hun gikk måtte hun regne med å ha dem rundt seg. De var blitt ekstra kjælne og folkekjære etter at turistene hadde dullet med dem hele sommeren. Hun fant litt mat som hun gav dem før hun gikk inn igjen.

«Så tidlig du er i dag,» sa tante Anna da hun fikk se den duggfriske Mette komme inn fra fjøset. «Jeg våknet tidlig,» sa hun, «så tenkte jeg at jeg like godt kunne gjøre meg ferdig med dyrestellet med det samme.»

Det tok litt tid før Mette greide å få fram det spørsmålet som hele tiden hadde ligget og brent i henne. Tante Anna hadde en hel masse å lire ut av seg før hun stoppet opp så pass mye at Mette kunne få slippe til. Men endelig fikk hun en anledning. «Hørte du noen her i natt?» Mette så spent på den gamle damen. Hun stirret forundret tilbake. «Var det noen her i natt? Nei, jeg hørte ingenting. Hørte du noen?»

Mette fortalte om stemmene hun hadde hørt, men hun sa ingenting om hva de hadde sagt.

«Det var nok Morten og karene hans som kom tilbake fra fjellet,» konkluderte hun rolig. «Jeg ser at bilen hans er borte, så han dro nok ned til bygda med dem. Det varer sikkert ikke så lenge før han er tilbake igjen. Gjestene kommer jo snart.»

Mette sa ikke mer. Det var tydelig at hun ikke var det minste urolig for Morten, og da ville heller ikke Mette påføre henne ekstra uro. Det var nok best at hun tok dette opp med Morten selv.

Hun satt en stund i egne tanker. Tante Anna gikk ut i melkeboden, så hun fikk anledning til å konsentrere seg om sine egne tanker et øyeblikk. Hun var forresten slett ikke sikker på om hun kom til å snakke med Morten om dette. Det var ikke sikkert at dette var noe han ville snakke med henne om. Kanskje det var best at hun bare så det hele an en stund. Det kunne jo godt hende at han selv brakte emnet på bane etter hvert.

Det varte enda en stund før de hørte bildur fra veien. Tante Anna holdt på med noe inne på værelset sitt, så Mette var alene i rommet da Morten kom inn. Han hilste åndsfraværende og gikk bort til komfyren for å skjenke seg en kopp kaffe. Med koppen i den ene hånden og en avis i den andre gikk han bort og satte seg ved bordet. Mette betraktet ham i taushet. Han åpnet avisen, men snart falt den ned i fanget igjen. Blikket hans søkte noe langt der utenfor vinduet. Dype rynker lå mellom de mørke øynene.

Mette tok opp igjen det hun hadde holdt på med da han kom inn. Igjen hadde han fått det åndsfraværende uttrykket som slett ikke innbød til noen slags samtale. Hun våget ikke å komme med de spørsmålene hun så inderlig lengtet etter å få svar på.

Plutselig lente Morten albuene mot bordkanten og støttet haken i hendene. Et tungt sukk unnslapp ham. Da han begynte å snakke, var stemmen like fjern som blikket. Den var også preget av et dypt alvor og oppgitthet. «Jeg har visst gjort noe forferdelig dumt ...»

Han tidde igjen og så rett på Mette. I åndeløs spenning ventet hun på at han skulle fortsette. Men så ombestemte han seg visst. Med en hoderisting som uttrykte en dyp fortvilelse reiste han seg brått og gikk ut.

Fortvilelsen som Mette hadde lest i øynene hans, var med ett smittet over på henne. Alle spørsmålene kom for henne igjen. Skulle hun aldri få svar på dem? Morten hadde altså gjort noe dumt. Hun la spesielt merke til den formuleringen. Han hadde ikke sagt galt. Kunne det ha en betydning? Hun håpet inderlig det.

I det samme kom tante Anna inn igjen. Hun hadde ikke merket noe til det som hadde skjedd der inne. Munnen hennes gikk i den vanlige duren. Det så heller ikke ut til at hun la merke til at Mette var særdeles taus.

Snart kom skoleklassen som de ventet på. Det ble med det samme en hektisk aktivitet for dem alle, men Mette hadde vanskelig for å konsentrere seg om det hun skulle gjøre. Tankene gikk hele tiden i andre retninger.

Da kvelden kom, følte hun seg helt utslitt. Hun lengtet bare etter å kunne slenge seg ned på senga. Likevel ble hun sittende ved bordet med kaffekoppen. Morten var ennå ikke kommet inn. Hun hadde et håp om at de skulle få seg en prat først på tomannshånd. Tante Anna hadde reist ned til bygda sammen med skoleklassen, så det var bare de to som var der oppe.

Etter en liten stund kom Morten, men han stoppet like innenfor døra. «Jeg må nok ned til bygda igjen,» sa han. «Har du noe imot å være her alene i natt?»

«Nei …» Hun dro litt på det. Å være alene om natta var hun ikke redd for, men hun hadde så inderlig håpet å få en prat med ham. Hun kunne heller ikke begripe hvorfor han måtte ned til bygda igjen. Skuffelsen føltes som en fysisk smerte. Det var så mye hun ville ha pratet med ham om.

Det så ikke ut til at Morten merket skuffelsen hennes. Det virket bare som om han var lettet over at hun var villig til dette. Dermed snudde han, sa adjø, og forsvant ut til bilen. Mette sto i vinduet og så etter ham mens tårene presset på bak øyelokkene.

Vel. Nå kunne hun i hvert fall gå og legge seg.

22 • Nye redsler

Fortumlet og skjelvende satte Mette seg opp i senga. Hun så seg forvirret rundt i rommet. Hva var det for noe? Hva var det som hadde vekket henne? Hun følte seg helt omtåket. Søvnen satt ennå i henne. En lyd i lufta gav henne en isende angstfølelse. Fortumlet gned hun seg i øynene for å bli skikkelig våken. Det var stummende mørkt i rommet, så hun skjønte at det var midt på natta. Denne gangen var det ikke stemmer hun hadde våknet av, det var hun i hvert fall sikker på. Men hva kunne det være?

Et skikkelig brak fikk henne plutselig til å hoppe høyt i senga. Samtidig slappet hun litt av. Det var et kraftig tordenbrak. Der hadde hun altså forklaringen. Selv om tordenvær kunne være skremmende nok, var det i hvert fall noe naturlig. Enda en natt skulle hun altså bli forstyrret av ubehagelige lyder.

Det varte ikke lenge før neste smell kom. Det var enda kraftigere enn det forrige, hadde hun inntrykk av. En stund ble hun sittende der i senga og lytte til rullingen mellom fjellene. Så kom et kraftig lynglimt, som i brøkdelen av et sekund lyste opp hele rommet. Ikke lenge etter fulgte et nytt brak.

Mette satt skjelvende og telte sekundene mellom lynet og braket. Hun visste at om det var mer enn sju sekunders opphold, så var det ingen fare for at det ville slå ned for nær. Men hun kom ikke lenger enn til fire før det braket løs. Og kraftigere glimt og smell hadde hun sjelden opplevd.

Snart var det en ny lyd som fylte lufta. Kraftige regndråper slo mot taket og vinduet. Det kunne forresten ikke være regn slik som det smalt. Det måtte uten tvil være hagl.

Bråket gjorde det umulig å tenke på å fortsette søvnen. Hun famlet etter lommelykta for å finne ut hvor mye klokka var. Så ergerlig at hun ikke hadde en med selv-lysende visere.

Da hun endelig fant lykta, så hun at klokka var nesten tre. En trykkende smerte i hodet fortalte at hun sårt hadde trengt denne nattesøvnen. Snart ble lyden på taket litt bløtere, men det virket som om intensiteten bare økte. Regnet øste formelig ned.

Plutselig rykket hun til der hun satt. Dyra … Hvordan gikk det med dyra i dette været? De måtte da være vettskremte. Sauene kunne jo gå inn i sauefjøset. Men de andre gikk ute, og fjøsdøra var lukket.

Raskt hoppet hun ut av senga og fikk på seg et par sko og en jakke. Regnfrakk kunne hun ikke finne i farten. Med lommelykta i handa åpnet hun døra og skyndte seg ut i det silende regnværet. Før hun nådde fjøset var hun våt til skinnet.

Utenfor fjøsdøra sto kyrne og kalvene tett sammen. De lutet hodene mot været mens de rautet urolig. Heldigvis var de der alle sammen. Hun åpnet døra, og snart ble det trengsel i åpningen. Alle ville inn på en gang. Det tok litt tid før hun greide å skille dem slik at de kunne gå inn en etter en.

I det svake lykteskinnet greide hun etter hvert å få bundet dem alle. Geitene kom også inn. Det var best at de alle var bundet, tenkte hun. Skulle de bli ytterligere skremt, kunne de lage et skikkelig spetakkel der inne i fjøset.

Sauene hadde klumpet seg sammen inne i sauefjøset, kunne hun se da hun kom ut igjen. Så gjennomvåt som hun likevel var, kunne hun like godt ta en tur bort og se til dem også. De var sikkert skremt, men de sto tørt og godt der inne. Alle var der. Heldigvis hadde ikke noen stukket av i redsel.

Hun løp fort tilbake til seterbua igjen. Før hun rakk døra, smalt det på nytt. Denne gangen kom lynglimtet og smellet samtidig. Mette stoppet et øyeblikk, stiv av skrekk. Dette smellet var annerledes enn de forrige. Det var mer som et børseskudd, tett etter-fulgt av en splintrende skrapelyd. Der slo det ned, tenkte hun og kikket seg redselsla-gen omkring. Hun kunne ikke se noe. Mørket lå tett omkring henne, for lyset fra lommelykta nådde ikke særlig langt. Det var i hvert fall ikke bygningene som var ram-met, greide hun å registrere.

Fort smatt hun inn døra igjen. Hutrende av kulde vrengte hun av seg det våte tøyet. Etter å ha tørket seg omhyggelig med et håndkle, fikk hun på seg nattkjolen og hoppet i seng igjen.

Været fortsatte like ille. Søvnen kunne hun visst se langt etter denne natta.

Snart dukket en ny uro opp i henne. Tenk om lynet slo ned i fjøset! Alt det tørre høyet som lå på høyloftet, ville lett kunne bli antent av en gnist. Selv om det regnet tett, så kunne det jo brenne lenge der inne før regndråpene greide å slukke ilden.

Hun slengte føttene ut av senga igjen og stakk dem i et par tøfler. Så trakk hun på seg en strikkejakke utenpå nattkjolen og gikk ut av soverommet sitt. Der tullet hun rundt seg et pledd og satte seg ved bordet. Vinduet over bordet vendte mot fjøset, så hun kunne holde fin utkikk derfra.

Mens hun satt der og stirret ut i mørket, kjente hun hvordan uhyggen igjen bredte seg i hennes indre. Dette var ikke moro. Lyn på lyn ble avløst av det ene braket etter det andre. Uværet herjet vilt over hodet på henne. De høye fjellene skapte ekstra lang-varige rullinger. Hun var redd … ja, hun var skikkelig redd.

Da var det at hun kom på bibelverset hun hadde lest natta før. I skinnet fra lom-melykta åpnet hun Mortens bibel som lå der på bordet. Raskt bladde hun seg fram til Salme nitti. Hun leste det femte verset langsomt gjennom.

Igjen kjente hun hvordan de kjære ordene gav henne ro og trøst. Du skal ikke frykte for nattens redsler ... Hun foldet hendene over den åpne Bibelen og takket Gud for at han var der hos henne.

Da hun igjen åpnet øynene, falt blikket på det niende verset. Hun lest: For du, Herre, er min tilflukt! Tårene begynte å renne i takknemlighet. Hun hadde ingenting å frykte. Disse enorme kreftene som raste der ute, var det ingen mennesker som kunne hamle opp med. Men hun visste at også lyn og torden måtte lystre Guds hånd. Disse kjempe-kreftene var bare bagateller for Hans allmakt. Nei ... hun hadde virkelig ingenting å frykte denne natta heller.

∘ ∘ ∘

Et dunk borte fra døren fikk henne til å hoppe på benken der hun satt. Forvirret så hun seg omkring. Det var helt lyst i rommet. Mette skjønte at det var morgen. Hun hadde sovnet der ved bordet. Ute var alt stille. Det forferdelige været var avløst av lette skyer som ble drevet forbi av en frisk bris, kunne hun se gjennom vinduet.

Plutselig sto Morten ved siden av henne. Sjokkert stirret han på den pjuskete skikkelsen som satt der ved bordet. Mette ble enda mer forvirret med det samme. Hun ville ikke akkurat at han skulle se henne slik i bare nattkjolen. Men Morten så ikke på den. Han viste oppriktig bekymring for henne.

«Har det hendt noe?» spurte han og satte seg ved bordet rett overfor henne.

Mette smilte sjenert. Så fortalte hun om nattas begivenheter.

Morten lyttet oppmerksomt. Et fortvilet drag gled over ansiktet hans da han skjønte hvilken natt hun hadde hatt.

Men Mette smilte igjen. Så skjøv hun Bibelen bort til ham. Den lå fortsatt oppslått på Salme nittien. Hun pekte på vers fem og sa med munter stemme: «Jeg hadde in-genting å frykte. Se bare her. Gud viste meg dette i natt. Hun holdt på å si i natt igjen, men tok seg i det. Det som hørte til forrige natt, var det nok best å ta opp ved en senere anledning.

Med dypt alvor leste Morten det korte verset. Stemmen hans var nesten ikke hør-bar da han sa: «Det er altså en som tar seg av sine når andre svikter.»

Mette kjente en inderlig medlidenhet med ham, men hun visste ikke hva hun skulle svare. Der var blitt så mye uklart mellom dem, syntes hun. Fortroligheten de en gang hadde hatt, var der liksom ikke lenger. I hvert fall følte hun seg så pass usikker at hun ikke greide å snakke så åpent som hun før hadde gjort.

«Bare ta det med ro, du,» sa Morten da hun reiste seg for å gå inn og kle på seg. «Jeg skal ta meg av dyra i dag.»

Hun så takknemlig på ham. «Takk skal du ha. Hodet mitt liker visst ikke slike netter,» svarte hun og gikk inn til seg selv. Den dunkende smerten der oppe hadde bare økt på.

Det var langt på dag da Mette igjen våknet. Uthvilt og opplagt spratt hun ut av senga. Snart ville nok alt dette urolige være over, og hun kunne nyte de siste par ukene hun skulle være der i fulle drag. Bare hun fikk snakke med Morten snart, så ville alt bli bra.

Det var ikke mye Mette så til Morten den dagen heller. Han hadde mange ting å ordne med ute. Oppe i fjellskråningen bak seterbua fant han et tre som var fullstendig splintret i stykker. Det var der lynet hadde slått ned.

Mette skalv litt da hun så hvor nær hun hadde stått. Hun hadde virkelig hatt engle-vakt den natta. Morten kom bort til henne da hun sto og så på det ødelagte treet der oppe. En stund sto de der sammen og så på det som lett kunne ha ført til en ulykke. Så snudde han seg brått mot henne. «Du kan ikke være her alene om nettene. Det er i hvert fall helt sikkert.» Stemmen hans var preget av det dypeste alvor. «Jeg skal be Ellen om å komme opp hit i kveld.»

Mette svarte ikke. Hun kikket bare litt forvirret på ham. På nytt kom uroen sigende innover henne. Skulle han ned til bygda i kveld igjen? Hun våget ikke spørre. Og så denne Ellen …

Det ble ikke sagt mer mellom dem. Morten snudde og gikk tilbake til det han holdt på med.

Da Mette gikk inn igjen i seterbua, var hun bare opptatt av én tanke. Hun måtte prøve å legge alle urolige tanker bort. De gav henne bare lidelser. Dette var egentlig ikke noe hun hadde noe med. Hadde det vært det, så hadde nok Morten snakket med henne om det. Litt ergerlig trampet hun i gulvet. Hvorfor skulle hun alltid være så følsom at hun tok alle slags bekymringer inn over seg?

Hun så ikke mer til Morten den dagen. En stund senere hørte hun bilen forsvinne nedover veien.

Ganske riktig kom Ellen en stund senere. Mette følte seg ikke særlig opplagt til så mye sosialt den kvelden. Etter at de hadde spist kvelds, unnskyldte hun seg med at hun hadde hodepine og gikk inn til seg selv. Det var slett ingen løgn hun kom med. Den kraftige dunkingen hadde tatt seg opp igjen, så hun følte bare for å gå til sengs.

23 • Månens avsløring

Ellen var så hyggelig som det gikk an å bli. Mette skammet seg litt over at hun ikke greide å vise henne mer fortrolighet enn hun gjorde. Både fjøsstellet og det som måtte gjøres i seterbua, deltok Ellen i på en helt naturlig måte. Mette behøvde ikke fortelle henne hvordan tingene skulle gjøres. Hun var godt kjent med det alt sammen, så det ut til. Også det gav Mette en nagende følelse av ubehag. Mistanken om at det kunne være et mer fortrolig forhold mellom henne og Morten, ble på en måte bekreftet ved dette, syntes hun.

Da de satt ved frokostbordet, ble plutselig Ellen svært alvorlig. «Det har jammen blitt noen leie greier dette.» Hun så litt betenkt ut i lufta. Mette kjente at hun stivnet til med det samme. Kom hun til å fortelle noe nå, tro? Mette visste plutselig ikke om hun ville vite sannheten. Det så ikke ut til at Ellen la merke til at hun reagerte.

Da hun fortsatte, skjønte Mette at Ellen trodde hun visste mer enn hun gjorde. «Jeg er jo havnet midt opp i dette,» fortsatte hun.

Med ett festet hun blikket rett på Mette. «Jeg tror faktisk det beste hadde vært om du reiste snart. Det vil sikkert være best for alle, ikke minst for deg selv. Hvis du velger å gjøre det, kan jeg godt overta for deg den stunden som er igjen av sesongen. Jeg er jo vant til å være her i dette arbeidet.»

Mette følte det som om kniver ble stukket inn i hennes indre. Hva var det egentlig denne damen satt der og sa? Ville hun ha henne vekk? Mette kunne ikke skjønne at hun hadde opptrådt på noen måte som Ellen kunne ha oppfattet som truende. Tusen spørsmål raste rundt i hodet hennes. Hun visste ikke hva hun skulle si. Til slutt greide hun å stamme fram et svar: «Hvis … det er det dere tror er best, så …»

Ellen falt i tanker igjen, og så ut i lufta. «Jeg vet ikke,» sa hun og sukket. «Jeg vet virkelig ikke.»

Det ble ikke snakket mer om saken. Mette følte bare behov for å komme for seg selv. Så fort hun syntes det virket naturlig, sa hun at hun ville ta en tur opp i lia for å se om hun kunne finne noen bær. De ventet ingen besøk den dagen, så det var ikke så mye for henne å gjøre før fjøsstellet til kvelden.

Aldri hadde hun følt seg så elendig som da hun trasket med bøtte og bærplukker oppover lia. Missi og Keiseren kom løpende da de fikk øye på henne. Så deilig det var med disse dyra. I deres hverdag var det ingen vanskelige spørsmål og umulige avgjørelser som måtte taes. Fikk de bare mat og stell, og så en god porsjon med kos, så var de fornøyd. Mette satte bøtta fra seg og la begge armene rundt den myke halsen til Keiseren. Denne kalven var noe helt spesielt for henne. Hun følte seg på en måte som en mor for den. Og slik så det nesten ut til at den oppfattet henne også. Den slikket henne på hånden og gned seg inn til henne. Den vekket så mange tanker og følelser i henne. Enda sto fødselen klart for henne. Kampen hun og Morten hadde kjempet sammen for å redde livet til denne lille skapningen. Andre følelser kom også fram. Øyeblikket der ute i vannet … Hun la hodet helt inn til kalvens og lot tårene renne ned i den myke pelsen. «Jeg må visst dra fra deg snart,» hikstet hun, «men jeg vet ikke hvordan jeg skal greie det.»

Missi kom også bort til henne. Den slikket tårene av kinnene hennes. Mette måtte smile. Det virket som om den ville trøste henne i denne fortvilelsen.

Lenge ble hun sittende der med kalvene. Det så heller ikke ut til at de ble lei av henne.

Da hun endelig reiste seg og gikk videre, fulgte begge to med. Hun lot dem komme. Det var godt å ha dem der. De gav henne en god trøst.

Øverst oppe i lia fant hun et sted hvor blåbærlyngen lavet av bær. Hun fylte bærplukkeren gang på gang. Altfor snart var bøtta full. At jeg ikke tok med meg ei bøtte til, tenkte hun. Hun hadde slett ikke lyst til å dra ned igjen ennå.

Oppe på en stein satte hun seg og så utover. Der nede så hun hele seterområdet. En ting var hun ikke i tvil om. Et vakrere sted hadde hun aldri sett. Sola blinket i tjernet. Rundt omkring kunne hun se at naturen laget seg til høst. Selv om ikke de vakre fargene hadde begynt å vise seg ennå, var bjørketrærne allerede ganske gule. Der hun satt kjentes lufta frisk, men sola gav nok varme til at hun ikke frøs. Temperaturen var ikke den samme som den hadde vært for noen uker siden.

Hun snudde litt på seg og så innover myrene og viddene som strakte seg bortover mot de majestetiske fjellene i horisonten. Noen høydedrag innimellom hindret henne i å kunne ta den virkelig store, og vidstrakte herligheten i øyesyn.

Et stykke lenger borte hørte hun den klukkende lyden fra en liten fjellbekk som rant mellom knausene. Noen ryper flakset forskremt opp da Missi og Keiseren kom for nær med sine byksende sprett.

Tiden sto formelig stille for henne der hun satt og betraktet de vakre omgivelsene. Klokka brydde hun seg ikke om å se på.

Til slutt reiste hun seg likevel motvillig og begynte å gå nedover igjen. Hun måtte bevege seg forsiktig, for bøtta var breddfull av bær. Kalvene svinset fortsatt rundt henne, så hun måtte være på vakt overfor dem også.

Alt virket øde og forlatt da hun kom ned til setra. Hun la merke til at Morten sin bil var der, så han måtte nok være et sted i nærheten.

I solveggen ved seterbua fant hun en lun plass. Der satte hun seg for å rense bærene. Da fikk hun se Ellen og Morten. De sto i ivrig samtale borte ved Marits campingvogn.

Morten pekte mot tjernet. Begge så interessert i den retningen. Mette vendte oppmerksomheten sin mot bærene igjen. Hva de der borte foretok seg, hadde hun ikke noe med, minnet hun seg selv om.

De spiste middag sammen utpå ettermiddagen. Om noen merket at Mette var eks - tra taus, så kommenterte de det ikke. De andre to pratet naturlig om alt mulig. Samtalen dreide seg mest om noen turister de hadde truffet i fjellet. Det var folk de ikke hadde sett på mange år, men som hadde bodd i bygda da de var barn. De hadde begge lekt med dem da. Den ene historien fra den tiden ble fortalt etter den andre. Hadde ikke Mette følt seg så nedtrykt, så hadde dette vært et riktig hyggelig måltid.

Så fort de var ferdige med å spise, gikk Mette ut til dyra. Hun hadde med noe ekstra godt til dem alle. Lammene var blitt ganske store etter hvert. De var ikke så lekne lenger som de hadde vært da hun kom, rett etter sankthans, men de var blitt mye mer fortrolige med henne. Med en gang de så henne, kom de løpende. Hun tok seg god tid med hvert av dem denne dagen. Nå var det jo slett ikke sikkert hun kom til å reise ennå. Antydningen Ellen hadde kommet med, var kanskje bare hennes ønske eller vurdering, men Mette kunne ikke fri seg fra at dette var en seriøs tanke. Bare hun kunne ha fått en prat med Morten ...

Melkingen tok hun seg også god tid med. Hun gikk fra den ene til den andre av kyrne, klødde dem bak ørene og klappet dem på halsen. De kjente henne så godt. Alle signaler viste at de satte stor pris på budeia de hadde hatt denne sommeren.

Etter at fjøsstellet var unnagjort, brukte hun lang tid på å bearbeide en del av melken. Både separering og koking av eggost ble gjort. Hun så ikke noe til de andre, og var egentlig glad til. Bilen sto der, så hun visste at de måtte være et eller annet sted. Kanskje de hadde tatt seg en liten fjelltur, eller de satt og pratet i campingvogna til Marit. Ellen brukte den jo som soverom mens hun var der på setra.

Den kvelden ble Mette liggende og kaste seg fram og tilbake i senga. Søvnen ville ikke komme. Tankene svirret rundt i hodet hennes og ble til et eneste kaos. Alt var stille i huset. Utenfor vinduet var skumringen gått over til mørke. Med vidåpne øyne stirret Mette rundt seg i rommet. Snart var det så mørkt at hun ikke kunne skimte noen av de kjære tingene som hun hadde blitt så kjent med. Senga i den andre enden av rommet sto full av saker og ting som hun hadde hatt med seg i kofferten. Kommoden var også ganske fullstappet. Utenfor kunne hun høre bjellene til sauene når de rørte på seg borte i sauefjøset. Den sprø klangen hadde alltid fått henne til å føle en sterk tilfredshet. I kveld fylte den henne bare med vemod.

Hun tente lampa og åpnet Bibelen. Kanskje hun kunne finne noen trøstens ord der. En stund ble hun liggende og bla fram og tilbake. Til slutt la hun den fra seg igjen. Det var umulig å konsentrere seg om det hun leste.

Tiden gikk. Minuttene ble til timer, men Mette lå like lys våken.

Plutselig slengte hun av seg dyna og satte beina på gulvet. Hun kunne like godt stå opp. Det nyttet likevel ikke å forsøke å sove. Raskt trakk hun en jakke utenpå nattkjolen, stakk de bare føttene i et par sko og gikk ut på vollen.

Hun hutret med det samme hun kom ut døra. Lufta var kjøligere enn hun hadde ventet. Oppe på himmelen var månen kommet til syne over fjellet i øst. Den gav så pass mye lys at hun kunne se hvor hun gikk. Gresset var vått av dugg. Hun gikk langs stien ned mot tjernet. Alt var stille. Dyra lå nok og sov hver på sin plass. Kun en svak susing kunne høres av vinden som strøk over tretoppene i sør.

Nede ved tjernet ble hun stående mens tankene strømmet på. Alle de stundene hun hadde tilbrakt på denne stranden! Noen ganger sammen med Morten, og andre ganger sammen med turister de hadde hatt på besøk. En skjelving gikk gjennom kroppen hennes. Det var ikke kulden i lufta som forårsaket den, skjønte hun. Denne sommeren ville hun alltid komme til å huske som noe av det mest fantastiske hun hadde opplevd.

Sakte gled månen bak noen skyer. Det ble stummende mørkt rundt henne. Bare en svak lysning over fjellene var synlig. Kulden begynte også å gjøre seg sterkt gjeldende i skoene og langs de bare beina under den lange nattkjolen.

Plutselig ble hun var en lyd. Den kom fra den andre siden av tjernet. Hun stirret intenst ut i mørket, men det var umulig å skimte noe som helst. Antakelig var det et dyr som ruslet der borte på bredden.

Der hørte hun noe igjen. Nå var det ute i vannet. Kunne det være et dyr som hadde lagt på svøm? Månen var fortsatt bak skyene. Hun kikket opp mot himmelen. Hvis den bare kom fram, ville hun sikkert kunne se hva det var. Sakte gled skyene forbi, men det ville nok ennå ta noen minutter før den kom helt fram igjen.

Det hørtes jevne plask ute i vannet. Faktisk hørtes det ut til at det kom nærmere og nærmere. Stiv av spenning ble Mette stående på bredden. Et øyeblikk vurderte hun å snu og løpe tilbake til seterbua. Men spenningen var for stor. Hva kunne dette være?

Hun lyttet til de jevne plaskene, og med ett gikk det opp for henne at det måtte være åretak fra en båt hun hørte. Det var altså folk som var ute på tjernet midt på natta. Lynraskt smatt hun bak noen busker i nærheten. Hun ville nødig bli sett der i bare nattkjolen. De måtte sikkert tro at hun var ute og gikk i søvne. Tanken på hva slags folk det var som streifet ute på denne tiden av døgnet, skremte henne også.

Der hørte hun at båten dunket mot bredden bare et lite stykke bortenfor der hun lå. Musestille krøp hun sammen bak buskene. I det samme kom månen fram igjen, og hele stranden lå badet i det klare måneskinnet. Da så hun tydelig to personer som krabbet ut av båten og fortøyde den ved bredden. Sjokket fikk bølger til å rase inni henne da hun fikk se hvem de to var. Den kjente skikkelsen til Morten var ikke til å ta feil av. Den andre, som han varsomt hjalp ut av båten, avslørte seg også fort. En klingende latter fortalte at det var Ellen Morten var sammen med denne natta ute på tjernet. De to hadde det visst svært så hyggelig. Gang på gang lød den glade latteren fra dem begge.

Mette ble liggende lenge etter at de var forsvunnet bortover stien. Aldri i verden om hun ville at de skulle oppdage henne der. Hun ville være helt sikker på at de var vel inne før hun gikk tilbake. Snart så hun et svakt lys i vinduet oppe under mønet. Da skjønte hun at Morten var kommet opp på hemsen. Enda en stund lå hun der. Det var så vidt hun hadde følelser igjen i tærne. Resten av kroppen var også iskald.

Endelig våget hun seg fram. Så lydløst hun kunne løp hun oppover stien. For sikkerhets skyld tok hun seg en tur innom utedoen ved fjøset før hun gikk inn. Hvis hun møtte noen, ville de sikkert bare tro at hun hadde hatt et ærend der.

Det tok lang tid før Mette fikk tilbake varmen i kroppen igjen. Og enda lenger tid tok det før hun greide å sove. En bunnløs fortvilelse vellet opp i henne. Plutselig var det som om noe klarnet oppe i hodet hennes. «Slik kan du ikke fortsette,» sa hun til seg selv. «Nå må du finne ut av dette, og så gjøre noe med det.» I det samme sto det helt klart for henne … grunnen til at hun følte denne uroen … hvorfor hun var så fortvilet over det hun hadde fått se i måneskinnet der ute i natta.

Mekanisk tente hun lampa. Hun grep en lapp som lå på nattbordet. Det var visst en kassalapp fra sist hun var i butikken. Med pennen hun hadde liggende i dagboka, skrev hun raskt ned fire ord: «… Jeg elsker deg, Morten …»

Lenge stirret hun på ordene mens tårene rant nedover kinnene. Nå var det sagt, og skrevet. Det var altså det som var hennes problem. Endelig våget hun å innrømme det for seg selv. Hun visste med en gang at dette ikke var noe som hadde hendt med henne akkurat da. Nei … slik hadde hun hatt det helt siden den første dagen … da hun fikk se ham ved det andre tjernet.

Gråten var i ferd med å overmanne henne helt. Hva nyttet det vel å innrømme noe slikt. Det hele var jo håpløst. Kunne det være klarere bevis enn dette på at det var et forhold mellom de to som hun hadde sett i båten der på tjernet? At hun måtte reise så fort som mulig, sto helt klart for henne. Hun ville aldri greie å fungere i arbeidet sitt med disse følelsene etter denne innrømmelsen. Det hun sikkert ville komme til å gjøre, var nok at hun ødela noe mellom Morten og Ellen, og det ville hun jo selvsagt ikke. Nei, hun måtte vekk, og det måtte skje fort. Allerede neste dag måtte hun snakke med Morten. Bestemmelsen var tatt.

Hele tiden glødet det et ørlite håp om at hun tok feil Det kunne jo være en misforståelse. I så fall ville hun få greie på det i morgen, tenkte hun.

Etter at denne avgjørelsen var tatt, greide hun å slappe litt mer av. Lappen hun hadde skrevet de fire ordene på, la hun inn i dagboka. Ingen måtte få se den. Hun kom nok snart til å brenne den opp … men ikke riktig ennå.

Etter hvert gled hun inn i en urolig søvn.

24 • Oppbrudd

Aldri hadde Mette følt seg så utkjørt som da hun våknet neste morgen. Kroppen kjentes enda stiv etter den kalde måneskinnsturen hun hadde hatt om natta. Mangelen på søvn merket hun best ved den dunkende hodepinen. Drømmene hadde vært urolige og vonde. Det føltes som om hun hadde ligget i helspenn hele natta. Bestemmelsen hun hadde tatt, sto likevel klart for henne. Hun måtte bare komme seg opp og få det overstått. Hun skjønte også at hun måtte si det hele som det var til Morten, samme hvor ydmykende det var. Han måtte få greie på den hele og fulle sannhet.

Med den bestemmelsen klart for seg sto hun opp og kledde på seg. Da hun kom ut, så hun ingen av de to andre. En ting kom hun i hvert fall til å være nøye på. Skulle hun snakke med Morten, så måtte hun være sikker på at de var alene. Dette var ikke noe for andre ører.

Jeg kan like godt begynne med melkingen, tenkte hun der hun sto, så er det unnagjort.

Hele tiden mens hun var i fjøset, kjempet hun med en vond klump nede i halsen. Gang på gang kom det for henne at dette kanskje var siste gang hun gjorde dette arbeidet. Aller verst ble det da hun sto og klappet Keiseren. «Jeg begriper ikke hvordan jeg skal greie meg i byen uten deg,» sa hun mens hun trakk den varme dyrekroppen tett inntil seg. Noen store tårer dryppet ned på den lille snuten.

Før hun gikk inn igjen, tok hun en tur bort til kilden ved fjellet for å vaske ansiktet litt i det kalde vannet. Kanskje hun på den måten kunne viske bort noen av de følelsesmessige sporene etter avskjeden med dyra.

Morten satt ved bordet og drakk kaffe da hun kom inn. Ellen var ikke å se noen steder, så Mette gikk ut fra at hun fremdeles sov ute i campingvogna. Hun hadde jo vært sent i seng kvelden før. Den første tanken som slo henne, var at nå måtte det skje. Situasjonen var ideell, og det var best å få det hele overstått.

Hun begynte litt famlende, men måtte stoppe opp. Hvordan i all verden skulle hun si dette? Morten så litt undrende på henne. Hun var tydelig nervøs.

«Jeg har tenkt på at det kanskje er best jeg reiser ...» Nei huff. Det var ikke slik hun skulle ha sagt det. Mette så ned i gulvet.

Morten stirret på henne. Så gled det en mørk skygge over ansiktet hans. En trekning gikk gjennom kroppen som om han kjente på en fysisk smerte. Stemmen var sterkt anstrengt da han svarte: «Ja, kanskje det er det beste. Jeg kan jo godt forstå at du må føle det slik.»

Mette så forvirret på ham. Kunne han forstå det? Hadde det vært så lett synlig? Betydde dette at hennes mistanker var riktige. Det ørlille håpet forsvant øyeblikkelig.

Morten knyttet hendene hardt sammen og pustet tungt før han fortsatte. «Jeg kan kjøre deg til stasjonen. Bare gjør deg klar, så skal jeg finne ut når toget går.»

Mette følte at hun holdt på å besvime. Hun fikk ikke sagt mer. Hvis hun åpnet munnen nå, ville garantert gråten sprute ut. En heftig nikking gav bare til kjenne at hun godtok løsningen. Så gikk hun raskt inn på rommet sitt.

Aldri hadde hun pakket så fort noen gang. Klær og andre eiendeler ble stuet ned i kofferten og ryggsekken. Hun hadde ikke tid til å tenke på at det skulle brettes pent sammen. Da hun gikk for å hente seg noe varmt vann så hun kunne få vasket seg litt skikkelig, så hun at Morten hadde gått ut. Lettelsen var stor over at hun slapp å treffe ham igjen riktig enda. Han var fremdeles ikke kommet inn da hun satte seg til bordet for å spise litt frokost.

Det var ikke før hun hadde gjort ferdig oppvasken, at han kom inn igjen.

«Toget går om to timer,» sa han uten å se på henne. «Kan du greie å bli ferdig til da?»

«Jeg er allerede klar,» svarte Mette og anstrengte seg til det ytterste for å virke noenlunde normal i stemmen.

«Det er bra,» sa Morten. «Hvis du henter bagasjen, så skal jeg bære den ut for deg.»

Mette gikk inn på rommet sitt igjen. Hun ble stående litt innenfor døra og puste tungt. Så tok hun et raskt blikk rundt i rommet for å se om det var noe hun hadde glemt. Der fikk hun se dagboka på nattbordet. En skjelving gikk gjennom henne da hun trev tak i den ene permen og slengte den ned i kofferten så bladene flagret. Det skulle ha tatt seg ut at hun glemte den igjen!

Det så ikke ut til at det var andre ting som lå igjen. Skulle de finne noe etter at hun var reist, kunne de jo bare sende det til henne. Raskt skrev hun adressen sin på en lapp og la den igjen på nattbordet. Hun skulle si til Morten hvorfor hun hadde lagt den der når de kjørte nedover.

Turen mot bygda opplevde hun som et mareritt. Det var ikke mye som ble sagt. Morten hadde riktignok aldri vært så snakkesalig. Men de hadde likevel alltid kunnet snakke naturlig og avslappet sammen. I dag var det så vidt han svarte når hun snakket til ham. Ansiktet så helt mørkt ut, og de mørke øynene var aldeles svarte. Dype rynker lå over pannen hele tiden. Dette uttrykket hans skremte henne. Han så nesten ti år eldre ut. Mette fant ikke på særlig mye å si hun heller. Inni henne raste det en storm som hun hele tiden kjempet med å holde der inne. Det føltes som om et utbrudd kunne komme når som helst. Og hvordan det ville arte seg, ante hun ikke.

Den vakre naturen langs veien hadde hun ikke øye for i det hele tatt. Det var bare da de kjørte forbi tjernet, der hun hadde badet på vei opp, at hun måtte snu seg og se ut. Morten snudde seg også og så mot vannet. En liten trekning gikk over ansiktet hans i det samme. Tenkte de kanskje på det samme? Ikke en eneste gang gjennom hele denne sommeren hadde han antydet noe om det møtet ... der han hadde sett henne stå naken for å kle på seg. Mette krympet seg fremdeles ved tanken.

At denne vidunderlige sommeren skulle slutte på denne måten, føltes nesten som en katastrofe for henne. Det verste var at hun hele tiden satt med en følelse av at det var en eller annen misforståelse inne i bildet. Men hun var aldeles ute av stand til å få rettet den opp. Det var altfor mange uklarheter til at hun kunne bringe emnet på bane. Det som plaget henne mest, var nok mistanken om at det var noen uhumskheter som ikke tålte dagens lys. Det var bare så ubegripelig at Morten kunne være med på noe slikt. Hun hadde jo hele tiden opplevd ham som ærligheten selv. En mer rettskaffen mann hadde hun ikke møtt. Heller ikke en bedre sjelesørger. Nei, dette var for vanskelig. Hun kunne ikke bringe det på bane. Det var helt umulig.

Stasjonen lå litt vest for handlesenteret, men det var ikke så langt unna. Morten stanset da de kom fram, og løftet bagasjen hennes ned på perrongen. Mette gikk ut. Hun visste ikke helt hva hun skulle gjøre eller si. Det var ennå en god stund igjen til toget skulle gå. Et øyeblikk sto Morten og så på henne. Hun så rett inn i det alvorlige ansiktet hans. Gang på gang svelget hun, men greide likevel ikke å si noe. Klumpen i halsen gjorde at det snørte seg helt til der nede. Og gråte ville hun ikke. Nei, det måtte ikke skje.

Morten kjempet også med noe, men hun forsto ikke helt hva det var. Det kunne se ut som han ville si noe. Men det kom ikke en lyd fra ham. Ansiktet trakk seg bare i et lidende drag. Mette greide ikke å tolke det. Hun hadde i det hele tatt ikke tanker som var klare nok til å forsøke.

Da han endelig åpnet munnen, tok han bare hånden hennes og sa: «Du må ha takk for i sommer, og farvel ...»

Han stoppet. Mette fikk også hvisket fram et farvel.

Plutselig snudde han og gikk. Ikke et blikk sendte han til-bake ... snudde bare bilen og kjørte. Så var han borte.

Aldri i sitt liv hadde hun følt seg så fortapt som da hun sto igjen alene der på perrongen. Klumpen i halsen begynte å verke. Hun kjempet og kjempet. Gråte ville hun bare ikke. Åååååå ... som hun lengtet etter å kunne få gråte skikkelig ut for seg selv. Hyle ... skrike ... rope ...

Hvis hun gjorde det hun følte for her på stasjonen, så ville hun garantert komme til å bli arrestert, det var hun sikker på.

Endelig kom toget. Så fort hun kunne gikk hun inn og fant seg en plass så langt vekk fra andre passasjerer som mulig. Hvordan hun skulle komme seg gjennom de timene hun hadde foran seg, kunne hun ikke begripe.

Senere husket hun denne turen som en eneste lang lidelse. Klumpen i halsen føltes som en byll som bare vokste og vokste. Ved bare den minste sinnsbevegelse var hun redd for at den ville briste. Av og til forsøkte hun å lese litt, men hun greide ikke å konsentrere seg. Hun måtte bare legge aviser og bøker fra seg igjen. Sove prøvde hun også å få til, men også det var umulig. Mat greide hun ikke tanken på i det hele tatt. Niste hadde hun tatt med, men den lå urørt hele veien.

Vel framme på Sentralbanestasjonen fikk hun tak i en drosje, og snart var hun tilbake i leiligheten sin.

En kald og innestengt luft slo imot henne da hun låste seg inn. Den lange sommeren da rommene hadde stått ubebodd, hadde satt sine spor. Hun åpnet et vindu i stua, men lukket det snart igjen. Det var for kaldt til å lufte. Været der i byen var grått og trist. Det stemte perfekt med humøret hennes. Temperaturen ute var også falt betraktelig etter at kalenderen skiftet fra august til september. Dessuten var ikke den eksosfylte lufta der ute noe å slippe inn i stua. Mette merket godt forskjellen fra den friske fjellufta som hun var blitt så vant med.

Etter å ha satt på litt varme, gikk hun inn på soverommet. Der sto senga oppreid akkurat slik som hun hadde forlatt den.

Endelig, tenkte hun. Nå er jeg alene. Ingen vet at jeg er kommet tilbake. Ingen kommer til å ringe på døra. Mobiltelefonen var slått av. Hun var alene … helt alene. Nå kunne hun … Med et hikst slengte hun seg på senga. Og så kom gråten.

Lenge lå hun der. I ukontrollerte hulk og hikst rant tårene ned og vætte hele puta. Hun brydde seg ikke om det, fortsatte bare å gråte. Så godt som det var å få hull på denne byllen. Men så vondt det også var å la alle disse vonde følelsene komme fram. Tankene svirret fram og tilbake. I øyeblikket tenkte hun mest på hvor synd det var på henne. Det verste var at hun greide ikke å finne noen skyldige i denne smerten. Hvem kunne hun egentlig gi skylden for alt dette vonde? Når hun begynte å tenke på det, gikk hun bare i stå. Alt var så forvirrende og kaotisk. Nei, hun ville ikke tenke på det. Skylden var nok bare hennes egen. Hvorfor i all verden skulle hun finne på å forelske seg i denne mannen? Hadde hun bare ikke gjort det, så hadde nok hele denne situasjonen vært annerledes. I hvert fall hadde hun ikke hatt det så vondt.

Langt om lenge stilnet gråten, og hun falt utmattet i søvn.

25 • Alene med tårene

Forvirret satte hun seg opp i senga. Hvor var hun? Det omtåkete hodet greide ikke å sortere tankene. Hun hørte trafikklyd utenfra, men hvordan kunne det henge sammen? Hvor var det blitt av sauene … og bjelleklangen? Og rautingen til kyrne som ville inn for å bli melket? Det var helt mørkt i rommet, men hvor i all verden var hun?

Sakte kom gårsdagens begivenheter tilbake til henne. Hun var jo i byen. Hvor lenge hadde hun sovet, tro? Det tok litt tid før hun fant lysbryteren på nattbordlampen. Da hun endelig fikk på lyset, så hun at klokka bare var tre om natta. Det kunne ikke nytte å stå opp ennå. Hun hutret litt, for hun hadde bare lagt seg til å sove oppå dyna. Fullt påkledd lå hun der.

Litt famlende fikk hun av seg klærne og krøp under dyna. Det var best å sove litt til. Hun følte seg forresten helt elendig. Hodepinen dunket sine taktfaste slag. Alle tanker på framtiden føltes som en lidelse. Hvordan skulle hun greie å takle jobben på kontoret igjen? Alle spørsmålene hun ville få. Forventningen hos venner og kollegaer. De var sikkert sprekkeferdige av nysgjerrighet. Da hun reiste, hadde de i all vennskapelighet mobbet henne med at hun ville komme tilbake i bunad og med skaut på hodet. Kanskje hun hadde med seg en gjetebukk eller to i bagasjen? Denne humoren hadde hun frydet seg over den gangen. Hun hadde til og med lovet å stille opp i full budeiemundur første dag på jobb.

Og så var det Tore … Hun sank ned i puta igjen. Visste han nå hvor det var hun hadde vært i sommer, tro? Hun hadde egentlig bestemt seg for å følge Mortens råd om ikke å bry seg om det han sa, men heller gi ham noen komplimenter i ny og ne. Men alle disse gode forsettene føltes nå bare som et uoverstigelig berg.

På nytt kom gråten. Det var ubegripelig at det fantes så mange tårer. Heldigvis skulle hun ikke begynne å jobbe før om en uke. Hun var også glad for at hun ikke trengte å være redd for at noen skulle dukke opp på døren. Det var jo ingen som visste at hun var der.

Utpå morgenkvisten falt hun igjen i søvn og våknet ikke før det var langt på dag. En gnagende følelse i magen fortalte henne at hun trengte frokost.

Møysommelig satte hun seg opp og gned seg i øynene. Hele ansiktet føltes stivt og rart. Jeg trenger nok en grundig vask, tenkte hun og gikk ut på badet.

Sjokket som møtte henne i speilet, fikk henne til å ønske at hun bare hadde blitt liggende i senga. Hvordan var det hun så ut? Hele ansiktet var hovent og rødflekkete. Øynene var også røde, i hvert fall det hun kunne se av dem mellom de hovne øyelokkene. Håret var pjusket. Det hadde sikkert blitt vått av å ligge på den tårevåte puta, og så hadde det tørket i den formen det lå der. Aldri i sitt liv hadde hun sett noe så avskyelig. Antakelig hadde hun grått mens hun sov også. Hadde ikke alt vært så tragisk, så hadde hun ledd. En ting var i hvert fall helt sikkert, hun kunne ikke gå ut slik. Hun var fullstendig innestengt i sin ensomhet der i leiligheten.

For utseendet sin del hjalp det ikke stort med en dusj. Likevel følte hun seg mer vel etterpå. Det var bare det inni henne som såpevann ikke greide å gjøre noe med.

Så var det frokosten. Det varte ikke lenge før konsekvensene av denne hurtige hjemreisen gikk opp for henne for alvor. Hun hadde jo ikke fått planlagt noe som helst. Det eneste spiselige hun fant i huset, var nisten hun hadde hatt med seg da hun reiste, og en pose havregryn som sto i skapet. Og så hadde hun jo vann i springen. Ikke engang kaffe kunne hun finne.

Mens hun spiste nisten, begynte hun å tenke på hvor lenge det egentlig var siden sist hun hadde fått seg noe mat. Det måtte være over et døgn siden. Hun hadde ikke spist noe på hele turen. Og da hun kom tilbake til leiligheten, hadde hun jo bare gått rett til sengs.

Fremdeles følte hun ingen sult. Men gnagingen i magen sa at hun måte få i seg noe. Slik som hun så ut, kunne hun ikke gå for å handle, så det måtte nok bare bli havregrøt til kvelds.

En ubegripelig følelse av motløshet kom over henne der hun satt. Om hun bare hadde hatt noen hun kunne betro seg til. Kanskje en venninne eller en slektning, men hun kom ikke på noen. Det var sikkert mange i omgangskretsen hun kunne ha snakket med, men hun greide ikke tanken på å skulle åpne seg for noen. Det hele var for ydmykende.

Mens hun satt der og grublet, kom tårene på nytt. Hun greide ikke å stoppe dem. Ikke så hun noen vits i det heller. Hun lot dem bare renne. Hvor var det blitt av livsgnisten og pågangsmotet hennes? Alltid pleide hun å ha noe som hun gledet seg over å holde på med. Det kunne være en eller annen hobby, et håndarbeid, eller rett og slett noe i forbindelse med jobben. Nå virket alt bare håpløst. Ingenting fristet henne til å ta fatt. Det eneste hun hadde lyst til, var å sitte der og gråte. Aldri i sitt liv hadde hun opplevd noe liknende.

Hun fant fram Bibelen fra kofferten. Kanskje det var et oppmuntrende ord der for henne. Apatisk bladde hun fram og tilbake, men hun greide fremdeles ikke å konsentrere seg om noen lesing. Til slutt la hun den fra seg. Kanskje også Gud har forlatt meg, tenkte hun. Han syns nok jeg er aldeles tåpelig, her jeg sitter og sturer. Tårene rant og rant.

Plutselig kom hun på en sangstrofe: Fortell Ham alt, så er det ei ditt eget ...

Fortelle Ham alt ... kunne hun det? Brydde Gud seg om dette, tro? Et øyeblikk ble hun sittende og tenke på det. Hun kunne jo prøve, men ...

Tvilende foldet hun hendene og begynte å forme tankene i ord. «Kjære Jesus ... jeg har det så vondt ... jeg føler meg aldeles ...» Famlende begynte hun å fortelle alt slik det var, og slik hun følte det. En lang stund satt hun dypt konsentrert i bønn. Etter hvert slappet hun litt av.

Men så kom det over henne igjen. Det var som et heftig sinne vellet opp i henne. «Hvorfor ble det slik? Hvorfor hindret du ikke dette i å skje? Du har jo all makt. Dette er da ingen vanskelighet for deg. Du kunne i det minste ha gjort det slik at jeg ikke ble så forelsket i denne fyren. Hvorfor gjorde du ikke det?»

Et voldsomt raseri fylte hele hennes indre. Hun kastet seg på kne ved stolen og lot raseriet få fritt løp. Igjen og igjen ropte hun spørsmålene ut. «Hvorfor ... hvorfor ... Kanskje du ikke finnes? Kanskje jeg har satset hele mitt liv på en bløff ...»

Sakte begynte raseriet å avta. Snart lå hun bare der helt utmattet. Hun hadde ikke mer å si ... ingen flere spørsmål. Alt var liksom rent ut av henne. Tankene gikk i surr. Hun lå bare der på kne foran stolen.

Da var det akkurat som hun kjente en hånd som varlig strøk henne over håret. Hun så fort opp, men der var ingen. Selvsagt var det bare en innbilning. Tårene fortsatte mens hun sank sammen igjen.

Der var det på nytt. Hun følte den varsomme berøringen. Forundret reiste hun seg sakte opp. Så merket hun, mer enn hun hørte, en stemme som sa: «Les Salme nittien.»

Skjelvende strakte hun seg etter Bibelen. Det tok litt tid før hun fant det rette stedet, for hendene fortsatte bare å skjelve.

Endelig lå Salme nittien oppslått i fanget hennes. Det var vers femten som øynene først falt på. Hun begynte å lese. «Når han kaller på meg, svarer jeg; jeg er med ham i nød og trengsel, jeg frir ham ut og gir ham ære.»

En lang stund ble hun bare sittende og stirre. Hun hadde ropt på Gud. Aldri i sitt liv hadde hun ropt mer inderlig på sin skaper. Men hun hadde faktisk bare følt det som om det var veggene hun ropte til. Hun hadde følt seg aldeles ensom og forlatt.

Men hun hadde ikke vært det. Mellom de veggene hadde Gud vært. Han hadde faktisk vært der sammen med henne. Dette var jo et tindrende klart bevis på det. Hun hadde kalt på Ham ... og Han hadde svart henne ... Ordet der i Bibelen var sannhet. Hun visste det ... ja, hun var overbevist ... Da måtte resten også være sannhet. Han var med henne i denne nøden. Hun var ikke alene. Hvorfor Han ikke hadde ført henne utenom disse lidelsene, skjønte hun ikke. Heller ikke hvorfor hun måtte være i den forferdelige uvissheten når det gjaldt Morten. Men én ting visste hun. Dette var ikke gått Gud hus forbi. Det var noe Han så, og som Han ville ta seg av på en eller annen måte.

Det var også et løfte i dette verset. Det var et løfte om utfri-else og ære. Det var mer enn hun kunne begripe der hun satt, men det gav henne litt mot. Kanskje det fantes en vei ut av dette.

Undringen fylte henne mer og mer. Hun tenkte på bønnen hun hadde bedt. Det var ikke akkurat en from og fin bønn. Det var jo faktisk et skikkelig raseriutbrudd. Mens hun tenkte på dette, ble hun fylt av en forunderlig fred. Denne bønnen hadde Gud hørt, og Han hadde svart på den. Men svaret hadde ikke vært i samme tone. Svaret hadde vært fylt av den mest vidunderlige kjærlighet. Gud tålte altså at menneskene raste mot Ham når livet tilsynelatende gikk dem helt imot?

Ja … det var slik Gud var. Hun visste det jo så godt, men akkurat i denne situasjonen hadde hun ikke greid å se det. Hun måtte nesten smile litt for seg selv. Tenk at hun kunne glemme så fort. Det var jo ikke lenge siden hun hadde opplevd så klare bønnesvar. Gud hadde svart henne like tindrende klart den natta hun var så redd der oppe på setra.

Og det var ikke bare de forsiktige og milde bønnene Han hørte. Nei, Han hørte like mye på dem som kom med sin inderligste nød. Og Han greide å takle de kraftigste følelsesutbrudd.

Litt etter litt falt kroppen hennes til ro. Sorgen og usikkerheten var der fremdeles, men den freden som denne opplevelsen hadde gitt, gav henne muligheten til å tenke klart igjen. Gråten som hele tiden hadde vellet opp i henne, stilnet også mer av.

Resten av dagen brukte hun til å pakke ut av bagasjen. En del klær trengte vasking, mens andre bare måtte legges bort. Sommertøyet kunne hun jo ikke bruke lenger. Det var allerede høst, og vinteren sto snart for døra. Det hjalp for tankene å være opptatt med noe, merket hun. Dette gjorde at hun fant på både det ene og det andre å gjøre. Vinduene trengte å vaskes, og kjøleskapet måtte også ha en rengjøring før hun kunne begynne å fylle det opp igjen.

Da kvelden kom, kjente hun at tungsinnet fremdeles satt ganske dypt. Rett som det var merket hun at tankene kretset om det vonde. Det var ikke fritt for at det dryppet noen tårer også. Men freden fra Salme nittien var der fortsatt. Det gjorde at hun den kvelden gikk til ro atskillig roligere.

26 • Fra drøm til virkelighet

Dagene som fulgte ble tunge og vanskelige. Kontakten med omverdenen måtte hun jo forsøke å ta opp igjen. På søndagen gikk hun for å besøke noen venninner. De undret seg nok litt over det dystre humøret hennes. Men hun forsøkte å forklare så mye av situasjonen at de skjønte der var et problem. Det var likevel ikke så lett. Hun ville ikke si noe om Morten og følelsene sine overfor ham. Og når det gjaldt resten av problemet, så var det jo så mye hun ikke forsto selv en gang.

Mandag morgen ringte hun til kontoret. Hun ville bare høre om det var mye å gjøre der. I så fall kunne hun gjerne komme på jobb litt tidligere enn avtalt, sa hun. Tanken på flere dager innestengt der i leiligheten med tårer og grublerier skremte henne nesten. Det ville nok bli mye bedre hvis hun kom i jobb og kunne konsentrere seg om noe helt annet.

Forslaget hennes ble møtt med begeistring. De hadde masse å gjøre. Hun kunne gjerne komme med det samme. Takknemlig gjorde hun seg i stand og dro på jobb.

Om hun hadde tenkt at jobben kunne løse alle problemer, så hadde hun nok tatt litt feil. Riktignok var det hyggelig å treffe igjen kollegaer, og Tore var – til hennes store lettelse – ute på reise. Hun risikerte altså ikke å treffe ham på en stund. Men konsentrasjonen hennes var det verre med. Gang på gang tok hun seg i å bare sitte der og se ut i lufta. Brevene hun skulle skrive måtte hun begynne på om igjen flere ganger. Det var nesten umulig for henne å samle trådene for planer og høstprogram som skulle settes opp. Dagen ble mer et slit enn en avkopling.

I lunsjpausen ble hun sittende alene en stund med ei av de andre damene på kontoret. Hun så oppriktig bekymret på Mette. «Hva er det som plager deg?» spurte hun. «Du ser jo aldeles hvit ut i ansiktet.» Hun hadde også lagt merke til at hun stadig falt i dype tanker mens hun arbeidet.

«Det oppsto litt kluss før jeg reiste fra den forrige jobben, men det ordner seg nok snart.» Mette ville ikke si mer. Hun orket ikke å begynne på noen slags forklaringer. Det var jo så umulig likevel. Kollegaen så granskende på henne en stund, men spurte ikke mer.

Etter endt arbeidsdag gikk hun rett hjem. Hun følte seg aldeles utslitt. Hvor i all verden var det blitt av livsgnisten og arbeidsgleden? Og kreftene som hun mente at hun hadde samlet i haugevis av denne sommeren – hvor var det blitt av dem?

Neste dag ble ikke stort bedre. Stadig måtte hun ta seg sammen og mobilisere alle de kreftene hun kunne oppdrive, for å konsentrere seg om den minste ting. Rett som det var oppdaget hun at ting som var helt opplagte, rett og slett hadde gått i glemmeboken. Og avtaler som hun gjorde, måtte hun skrive ned med det samme, ellers gikk de samme vei.

«Situasjonen er jo helt fortvilet,» sa hun til seg selv da hun slengte seg ned i en stol etter endt arbeidsdag. «Dette går bare ikke lenger.» En liten gnist av vilje og tross flammet opp i henne. «Dette må jeg gjøre noe med. Jeg kan ikke fortsette på denne måten.» Men så kjente hun at det hele på en måte rant ut av henne igjen, for hva kunne hun vel gjøre? Hun visste selvsagt at hun kunne ringe til Morten og få ham til å forklare alle de tingene som skapte slik uro i henne. Alle de mystiske begivenhetene og antydningene som hun hadde blitt så forvirret av. Men hun greide det bare ikke. Det motet som skulle til for å møte de svarene som hun da regnet med at hun fikk, det hadde hun slett ikke.

Aldeles oppgitt lente hun seg tilbake i stolen. Hun så på klokka. Nå skulle snart kyrne melkes. Hun lurte på om Ellen fikk gitt sauene de godsakene som de forventet på denne tiden. Og Keiseren … tok hun seg nok tid med ham, tro? Den likte så godt å bli klappet og klødd bak ørene. Og så ville den alltid suge en stund på fingrene hennes.

Så var det geitene. Fikk hun passet på slik at de ikke smatt inn i melkeboden? Med skrekk tenkte hun på hva de kunne greie å få i stand der inne blant all melkematen.

Plutselig reiste hun seg opp og gikk bort til et skap. Der tok hun ut ei stor bunke med fotografier. Alle bildene hun hadde tatt gjennom sommeren, hadde hun bare lagt inn der. Ikke en eneste gang etter at hun kom tilbake, hadde hun sett på dem. Nå ville hun gå gjennom dem. Kanskje hun da ville komme på noe hun kunne gjøre for å bli litt mer rolig inni seg.

Det var ikke mange bildene hun hadde sett på før hun forsto at dette slett ikke var den rette måten å glemme på. Følelser og tanker kom veltende innover henne igjen. Der så hun bildene hun tok da Missi ble født. Gutten som falt bakover i høyet på fjøsgulvet da kalven plutselig sprutet ut. Hun hadde greid å fange inn et øyeblikk av forbauselse og latter, samtidig med at noe fantastisk skjedde. En liten skapning kom til verden … Det var som om hun kunne høre den muntre latteren til Morten der ved siden av.

Så var det tante Anna. Det runde fjeset strålte mot henne fra bildene. Langt inne i noen sprekker i ansiktet skimtet hun to øyne som bare var godheten selv. Videre så hun bilder fra stevnet, og andre arrangementer.

Forunderlig så mange bilder hun hadde av Morten. Den solbrune huden fikk henne selv til å virke litt blek ved siden av. Faktisk hadde hun fått ganske mange bilder der han og hun var sammen. Det hadde aldri vært vanskelig å få folk til å hjelpe med fotograferingen. Smilet han sendte henne fra bildene, fikk det igjen til å skjelve inni henne. Tårene ville hele tiden fram. Sakte sank bunken med bilder ned i fanget. Tankene begynte å vandre. Snart fikk de frie vinger. Hun var tilbake på setra. Bjelleklangen og susingen fra vinden som feide nedover fjellet, fylte henne med den lenge etterlengtede roen. Der kom Keiseren løpende mot henne. Hun fanget ham inn i armene sine, og så rullet de rundt på vollen. Geitene kom også og ville være med på leken. Tante Anna sto i døra og lo mot dem. Snart var der fullt av barn som frydet seg med i den viltre leken.

Snart kom en bil kjørende oppover veien. Det var Morten. Da han så den elleville leken, ville også han være med. Han trykket inn bilhornet så dyr og barn skvatt til alle kanter. Med en trillende latter trykket han på bilhornet igjen.

Plutselig føltes ikke den skingrende lyden like behagelig. Hun ristet litt fortumlet på hodet. Hvor var hun? Hun var da slett ikke på setra. Nei, hun satt og sov i stolen sin i leiligheten. Den deilige følelsen hun nettopp hadde hatt, forsvant gradvis. Det var altså bare en drøm. Der kom den skingrende lyden igjen, men det var ikke noe bilhorn. Det var dørklokka. Forskrekket samlet hun sammen bildene og la dem på bordet. Noen av dem hadde falt ned på gulvet.

Idet hun gikk forbi speilet, snudde hun seg for å se om hun i det hele tatt så slik ut at hun kunne ta imot folk. Utseendet var ikke akkurat noe å skryte av, men det var nok bare en av naboene som kom innom et ærend, så det fikk våge seg at hun ikke så særlig tiltalende ut.

Da hun åpnet døra, ble hun bare stående og måpe. Drømte hun ennå, tro? Et par ganger måtte hun blunke for å være helt sikker. Nei, hun tok ikke feil. Det var Morten som sto der.

Noen lange sekunder ble de bare stående og stirre på hverandre. Til slutt smilte han et litt usikkert smil og sa: «Får jeg lov til å komme inn?»

«Jo …» Mette kremtet. Stemmen ville ikke bære. Hun prøvde på nytt: «Ja, bare kom inn.» Stemmen var ikke mer enn en hvisking. Hun åpnet døra på vidt gap og slapp ham inn.

Etter at hun hadde gjenvunnet det meste av fatningen, fikk hun vist ham til rette i stolen hvor hun nettopp hadde sittet. Selv satte hun seg i sofaen ved siden av. En flyktig tanke streifet henne om at hun burde sette på noe kaffe … Men hun slo den vekk. Aldri i livet om hun hadde greid å koke kaffe akkurat da.

En stund ble de bare sittende der. Ingen sa noe. Tankene raste rundt i hodet på Mette. Hva kunne det være som hadde fått Morten til å reise alle disse milene og alle disse timene for å besøke henne? Kunne det være noe galt? Da måtte det være noe forferdelig galt.

En isende redsel begynte å spre seg gjennom kroppen hennes.

Endelig kremtet Morten. Det var tydelig at dette var et vanskelig øyeblikk også for ham. «Jeg måtte bare snakke litt med deg,» begynte han. «Jeg er redd for at det oppsto en del misforståelser før du reiste.»

Mette stirret forundret på ham. Hva kunne dette være? Hun greide ikke å si noe … ventet bare på at han skulle fortsette.

Han så ned på hendene sine, som lå hardt knyttet i fanget, mens han fortsatte. «Vi snakket om det da du var reist … altså Ellen og jeg … Det kan hende det oppsto en misforståelse. Hun fortalte at hun hadde anbefalt deg å reise. Jeg ante ingenting om det da. Jeg trodde det var ryktene du syntes ble så ubehagelige at du ikke orket å være der lenger.» Stemmen hans var svak og anstrengt. Det så ut til å være en hard kraftanstrengelse for ham å greie å si noe i det hele tatt.

314

Mette stirret enda mer forundret på ham. Forvirringen hennes var total. Hva var det han snakket om? Endelig greide hun å presse fram en lyd. «Ryktene!?»

Morten smilte et blekt smil. «Så du visste altså ikke noe om dem?»

Hun ristet bare på hodet. Dette var aldeles ubegripelig for henne.

Plutselig forsvant smilet hans, og de dype rynkene grov seg ned mellom øynene. «Men hvorfor reiste du da?» De mørke øynene stirret intenst på henne.

Mette følte seg aldeles som lammet innvendig. Hva skulle hun si? Blikket hans krevde et svar, og det nokså snart. Hun kremtet. Stemmen ville fremdeles ikke virke helt. Det var nok ingen annen råd enn å si alt som det var. Hun kunne ikke sitte og skjule noe. Det ville bare føre til enda flere lidelser. Nei, sannheten måtte fram.

Hun tok sats og mobiliserte alle sine krefter før hun svarte. «Jeg forsto det slik at Ellen helst ville at jeg skulle dra.»

Forbauselsen lyste ut av øynene til Morten i det samme ordene var sagt. «Hvorfor i all verden skulle hun ville det?»

Nå var det Mette som knyttet hendene i fanget. Blikket hennes fulgte hver bevegelse der nede. Da hun fortsatte, var stemmen hennes nesten ikke hørbar. «Jeg regnet med at hun syntes det var litt ubehagelig at jeg …» Hun stoppet opp. Men så tok hun sats igjen. Dette måtte hun bare få sagt. «Jeg mener, jeg tenkte at hun sikkert ikke likte at jeg var der … når du var der.» Det hele gikk i stå for henne.

Morten lente seg framover og støttet albuene mot knærne. De hevede øyebrynene gav henne en oppfordring til å fortsette. Igjen tok Mette sats. Dette ble bare noe rot. Med en stemme som var kvassere enn hun mente det, sa hun: «Jeg forsto jo at det er et forhold mellom dere, og da er det jo ikke så rart at hun syntes det var dumt å ha deg der alene sammen med en annen kvinne.» Puh, nå var det sagt. Mette falt sammen litt og kikket forsiktig opp på ham.

Sjokket som lyste ut av øynene hans, fikk henne igjen til å føle en total forvirring. «Hvordan i all verden kom du på den tanken?» Han ropte nesten ordene mot henne.

Igjen kom tanken til Mette om at nå måtte alt fram. Hun begynte å fortelle om hvordan hun hadde lagt merke til deres nære forhold. Måten de snakket til hverandre på, og interessen de viste for hverandre. Til slutt fortalte hun om det som hadde bekreftet det hele for henne, nemlig episoden ved tjernet den natta.

Morten satt i taushet og lyttet. Ikke med en mine viste han hva han følte. Da hun var ferdig og hadde fortalt alt, ble hun sittende stille igjen og se ned i fanget.

Morten satt også stille en stund. Så brast han plutselig i latter. Mette følte med det samme at hun kunne ha slått ham. Han lo altså bare av det. Det stramme uttrykket hennes fikk fort latteren hans til å stilne.

Så var det Mortens tur til å snakke. Han fortalte at Ellen var naboen hans nede i bygda. Det hadde hun vært så lenge han kunne huske. De hadde lekt sammen som barn. Et år, da Ellen var ganske ung, hadde hun jobbet en hel sommer som budeie sammen med moren hans der oppe på setra. Og fremdeles hjalp hun tante Anna rett som det var når det trengtes. Arbeidet der oppe var hun vel kjent med. Hvis de hadde ønsket å gifte seg med hverandre, så hadde de gjort det for lenge siden. Nei, de tankene hadde aldri streifet dem. De var bare gode venner.

Mette så litt skamfull framfor seg. «Men hva med den natta på tjernet?» Hun måtte spørre om det …

Morten lo litt igjen. «Husker du at vi snakket om at vi hadde møtt noen gamle venner i fjellet?»

315

Mette nikket.

«De leide Fjellbusetra. Du vet den på den andre siden av tjernet. Den kvelden bestemte vi oss for å dra bort og besøke dem. Det ble sent før vi brøt opp igjen, så vi fikk låne en pram. I det ustabile måneskinnet var det lettere å ro over vannet enn å lete oss fram langs stien ved bredden.»

Mette kjente at en lettelse – sammen med en stadig økende spenning – gjorde at hun skalv innvendig. Det var godt å få en oppklaring når det gjaldt hans forhold til Ellen, men det var mer. Det var enda mange ubesvarte spørsmål.

«Jeg skjønner at jeg har trukket litt forhastede slutninger,» sa hun. «Jeg beklager hvis jeg laget vanskeligheter for dere.» Så kikket hun opp på ham igjen. «Du sa noe om rykter. Hva mente du med det?»

Morten ble mørk i ansiktet med det samme. «Husker du at Ellen kom nokså opprørt opp på setra igjen etter at hun hadde fulgt de russiske gjestene ned til bygda?»

Mette nikket. Hun husket godt det. Det var jo da alle plutselig forsvant. Faktisk var det da alt det skumle begynte.

«Da de skulle gå om bord i bussen, viste det seg at ei av damene i selskapet ikke var der,» fortsatte han. «De kunne ikke finne henne, så bussen måtte bare reise. I hui og hast måtte vi sette i gang en leteaksjon. Vi fant damen hjemme hos en av dem som hadde vært på flittige besøk hos dem da de var på setra. Det viste seg at hun hadde fått kontakt med en mann forrige gang de var på besøk. De hadde faktisk holdt kontakten hele tiden. Nå tilbød han henne ekteskap, og hun regnet med at hun bare kunne bli igjen. Det ble ganske mye kluss ut av det, ikke minst på grunn av at det snart viste seg at mannen ikke var snill med henne. Det ble mange ting som vi måtte hjelpe denne kvinnen med. Hele situasjonen så litt mørk ut en stund. Spesielt Ellen tok dette veldig hardt. Det var jo hun som hadde fått disse folkene til å komme. Heldigvis fikk vi ordnet opp i tingene etter en stund. Men dette førte til at det begynte å svirre en del rykter. Ryktene hadde forresten allerede begynt da russerne var der sist, for flere visste om kontakten mellom disse to. Hele virksomheten ble regnet for å være noen snuskete greier. Også seterdriften min ble satt i et negativt lys. Noen så visst på det hele som rene bordellvirksomheten. Jeg visste ikke noe om dette før etter at denne episoden fant sted.»

Plutselig stoppet han opp. Han sukket og ristet på hodet. «Det er helt forferdelig som folk kan få tingene til å arte seg når fantasien får fritt spillerom,» sa han stille.

En stund ble de sittende uten å si noe. Mette tenkte på det han hadde sagt. Brikkene begynte å falle på plass, men enda var det noe hun ikke forsto. Samtalen hun hadde hørt den natta virket fremdeles uforståelig for henne. Da var jo også hun blitt trukket inn i bildet. Og dagen etter hadde Morten sagt at han hadde gjort noe dumt. Hva kunne dette bety? Hun måtte spørre.

Morten smilte et skjevt smil. Det tok litt tid før han svarte. Det så ut som han kjempet med hva han skulle si. Mette ventet spent. Var det likevel noe grums? Hun måtte bare vite det.

Morten kremtet litt. Da han begynte å snakke, virket det som han helst ville ha sluppet å si akkurat det. Men blikket til Mette presset ham videre. «Ryktene ble jo ikke bedre av at jeg ansatte ei kvinnelig budeie. Noen var visst svært opptatt av det, spesielt da de så at det var ei ung og vakker kvinne, og ikke ei eldre dame som vi først trodde det var vi ansatte. Og da episoden med den russiske damen skjedde, tok alle ryktene helt fyr. En sen kveld fikk jeg besøk av noen fra bedehuset. De mente jeg måtte trekke meg fra styret der. Ingen visste jo hva som var sannhet eller løgn. De regnet med at det til og med kunne bli snakk om politianmeldelser i saken. Det var noen forferdelige dager.» Morten så ut i lufta og ristet på hodet.

Der fikk Mette svar på hva det var hun hadde hørt om natta.

«Jeg bestemte meg fort for at jeg måtte holde meg mest mulig nede i bygda,» fortsatte Morten. «Jeg tenkte at ryktene kanskje ville dabbe litt av hvis de så at jeg aldri var på setra uten at det også var andre mennesker der.» Han smilte litt sjenert før han tilføyde: «Det ble fort lagt merke til hvis du og jeg var alene der oppe.»

Hvilke kvaler han hadde lidt. Mette syntes plutselig veldig synd på ham. Morten fortsatte å snakke igjen: «Det var øyeblikk da jeg angret på at jeg hadde ansatt deg. Jeg regnet med at jeg ved dette hadde påført også deg store ubehageligheter. Det var derfor jeg sa at jeg nok hadde gjort noe dumt.»

Plutselig kom det et humoristisk glimt i de alvorlige øynene. «Men jeg angrer ikke så veldig mye på det. Det var jo hyggelig å bli kjent med deg også.»

Mette måtte le. Hun pustet ut. Nå var alle de vonde spørsmålene besvart. Hun forsto det alt sammen. Antydningen fra mennene hun hadde hatt konfrontasjonen med der oppe tidlig på sommeren, og advarselen fra mannen på stevnet. Samtalen hun hadde overhørt på butikken. Og til slutt Ellens antydning om at det beste for henne var at hun reiste.

Å, hvilken lettelse det var. Nå var den delen av problemet løst.

27 • Fra mørke til lys

Lenge ble de sittende og prate om det som hadde hendt. Mette slappet mer av, og det gjorde tydeligvis Morten også. Han fortalte mer om det som hadde skjedd etter at hun var reist. Han og Ellen hadde altså hatt en lang prat. Det ble klart for dem at årsaken til Mettes hurtige oppbrudd kunne være en misforståelse. Den kvelden hadde Morten slått opp i Bibelen og lest det verset i Salme nitten som Mette hadde vist ham den morgenen etter tordenværet. Men det var ikke ordene om at man ikke skulle frykte for nattens redsler, som han hadde festet seg ved. Det var den siste delen av vers fem som ble så sterkt for ham. Der sto det: ... *for pilene som flyr om dagen* ...

Han skulle altså ikke frykte for pilene som flyr om dagen. For ham ble det slik at pilene var et bilde på ryktene. Disse ryktene ... pilene ... hadde han virkelig fått erfare. Og han hadde blitt redd. Han hadde forsøkt å flykte fra dem ved å holde seg borte fra setra så mye som mulig. Og så hadde han forsøkt å få dem til å dø ut ved å tie. Hvis han ikke sa noe om dette til noen, så ville de kanskje stoppe opp. Men slik hadde det ikke gått.

Da han leste det verset, forsto han at han var slave under ryktene så lenge han fryktet dem og flyktet fra dem. Nei, han måtte møte dem med oppriktighet og ærlighet. Derfor hadde han innkalt til et møte i bedehusstyret, der han hadde orientert om saken. Alt hadde han fortalt, og alle fikk anledning til å si det de følte i saken. Det ble mange følelser og meninger som kom på bordet den kvelden. Men dette gjorde at lufta ble renset. Han hadde også sagt at han kom til å reise inn til byen for å prate med Mette. «Jeg var faktisk også helt ærlig der,» sluttet han og så litt sjenert ned i gulvet.

Mette satt og lyttet i undring. Han hadde virkelig et ubegripelig mot. Tenk om hun selv hadde hatt bare en smule av det! Da hadde hun kanskje ikke behøvd å gå hele denne tiden med denne smerten. Ikke en eneste gang hadde hun våget å snakke med Morten om uroen sin der oppe på setra.

Det ble stille igjen mellom dem. De så på hverandre. Mette kjente at hjertet banket hardt. Morten så ut som han ville si noe mer, men så ble det visst ikke noe av det likevel. En svak rødme spredte seg over ansiktet hans. Det var noe mer ... Mette kunne se det. Hun smilte litt for å oppmuntre ham til å fortsette.

«Jeg kom egentlig ...» Han kremtet litt før han fortsatte. «Egentlig kom jeg fordi jeg fant noe som du hadde glemt.»

Mette så forundret på ham. «Men hvorfor sendte du det ikke bare i posten? Det var jo derfor jeg la igjen adressen.»

Morten vred litt på seg. «Jeg kunne ikke det,» svarte han. «Jeg måtte snakke med deg, for det var noe ved det som jeg måtte spørre deg om.»

Dermed trakk han opp noe av lommen som han rakte henne. Mette stivnet i hele kroppen da hun fikk se den lille hvite kassalappen. I et glimt så hun for seg dagboka da hun hadde slengt den flagrende ned i kofferten. Ikke et øyeblikk hadde hun tenkt på den lille lappen som lå i den.

Han behøvde ikke vise henne den. Så altfor godt kjente hun til de fire ordene som sto på den. Hun ønsket bare at hun kunne ha falt gjennom gulvet. Ikke ett ord greide hun å få fram. Morten så også nervøs ut. «Jeg måtte bare spørre deg om det som står på den lappen, er sant,» sa han med en stemme som kunne briste hvert øyeblikk.

Igjen forsto Mette at hun måtte si sannheten. Men hun greide ikke å få lyd i stemmen. Svaret ble bare en svak nikking. Morten reiste seg og kom bort og satte seg ved siden av henne i sofaen.

«Det er bare det,» fortsatte han. «Hvis det er sant det som står her, så vil jeg spørre deg om du kunne tenke deg å komme tilbake ... som min kone ...»

Mette stirret på ham et øyeblikk i stiv spenning. Tøyset han med henne, tro? Nei. De vidunderlige øynene var bare fylt av en inderlig spenning. Det var som om alt det som betydde noe for ham her i denne verden, var svaret på det spørsmålet.

Et strålende smil spredte seg over ansiktet hennes mens tårene begynte å renne. Sakte gled hodet hennes ned mot skulderen hans. Ordene hun hvisket mot halsen hans kunne ikke misforstås. Varsomt lukket armen hans seg om skuldrene hennes, og slik ble de sittende en lang stund. Skjortekragen hans ble etter hvert gjennomvåt av tårer. Men denne gangen var det ikke smertens tårer. I så fall var det de siste rester av dem som nå rant ut. Etter dette ville det bare bli gledestårer. Det var Mette sikker på.

Plutselig trakk Morten henne litt ut fra seg og så henne inn i øynene. «Det er en ting til jeg må si.» Bak det alvorlige uttrykket spilte det et humoristisk glimt. Mette ventet i spenning på hva det kunne være for noe mer nå. «Jeg må bare be om tilgivelse fordi jeg sto og kikket på deg da du badet ved det tjernet den gangen ... Jeg har skammet meg over det i hele sommer.»

Mette stirret først på ham, så begynte hun å le. «Og jeg som har skammet meg slik over at jeg kunne være så lettsindig!» De lo begge to.

«Men én ting vet jeg i hvert fall,» sa Mette. «Det var da det skjedde for min del.» Hun pekte på lappen som lå på bordet. «Det skjedde nok noe hos denne karen også den gangen,» sa Morten og humret.

Så ble han alvorlig og så på henne igjen. «Jeg trodde jeg skulle ha dødd da jeg forlot deg på stasjonen. Det er det verste jeg har opplevd. Jeg trodde jo ikke jeg skulle få se deg mer igjen. Derfor måtte jeg skynde meg av sted så ingen skulle få se …» Han stoppet opp litt før han fortsatte med en mye svakere stemme: «… at jeg gråt.»

Mette trykket seg inntil ham. Igjen ble de sittende og nyte hverandres nærvær.

«Åååå … som jeg har lengtet tilbake …» Mette så drømmende ut i lufta «… til setra … og dyra …»

Morten stirret på henne tilgjort fornærmet. «Dyra!?»

Mette lo en trillende latter. «Ja, dem også …» •

I 1890-årene tok den svenske fortgrafen, Axel Lindahl, dette bildet av den lille bygda, Homme, i Valle sokn, Setesdal. Fjellet i bakgrunnen heter Einang.

28 • Onkel Torkel

En piskende vind feide mot vindusruten, og et tett snødryss fulgte med. Mette strakte seg og tittet over kanten på den varme dyna. Med et lite grøss rullet hun seg sammen igjen, glad for at hun ikke var nødt til å gå ut i det ufyselige været. Hun var faktisk ikke nødt til å stå opp i det hele tatt ennå. Ingen jobb ventet på henne der ute i vinterværet. Hun kunne bare ligge der i den varme senga og dra seg så lenge hun ville. Hvilken deilig tilværelse, tenkte hun og smilte for seg selv mens hun og nøt den behagelige varmen under dyna. Morten hadde dratt på jobb for en god stund siden. Han pleide ikke å vekke henne om morgenen. Siden hun ikke måtte opp for selv å rekke en jobb, syntes han at hun bare måtte nyte disse morgenene i fred og ro så lenge det varte. Den siste tiden hadde jammen vært stressende nok for henne.

Mette så på klokka. Den var snart halv ni. Hun strakte seg igjen, men følte seg slett ikke fristet til å stå opp til en slik kald og mørk dag. I stedet ble hun liggende mens tanken vandret tilbake til de siste ukers begivenheter. Det var helt ufattelig å tenke på at nå var hun gift med den vidunderlige mannen som hun hadde blitt så forelsket i på setra der hun jobbet i sommer. Den jobben hadde hun tatt for å få litt avveksling en stund – fra et stress som hadde begynt å slite litt for mye på henne. Hun jobbet ellers på kontoret til en kristen organisasjon i Oslo. Og dit hadde hun absolutt tenkt å dra tilbake etter sommeren, noe hun da også hadde gjort. Men så viste det seg altså at de følelsene som var satt i sving den sommeren, ikke ville forsvinne så lett.

Den litt innesluttede og tause, men tvers igjennom snille og gode Morten hadde nå vært hennes ektemann i to uker allerede. De bodde sammen i det store huset på gården hans i den lille fjellbygda som hadde blitt så kjent og kjær for henne den tiden hun arbeidet med dyrene på setra hans.

Etter at bestemmelsen om at de ville gifte seg var tatt, tok det ikke lang tid før de begynte å planlegge bryllup. Ingen av dem hadde lyst til å dra ventetiden ut mer enn nødvendig. De bodde så langt fra hverandre at de ikke kunne besøke hverandre så ofte som de gjerne ville. Og da Mette fikk ordnet en avtale med organisasjonen hvor hun arbeidet, om å gå inn i deres arbeid lokalt der hvor hun nå skulle flytte til, så syntes verken hun eller Morten at der var noen grunn til ikke å begynne og planlegge bryllup. De fant ut at påsken måtte være en ideell tid for en slik begivenhet. Lørdag før palmesøndag ble valgt som bryllupsdag.

Da den store dagen opprant, ankom Mette sammen med en hel gjeng familie og venner som var bedt til bryllupet. Den tidlige vårdagen hadde vært fin og klar, selv om det var ganske kaldt i luften. Selve bryllupstilstellingen hadde ikke Mette hatt noe med. Det var Marit, Mortens søster, og Ellen, venninna hennes, som hadde insistert på å ta seg av den. Så den overdådige og flotte festen hadde vært en skikkelig overraskelse for henne. De hadde feiret det hele i huset som nå var hennes hjem. Over femti gjester var benket til bryllupsmiddag i den store stua.

Mette smilte for seg selv der hun lå i den brede, gamle ektesengen og tenkte tilbake på den dagen. Foreldrene hennes hadde vært der. Det samme hadde søsteren hennes med familie, og en del tanter, onkler og venner fra hjembygda hennes på Sørlandet. Noen venner og kollegaer fra kontoret i Oslo var også kommet. Så hadde der vært en god del av Mortens familie og venner fra fjellbygda. En fantastisk dag som hun frydet seg over når hun tenkte på den.

Hun måtte nesten le for seg selv når hun tenkte på Mortens forlover. Han hadde studert fælt på hvem han skulle spørre til den oppgaven. De hadde hatt en lang telefonsamtale i sakens anledning. Han hadde så mange gode venner i bygda, men han syntes ikke at han kunne plukke ut en spesiell person til dette. Det var vanskelig for ham å skulle stille en foran de andre. Det var da Mette hadde foreslått at han skulle spørre Ellen om å være forloveren hans. Morten hadde ledd godt av forslaget, men Mette hadde ikke gitt seg. Til slutt hadde han gått med på det, på den betingelsen at Mette spurte henne. Han ville ikke gå til Ellen med et slikt forslag, sa han. Mette hadde mer enn gjerne påtatt seg å gjøre det. Han skjønt jo hva som lå bak Mettes forslag uten at han kommenterte det noe. Hun ville med dette be om tilgivelse for at hun hadde opptrådt litt avvisende mot Ellen den sommeren. Mette hadde nemlig trodd at der var et forhold mellom Morten og Ellen, og det hadde ikke Mette greid å takle, selv om hun på det tidspunktet ikke var villig til å innrømme at hun selv var forelsket i Morten. Da hun forsto at der ikke fantes noen forhold mellom disse, hadde hun vært litt flau over de slutningene hun så raskt hadde trukket.

Dette syntes hun måtte være en fin måte å gjøre godt igjen alt i den forbindelse. Ellen hadde også ledd godt da Mette ringte og spurte henne. Men hun hadde sporty og humoristisk svart at det ville hun gjerne gjøre for Morten. Og Mette merket at hun med dette fikk et godt og fortrolig forhold til Ellen. Det var hun svært glad for. De bodde jo så nær hverandre at de nok ville få mye med hverandre å gjøre i tiden som kom. Og så var de jo også så like på alder, i begynnelsen av trettiåra, alle tre.

Motvillig satte hun seg opp på sengekanten. Det var nok best å komme seg opp. Hun kunne ikke ligge slik og dra seg hele dagen. Der var en del å gjøre i huset, så hun var ikke arbeidsledig selv om hun ikke behøvde å tenke på jobb enda. Hun hadde fått fri et par uker etter påske for at hun skulle få anledning til å komme skikkelig i orden i sitt nye hjem.

Hutrende stakk hun føttene i et par tøfler og gikk ut på badet. Det store huset hadde seks soveværelser i andre etasje. I tillegg var der et stort bad og et lagerrom. Aldri hadde hun hatt så god plass noen steder hun hadde bodd. Det var rene drømmehuset, syntes hun. Selv om det var ganske gammelt, var det godt vedlikeholdt, og det var også oppusset og modernisert for ikke så altfor lenge siden.

Etter en rask dusj gikk hun ned på kjøkkenet for å spise frokost. En lun varme slo imot henne da hun åpnet kjøkkendøra. Morten hadde fyrt i ovnen der før han gikk, så hun kunne stå opp til en behagelig temperatur, på tross av kulden utenfor. Kaffekanna sto også full av varm kaffe. Raskt smurte hun seg et par brødskiver og satte seg for å spise.

Plutselig ringte det på døra. Mette hoppet på stolen så kaffen skvatt ut av koppen hun holdt i hånda. Hvem kunne det være som kom så tidlig på morgenen i dette været? Raskt reiste hun seg og gikk for å åpne. Utenfor sto ei nokså hutrende og nedsnødd Marit.

«Kom inn,» sa Mette forskrekket. «Hva er det som bringer deg ut i dette forferdelige været så tidlig på morgenen?»

Marit trådte innenfor døra, men hun gjorde ikke tegn til å ta av seg yttertøyet. I stedet la Mette merke til et bekymret drag i det rødflekkede ansiktet. «Jeg må gå igjen,» sa hun, «jeg må være på skolen klokka ti, men jeg måtte bare snakke litt med deg.» Mette visste at hun jobbet som lærer på en skole i nabobygda. Og hvis hun måtte være der klokka ti, skjønte Mette at hun ikke hadde tid til å stoppe særlig lenge. På dette føret kunne det ikke være lett å kjøre, så hun måtte nok beregne god tid.

«Det gjelder onkel Torkel,» skyndte Marit seg å forklare. «Jeg var innom ham i går en tur, og da følte han seg så uvel. Han så slett ikke bra ut heller, men han påsto at det bare var en forkjølelse, som det ikke var noe å bry seg om. Jeg tenkte at jeg ville høre hvordan det sto til med ham i morges, derfor ringte jeg til ham. Og det er det som bekymrer meg, for der var ingen svar å få. Jeg kan ikke begripe at han kan ha gått ut i dette været så skrøpelig som han var i går. Jeg prøvde å ringe ham to ganger, men ingen tok telefonen. Dette bekymrer meg litt. Selv om han alltid har vært frisk og sprek, så er han jo tross alt åttifem år … nei … jeg liker det ikke.»

Dyp bekymring preget hele kvinnen der i døra. «Hadde det ikke vært fordi jeg absolutt må på skolen i dag, så hadde jeg tatt meg fri og dratt opp til ham. Men jeg har bare ikke anledning til det nå. Derfor tenkte jeg at kanskje du kunne ta en tur opp å se til ham.» Hun så spørrende på Mette.

«Selvfølgelig kan jeg det,» svarte Mette, glad for å få spørsmålet. Det skulle bare mangle at hun som gikk der uten å ha noen slags forpliktelser, ikke kunne ta en tur for å se til denne gamle onkelen. Hun visste hvor han bodde. Morten hadde vist henne det en gang de hadde tatt en kjøretur rundt i bygda for at hun skulle bli litt mer kjent med sitt nye hjemsted. Hun hadde også hilst på den gamle mannen et par ganger, men Morten hadde ikke fortalt noe særlig om ham. Mette hadde heller ikke kommet på å spørre om så mye.

«Jeg kan gå med det samme,» sa hun til Marit, som tydeligvis svært gjerne ville komme seg videre igjen så fort som mulig.

«Takk skal du ha,» sa Marit lettet. «Det er ikke så lett å ha tilsyn med en mann som han.» Hun lo litt og ristet på hodet. «Du vet hvor sta han kan være. Men jeg synes ikke vi bare kan la han sitter der oppe i Lia alene hvis han er syk. Vi må i hvert fall ha et øye med ham, synes jeg.»

Mette nikket. Hun visste slett ikke hvor sta onkel Torkel var. Morten hadde ikke fortalt noe som helst om det, men hun forsto at det ikke var noen vits i å bemerke det akkurat da. Marit måtte på jobb, og hun måtte en tur opp i Lia. Det var best å komme seg av gårde.

Marit løp ut i snøværet igjen. Hun hadde parkert bilen borte på hovedveien. Det var derfor hun var så full av snø. Hun hadde gått bort til huset, for veien inn var jo ikke brøytet. Mette så at det kom til å bli en drøy jobb med snømåking før hun kunne komme ut med bilen sin, men det skulle nok gå, tenkte hun.

Morten hadde ikke behøvd å tenke på snømåking om morgenen, for han pleide bare å spasere til jobb. Banken hvor han jobbet, lå ikke lenger unna enn at han kunne gå. Forresten hadde nok det meste av denne snøen kommet etter at han var dratt.

29 • Det tause huset

Mette kjørte i sneglefart oppover bygdeveien. Brøytemannskapene hadde ikke kjørt der på en god stund, så snølaget i veien gjorde føret både sleipt og glatt. Vinden hadde også økt på, så selv om det ikke snødde like tett, var snødrevet likevel vanskelig å orientere seg i. Et par ganger trodde hun at hun hadde kjørt forbi avkjørselen til det lille småbruket som ble kalt Lia. Men så kom hun forbi steder som hun greide å kjenne igjen, og da forsto hun at hun ennå ikke var kommet fram.

Et slikt vær var visst ikke så uvanlig her oppe, selv om de nå var kommet et stykke ut i april. Selv var hun vant til, fra Sørlandet, at påskeliljer og krokus blomstret på det fineste på denne tiden. Men så høyt til fjells som hun var her, var situasjonene ofte en annen, hadde hun raskt fått erfare.

Hun prøvde å huske det lille Morten hadde fortalt om denne gamle mannen, og gården han bodde på. At han var bror til Mortens morfar, hadde hun i hvert fall fått med seg. Så det var egentlig Mortens mor han var onkel til. Men det var visst slik der i distriktet at onkler og tanter til foreldrene også ble kalt det av barna. I hvert fall de onkler og tanter som ikke var gift. Og onkel Torkel hadde visst aldri vært gift, men bodde alene i det huset hvor Mortens mor kom fra. Hvis hun ikke husket feil, hadde han overtatt garden etter at broren døde. Den broren som altså var morfar til Morten. Noe mer enn det kunne hun ikke komme på at hun hadde hørt om ham.

Plutselig stoppet hun bilen og stirret ut av bilvinduet. Der borte måtte da avkjørselen være. Et stykke fra veien lå det et lite, gammelt hus. Det måtte være der onkel Torkel bodde. Men veien bort til huset var ikke brøytet, så hun forsto at hvis hun skulle komme seg dit, måtte hun ta bena fatt.

Etter litt strev fikk hun parkert bilen så pass langt utenfor veien at hun tenkte brøyteplogen kunne greie å passere. Så var det bare å legge i vei. Hun var glad for at hun hadde tatt på seg gummistøvler, og selv dem kunne til tider føles snaue nok. Den lette snøen skvatt opp for hvert skritt hun tok. Rett som det var havnet noen klatter ned i støvlene.

De nær to hundre meterne hun måtte gå, føltes som en evighet å få lagt bak seg, syntes hun. Snøen og vinden som pisket henne i ansiktet, gjorde at hun nesten ikke greide å se noen ting.

Da hun kom så nær at hun kunne ta stedet i nærmere øyesyn, stoppet hun og stirret bekymret på det gamle huset. Ingen ting tydet på at noen hadde vært ute i snøen den dagen. Verken veien mot uthuset eller trappa var måket. I vinduene var det helt mørkt, og fra pipa var det ingen tegn til røyk som steg opp.

En skjelving gikk gjennom kroppen hennes. Hva var det hun hadde gitt seg ut på? Hva ville hun egentlig møte der inne? En plutselig panikk grep henne, og hun fikk lyst til å snu og dra tilbake for å hente noen som kunne bli med henne inn. Men så begynte hun å tenke på hvem det skulle være. Morten var jo på jobb. Det var sikkert ikke lett for ham å komme fra. Verken Marit eller mannen hennes var hjemme. Tante Anna, den gamle trivelige tanta til Morten som hun hadde blitt så godt kjent med i sommer, kunne hun ikke dra ut i dette været. Det var helt opplagt. Nei … hvem i all verden skulle hun gå til for å be om hjelp?

Med besluttsomme skritt gikk hun mot bislagdøra på baksiden av huset. Dette måtte hun bare gjøre på egen hånd. Hun kunne ikke løpe og gjemme seg nå. Forsiktig ban-

323

ket hun på ytterdøren. Så ventet hun et øyeblikk i åndeløs spenning. Ingen reaksjon var å spore der inne fra. Igjen banket hun. Denne gangen litt hardere, men fremdeles var der helt stille der inne. Hun tittet inn av et vindu. Det måtte være kjøkkenvinduet, forsto hun. Der inne så det ikke ut til å ha vært noen den dagen. Uroen inni henne økte på. Hjertet banket fortere mens redselen virkelig begynte å gripe fatt i henne. Han måtte jo være der inne. Hvis han hadde gått ut denne dagen, ville hun ha sett det i snøen. Men der var ingen antydninger til at noen hadde vært ute av døra etter at det begynte å snø. Riktignok hadde det vært bart dagen før, men da hadde jo Marit vært der og sett at han var hjemme.

Forsiktig skjøv hun ned dørhåndtaket. Døra gled opp med det samme. Den var altså ikke låst. Raskt smatt hun inn i bislaget og lukket døra etter seg. Så åpnet hun kjøkkendøra og gikk inn. Ingen tegn til liv kunne hun se noen steder. På kjøkkenbenken sto det noen skitne kopper, men de var ikke brukt den dagen, det kunne hun lett se. I en krok på den motsatte veggen sto det en ovn. Hun gikk bort og la hånen på den. Det var som hun tenkte. Den var helt kald. Og vedkassen ved siden av var tom. Nei, temperaturen der inne var ikke særlig høy, kunne hun kjenne.

Det var to dører til i rommet. Rett overfor bislagdøren var det ei som hun gikk ut fra ledet ut i en gang. De fleste hus av denne typen var bygget på samme måte. To stuer med en gang i midten. Så et kjøkken, og gjerne et lite kammers på baksiden. Bislaget var bygget på inn mot kjøkkenveggen som et lavere utbygg.

Mette rettet blikket mot døra i enden av kjøkkenet til venstre. Kanskje han brukte det som soveværelse. Så stille hun kunne gikk hun over gulvet og banket på døra. Et øyeblikk ble hun stående og lytte. Da hørte hun en lyd der inne fra. Det var noen som hostet. En lettelse blandet med stigende uro fylte henne da hun forsto at det tross alt var liv i huset.

Forsiktig skjøv hun opp døra og tittet inn. En stram, tett lukt slo imot henne med det samme. Der fikk hun øye på ei seng med en haug av sengetøy oppi.

«Hallo! Er det noen her?» spurte hun. En bevegelse borte i senga fortalte at det ikke bare var sengeklær som lå der.

«Hvem er det som kommer rekende rett inn i huset på denne måten?» kom det fra en skurrete og anstrengt stemme, mens et pjuskete hode lettet seg litt fra puten. Mette måtte smile litt over den bryske mottagelsen. Men hun følte seg faktisk også som en frekk inntrenger, så det var en nokså forsiktig og svak stemme som svarte:

«Det er bare meg, Mette. Marit var litt bekymret for deg. Jeg lovet å stikke innom for å se hvordan det sto til med deg.»

To mørke øyne stirret opp på henne da hun kom nærmere senga. Utrykket i ansiktet fortalte at hun slett ikke måtte regne seg for å være altfor velkommen. Den første tanken som slo henne, var at de mørke øynene nok måtte være noe som lå til slekten. Morten kom nok også til å se slik ut når han ble åttifem, for det var de samme øynene, og den samme ansiktsformen som lå der på den fuktige puten. Hadde ikke situasjonen vært så alvorlig hadde hun sikkert begynt å le av slike tanker og observasjoner. Men hun var ikke kommet for å betrakte et par mørke øyne under noen kraftige pjuskete grå øyenbryn i et magert ansikt. Faktisk kunne situasjonen være ganske alvorlig. Det var best hun fant litt mer ut av dette før hun ble kastet ut.

«Hvordan er det med deg?» spurte hun bekymret. «Du ser nokså skrøpelig ut.» Det kom et grynt fra senga. «Litt snue har da aldri fått folk til å krepere, så vidt jeg vet,» svarte han grettent.

«Men … det må da være mer enn litt snue som plager deg.» Mette så urolig på det gulbleke ansiktet på puta.

«Du kan bare hilse Marit og si at jeg er på bena igjen om et par dager. «Flonsa» har aldri pleid å ri meg lenger enn det tidligere, så den gjør nok ikke det denne gangen heller.»

Det så ut som han mente samtalen var over, og at hun med det bare kunne gå igjen. Men Mette ville ikke la seg avfeie så lett. Hun så godt at mannen ikke var frisk. Sannsynligvis kunne han ikke greie å komme seg opp av senga. Hvordan skulle han greie å få i seg mat, for ikke å snakke om drikke?

«Du har det kaldt her,» sa hun. «Skal jeg ikke fyre litt i ovnen for deg før jeg går?» Igjen kom det bare et grynt fra senga. Han ville nok helst ha protestert, men av en eller annen grunn ble det ikke sagt noe mer. Mette ventet ikke på nærmere svar. Hun snudde bare og gikk ut igjen for å finne ved.

I bislaget fant hun ei snøskuffe. Det tok litt tid før hun fikk skuffet seg veg bort til vedskjulet som hun skjønte måtte være i uthuset. Det ble ikke rare veien, men hun gav seg ikke før hun hadde hentet inn nok ved til å fyre opp både i kjøkkenovnen og i ovnen inne i kammerset. Hun fylte også opp vedkassene så der skulle være litt ved å fylle på med etter hvert. Snart brant det lystig i begge ovnene. Borte i senga var der få bevegelser å spore. Et øyeblikk trodde Mette at han hadde sovnet. Men så kom det en kraftig hostebølge igjen. Mette gikk ut på kjøkkenet og fylte et glass med vann. Kanskje det ville hjelpe ham litt. I hvert fall visste hun at han burde få i seg drikke.

«Her er litt drikke til deg,» sa hun da hun kom inn i kammerset igjen. En skjelvende hånd strakte seg etter glasset. Han svarte ikke, men hun syntes å merke en slags takknemlighet.

Da han heiste seg litt opp på puta for å drikke la hun merke til at han lå fullt påkledd i senga. Hun sa ikke noe, men registrerte det bare med forundring. Kanskje han frøs. Det bleke ansiktet med de røde flekkene kunne tyde på at han hadde feber. Eller kanskje han rett og slett ikke hadde greid å få av seg klærne før han la seg. Det så ikke ut til at det var særlig mye krefter i den magre kroppen der under dyna.

På et lite bord som tjente som nattbord ved senga, la hun merke til at det sto en telefon. Igjen undret hun seg over det Marit hadde sagt om at hun ikke hadde fått svar da hun hadde ringt ham om morgenen. Han kunne da lett ha nådd røret fra senga. Hvor syk var han egentlig? Igjen kjente hun uroen stige inni seg. Kunne hun bare la ham ligge slik? Nei, avgjorde hun raskt. Han måtte ha hjelp. Men hva kunne hun gjøre?

«Marit sa at hun forsøkt å ringe deg i morges?» Hun sa det som et spørsmål for kanskje å få greie på hva som hadde skjedd om morgenen.

Han tittet opp på henne med rynkede bryn. «Ja, jeg kunne vel tenke meg at det var henne,» svarte han bryskt. «Det går da ikke an å prate i telefonen når hele kveldsmaten er i ferd med å returnere.» Han gjorde et lite kast med hodet mot ei bøtte som sto under bordet.

Ja vel, tenkte Mette. Der var altså forklaringen. Han hadde strevd med å kaste opp da telefonen ringte. Det forklarte også den stramme luften i rommet. Hun hadde lyst til å åpne et vindu, men våget ikke. Det ville jo bare gjøre det enda kaldere der inne for den syke mannen. I stedet lot hun døra til kjøkkenet stå åpen.

«Er det noe mer jeg kan gjøre for deg?» spurte Mette. «Kanskje jeg skal ringe …?» Hun ble avbrutt av en ilter protest fra senga. «Jeg har ikke bedt deg om å gjøre noe som helst, og det har jeg ikke tenkt å gjøre heller. Et par dager, sa jeg. Hils Marit og si det. Da er jeg på bena igjen. Adjø!»

Beskjeden var klar nok. Nå måtte hun gå. Men kunne hun bare forlate ham her? Hun så et øyeblikk på den spinkle skikkelsen i senga. Han så helt medtatt ut. Sannsynligvis var det akkurat det han var, så hun kunne egentlig godt forstå at han gjerne ville ha henne ut. Hun hadde lyst til å ta telefonen der på bordet og ringe til Morten, men hun våget ikke. Beskjeden hun hadde fått var klar nok. Kanskje hun bare ville gjøre det enda verre for ham med å trosse seg fram. Nei, hun hadde slett ikke lyst til å hisse denne gamle mannen opp mer enn nødvendig.

Uten å si noe mer snudde hun og forlot rommet. Det ville ikke nyttet å diskutere mer med ham uansett. Nå forsto hun i hvert fall hva Marit hadde ment med at han var sta og vanskelig å ha med og gjøre. Hadde hun bare vært litt mer kyndig i sykepleie, så kunne hun kanskje ha vurdert situasjonen mer fornuftig. Det eneste fornuftige hun i øyeblikket kunne komme på, var å gå. Men hun ville kjøre rett bort til Morten i banken og rådføre seg med ham om hva de burde gjøre.

Idet hun rundet hushjørnet for å ta fatt på tilbakeveien, fikk hun se brøyteplogen som suste forbi borte på veien. Takknemlig tenkte hun at nå ville turen tilbake bli atskillig lettere. Det snødde ikke lenger fullt så tett, men vinden var like kraftig. Bøyd mot den piskende snøføyka kjempet hun seg tilbake til bilen.

Tilbakeveien ble, som hun hadde tenkt, mye lettere. Snart stoppet hun utenfor handlesenteret som banken var en del av. Et øyeblikk ble hun sittende og se seg om. Hvor ofte hadde hun ikke vært der i sommer da hun jobbet som budeie for Morten oppe på setra hans. Da var det varmt med gress og blomster, og løv på trærne. Nå var det snø og kulde. Hun syntes bygda var like vakker i vinterdrakt som den hadde vært i sommerens fortryllende skjønnhet. Den gang hadde hun ikke ant at dette skulle bli hennes permanente hjem. Så annerledes alt var blitt!

På grunn av været kunne hun ikke se gården hvor hun nå bodde. Hun kunne heller ikke se gården til Petter, naboen som hjalp Morten med å stelle dyrene om morgenen når han selv var på jobb. Han hadde også hjulpet dem en del der oppe på setra i sommer, så hun var blitt ganske godt kjent med ham. Et øyeblikk lurte hun på om hun skulle kjøre bort for å se om han var hjemme. Han kunne sikker hjelpe henne. Men så bestemte hun seg for heller å gå inn og snakke med Morten.

Raskt gikk hun inn i det varme og koselige banklokalet. Morten kikket forundret opp da hun kom inn. Han smilte til henne, men henvendte seg straks tilbake til en kunde som han i øyeblikket var opptatt med. Mette slo seg ned i en stol et stykke unna. Det var best å vente til han var ledig.

Etter noen minutter snudde kunden seg og gikk ut. Mette så at nå kunne hun få snakke uforstyrret med Morten, så hun reiste seg og gikk bort til skranken. «Hva kan jeg hjelpe denne fortryllende damen med?» spurte han i en tilgjort høytidlig tone. Mette var øyeblikkelig med på notene. «Jeg skulle bare ta ut et par millioner fra en konto,» sa hun i det dypeste alvor. Morten hevet øyenbrynene og stirret sjokkert på henne. «Og hvilken konto skal dette taes fra da?» spurte han mens han forsøkte å kvele en latter. Mette sto der fortsatt like alvorlig. «Det må jo selvsagt bli fra kontoen til min mann,» svarte hun kjapt.

En mann som satt et stykke unna og arbeidet, hadde hørt hele samtalen. Nå brast han i latter og sa: «Der ser du, Morten. Var det ikke det jeg sa. Du hoppet altfor fort inn i det ekteskapet. Og nå sitter du der. Kom ikke og si at jeg ikke advarte deg. Kvinnfolk …» Dermed brast de i latter alle tre.

326

Etter at de fikk pusten og talens bruk tilbake igjen, spurte Morten. «Vel, jeg går ut fra at det var noe mer du ville. Eller kanskje du bare ville seg meg … litt sånn … midt på dagen?» Han blunket til henne mens smilet lå over hele ansiktet hans. Mette smilte tilbake. «Ja det er klart jeg vil se deg,» svarte hun. «Men akkurat i dag er det noe spesielt jeg må snakke med deg om.» Hun ble alvorlig med det samme.

«Marit var innom i morges før hun dro på jobb. Hun var svært bekymret for onkel Torkel. I går var hun borte hos ham en tur. Da var han ikke helt i form, så hun ville ringe ham igjen i dag før hun gikk på jobb for å høre hvordan det sto til. Men da hun ringte, var det ingen som svarte. Hun hadde ikke anledning til å stikke bort igjen da, derfor spurte hun om jeg …» Hun stoppet brått og så forvirret på Morten. Han satt stiv i stolen og stirret rett fram for seg. All farge var forsvunnet fra ansiktet hans. Kjevemusklene svulmet på hver side i et krampaktig bitt. Den høyre hånden holdt så hardt rundt en kulepenn at hun var redd den skulle brekke rett av. En ising av redsel fòr nedover ryggen hennes. Hva kunne dette bety?

Plutselig rettet Morten seg opp i stolen og la pennen på skranken med et smell. Det mørke håret, som alltid lå så velstelt, fikk med ett noe vilt over seg. Det var som om han våknet opp av en søvn.

Da han igjen begynte å snakke, virket han nesten som før igjen. «Har du vært borte hos ham?» Mette nikket. «Han så svært skrøpelig ut,» svarte hun.

Morten så på klokka. «Jeg skal ta meg en tur bort til ham så fort jeg kan komme fra her.»

Mette pustet lettet ut. «Da setter jeg igjen bilen, så kan du ta den når du drar,» sa hun og la nøklene på skranken. Med et takknemlig smil snudd hun og gikk mot døra. En annen kunde var kommet inn mens de snakket. Han sto og ventet på å komme til ved skranken hos Morten.

Mette kikket bort på Morten igjen før hun gikk ut. En dyp rynke hadde lagt seg mellom øynene hans. Det var noe som plaget ham, men hun skjønte ikke hva det kunne være.

Forvirrede tanker kretset rundt i hodet på henne der hun trasket hjemover i den isende vinden. At Morten var en taus mann som bar tanker og følelser langt inni seg, hadde hun smertelig erfart for lenge siden. Hvor mange ganger hadde hun ikke lidd de verste kvaler der oppe på setra i sommer på grunn av dette. Men hun visste at hun egentlig ikke kunne klandre ham så mye, for dette var nok bare en del av hans natur. Hadde hun bare ikke selv vært så følsom og ømskinnet, så hadde sikkert ikke dette hatt noen betydning. Men hun greide ikke å distansere seg fra det hele når slike vonde anelser dukket opp. Og nå hadde det skjedd igjen. Hadde hun bare fått snakket med ham der i banken, men med kunder og andre funksjonærer rundt seg kunne hun ikke komme seg til å spørre om noe. Uroen begynte å arbeide inni henne. Der var noe … men hva det var … nei, hun ante det bare ikke.

30 • Mørke skyer

Minuttene sneglet seg av sted og ble til timer. Mette tenkte hele tiden på den syke gamle mannen borte i Lia. Hvordan gikk det med ham, tro? Flere ganger var hun fristet til å ta på seg for å dra bort og se til ham. Men så husket hun på den avvisende holdningen han hadde hatt til henne. Det var nok mye bedre at Morten dro. Han kjente ham bedre, så han aksepterte nok ham lettere.

Hun forsøkte å gjøre noe for å få tiden til å gå, men det var vanskelig å konsentrere seg om arbeidet. Rett som det var kikket hun på klokka. Mon tro når Morten greide å komme fra?

Ute blåste det like ille. Snøen økte på igjen og la seg i stadig større fenner rundt omkring. Brøyteplogen fòr forbi med jevne mellomrom, hadde Mette registrert, så kjøreforholdene var nok ikke av de aller beste.

Plutselig hørte hun en bil som stoppet borte ved innkjørselen til gården. Raskt gikk hun til døra for å se hvem det kunne være. Snart fikk hun øye på en skikkelse som løp mot låven. Det var Morten. Etter noen minutter hørte hun en traktor som ble startet, og snart kjørte han av sted igjen med den. Det så ut til at han hadde det travelt, for han kjørte fortere enn hun syntes var forsvarlig på det glatte føret. Hva kunne det være som sto på nå tro? Hva var det Morten trengte traktor til? Et par ganger forsøkte hun å få tak i ham på mobiltelefonen, men der var det ingen svar å få.

En plutselig innskytelse fikk henne til å ringe Marit. Det var bare den eldste sønnen som svarte. Marit var i Lia hos onkel Torkel. Hun hadde kommet hjem tidligere fra jobb og dratt rett bort dit kunne han fortelle. Da var det altså noe som skjedde der borte i hvert fall.

Hun begynte å forberede middagen for å ha noe å gjøre, men rett som det var stoppet hun midt i arbeidet og ble stående å stirre ut av vinduet.

En skarp ulelyd skar med ett gjennom stillheten. Og snart fòr en bil med blinkende blålys forbi i stor fart. Sykebil! Mette kjente at hun skalv. Situasjonen der borte var nok verre enn hun hadde trodd. Kanskje hun hadde handlet galt? Kan hende hun burde ha ringt doktor med en gang, uten å ta hensyn til den egenrådige gamle mannen. Urolig gikk hun fram og tilbake på gulvet. Hun vred hendene mens hun grublet over den alvorlige situasjonen.

Det gikk en halv times tid før sykebilen kom tilbake igjen. Fremdeles hadde den blålys på, men sirenen var taus. Kanskje det kunne bety at ikke situasjonen var fult så alvorlig … eller … kunne det bety at der ikke var mer å gjøre … «Nei, så alvorlig var det da ikke!» sa hun høyt til seg selv og treiv kaffekanna som sto på kjøkkenbordet. Hun skjenket i en kopp og satte seg ved bordet for å forsøke å roe seg litt.

Etter det varte det ikke så lenge før hun hørte traktoren til Morten igjen. Helt nummen av spenning ventet hun på at han skulle komme inn. Men det var ikke før han hadde skuffet vekk snøen på hele gårdsplassen at han endelig kom inn i det varme kjøkkenet. Han virket mørk i ansiktet, og hele skikkelsen bar tydelig preg av at det var en alvorlig situasjon han hadde hatt med å gjøre.

«Hvordan står det til med ham?» spurte Mette spent. Morten svarte ikke med det same. Det virket nesten som om han ikke hørte hva hun sa i det hele tatt. Mette så på ham med stigende uro. Han satte seg tungt ned på en stol mens han så fjernt fram for seg.

«Han måtte på sykehus forsto jeg?» forsøkte Mette igjen.

Plutselig så Morten på henne. Det var som om han først da så at hun var der. «Ja,» sa han. «Ja … han var ikke særlig mye til kar …» Han sukket. Hun kunne se at han skalv på hendene, og ansiktet var svært blekt. Igjen undret hun seg over reaksjonen hans. Han pleide da aldri å ta slik på vei bare på grunn av en litt kritisk situasjon. Den solide og stødige mannen hennes var ikke til å kjenne igjen i det hele tatt.

Etter hvert så det likevel ut til at han roet seg litt, og han begynte å snakke. «Da jeg kom bort til ham, hadde han ganske høy feber kunne jeg se. Han lå nesten bare og sov. I hvert fall lå han som i en døs. Jeg ringte doktoren med det samme. Marit kom også så fort hun kunne. Da doktoren kom, fant han fort ut at det måtte være lungebeten-nelse, og det er jo ikke noe å spøke med i den alderen. Der var ikke noe annet å gjøre enn å få ham på sykehuset.»

«Hva var det du måtte bruke traktoren til?» spurte Mette etter en stund. «Det så ut til at du hadde det svært travelt, så fort som du kjørte.»

«Ja, jeg måtte skynde meg å få måket opp veien slik at ikke ambulansemannskapene skulle bli nødt til å bære den syke mannen helt bort til veien. Det var ille nok bare å få ham ut i bilen i denne snøføyka.»

«Hvordan tror du det går med ham?» Mette var bekymret. Morten ristet betenkt på hodet. «Det så ikke bra ut, men nå får han i hvert fall god behandling. Vi får bare håpe at det går bra.»

Mette følte seg fremdeles lite til pass. Kunne hun ha hindret at det ble så ille, tro, hvis hun hadde fått tak i doktor med det samme? Hun måtte spørre hva Morten mente.

«Nei,» svarte han da hun spurte. Et mildt drag gled over ansiktet hans da han så det forpinte utrykket hennes. «Du gjorde en god jobb.» Han smilte til henne. «Man må kjenne onkel Torkel godt for å greie å hamle opp med ham. Og selv mange av dem som kjenner ham, har problemer med det. Jeg kan tenke meg at det ikke var den varmeste velkomst du fikk. Du gjorde det helt rette. Du må ikke tenke på noe annet.»

Mette pustet ut, takknemlig for det han sa. Der var nok ikke noe hun behøvde å be-breide seg. Dessuten trengte de jo å få brøytet veien for å få pasienten av gårde. Det måtte jo Morten ha tatt seg av uansett. Nei, det var nok ikke noe hun kunne ha gjort annerledes.

«Er det Marit som pleier å ha tilsyn med ham?» spurte Mette. Hun gikk bort til kom-fyren for å øse opp middagen. Kun et kort ja fikk hun til svar. Forundret stoppet hun midt i arbeidet og kikket på ham. Det mørke, innesluttede utrykket var igjen kommet over ham. Han satt bare der uten å si noe mer.

Mette ble stående et øyeblikk å stirre på ham. «Er det noe galt?» Den forpint stem-men hennes fikk Morten til å rette seg opp med et rykk. Øynene deres møttes i et in-tenst blikk. Så gled det et smil over ansiktet til Morten mens ansiktsutrykket ble mer avslappet. «Nei … nei, det er ingenting galt. Det er bare meg som er litt … litt dum.» sa han med en litt anstrengt latter.

Mette skjønte at han ikke hadde lyst til å si mer om det. Kanskje han ikke hadde så lett for å takle sykdom slik på nært hold. Det var visst mange som hadde det slik. Nei, det var nok ikke noe å bry seg om.

Selv om atmosfæren ble taus og litt trykket der i kjøkkenet, så var det ingen vond atmosfære, i hvert fall ingenting vondt mellom dem. Det var nok ikke så mye hun kunne gjøre for ham. Men en ting kunne hun gjøre, og det kom hun til å gjøre desto mer. Hun kunne be. Ikke minst onkel Torkel trengte forbønn. Hun hadde lyst til å spørre hvordan det sto til med den gamle mannen når det gjaldt hans åndelige tilstand. Men heller ikke det ville hun ta opp nå. Det var i det hele tatt ikke mer å si om situasjonen, fant hun ut. Det var best å la det hele ligge til de fikk høre hvordan det gikk på sykehuset.

31 • På glattisen igjen

Snøstormen la seg forholdsvis fort. Det var forhåpentligvis bare vinterens siste krampetrekninger før den helt gav herredømmet over til våren med varme, liv og frodighet. Neste dag regnet det, og snøen ble omgjort til vasstrukne sørpedammer. Veien ble enda mer sleip og ufremkommelig. Mette var glad for at hun ikke hadde behov for å ta ut med bilen i hvert fall. På et slikt føre kunne hun like godt regne med å havne i grøfta, tenkte hun

I stedet tok hun fatt på en del kasser som sto i gangen. Det var ting hun hadde hatt med seg på flyttelasset fra byen, men som hun ennå ikke hadde fått plassert i skap og skuffer. I det store huset var det rikelig med plass, det var bare å få ryddet det hele til slik at det ble greit og praktisk. Hun måtte tenke seg litt om før hun bestemte seg for hvor hun skulle sette tingene. I stua sto det en del gamle møbler. En stor skjenk hadde plass til det meste av finserviset. Den var en del av et gammelt spisestuemøblement som Morten hadde arvet etter foreldrene. Et nydelig trearbeid i eik. Den, sammen med det kraftige bordet og de solide stolene, gav hele stuen et majestetisk preg. Alle ben og stolrygger var nydelig utskåret. Og skjenken, med sine romslige skap og skuffer, dekket nesten halve endeveggen i den store stuen.

I den andre enden av rommet sto en nyere skinnsalong. Men alt passet fint sammen, så der var ingen stilkollisjon mellom nytt og gammelt. Morten hadde vært nøye med det når han anskaffet noe nytt til huset.

De møblene Mette hadde hatt inne i byen, hadde hun solgt. De ville ikke ha passet inn i et slikt stilfullt hus. Og dessuten var det like greit å kvitte seg med det, så slapp hun i hvert fall den frakten. Morten hadde jo det som trengtes likevel.

Midt på den lange ytterveggen i stuen var det ei stor, dobbel dør. Tidligere hadde det vært to stuer der med en gang i midten. Denne døra var da utgangsdøra som ledet ut mot hagen. Men så var de to stuene og gangen gjort om til ei hel stue. Derfor var det at stuen var så stor. Faktisk hadde den vært enda større, for i den ene enden hadde de delt av et rom til soverom. Det var da mor til Morten var syk at det ble gjort. Det var vanskelig å ha en sengeliggende pasient å stelle når de måtte helt opp på loftet. Derfor hadde de laget til et rom ved siden av kjøkkenet som hun kunne ha. Det rommet hadde Morten innredet til kontor, og Mette syntes det var en praktisk og grei løsning.

Langs den andre ytterveggen var kjøkkenet plassert. Også det hadde forholdsvis ny innredning med rikelig plass i skap og skuffer. I enden av kjøkkenet var det en stor gang med trapp opp til loftet og hovedinngang utenfra. Ved siden av hovedinngangen var det også i senere tid innredet et moderne bad, hvor det tidligere hadde vært et kammers.

Men der var også en inngang til kjøkkenet. Det var den de brukte til daglig. Der var et lite påbygg med vaskerom og plass til skifting av arbeidstøy. Det utbygget var heller ikke så veldig gammelt. Der gikk også trappen ned til kjelleren.

Mette gikk fra rom til rom og fra skap til skap. Etter hvert fikk hun tømt den ene kassen etter den andre. I gangen nede, og også oppe på loftet, var det plassert garderobeskap, så hun kunne bare stue inn. Hun nynnet og sang mens hun arbeidet.

Plutselig skvatt hun til. Det var telefonen som ringte. Stillheten rundt henne, og den dype konsentrasjonen hun var i, gjorde at hun ikke var forberedt i det hele tatt på et signal fra omverdenen. Men da hun tok av røret og hørte at det var fra sykehuset, kjente hun at hjertet begynte å slå enda raskere. Onkel Torkel var blitt dårligere, kunne de fortelle. Det så faktisk ganske kritisk ut. Mette takket for beskjeden og sa at de skulle komme til sykehuset så fort de kunne.

Etter at hun hadde lagt på, ble hun stående et øyeblikk for å summe seg. Hun skalv lett. Hva skulle hun gjøre? Hun måtte prøve å få tak i Marit, tenkte hun. Morten måtte hun nok også si fra til, men hun gruet for det. De merkelige reaksjonene hans skremte henne litt. Men kunne hun gjøre noe annet? Nei, han måtte få greie på dette.

Til hennes forbauselse var det ingen reaksjon å spore i stemmen til Morten da hun ringte ham. I hvert fall ikke annet enn dyp bekymring for den gamle onkelen. «Jeg skal dra med det samme,» sa han.

De ble enige om at han og Marit skulle dra inn til sykehuset. Han skulle ringe henne med det samme. Mette var glad for at hun slapp å ta ut på det vanskelige føret, men hun var også litt bekymret for Morten, selv om hun visste at han var mye mer vant til slike forhold enn henne. Hun var også urolig for onkel Torkel, men hun forsto at det nok ikke var så mye for henne å gjøre der. Det var best at det ikke kom for mange og uroet ham.

Resten av dagen hadde Mette vanskelig for å konsentrere seg om arbeidet hun holdt på med. Tankene var hele tiden på sykehuset hos den syke mannen. Hvor kritisk var det egentlig med ham? Hadde han mye vondt? Var han i det hele tatt bevisst? Ingenting av dette hadde hun kommet på å spørre om da de ringte fra sykehuset. Eller hvordan var det med hans åndelige liv? Heller ikke det hadde hun fått snakket med Morten om. Var han beredt til å dø? Det spørsmålet ble plutselig så viktig for henne der hun gikk fram og tilbake i stuen. Hendene hennes var hardt sammenkneppet. Bønn og tanker gikk om hverandre.

Onkel Torkel var en litt gretten og sta person, hadde hun forstått. Men det behøvde ikke bety at han hadde et vanskelig og grettent forhold til sin Gud. Riktignok oppfordrer Bibelen menneskene til å være gode og omsorgsfulle mot hverandre, men nå er det jo slik at vi mennesker er så forskjellige. Og når det gjelder spørsmålet om frelsen og det evige livet, så dømmes vi ikke ut fra hva slags gjerninger vi greier å prestere. Nei der er det kun forholdet til den Herre Jesus Kristus som teller. Den som har tatt imot Ham, og tror det Bibelen sier om Ham, den har løfter om å få del i den herlighet som loves etter at dette livet her på jorden er slutt.

Men hvis han nå ikke hadde ordnet med dette, hva da …? Hvis han ikke hadde brydd seg om Jesus i det hele tatt, og nå var bevisstløs. Kanskje han ikke kom til bevissthet igjen i det hele tatt, hva da? Mette grøsset der hun gikk. Mange slags groteske fremstillinger av helvete hadde hun sett og hørt om, men hun var slett ikke så sikker på at det var det rette bildet av fortapelsen. Men at der finnes en fortapelse, det visste hun at Bibelen sa. Hvordan den kom til å arte seg, var nok ikke så lett for menneskene å forstå, men en ting visste hun i hvert fall at Bibelen sa klart, og det var at der vil man være skilt fra Gud i all evighet.

Hvordan tilværelsen vil bli uten Gud, er det nok heller ikke lett for et menneske å forestille seg. Her i verden kan vi nok oppleve mye vondt og vanskelig, vi har jo de onde kreftene som hele tiden gjør seg gjeldende både inni oss og imellom oss, men Gud er her også og har en sterk innflytelse. Så hvordan vår verden hadde sett ut uten den innflytelsen, vil det nok heller ikke være så lett å se for seg.

En ting var i hvert fall Mette helt sikker på, og det var at det var uhyre viktig for menneskene å få ordnet sitt forhold til Gud mens de ennå levde i denne verden. Og hvor lenge de lever, er det ingen som vet noe om. Hvis ikke dette hadde vært så viktig, så hadde jo ikke Gud behøvd å gjøre så mye for å ordne denne frelsesveien som Bibelen forkynner om. Han hadde ikke behøvd å sende sin eneste sønn ned til denne onde jorden for å ta oppgjøret med synden. Han hadde ikke behøvd å sende sin sønn i døden for å ta den dødsstraffen som menneskene hadde pådratt seg ved sine synder og gale gjerninger mot Gud.

En bølge av takknemlighet skyllet med ett innover henne ved tanken på nettopp dette. Tenk at der ikke var noe hun behøvde å gjøre for å få denne frelsen annet enn å ta imot det som ble gjort den gangen på korset. De gale tingene hun hadde gjort, de som ble kalt synd, fortjente alle dødsstraff i Guds øyne. Denne straffen visste hun var ufravikelig, for ingen synd kan komme inn i Guds rike. Men denne dødsstraffen var det altså Jesus var villig til å ta i hennes sted. Alt som måtte gjøres, hadde Jesus gjort. Bare onkel Torkel også hadde forstått det, og så tatt imot det!

Tankene fortsatte å kretse mens tiden sneglet seg avsted. Etter hvert begynte hun å stelle til litt middag, men hun ante ingenting om når hun kunne vente Morten hjem igjen.

32 • Skjult smerte

Klokka var over åtte før en bildur utenfor huset fortalte at Morten var tilbake igjen fra sykehuset. Han virket sliten da han kom inn og satte seg ved kjøkkenbordet. Med en trett bevegelse dro han hånden gjennom det tykke, mørke håret. Dype rynker lå over de nesten svarte øynene. Mette så alvorlig på ham. «Hvordan står det til med onkel Torkel?» spurte hun spent. Morten ristet sakte på hodet. «Det ser ikke så bra ut. Marit blir hos ham i natt, men det er ikke sikkert han greier så mange timene til. Det viste seg at det var kreft, med spredning til lungene, som forårsaket lungebetennelsen. Han må ha gått med det en stund uten å ha vært klar over det. Når det nå ble lungebetennelse av det var der ikke så mye de kunne gjøre.»

Et dypt alvor preget hele atmosfæren der inne på kjøkkenet. Mette sa ikke mer. Hun fant bare fram noe mat til Morten. En lang stund ble de sittende der i taushet. Der var liksom så lite å si. Døden må jo komme en eller annen gang til alle, men når den kommer, er den ikke akkurat ventet, samme om alderen nok kan tilsi det.

Det var ikke før de skulle legge seg at Mette greide å komme fram med det spørsmålet som hadde kvernet rundt i hodet hennes hele dagen, det om den åndelige situasjonen for den gamle mannen. Morten tenkte seg om en stund før han svarte. «Nei, sannelig om jeg vet. Han var jo ikke akkurat så meddelsom når det gjaldt slike personlige ting, men jeg tror nok han hadde en viss respekt for det hellige. Han vokste i hvert fall opp i et kristent hjem, og fikk den oppdragelsen som hørte med. Men ... nei ... noe mer vet jeg dessverre ikke. I dag var han ikke i stand til å snakke i det hele tatt. Jeg vet ikke om han merket at vi var der, så vi fikk ikke snakke med ham om noe slikt.»

Mette sa ikke noe mer. Et tungt vemod fylte henne. Så viktig det var å ha de tingene klart før man kom så langt ... Hun sukket. Men der var jo selvsagt en mulighet for at han hadde forholdet i orden. Det var jo kun en sak mellom ham og Gud, og den var det ikke så lett for dem som mennesker å dømme om.

Tidlig neste formiddag kom Marit. Hun bar tydelig preg av å ha ei våkenatt bak seg. Det at det var en slik alvorlig situasjon, gjorde det ikke lettere, for hun kunne fortelle at onkel Torkel hadde sovnet stille inn utpå morgenkvisten.

332

Det ble med ett en hektisk aktivitet. Mange ting måtte ordnes, og beskjeder måtte gies både til den ene og den andre. Samtaler med både begravelsesbyrå og presten måtte også til. Heldigvis var det lørdag, så ingen trengte å tenke på at de måtte på jobb.

Begravelsen ble bestemt til onsdag uka etter. Marit var nok den som tok det meste av forberedelsene, men Mette og Morten hjalp til så godt de kunne.

Begravelsen forløp på tradisjonelt vis, men de hadde ingen minnestund etterpå. Seremonien ble bare avsluttet ved graven. Det var en litt kjølig dag, men snøen og slapset etter siste snøstorm hadde nesten forsvunnet. Marka og skogen begynte tydelig å lage seg til vår, selv om det ikke akkurat hadde begynt å spire så mye. Trekkfuglene var i hvert fall på plass med sitt yrende sangkor i liene. Bekkene gikk brusende og svulmende ned fra fjellet. Der oppe lå der enda igjen ganske mye snø, men den tinte godt dag for dag.

Da de gikk hjem igjen fra kirka, ble Mette stående en stund og se oppover mot fjellet i nord. Der oppe lå setra. En ilende følelse av spenning og forventning fôr gjennom henne med tanken på at nå nærmet det seg tiden da de kunne begynne å forberede seg på seterdrift igjen. De hadde snakket om det av og til, og hun gledet seg som et barn. Den alvorlige og dystre situasjonen de nettopp var kommet fra, greide ikke å kvele den yrende gleden som hun følte ved tanken på den forestående sommeren. Hun hadde ordnet det slik med jobben sin at hun skulle være permittert den tiden hun var på setra. Ikke minst gledet hun seg til å arbeide sammen med tante Anna igjen.

Den gamle tanta til Morten var like forventningsfull som henne, det visste hun. Rett som det var hadde Mette tatt seg en tur bort til henne for å slå av en prat. De bodde jo ikke så svært langt fra hverandre. Tante Anna hadde pratet og skravlet i vei på sin vanlige måte, og Mette hadde storkost seg. Mange planer hadde de allerede lagt for den forestående sesongen. Mat de skulle lage, og demonstrasjoner de skulle ha for turistene som kom for å besøke setra, var nøye gjennomgått.

Den gamle kvinna var nok ikke så sprek som hun engang hadde vært, det hadde Mette lagt merke til allerede året før, og bedre var hun nok ikke dette året. Men Mette hadde nå lært så mye av henne at hun kunne greie mye av arbeidet på egen hånd. Hun kom til å passe nøye på så det ikke skulle bli for hardt slit for henne. I mange tilfeller var det nok bare at hun var der og kunne gi veiledning og råd. Og var det noe tante Anna var flink til, så var det nettopp det. Munnen og hodet hennes så det i hvert fall ikke ut til å være noe i veien med ennå.

Dagene som fulgte ble igjen fylt med de vanlige gjøremålene. Mette hadde begynt å jobbe igjen. Rett som det var måtte hun ut på et møte, eller være med å arrangere en fest eller en barnesamling på et bedehus et eller annet sted i distriktet. Luften ble varmere og kveldene lysere for hver dag. Når hun var ute og gikk, måtte hun ofte bare stoppe opp for å trekke inn den friske vårluften. I hagene begynte vårblomstene å titte fram. Hjemme på Sørlandet hadde de nok blomstret lenge allerede. Her var allting mye senere, naturlig nok, men så gikk det mye fortere når det først begynte, syntes hun.

En ettermiddag møtte hun Marit på butikken. De pratet sammen en stund. «Det er nok best at vi får ryddet litt borte i Lia,» sa Marit idet hun skulle til å gå. «Jeg har snakket med Ellen, hun er villig til å hjelpe meg. Jeg tror vi tar en tur bort på lørdag for å se litt gjennom huset. Arveoppgjøret må jo også gjøres, men det kan vi sikkert ta litt etter hvert …» Hun nølte litt før hun fortsatte: «… men jeg skal ta meg av dette.» Det siste kom raskt og avgjort.

«Du kan da skjønne at vi blir med for å hjelpe, skulle bare mangle.» Mette ble ivrig.

«Nei, nei. Dette greier vi. Ikke tenk på det.» Marit ble nesten heftig. Et øyeblikk ble de stående å stirre på hverandre. Mette undret seg. Det virket nesten som om Marit helst ikke ville si til henne at de skulle gjøre dette. Men det var da like mye henne og Morten sin jobb som det var Marit sin. Det var de tre søsknene, Marit, Morten og Siri som var de nærmeste arvingene, hadde Mette forstått. Siri bodde i Trondheim med sin familie, så det var ikke så lett for henne å hjelpe til så mye. Derfor ble det Morten og Marit som måtte ta seg av det meste. Men det betydde jo ikke at Marit skulle gjøre alt.

«Jeg kan snakke med Morten om det,» sa Mette til slutt. Marit ble synlig urolig igjen. «Det behøver du slett ikke …» Så stoppet hun og tenkte seg om litt. «Ja, ja, du får gjøre som du vil,» sa hun trett. Dermed snudde hun og gikk.

Mette ble stående å se etter henne en stund i undring. Så rart hun hadde oppført seg. Hva kunne det bety? Det var nok best hun gikk hjem og snakket med Morten. Kanskje han kunne forklare det.

Det tok imidlertid lenger tid enn hun hadde regnet med før hun fikk snakket med ham om saken. Det skulle arrangere Tomasmesse i kirka samme lørdagskvelden, så Morten, som satt i menighetsrådet, var på møte der for å planlegge arrangementet. Det var ikke før han kom hjem fra jobb på fredag at hun fikk anledning til å nevne ryddingen borte i Lia. De satt ved kjøkkenbordet for å spise middag da hun plutselig kom på det. «Marit vil ta en tur bort til Lia for å rydde litt i huset. Jeg foreslo at vi kunne komme bort og hjelpe til. Vi må jo få det gjort snart.»

Morten hadde øst opp en diger porsjon med lapskaus på tallerkenen. Gaffelen hans stoppet halvveis til munnen, og falt ned igjen på tallerkenen. «Ja … vi må jo det … snart.» Stemmen hans var nesten ugjenkjennelig, hes og forpint. Ansiktet var på et øyeblikk blitt helt hvitt. Han pustet tungt et par ganger før han brått reiste seg, og nesten løp inn på kontoret.

Sjokkert og forvirret ble Mette sittende igjen ved bordet. Lapskausen hennes var også glemt. Inne fra kontoret kunne hun høre raske skritt som gikk fram og tilbake på gulvet. Der var noe galt … noe forferdelig galt. Men hun ante ikke hva det kunne være. Han hadde det vondt, det kunne hun forstå, men hva det var som smertet, hadde han aldri nevnt et ord om. Det kunne nesten se ut som om han var livende redd for noe.

Dette måtte sannsynligvis Marit ha kjennskap til. Kanskje hun trodde at Mette også kjente til det.

Plutselig følte hun seg liten og utenfor. Helt hjelpeløs ble hun sittende der ved bordet. Matlysten var helt borte. Minuttene gikk mens hun bare satt der. Situasjonen var blitt så underlig … skremmende var det. Helt som lammet satt hun der … ante ikke hva hun helst burde gjøre.

Plutselig reiste hun seg. «Nei, dette går ikke lenger,» sa hun bestemt til seg selv. Forsiktig gløttet hun på døra til kontoret. Morten sto foran vinduet, men hun var slett ikke sikker på om han så noe der ute. Ansiktet, ja hele skikkelsen så ut som om den var blitt tretti år elder på noen minutter. Smerten som tegnet seg i hvert trekk og hver muskel så ut som om den hvert øyeblikk kunne kvele ham.

«Hva er det …?» Stemmen hennes var bare en visking. Men den utrykte likevel en intensitet som kom fra hennes innerste sjel.

Morten reagerte øyeblikkelig og kom bort til henne. Han la begge hendene på skuldrene hennes og så henne dypt inn i øynene. Det var som om blikket hans tryglet henne om noe … om hjelp ? «Mette …!» Det ene ordet kom som et stønn. Før hun rakk å si noe la han en skjelvende arm rundt henne og ledet henne ut på kjøkkenet. Der satte han seg tungt ned ved bordet igjen. Mette satte seg ved siden av ham.

Han begynte ikke å spise. Maten var sikkert kald også nå.

Da han begynte å snakke var det nesten som om han var henført i en annen verden. Blikket var fjernt, og stemmen var svak og ustø..

«Det er snart fjorten år siden … vi skulle hjelpe onkel Torkel med noe høy. Vi var der alle sammen, mor, far, Siri, Marit, meg og … Even …» Stemmen hans døde helt hen. Musklene i kjevene arbeidet febrilsk. Han var helt askegrå i ansiktet.

Mette kjente at hun skalv. «Even …?» Spørsmålet kom bare som en hvisking. Hun greide ikke å si mer. Morten pustet tungt. Så var det som om han tok sats igjen og fortsatte. Hun visste ikke om han hadde hørt spørsmålet hennes, for han fortsatte som om han ikke var blitt avbrutt i det hele tatt.

«Det var varmt, og vi arbeidet hardt alle sammen. Ingen la merke til at Even ble borte. I hvert fall ikke før det hadde gått en tid … hvor lenge vet jeg ikke.

Da vi hadde ropt på ham noen ganger uten å få svar ,begynte vi å lete. En elleve år gammel gutt kunne da ikke bare bli borte sånn i løse luften …

Det var jeg som fant ham.» To store tårer begynte å renne nedover det forpinte ansiktet. Kniven og gaffelen ble knuget inni hendene hans så knokene hvitnet. Mette svelget, men hun sa ingenting.

Da Morten fortsatte, var det som om noe løsnet litt. Stemmen ble klarere, men den skalv, og tårene rant fritt. «Det var min skyld. Jeg skulle ha advart ham, for jeg visste om det råtne lokket over den gamle brønnen. Han hadde falt gjennom. I fallet må han ha slått hodet mot en stein og besvimt, for ellers hadde han sikkert greid å komme seg opp. I hvert fall hadde han kunnet rope om hjelp.

Han lå med hodet under i vann. Jeg fikk ham ganske raskt opp, men det var for sent …»

Mette hadde reist seg. Hun la varsomt begge armene rundt halsen til den kjære mannen sin, og sank ned på fanget hans. Han la armene sine rundt livet hennes, boret ansiktet inn mot den skjelvende kroppen hennes, mens hulkene kom i såre hikst.

Å, hvilken smerte han hadde lidd i alle disse årene. Ikke en gang til henne hadde han nevnt dette før. Ikke en eneste gang hadde han nevnt Even. Dette var første gang hun hørte om ham. Ingen av de andre i familien hadde heller nevnt noe om ham … ikke engang den skravlete tante Anna. Mette følte smerten dypt inn i sitt eget indre. Håret hans ble vått av tårene hennes.

Etter en stund kjente hun at kroppen hans slappet litt av. «Kanskje vi skulle prøve å spise litt,» sa han med et skjelvende smil. Mette smilte også til ham. «Ja, la oss gjøre det.» Hun strøk ham over kinnet og det kortklipte skjegget, og kysset varsomt de våte øynene, før hun reiste seg og satte seg på plassen sin igjen. Aldri hadde hun sett ham så vakker som i dette øyeblikket. De var med ett kommet hverandre så inderlig nær ved denne betroelsen. Mette kjente mannen sin så godt at hun skjønte hva det hadde kostet ham å snakke om dette. Men du verden så glad hun var for at han hadde gjort det.

Det virket nesten som om en mur var brutt, ikke bare imellom dem, men også i Mortens indre. Mens de spiste den kalde lapskausen, fortsatte Morten å snakke. Han fortalte om foreldrene som hadde sørget dypt etter at Even døde, og hvordan han selv hele tiden hadde følt at det var hans skyld som ikke hadde advart Even mot den farlige brønnen. Etter det hadde han nesten ikke greid å dra bort til Lia i det hele tatt. Bare tanken på den lille gården der borte fikk det til å snøre seg helt til inni ham.

Han snakket også om faren som døde så altfor tidlig av hjerteinfarkt, og moren som hadde vært sykelig i lang tid etter dette, før også hun for noen få år siden døde. «Jeg tror hun sørget seg syk,» avsluttet han stille.

Selv om Morten endelig hadde greid å snakke om dette, så Mette at han fortsatt hadde det svært vondt. Hun led med ham, men visste ikke helt hva hun skulle gjøre eller si. At Marit også hadde det vondt, kunne hun jo godt forstå, men det virket ikke som hun hadde det like vanskelig i forhold til Lia. Det var likevel tydelig at hun visste om hvordan Morten hadde det. Nå forsto Mette godt hvorfor hun hadde reagert som han hadde gjort.

Nei, Mette kom ikke til å presse Morten til å være med på rydding i Lia. Det måtte han gjøre som han selv følte for. Men det var vondt å tenke på at han skulle gå og lide slik. På en eller annen måte burde han få bearbeidet denne sorgen slik at han kunne greie å forholde seg til disse tingene på en mer avslappet måte.

33 • Det mørke hullet

Selv om Mette våknet ganske tidlig neste morgen, var Morten allerede stått opp. Om det var fordi det var lørdag, og hans ansvar å stelle dyrene i fjøset, eller det var andre grunner til at han ikke fikk sove, det visste hun ikke. Hun skyndte seg bare å få på seg klærne, og gå ned på kjøkkenet. Der satt Morten med kaffekoppen og stirret ut av vinduet. Han så på henne og smilte da hun kom inn, men så var han tilbake i sine egne tanker igjen. Mette sa ingenting. Hun begynte bare å stelle til frokost til seg selv. Morten hadde allerede spist, kunne hun se. Det var tydelig at noe arbeidet hardt inni ham. De mørke skyene over ansiktet var ikke helt borte. Nei, gårsdagens hendelse satt nok ennå dypt i ham. Så viktig det var, tenkte Mette, at sorg ble bearbeidet så tidlig som mulig. Ubearbeidede følelser kunne lett få slike konsekvenser. Hvis det bare ble stengt inne, eller dysset ned i taushet, så ble det liggende der like friskt. Det var som en hermetikkboks. Så lenge den var lukket og uåpnet, så kunne det virke som det var helt dødt og borte. Men med en gang man begynte å pirke litt hull på den, så var innholdet akkurat like friskt som da det ble lagt ned. Disse følelsene til Morten var akkurat like friske og vonde nå når det ble «pirket bort i dem» som de var da det vonde skjedde.

Plutselig reiste Morten seg. Han drakk opp den siste kaffeslurken fra koppen og gikk mot døra. «Jeg blir med bort i Lia i dag,» sa han idet han åpnet døra. «Jeg må bare ta fjøsstellet først.» Så lukket han døra og gikk.

Mette satt igjen i undring, men hun var glad for at han ville gjøre dette. Kanskje det kunne være med på å lette ham litt for alt det vonde som hadde plaget ham så lenge. Eller … hun ble alvorlig igjen. Kanskje det bare ville gjøre det enda verre for ham? Nei, dette måtte han bare gjøre som han selv ville med. Hun visste slett ikke hva som ville være det beste for ham. Litt nervøs begynte hun å vaske opp etter frokosten mens hun ventet på at Morten skulle komme inn igjen fra fjøset.

De dagene han ikke var på jobb, var det han som stelte de dyrene de hadde i fjøset. Ellers hadde han en grei avtale med naboen, Petter. Når Morten var på jobb, var det Petter som stelte dyrene for ham. Eller rettere sagt sønnen hans. Mette hadde sagt at hun godt kunne gjøre det når hun var hjemme, hun var jo så ofte i fjøset likevel. Rett som det var måtte hun ut og se til dyrene, og kose litt med dem. Og hadde hun noen matrester som hun visste at de likte, så var hun ikke sen om å gå med det til dem.

Men Morten hadde sagt at det arbeidet ville svært gjerne sønnen til Petter ha, for da tjente han de kronene.

Det var ikke vanlig seterdrift Morten drev med. Driften hans var kun for å vise turister hvordan seterlivet var i gamle dager. Mengder av turister, skoleklasser og leirskoleklasser kom opp dit gjennom hele sommeren og til langt ut på høsten. Det var til denne setra Mette hadde kommet sommeren før etter å ha søkt på en jobb hun fant avertert i en avis. Denne jobben tenkte hun måtte være den ideelle avveksling for henne, derfor hadde hun søkt permisjon fra jobben sin og reist til fjells for sommeren. Hun hadde ingen anelse om hvem det var hun kom til. Egentlig trodde hun at det var et gammelt ektepar hun skulle arbeide for, men så viste det seg altså at det var Morten som var bonden der. Og så var det tante Anna, søster til Mortens far, som sto for mye av arbeidet. Siden tante Anna var blitt så pass gammel og skrøpelig at hun vanskelig kunne greie alt arbeidet med dyrene, demonstrasjonene de hadde for turistene, og matlagingen, hadde han søkt etter mer hjelp.

Så hadde altså dette hendt. Hun smilte for seg selv. Hun hadde greid å forelske seg i denne bonden med det samme hun så ham.

Men den dramatikken ville hun ikke tenke på nå. Det hadde vært både godt og vondt. Nå var i hvert fall alt godt mellom dem. Bare nå også Morten kunne få det så godt at han greide å forholde seg naturlig til de vonde tingene fra fortiden.

Litt ut på formiddagen dro de begge oppover mot Lia. De kjørte i taushet. Mette kjente at hun var anspent i hele kroppen. Det var tydelig å merke at også Morten slet hardt.

Nå som det var bart for snø, kunne de kjøre helt bort til huset. Det sto en bil der fra før, så de forsto at Marit og Ellen allerede var kommet.

Morten gikk raskt ut av bilen, men han gikk ikke rett mot kjøkkendøra. I stedet gikk han mot skogen i enden av uthuset. Mette fulgte tett etter. Under noen trær der i bakken fikk hun se en stor haug med stein og stokker. Morten begynte å lempe vekk stein etter stein. Mette sto og så på i dirrende taushet. Hun skjønt bare så altfor godt hva det var. Der var brønnen …

Snart kom noen bølgeblikkplater til syne. Flere stykker lå oppå hverandre. Skal si den brønnen var godt sikret … men hun forsto jo godt hvorfor. Morten begynte å lempe bort platene. Før han tok bort de siste ble han stående litt. Mette svelget. Hun hadde mest lyst til å løpe vekk … snart ville et mørkt hull komme til syne … ville hun greie det. Og Morten … hvordan ville han reagere …?

Stiv av spenning så hun på da han løftet bort den siste platen. Hun gikk et par skritt nærmere. Et mørkt hull gapte imot dem. Hun kjente at hun ble kvalm. Morten sto stille og stirret ned i mørket. Hun så at han skalv. Et par snufs gjorde henne oppmerksom på at tårene hans rant fritt. Heller ikke hun greide å holde dem tilbake.

Over trekronene strålte sola. Den vakre vårdagen med fuglesang oppover lia, og yrende liv som spratt og spirte rundt dem på alle kanter, hadde de ikke syn for i det hele tatt. En frosk kvekket og hoppet bort mellom det visne løvet. Et vrimlende hav av maur strevde med hyttebyggingen sin like i nærheten. Ingen ting av dette … vårens under av nytt liv og vekst … ble registrert av de to som sto der og stirret ned i det svarte hullet. Det var døden de så der. Det var døden deres sinn, tanker og følelser var fullstendig preget av. En liten gutt på elleve år som hadde lekt og moret seg der en vakker som-

337

merdag ... og så med ett var det slutt ... det friske, sprudlende ungdomslivet ... det var med ett over ... der nede i mørket ...

Plutselig begynte Morten å bevege seg igjen. Sakte gikk han ut på brønnkanten, bøyde seg og begynte å klatre ned i mørket. Helt til bunns klatret han. Der nede hadde han vært en gang før ... Mette holdt pusten. I noen lange sekunder så hun bare hodet hans der nede. Blikket hans så ut til å saumfare hver stein og krok i den dystre graven ... graven, ja det var akkurat det hun følte at det var. Et gufs av våt, innestengt jord slo mot henne da hun strakte seg over kanten for å se bedre. Et dryss av tørt løv og rusk raste i det samme ned i dypet og traff Morten over skulderen, men han enset det ikke. Der bøyde han seg ned og strøk hånden over en stein. Det var så vidt hun kunne skimte konturene av bunnen og steinene oppover langs sidene, men Morten hadde tydeligvis ingen problemer med å skjelne den ene fra den andre. Den steinen ... En gang var den dekket av blod. Noe hardt hadde truffet den ... Resultatet ble skjebnesvangert. Den gang var det vann der nede, men den steinen hadde ikke stått under vann. Den hadde båret tydelig merke etter sammenstøtet. Morten hadde fortalt det i detalj. Han husket alt som om det skulle ha vært i går. Det virket som om bildet fra den dype brønnen var klistret til netthinnen hans med tindrende klare farger i detaljert nøyaktighet.

Dette var et viktig øyeblikk. Hun visste det. Ikke med en lyd ville hun forstyre ham i det som han nå gjennomgikk. Hvordan opplevde han det tro? Mette trakk seg stille tilbake mens hun ventet i intens spenning. Sekundene tikket og gikk, men hun følte at hun ikke hadde noe begrep om tid og klokke. Stillheten ble bare brutt av en svak susing i løvverket over dem, og den ivrige fuglekvitringen oppover i lia. Hun følte det nesten som om hele verden sto stille de lange minuttene til lyden av Mortens klatring oppover brønnkanten igjen kunne høres.

Da han kom opp, satte han seg på marka et lite stykke unna brønnen. Mette satte seg ved siden av ham. Han la armen rundt henne, men utrykket i øynene hans var ikke så mørkt lenger. Blikket hans søkte oppover mot de ruvende trekronene over hodet på dem. Noen klare solstråler banet seg vei gjennom de tette grenene og traff dem der de satt.

«Der oppe ... et sted over solstrålene ... der er Even nå.» Stemmen til Morten var svak, men den var lys og stø. «Han er hos Jesus nå. Han var ikke der nede i brønnen ... jeg så det ... blodet var også borte ...»

Et underlig smil la seg over ansiktet mens tårene fortsatte å renne. «Der er visst ingen grunn til å frykte for den lenger.» Det siste kom som et sukk, mer til seg selv enn til henne.

Sakte ristet han på hodet mens han rotet med en pinne i marka. «Jeg mente at døden hørte de gamle til. De unge, og i hvert fall barna, skulle leve.» Ordene hans rant liksom ut av ham der han satt. Mette sa ikke noe. Hun la bare hodet mot skulderen hans og knuget den ene hånden hans mellom begge sine mens tårene hennes fortsatte å renne.

«Jeg kunne ikke begripe,» fortsatte han, «at Gud kunne være med på noe slikt. Nei, det var lenge jeg mente at Han slett ikke var det heller. Det hele hadde skjedd kun fordi jeg hadde vært så tankeløs at jeg ikke kom med noen slags advarsler om faren her inne mellom trærne.

Og da jeg så hvordan mor og far sørget ... ja søsknene mine også for den sak skyld, så ...» Stemmen døde hen. Blikket søkte mot brønnen igjen. Tausheten senket seg atter over stedet.

Mette så på ham. Den inderlige kjærlighet hun følte for denne mannen gjorde at hun sanset hvert ord han sa men hver fiber i sin egen kropp. Alt han sa opplevdes nesten som en intens fysisk smerte for henne.

Forsiktig strøk hun ham over kinnet mens hun forsiktig spurte: «Mener du fremdeles at det er din skyld det som hendte?»

Han svarte ikke med det samme. Satt bare og stirret ut i luften en stund. Så snudde han seg brått mot henne og svarte med et svakt smil: «Nei. Jeg mener ikke det er min skyld. Jeg vet også at det ikke er det. Det føles bare slik. Men nå vil jeg forsøke å la vissheten få overtaket over følelsene. Håper bare det vil lykkes.» Det siste kom som et sukk.

Enda en stund ble de sittende før de reiste seg for å legge platene og hele haugen med stein og stokker over brønnen igjen. Ingen skulle få sjanse til å falle ned i den, verken folk eller dyr.

Da arbeidet var unnagjort ble de igjen stående å se på den store haugen med stein og stokker. Mette knuget seg inntil Morten. Han holdt også et godt tak rundt henne. De søkte liksom trøst og trygghet i hverandre der de sto og så på den store haugen foran seg. I hjelpeløs svakhet sto de der. Men også med en visshet om at de, i deres svakhet, var i hendene på en allmektig Gud. At han var en god og inderlig kjærlig Gud, det var de ikke i tvil om. Men hans veier var av og til nokså ubegripelige for dem som menneske.

Plutselig snudde Morten seg. «Jeg må se å få gravd igjen dette hullet,» sa han med fast beslutsomhet. Den brukes jo ikke lenger likevel. De snudde seg og begynte å gå tilbake mot huset igjen.

Da ble de oppmerksomme på to skikkelser som sto på baktrappen. Det var Marit og Ellen. De sto helt stille. Men da Mette og Morten kom nærmere, så de at begge to var helt oppløst i tårer. De forsto godt hva som hadde foregått der oppe i skogkanten denne formiddagen. Det hadde vært et viktig øyeblikk, ikke bare for Morten, men også for søsteren og venninnen hennes. Begge disse hadde jo også vært stekt involvert i tragedien. Kanskje dette kunne bære bud om en lysere og lettere fremtid for dem alle, i hvert fall når det var snakk om minnet etter Even.

Lenge ble de tre sittende på kjøkkenet og snakke sammen. Der var så mye usnakket. Endelig var der kommet et lite hull på den vonde byllen. Kanskje den verken som hadde samlet seg der gjennom disse årene snart nå kunne bli renset ut. Minnet etter Even ville nok alltid være der som noe sårt og trist, men den låste og tillukkede smerten ville kanskje nå kunne bli borte.

Mette tok seg en tur rundt i huset for å se seg litt om. Hun ville la dem få ha denne stunden alene for seg selv. De trengte å prate sammen … de tre der … alene.

34 • Endelig farvel

Det gamle huset var virkelig verdt en oppdagelsesferd. Selv om tankene hennes var nokså oppskaket etter formiddagens begivenhet, ble hun likevel fort oppslukt av alle de interessante tingene som fantes der i Lia. Gamle, forseggjorte møbler i alle rom. Det meste var sikkert håndlaget en eller annen gang i fortiden. Kister, skap og stoler i solid treverk. En stor himmelseng med en nydelig kommode ved siden av sto inne på et av værelsene i andre etasje. Det sto også en vaskevannsstol med fat og mugge i vakkert, mønstret porselen. Under senga sto ei nattpotte i samme stil. Mette måtte smile. Her var jammen alt på plass.

I rommet ved siden av fant hun ei stor rosemalt kiste. Nysgjerrig åpnet hun det tunge, buede lokket. Den var full av sengetøy og gamle duker. Forsiktig løftet hun opp en hvit, stor linduk. Den var håndsydd, kunne hun se. Et nydelig arbeid i hardangersøm. Hun ble bare stående og stirre da hun brettet den ut. Her hadde flittige hender arbeidet tålmodig i pinlig nøyaktighet. Huller og bitte små knuter var strødd utover tett i tett. Tenk om hun selv kunne ha lært denne kunsten. Hun sukket. Det hadde vært moro, men hun hadde vel ikke hatt nok tålmodighet til å fullføre et slikt arbeid.

Forsiktig brettet hun den sammen igjen og la den på plass. Så åpnet hun lokket på leddiken, det lille rommet i enden av kista. Enda mer nysgjerrig ble hun stående og stirre. Den var fylt av en mengde gamle gulnede brev. Hun tok opp et par og kikket på adressene. Til Maren Lia sto det. Mette visste at Maren var mormor til Morten, og gift med bror til onkel Torkel. Forsiktig snudde hun den skjøre konvolutten for å se på avsenderen. Gunhild sto det der. Etternavnet kunne hun ikke tyde skikkelig, men det var i hvert fall sendt fra Amerika. Varsomt løftet hun opp ei bunke av brevene. Det måtte være nærmere hundre av dem. Alle var sendt fra Amerika, men noen var adressert til Tomine. Mette visste ikke hvem det kunne være, men poststempelet viste at de eldste var rundt åtti år gamle.

Dette var interessant, Mette glemte helt tid og sted. Brev etter brev tok hun fram og la dem på et lite bord som sto ved siden av kista. Nederst i leddiken lå ei bunke som var bundet sammen med en hyssing. De brevene så ut til å være enda eldre enn de andre. Hun åpnet ikke hyssingen, men så bare på adressene. Også disse var sendt fra Amerika, men navnene var ikke de samme. Til Gunhild sto det, men det måtte være en annen Gunhild, for datostempelet var mye tidligere. Avsenderen på det bakerste brevet var Theodor Evensen Lia. Og det var sendt fra Nord Dakota.

Noe så spennende! Hun hadde ikke hørt noe om at de hadde slekt i Amerika. Dette måtte hun snakke med Morten og Marit om. Hun tok alle brevene og pakket dem forsiktig inn i et håndkle som hun fant i kista, for disse ville hun ha med seg hjem og studere nærmere.

Da hun kom ned i første etasje igjen, var de tre andre i full gang med arbeidet. Ellen ryddet ut gamle matvarer og ting i kjøkkenet som bare måtte kastes. Marit holdt på med noen klær. Det meste av dem måtte også bare kastes. Morten var inne i stuen og gikk gjennom en del papirer i et gammelt skatoll.

«Jeg må bare se gjennom dette. Kanskje her er verdisaker og papirer som vi må vare på,» sa han da Mette kom inn. «Booppgjør, med deling og slikt, må vi ta senere. Siri må jo også være med på det.»

«Hvor mange arvinger er det?» spurte Mette.

«Det er bare oss tre søsken,» svarte han. «Onkel Torkel hadde ingen barn. Og bror hans, som altså var min morfar, hadde bare mor. Der er ingen annen slekt etter dem.»

Det ble en travel dag. Ute på gårdsplassen tente de opp et bål hvor de brente alt rot og rusk som ikke kunne brukes, eller hadde noen verdi. Alle verdisaker, både inne i huset og ute i uthuset, ble omhyggelig plassert på steder hvor de kunne låses inne. Alle arbeidet iherdig, så det var ikke fritt for at de var ganske slitne da de kjørte hjemover utpå ettermiddagen.

Det var ikke før de satt hjemme i stuen igjen at Mette fikk anledning til å nevne brevene. Hun hadde tatt med seg håndklepakken da de dro. Morten ble også forbauset da han så alle de gamle amerikabrevene. Mette brettet ut håndkleet på spisebordet. Morten tok opp et brev og studerte det i taushet. Så tok kan opp et brev til, snudde og vendte på de, før han dro ut arket som lå inni konvolutten.

«Dette var litt overraskende,» sa han da han hadde lest en stund. «Når jeg tenker meg om, husker jeg nok at mor fortalte om noen gamle slektninger som reiste over til Amerika på begynnelsen av århundret, men jeg tror ikke hun hadde noe forbindelse med noen der borte. Dette er et brev fra hennes tante. Hun het visst Gunhild. Faktisk trodde jeg at hun hadde en tvillingsøster som også reiste over, men jeg husker ikke hva hun het.

Uansett, dette er så gamle ting at der er nok ingen av dem som lever lenger. Vi får studere mer på det senere. Nå er jeg trett. Skal jeg komme meg på Tomasmesse i kveld er det best jeg slenger meg nedpå litt.» Mette følte også for en hvil etter dagens strabaser. Messen begynte jo ikke før klokka åtte.

○ ○ ○

Mette trakk inn den friske vårluften i fulle drag da hun gikk ved siden av Morten langs bygdeveien mot kirka. De gikk hånd i hånd og nøt freden og roen omkring dem. Kvelden var lys og stille. Langs veikanten sto hvitveisene og nikket med sine lyse hoder, og selja raget opp over krattet med et dryss av grågule gåsunger. Knoppene på bjørka sto bristeferdige og ventet på at gradestokken skulle krype enda et par grader oppover. På fjelltoppene i nord lå ennå snøen som ei hvit kappe og gjenspeilte de siste strålene fra sola som var i ferd med å finne ei lagelig kløft å dale ned i der borte i vest. Hele bygda lå liksom i spent forventning mot den store forvandlingen som snart ville skje. Liv i skog og mark, så vel som i hage og åker, ville snart omdanne alle disse omgivelsene til et fantastisk frodige mangfold.

Bil etter bil kjørte forbi dem der de gikk. Det så ut til å komme mange til kirka denne fine vårdagen. I det samme ble hun oppmerksom på ansiktet til Morten. Det hadde fått noe av det dystre og tunge over seg igjen. Stakkars mann, han tenkte nok fremdeles på hendelsen borte i Lia. Dette var nok ikke ting som bare kunne viskes bort slik i en fei. Det ville nok ta litt tid, men hun var overbevist om at han ville få det bedre nå etter at han hadde greid å åpne seg litt om dette.

Inne i kirka ble de møtt av en ekstra hellig og fin stemning. Orgelet spilte mens folk samlet seg, og midt i krysset sto den store lysgloben. I midten brant et stort lys, og rundt, i kransen omkring, sto det små lys klar til å bli tent av dem som på den måten ønsket å konkretisere sin bønn og sine følelser for Gud.

På alteret var også lysene tent. De sto der og lyste opp den vakre altertavlen som hadde stått der og prydet den gamle stokkebygde korskirken i snart to hundre år. Her hadde Morten blitt døpt og konfirmert, og her hadde de to også blitt viet for bare noen uker siden. Men mange flere begivenheter enn dette hadde disse tykke stokkeveggene vært vitne til. Her hadde både mor og far til Morten blitt døpt og konfirmert, og siden viet. Også de som for over åtti år siden reiste over til Amerika, hadde en gang blitt båret til dåpen i denne kirken, gikk hun ut fra. De aller fleste som bodde i bygda hadde på en eller annen måte vært innom disse dørene i et for dem betydningsfullt ærende. Og fra koret der framme hadde Even for fjorten år side blitt båret ut mot ei grav et eller annet sted på utsiden. Hun måtte spørre Morten hvor den graven lå. Kanskje de kunne besøke den sammen en gang … Hun håpet i hvert fall det.

Tause satte de seg ned på en benk midt i kirkeskipet. Snart begynte seremonien. Hele menigheten reiste seg da presten, sammen med en del andre medhjelpere, kom inn i høytidelig prosesjon. Orgelet satte i gang sitt brusende tonevell, og menigheten stemte i med åpningssalmen. Den vakre sangen fylte hele det store rommet og hevet seg helt opp under den mektige hvelvingen under taket.

Så snart tonene døde hen, gikk presten fram i kordøren og ønsket menigheten velkommen. Før han begynte på liturgien, forklarte han litt om hvordan denne spesielle messen skulle foregå. Det var særlig forbønnsdelen som var litt utenom det vanelige. De kom til å bruke en god del tid på den. Da ville menigheten få anledning til å bevege seg fritt rundt i kirkerommet. Det var satt opp stasjoner på forskjellige steder hvor de som ønsket det, kunne gå for å be eller søke forbønn. Et sted kunne de skrive en lapp med bønneemner og legge den i ei skål. Presten ville etterpå be for det som var skrevet der. Så ville lappene bli brent. Ved lysgloben kunne de tenne et lys og be for det som opptok dem. Og ved alterringen kunne de komme og knele ned. Presten ville da be for dem med håndspåleggelse.

Hele denne tiden ville selvsagt også den enkelte bare kunne sitte stille i benken og be for seg selv.

Så begynte han på liturgien som også var litt spesiell. Den ble framført som en fin veksling mellom liturg og menighet.

Mette satt og kjente på en stille fred i sitt indre. Det var godt å kunne sette seg ned der og motta det gode budskapet om hjelp og trøst for dem som lider. Akkurat dette med lidelse var noe hun følte at hadde kommet henne litt for nær denne dagen. Hvordan Morten følte det, visste hun ikke. Han satt bare der i dypt alvor.

Da det ble invitert til forbønnshandling, var det straks noen som reiste seg og gikk bort til lysgloben. I taushet ble de små lysene tent ett etter ett. Snart var det flere som fulgte etter. En stille strøm av folk begynte å bevege seg rundt i rommet. Orgelet spilte. De myke tonene fløt liksom rundt og mellom dem alle sammen. Mette satt med fold-ede hender. Hun følte at hun ikke helt greide å forme tankene til konkrete bønner, men hele hennes indre var vendt mot Gud i et eneste rop … et rop om hjelp og trøst for dem.

Plutselig reiste Morten seg. Sakte begynte han å bevege seg bort mot lysgloben. Mette reiste seg også og fulgte med. Foran lysene ble han stående stille et øyeblikk. Hele ansiktsuttrykket viste at det var noe vondt som lå sterkt på ham. Med ei skjel-vende hånd tok han et lite lys og holdt det bort mot det store for å få fyr på det. Mette visste bare så inderlig godt hva som rørte seg inni ham. Hun sto bare der … ved siden av ham. Ville bare være der nå … være nær ham. Da lyset var tent, ble han enda stående litt. Han tok hånden hennes og klemte den hardt, men blikket var hele tiden vendt mot lysflammen. Det skalv rundt munnen hans, og øyenbrynene var trukket helt sammen i et krampaktig drag.

Med ett begynte han å gå igjen mens han hele tiden holdt henne i hånden. Hun fulgte med. Han slapp ikke hånden hennes før han sank ned på kne ved alterringen. Der

342

bøyde han seg frem og gjemte ansiktet i hendene. Mette knelte stille ned ved siden av. I det samme var presten der. «Er det noe spesielt dere vil jeg skal be om?» spurte han med lav, vennlig stemme. Det tok litt tid før Morten greide å svare. Men så kom det som et hulk: «Even …» Det var det eneste han greide å si. I det samme la Mette merke til en skikkelse som sank ned på den andre siden av Morten. Det var Marit. Hun gjorde ingen forsøk på å skjule tårene.

Fra øyekroken fikk Mette i et glimt se ansiktet til presten. Det ene ordet fra Morten var tydeligvis mer enn nok. Presten var en aldrende mann som hadde vært der i menigheten i mange år. Han kjente Morten og familien hans svært godt. Og spesielt tragedien med Even kjente han til. Det var han som hadde forrettet ved begravelsen.

Nå sto han der tydelig beveget og kjempet med noe nede i halsen. Øynene var blanke og munnen skalv. Morten skalv også der han lå. Mette kjente at noe dirret langt inne i henne selv også. Hennes tårer var allerede i ferd med å bløte opp det vakre skinnet som alterringen var polstret med.

Da presten endelig fikk så pass kontroll over stemmen at han kunne begynne å be, var det underlig å merke den trøst, omsorg og medfølelse han greide å formidle ved bønnen sin. Og for Mette føltes det som om Gud selv sa de trøstende ordene. Ja … det var vel egentlig slik det var. Gud var der hos dem i det øyeblikket. Han var dem nær, ikke fordi de tilfeldigvis var der i kirken, men fordi de hadde søkt hen til Ham med sin sorg og nød. Han avviste dem ikke, eller forholdt seg taus og likegyldig, nei han var der … og han led med dem, det var hun sikker på. Der lå de alle tre og gråt ut sin sorg for Gud. Men Mette var sikker på at det var flere enn dem som gråt. Hun husket jo beretningen om Marta, Maria og Lasarus. Da Jesus kom til dem, var Lasarus allerede død, og søstrene gråt. Jesus kom for å vekke Lasarus til live igjen, men likevel delte han sorgen med de to søstrene. Han gråt sammen med dem.

Nå var Even i himmelen sammen med Jesus og hadde det godt, men Jesus så allikevel de som var tilbake i sorg og savn. Han følte med dem, det var hun overbevist om, og hun var sikker på at han nå gråt sammen med dem.

Da de reiste seg etter bønnen, la Morten et øyeblikk en arm rundt hver av dem og klemte til. Så gikk de tilbake til plassene sine igjen.

Etterpå var det nattverd. Det var så godt å være der og ta imot brødet og vinen. Enda et konkret tegn på Jesu nærhet. Mette så på den fulle ringen med knelende nattverdgjester. Det var bare en halv sirkel der foran alteret. Men hun visste at dette egentlig skulle symbolisere enheten med dem som allerede var reist foran inn i evigheten med Jesus. I dette øyeblikket lå der en full sirkel med knelende nattverd - gjester. Den andre delen av sirkelen var i himmelen, og der lå Even. Han var der … sammen med dem … i nattverdmåltidet.

Da messen var over, ble de stående litt utenfor kirken. Marit var der sammen med dem, men ingen sa noe særlig. Alle var ennå preget av den sterke opplevelsen de hadde hatt. Det var som om de var redde for at den hellige fornemmelsen skulle forsvinne for raskt hvis de begynte å snakke.

Plutselig begynte Morten å gå bortover kirkegården. Han stoppet ved ei grav borte ved muren. Mette og Marit fulgte med. Det var Evens grav. Morten knelte ned og stelte litt med det allerede plettfrie gravstedet.

«Nå tror jeg endelig jeg kan greie å si farvel til Even,» sa han. Selv om ordene kom stille og forsiktig, var det likevel noe trygt og solid over det han sa. Han gråt ikke lenger, og ansiktet hadde også fått et lysere og lettere preg.

Marit tørket bort noen tårer mens hun snufset. «Å, så glad jeg er for dette,» sa hun. «Det har vært så vondt å se hvordan du led.»

Det ble heller ikke sagt så mye da de gikk hjemover, men den befriende atmosfæren de følte, bar bud om lysere tider, og fornyet styrke, om nye motganger skulle komme.

35 • Amerikabrevene

Over hele det store spisebordet i stua lå det gamle amerikabrev. Mette hadde sortert dem etter stemplingsdato og avsenderadresse. De aller fleste var skrevet av Gunhild. Men det var også noen fra ei som het Tomine, eller Mina som hun også av og til kalte seg. Mette gikk ut fra at det var den tvillingsøstera som Morten hadde snakket om. Bunken med de eldste brevene, de som var bundet sammen, hadde hun ikke åpnet ennå. Det var best å gjøre dette systematisk, tenkte hun, og ta litt av gangen.

Dypt konsentrert satt hun i sofaen og leste. Med ett var hun forflyttet over åtti år tilbake i tiden. En hel livshistorie brettet seg ut for øynene på henne etter hvert som hun la det ene brevet etter det andre fra seg igjen. Skriften var ikke alltid så lett å forstå, men som regel forsto hun meningen av sammenhengen.

En merkelig følelse fylte henne der hun satt. Alle disse brevene var blitt omhyggelig lest og tatt vare på. De fleste var skrevet til Tomine, eller mor som hun skrev. Ei mor som hadde opplevd å se sin to barn reise. Der hjemme satt de igjen med vissheten om at de kanskje aldri ville få se hverandre mer. Hva et morshjerte måtte føle, kan man vel knapt forestille seg. Ikke rart at denne brevskatten var blitt så omhyggelig og kjærlig tatt vare på. Det var det eneste de hadde igjen etter barna sine. Det eneste tegn på at der tross alt var et liv som pulserte og virket langt borte på den andre siden av det store havet. Men liv … Mette stusset litt. Hvordan ble det med det etter hvert, tro. Da hun snakket med Morten om dette dagen før, så hadde han ment at de antakelig var døde, og at det ikke kunne være noe mer slekt etter dem siden kontakte etter hvert var blitt helt brutt. At Tomine og Gunhild var døde, gikk hun ut fra. De måtte jo ellers ha vært hundre år nå, men var det så sikkert at det ikke var barn igjen etter dem … eller barnebarn?

Sannsynligvis hadde Morten rett i sitt resonnement, men Mette kunne ikke fri seg fra tanken på en annen mulighet. Det var derfor hun så systematisk ville gå gjennom disse brevene. Her måtte jo svaret i tilfelle ligge.

Det var ikke bare av egen nysgjerrighet hun ville gjøre dette. Det var like mye for å få avklart slektsforholdene. Tenk om de etter en stund skulle finne ut at de hadde gjort en fatal feil, for hvis der fantes slekt borte i Amerika, så var jo de berettiget å få en arv etter onkel Torkel. Og etter hva hun forsto på Morten, så var ikke den så rent liten. Det var ikke bare gården og eiendelene hans det var verdi i, men han hadde faktisk også spart seg opp penger. En del salg av attraktive hyttetomter i fjellet hadde spedd godt på formuen, og så hadde han visst vært så frisk og sprek helt til det siste, at han hadde hogget en masse ved for salg hvert år. Den gamle mannen hadde slett ikke greid å bruke opp særlig mye av det han hadde tjent. Det var ikke bare sta og bestemt den enslige gubben i Lia hadde vært. En god porsjon gjerrighet hadde han også vært kjent for. På seg selv hadde han ikke brukt mer enn det aller nødvendigste.

Etter hvert som Mette leste, ble en ny verden og en annen tilværelse åpnet for henne. Tomine og Gunhild hadde reist over til Amerika i 1921. Forholdene hjemme var vanskelige for unge mennesker, og ryktet om et eventyr der borte på det store kontinentet over havet fristet visst de fleste. Disse to jentene hadde tatt av sted allerede som attenåringer. Men de reiste ikke bare på lykke og fromme. Mette hadde ikke lest så lenge før hun forsto at de hadde to onkler som hadde reist over mer enn tjue år tidligere. Det var til disse, som da bodde i Nord Dakota, at jentene skulle reise.

Det var som om Mette helt levde seg inn i det hun leste, om sjøreisen og den store amerikabåten. Alle de forventningsfulle menneskene om bord – i alle aldre og fra alle samfunnslag – drømte om en fremtid i medgang og lykke. Kanskje ikke alle akkurat var så virkelighetsfjerne, men håpet var i hvert fall at livet der over skulle kunne by dem mer enn hva de kunne forvente hjemme i Norge.

«Sjøreisen har gått ganske bra,» leste hun, «selv om vi nok av og til fikk merke hva en sjøreise også kan være når det gjelder været. Nå skinner i hvert fall sola, og vi vet at vi nærmer oss innseilingen til New York. Det skal bli godt å sette føttene på fast grunn igjen. Men det kommer til å bli litt vemodig å skilles fra alle disse om bord som vi er blitt så godt kjent med på reisen. Det verste kommer nok til å bli avskjeden med den familien som Mina har hatt så mye med å gjøre. Det er et ektepar med fem barn. De har ikke hatt det så altfor lett på denne turen. Det minste barnet er bare to år, og det eldste er ni. Minstemann har krevd svært mye av moren denne tiden. Hun ser helt utslitt ut. Nummer tre, som bare er fem år, har også vært mye syk. Hun tåler visst ikke så godt sjø. Men Mina har tatt seg mye av henne. Nesten hver dag har lille Karen sittet i fanget hennes. Mina har blitt svært glad i den spede, bleke lille jenta. Du vet hvordan hun er, så omsorgsfull og øm. Det blir nok en del tårer når avskjedsstunden kommer, kan jeg tenke meg.»

Så kom det et markert avsnitt. Resten av brevet var skrevet etter at de var kommet i land i New York. Datoen var femte juni 1921.

«Mina er helt oppløst i tårer i dag. Avskjeden med lille Karen og familien hennes ble mer dramatisk enn vi hadde tenkt. Vi reiste jo alle på tredje klasse, så vi ble ikke kontrollert om bord slik som første og andre klasse ble. Vi måtte innom immigrasjonskontoret på Ellis Island. Der viste det seg at det var tuberkulose den lille var rammet av. Og folk med slike sykdommer vil de visst helst ikke slippe inn i landet. Det ser riktig mørkt ut for den rammede familien. Vi vet ikke hvordan det går med dem, og ikke kan vi få gjort så mye for dem heller, for vi må straks reise videre. Vi skal følge med en gruppe nordmenn som også skal lenger vestover.»

Resten av brevet var en beskrivelse av den yrende aktiviteten på kaia, og hvordan deres egen immigrasjonsprosedyre hadde forløpet. De var kommet greit gjennom det alt sammen. Så bad de mor hilse til alle de andre der hjemme. En spesiell hilsen sendte de til «Gomo» Gunhild og «Gofar» Even. Nå ville de snart være hos farbror Wilhelm og farbror Theodor i Nord Dakota.

Så besteforeldrene til disse jentene het altså Gunhild og Even. Det forklarte hvem de innebundne brevene var skrevet til. Og de var åpenbart sendt fra sønnene deres som hadde reist over til Amerika allerede før århundreskiftet.

Reisen vestover for de to tvillingsøstrene kunne lett følges. Mette fant fram et amerikakart hun hadde. De hadde sendt brev hjem fra flere av de byene der toget stoppet underveis. Mina skrev også litt, men som regel var det Gunhild som sto for brevskrivingen. Gunhild så ut til å være den praktiske som forklarte hvordan de hadde det, og hvordan reisen forløp. Og hun skrev om hvilke byer de passerte på reisa. Det var Albany, Rochester, Buffalo og Cleveland.

Mina virket mer drømmende. Hun beskrev helst det de så på reisen, eller episoder som utspant seg, og som hun ble betatt av. En gang beskrev hun i et langt brev et slagsmål de hadde vært vitne til. Både kniver og skytevåpen hadde vært inne i bildet. En skikkelig skremmende opplevelse, som hadde fått dem til å forstå at nå nærmet de seg virkelig den ville vesten.

«Neste stopp er Chicago,» skrev Gunhild i et brev. «Der kommer vi til å bli noen dager. Følget vårt kommer også til å bli mer oppdelt da. Noen skal stoppe der for godt, og noen skal videre vestover mot Iowa og Nebraska. Men heldigvis er det fortsatt noen flere som skal til Nord Dakota, så vi vil ennå få følge videre. Det verste er at jeg er litt bekymret for Mina. Hun sier ikke så mye, men jeg forstår at hun ikke er helt bra. Det ser ut som hun brygger på en influensa. Håper det ikke blir altfor anstrengende for henne med denne reisingen.»

Neste brev var også sendt fra Chicago, men det var datert tre uker senere. Der fortalte Gunhild at Mina hadde vært svært dårlig. Selv hadde hun også vært syk. De måtte stoppe igjen der i byen mens resten av reisefølget dro videre. Så syke som de var, greide de ikke å fortsette reisen.

Det hadde vært en tung tid, men heldigvis hadde de fått hjelp av noen nordmenn som de var blitt kjent med i ei Norsk kirke der i byen. Snart håpet de på at de kunne dra videre. Men Mina var fremdeles svært svak, så de ville vente litt ennå.

Etter hvert som Mette leste videre, ble hun mer og mer oppslukt av historien. Hun så nå at flere brev var sendt fra Chicago, og disse var ikke sendt så tett som de første. De to jentene fikk et langt opphold der i den store byen. Mina ble liksom ikke helt bra, så de ville ikke belaste henne med den anstrengende reisen. De fikk leid et rom der, og Gunhild fikk jobb som kjøkkenhjelp på et hotell.

Hele vinteren ble de der. Mina ble bare dårligere, og etter hvert ble det klart at hun hadde fått tuberkulose. Det var nok ingen tvil om at lille Karen hadde smittet henne på båten. For dem begge må det ha vært ei tung tid, men de beklaget seg ikke så mye til foreldrene der hjemme i Norge. De ville vel ikke at de skulle ha altfor store bekymringer for dem.

Så kom det er brev fra Mina. Mette kjente at hun ble beveget da hun leste det.«I dag føler jeg mer litt kjekkere, så jeg vil forsøke å skrive litt til dere, kjære foreldre. Jeg innser nå at vi aldri kommer til å se hverandre igjen her på jord. Hele tiden på denne reisen har der ligget et håp i mitt hjerte. Og det håpet har vært at vi en gang i fremtiden skulle få anledning til å komme hjem igjen til dere. Hjemmet der i Lia står jo for meg som det kjæreste på jord. Men nå har jeg begynt å lengte til et annet hjem. Et hjem som faktisk har rykket meg så mye nærmere. Det er det strålende hjemmet der i Himmelen. I går aftes trodde jeg at Jesus kom for å hente meg. Jeg hørte slik nydelig englesang, en vidunderlig fred fylte hele min sjel, og alt det vonde var liksom forsvunnet. Der var også en stemme som talte til meg. Den sa:«Jeg kommer snart!» Da fyltes mitt hjerte med et eneste rop:«Ja kom, Herre Jesus.» Nå er jeg snart hjemme, tenkte jeg, og den gleden som jeg da opplevde, sitter ennå i meg.

Etterpå forsto jeg ikke hva det var, om det var en drøm eller det var noe Jesus ville vise meg for at jeg ikke skulle ligge her og grue for døden. I hvert fall skapte dette en sterk himmellengsel i meg … en himmellengselen som på en måte visket bort all dødsangst. Men da jeg i dag lest Åpenbaringen 22,20, forsto jeg at dette var Guds Ord. Det var Han som talte til meg. Tenk så vidunderlig. Snart kommer Jesus for å hente meg.

Lov meg en ting, dere kjære der hjemme. Sørg for at ingenting skal hindre dere i å komme etter. Vi må møtes igjen der oppe. Og lille Torkel … jeg lengter slik etter ham. Vis ham dette brevet når han blir gammel nok til å forstå, og lær ham den rette veien.

Nå orker jeg ikke å skrive mer. Farvel, kjære mor og far, Even og Torkel, og på gjensyn.»

Med skjelvende hender la Mette brevet tilbake i bunken. Hun ble sittende en stund fordypet i tanker. Den lille Torkel, som Mina skrev om, måtte jo være onkel Torkel som de nettopp hadde fulgt til graven. Slik kjærlighet og omtanke som Mina hadde hatt for ham! Men det var nok ikke så rart. Han var jo bare tre-fire år da de reiste. Lengselen etter denne lillebroren hadde sikkert sittet svært dypt i dem. Igjen lurte hun på dette med hans åndelige tilstand før han døde. Var han nå forent med søsteren «der hjemme»?

Det neste brevet hun leste, var datert bare et par uker senere. Det var beskjeden fra Gunhild om at Mina var død. Hun beskrev ikke den siste tiden så nøye, men det var tydelig at den hadde vært hard, både for den døende, og for søsteren som fulgte med i lidelsene hennes.

Når det gjaldt selve begravelsen, hadde hun fått god hjelp av presten og vennene i kirken. Alt ble ordnet på beste måte. Nå lå den kjære søsteren hennes begravd på den norske kirkegården i Chicago.

En stund hadde visst Gunhild vurdert å reise tilbake igjen til Norge, men så ble det til at hun fortsatte reisen mot bestemmelsesstedet.

Etter dette ble det lenger mellom hvert brev. Det så nesten ut som om Gunhild mer og mer fant seg til rette med sin nye tilværelse. Hun ble godt mottatt hos slektningene i Nord Dakota. Onkler, tanter og søskenbarn tok imot henne med varme og kjærlighet. Hun ble inkludert i familien med den største selvfølgelighet, men den harde tilværelsen som prærielivet krevde, fikk også hun smake sin del av. Hardt arbeid og mange forsakelser måtte hun lære å forsone seg med.

Etter hvert kom det brev som fortalte om lysere tider. Navnet Nils ble stadig nevnt, en kjekk nordmann med egen farm et stykke vest for hovedstaden, Bismarck. Det ble bryllup og nye omveltninger for den norske jenta. Brevene kom nå helst til jul og ved spesielle anledninger. Etter hvert kom det også beskjed om en liten Robert som var født.

Brevet falt ned i fanget da Mette leste dette. Her sto det jo noe vesentlig. Kanskje var allerede hennes mistanker bekreftet. Nå visste hun jo slett ikke om barnet vokse opp, eller om det kom flere barn. Men muligheten var absolutt til stede. Det kunne vær slekt i Amerika som var arveberettiget. Dette måtte de studere nærmere og forsøke om de kunne finne ut av.

36 • Hilsen lillebror

S elv om våren så ut til å ligge like rundt hjørnet, lot varmen likevel vente på seg. Stadig kom det nye kuldeperioder med snø i lufta og frost på marka. Innover i fjellet lå det ennå snøskavler, selv om det var langt ut i mai. Ikke en eneste gang hadde Mette fått anledning til å komme opp på setra. Veien dit var fremdeles ufremkommelig. De kunne selvsagt ha tatt snøskuteren, men Morten hadde vært svært opptatt den siste tiden. Mange arrangementer, både i kirka og på bedehuset, hadde han ansvar for. Og i forbindelse med jobben var det også stadig møter eller andre ting som tok tiden hans. Hun var avhengig av å ha ham med hvis hun skulle bruke den, for hun var ikke vant til slik en kjøredoning.

De hadde ikke vært gift særlig lenge før de merket dagliglivets stressende jag igjen. Selv var hun også stadig på farten i forbindelse med jobben. Arbeidet var interessant, så hun stortrivdes med det, men etter hvert begynte hun å lengte intenst etter setra igjen. Stadig tok hun seg en tur borte til tante Anna for å prate om den forestående sommeren. Selv om tante Anna ikke lenger var så sprek som hun tidligere hadde vært, så var hun fullt bestemt på å være med der oppe. Matlagingen lå liksom i blodet hos henne. Mette tenkte at hun sikkert kom til å ende sine dager ved grøtgryta. Hun måtte smile litt for seg selv. Etter den tiden de hadde kjent hverandre forsto hun at en slik ende på livet måtte ha vært det den gamle dama aller helst kunne ønske seg.

På det trivelige kjøkkenet til tante Anna hadde de lagt planer for hva slags mat de skulle lage for turistene, og hva slags oppskrifter de skulle prøve. Den ivrige dama fikk stadig nye ideer og nye oppskrifter som hun straks ville prøve ut. Alt var gamle tradisjonsrike retter som hun fikk fra forskjellige deler av landet.

En dag sto de sammen i kjelleren hennes og bakte flatbrød. «Vi må ha masse flatbrød med oss,» sa tante Anna. «Det er jo så greit å servere til det meste av melkematen vi lager.»

Mette kunne ikke hjelpe henne så mye, for dette var en vanskelig kunst, men hun forsøkte å lære seg litt etter hvert. Tante Anna var forresten en dyktig læremester. Hele tiden mens hun arbeidet, gikk munnen i ett sett. Alt hun gjorde ble forklart i detalj, og mange historier fra gamle dager ble fortalt innimellom. Det var helt utrolig så mye kunnskaper denne kvinnen satt inne med. Mette frydet seg igjen, slik hun hadde gjort i sommer da de hadde stått slik og arbeidet sammen så mange ganger. Den ustoppelige ordflommen hadde forunderlig nok aldri trettet Mette en eneste gang etter hva hun kunne huske. Det at denne kvinnen var i stand til å arbeide så effektivt, samtidig som ordene fosset ut, hadde forbløffet Mette mer enn en gang.

Tante Anna satte rett som det var Mette til å gjøre nye ting. Den beste måten å lære på var å gjøre det selv, pleide hun å si. Også kjevlingen av flatbrødet måtte prøves, men Mette følte seg nokså klossete og overlot snart kjevlet til den gamle igjen. Det eneste hun følte seg trygg på, var potetskrellingen, og malingen av de kokte potetene som de trengte masse av til flatbrødbakingen.

En stor stabel med tynne, sprø flatbrødleiver lå på kjellerbordet da dagen var omme. Tante Anna og Mette satte seg ned for å puste ut ved kjøkkenbordet. De drakk varm kaffe med nystekt flatbrød til. Tante Anna hadde funnet fram smør og selvlaget gome som de smurte på flatbrødet i tykt lag.

Hun fortalte også at hun allerede hadde forberedt sommeren ved å bake en masse lefser. «Hele fryseboksen min er full,» sa hun og lo så hun ristet. Mette hadde sett henne bake lefser tidligere. Hun kunne ikke tenke seg noe deiligere enn de tynne, myke potetlefsene til tante Anna.

«Ja, nå gleder jeg meg virkelig til sommeren,» sa Mette og lo sammen med henne. Plutselig kom Mette på de gamle amerikabrevene hun hadde sittet og lest. Kanskje tante Anna kjente til disse menneskene? Dagen før hadde hun lest videre i brevene. Da hadde hun funnet ut at Gunhild og Nils fikk to barn til. En het Willy, og en het Mical. Den siste av dem var visst nokså svakelig. Det kunne tyde på at han var sterkt funksjons-hemmet.

Tante Anna ble ivrig da Mette brakte emnet på bane. «Kan skjønne jeg har hørt om disse,» sa hun. «Tomine, mor til Torkel, snakket ofte om familien der borte i Amerika. Hun sørget visst svært etter at den ene av tvillingene døde. Ja …» hun så tankefull ut i luften. «… man kan jo godt forstå at det må ha vært tungt å få en slik beskjeden. Tenk, ei nitten år gammel datter ligger syk, og så dør, langt borte i et fremmed land. Og så har man ingen mulighet til å kunne besøke graven hennes engang. Ja, stakkars Tomine, hun hadde det nok ikke så lett.»

Et øyeblikk ble de sittende i taushet. Vemodet og alvoret senket seg liksom inn over dem begge. Med ett ble de harde realitetene fra en fjern fortid rykket dem helt nær. Og brutaliteten i tilværelsen fra den tiden ble ekstra forsterket for dem der i kjøkkenet da tante Anna igjen begynte å snakke:

«Jeg tror de hadde det ganske vanskelig der borte i Lia på begynnelsen av århundret. Garden var jo ikke så stor, og andre muligheter til å skaffe seg inntekter hadde de ikke. Det var først da Even, Mortens morfar, overtok, at det gikk litt bedre. Han greide å skaffe litt ekstra penger ved å lage møbler for salg. Han var en dyktig møbelsnekker.»

«Da er det vel han som har laget alle de fine gamle møblene som står der borte i huset?» spurte Mette ivrig. «Ja, der har dere virkelig en skatt å ta vare på,» svarte tante Anna. «Men før han begynte med snekringen, så det ikke så rart ut der i gården. Jeg husker min mor fortalte at hun måtte bort til Tomine et ærende en dag. Da undret hun seg over at ingen av barna var å se noen steder. Hun var der ganske lenge, men hun så ingenting til noen av dem. Siden fikk hun greie på at Tomine ofte gjemte barna vekk oppe på loftet når det kom fremmedfolk til gards, for hun ville ikke vise for bygda de dårlige klærne de hadde.»

Mette grøsset der hun satt. At det gikk an å leve under så fattigslige forhold. Det var slett ikke rart at så mange reiste over til Amerika. Der var det i hvert fall håp om en bedre tilværelse en gang i fremtiden, selv om slitet ikke ble noe mindre der borte enn det de hadde vært vant med i gamlelandet.

«Men,» fortsatte tante Anna, «det var nok ikke bare dem som hadde det vanskelig. Vi fikk merke det i vår familie også. Men på en eller annen måte greide vi oss uten å måtte ta av sted ut i det ukjente.

«Jeg var ikke født da disse jentene dro av sted, så jeg husker dem ikke, men jeg har forstått at Maren, mormor til Morten, lenge hadde kontakt med familien i Amerika. Hva som var årsaken til at kontakten ble brutt vet jeg sannelig ikke. Sannsynligvis er det ikke flere igjen der borte av den familien. Jeg har i hvert fall ikke forstått at Torkel hadde noen kontakt med dem.»

Mette satt og grublet en stund. «Du tror ikke at det kan ha vært språket som førte til at det ble vanskelig å opprettholde kontakten?» spurte hun litt betenkt. Hun ville ikke helt gi opp håpet om at der kunne finnes slekt i Amerika.

Tante Anna ristet svakt på hodet. «Nei, sannelig om jeg vet …» hun tenkte seg litt om før hun fortsatte, «… men det er jo selvsagt mulig at det var det som var problemet.»

En stund ble de sittende og diskutere de gamle brevene, men så måtte Mette dra hjem igjen. Det var ikke så lenge til hun måte begynne på middagen, og senere på kvelden skulle hun på et møte.

En plutselig innskytelse fikk henne til å kjøre oppover mot Lia etter at hun hadde svingt ut av tunet til tante Anna. Bare en liten titt, tenkte hun. Husnøkkelen hadde hun hengende på knippet sitt, så det var bare å låse seg inn da hun kom fram. Hva hun ventet å finne der i det gamle huset, visste hun ikke, men hun ville se om der kunne være noe som gav nye spor i saken.

Det var med enda større interesse hun nå betraktet de gamle møblene i huset. Helt betatt ble hun stående foran det store skatollet i stuen. De fire bena var skåret ut som en slags S, og oppover langs skapdørene var det søyler av vridd tre, så det ut som. Dørene i overskapet hadde tynne, firkantede spiler. Mellom spilene var det åpent inn i skapet, men på baksiden av dørene var det trukket et rødt tøystykke som gav en nydelig effekt til det gul-brune treverket. På toppen av skatollet sto det to kuler med en tynn spiss øverst. Kulene var plassert en på hvert fremre hjørne.

At det gikk an å lage noe så vakkert! tenkte Mette der hun sto. Dette hadde han nok gjort bare med kniv, høvel og sag. Hun gikk fra den ene tingen til den andre og strøk forsiktig over lister og flater med hånden. Fra rom til rom gikk hun. Hun kunne ikke gå gjennom alt som lå i skuffer og kasser, Det måtte de vente med til de skulle ta fatt på delingen.

Men først måtte de altså finne ut om der var flere enn Morten og hans to søstre som hadde rett til arv.

Et øyeblikk lurte hun igjen på hvorfor hun egentlig hadde kommet hit. Det var jo helt umulig å vite hvor man skulle lete etter noe som kunne gi viktig informasjon om slekta i Amerika. Litt motløs gikk hun inn i kammerset, der hun hadde funnet onkel Torkel så syk den dagen. Senga sto der ennå, men sengeklærne var borte. Marit hadde nok tatt dem med hjem for å vaske dem.

Ved den ene veggen sto en skjenk med ei bokhylle over. Også denne var i den samme sirlige stilen som de andre møblene i huset. Blant bøkene som sto i hyllen, ble oppmerksomheten hennes fanget av en stor, gammel bibel. Forsiktig løftet hun boka ned og la den bort på bordet. Det var en velbrukt bibel, det kunne hun lett se, men de skinninnbundne permene holdt fremdeles de dyrebare arkene forsvarlig på plass. Og gullskriften på bokryggen var det også mye igjen av.

Forsiktig åpnet hun Bibelen. En eim av gammelt papir slo mot henne i det samme. På første side sto det Bibelen eller Den Hellige Skrift indeholdende det Gamle og Nye Testamentes kanoniske Bøger, med sirlige gotiske bokstaver. Nederst sto årstallet 1876.

Dette var altså familiebibelen som hadde fulgt disse menneskene opp gjennom slektene. Hun begynte å bla i de skjøre arkene. Noen steder var sidene nesten helt slitt i stykker. Et par steder var det brukt nål og tråd for å reparere de største skadene.

Plutselig ble hun oppmerksom på noe som var skrevet på første side. Den var helt tettskreven. Også siste side så hun at det var skrevet mye på. Skrifta var nokså vanskelig å tyde, men hun kunne se at det var navn og årstall som var skrevet ned der. Ivrig begynte hun å lese. Det var jo hele slekta som var nedskrevet. Kunne det kanskje finnes et svar her?

Raskt lukket hun bibelen og stakk den under armen. Dette ville hun studere nærmere når hun kom hjem.

Forskrekket så hun på klokka. Var den alt blitt så mye? Nå skulle middagen ha vært på kok for lenge siden. Det var best å komme seg av gårde så fort som mulig.

Det ble en lettvint middag den dagen, men Morten klagde ikke over det. Han var like spent som Mette på å finne ut mer om den gamle slekta.

Etter middag ble de begge sittende i sofaen med den gamle bibelen på fanget. Med felles anstrengelser greide de å tyde navn etter navn. Bibelen hadde visst opprinnelig tilhørt en som het Even Lia. Han var gift med ei som het Gunhild.

«Her er det jammen mange av de samme navnene som går igjen,» sa Mette. «Ja.» Morten smilte. «Det ser ikke ut som at de hadde så mye fantasi i så måte. Men det kommer nok helst av at navnetradisjonene var slik på den tiden. Foreldre og besteforeldre skulle kalles opp. Man hadde liksom ikke noe valg der.»

Barna til disse to var Theodor født 1877 og Vilhelm født 1878, begge emigrert til Amerika i 1898. «Her har vi det,» ropte Mette ivrig.

Morten fortsatte å lese. Ola født 1880, gift med Tomine født 1882. Disse overtok garden. Så var det Berta og Matilde. Også disse emigrerte, men det sto ingen årstall der.

De neste som var nedskrevet, var barna til Ola og Tomine. Først var det tvillingene Gunhild og Tomine. De ble født i 1903, men i 1921 dro de over til Amerika. Ved siden av disse navnene var det tilføyd en del med mindre skrift. Det var dødsdatoen for Tomine. Årstallet var 1922. Så sto det navnet på Gunhilds mann, som het Nils. Deretter var tre navn føyd til. Det var Robert, Willy og Mical.

Mette så litt skuffet opp på Morten. «Her står det jo ikke stort annet enn det vi allerede vet,» sa hun. «Nei, sa Morten, men det er nå ganske interessant likevel. Jeg har i hvert fall ikke visst så mye om slekta før. Se, her står det videre om morfar. Han var jo bror til tvillingene, og det var altså han som overtok garden i Lia. Even het han og var født i 1905. Kona hans, som het Maren, var født i 1908. Så var det altså Torkel som ble født i 1917. Han overtok gården da morfar døde i 1966.

Even og Maren fikk bare ei jente, og det var min mor som het Berta. Hun ble gift med Sivert, min far, og han var jo bror til tante Anna.»

«Dette var i hvert fall mange navn,» sa Mette med et sukk. «Jeg må nok studere dem en stund før jeg greier å sortere alt.»

Morten trakk bibelen litt nærmere og begynte å bla i den. «Se her så slitt den er. Dette er nok et sted de har vendt tilbake til ofte. La oss se hva som står der.» Han begynte å lese et sted hvor ordene var understreket med en tykk strek: Herre! Hør min Røst naar jeg raaber, og vær mig naadig og bønhør mig! Det var Salme 27,7. Mette følte med det samme at hun igjen kjente noe av nøden fra den fjerne fortiden. Her var et nødrop steget opp til Gud. Et rop om hjelp kanskje. En hjelp som de sårt trengte for å greie og opprettholde livet i den karrige fjellbygda. Og hvordan var det med bønnesvaret, tro? I hvert fall hadde slekta her fortsatt, det var jo Morten et bevis på. Men de der over i Amerika, hvordan hadde det gått med dem? Det visste de ikke ennå. Ville de noen gang få greie på det?

Plutselig falt noe ut av bibelen og landet i fanget til Morten. Forsiktig løftet han opp en hvit konvolutt. Det var ingen adresse utenpå, men inni lå det to store ark. Morten dro dem ut og begynte å lese.

Kjære Mina. Jeg får aldri sendt dette brevet til deg, men jeg har tenkt så mye på deg i det siste. Jeg var bare fire år da dere reiste, men jeg husker det som om det var i går da vi sto der ved kjerra og tok farvel. Smerten sitter ennå i meg.

Det var ikke mye dere fikk med dere til den nye verden, men så var det heller ikke så mye du fikk bruk for.

Nå er du i en annen verden, og der trenges ikke noe av dette som vi her i verden sliter helsa av oss for å skaffe til veie. Du får også slippe all den hjertesorg som denne verdens mennesker sjelden blir skånet for.

Du slipper å se mors tårer, og du slipper å se fars bekymrede blikk. Dere er nå sammen i glede. Å, som jeg lengter etter å møte dere alle.

Du gav meg en hilsen før du reiste over der du er nå. Mor og far fikk beskjed om å overbringe den til meg når jeg ble gammel nok til å forstå. De gjorde som de ble bedt om, men jeg forsto nok likevel ikke så mye av det da. Det er først nå, i den senere tid, at tankene har kretset om den hilsenen.

Kjære søster, jeg vil så gjerne se deg igjen. Alle disse årene har jeg lengtet så jeg nesten ble syk etter dere, og da spesielt deg. Du var alltid så god mot meg. Selv om vi ikke hadde så mye at vi en gang kunne spise oss mette, så greide du ofte å finne noe godt til meg. Jeg har en mistanke om at du selv heller sultet litt ekstra for at jeg skulle få ditt.

Ja, jeg lengter etter dere, men i det siste er det en jeg lengter enda mer etter å få møte, og det er Jesus. Tenk, jeg som vel er den største synderen i hele fjellbygda, fikk lov til å begynne på nytt. Jesus tok all den elendigheten som fantes her inne i den skranglete skrotten, og så renset Han det bort. Nå er veien klar også for meg. Jeg vet ikke hvor lenge jeg har igjen å leve her. Helsa mi har vært særdeles god, må jeg vel si, men aldri har jeg tenkt på at jeg burde takke Jesus for det. Ikke før nå når jeg så inderlig gjerne skulle ønske at jeg fikk reise Hjem. Men jeg nærmer meg snart åtti år nå, så Gud kan vel ikke drøye så altfor lenge med å hente meg, vil jeg tro. Her i Lia har jeg ikke mer å gjøre. Og bygda vil nok ikke savne meg noe særlig, vil jeg tro. Jeg greier ikke å leve slik jeg burde. Det gamle henger så altfor fast i meg, men heldigvis er det en nådig Gud jeg har møtt.

Jeg ville bare skrive dette brevet, vet egentlig ikke hvorfor. Men jeg sier på gjensyn til både deg og Gunhild. Og så til den stakkars Nils som ble så ille medfaren. Willy og Mical skal det også bli fint å få møte. Håper vi kan forstå hverandres språk der oppe i himmelen, om vi ikke greide det her på jord. Hjertelig hilsen Lillebror.

De ble sittende tause en lang stund. Mette måtte tørke bort noen tårer, og Morten var heller ikke helt stø i stemmen. «Der fikk vi i hvert fall svar på et vesentlig spørsmål,» sa Mette med skjelvende stemme. Onkel Torkel er i Himmelen, ingen tvil om det.

«Ja,» svarte Morten, «og vi fikk også svar på at både Willy og Mical er døde.»

«Men Robert?» Mette stirret fjernt ut i luften.

Morten så også betenkt ut. «Nei, vi kan ikke slutte å lete ennå,» svarte han. «Der er nok fortsatt en mulighet for at Robert, eller eventuell slekt etter han, lever.»

37 • Det gamle skrinet

En mild vind feide over tunet og rusket opp i det lyse, kortklipte håret til Mette. Hun sto på trappa og speidet oppover lia i nord der veien mot setra gikk. Endelig var våren kommet med sol og varme, men snøen der oppe så virkelig ut til å være seiglivet. På fjelltoppene kunne hun se ei hvit kappe som hang ganske langt nedover. Nå må det da snart gå an å komme opp til setra? tenkte Mette der hun sto. De varme solstrålene gav henne en ekstra sterk lengsel etter livet der oppe.

Varmen hadde kommet for fullt for et par dager siden. Nede i dalen begynte løvet å spire fram på de nakne bjørkekvistene, og fuglene var i full gang med sitt yrende liv, med reirbygging og matsanking. Sang og kvitter fylte luften fra tidlig morgen og til langt på kveld. Nedover fra fjellet kom bekkene brusende med et vell av grått og grumsete vann. Elva gikk stor og mektig forbi gården og stupte tordnende ned i kulpene ved de store strykene. Snøsmeltingen oppe i fjellet gjorde seg sterkt gjeldende der i bygda. Våren kom nesten som en eksplosjon, syntes Mette.

Dagen før hadde de feiret 17. mai. Det var jo den første 17. maifeiring hun hadde vært med på der i bygda. Med undring hadde hun lagt merke til hvordan alle var med på å yte sitt for at det skulle bli en riktig festlig dag. Den intime og fortrolige atmosfæren gjorde at hun følte seg ekstra vel, selv om barnetoget og festsalen på skolen ikke var så full av folk som hun var vant med fra Oslo.

Morten kom gående mot henne over tunet. Han smilte og fulgte blikket hennes oppover mot fjellet. «Er du snart reiseklar?» spurte han ertende da han så lengselen i blikket hennes. «Å ja,» svarte Mette. «Hvor lenge vil det vare før vi kan ta oss en tur opp dit, tror du?» «Jeg håpet at vi kunne komme opp en tur i dag,» sa han. «Veien er nok litt ødelagt etter vinterens herjinger, men forhåpentligvis vil den være så pass fremkommelig at vi greier å ta oss frem med bil. Jeg har nemlig fått forespørsel fra en mann som ønsker å leie seterbua et par uker fremover nå. Vi kan jo ikke begynne seterdrifta ennå likevel, så sen som våren er i år, så jeg tenkte at vi like godt kunne skaffe litt penger ved å leie den ut.»

«Men da må vi vel gjøre den litt i stand,» sa Mette ivrig. «Ja, det var derfor jeg tenkte vi måtte forsøke å ta oss opp dit i dag,» svarte Morten.»

Med ett var Mette i full aktivitet. Hun fant raskt fram de tingene hun mente de måtte ha med, og snart satt de i bilen på vei oppover.

Jevnt og trutt klatret den solide, firehjulsdrevne bilen til Morten oppover de bratte kleivene mot myrområdene som strakte seg milevis innover. Veien viste seg å være svært bløt, og flere steder lå det fortsatt litt snø igjen i veibanen, men det var ikke verre enn at de greide å komme fram. Det var ikke før de kom til den siste svingen, der landskapet åpnet seg mot seterområdet, at de måtte stoppe. Der hadde en bekk gått over sine bredder og gravd et stort hull i veien.

«Jeg må nok sette i gang med veiarbeid her, ser det ut til,» sa Morten. Men Mette hørte ikke etter. Hun var alt ute av bilen. Snart sto hun og betraktet det vidunderlige synet som hun hadde blitt så betatt av sommeren før. Det var setra som lå der så fredfullt under fjellskrenten mot nord. Og så var det vollen som strakte seg oppover mot lia i vest, og nedover mot det blanke, men mystiske tjernet i øst. I sør, der hvor hun sto, strakte furuskogen seg et godt stykke nedover. Tvers over den åpne plassen gikk kjøreveien helt bort til seterbua. På østsiden av den lå campingområdet, der hvor turistene pleide å holde til om sommeren.

Nå lå hele området badet i solskinn. Mette snappet etter pusten. Endelig var hun her igjen, og stedet var like vakkert som hun husket det fra i fjor sommer. Det eneste som var annerledes, var snøflekkene langs jordet til høyre, der hvor de hadde hesjet høy, og de bare løvtrærne oppover skråningen i nord, som i fjor hadde stått fulle av løv.

Hun gikk sakte oppover mot bua mens hun hele tiden trakk inn den friske fjelluften i lange drag. Også her var fuglene i full aktivitet.

Stadig vekk måtte hun stoppe for å studere noe nærmere. Fjøset og sauehuset lå der de hele tiden hadde ligget, til venstre for seterbua. Gjerdet, som gikk langs veien fra furuskogen og opp til fjøset, var også stort sett i orden. Kun noen få stolper måtte repareres her og der.

En innestengt, muggen lukt slo imot henne da hun åpnet budøra. Den gamle stokke- bygde bygningen hadde stått solid gjennom hele vinteren, ja, gjennom mange vintre der oppe i fjellet. Men eimen av det grove treverket gav klare signaler om tid og elde.

Alt var som det hadde vært da hun forlot stedet der i høst. Et sting av smerte fòr gjennom henne ved tanken på den opplevelsen. Misforståelser, rykter og vonde følelser hadde gjort at avskjeden ble både dramatisk og smertefull for henne. Men heldigvis hadde det hele ordnet seg etter hvert. Hun ville ikke tenke mer på det. Nå var det en ny tid og et nytt år.

Blikket hennes fòr over rommet. Der til høyre sto den store vedkomfyren. Der hadde de stekt lappekaker på den store hella, og der hadde de kokt både grøt og andre ting. En propankomfyr sto lenger borte. Det var der de pleide å koke kaffen om mor- genen.

Så var det trappa opp til hemsen der hvor Morten hadde hatt sitt soverom. Den trappa var egentlig ikke mer enn en stige, men Morten hadde ingen problemer med å komme seg opp og ned. Der hadde han visst klatret siden han var en liten gutt.

Til venstre under vinduet sto spisebordet. Mette tenkte på alle de samtalene de hadde hett der over en rykende kopp kaffe. Spesielt husket hun den uværsnatta hun hadde sittet og passet på fjøset som hun godt kunne se fra vinduet. Lyn og torden hadde skremt både henne og dyrene. Og hun var livredd for at lynet skulle slå ned i det tørre høyet på høyloftet. Hun måtte smile litt av minnene. Men opplevelsen hadde vært dramatisk nok. Da hun midt på natta måtte ut for å få inn dyrene i det forferdelige regnværet, hadde lynet slått ned i fjellskrenten rett bak seterbua. Et tre var blitt helt splintret opp. Skrekken hadde sittet i henne lenge etterpå.

Det var tre rom til i huset. Under hemsen var tante Anna sitt soverom. Der oppbe- varte hun også alt av ull og andre ting som hun trengte til demonstrasjonene hun hadde for turistene. Så var det soverommet på baksiden, det som hun selv hadde brukt. Og så var det melkeboden ved siden av.

Mette gikk over gulvet og inn i melkeboden. Det var det eneste rommet som hadde elektrisk strøm der på setra. Den kom fra et solcellepanel ute på buveggen. De trengte strøm der for å kunne oppbevare melk og annen mat forsvarlig. Hun la merke til at seterbua ikke hadde vært helt ubebodd gjennom vinteren. Noen små svarte kuler på benkene viste at musene hadde vært flittige gjester. «Her må jeg i hvert fall vaske,» sa hun til seg selv da hun tømte ut muselort av et fat. Men først ville hun se seg litt mer omkring. Hun gikk ut bakdøra og ble stående og speide oppover skråningen der bak. Treet som lynet hadde ødelagt, var nå helt veltet. Rota lå med sine lange antenner og pekte rett til værs. Snøen hadde nok hjulpet til slik at den ble enda mer istykkerrevet.

Raskt begynte hun å klatre oppover skråningen. Treet sto sannelig ikke langt fra huset, tenkte hun da hun så ned igjen fra der lynet hadde slått ned. «Der mellom bua og fjøset sto jeg,» sa hun halvhøyt. Hun grøsset ved tanken på at hun hadde vært så nær en katastrofe.

Der rota til det veltete treet hadde stått, lyste det nakne berget mot henne Både lyng og mose var revet med i fallet.

Plutselig ble hun oppmerksom på en dyp grop ved siden av rota. Hun bøyde seg ned for å se litt nøyere på den. Da la hun merke til et hull som gikk fra gropen og vannrett innover i fjellet. Åpningen var faktisk ganske stor. Mette krabbet ned og strakte hånden inn i hullet for å se hvor langt inn det gikk. Men hun nådde ikke enden på det, enda hun nesten hadde inne hele armen.

«Et forunderlig fenomen,» tenkte hun og følte seg frem rundt kantene. Med ett kom hånden bort i noe som skrapte mot fjellet. Det var et eller annet der inne. Forsiktig følte hun seg fram igjen. Der var det. Varsomt trakk hun ut noe. Da hun fikk det ut i lyset, så hun at det var et gammelt skrin, eller en boks, nesten på størrelse med en iskremboks. Den var av et metall som hadde rukket å ruste skikkelig den tiden den hadde ligget der i hullet. En stund ble hun stående og studere den. Hun kunne tydelig merke at det var noe inni, men det var ikke noe tungt eller skranglete noe.

Lokket satt aldeles fast, så hun fant ut at hun heller måtte ta det med seg ned i bua. Kanskje Morten kunne få det opp når han kom inn.

Det viste seg at skrinet ble vanskeligere å få opp enn de hadde trodd. Morten var også svært spent på hva som kunne skjule seg der inne. «Kanskje det er noen papirer,» sa han. «Eller penger,» foreslo Mette ivrig. Morten lo. «Ja det kan godt hende, men da er det nok ikke penger som vi kan gjøre oss nytte av. Dette skrinet har nok ligget der oppe ganske lenge, vil jeg tippe.»

«Tror du det kan vært så gammelt?» Mette stirret forbauset på den rustede boksen. Morten snudde og vendte på den. «Jeg vet ikke, men så stor som den rota der er, så må den i hvert fall ha ligget en god stund.»

De greide ikke å gjøre mer med skrinet. For at ikke innholdet skulle bli ødelagt, fant de ut at de heller måtte vente med å åpne det til de hadde andre redskaper å hjelpe seg med. De satte det bare inn i skapet borte i hjørnet, og så tok de fatt på vaskingen.

Det ble sent på dag før de, trette og slitne, kunne reise hjem igjen, og da var hele skrinet i skapet glemt.

38 • Den første turisten

En uke med strålende vær hadde forvandlet bygda fra å være en kald og naken vinterbygd, med snø og is oppover i liene, til et varmt og frodig sommerparadis. Løvet var nesten helt utsprunget på bjørkekvistene, og gresset spirte grønt over jordene. Aldri hadde Mette opplevd noe liknende. Hun hadde for noen dager siden tenkt på denne våren som en eksplosjon, men den var nesten mer enn det. Det var så det helt tok pusten fra henne. Alt skulle skje denne korte tiden. Bøndene kjørte gjødsel og pløyde åkrer nesten natt og dag. Morten hadde også hendene fulle. Selv om han ikke drev gårdsbruk på samme måte som de andre bøndene, så hadde han likevel mye av det samme som måtte gjøres. Eiendommen skulle holdes i hevd, og det var et arbeid som i vesentlig grad falt på denne korte årsperioden.

Veien opp til setra hadde tørket betraktelig opp, og Morten hadde reparert alle de stygge hullene, så nå var det ingen problemer med å ta seg fram dit opp.

Mette satt på verandaen og nøt den behagelige temperaturen. Over hodet hennes hadde ei linerle et hektisk arbeid med reiret sitt. Av og til tok den en sving over tunet. Da svevde den så lavt at den nesten snertet bort i Truls, den store hannkatten, som lå der og vaktet på den. Rett som det var bykset Truls i været. Den hadde vel håp om å få seg en lekkerbisken i en fart, men det så det ut til å bli problemer med. Linerlen var alltid høyt oppe i lufta igjen før den feite hannkatten var kommet i bevegelse. Mette lo der hun satt og betraktet spillet. «Nei, du får nok vente til vi kommer opp på setra. Der skal du få så mye fløte og godsaker som du bare kan greie å legge i deg,» ropte hun etter den. Ikke for det, Truls trengte nok ikke mer godsaker enn det han fikk der på gården. Det var størrelsen et tydelig bevis på. Men Mette likte nå allikevel helst den tanken at der oppe på setra var de aller beste tingene å få tak i, i hvert fall for et dyr.

Plutselig svingte en bil inn på tunet. En mann steg ut og kom bortover mot henne. Han hilste og presenterte seg som Arvid. Da forsto Mette at det var han som skulle leie setra. Morten var på jobb, så det ble nok henne som måtte vise ham veien opp.

«Jeg kjører foran, så kan du bare følge etter,» sa Mette etter at de hadde vekslet noen ord. «Vi er der oppe om vel et kvarter, vil jeg tro.» Hun satte seg inn i bilen sin og svingte raskt ut på veien.

Oppe på setra så alt mye frodigere ut nå enn sist de hadde vært der, selv om det nok ikke var så grønt der som nede i bygda. Men snøen på vollen var i hvert fall borte. Det var bare på de aller høyeste toppene i det fjerne de fremdeles kunne se noen hvite flekker.

Gjesten var tydelig begeistret for det nye losjiet sitt. En mer idyllisk plass kunne han visst ikke ha funnet. Mette viste ham rundt i seterbua og ellers i området rundt. Etterpå satte de seg på en benk ute i solveggen for å prate litt.

Arvid kunne vel være midt i trettiårene, gjettet Mette. Han var en helt annen type enn Morten, la hun merke til. Han var nesten like lys i håret som henne selv, og ansiktet hans var kraftig, men velformet. Håret lå i bølger over kronen, men nakken var helt kortklipt. Ellers var han ganske høy og slank. Øynene var en blanding av grønt og brunt. En virkelig kjekk mann. Tanken kom så brått over henne at hun ble blussende rød og vendte blikket flakkende bortover mot tjernet. Hva slags tanker var det hun satt med? Hun skjente litt på seg selv i sitt indre før hun igjen fant roen og fortsatte samtalen.

Arvid viste seg å være en hyggelig mann som det var lett å komme i prat med. «Har du hørt om sagnet,» spurte hun etter en liten stund, «det sagnet som har gitt setra her navn?»

«Nei, jeg har ikke hørt så mye om denne setra i det hele tatt,» svarte han. «Er der et sagn knyttet til stedet? Det høres jo spennende ut.»

«Ja,» svarte Mette ivrig. Så fortalte hun om Silja, som en gang i tiden skulle ha blitt forvist til denne setra av familien, fordi hun var blitt med barn uten å være gift. Denne skammen ville de forsøke å skjule så lenge som mulig, ikke minst på grunn av ryktene som gikk om at det var sønnen til selveste storbonden i ei av nabobygdene som var barnefaren. Denne ville imidlertid ikke vite noe av forholdet, derfor fryktet familien at de kunne få store ubehageligheter fra den kanten.

Utpå høsten ble det klart at noe var galt på setra. En av hundene kom ned til gards og var aldeles på styr. Folk dro straks opp for å se etter hva som kunne ha skjedd. Da fant de bare en urolig dyreflokk utenfor fjøsdøra, men ingen budeie.

«Det ble jo ei intens leting,» fortsatte Mette. «Til slutt fant de henne i tjernet. Hun hadde druknet. Men det forunderlige var at liket ikke bar noe barn. Etter det har dette sagnet, på en måte, hvilt over denne setra. Derfor heter tjernet Siljatjernet, og stedet her Siljatjernsetra,» sluttet hun.

Arvid lyttet oppmerksom hele tiden. «Det var jammen litt av ei historie,» sa han og lo. En stund ble de begge sittende i taushet og stirre bortover mot den mørke vannflaten. Fortidens skygger gav liksom et lite gjenspeil i dypet der, kunne de nesten føle.

«Nei, la oss ikke sitte her og sture over gamle skrøner som sikkert bare er kommet opp i fantasien til bygdas sladrekompani.» Det siste ordet sa Mette med ekstra trykk. Selv hadde hun jo fått føle akkurat det med sladder forrige sommer, så den slags konversasjon hadde hun ikke mye til overs for. «La meg heller få høre hva som har ført deg, helt alene, langt hit opp i ødemarken,» sa hun muntert.

Smilet forsvant fra leppene hans mens en skygge la seg over ansiktet. Han flyttet ikke blikket fra tjernet. Da han begynte å snakke, var det en vemodig, nesten bitter, klang i stemmen hans. «Jeg er nettopp blitt separert,» sa han enkelt. «Kona stakk av med en annen mann. Det er det hele. Jeg måtte bare vekk.»

«Å, så leit.» Mette så fortvilet bort på ham. «Så vondt du må ha det. Jeg beklager at jeg spurte om dette ...»

«Nei, det gjør ingenting,» svarte han i en lettere tone. Først nå så han på henne igjen. Et trist smil gled over leppene hans. «Jeg kan like godt snakke om det. Dere må jo få greie på det likevel, synes jeg. Håpet mitt var at jeg skulle greie å komme litt mer til hektene igjen her oppe i fjellet. Turer med frisk luft og vakker natur har alltid virket oppløftende og avslappende på meg. Og kan jeg i tillegg ta med fiskestanga, så burde alt ligge til rette for den beste behandling.»

Han tidde mens han ristet svakt på hodet. Stemmen var nesten ikke hørbar da han igjen begynte å snakke: «Den siste tiden har vært så hard at jeg nesten ikke trodde jeg skulle greie å komme gjennom det. Metoden til denne Silja her har streifet meg mer enn en gang.»

Mette grøsset. Stakkars mann, tenkte hun. Der og da bestemte hun seg for å prøve og gjøre tilværelsen så trivelig som mulig for ham ... hvis det var noe hun kunne gjøre.

Det ble ikke sagt så mye mer mellom dem. Arvid takket for hjelpen, og Mette sa farvel etter at hun innstendig hadde bedt ham om å si fra hvis det var noe de kunne hjelpe ham med.

«Har du mobiltelefon?» spurte hun idet hun satte seg inn i bilen igjen. «Ja …» Han dro litt på det. «… Men er det dekning her oppe da?»

«Ja,» sa Mette. «Her rundt setra pleier det i hvert fall å gå bra. La meg få nummeret ditt. Det kan være greit, så kan vi få tak i deg hvis det er noe. Jeg går ut fra at du har vårt?»

Han nikket og skrev ned nummeret i en fart på en lapp som Mette fant i bilen.

Det var ei nokså tankefull Mette som kjørte nedover veien mot bygda den ettermiddagen. Medlidenheten med den hardt prøvede mannen fylte hele hennes indre. Tenk at han hadde gått med så håpløse tanker. Kunne han virkelig ha vurdert selvmord? Så grusomt han måtte ha det.

Tankene hennes var så opptatt med alt dette vonde som han hadde snakket om, at hun ikke helt greide å konsentrere seg om kjøringen. Uten at hun merket det tråkket hun inn gasspedalen enda et hakk. I det samme som farten økte opp, ble hun oppmerksom på en rev som hoppet ned fra en skrent og havnet i veien rett foran bilen.

I et kaotisk øyeblikk skjønte hun ikke riktig hva som skjedde. Bilen snurret rundt og havnet ute i ei myr et godt stykke nedenfor veibanen, med hjulene oppe i luften. Bare i brøkdelen av et sekund skimtet hun reven som lynraskt hoppet over noen tuer i myra, og forsvant mellom krattet på den andre siden. Det tok enda noen sekunder før hun fikk summet seg så mye at hun registrerte sin egen situasjon. Der satt hun altså … eller rettere sagt hang i sikkerhetsbeltet, med hodet ned, og med intense smerter i den ene skulderen.

39 • En enslig rev

«Jeg må komme meg ut herfra, men hvordan?» Mette kjente at panikken ikke var langt unna. Den venstre armen greide hun nesten ikke å røre. Bare den minste bevegelse fikk smertene til å jage gjennom kroppen.

Etter litt strev greide hun likevel å få ålet seg rundt så pass at hun i hvert fall hadde hodet den rette veien. Hun fant også fort ut at ingen av dørene var til å rikke, men frontruta var knust. «Kanskje jeg kan komme meg ut der?» sa hun halvhøyt og begynte å lete etter noe hun kunne slå vekk glassbiter med. Det eneste hun fant, var skoen. Med den greide hun å lage en åpning.

Etter enda mer strev og mange smertestønn satt hun endelig på ei tue i myra.

Hva nå? Et intenst raseri fylte henne med ett. Hva skulle den hersens, skabbete revepelsen labbe rett ut i veibanen etter? Revene skulle jo flykte for folk … de skulle jo være redde … Ja, redde skulle de være. Den måtte da høre at hun kom.

Og så ble den ikke skadet engang. Den skulle ha ligget dau der oppe i veien. Ja, det var akkurat det den skulle … dau … som et fenalår. Hadde hun bare hatt ei børse, så skulle hun ha plaffet løs på den første reven hun så … Ja, det skulle hun gjøre på et øyeblikk, selv om hun aldri hadde løsnet et skudd før i sitt liv. Og dau skulle den bli, det skulle hun i hvert fall sørge for. Hun slengte ut den friske armen med det samme, som om hun ville kaste noe etter den der borte mellom krattet. Men resultatet av den heftige bevegelsen ble bare et intenst smerteskrik, etterfulgt av noen lange såre hulk.

«Å, hva skal jeg gjøre?» hulket hun. Sinnet rant av og gikk over i fortvilelse. «Her sitter jeg. Bilen er smadret. Venstre armen er ubrukelig, og ....," hun stønnet igjen. Det var vondt å puste. Hvor skadet var hun egentlig? Øm følte hun seg over hele kroppen.

Etter hvert begynte tankene å arbeide mer normalt. «Jeg må få tak i hjelp ... mobiltelefonen!»

Møysommelig kom hun seg på bena igjen, og mobiltelefonen fant hun også snart. Men det var ingen som tok telefonen hjemme. «Morten er nok ikke kommet hjem ennå ...» Hun så på klokka. «Kanskje han jobber overtid. Jeg får ringe til banken.» Men så var det nummeret til banken da. Samme hvor mye hun vred hjernen sin, så kunne hun bare ikke komme på det. Tankene hennes var i det hele tatt nokså kaotiske. Hun begynte å skjelve der hun satt. Enda det var varmt i lufta, så skalv hun som i de verste frostrier. Smertene i skulderen var også så intense at hun hadde vanskelig for å konsentrere seg.

«Hvem kan jeg ringe til?» Hun kom ikke på noen i det hele tatt. I hvert fall ikke noen som hun kunne huske telefonnummeret til. Nødnumrene til legevakt eller politi hadde hun selvsagt, men hun kunne da ikke bry dem med dette?

Plutselig kom hun på lappen der Arvid hadde skrevet mobilnummeret sitt. Arvid, ja, han måtte da være den nærmeste å ringe til. Men hvor var lappen? Hun ville ikke klatre inn igjen for å lete etter den.

Etter en stund fikk hun se den gjennom vinduet. Hun greide ikke å få tak i den, men hun kunne så vidt skimte tallene som sto der.

Arvid svarte nesten med det samme, og han oppfattet raskt situasjonen. Det varte ikke mange minuttene før han var ved ulykkestedet.

«Hva i all verden er det som har skjedd her?» spurte han sjokkert da han klatret ned skråningen mot myra. Mette greide ikke å svare. Gråten overmannet henne helt. Raskt oppfattet han den skadede skulderen. Armen hang litt underlig ned. «Du må komme deg til lege,» sa han. «Jeg skal hjelpe deg.»

Varsomt hjalp han henne opp på veien og inn i bilen sin. Mette skalv fremdeles, men det var deilig å slippe å tenke på noe annet enn å sitte der.

Det var ikke så mye som ble sagt på turen, men hun la merke til at Arvid stadig så på henne med et granskende blikk. Han viste tydelig medfølelse i alt det han sa og gjorde. Mette kjente at det gjorde henne usigelig godt å legge merke til denne omsorgen. Uroen for at hun kunne være mer skadet begynte også å sige innover henne, for hun fikk mer og mer problemer med å puste. Det stakk i siden hver gang hun innåndet.

Plutselig begynte tårene å renne igjen. Tanken på at kanskje hele sommeren ville bli ødelagt for henne fikk enda kraftigere skjelvinger til å gå gjennom kroppen hennes. Noe som igjen fikk smertene til å øke på.

«Du har det visst fryktelig vondt,» sa Arvid med sterk bekymring i stemmen. Mette ville smile til ham, men hun greide det ikke. Fortvilelsen inni henne var for sterk. Hvorfor måtte dette hende? Et nytt raserianfall begynte å arbeide seg opp. «Gud, hvorfor kunne du ikke hindre at dette hendte?» Hun sa det ikke høyt, men for henne selv opplevdes det allikevel som et skrik. «Du kunne da ha hindret den reven i å hoppe ut i veien?»

I det samme var det som en helt ny tanke kom til henne. Ja det var nesten som en stemme utenfra: «Ja, jeg kunne ha hindret reven, men kunne jeg ha hindret deg i å tråkke gasspedalen lenger inn? Hva med konsentrasjonen din om kjøringen?» Mette ristet på seg så en ny smertebølge fòr gjennom henne. Hun sank tilbake i setet men et stønn. Konsentrasjonen? ... Tankene? ... Hun ville ikke tenke mer. Hun ville ikke høre flere stemmer ...

Arvid så enda mer bekymret på henne og økte farten. Han sa ikke noe, men han tolket visst stønnene hennes slik at hun trengte legebehandling, og det brennkvikt.

Snart var de nede i bygda. Morten var kommet hjem, og sjokket over det som hadde hendt, preget straks hele mannen. Han takket Arvid hjertelig for hjelpen, og så overtok han ansvaret for den skadede kona si.

Det var en ubeskrivelig lettelse for Mette å komme til sykehuset og få hjelp. Det viste seg at det var kragebenet som var brukket, og så var det noen brukne ribben også. Ikke noe alvorlig, heldigvis. Men en tid framover måtte hun ta det helt med ro.

«Du er nok helt bra igjen til du skal på setra,» sa legen til henne da hun uttrykte sin bekymring. «Du skal se at du er den samme gamle igjen om noen uker.»

o o o

Det ble en stille tid for Mette. Men hun nøt også roen etter det hektiske jaget hun hadde vært inne i så lenge. Arvid kom rett som det var innom for å se hvordan det gikk med henne. Lange stunder kunne de sitte sammen over en kaffekopp på kjøkkenet og prate. De ble svært godt kjent denne tiden. Også Morten likte den nye leieboeren. Et par ganger dro de sammen innover i fjellet på fisketur. Men det var helst når Arvid og Mette var alene, at han åpnet seg og fortalte om sine egne problemer. Mette syntes inderlig synd på ham. Hun skjønte at han hadde behov for å prate om det av og til, og det lot hun ham så gjerne får lov til.

Denne tiden fikk Mette også god tid til å studere de gamle amerikabrevene. En del nye opplysninger kom fram. Hun fant ut at Robert studerte til lege i Minneapolis og fikk jobb på et sykehus der. Gunhild kom etter hvert på en institusjon i Bismarck. Der døde hun i 1967. Etter dette ble kontakten med Amerika brutt, så det ut til.

Det var bare Maren, Mortens mormor, som hadde hatt kontakt med slekta der over på den tiden.

Mulighetene for at det kunne finnes slekt der borte, syntes de nå var helt klar. Morten satt en ettermiddag borte i banken og arbeidet med saken. Han tok kontakt med en del bankforbindelser de hadde, både i Minneapolis og i Bismarck, for om mulig å få greie på noe mer. Men det så nytteløst ut. Han ringte til og med til institusjonen hvor Gunhild hadde bodd. Der kunne de bekrefte at ei ved navn Gunhild Ånensen hadde vært beboer der, men de ante ingenting om slekta hennes.

Mette følte en usigelig motløshet da Morten kom hjem og fortalte om det negative resultatet av undersøkelsene. Hvordan i all verden skulle de finne denne mannen når de ikke ante noe som helst om ham?

«Har du funnet ut om han er gift?» Morten brøt inn i tankene hennes.

«Ja, det tror jeg da virkelig at jeg leste et sted.» Hun gikk inn i stua, og straks kom hun tilbake med et brev. «Her tror jeg det står noe som kan tyde på det.» En stund sto hun i taushet mens øynene fòr nedover linjene for å finne det rette avsnittet.

«Her må det være,» sa hun ivrig etter en stund. Hun begynte å lese: Det er ikke så ofte jeg får besøk nå. Etter at Carl solgte farmen og dro vestover, er her ingen av Nils sin familie igjen. Men Robert og Nancy var her for en uke siden. Det var godt å se dem, selv om de ikke hadde barna med seg. Det er ikke så ofte han får anledning til å besøke meg. Han er jo så opptatt på sykehuset, og Nancy arbeider visst også så mye på kontoret sitt at det ikke blir så mye fritid for dem. Men beboerne og personalet her er hyggelige ...

«Nancy må vel være kona hans.» Mette fortsatte å lete nedover linjene for å se om der kunne finnes flere viktige opplysninger. Men til slutt la hun fra seg brevet og ristet på hodet. «Noe særlig mer om dem har jeg ikke funnet. Hvem denne Carl er har jeg heller ikke funnet ut, men det kan jo se ut som at det er noen av slektningene på Nils sin side.

At de har barn, ser det jo også ut til her, men hva de heter, har jeg ikke sett noe om. Kanskje vi kan høre med Frelsesarmeen. De er jo flinke til å oppspore folk rundt omkring i verden.» Hun så ivrig på Morten. Han smilte, men ristet svakt på hodet. Et øyeblikk ble han igjen sittende i dype tanker mens smilet hele tiden lekte om munnen hans.

Til slutt så han bort på henne. «Kanskje vi skulle ta oss en tur over selv for å se om vi kan finne ut noe?»

Mette falt ned på stolen mens de lyseblå øynene så ut som de holdt på å falle ut av hodet på henne. «Hva sier du? Vi … skal vi begynne å lete der borte i det enorme landet etter en mann som vi ikke en gang aner noe om? Er du gått helt fra vettet?»

Morten lo. «Hvorfor ikke? Vi har da en del vesentlige opplysninger. På det sykehuset i Minneapolis må der da finnes opplysninger om hvem som jobber der, eller …» han tenkte seg om litt igjen, «… eller har jobbet der. For denne mannen er nok allerede blitt pensjonist.»

«Jeg vet ikke når legene blir pensjonister der borte,» svarte Mette litt oppgitt. Men han må jo være i syttiårene nå. Kanskje han allerede er død …»

«Ja.» Morten smilte fortsatt sitt lune smil, «Kanskje han er død, men det hadde da vært moro med en tur?»

Mette måtte også smile. Akkurat det var hun helt enig med ham i.

Mer ble det ikke sagt om saken den dagen.

40 • Kuslipp

«Nå må jeg nok dra hjemover igjen.» Arvid stakk hodet inn av kjøkkendøra. «Jeg kom bare innom for å si farvel. Sykemeldingsperioden min løper snart ut, så jeg må tilbake til arbeidet mitt igjen.» Han så oppriktig lei seg ut der han sto. Mette følte seg også vemodig med det samme. Det hadde vært så hyggelig å ha ham der opp. Og alle de koselige samtalene de hadde hatt, ville hun virkelig savne. At han etter hvert hadde passet på å komme når han visste at Morten var på jobb, det ville hun ikke dvele ved. Det var sikkert bare tilfeldig. Hyggelig hadde det i hvert fall vært.

«Så leit,» svarte hun. «Da ser vi vel ikke noe mer til deg?» Han sto en stund og så på henne. Blikket var fullt av noe hun ikke helt kunne tolke. En slags indre smerte, samtidig som det også så ut til å være beundring. Men han hadde jo hatt det så vondt, stakkar. Ikke rart at blikket kunne fylles med smerte da.

Hun gikk bort til ham og tok hånden hans til farvel. Impulsivt gav hun ham en klem. Hun kjente at han rykket til med det samme, men han gjengjeldte avskjedsklemmen.

«Jeg har tenkt litt på om jeg skulle tilbringe sommerferien min på setra,» sa han plutselig idet han skulle til å gå. Kanskje dere kan få plass til ei campingvogn til på området der oppe?»

«Å ja.» Mette viste tydelig begeistring over spørsmålet. «Du er hjertelig velkommen!»

Arvid smilte og vinket til henne idet han gikk mot bilen. «Jeg går innom banken og tar farvel med Morten,» ropte han tilbake. «Så kan jeg jo betale leia med det samme.»

Mette ble sittende igjen med en underlige uroen inni seg. Hun ville virkelig savne denne mannen. Men ... der kunne da ikke være noe galt i det? Nei, hun hadde ingenting å angre på i forholdet til Arvid. Likevel følte hun at noe ikke var som det skulle. Men de hadde jo hatt det så fint, og han trengte virkelig noen å snakke med i den vonde situasjonen som han var. Nei, hun ville ikke tenke mer på dette. Nå var han reist. Og kom han tilbake til sommeren, så hadde han sikkert kommet over hele greia.

o o o

Dagene ble stadig varmere. Gresset sto langt og frodig på enga bak låven. Bøndene rundt om i bygda hadde allerede sendt saueflokkene sine til fjells. Det spirte og grodde så man nesten kunne høre det alle steder. Mette kjente også at armen hennes var blitt mye bedre. Snart kunne hun bruke den nesten som før. Morten hadde sagt at de kunne vente de første turistene til setra allerede før sankthans, og det var i neste uke. Mette gledet seg som et barn. Hun hadde vært borte hos tante Anna flere ganger de siste dagene. Alt var klart til en ny sesong. Nå var det bare å komme seg opp og få installert seg med folk og dyr.

Morten hadde en grei avtale med Petter. Når en sesong på setra var over, kjøpte han de kyrne som melket, og som ikke Morten på grunn av manglende melkekvote kunne ha om vinteren. Og når så en ny sesong begynte, fikk han kjøpt dem tilbake igjen. Det var forresten ikke alltid de sammen kyrne han fikk igjen. Petter pleide plukke ut noen som han mente ville passe greit der oppe. Det var viktig at det var noen rolige og folkekjære dyr. De skulle jo helst være mest mulig sammen med turistene. Og til Petters fordel gjaldt det også at de ikke melket så mye. Det ble som regel vanskelig nok å få brukt opp all melken når de ikke kunne sende noe til meieriet.

To av kyrne som de hadde hatt på setra året før, skulle bli med denne sommeren også. De var så rolige og greie, og så aksepterte de så greit håndmelking. De fleste kyrne til Petter ville ikke vite av annet enn melkemaskin.

De hadde også blitt enige om å ta med ei kvige som snart skulle kalve. «Det er første kalven,» sa Petter, «så den har aldri vært melket før. Men den er snill som et lam, så jeg tror den vil passe perfekt hos dere. Barna mine har kjælt ekstra mye med den i vinter, så den er fortrolig med både barn og voksne.»

Morten var godt fornøyd med kjøpet, så nå mente han at alt var klart for en ny sesong.

Det som Mette sørget mest over, var at Keiseren ikke kunne bli med opp. Det var den kjære oksen hennes, som hun i fjor sommer hadde vært med på å hjelpe til verden. En skikkelig dramatisk historie. De hadde funnet moren hans ute i et vann. Den hadde falt ned fra et fjell, og var stygt skadet. Etter mye strev greide de å få den på land, men der måtte de avlive den. Morten greide imidlertid å berge kalven ved å foreta et keisersnitt på den døde kvigen.

Etter det ble denne kalven en ekstra kjær og kjælen venn for dem alle, og da spesielt Mette. Det var også hun som hadde gitt ham navn. Hun syntes at Keiseren måtte være et passende navn siden han kom til verden ved keisersnitt. Rett som det var hadde Mette tatt seg en tur bort i fjøset i løpet av våren for å snakke med den og klø den bak ørene.

Selv om hun hadde vært borte fra den ganske lenge i vinter, mente hun bestemt at den kjente henne igjen da hun kom til gards.

362

Nå var Keiseren blitt en stor og kraftig ungokse. Og slike store okser var det ikke lov å slippe fritt ut på beite om sommeren. Derfor måtte den bli hjemme. Men Missi skulle få bli med. Den sto også i deres eget fjøs. Det var den andre kalven som ble født der oppe den sommeren. Nå var også den blitt ei ganske stor kvige.

Hun visste i hvert fall en ting, og det var at disse kvigene ikke skulle få reke for langt inn i fjellet. Det skulle hun passe på. Hun ville ikke risikere at noe dramatisk skulle skje med dem også.

Så var det sauene og geitene. De skulle jo selvsagt også bli med. Seks sauer og elleve lam gikk der i fjøset og trippet av lengsel etter det saftige og frodige fjellbeitet. De hadde gått litt rundt på jordene ved låven, men for dem var det fjellet som lokket mest. Også de to viltre geitene, som hadde laget så mye brudulje året før, skulle få en ny sjanse dette året. Mette smilte for seg selv når hun tenkte på alle de gangene hun måtte jage dem ut av melkeboden eller fra campingplassen når de ble for innpåslitende for turistene.

○ ○ ○

Lørdag morgen var Morten og Mette klar til buføring. Mette hadde vært oppe med en god del forsyninger dagen før. Rene håndklær og sengetøy måtte jo til, og mange ting trengtes også til matlagingen. Nå var både skuffer og skap fylt opp.

Denne dagen var det dyrene som skulle flyttes. Morten fikk låne en hestetilhenger som de kunne kjøre dem i. Det var jammen bra at de ikke lenger trengte å jage dem oppover langs stier i myrer og fjell for å få dem til seters, tenkte Mette. Morten hadde fortalt hvordan dette pleide å foregå i gamle dager. Selv hadde han aldri behøvd å gå i tresko en lang dag med en kjepp etter dyreflokken når de buførte. Men far hans hadde fortalt ham om hvordan dette foregikk i hans barndom. Da hadde de fraktet forsyningene opp på hesteryggen, mens folk og dyr måtte gå. Denne dagen var en helt spesiell dag i året. En dag mange så frem til og lengtet etter. Men også en dag som noen gruet for. Det var nok ikke alle som var like glad i gjetingen og traskingen inne i fjellet. I den tiden foregikk forresten dette atskillig senere på sommeren. Det var bare sauene som ble sendt opp på forsommeren. Men nå var det ikke arbeidet med slått og høying i fjellet, eller hensynet til det øvrige arbeidet nede på garden, som var avgjørende. Nå var det bare turistene som styrte timeplanen deres.

Tante Anna og Mette dro først av sted. De skulle være der oppe og hjelpe til med å få dyrene på plass når de kom.

Mette ble stående noen øyeblikk i taus beundring og se utover vollen da de endelig var oppe. Sommeren hadde pyntet både mark og fjell med sin sterke grønnfarge. Igjen ble hun slått av de intense fargene som spilte i den storslåtte naturen der i fjellet. Gress og løv var liksom så mye grønnere, og det blanke tjernet så mye blåere. Selve himmelen virket mye høyere og klarere enn nede i bygda, syntes hun. Enga på vollen hadde spirt godt, men gresset var ikke særlig langt ennå. Det ville nok vare en tid før de kunne begynne å slå det. Men på campingområdet måtte de snart begynne å slå, for der skulle det jo bare være vanlig plen.

Sola varmet godt, kjente hun der hun sto, men det var likevel et friskt og kjølig drag i lufta. Hun var glad for at hun hadde tatt med godt med klær.

Plutselig skar stemmen til tante Anna gjennom stillheten. Hun hadde allerede vært inne med ei bør av forskjellige ting. Der kom hun ut igjen til bilen for å hente mer: «Skal si dere har gjort det koselig her inne. Og så rent og friskt det dufter! Ja, her skal vi virkelig få det trivelig i sommer. Håper bare ikke geitene spiser opp for mye av forsyningene våre inne i melkeboden.» Det siste ble sagt mens latteren trillet ut av henne så den store, runde kroppen ristet. Øynene forsvant nesten helt bak de runde kinnene.

Mette lo også. Hun ble stadig like forbauset over hvor mange ord som kunne renne ut av den blide munnen på et øyeblikk, når hun var begeistret. Forresten var det ikke bare når tante Anna var begeistret, at munnen gikk som ei kvern. Det gjorde den jo nesten hele tiden.

Det varte ikke lenge før Morten og Petter svingte inn på vollen med de første dyrene. Gode gamle «Plomma» var den første som ble leid bort til fjøset. Morten hadde fortalt henne at han hadde gitt den det navnet en gang fordi han syntes den var så rund på midten, og så lignet den så på en plomme på fargen. Året før hadde de ikke brukt så mye navn på de gamle dyrene, men Mette syntes at det ble mye mer personlig hvis de gjorde det. Derfor hadde hun bestemt seg for å bruke kunavnene mer dette året.

Plomma viste tydelig at den var kjent der fra før. Den gikk lydig bortover mot fjøset, men det var også klart at den forsto at nå var friheten og herligheten begynt. Rett som det var tok den noen viltre sprett bortover. Den satte hodet i bakken og slengte bakbena til værs mens halen svinset rundt i luften. Mette frydet seg der hun sto og så på. «Jeg lar den bare gå her, så får den rent litt av seg,» sa Morten og gikk for å hente den andre kua som de hadde med. Det var den nye kviga. Petter løsnet tauet den var bundet med, og så dro han for å få den til å gå ut av hengeren. Men det så ikke ut til at den hadde tenkt seg ut i det hele tatt. Med stive ben strittet den imot alt den kunne. «Kom nå her!» ropte Petter. Morten gikk inn og dasket den mot halsen for å få den til å snu seg rundt, men ingenting så ut til å hjelpe. Kviga ville bare ikke rikke seg.

Petter brølte og Morten dasket mens de hele tiden nøkket og dro i tauet, men kvigen var like sta. Den ville ikke en gang rikke på et ben.

Plutselig skar en intens og skingrende lyd gjennom lufta. Det var tante Anna som satte i med en kulokk, og det en av skikkelig høyfrekvens. Mette skvatt så hun nesten ramlet bakover. Det samme gjorde visst Petter og Morten også. Men det som ikke brølene og sparkene til mannfolkene hadde greid, det greide tante Anna med den veltrente stemmen sin. På et blunk var kviga ute av hengeren. Petter fikk ikke summet seg før den var langt nede på jordet. Med hodet høyt hevet og halen rett til værs løp den som en gal mot skogen. Tauet slang og dinglet i marka etter den.

«Vi må få tak i den før den forsvinner over alle hauer,» ropte Morten og satte etter i fullt firsprang. Petter satte også etter så fort de knubbete bondebeina kunne bære ham.

Det gikk atskillig raskere med Morten, så Mette. Den slanke og spenstige kroppen la fort den grønne enga bak seg. For Petter så det mye tyngre ut. Både baken og magen bar nok tydelig preg av å ha sittet for mye bak traktorrattet, tenkte hun med et smil. Kjeledressen og gummistøvlene gjorde det slett ikke lettere.

Snart var kviga helt forsvunnet mellom trærne der langs jordekanten. Men det varte ikke lenge før de fikk se den igjen. Da kom den styrtende ut av krattet mye lenger oppe. Med hodet og ørene rett til værs kom den farende med kurs rett mot seterbua. Mette løp mot bilen for å komme ut av veien for den. Hun la merke til utrykket i øynene på det løpske dyret. De så helt ville ut. Det hvite lyste mot henne, og fra nesen oste det damp og røyk. Lynraskt smatt hun inn i bilen. I det samme hørtes en ny gjennomtrengende lyd, men denne gangen var det mer som et dødsskrik. Skriket kom fra tante Anna som var blitt klar over den overhengende faren hun plutselig befant seg i.

Aldri hadde Mette trodd at den runde, vaggende kroppen kunne bevege seg så fort.

På et øyeblikk smatt hun inn i seterbua. Døra gikk igjen med et smell, og Mette kunne høre hvordan slåen på innsiden ble slengt på.

Kviga fortsatte sin ville ferd bortover mot fjøset. Den hoppet over gjerdet, men greide ikke å komme helt over. To stolper spratt i været, og tråden ble brutalt revet av i spranget.

Der sto Plomma og betraktet galskapen. Med et redselsbrøl satt også den plutselig av sted. Fire stolper ble dratt bortover vollen etter tråden da den sprang over gjerdet i motsatt retning.

Der kom Morten og Petter pesende tilbake. De stoppet et øyeblikk for å få pusten igjen mens de så på dyrenes ville ferd. Plomma som brølende hadde satt kurs mot tjernet, og kviga som allerede var borte i lia der i vest. Den snudde raskt da motbakken ble for tung, men farten så det ikke ut til at den ville senke noe på. Før de to dyrefangerne helt fikk summet seg, styrtet den forbi dem igjen. Gjerdet lå nå nesten helt flatt. Plomma hadde stoppet og sto nede ved tjernet og peste. Da ble den oppmerksom på kviga som igjen var på vei rett mot den. Et nytt brøl, og noen kraftige sprett fikk kviga til å gjøre en brå sving slik at den snart var på vei tilbake mot fjøset igjen.

Mette smatt ut av bilen og gikk bort mot mennene. «Hva skal vi gjøre?» spurte hun fortvilet.

Morten kløddde seg i håret. De mørke øynene speidet etter kviga. Noe trassig og bestemt lå over utrykket hans. «Hvis dere to går bortover mot tjernet, en på hver side av enga, så skal jeg se om jeg kan få jaget den ned til bredden. Ta med dere gode kvister som dere kan jage med hvis den vil svinge av. Kviga skal på vann!» Det siste ble sagt mellom innbitte tenner.

Mette og Petter var allerede på vei bortover. Raskt brakk de seg hver sin kvist av ei bjørk som sto i jordekanten. Mette gikk mot venstre og Petter mot høyre. Et stykke fra vannkanten stilte de seg opp klar til å jage det ville dyret ut i tjernet.

I mellomtiden hadde den igjen snudd oppe i lia, og var på vei tilbake. Plomma så de ikke noe til. Den hadde vel søkt dekning et eller annet sted mellom trærne. Morten sto ubevegelig og stirret det løpske dyret rett inn i øynene mens den nærmet seg i rasende fart. De to nede ved vannkanten kunne ikke riktig se hva som skjedde, men plutselig hadde Morten greid å få tak i tauet som hele tiden dinglet etter den. Fast bestemt på ikke å slippe fulgte han med i den ville ferden.

«Dette må gå galt!» skrek Mette vettskremt. I det samme så de at Morten mistet fotfestet og falt framover, men han slapp ikke taket i tauet. Som en lekeball ble han trukket på magen etter dyret.

Da kviga så vannkanten, ville den svinge mot venstre. Men Mette sto der og skrek mens hun viftet med både armer og bein, så den tok ikke sjansen på den retningen. Den snudde fort mot høyre, men der var Petter. Den kraftige rødhårede mannen med den buldrende stemmen var visst heller ikke å foretrekke. Nå var der ikke så mange muligheter igjen. Og farten gjorde at den ikke hadde tid til å vurdere så mange flere heller. Med et fossende plask styrtet den ut i tjernet med Morten i tauet rett etter.

Det ble en plasking og spruting et øyeblikk som så ut til å ta pusten fra dem begge, men så roet det hele seg ned. Morten krabbet raskt på land og dro inn tauet. Kviga fulgte straks med.

Det så ut til å være et helt annet dyr de fikk opp av tjernet. Helt utmattet la den seg ned på bakken. Der ble den liggende og pese mens dampen oste av den.

«Der fikk vi tatt deg,» sa Morten mens tennene klapret i munnen på ham. Det kalde vannet hadde ikke akkurat vært en fornøyelse å bade i.

«Denne kviga kan du bare ta med deg hjem igjen,» sa han henvendt til Petter. «Noen flere slike basketak kan jeg ikke si at frister.»

Nå tok det ikke lang tid før kviga var tilbake i hengeren igjen. Petter bakket den så langt ned mot tjernet som han kunne komme. Og med forente anstrengelser fikk de inn det utmattede dyret.

Plomma kom også luskende etter hvert. Snart gikk den fredelig og beitet på vollen.

Etter at Morten hadde fått på seg tørre klær, ble han stående sammen med Mette og betrakte det ødelagte gjerdet.

«Jeg syntes Petter sa at dette var slik ei snill og rolig kvige,» sa Mette undrende. «Hvordan kunne den oppføre seg slik da?»

Morten ristet på hodet. «Disse dyrene er det ikke alltid så lett å forstå seg på. Noen ganger hender det at de oppfører seg helt annerledes enn forventet. Og får man først slike vanskeligheter med et dyr, så kan du være sikker på at problemene vil fortsette. Jeg vil i hvert fall ikke ta slike sjanser.

Men nå er det vel best jeg kommer meg ned igjen til gården for å hjelpe Petter med resten av dyrene. Håper vi slipper flere slike episoder.» Han hoppet inn i bilen som Mette og tante Anna hadde brukt, og snart var han forsvunnet nedover veien.

41 • Hvile

Tante Anna sto og trallet og sang inne i melkeboden. Mette visste ikke helt hva det var hun holdt på med, men det var i hvert fall trivelig å høre de velkjente lydene der inne fra. Ute var det kjølig med tåke og litt regn i lufta. Morten hadde dratt til bygda for å ta imot en gruppe med turister som de ventet.

Både dyr og folk hadde roet seg der på setra etter den strabasiøse flyttingen. De hadde fått opp ei ny kvige som var mye roligere. Også den skulle kalve, men ikke før litt senere utpå sommeren. Barna til Petter hadde gitt den navnet «Silkedokk», sikkert fordi de syntes den var så silkemyk og god. Den andre av de gamle kuene het «Stjerna». Den var svart med ei hvit stjerne i panna, og derav navnet. I tillegg hadde de fått med opp en fire måneder gammel kalv. Den hadde de ikke kjøpt, de skulle bare ha den der for at turistene skulle få kose seg med den. Petter var bare glad for å slippe stellet med den om sommeren. Og for turistene oppe på setra var det alltid populært med mindre dyr. Den hadde fått navnet Pia.

Mette satt ved vinduet i seterbua. Et øyeblikk lot hun blikket gli over dyreflokken som gikk der ute på vollen og beitet så fredelig. Også sauene hadde funnet seg godt til rette. Den sprø bjelleklangen nådde helt inn til henne der hun satt. Oppe i lia hadde de funnet seg et godt, saftig beite. De kjære lydene fikk henne til å sukke av lykke. «Så deilig det er å være her,» sa hun og smilte for seg selv.

Det så ikke ut til at noen av dyrene der ute brydde seg om det ruskete været. Bare de fikk være på fjellet og fråtse i det deilige fjellbeitet, så var det visst det eneste som betydde noe for dem. Lammene svinset rundt mødrene mens halene snurret som små propeller etter dem. Der, under de nyklipte magene til søyene, fant de alt de hadde behov for. Lykken så ut til å være fullkommen også for dem.

Det var likevel ikke så lenge Mette lot seg henføre med å se på dyrene. Snart var oppmerksomheten hennes igjen vendt mot det hun hadde foran seg på bordet. Det var nemlig det gamle skrinet som hun hadde funnet i hulen oppe i fjellskråningen. I strevet med flyttingen og ellers alt det som hadde skjedd, hadde hun helt glemt det vekk. Det var ikke før hun skulle hente noe inne i hjørneskapet at hun kom på det, for der sto det jo. Nå satt hun med det foran seg og studerte på hvordan hun skulle greie å få det opp. Nysgjerrigheten hennes var helt sprekkeferdig. Hva kunne skjule seg under det gjenstridige lokket? Hun hadde forsøkt å smøre kanten inn med olje, og så hadde hun pirket og skrapt vekk rust med en skarp kniv, men det så ikke ut til at noe ville hjelpe. Det satt fremdeles bom fast.

Med ett kom tante Anna inn fra melkeboden. «Hva er det du sitter og plundrer med?» spurte hun da hun så hvor konsentrert Mette var.

«Det er dette skrinet,» sa Mette og viste henne blikkboksen. «Jeg begriper bare ikke hvordan jeg skal få av lokket.»

Tante Anna kom nærmere og myste nysgjerrig. «Hvor har du funnet dette?» spurte hun. Mette fortalte om hulen hun hadde funnet der oppe under den veltede rota. Forsiktig løftet tante Anna opp skrinet og ristet på det. «Det er noe inni,» sa hun. «Dette var da underlig. Aldri har jeg visst at det fantes ei hule der oppe, og så ofte som jeg krabbet rundt i knausene her som barn. Dette må være skrekkelig gammelt.»

Mette kjente at spenningen steg enda noen hakk. Kunne hun bare begripe hvordan de skulle greie å få opp lokket uten å ødelegge det som var inni!

I det samme hørte de bildur utenfra. Flere biler og campingvogner kom kjørende bort mot campingområdet. «Der kommer turistene,» ropte Mette. Hun satte raskt skrinet tilbake i skapet og løp ut.

Det ble med ett en hektisk aktivitet. Turistene var en gruppe tyske familier som skulle tilbringe flere dager på setra. Mat skulle de holde selv, men tante Anna pleide alltid å servere noe godt, enten som velkomst eller til spesielle arrangementer som de stelte til der oppe. Nå var det flatbrød, spekemat og mye annet godt, som hun hadde forberedt. Smør hadde hun kjernet tidlig på morgenen, og gome, dravle, søtost, og flere andre forskjellige slags oster sto klart til å bli servert.

Mette hjalp henne med å få alt fram. De måtte sette det på bordet i seterbua på grunn av det ustabile været. Så ble turistene bedt om å komme inn og forsyne seg etter hvert som de hadde fått installert seg på campingplassen.

Det var egentlig ingen tradisjonell campingplass de drev der oppe. Det var bare ryddet til et område slik at det var mulig å plassere en del campingvogner der. Og det eneste sanitæranlegg som fantes på setra var utedoen ved fjøset, og tjernet som badekar. Men de fleste campingvognene som turistene kom med var så godt utstyrt at dette som regel ikke ble noe problem. Poenget for dem var bare å få være der å ta del i seterlivets daglige gang. I tillegg til det fikk de jo også anledning til å ta turer, både til fiskevann og ellers innover i fjellet.

Nå kom åtte familier i tur og orden inn i seterbua for å smake på godsakene der. Tante Anna smilte fra øre til øre over de mange godordene hun fikk. Alt som var satt fram ble mottatt med stor begeistring og glupende appetitt. Der var nok et og annet som ikke helt falt i smak hos de aller minste, men da fikk gjerne tante Anna seg en ekstra god latter. Det var jo ting som kunne smake litt skarpt og spesielt for de sarte barneganene. Ute på vollen boltret barna seg allerede i vilter lek. Seterferie var jo en spesiell og eksotisk opplevelse for dem.

Etter at de hadde spist, sa Mette at de kunne få lov til å gå bort til dyrene, men de måtte bare være nøye med å lukke grindene etter seg. En flokk med barn løp snart over beitemarka. De fleste av dyrene var så kjælne og folkekjære at de straks kom dem i møte. For enkelte av de minste barna ble nok de store kyrne en litt for skummel opp - levelse. To små jenter kom hylende tilbake igjen mens de ropte på mamma. Mette ble med dem og mødrene deres bort til noen av de minste lammene. De var mye tryggere, syntes de visst.

I frydefulle hyl gikk leken mellom sau og ku. Dyrene fulgte villig med i sprettene, i hvert fall de yngste av dem. Pia ble snart favoritt-lekekameraten deres. Hvor de sto og gikk fulgte hun med.

Noen av barna sto som trollbundet og klappet og strøk de myke pelsene. Spesielt lammene var så deilige å ta på, og det så slett ikke ut til at de ble lei behandlingen.

Utpå ettermiddagen så det også ut til at været bedret seg. Tåken forsvant litt etter litt, og sola viste seg av og til mellom de flyktende skyene. Temperaturen var ikke akkurat den beste til å være sommer, men det så ikke ut til at noen sørget over det.

Da Mette fant fram bøttene og gikk mot fjøset for å melke, ble det straks trangt rundt henne. «Dere må hjelpe meg å få inn dyrene,» sa hun. I det samme ble det liv i flokken. Med rop og sprett var snart alle kyrne inne i fjøset. Mette bandt dem fast, en i hver bås. Og så fant hun fram kraftfôr til dem. Barna fikk lov til å dele ut fôret. Det ble straks kamp om hvem som skulle gjøre jobben.

«Nå må dere være litt rolige,» sa hun da hun satte seg på krakken for å melke. «Det kan hende de ikke vil slippe ned melken hvis der er for mye forstyrrelse rundt dem.» Mette var glad for at hun så godt mestret det tyske språket. Det med språket var noe Morten hadde lagt ekstra sterk vekt på da han ansatte henne året før. Det at hun mestret både engelsk, tysk og en god del fransk, var nok sterkt medvirkende til at nettopp hun fikk jobben.

Litt roligere ble det nok i barneflokken, men iveren og spenningen gjorde det visst nesten umulig å greie å stå stille. Mette måtte le av de ivrige barneøynene som fulgte med i alt hun foretok seg.

Den store hannkatten Truls, som selvsagt også var blitt med til seters, kom i det samme luskende inn av fjøsdøra. Den visste at der nå kunne vanke en varm melkedråpe.

«Pus, pus.» Mette kalte på katten. Den kom straks bort til krakken hennes. «Se nå her,» sa hun til barna, og så melket hun en lang stråle ut i lufta. Truls bykset øyeblikkelig fram og fanget den deilige varme melka med tunga. Gang på gang sendte Mette melkestråler mot katten, og hver gang fanget den dem opp. Barna lo av forbauselse og begeistring. Straks ble katten den som fikk hele oppmerksomheten deres.

Den kvelden hørte de barnelatter og elleville rop til langt på kveld. Mette og tante Anna satt lenge med kaffekoppen etter kveldsmaten. De frydet seg over livet der ute på vollen.

Morten gikk ganske tidlig til sengs. Han hadde vært oppe grytidlig om morgenen, så da de satt og spiste kvelds, holdt øynene hans nesten på å falle igjen.

Mette listet seg stille inn på soveværelset da det begynte å skumre ute. Stor ble hennes forbauselse da hun så at Morten fremdeles lå våken. Parafinlampa på nattbordet var tent, og han lå tydelig fordypet i noe han leste.

«Sover du ikke? Du så jo stuptrett ut ved kveldsbordet.» Mette satte seg på sengekanten og begynte å kle av seg.

368

Morten kikket opp på henne og smilte. «Jo, det skal være sikkert at jeg var trett,» sa han, «men så begynte jeg å lese her, og da var det som om jeg våknet til igjen.» Da la Mette merke til at det var Bibelen han lå og leste i. «Hør her hva som står i 2. Mosebok sytten.»

Han begynte å lese om en trefning israelittene hadde hatt med amalekittene under ledelse av Josva. Moses hadde, sammen med Aron og Hur, gått opp på en høyde der de hadde god utsikt over kampområdet.

Mette dro på seg nattkjolen mens hun lyttet, og krøp under dyna.

«Hør her hva som står videre.» Iveren i stemmen hans fikk Mette til å lytte ekstra oppmerksom. Da gikk det slik til at så lenge Moses holdt hånden i været, hadde israelittene overtaket. Men så snart han lot hånden synke, var amalekittene de sterkeste. Men så begynte Moses å bli trett i hendene. Da fant de en stein og la den til rette for ham; den satte han seg på, og Aron og Hur støttet hendene hans, en på hver side. Så var hendene hans støe helt til solen gikk ned. Slik vant Josva over amalekittene og deres hær med kvasse sverd.

Morten stoppet og så på henne. I øynene lyste det en glans som om han hadde sett noe riktig vakkert. Mette var litt usikker. Hun skjønte ikke riktig hva det var han hadde sett i de versene.

Plutselig sank han tilbake mot puten og stirret tankefull opp mot taket. Stemmen hans virket trett da han igjen begynte å snakke:

«Jeg har følt meg så sliten denne våren. Alt arbeidet som måtte gjøres de korte ukene, fra snøen gikk og til sommeren var her, gjorde nok sitt, men jeg tror ikke bare det er det. Dette med Even, og alle følelsene som kom fram igjen der borte i Lia, har nok slitt på meg mer enn jeg har forstått. Spesielt syntes jeg det ble tungt med alt det ansvaret jeg hadde på bedehuset og i kirka, midt oppi dette.

Og så kom skyldfølelsen. Jeg ønsker jo så inderlig å få være med i det kristne arbeidet, men når jeg ikke helt synes at jeg orker alt det jeg har ansvar for, så tenker jeg at det i hvert fall ikke bør gå ut over arbeidet i Guds rike.»

Han sukket. Mette strøk ham over håret. Stakkars mann. Hun ante ikke at han hadde slitt på denne måten. Men så var jo Morten slik at man sjelden kunne se utenpå ham hva som rørte seg inni.

«Har du ikke snakket med noen av de andre i menigheten om dette?» spurte hun mykt. «Det må da kunne gå an å få avløsning i et og annet?»

«Ja …» Morten dro på det. «Jeg har nok nevnt det, men jeg vet ikke om jeg har ønsket å få avløsning. Jeg har jo følt det som et kall, denne tjenesten, så da var jeg ikke sikker på om det var Guds vilje at jeg skulle si det fra meg.»

Han lå der taus et øyeblikk. Enda et sukk slapp fra ham før han fortsatte: «Til og med bønnen ble tung for meg. Det å ta en stille stund i «lønnkammeret» greide jeg simpelt hen ikke å få til. Ofte sukket jeg til Gud om å få krefter, og kraft, til å greie det, men jeg har liksom ikke fått noe svar på den bønnen.

Disse versene som jeg leste her i 2. Mosebok har ligget som en svepe over meg. Der ser vi jo hvor viktig bønn er. Hvis armene til Moses begynte å synke, fikk jo fienden overtaket. Slik jeg ser det, har vi der et tydelig eksempel på hvor viktig det er å holde ut i bønn. Svikter vi, eller slurver med de stille stundene, så må vi regne med at arbeidet i Guds rike stagnerer. Ja kanskje det til og med kan gå tilbake og dø.»

«Men …» Mette heiste seg opp på albuene og så ham inn i de mørke øynene. «Det kan da ikke bety at man må slite seg aldeles ut. Vi er jo bare mennesker, det vet jo Gud også. Vi må da kunne få lov til å ta pauser for å få hvile litt?»

Plutselig kom det iver i øynene til Morten igjen. «Ja, det var nettopp det jeg fikk se i disse versene her i Bibelen. Moses ble også trett. Ja, han ble så trett at han ikke orket mer. Men hva skjer så? De to hjelperne hans kunne jo ha lagt seg på kne og bedt Gud om å gi Moses kraft til å holde hendene oppe. Og jeg er ikke et øyeblikk i tvil om at han også kunne ha gitt ham det. Han kunne ha gitt Moses styrke i armene slik at han hadde greid å stå rakrygget hele dagen uten i det hele tatt å kjenne det i musklene. Men Aron og Hur ba ikke om styrke for Moses. Nei, i stedet la de tingene til rette slik at han kunne få hvile mens han gjorde sin tjeneste. Og disse to vennene hans tok også mye av børa hans.»

Mette smilte der hun lå ved siden av ham og kjente den gode varmen fra kroppen til den kjære mannen. Endelig begynte hun å forstå hva som hadde fått søvnen til å vike denne sene kvelden. Gud hadde begynt å tale til ham om hvile. Morten trengte hvile … og da helst hvile fra det åndelige ansvaret. Det ansvaret som Gud selv hadde gitt til denne særdeles pliktoppfyllende mannen.

«Det ble så befriende godt for meg dette,» fortsatte Morten mens Mette krøllet seg sammen i armkroken hans. «Hvilen, den vil jeg finne her oppe på setra. Det er ikke akkurat hvile fra arbeid jeg søker, men heller hvile fra et stadig økende stress. Her oppe kan jeg ta lange turer i fjellet, gjerne sammen med turister. Slike turer har alltid virket avstressende og beroligende på meg. Og mens jeg går der, da helst alene, kan jeg jo snakke med min Himmelske Far. Aldri vil jeg vel få bedre tid, og mer krefter til akkurat det. Det beste lønnkammeret mitt har alltid vært fjellet. Og så kan de andre i menigheten ta seg av de praktiske tingene der nede i bygda.»

En ubeskrivelig fred og lykke fylte Mette der hun lå. Så fantastisk at de hadde en levende Gud. En som så til sine barn i alle situasjoner, og som slett ikke påla noen mer enn de kunne makte. Riktignok var det et livsviktig arbeid de sto i. Sjelevinningsarbeidet, som de begge var så engasjert i, så de på som det viktigste de kunne være med på. Og de var overbevist om at også Gud så det som det viktigste. Men det som var så fantastisk, var at Han hadde veier og metoder i arbeidet som slett ikke skulle ta både mot og krefter fra arbeiderne. All denne trøst og hjelp fantes i Ordet.

«Så var hendene hans støe helt til solen gikk ned,» siterte Morten stille etter hukommelsen. «Det ser ut til å være en livslang tjeneste vi er satt inn i, men Han vil sørge for at våre hender er støe helt til sola går ned, og vi er hjemme i Himmelen.»

«Ja,» sa Mette. «La oss bare ta en dag av gangen, så skal du se at vi skal komme gjennom.»

«Og så må vi være lydhøre for den stemmen som taler til oss fra disse bladene her,» la Morten til og klappet på de sorte skinnpermene. «Vi må la Han få lov til å styre oss i alle ting.»

Det ble stille der inne i soverommet. Freden fylte på en måte hele rommet. Gud var der hos dem, det var de ikke i tvil om. Og var bare Han sammen med dem, så kunne hva som helst hende, tenkte Mette før øynene hennes gled igjen.

Snart sov de begge fast.

42 • Med hest og trille

De tyske turistene så ut til å stortrives på setra. Flere av de voksne tok rett som det var turer i fjellet sammen med Morten, mens Mette og tante Anna holdt barna i aktivitet på vollen. Tante Anna hadde mange artige historier på lager. Selv om hun trengte Mette som tolk, greide hun å fengsle selv de minste ved sin engasjerende måte å fortelle på. Hvor hun sto og gikk fulgte det stadig en hale av barn etter henne. Hun lot dem få lov til å prøve både separatoren og smørkjernen. I melkeboden fantes det en masse ting som var spennende for dem å studere.

Dyrene fikk nok likevel mest oppmerksomhet. Truls ble stadig klappet og kost med. Det hendte at Mette fant den langt inn under spisebordet. Der hadde den gjemt seg for å få noen øyeblikks fred. Selv om den var særdeles kjælen og folkekjær, så det ut til at det til tider ble i meste laget for den.

Lammene fikk også rett som det var besøk, men de kunne visst ikke få nok selskap, så det ut til. De svinset begeistret rundt så snart det var noen som ville være med på leken. Likedan var det med geitene. De fulgte med overalt. Gjerdet, som nå var blitt grundig reparert, tok ikke disse spretne villstyringene særlig mye hensyn til. Og rett som det var kunne de se dem høyt oppe i fjellskråningene. Men de dro aldri langt av sted. De var altfor folkekjære til det. Snart var de ved foringsplassen igjen. Der vissete de nøyaktig når maten kunne ventes. Det så ut som om de hadde god forstand på tid og klokkeslett.

En dag kom Morten med en hest. Han hadde fått låne en rolig og snill fjording av en bonde nede i bygda. Det var en hest som var godt vant med både barn og voksne. I tillegg var den en dyktig arbeidshest. Både arbeid på jordene om sommeren, og hogstarbeid i skogen om vinteren var den vant til. Petter hadde ofte lånt den til arbeid på gården sin der det var vanskelig å komme til med traktor.

Morten tenkte at det kunne være interessant for turistene å se hvordan gårdsarbeid ble utført i gamle dager da de ikke hadde traktorer og andre maskiner å hjelpe seg med. Han tenkte også at det kunne være moro, både for barn og voksne, å få en kjøretur i vogna. Han hadde fått med ei fin trille som de kunne ta kjøreturer nedover langs veien med.

Mette var slett ikke vant til hester, men denne ble hun snart fortrolig med. Det varte ikke lenge før hun greide både å få på seletøyet og manøvrere dyret

Rett som det var tok de turer nedover veien med trilla full av barn. Som regel var det Morten som satt med tømmene. Hesten spaserte alltid rolig og støtt langs veien. Snart ble den så kjent med ruten de pleide å ta at den ikke behøvde å styres i det hele tatt. Når de kom til utkjørselen der de måtte snu, stoppet den automatisk.

○ ○ ○

Tiden for avreise for tyskerne nærmet seg. Barna sørget over at de måtte forlate de kjære dyrene. Flere av dem viste klart at de kjente barna igjen når de kom løpende langs beitet. Den kontakten de hadde fått, var det helt rørende å legge merke til.

«Kan vi ikke ta en siste tur med hesten før vi drar?» spurte en av guttene. Det var en livlig åtteåring som hele tiden hadde vist spesiell interesse for den rolige gampen. «Det kan vi gjerne,» sa Morten muntert og rusket den ivrige gutten i håret.

Snart begynte han å sele på hesten. Gutten hoppet begeistret opp og ned mens han utålmodig ventet på at alt ble klart til kjøreturen.

«Jeg må bare inn for å hente mobiltelefonen, og ordne noen saker først,» sa Morten da han var ferdig. «Jeg er tilbake om et øyeblikk. Bare vent her så lenge.» Han bant hesten til en stolpe i gjerdet og løp inn i melkeboden. Gutten, som var helt sprekkeferdig av forventning, løp bort og treiv tømmene. «Jeg kan passe hesten!» ropte han ivrig. Men Morten var allerede forsvunnet gjennom døren så han hørte ingen ting. Gutten fikk imidlertid raskt opp knuten rundt stolpen. Snart satt han stolt i vogna og slengte med tømmene. Han hadde sett Morten gjøre det på den måten, så han mente visst at han visste hvordan en hest skulle behandles. Men det han ikke visste var at nettopp det var tegnet Morten brukte for å få hesten til å gå. Med et rykk satte både hest og vogn seg i bevegelse. «Stans!», ropte gutten og slengte enda mer med tømmene. Hesten, som trodde det betydde at den måtte gå fortere, satte straks opp farten. Før noen riktig fikk sukk for seg var de forsvunnet rundt svingen nede ved skogholtet.

Morten kom løpende ut da han forsto hva som hadde skjedd, men han så fort at han aldri ville greie å ta dem igjen ved å løpe etter. Mette hadde også lagt merke til at både hest og vogn var borte uten at kjørekaren var blitt med. Morten løp bort til bilen og startet opp. Mette satte seg raskt inn ved siden av ham. Da de svingte ut på veien, kunne de høre hylene til guttens mor som var blitt oppmerksom på at hesten og barnet var borte.

De hadde ikke kjørt så langt før de fikk se hesten og trilla foran seg. Det var et nokså kaotisk skue som utspant seg der på veien. Gutten sto halvveis oppe mens han deljet og slo med tømmene mot hesteryggen. Hesten som trodde at den hele tiden måtte øke farten var nesten i fullt sprang.

«Dette kommer til å ende med ei ulykke,» sa Mette skrekkslagen. «Hva kan vi gjøre?» Hun forsøkte å rope til gutten gjennom det åpne bilvinduet, men det så ikke ut til at han hørte noe i det hele tatt. Morten sa ikke noe. Han var dypt konsentrert om det som foregikk der framme, samtidig som han forsøkte å komme så nær opptil som mulig med bilen.

Snart måtte de runde en sving. Da så det ut til at hesten ble oppmerksom på bilen som fulgte etter. Den satte i et ekstra byks og slengte med hodet mens den styrte enda lenger mot veikanten. Morten saknet farten med det samme. «Vi må ikke kjøre så nær at vi skremmer hesten heller,» sa han. «Hadde vi bare greid å få kontakt med gutten, men det ser jo ikke ut til at han er mottakelig for noen slags beskjeder.» Dype rynker lå over øynene hans, og munnen ble presset sammen i et krampeaktig bitt mens det tydeligvis foregikk en hektisk aktivitet oppe i hodet hans.

Mette var på randen til hysteri. Hun satt med hodet nesten helt framme i frontruten. Sikkerhetsbeltet hadde hun fjernet, klar til å hoppe ut så fort en anledning bød seg. Men det så slett ikke ut til at noen slik anledning ville komme, for hesten ble bare mer og mer urolig. Den slengte stadig med hodet. Forvirringen over den uventede behandlingen fikk den til å oppføre seg temmelig ukontrollert. Farten var også blitt faretruende høy. Ingenting så ut til å kunne stoppe den ville ferden.

«Vi må gjøre noe!» skrek Mette. «Han kommet til å bli drept. Tenk hva som vil skje når de kommer ned mot de bratte kleivene. Der vil de aldri greie å holde seg på veien med en slik fart!»

«Hadde vi bare greid å komme forbi ham,» sa Morten, «da skulle jeg nok ha fått stoppet den, men her er veien altfor smal til det.»

«Kanskje vi kunne få noen nede i bygda til å møte ham?» sa Mette med et glimt av håp i øynene. Morten ristet tvilende på hodet. «Det skal noe til at de rekker å komme opp kleivene før hesten er der nede.»

«Det er i hvert fall et forsøk verd,» sa Mette og treiv mobiltelefonen. «Forsøk Petter,» sa Morten og gav henne nummeret.

«Pappa er ikke hjemme,» sa barnestemmen som svarte da Mette spurte etter Petter. «Er det noen andre voksne der?» Stemmen hennes var nesten febrilsk. Hun forklarte i rasende fart situasjonen og ærendet deres.

Gutten ble tydelig oppskaket, kunne hun høre. «Det er bare jeg og Birger som er hjemme,» sa han, «men jeg skal høre med Birger.» Dermed ble forbindelsen brutt. Han hadde tydeligvis lagt på.

«Det ser ikke ut til at vi kan få tak i hjelp,» sa Mette og brast i gråt. Ferden der framme fortsatte bare i samme ville farten. Morten bremset opp litt. «Jeg er redd for at vi bare skremmer opp hesten mer med å følge etter på denne måten,» sa han, «men jeg ville helst ha vært i nærheten …» Han stoppet litt mens et smertedrag fòr over det anstrengte ansiktsutrykket hans. Etter et sukk fortsatte han: «… hvis noe skulle skje.»

Stadig så de at gutten snudde seg mot dem. Han skrek og viftet med armene mens skrekken lyste ut av øynene hans.

«Hilfe, Mutti, Mutti … hilfe …!» De tyske ordene rant ut av ham, men det hjalp ikke det minste. De var rett og slett ikke i stand til å gi ham hjelp. Et par ganger så det ut til at vogna skulle kantre. Mette skrek opp og treiv tak i bildøra for å komme ut. Men så greide den allikevel å følge etter den ville hesten, med hjula på veien. Sving etter sving ble tilbakelagt mens de to i bilen fulgte dramaet med stadig større uro. De så at snart kunne ferden være slutt, og da torde de ikke tenke på hva som kom til å skje.

«Nå er vi snart ved kleivene,» sa Mette. Stemmen var forpint til det ytterste, mens tårene rant hele tiden.

«Bare den ikke tar ut der hvor de høye skrentene er,» sa Morten. Mette grøsset med det samme. Hun så for seg steinura nedenfor veikanten. Bratt var der også. Akkurat der gikk veien i ekstra skarpe svinger. Dette måtte gå galt … Tanken sto klart for henne med det samme.

En underlig ro fylte henne midt i panikken. «Gud, nå overgir jeg dette barnet i dine hender.» Hun visste ikke om hun hadde bedt høyt, eller det bare var et sukk som steg opp fra hennes indre. Mer fikk hun ikke formet til bønn.

Da var det som om hun fikk se en åpenbaring. I neste øyeblikk ble hun klar over at det slett ikke var noe overnaturlig, men et menneske som sto der framme på veien. Rolig og stø sto han midt i veibanen med begge armene i været. Hesten vrinsket og slengte med hodet, men snart hadde personen der borte fått den under kontroll. Skummende av svette sto den og snøftet, mens den ble klappet og godsnakket med av redningsmannen.

Mette var ute av bilen før Morten hadde greid å bremse helt ned. På et øyeblikk var hun borte hos gutten som gråtende og skjelvende falt ned i armene hennes. Hun bar ham bort til bilen mens hun hele tiden snakket beroligende til ham. Tårene rant like stritt hos dem begge.

Da Mette hadde fått gutten inn i bilen, fikk hun omsider anledning til å se bort på redningsmannen. Morten var allerede borte hos ham. Det var Birger, den tolv år gamle sønnen til Petter. Borte i veikanten sto en firehjuling parkert. En følelse av ærefrykt og beundring fylte henne helt der hun satt. Det var ingen tvil om at gutten der borte hadde reddet et menneskeliv den dagen. Sannsynligvis hadde han også reddet livet til hesten. Hun kunne se at Morten klappet gutten på skulderen. Kjente hun Morten rett, ville nok ikke det bli den eneste takken han fikk for denne bragden.

Hesten hadde roet seg, men den bar ennå preg av den ville ferden. Birger og hesten så ut til å kjenne hverandre godt. Med sikre bevegelser tok han seg av det slitne dyret.

Morten kom tilbake til bilen.

«Birger vil ta med seg hesten opp til setra, så da kan vi bare kjøre i forvegen,» sa han og satte seg inn.

Det ble stor glede da de kom tilbake igjen med gutten, selv om de der oppe ikke hadde sett hvilken alvorlig fare han hadde vært i. Morten forsøkte, på en forsiktig måte, å få foreldrene til å skjønne alvoret. Han ville at de skulle forstå hvilken bragd Birger hadde utført.

Senere på dagen fikk Mette greie på at guttens foreldre virkelig hadde forstått det, for de hadde gitt Birger et stort pengebeløp som takk.

Da kvelden kom, kjente Mette at påkjenningen den dagen hadde tatt hardt på henne. Men hun var likevel lykkelig over at det hele hadde endt så godt. Birger hadde gjort en kjempejobb, men hun så klart at han hadde vært styrt av en høyere makt. Fremdeles satt den underlige følelsen i henne som hun hadde kjent i det øyeblikket hun overgav hele problemet til Gud der i bilen. Det var en følelse av fullstendig maktesløshet overfor en uunngåelig katastrofe, samtidig som vissheten var der om en makt som var sterkere enn alle naturkrefter. Det var til denne makt hun hadde overgitt problemet, og Gud hadde grepet inn.

Nå visste hun godt at det slett ikke var ved alle ulykker Han grep inn så konkret som dette. Det var jo Even et tydelig eksempel på. Så ofte led jo mennesker i sorg og smerte, og i mange av de situasjonene kunne det også ha blitt bedt på det inderligste om hjelp. Men hjelpen så ikke ut til å komme.

Dette var et vanskelig problem, tenkte Mette der hun gikk og puslet rundt dyrene om kvelden. Men en ting visste hun i hvert fall, og det var at i dag hadde Gud grepet inn på en forunderlig måte, og det takket hun Ham for.

Og så bad hun om hjelp til å akseptere at det slett ikke var alle ulykker Han lot menneskene unngå å komme opp i. Der var jo så mye de ikke forsto. Igjen sto det klart for henne at Guds tanker så ofte var helt annerledes enn menneskers tanker. Det som et menneske så som en ulykke, var ikke nødvendigvis det i Guds øyne. Kanskje det bare var en litt tidligere «forflytning til Herligheten». Igjen var tankene hos Even.

43 • Menighetstur

Turiststrømmen til setra økte stadig på etter som dagene gikk. Varmen var også kommet med full styrke. Noen kom gruppevis, og hadde gjort avtaler om forskjellig slags opplegg på forhånd. Men mange kom også bare opp for å se på setra og dyrene. Og var det ledig plass slik at de kunne få plassert ei campingvogn eller et telt, så fikk de være der så lenge de ønsket. Leien var kanskje litt høy, men så fikk de også mye for pengene. Demonstrasjoner av forskjellige slag hadde de rett som det var. Tante Anna kokte ost i en stor kjele over vedkomfyren inne i seterbua, og hun stekte lapper og pannekaker på hella der. Karding og spinning av ull viste hun også, og mange slags gamle redskaper og gjenstander hadde hun å vise fram.

Mette hadde stadig en flokk med barn og voksne rundt seg når hun satt med bøtta mellom knærne og melket de godmodige kuene. Noen av barna fikk også prøve seg, men det var ikke lett å få ut melken av spenene. Det måtte en spesiell teknikk til.

En søndag ventet de ekstra storinnrykk. Det var en kirke i nabobygda som skulle ha menighetstur. Borte ved tjernet gjorde Morten i stand til gudstjeneste. Der ble verken alter eller prekestol. Kirkebenkene måtte de også unnvære, men de regnet med at folk selv brakte med seg noe å sitte på. Høyttalere hadde i hvert fall Morten rigget opp nede ved vannkanten. De var koblet til en liten lastebil som han hadde fått låne. Den hadde han greid å kjøre nesten helt bort til stranden.

Dagen før hadde Mette ryddet stranden for rusk og rask som hadde reket inn med vannet i løpet av våren, så nå så den så fin ut som det reneste kirkegulv. Vannet var også blitt mye varmere de siste dagene. Hun hadde allerede prøvd det et par ganger. Siden de ikke hadde dusj i seterbua, måtte de jo ty til tjernet når det trengte et bad. De første dagene de var der oppe, hadde vannet vært for kaldt til å bade i, så da hadde de dratt ned til gården når de trengte en dusj.

Geitene kom byksende bort til henne der hun satt på den store, firkantede steinen som tjente som benk der på bredden. De strakte snutene opp i fanget hennes. «Tror dere at jeg har noe godt til dere her?» spurte hun og klødde dem i ragget. De likte alltid å få noen godord og klapp. Men aller best likte de når hun stakk til dem noe de kunne spise, og det gjorde hun visst så altfor ofte.

Morten hadde vært litt bekymret for hvordan det skulle gå med alle folkene og bilene når disse to løp rundt med sin utrolige frimodighet og nysgjerrighet. Men Mette mente at de bare kunne stenge dem inne i fjøset den tiden gudstjenesten pågikk, så ble de nok ikke til noe problem.

Året før hadde de arrangert et misjonsstevne på setra, og da ville ikke Morten ha geitene der i det hele tatt den dagen. Men i år hadde Mette insistert på å få ha dem på setra helt fra begynnelsen av. Hun skulle nok greie å passe dem, mente hun.

Dette året hadde de også planlagt misjonsstevne, men akkurat den dagen det skulle gå av stabelen, regnet det så kraftig hele dagen at det bare måtte avlyses. Derfor var de glade for denne anledningen til å kunne samle folk på setra rundt forkynnelsen av Guds Ord.

«Det er nok best å få dere inn i fjøset,» sa Mette med et siste klapp før hun reiste deg, «for snart begynner bilene å komme.»

Straks hun begynte å gå fulgte de livlige dyrene villig med.

Denne dagen så i hvert fall ut til å bli varm og fin. Vinden var heller ikke så kjølig som den hadde vært for en tid siden. Mens hun gikk bortover, så hun at enga hadde vokst ganske mye den tiden de hadde vært der.

Ikke før var geitene inne i fjøset, så begynte bilene å komme. En etter en ble parkert på vollen og nedover langs veikanten. Flokken ved tjernet ble ganske stor etter hvert. Mange barn var der også som straks løp rundt for å leke. De fikk beskjed om at de kunne få lov til å gå bort til dyrene når gudstjenesten var over.

Presten var en hyggelig, litt eldre mann. I sin stilfulle kappe steg han fram og ønsket forsamlingen velkommen. Liturgien ble fulgt på samme måte som i kirka, men de måtte unnvære orgelet. I stedet hadde de med seg to som spilte trekkspill.

Gudstjenesten der ute i det fri ble en ny og fin opplevelse, syntes Mette. Presten talte så varmt om Guds omsorg og kjærlighet, men han la også sterk vekt på at skulle menneskene få nyte godt av alle de godene som Han, ved sin stedfortredende gjerning på Golgata, hadde tilveiebrakt, så måtte de også ta imot det. Det var ikke noe som automatisk ble gitt den enkelte i det øyeblikket de ankom denne jord. Nei, de måtte akseptere Jesus som sin Herre og Frelser. Ja, ikke bare det, de måtte lukke Ham inn i sitt liv og la Ham få lov til å rense bort all synd som var der. Det var det Jesus kom til jord for å ordne, og det var det han nå så gjerne ønsket å gjøre med den enkelte, også denne dagen.

Det var ingen lang tale han holdt, men budskapet var enkelt og forståelig.

Etter prekenen syntes Mette det ble enda mer høytidelig, for da skulle et lite barn bæres til dåpen. Sterkt beveget satt hun og så på at presten tok vann fra tjernet på det lille barnehodet. Tenk at et lite barn skulle bli døpt der i deres tjern denne dagen. Så fint, og så stort.

At disse foreldrene bar dette lille barnet til dåp her i dag, var en handling som skulle vise at de ønsket at barnet skulle være overgitt i Herrens hender. I hvert fall ville livet senere vise om det var det de ønsket, for da ble det klart om de fulgte, og også selv levde denne troen ut, slik at barnet kunne bli kjent med den Herre Jesus i det daglige livet.

Så altfor godt visste Mette at det slett ikke alltid var dette ønsket som drev foreldrene til å bære barna til dåpen. Det hele ble gjort bare som en fin tradisjon. Likevel visste hun at Guds gjerning i dåpen var like viktig for barnet. Det ble tatt imot i Himmelen. Skulle så ikke opplæringen i den kristne tro bli fulgt, ville denne dåpen bli til lite nytte for den lille senere i livet. Troen måtte også være til stede for at dåpen skulle ha sin virkning.

Men denne dåpen var et tegn som Gud gjorde en gang for alle. Og skulle dette mennesket en gang senere i livet ta imot troen igjen, så ville det som skjedde der ved vannkanten denne dagen, igjen få sin fulle betydning og virkning.

Mens dåpssalmen tonet utover vannet mot fjellene der borte i øst, vanket tankene til Mette sine egne veier. Hun kom til å huske den samtalen hun hadde hatt med en konfirmant nettopp der ved tjernet året før. Det var også dåpen det dreide seg om den gangen.

Hvis nå dette barnet skulle komme til å dø før det rakk å bli døpt, hva ville da skje? Tankene fortsatte å spinne.

Svaret sto klart for henne i det samme. Hun husket et vers fra Bibelen. Det var vers 16 i Salme 139. Du så meg den gang jeg var et foster, i din bok ble alt skrevet opp; mine dager ble dannet før en eneste av dem var kommet.

Der står det jo klart at Gud er med i alt som skjer med et menneske helt fra unnfangelsens øyeblikk, ja, faktisk før det. Dette mennesket har Han en plan med. Men menneskene har ved syndefallet forkludret denne planen. Da synden kom inn i verden, ble også den alle mennesker til del, også de små barna.

Men dersom foreldrene overgir barnet i Guds hender helt fra begynnelsen av, så ser Gud i nåde til dem på grunn av foreldrenes tro. Denne troen viser de i handling ved at de bærer barnet til dåpen. Denne dåpen er jo noe Gud selv har foreskrevet, men han er nok ikke avhengig av en tid og et øyeblikk for sin innlemmelse av barnet i himmelens bok. Hans nåde er så ufattelig rik at han slett ikke er avhengig av at vi rekker å få båret barnet til dåpen. Det som teller, er vår tro, altså foreldrenes tro og ønske for barnet. Og denne tro legger også Gud ned i barnet som en gave.

Men skulle derimot foreldrene si at de ikke ønsket å bære barnet til dåpen, for Gud tar jo imot det allikevel, da er det et tegn på vantro og mistillit til Guds forordning.

Mette tenkte seg litt om der hun satt. Hun visste at mange praktiserte dåpen på en annen måte. At også de var Guds barn, var hun ikke i tvil om. Nei, Gud var nok så stor at han ikke innskrenket dette til en liten begrenset bås. Men troen og overbevisningen om hvordan dette skulle gjøres, la han også ned i hver enkelt, og da var det nok viktig å følge det man så som rett.

Plutselig begynte folk å reise på seg. Mette hadde vært så langt borte i tankene at hun hadde gått glipp av hele avslutningen.

Straks ble det livlig rundt henne. Barna løp bortover vollen for å se på dyrene. Noen av de voksne rigget til en stor grill, og snart kjentes duften av nystekte pølser og koteletter. Praten gikk høylydt mens folk satte seg rundt i klynger for å spise.

Morten og Mette satt sammen med ei gruppe litt eldre folk. Presten var også sammen med dem. Snart kom samtalen inn på sagnet. En gammel mann i flokken hadde visst god kjennskap til det. «Det sies at Silja ble begravd ved kirka her i bygda,» sa han, «men siden de regnet med at det var selvmord hun hadde begått, begravde de henne utenfor kirkegårdsmuren. På den tiden var de nøye med at de som begikk en slik udåd, ikke måtte begraves i innvidd jord. Graven skal visst ha vært på nordsiden av kirken, mellom kirkegården og elva.»

Alle rundt ham satt tause og lyttet oppmerksomt til det han sa. Alltid hadde dette sagnet skapt interesse, og Mette forsto klart at det fremdeles gjorde det. Morten lyttet ekstra nøye til det den gamle mannen fortalte.

«Nå hadde det seg visst slik,» fortsatte han og humret litt for seg selv, «at rett etter begravelsen ble det et forferdelig uvær. Hele natta raste stormen over bygda. Regnet styrtet ned mens lyn og torden slo i ett. Det skal visst ha vært så ille at ingen mann våget seg ut før langt ut på neste dag. Da kom en mann likblek av sjokk styrtende til presten. «Dere må gjøre noe … straks … Silja kommer!» skrek han. Presten fikk med seg klokkeren, og sammen løp de bort til kirkegården. Der fikk de se kista til Silja stå halvveis oppe av gravhullet.

Denne episoden skapte skrekk og uhygge i hele bygda. Noen mente at det var jenta som ville hevne seg fordi hun ikke var blitt lagt i innvidd jord, mens andre mente at det var den Onde selv som var på ferde.

Kisten ble i hvert fall gravd ned igjen, men ikke lenge etter ble det et liknende uvær. Da regnet gav seg så pass at folk igjen tok ut, fikk de se at det samme hadde skjedd igjen. Kista sto halvveis på ende med hodeenden oppe av jorda.

Dette skapte en slik skrekk hos dem som hadde foretatt begravelsen, at de straks tok med seg kista og begravde den innenfor kirkemuren. Etter det har visst Silja hvilt i ro, for det skjedde ikke noe mer med den kista.»

Mette grøsset der hun satt. Selvsagt var dette bare gammel fantasi og overtro, men det var likevel uhyggelig å høre slike fortellinger.

En annen mann, som hadde fulgt fortellingen med stor interesse, kom straks med flere spørsmål om hvor det var de først hadde begravd den kista. Fortelleren så ut til å ha god kjennskap til dette, så han forklarte nøyaktig der det skulle ha vært. Den andre ble sittende og tenke et øyeblikk i det dypeste alvor.

«Jeg har ofte hørt historien om Silja,» sa han etter en stund, «og jeg har alltid regnet det hele for å være noe oppspinn fra gamle dager. Men etter å ha hørt dette begynner jeg faktisk å lure på om den allikevel kan være sann.»

«Sann! Hva mener du med det?» Morten så forbauset på ham. «Det går da ikke an å finne ut noe slikt så lenge etterpå.»

«Jo, du skjønner det,» sa mannen mens han bøyde seg nærmere flokken og støttet albuene på knærne. «Jeg har vært graver der på kirkegården i snart tretti år. Der finnes ikke en centimeter av grunnen der som ikke jeg kjenner til, tror jeg. Det stedet som du beskrev, ligger ganske lavt, og nær elva. Det området av kirkegården som ligger nærmest muren der, har vi sluttet å bruke på grunn av at elva lett går så høyt opp. Grunnvannet stiger slik at vi vanskelig kan få gravd ei dyp nok grav. Hvis vi allikevel har gjort det, så risikerte vi nettopp at kista kom opp igjen. Oppdriften blir så kraftig at den sprenger seg vei helt opp i dagen igjen. Dette er jo en helt naturlig foreteelse. Og slik som du fortalte, så var det uvær og regn hver gang før dette hendte. Ja, jeg vil faktisk si det slik at man umulig kunne greie å beholde ei kiste under jorda der hvor den ble begravd. Det var jo enda nærmere elva.»

Det ble en underlig stemning i flokken. Disse nye opplysningene hadde nok de fleste ønsket bare å kunne avfeie som eventyr og oppspinn. Men en slik forklaring gjorde det hele så opplagt og forståelig. Og da var det vanskelig å bortforklare det hele.

Mette lot blikket gli over den mørke vannflaten. Igjen kjente hun den samme uhyggen som hun hadde kjent den første gangen hun fikk høre om sagnet. Selv om alt kunne forklares på en naturlig måte, så hvilte det allikevel mye mystikk over det. Uff, hun syntes nesten hun frøs der midt i solsteiken. Så underlig at slike ting, som var så nær knyttet til overtro og overnaturlige begivenheter, hadde så sterk tiltrekningskraft. Det var som om en usynlig makt trakk oppmerksomheten deres mot de uhyggelige. Dette var de onde makters spill. Det sto helt klart for henne i det samme. Folk hadde opp gjennom tidene tillagt det overnaturlig betydning. Og da var ikke de onde makter sene om å være med på leken. Historien hadde etterlatt seg mye redsel og gru i sitt spor.

44 • Nåde og tilgivelse

Enda en stund var den lille gruppen opptatt av det gamle sagnet. Selv om de fleste var fra nabomenigheten, så hadde disse eldre menneskene hørt om det i en eller annen variant. Flere hadde detaljer å føye til som de syntes var spennende.

«Tenk å ende sine dager på en slik måte,» var det plutselig en som sa. Han ristet på hodet og sukket. «Selvmord … det siste hun gjorde her i verden var et drap.» Ordene ble hengende i lufta som noe uhyggelig.

«Å … nå er det vel det samme hvordan man ender sine dager,» sa presten på sin lune og rolige måte. «Hvis man ikke har sitt forhold til Gud i orden, så er det uansett en alvorlig sak. Og hvordan det sto til med denne jenta i så måte, er det vel ingen som vet.»

«Nei, det er så,» sa mannen, «men selvmord er mord, det mener nå jeg. Og hvordan kunne hun få gjort opp for denne udåden?» Et megetsigende blikk mønstret prestens rolige skikkelse.

Hva presten svarte, fikk ikke Mette med seg, for hun ble plutselig oppmerksom på ei kvinne som raskt reiste seg. I et glimt så hun et likblekt ansikt med et forpint utrykk, før hun snudde ryggen til gruppen og begynte å gå med raske skritt mot vollen. Mette reiste seg også. Det så ikke ut til at resten av gruppen la merke til at de to kvinnene forsvant. De var allerede fordypet i det alvorlige emnet.

Mette fulgte etter kvinnen og tok henne igjen borte ved campingområdet. «Har du problemer?» spurte hun forsiktig og la hånden varsomt på skulderen hennes. Et snufs gav klart til kjenne at hun gråt.

«Huff da, jeg er bare så dum,» sa hun og forsøkte å smile. Men smilet nådde ikke øynene. Der kunne Mette ane den dypeste fortvilelse. Smilet forsvant også brått mens tårene fortsatte å renne.

«La oss sette oss der borte,» sa Mette og pekte mot benken som sto ved veggen til seterbua. Tause gikk de bort og satte seg. Kvinnen snufset igjen. Hun trakk fram et lommetørkle og pusset nesen før hun begynte å snakke.

«Det ble bare så vanskelig for meg der borte.» Stemmen hennes var svak og skjelvende. Hodet hennes lå litt på skakke som om hun ikke orket å bære det. «Du skjønner … de snakket om selvmord som den største forbrytelsen noen kunne gjøre. I hvert fall oppfattet jeg det slik at en som gjør noe slikt, ikke kan komme til himmelen.» Stemmen var nesten helt på bristepunktet, men hun fortsatte snart igjen.

«Sønnen min tok livet sitt for snart ett år siden. Jeg trodde at jeg begynte å fungere litt mer normalt igjen nå, men dette fikk alt det vonde fram igjen. Åååå …» Et sårt hulk unnslapp henne. «Det verste for meg i denne tiden etterpå har vært nettopp spørsmålet om hvor han er nå.»

Hun stoppet. Smerten som tegnet seg i ansiktet, var nesten ufattelig. Mette syntes skrekkelig synd på henne. Stakkars menneske. Hvilke lidelser hun hadde gjennomgått. Hun skulle ønske at hun kunne ha tatt ei diger gresstuste og kylt inn i munnen på den eldre herren der borte. At det gikk an å snakke på den måten! Hvilke fordommer og holdninger som enkelte kunne gå med! Ansiktsuttrykket hans hadde egentlig talt mer enn ordene. Hun grøsset, men nå måtte hun forsøke å ta seg av denne stakkars kvinnen.

«Hvor gammel var sønnen din?» spurte hun mildt. Kvinnen pusset nesen igjen før hun svarte. «Han var nitten år.» Mette kjente smerten langt inni seg når hun så kjærligheten som lyste ut av de lidende øynene.

«Han var slik en god gutt,» fortsatte hun. «Alltid hjelpsom og snill. Og så var han så glad i Jesus.» Da hun sa det siste, brast stemmen helt. Det tok en god stund før hun greide å fortsette. Mette satt taus og strøk henne over hånden. Det så ikke ut til at noen la merke til dem der de satt. Noen av gjestene hadde tatt seg små turer rundt i området, mens andre prøvde vannet. Barna løp og skrek av fryd mens de lekte med dyrene.

Da kvinnen fortsatte igjen, var hun blitt litt roligere. «Det var bare det at det skjedde noe med ham. Plutselig begynte han å snakke så rart. Til å begynne med var det bare noen korte øyeblikk det varte, senere ble det mer. Han kunne se eller høre underlige ting. Noen ganger fikk han det for seg at han måtte gjøre noe som var helt merkelig. Skulle han reparere noe, det kunne være en ganske enkel liten ting, ja, så kunne han like godt ødelegge det. Det hendte også at han kunne ta en ting, for eksempel mobiltelefonen, og så sende den i veggen. Etterpå sto han helt overrasket og spurte: «Hvorfor gjorde jeg det?»»

Hun stoppet igjen. Det virket som hun satt og tenkte. Mette forsto at hun hadde behov for å snakke om dette, så hun sa ikke noe, ventet bare på fortsettelsen. Det varte heller ikke lenge før den kom:

«Det verste var at noen mente at det var religionen som hadde gått til hodet på ham. Det var nemlig noen ganger at han mente Gud snakket til ham. En gang trodde han at han selv var apostelen Paulus. Da ville han av sted for å holde tale.»

«Fikk han noen form for legehjelp?» Mette var i tvil om hun våget å spørre, men så gjorde hun det likevel.

«Å ja,» kvinnen ble ivrig med det samme. «Han var til lege flere ganger, men det

379

virket ikke som om de forsto hvordan han hadde det, for når han kom dit, var han jo slik som han pleide. Da husket han heller ikke så mye av hvordan han hadde vært. Jeg skulle ha gått med ham,» sukket hun sårt, «men en voksen, myndig gutt vil helst ikke ha mamma med seg til lege.

De merket riktignok at han var nokså nedfor, men … der var noe mer … åååå … han hadde det så skrekkelig vondt.» Hun stoppet. Gråten tok overhånd igjen. Denne gangen varte det lenge før hun greide å fortsette.

Da ordene endelig ville forme seg for den oppskakete kvinnen igjen, kom de nesten bare som en visking: «Vi rakk aldri å finne ut av det … en kveld … han kom ikke inn … vi fant ham på låven … i et tau.»

Mette kjente at hun skalv lett, men hun prøvde å holde seg så rolig hun kunne. Noe så skrekkelig.

Kvinnen hadde sunket sammen. Hun ristet av grått. Mette la armen om henne og trakk henne inn til seg. Det var det eneste hun i øyeblikket greide å gjøre.

Plutselig rettet kvinnen seg opp igjen. Hun stirret på Mette med et intenst blikk. Fortvilelsen lå som en bunnløs sjø bak de opphovnede øyelokkene. «Hvor er han nå?! …» Spørsmålet kom nesten som et skrik fra den forpinte strupen.

Mette så rolig på henne. Hun svarte ikke med det samme. I brøkdelen av et sekund steg det opp et ordløst sukk til Gud om hjelp til å svare rett.

«Sønnen din var syk,» sa hun. Kvinnen nikket, men hun fortsatte å stirre. Det så ikke ut til at hun syntes det var noe svar. Var det noe hun selv var klar over, så var det nettopp det. Mette renset stemmen før hun fortsatte:

«De tingene han sa og gjorde, var et resultat av sykdommen. Det er vel slik at lidelser av dette slag ofte arter seg på den måten at de overreagerer på enkelte ting. Der er noe i hodet som kommer i uorden, og da blir reaksjonene nokså underlige. Dette er nok ikke det eneste tilfellet der religionen får skylden for lidelsen. Men sannheten er nok heller den at når man blir syk på denne måten, så er det de tingene man ellers er interessert i, og opptatt av, som også de syke tankene kretser om. Hadde han vært sterkt politisk interessert, så kan det godt hende at det var politiske ting det hadde dreid seg om. Kanskje han da hadde trodd at han var statsministeren, eller Hitler, for den saks skyld.»

Kvinnen nikket svakt, men hun svarte ikke noe. Satt bare og ventet på at Mette skulle fortsette.

«Kan du vente her et øyeblikk,» sa plutselig Mette. «Jeg skal bare hente Bibelen min. Der er noe der jeg vil vise deg.»

På et øyeblikk var hun inne i seterbua, men snart kom hun tilbake igjen. Raskt slo hun opp i Romerbrevet. Der begynte hun å lese fra vers 33 i kapittel 8: «Hvem kan anklage dem som Gud har utvalgt? Gud er den som frikjenner, hvem kan da fordømme? Kristus Jesus døde, ja, mer enn det, Han sto opp og sitter ved Guds høyre hånd, og han går i forbønn for oss. Hvem kan skille oss fra Kristi kjærlighet? Nød, angst, forfølgelse, sult nakenhet, fare eller sverd?

Og lenger nede her står det også: For jeg er viss på at verken død eller liv, verken engler eller krefter, verken det som nå er eller det som kommer, eller noen makt, verken det som er i det høye eller i det dype, eller noen annen skapning skal kunne skille oss fra Guds kjærlighet i Kristus Jesus, vår Herre.»

Mette så opp på kvinnen som satt der så oppmerksom og lyttet. «Her står det klart. Ingenting kan skille et menneske fra Jesus. Ikke engang Djevelen kan det. Den eneste som kan skille oss fra Jesus, er vi selv, og vårt eget valg om å følge verdens lyster og fristelser i stedet for Ham.

Du sa jo at han var så glad i Jesus?»

«Å ja.» Hun knyttet hendene i fanget mens blikket flakket mot fjelltoppene i øst. Sola stekte på dem der de satt, og barna fortsatte sin lek rundt på vollen. Men det så ikke ut som hun la merke til noe av det. Hun var tilbake hos sønnen i tankene.

«Da disse vonde turene kom over ham, så tryglet han Jesus om hjelp.» Plutselig så hun rett på Mette igjen: «Du skjønner, han fikk slike forferdelige angstturer.»

Mette fortsatte mens hun så inn i det herjede ansiktet: «Heller ikke denne sykdommen kunne skille ham fra Jesus og Hans kjærlighet.»

«Nei …» Kvinnen stirret tvilende ned på de knyttede hendene i fanget. «Kanskje ikke sykdommen, men …»

Mette skjønte hva hun tenkte på. «Det han gjorde, var et resultat av sykdommen. Det vil aldri bli tilregnet ham.»

«Hvordan kan vi vite det så sikkert?» Noe intenst kom over henne i det samme hun uttalte ordene. Det intense blikket boret seg inn i Mette der hun satt. Et øyeblikk ble de bare sittende og stirre på hverandre.

Da var det Mettes tur til å la blikket gli langs horisonten, mens tankene hennes begynte å forme seg i ord: «Den som er et Guds barn, og det forstår jeg at sønnen din var …» Et raskt blikk på kvinnen oppfattet en heftig nikking som svar, «… den lever i Guds nåde og tilgivelse. Og tilgivelse er der å få for alle synder, samme hvor store og alvorlige de er.»

«Ja, men han rakk jo aldri …» Det fortvilede utrykket lå nå nesten nedgravd i hver pore i ansiktet hennes.

Mette tok plutselig hånden hennes i begge sine og så henne rett inn i øynene: «Hva er tilgivelse, tror du? Er det noe man kun får etter at man har greid å hviske fram en bønn om det, gjerne under dynen om kvelden, etter at man har gjort noe man ikke skulle? Nei, jeg skal si deg hva tilgivelse er. Tilgivelse er noe som ble ordnet på Golgata en gang for to tusen år siden. Der ble soningen for alle våre synder gjort. Det var ikke bare for de syndene som allerede var begått, men også for dem som siden kom til å bli begått av menneskene. Alt ble sonet der. Den som er et Guds barn, lever i tilgivelsen. Nåden kaller vi det. Og denne nåden fikk din sønn erfare i det øyeblikket synden hans ble begått. På grunn av det Jesus gjorde på Golgata gikk han rett til Jesus den gangen for et år siden.»

Kvinnen stirret på henne med halvåpen munn. Tårene rant, men øynene hadde fått et mer åpent utrykk. Hun svarte ikke noe med det samme, satt bare og stirret. Så begynte hun å snakke. Det virket som om ordene var mer til henne selv enn til Mette:

«Slik har jeg aldri tenkt på det. Men det er jo rett. Det er jo slik Bibelen sier det.»

En stund så det ut til at disse nye tankene arbeidet rundt i hodet hennes, men så var smerteutrykket tilbake igjen.

«Det er bare så vondt å ha mistet ham. Hvorfor … Jeg ba jo så inderlig for ham i den tiden da han gikk der og led. Jeg ba om helbredelse. Hver dag ba jeg om det, men …» Hun ristet fortvilet på hodet.

Mette så på henne med den dypeste medfølelse. «Det er ikke alltid lett å forstå slike vonde ting som skjer,» sa hun. «Og så altfor mange hvorfor vil vi nok aldri få svar på her i verden. Men noe kan vi kanskje prøve å forstå. La oss forsøke å sette oss litt inn i Guds sted. Du gråt over sønnen din som led. Hvor mye mer tror du ikke Gud gråt, Han som ser alt. Han så hvert lidelsestrekk i den unge kroppen, og han så hver angstbølge som skaket ham. Så vondt det måtte være for Gud å oppleve det. Dette var jo barnet hans som han hadde så inderlig kjært.

Foreldre reagerer jo når barna lider. Det vet jo du det meste om. La oss tenke oss en situasjon. Dette er nok et haltende bilde, men jeg syntes likevel det sier noe: Tenk om naboen din kom hjem til deg en dag i den tiden da gutten din var liten, og sa at han hadde sett ham nede i vegen. Der hadde han falt og slått seg, og hadde det forferdelig vondt. Hadde du da sagt: «Se her er noe bandasje og noe salve, ta det og stell godt med ham, så blir han nok frisk igjen»? Nei, du hadde ikke sagt det. Du hadde løpt av sted med en gang og båret barnet hjem i armene dine.

Det var det Gud gjorde med sønnen din. Han kunne ha helbredet ham, men det hadde bare vært det nest beste for ham. Han måtte ha fortsatt å leve her i denne vonde verden, og kanskje han senere i livet kom til å oppleve mer vondt. Nå syntes Gud at denne gutten hadde lidt nok. Han ville ikke at han skulle ha mer vondt … ikke i alle evighet. Derfor tok han ham hjem. Han har det godt nå. Ingen flere lidelser. Ingen sorger. Ingen nød. Skal vi ikke la ham få lov til å eie den lykken?»

Kvinnen så på henne med et underlig blikk. Hun svarte ikke noe med det samme. Satt bare som i dype tanker.

«Og så må du huske at Gud også ser deg,» fortsatte Mette. Han ser dine tårer og han ser din smerte. Kanskje han også gråter fordi han ser at du har det så vondt. Han elsker deg like høyt som han elsket sønnen din. Nå ønsker han å trøste deg. Han vil også bære deg i armene sine, men kanskje du må være her i verden en stund til.

«Ja …» Det kom som et tungt stønn fra den lidende kvinnen. «Det er bare så vanskelig å gripe. Jeg har jo selvfølgelig merket hans hjelp og trøst mange ganger denne tiden, men så er de vonde tankene der igjen. Det har vært som en evig runddans.»

Plutselig så hun på Mette og smilte. Denne gangen nådde smilet øynene. «Takk skal du ha. Du må unnskylde at jeg har plaget deg med dette på denne fine dagen.» Det var som om de med ett ble klar over den varme solen og det yrende livet rundt dem.

Mette la armen rundt henne og gav henne en klem. «Du har slett ikke plaget meg. Det er jo bare så godt hvis vi kan være til litt hjelp for hverandre.»

«Du har virkelig vært til god hjelp for meg,» sa kvinnen og gjengjeldte klemmen. Jeg er overbevist om at det er Gud selv som har snakket gjennom deg i dag. Slik føler i hvert fall jeg det.»

Hun pusset nesen og reiste seg fra benken. «Du har ikke et sted hvor jeg kan få vasket fjeset mitt litt?» spurte hun og dro håndbaken over øynene.

Mette viste henne vannkranen inne i melkeboden før hun igjen gikk tilbake til de andre gjestene. Men hun greide ikke å følge skikkelig med i samtalene der, for tankene hennes var fremdeles hos kvinnen hun nettopp hadde snakket med.

Snart så hun en bil som kjørte nedover veien, og hun skjønte at hun allerede var dratt.

45 • Besøk fra fjellet

Halvt omtåket og fortumlet satte Mette seg opp i sengen. Hun gned seg i øynene mens hun krampaktig forsøkte å komme til så mye klarhet at kunne forstå hva det var som hadde vekket henne. Morten begynte også å røre på seg. «Hva er dette for slags spetakkel?» spurte han og vred seg rundt så han kunne sende et sløret blikk mot vinduet.

Da hørte Mette det ganske klart. Utenfor var det noe som foregikk. Sauene breket og kyrne rautet. Den intense lyden til sauebjellene fikk nesten hele luften til å dirre. Det var et voldsomt oppstyr der ute.

Fort spratt hun opp av senga og tittet ut av vinduet. Ute lå det en grå tåkedis. Sola hadde ikke greid å jage den på flukt ennå. Et raskt blikk på klokka fortalte at det fremdeles var den tiden da de skulle ligge under dyna. Den var bare halv fem.

Borte ved sauefjøset kunne hun se noen av sauene. De løp forvirret rundt mens lammene forgjeves forsøkte å finne igjen de rette mødrene sine. En hadde klatret høyt opp i skråningen og forsøkte febrilsk å finne et trygt tilfluktsted på det bratte berget.

Morten spratt også opp og fikk på seg noen klær. Han var ute av døra før han hadde kneppet buksa. Mette tok seg ikke bryet med å få på seg mer klær. Hun løp ut i bare nattkjolen.

Ute på vollen ble de møtt av et forvirrende syn. I den dimme disen kunne de se sauer som hoppet og spratt over alt. Til og med på campingområdet var det flere som hadde funnet veien inn imellom vogner og biler. Noen av turistene var allerede ut for å forsøke å jage dem vekk. I enga gikk der også mange og forsynte seg grådig av det saftige gresset.

Mette styrtet inn igjen og fikk på seg noen klær før hun igjen løp ut på vollen.

«Vi må forsøke å få samlet dem, og så jage dem inn i fjellet igjen,» sa Morten. «Det er flokken til en av naboene nede i bygda, ser det ut til. Det er ikke ofte at så store flokker har trukket ned hit til setra. De liker som regel ikke så godt å komme i nærheten når der er sauer og andre dyr her fra før.»

«Men hvordan skal vi nå gripe dette an?» spurte Mette forvirret. «Og se på enga, den som vi snart skulle slå.» Morten stirret også bekymret på det fine og frodige gresset som nå ble tråkket ned av en mengde små klauver, samtidig som de la fra seg den ene ladningen av møkk etter den andre.

«Se på våre dyr.» Mette ble enda mer bekymret «De er jo helt vettskremte. Bare de ikke flykter til fjells.»

«Hvis du prøver å få med deg dem borte ved campingvognene, så skal jeg ta meg av dem i enga,» sa Morten. «Vi må prøve å jage dem bort til stien ved tjernet. Der tror jeg vi lett kan lede dem inn i fjellet igjen.»

Det ble en hektisk aktivitet ute på vollen. Flere av turistene kom også for å hjelpe til. Etter en stund hadde de samlet flokken så noenlunde. Morten jaget noen i forveien bortover mot stien, og da fulgte snart resten etter. Mette gikk bakerst for å se at alle ble med.

Plutselig var det en som stakk ut fra flokken med kurs rett mot tjernet. «Skynd deg å hente den inn igjen!» ropte Morten. «Så forvirret som den er kan den fort løpe på vann, og da er det nok ikke lenge før den drukner.»

Mette løp så fort bena kunne bære henne. Heldigvis greide hun å få snudd sauen før den nådde vannet.

I yrende mylder av breking og svinsing beveget hele flokken seg ut av seterområdet og oppover lia mot fjellet. Morten ledet an med noen av dyrene, og så måtte Mette se etter at resten fulgte greit med. Det ble en del springmarsjer og lynspurter for henne før de endelig var kommet så langt inn at de syntes de kunne forlate flokken. Sola var da kommet godt opp på østhimmelen. De varme strålene gav dem nesten mer enn de behøvde, for marsjen hadde gitt dem den varmen de trengte og vel så det. Svettestriper rant nedover skjorteryggen til Morten, og Mette kjente at hun selv også var blitt ganske fuktig. Heldigvis var der enda så pass mye kjølighet igjen i den tidlige morgenluften at det svalet forfriskende.

«Jeg får håpe at de nå vil holde seg her oppe,» sa Morten og betraktet de hvite ullnøstene som snart spredte seg ut over i det vidstrakte området.

Mette og Morten satte seg på en stein for å puste litt ut. Mette lot blikket gli over det inntagende landskapet. Lengst borte i nord tegnet fjelltoppene seg majestetisk mot den klare himmelen. All tåke og dis var forsvunnet. Bare noen få skydotter seilte dovent over den mektige hvelvingen høyt over hodet på dem.

Begge satt de i taushet og bare nøt synet av naturens gigantiske panorama. Plutselig ble Mette oppmerksom på ei ørn som svevde høyt der oppe. Bare den ikke var på leting etter et passende bytte der i saueflokken. Dyrene hadde roet seg og gikk fredelig og beitet mellom fjellknauser og kratt. Den klare bjelleklangen gav en helt spesiell fjellstemning, syntes Mette.

Ørna seilte i store sirkler over området. Det var tydelig at den hadde sett seg ut et bytte langt der nede i lyngen. Utrolig at den kunne ha et slikt kikkertblikk, tenkte hun der hun betraktet adferden til den store fuglen. Plutselig stupte den ned mot marka, men på et øyeblikk var den i lufta igjen. I klørne kunne hun se at det hang noe og dinglet, men heldigvis var det ikke et lam den hadde tatt. Stakkars småkryp som løp der nede i lyngen. Det kunne ikke være lett for dem å berge seg for slike lynangrep. Snart var ørna forsvunnet mot fjellene i det fjerne. Den hadde vel et rede der et sted med noen små hjelpeløse unger som skrek etter mat. Det var jo klart at fuglen måtte jakte. Men så underlig naturen var laget. Her var virkelig ordtaket: den enes død er den andres brød, en realitet.

Mette tok hånden til Morten. Så godt det var å sitte der ved siden av den kjære mannen sin. Han vendte blikket mot henne og smilte. Øynene hans gjenspeilet hennes egne følelser på en inderlig og fortrolig måte. Hjertet hennes begynte å banke fortere. Stillheten og freden rundt dem gav en forsterket stemning til de varme følelsene inni henne.

Morten la armen rundt henne og trakk henne inn til seg. De var helt alene der i Guds frie natur, kun med sauene som nokså uinteresserte tilskuere. Varsomt tok han hodet hennes i begge hendene sine og kysset henne. Hun trykket seg inntil han og ønsket at de kunne sitte der i all evighet. Følelsene bruste i hennes indre. Varsomme, kjærlige ord ble som kjærtegn for sjel og sinn hos dem begge. De satt der … lenge … klokka enset de ikke. Sola varmet mer og mer etter som den steg høyere og høyere på himmelen. Fuglene kvitret og sang. Tonene blandet seg med sauebjellene som ble svakere og svakere etter hvert som de beveget seg lenger og lenger utover i området på leting etter mer mat. Harmonien og freden der i fjellet fylte dem helt inn i det innerste, en atmosfæren perfekt for ømhet og kjærlighet.

Da de endelig reiste seg var det med nokså motvillige bevegelser. Fremdeles var tankene og følelsene mest opptatt med den andre. Hånd i hånd begynte de å gå tilbake samme vei som de var kommet. Turen gikk atskillig roligere nå. De nøt den deilige dagen og den friske morgenluften i fulle drag

Et nytt oppstyr møtte dem da de endelig kom tilbake til setra igjen. Flere av turistene hadde samlet seg under fjellskråningen bak seterbua. Noen forsøkte å klatre oppover det bratte berget. Roping og støy kunne høres lenge før de to fjellvandrerne nådde bort på vollen.

Det viste seg snart at det var den sauen som hadde klatret opp der tidlig i morges, som skapte oppstyret. Den sto nå på ei smal fjellhylle ute av stand til å komme verken opp eller ned. Fra flere kanter var det barn og voksne som forsøkte å komme den til hjelp, men fjellet var ekstra sleipt og vanskelig akkurat der. Ingen av dem greide å komme helt fram til dyret. Sauen sto bare og trippet fram og tilbake. Det redde blikket flakket snart fra den ene til den andre av de ivrige redningsmennene.

«Hva er det de gjør?» sa Morten bekymret da han kom nærmere. De skremmer jo vettet av den stakkars sauen med all den ropingen og støyen. Raskt var han borte hos turistene og forsøkte å roe dem ned, men det var slett ikke så lett. De oppskakede barna løp rundt mens de ropte og skrek. Alle ville gjerne hjelpe til, og alle hadde sine meninger om hvordan dette burde gjøres. De voksne var slett ikke bedre enn barna.

Sauen der oppe på hylla ble bare mer og mer urolig. En av de voksne var kommet nesten helt bort til den. «Kom hit!» ropte han plutselig med kraftig røst. Den vettskremte sauen kvakk til i det samme, og dermed gjorde den et voldsomt byks rett ut i lufta.

Fra flokken nede på marka hørtes det et redselsskrik idet den hvite bylten landet på fjellet flere meter under. Derfra rullet den kast i kast nedover skråningen. Den ble liggende mellom lyng og mose i ei lita fjellkløft ikke langt fra der turistflokken sto. På et øyeblikk var de borte hos den. Et nytt skrik kunne høres da den ble tatt i nærmere øyesyn. «Død! … Den er død …» Flere av barna gråt, og Mette greide heller ikke å holde tårene tilbake da hun så den kjære sauen deres ligge der livløs.

«Det var dette jeg var redd for,» sa Morten med et mørkt blikk. «Sauer som går seg fast slik kan lett bli så redde at de bare hopper uten å tenke på hva slags konsekvenser det kan ha. Derfor må vi alltid være rolige og forsiktige når en slik redningsaksjon skal utføres. Disse turistene har tydeligvis ikke mye greie på slikt,» sa han og ristet på hodet.

Det ble en sorgens dag, ikke minst for alle barna som hadde blitt så glade i de godmodige sauene. Nå var det også to lam som ikke lenger hadde en mor å ty til. Disse fikk ekstra mye kos og oppmerksomhet. Det kunne lett merkes at de lengtet etter moren som var borte. Stadig gikk de brekende på leting etter maten sin. Tante Anna fant ei flaske som hun helte litt lunket melk på. Så trakk hun en smokk over flaskeåpningen. Dermed hadde hun den perfekte tåteflaske. Snart lå det ene lammet i fanget hennes og sugde begjærlig. Det andre lammet var mer skeptisk til den nye «moren». Men etter litt godsnakking og klapp greide hun også å få den til å drikke. Snart var alle barna opptatt med mating av de stakkars morløse lammene.

Morten tok med seg den døde moren ned til bygda, mens Mette satte i gang med fjøsstellet. Det var blitt ganske langt på formiddagen, så kuene sto alt ved fjøsdøra og rautet. Den vidunderlige følelsen av ro og harmoni, som hun hadde følt der oppe i fjellet, var blitt brutalt forstyrret her i kaoset på setra denne formiddagen. Men da hun satt med hodet inn til den varme kumagen og melket, kjente hun at de varme følelsene enda satt der dypt inni henne. Det var en fred og en trygghet av godhet og kjærlighet som varmet, og gav håp om en lykkelig framtid for dem begge.

Snart var melkingen unnagjort, og kyrne ute på beitet igjen. Mette tok melkebøttene og gikk mot melkeboden. Da fikk hun se tante Anna borte ved bekken. Hun kom bærende på et fang med et eller annet som hadde ligget der i vannet. «Er det veden du har lagt i bløt der borte?» spurte Mette med et muntert blikk. Det så akkurat ut som et vedfang hun kom med.

«Tenk, ved du,» sa tante Anna og lo så hun nesten mistet alt hun bar på. «Dette er fisk … Stokkfisk er det,» sa hun og lo enda mer da hun så det forbausede utrykket til Mette. «Det er torsk som har hengt til tørk oppe i nord et eller annet sted. Og nå har jeg hatt den liggende i bekken en tid i bløt, for her skal det bli lutefisk.»

«Ja vel,» sa Mette, «men er det ikke litt tidlig med lutefiskproduksjon nå. Jeg trodde det var noe man laget til jul?»

Igjen lød den trillende latteren til den gamle dama. «Ja, men du vet at her oppe på setra følger vi ikke alltid timeplanen på den måten. Er det noe vi vil lage for turistene, så lager vi det, selv om det ikke er den rette årstiden for det.»

Mette kom nærmere for å se på de lange tynne stokkene som lå der over armene hennes. «At dette kan bli mat,» sa hun og vred på nesen mens hun studerte de skrukkete pinnene.

«Dette blir mat, skal jeg si deg, og det skikkelig også,» sa tante Anna ivrig. «Når denne er ferdig behandlet, skal du se at det ikke er mye igjen av de tynne stokkene. Nå skal den lutes og vannes ut, og når hele prosessen er unnagjort, så er fisken blitt fem til sju ganger så stor.

Mette sperret øynene opp. «Hva gjør du for å få det til?»

«Nå skal du se,» sa hun og vagget bortover mot melkeboden. «Først må vi kappe opp dette i passende stykker. Det kan du hjelpe meg med.»

Mette fulgte etter inn i boden og begynte ivrig med arbeidet etter at hun hadde satt melka til kjøling i kulpen. Den fikk vente til senere. Flere av turistene kom også for å se hvordan fisken ble behandlet. Mange hadde hørt om lutefisk, og noen hadde til og med smakt det, men ingen hadde noen gang vært med på tilberedelsesprosessen.

Da all fisken var skåret i tommetykke skiver, la tante Anna alle stykkene i et stort kar. Så tok hun ei bøtte som det var noe flytende oppi. «Dette er lut,» sa hun. «Jeg renset komfyren der inne for aske i går. Den helte jeg kokende vann over, og rørte godt rundt. Så lot jeg det hele stå til i dag. Da var det bare å øse opp den klare luten som hadde dannet seg på toppen av asken. Det er forresten bjørkeaske som er det beste til dette bruk,» la hun til og helte væsken over fisken. Så helte hun på enda mer vann. Hun prøvde med fingrene om luten var «glatt» nok.

Mette skjønte at der trengtes en god porsjon erfaring for å få dette riktig, og var det noe tante Anna hadde, så var det nok akkurat det.

«Nå må dette stå til luting to–tre døgn. Men vi må nok bære det bort til kulpen i bekken igjen, for det må stå kaldt,» sa hun.

«Når lutingen er ferdig, må fisken vannes ut,» fortsatte hun for å forklare resten av prosessen, «da er stykkene blitt tykke og nesten geleaktige. Utvanningen må også pågå et par dager. Vannet må skiftes flere ganger, og det må hele tiden stå kjølig.

Egentlig skal man ikke lage lutefisk når det er så varmt i været som det er nå, men jeg har før greid å få det til med å kjøle det i kulpen. Jeg håper det vil gå bra denne gangen også,» avsluttet hun.

Tante Anna fortsatte å snakke mens de bar karet bort i kulpen. Flere av turistene hadde spørsmål å komme med, og tante Anna hadde svar på det meste.

Etterpå satte de seg ved hagebordet utenfor seterbua med en kopp kaffe.

En stund senere kom Morten tilbake igjen. Han kom raskt bort til de to som satt ved hagebordet. Det lyste iver og begeistring av hele ansiktet hans.

«Nå skal dere høre,» sa han og slengte seg ned i en ledig hagestol. «Jeg fikk en interessant telefon i dag. Det var noen amerikanske turister som ønsker å komme hit om et par uker. De vil gjerne være her noen dager. De er i Norge for å oppspore sine norske røtter. Nå har jeg flere ganger hatt slike turister her. Det er gjerne folk som ønsker å se det landet som slekta kom fra. Men det interessante med disse er at de kanskje kan bli til hjelp for oss. De skal besøke flere bygder og gårder hvor de vet at deres fjerne slektninger kom fra. En av dem har hatt slekt som er kommet fra en gard i ei av nabobygdene her. Jeg lovet å vise dem stedet, og så kjøre dem litt rundt i distriktet så de kan få se litt av det «Gamlelandet» som de visst har hørt så mye om.

Da jeg snakket med dem, så nevnte jeg vårt problem. De var straks villige til å hjelpe oss hvis det var noe de kunne gjøre. Nå kommer ikke akkurat disse fra Minneapolis, men de er godt kjent med den norsk-amerikanske historien, og de er også godt kjent i mange av de områdene hvor det vil være aktuelt for oss å lete. Så jeg tenkte …» Han stoppet litt og smilte igjen mens han dro fram et ark hvor han hadde skrevet noe.

«Kanskje …» Han så rett på Mette. «Kanskje vi skulle ta oss den turen som vi snakket om i vår, hva synes du?»

Mette smilte også begeistret tilbake, men så kom det noe tvilende over henne. «Hvordan mener du vi skal få ordnet det?»

Morten la arket på hagebordet og pekte ivrig på noe han hadde skrevet. «Jeg ringte et reisebyrå i dag,» sa han. Det viser seg at det ennå er noen få plasser igjen på det flyet som disse turistene skal reise tilbake med. Hvis vi drar da, kan jeg ordne det slik at det ikke blir så mye aktivitet her oppe på setra mens vi er borte. Jeg har også snakket med Ellen om muligheten for at hun kan være her den tiden og ta seg av dyrene. Det var hun villig til.»

Tante Anna brøt begeistret inn med det samme: «Dette må dere absolutt få til. Så moro det må bli å komme vekk litt, og så slik en tur. Dere må slett ikke nøle med å hoppe på dette. Ellen og jeg greier fint det som må gjøres her. Bare dra, dere.»

Mette så begeistret fra den ene til den andre. «Jeg kan jo ikke si annet enn at dette høres skrekkelig spennende ut,» sa hun.

«På reisebyrået fikk jeg dem til å holde av et par billetter,» fortsatte Morten. «Så da sier vi det, eller hva?» Mette nikket mot det ivrige blikket hans. «Så sier vi det!»

Alle tre begynte å snakket i munnen på hverandre av opphisselse. Planer og forberedelsene måtte straks settes i gang. En del av det programmet som var fastlagt, måtte endres litt, men Morten trodde ikke det ville by på noen problemer.

Mette kjente ilinger gjennom hele kroppen av spenning, men hun så nok allikevel litt mørkt på det med å finne slektningene. «Om vi ikke finner dem, så får vi i hvert fall en fin tur,» trøstet Morten henne da hun uttrykte sin bekymring. Tante Anna sa seg helt enig med ham.

Etter denne bestemmelsen kom det en helt ny og forventningsfull stemning inn i den daglige tilværelsen deres. Stadig snakket de om de gamle brevene og slekta der over. Ville de noen gang finne dem? Var det i det hele tatt slekt å finne der borte? Hva slags folk var det i så fall? Tusen spørsmål kvernet rundt i hodet til Mette etter som dagene gikk og avreisen nærmet seg. Spenningen økte også, ikke minst til den amerikanske turistgruppa skulle komme. Hva slags opplysninger og hjelp kunne de folkene bidra med tro? Stadig vekk fant hun fram brevene. Også de eldste av dem ble gjennomgått.

387

Det var ikke så lett å finne en tråd i livet og tilværelsen til dem i det nye landet, for det så ut til at det bare var noen av brevene deres som var blitt oppbevart. Det eneste Mette klart kunne skjønne, var at de kom til Nord Dakota etter først å ha vært en tid i en by som het Beloit i Wisconsin. Der hadde de fått hjelp av en mann som de kalte Sjur. Han hadde utvandret fra Norge nesten femti år tidligere og blitt en betydelig skikkelse i den norske kolonien. I lang tid drev han en slags transittvirksomhet. Mange av nordmennene som utvandret i den tiden, kom i kontakt med nettopp ham. Siden han var fra omtrent samme distrikt i Norge som dem selv, hadde det vært naturlig også for dem å slå seg sammen med ham og familien hans.

Senere hadde de reist til Nord Dakota, hvor de hadde skaffet seg egen jord. Også sønnene til Sjur ble med dit for å skaffet seg jord. Siden kom gamle Sjur selv.

De fire søsknene hadde etter hvert slått seg ned på forskjellige steder i samme distrikt.

I disse brevene var det lite opplysninger om slektens gang. Nå var det heller ikke disse Mette og Morten først og fremst skulle besøke. Dette var en enda eldre generasjon, så de trengte nok flere opplysninger om de skulle greie å oppspore noen av dem.

46 • Høyslått på vollen

Mette gikk og nynnet for seg selv mens hun puslet rundt sauene borte i sauefjøset. Det var bare et lite skur som sto et stykke bakenfor fjøset. Døra sto åpen hele tiden så dyrene kunne gå ut og inn som de ville. For det meste holdt de seg ute i den friske fjelluften og det frodige gresset i liene. Men Mette la hver dag inn noe godt til dem der i skuret for at de skulle holde seg rundt setra og ikke stikke til fjells. Etter hvert var de også blitt så folkekjære at de kom løpende så fort noen kom i nærheten. Lammene hoppet og svinset rundt henne. De snappet nesten maten ut av hendene hennes. Etter at de to lammene ble morløse hadde det ikke vært noe problem å få hjelp med matingen. Barna var øyeblikkelig parat når de så at Mette kom med tåteflaskene. Mette smilte til de to jentene som for øyeblikket satt med hver sitt lam borte ved fjøsveggen. Lammene sudde begjærlig i seg den varme drikken.

Stemmen til tante Anna kunne også høres. Hun sto borte ved kulpen i bekken og skiftet vann på lutefisken. Noen av lammene hoppet rundt henne i håp om at også hun hadde noe godt å komme med. Hun lo og snakket til dem som om det var en barneflokk hun hadde der.

Med denne foringen fulgte også en god porsjon klapping og kos. Både Mette og dyrene frydet seg der de puslet rundt hverandre og lot klokke være klokke. Ingenting stresset dem opp denne dagen.

Mette rettet seg opp og lot blikket gli over det velkjente området. Også dette så ut til å bli en deilig dag. Sola varmet allerede godt, selv om det ennå var tidlig på formiddagen. Borte i lia kunne hun se kyrne. De gikk og beitet så fredelig oppover skråningen i vest. Fuglene kvitret hektisk over hodet hennes og hadde det visst mye mer stressende enn henne. Rett som det var så hun en som fløy inn gjennom gluggen til høyloftet over fjøset. Straks kunne hun høre en intens kvitring. Fugleungene i reiret der inne kjempet nok en intens kamp om å få den første matbiten.

Et tilfreds sukk unnslapp henne der hun sto. Freden og harmonien som hun så ofte hadde følt der på setra, gav henne igjen en vidunderlig lykkefølelse. Alle de kjente lydene, synsinntrykket som den mektige naturen rundt gav, og så ikke minst duften av mark og fjell blandet med dyrenes sterke lukt, gav henne en helt eiendommelig følelse.

Borte på vollen holdt Morten på å forberede høyslått. En stor flokk med turister sto langs stien for å se på det som foregikk. Han hadde rotet fram en gammel hesteslåmaskin fra låven nede i bygda. Nå strevde han med å få spendt den til hesten. Mette gikk nærmere for å se. Hun var spent på om han ville få dette til. I lang tid hadde han arbeidet med å klargjøre det gamle redskapet. Knivene hadde han tatt med seg inn i seterbua kvelden før. Der hadde han sittet og slipt dem møysommelig med et bryne.

Forsiktig ble hesten manøvrert ut på jordet. Morten satte seg opp på det runde setet som Mette syntes så nokså vaklende og ukomfortabelt ut. Forsiktig løsnet han spaken som holdt knivene oppe, og hele det lange knivsettet ble lagt ned i gresset. Med et rykk satte hesten seg i bevegelse på Mortens kommando. Og straks begynte gresset å falle der hvor kniven skar seg igjennom. En intens knitrende og svitsjende lyd kunne høres når knivbladene ble dratt mot hverandre, og gresset ble kuttet.

Hesten dro slåmaskinen i jevn fart bortover jordet. De tynne stålhjulene laget små striper etter seg i enga.

Mette tok ei rive og begynte å rake vekk det nyslåtte gresset der hvor neste rad skulle slåes. Hun visste at det ikke var lett å få slått hvis der lå for mye løst gress fra før.

Runde etter runde dro hesten den skranglete gamle maskinen, mens gresset falt i lange ranker. Flere av turistene hadde med filmapparat. Dette var visst noe spesielt som de ville forevige.

Etter en stund stoppet Morten for å ta seg en pause. «Kan ikke jeg få lov til å forsøke,» ropte Mette ivrig. «Det ser jo ut til at hesten nesten greier jobben på egen hånd likevel?»

Morten så litt tvilende på henne. «Det er ikke akkurat så lett, og setet her er nokså ustøtt. Jeg greide ikke å få montert noen sikkerhetsbelter.» Mette lo godt av den muntre bemerkningen. På setet der oppe var det ikke en gang noe å holde seg i. Men hun så ikke det som noe problem. Hesten hadde jo gått så rolig og støtt, og så var jo farten så lav.

«Du kan jo prøve litt,» sa Morten, «men vær forsiktig med de skarpe knivene.»

Raskt krøp hun opp på det runde metallsetet. Hun la merke til at det var ganske glatt å sitte på, for det var ingen pute der. Forsiktig greide hun å senke kniven, og så var det bare å sette i gang. Hun ble oppmerksom på at turistene sto ekstra ivrige med film - apparatene sine.

Med et rykk satte hesten i gang. Hun sjanglet litt med det samme, men snart fant hun balansen igjen. Rolig og sikkert ble maskinen trukket framover, men farten var jammen høyere enn hun trodde.

Meter etter meter ble gresset kuttet og lagt i ranke etter henne der hun fòr fram. Hun holdt tømmene i et sikkert grep med venstre hånd, og høyre hånd hadde hun på spaken til knivene, klar til å løfte dem hvis noe skulle skje.

Plutselig kom det et kraftig rykk i maskinen, og hesten med hele maskineriet, ble stående bom stille.

Mette ikke fikk summet seg før hun fòr i en bue og landet på marka foran hestebeina. Hesten sto urolig og rykket i drettene.

«Hvordan gikk dette?» Morten kom styrtende til mens hun forumlet forsøkte å komme seg på bena igjen. «Har du skadet deg?» Han tok et fast tak i armen hennes for å hjelpe henne vekk fra de urolige hestebena.

«Jeg tror ikke det,» svarte hun forvirret. Flere av turistene kom også til for å se om det var noe de måtte hjelpe med.

«Det gikk bra,» sa hun og børstet gress av klærne, «men jeg begriper bare ikke hva som skjedde.»

Morten tok en tur rundt maskinen for å undersøke. «Her har vi det,» sa han. «Kniven har stoppet i en stokk. Det er nok endepålen til hesja vi hadde her i fjor som vi ikke har fått opp.»

Det ble ikke mer høyslått på Mette den dagen. Morten tok seg av resten. Men han måtte innrømme at hvis det ikke hadde vært hun som satt der på det glatte setet akkurat da det skjede, så hadde det nok vært han som hadde ligget der mellom hestebeina. Den stokken ville nok heller ikke han ha klart å oppdage.

Heldigvis var hun ikke skadet på noen måter, men hun følte seg nokså mørbanket. Og for turistene hadde det jo blitt en spesiell ekstra oppvisning, i hvert fall for dem som filmet.

Hele den dagen var de opptatt med hesjing. Morten satte de lange stokkene ned i jorda og bant på ståltråd mellom dem. Så hjalp Mette til med å henge gresset opp på tråden for at det skulle tørke. Flere av turistene hjalp også ivrig til. De arbeidet iherdig mens sola stekte ubarmhjertig på de svetten kroppene.

Da de endelig var ferdig, ble hele flokken buden på rømmegrøt på vollen. Tante Anna hadde kokt ei diger gryte som hun satte ut. Der kunne alle forsyne seg så mye de ville. Det var deilig med mat og en hvil etter det harde arbeidet hele dagen. Mette pustet ut der hun satt.

Plutselig kom en bil med ei campingvogn kjørende opp langs veien og stoppet like ved dem. Da Mette fikk se mannen som hoppet ut, glemte hun både maten og hele trettheten. Det var nemlig Arvid som kom.

«Hjertelig velkommen,» ropte hun og gikk ham i møte. «Det var skikkelig koselig å se deg igjen.»

«Nå lengtet jeg slik at jeg måtte tilbake,» svarte han og lo. Morten kom også for å hilse på ham. Tante Anna kom kvitrende med ei skål rømmegrøt før han hadde fått satt seg.

Det ble en munter stemning rundt bordet. «Du har gått glipp av opptrinnet mitt i dag,» sa Mette og lo. De andre lo også og fortalte om den luftige ferden hun hadde foretatt.

«Det skulle jeg gjerne ha sett,» sa Arvid muntert mens han betraktet henne med et intenst blikk. Mette så fort opp på ham, men senket snart blikket igjen. Det var noe ved denne mannen som gjorde henne urolig. Der bygget seg liksom raskt opp en indre spenning som hun ikke helt kunne tolke. De hadde hatt mange samtaler da han var der sist. Han hadde trengt noen å snakke med, og hun hadde mer enn gjerne gitt ham den hjelpen han trengte. Men hvordan var det nå? Var det fortsatt for å få hjelp og hvile i en vanskelig tid som var grunnen til at han kom? Mette kjente seg med ett splittet i sitt indre. Var det ønsket om å hjelpe ham som gjorde at hun gledet seg slik over å se ham igjen, eller var det noe annet? Det var dette som uroet henne. Og hvordan var det med ham? Blikket han sendte henne, gav henne en enda sterkere uro. Men hun ville ikke tenke på det nå. De hadde det jo så hyggelig der alle sammen.

Etter at de hadde spist, hjalp Morten Arvid med å finne en grei plass hvor han kunne sette vogna si, og så gikk de alle sammen til tjernet for å bade.

47 • Tilbake til gamlelandet

Endelig var dagen der da de kunne vente de amerikanske turistene. Morten hadde ordnet med leie av flere campingvogner som amerikanerne skulle bruke mens de var på setra. Tante Anna hadde stelt ferdig lutefisken. Den lå nå glinsende og fin ute i melkeboden. Hun ville servere dem et skikkelig lutefiskmåltid den første dagen de var på setra.

Morten dro tidlig ned til bygda for å ta imot gjestene. De skulle komme med toget utpå formiddagen. Han trengte også hjelp med transport av både folk og campingvogner, så han hadde en del som måtte ordnes.

Etter at Mette var ferdig med fjøsstellet, og dyrene var sluppet ut på beite igjen, satte hun seg ved hagebordet ute på vollen. Sola steikte ikke slik som den hadde gjort noen dager tidligere, men det var likevel varmt og deilig. Gresset var fremdeles fuktig etter en regnskur tidlig på morgenkvisten.

Mens hun satt der og nøt den friske luften, kom Arvid slentrende bort til bordet. «Så budeia sitter bare her og drar seg i dag,» sa han muntert og satte seg rett overfor henne. Mette smilte, men så ble hun alvorlig igjen. «Hvordan går det med deg?» Det var sterk medfølelse og omsorg i stemmen hennes. De hadde ikke fått anledning til å snakke så mye på tomannshånd ennå.

Arvid forsto med en gang hva hun mente, og han ble også alvorlig. Et trett utrykk falt over ansiktet. «Det fungerer jo på et vis, men …» Han stoppet og så på henne. Blikket var igjen fylt av det intense som skapte slik uro hos henne. «… det er ikke alt som er så lett.» Han sa ikke mer. Satt bare der og så på henne.

Mette følte en inderlig medlidenhet med ham. Så gjerne hun skulle ha hjulpet ham … hvis hun bare kunne …

«Det er så mye folk her,» sa han etter en liten stund. Et skjevt smil gled over munnen. «Det er ikke så lett å snakke …»

Mette forsto hva han mente. Så fortrolige samtaler som de hadde hatt sist da han var der, var det nesten umulig å få nå.

Plutselig tok han hånden hennes som lå på bordet og så henne ivrig inn i øynene. «Kunne vi ikke ta oss en tur innover i fjellet en dag … bare vi to … da kunne vi ha fått pratet om så mye …»

Mette kjente en dirrende følelse langt inni seg. Så fint det hadde vært. Bare de to, helt alene. Så mye de da kunne få snakket om. Hånden hans lå fremdeles over hennes. Hun lot den ligge. Blikket hans som søkte i øynene hennes etter et svar, var fulle av spent forventning. Dette var noe han virkelig ønsket, kunne hun se. Hva slags behov var det han hadde? Tanken kom brått, men hun skjøv den like fort vekk igjen. Det var hjelp han trengte, minnet hun seg selv om, kun en å snakke med. Men følelsene som raste inni henne greide hun ikke verken å styre eller å tolke. Det eneste som i øyeblikket sto klart for henne, var at akkurat det hadde vært så fint. Bare det to … alene … langt inne i fjellet.

Sakte gled et smil over leppene hennes mens hun nikket forsiktig. «Ja,» sa hun. «La oss gjøre det.»

Et strålende smil spredte seg over hele ansiktet hans mens han klemte hånden hennes. Nå var uroen hennes i ferd med å vike til fordel for en intens spenning. Hun så bare inn i de strålende vakre øynene hans, og la den andre hånden sin over hans. Et øyeblikk ble de sittende der mens noe dirret mellom dem.

«Når skal vi dra?» spurte han med litt uklar stemme. Mette kremtet for å rense stemmen sin før hun svarte: «I dag er det tirsdag,» sa hun mens hun tenkte seg om. «Jeg tror ikke jeg får anledning før torsdag.»

«Torsdag er fint,» svarte han og reiste seg. «Da sier vi det.» Han sendte henne et varmt og fortrolig smil mens han blunket litt med det ene øyet. Så snudde han seg og gikk tilbake til vogna si.

I det samme kom tante Anna ut. Hun snakket i vei uten å legge merke til de blussende kinnene til Mette. «Nå har vi nok snart gjestene her,» sa hun. «Jeg har kjernet en masse smør som vi kan ha til lutefisken i ettermiddag. Håper Morten husker å gå innom hos meg og hente lefsene i frysen. Det blir jo ikke noe lutefiskmåltid uten lefser. Og så tror jeg du snart må sette i gang med potetskrellingen. Vi må koke masse poteter.»

Mette reiste seg raskt og var glad for å få noe å gjøre. De forvirrende tankene hadde nesten fått henne helt ut av likevekt. Nei, nå måtte hun sannelig sanse seg. Arbeide var det hun skulle gjøre, ikke sitte der og drømme.

Ikke lenge etter var hun i full gang med potetskrellingen. Det var jo en fin jobb å sitte med der ute på vollen. Snart kom det noen barn bort til henne for å se på. De lurte sterkt på hva hun skulle bruke så mange poteter til. Mette fortalte om amerikanerne de ventet, og middagen som skulle serveres til dem senere. Hun mente at det sikkert ville bli litt lutefisk til barna også hvis de ville smake.

Klokka var nesten tolv før de første bilene begynte å komme. Det var ei gruppe på femten mennesker. De fleste av dem var nokså oppi årene. «Det er vel helst folk i den alderen som interesserer seg for så gamle ting,» tenkte Mette der hun sto og betraktet gruppen mens de fant seg til rette i campingvognene.

Selv om gjestene hadde passert «middelalderen», så var det likevel en sprek og sprudlende gjeng. Med iver og begeistring gikk de rundt på området og betraktet alt de så av både bygninger, utstyr og dyr.

«Se her,» sa en av de ivrigste blant dem. Han pekte på de grove stokkene som seterbua var bygget av. «Det er tydelig at de som emigrerte over til Amerika herfra midt på attenhundretallet, tok byggeskikken med seg. Akkurat slike stuer er det vi finner blant de eldste bygningene der over også. Men de gjorde det litt annerledes her,» sa han og betraktet et av hushjørnene nøye. «Her ender hver stokk akkurat i hjørnet.» Han pekte på de sirlig tilkuttede endestokkene. De lå i hverandre, nøyaktig tilkappet, og kuttet slik at det ble et fint hjørne på bygningen. «På de gamle husene i Amerika stikker hver stokk litt lenger ut i hjørnet. Bare legg merke til det når dere ser westernfilmer på fjernsyn.»

Han fortsatte å studere veggen. «Her tror jeg det er brukt mose som isolasjon mellom stokkene.»

«Ja,» sa Morten, «det ble dyttet inn mose i alle sprekker så ikke vind og kulde skulle trenge inn mellom stokkene, og den har vi rett som det er måttet skifte ut litt her og der.»

«Der over,» fortsatte mannen, «i hvert fall i det området hvor jeg er kjent, så ble det brukt en slags leire som isolasjon mellom stokkene.»

En god stund fortsatte de å betrakte det gamle byggverket. Og iveren ble ikke mindre da de kom inn og fikk se den gamle innredningen. Spesielt komfyren vakte sterk begeistring. «Slike ble også brukt på prærien i gamle dager.» Det var den samme mannen som snakket. Han lo litt der han sto bøyd over den gamle ovnen. «Det hendte rett som det var at de tok slike ovner med ut på jordet,» fortsatte han. «Når de arbeidet ute på de store præriejordene, var det altfor langt å dra hjem for å få seg mat. Derfor tok de heller med seg ovnen ut, og så kokte de maten der ute hvor de arbeidet.»

Mette lo og kikket ut på vollen. «Det problemet hadde de nok ikke her.»

Etter en grundig omvisning med mange forklaringer og kommentarer på både det ene og det andre, dro gjestene til vognene sine for å stelle seg litt før middagen. Mette og tante Anna dekket et langt bord inne i seterbua. Det var så vidt de greide å få plassert alle sammen, men siden de skulle servere, unnlot de å dekke til seg selv. Da gikk det akkurat.

Midt på bordet satte tante Anna ei fin gammel tine med det nykjernede smøret i. Den var i nydelig utskåret tre. På innsiden av lokket var der også dype utskjæringer. «Det er for å lage et fint mønster på toppen av smøret,» forklarte tante Anna og tok av lokket for å vise kunstverket sitt.

«Så flinke folk var før i tiden, og så nøye de var med å lage alle ting så vakkert og tiltalende,» sa Mette beundrende.

«Å ja,» svarte tante Anna, «det skulle være vakkert, og så skulle det smake godt. Festmaten i den tiden var ingen slankekost, men så spiste de jo ikke så mye av verken fett eller søtt til hverdags, så de tok nok ingen skade av det.»

Snart begynte gjestene å komme. Tante Anna viste dem høytidelig til bords mens Mette øste opp potetene. Et digert trefat med rykende varme poteter ble plassert på bordet. Og så begynte tante Anna å ta opp fisken. Stor var begeistringen da de fikk se hva det var de skulle få servert. De fleste hadde hørt om lutefisk, og noen hadde også smakt det. Nettopp denne retten var noe de forbandt ekstra sterkt med Gamlelandet. Men hvordan den skulle spises, var de likevel nokså uvitende om. Tante Anna måtte ha et lite lynkurs for dem før de kunne sette i gang måltidet. Mette sto trofast ved hennes side som tolk. Selv om de alle sammen var av norsk opprinnelse, kunne de ikke så mye norsk.

«Lutefisk kan tilberedes og spises på litt forskjellige måter,» begynte hun, «men her i distriktet har det fra gammelt vært mest vanlig å gjøre det på denne måten». Hun tok en lefse som var kuttet i en trekant. Den var helt tynn og så nok helst ut som en blekgul serviett for de utenlandske gjestene. Så smurte hun et tykt lag smør på lefsa. Deretter la hun en god porsjon opphakket poteter og lutefisk på smøret. Det hele rullet hun så sammen til ei tykk pølse. Så skulle pølsa spises, og det med bare fingrene.

Etter tante Annas veiledning satte gjestene i gang med iver og begeistring. Hvordan de syntes den sterke lutefisken smakte, var det ikke så mange som sa så mye om, men det skapte i hvert fall stor munterhet. Både den fremmede måten å spise på og den dirrende, geleaktige fisken ble livlig kommentert.

Til dessert fikk de servert multekrem, også det til stor begeistring for gjestene. Tante Anna fortalte at multene var plukket i fjellet rundt setra. «Men jeg forteller ikke hvor,» sa hun og lo godt. «Multestedene er alltid hemmelige,» fortsatte hun. «Hvis noen kommer og spør om det er mye multer i fjellet, så får de som regel det svaret at:«dette året har nok multehøsten slått aldeles feil». Men det underlige er at når jula kommer, så er det multer på hvert bord i hele bygda.» Hun lo så hun ristet der hun sto og fortalte. Munterheten spredte seg blant gjestene. Den festlige måten hun hadde å fortelle på fikk stemningen der i seterbua til å stige helt til topps.

«Nei, vær trygg du, vi skal ikke komme og spise opp multene for dere til høsten,» var det en godmodig gubbe som forsikret.

Etter at de hadde spist, ble de sittende lenge ved bordet og snakke. Mange hadde historier som de hadde fått fortalt fra sine foreldre og besteforeldre. Det var historier om trange kår i Gamlelandet og om farefulle reiser ut i det ukjente, i håp om å få en bedre tilværelse. Men ikke alle hadde møtt lykken der på den andre siden av havet. For noen ble det også nød og armod, og enkelte gikk under på grunn av alkohol og pengespill. Vær og klima, da spesielt i nord, ble også en farlig fiende. De trengte å lære seg tilpasning i dette ugjestmilde landet. Derfor var det noen som nettopp så dette som sin oppgave. De tok imot dem som kom nye og uvitende over fra Norge. Og så gav de dem den nødvendige hjelp og veiledning så de kunne få en bedre mulighet til å greie seg på egen hånd.

Han som hadde vist slik interesse for tømmerhuset da de kom, viste seg å hete Frank. Det var han som hadde slekta si fra en av nabobygdene der i distriktet. Han bodde nå på en farm i Nord Dakota, og slekta hans hadde bodd der i distriktet i over hundre år. De hadde funnet ei dagbok som den første settleren i slekta hadde skrevet. Derfor kjente de ganske godt til slektens historie. Han het Sjur og kom fra en stor gård i Norge. Morten visste godt hvilken gård det var, så han lovet å ta alle sammen med dit neste dag.

«Denne Sjur stammet egentlig ikke fra den gården,» fortsatte Frank. «Han arbeidet bare der som gårdsgutt, men han visste ikke hvor han stammet fra. Moren hans kom til den gården som spedbarn. Moren hennes var antakelig død. Det var jo mange som døde i barselseng i den tiden. Og faren måtte sannsynligvis også være død. Så trengte de vel en amme. Det fant de blant tjenerne på denne storgården. Der var det ei som hadde et lite barn, og som også hadde melk nok til å berge dette andre barnet. Noe mer om slekta hennes visste han ikke.

Moren vokste opp der på gården og ble tidlig regnet som en av tjenerne. Hun fikk imidlertid ikke den beste behandling. Utnyttelse og overgrep hørte visst til dagliglivet. Det kunne nesten virke som hun ble brukt som et leketøy av de voksne mennene der.» Frank grøsset før han fortsatte. Alle de andre satt i spenning og lyttet til beretningen hans. Fortiden hadde jammen ikke vært lett verken for den ene eller den andre.

«Resultatet av «leken» ble altså denne Sjur.» Frank fortsatte mens han ristet alvorlig på hodet. Hele sin oppvekst ble han så gående der på gården med tilnavnet Lausungen. Både dårlig mat, spark og slag måtte han tåle. Han skrev selv at hestene der på gården hadde det mye bedre enn han.

«Dette er langt tilbake i tiden.» Frank rynket brynene og tenkte seg om. «Jeg tror han måtte ha blitt født i 1820-årene. I hvert fall reiste han over til Amerika i 1853, og da var han rundt 30 år. Han fikk kontakt med noen haugianere som ville reise over. De hadde så mye problemer på grunn av sin religiøse tro at de hadde valgt å emigrere. Disse slo Sjur seg sammen med og kom over til New York med et emigrantfartøy. Derfra reiste han vestover og slo seg ned i en by som het Beloit. Der giftet han seg og fikk familie. Og det var også der han etter hvert begynte sin transittvirksomhet.

Plutselig kom det liv i øynene til Mette. «Var det Beloit du sa?» Raskt var hun borte i hjørneskapet hvor hun hadde lagt de gamle brevene. Det varte ikke lenge før hun fant det hun lette etter. «Her står det,» sa hun ivrig. «De eldste av slektningene dine, Morten, slo seg også ned i Beloit for en tid, og det var nettopp hos en mann som het Sjur. Han drev transittvirksomhet der. Det må da være den samme mannen?»

Med ett ble det liv i Frank også, og resten av gruppen fulgte interessert med i det som ble sagt. De fant fort ut at det virkelig var snakk om den samme personen, og det som de syntes var enda mer interessant, var opplysningene i brevet om at de etter hvert reiste til Nord Dakota og slo seg ned der sammen med sønnen til Sjur. Det måtte jo bety at der var muligheter for å finne eventuelle slektninger der ved hjelp av denne Frank.

Etter hvert begynte gjestene å reise seg fra bordet. De takket hjertelig for maten og gikk ut til vognene sine. Etter den lange reisen, og tidsforskjellen, var de ganske trette. En god middagshvil kunne de visst trenge alle sammen. Men Frank ble sittende enda en stund og snakke med Morten og Mette. De nye opplysningene skapte spenning og nysgjerrighet hos dem alle tre.

48 • Fristelse og kamp

I den gamle dobbeltsenga inne på soveværelset ved siden av melkeboden lå Mette og vred seg fram og tilbake. Hun fikk ikke sove. I nesten en time hadde hun ligget der, men søvnen ville ikke komme.

Det hadde vært en hektisk dag, så hun hadde gått tidlig til sengs med påskudd om at hun var trett og sliten. Ja, det hadde hun virkelig også opplevd at hun var, men etter som minuttene sneglet seg av sted, gikk det mer og mer opp for henne at det kanskje var noe annet som hadde forårsaket ønsket om stillhet og ro. Der var nemlig noe inni henne som skapte uro. Der var tanker som hun helst ikke ville slippe fram. Hun ønsket bare å sove det bort alt sammen. Men tankene ville ikke slippe taket. Hele den lange, hektiske onsdagen hadde de ikke vært særlig plagsomme. Hun og Morten hadde dratt av sted ganske tidlig på dagen, sammen med de amerikanske turistene, til den gården som slekta til Frank kom fra. Det hadde vært en særdeles interessant dag. Familien som bodde på gården, hadde tatt imot dem med stor begeistring. Det var tydeligvis ingen ting igjen av de gamle vonde forholdene som denne Sjur hadde beskrevet i den gamle dagboken som Frank hadde sitert fra. Men de kunne bekrefte at det var den samme slekta som fremdeles bodde der. Derfor hadde besøket vært ekstra sterkt og følelsesladet. Mange ting på gården sto fremdeles igjen fra den tiden da det var en skikkelig storgård. Familien som bodde der nå, visste imidlertid ikke særlig mye om de gamle slektene, så dagboka til Frank ble studert med stor interesse.

Det var på vei hjemover igjen at Mette hadde begynt å føle på en sterk uro. Først hadde det vært en pirrende spenning og forventning med tanke på neste dags utflukt. Men etter hvert hadde dette utviklet seg til noe som bare lå og gnagde der langt inni henne et sted.

Hun var trett … ja, det var bare det hun var … men hvorfor fikk hun ikke sove?

Morten var ikke kommet hjem ennå. Han hadde dratt innover i fjellet sammen med noen av de andre turistene nesten med det samme de kom tilbake. Hun visste i det hele tatt ikke om han kom igjen den kvelden. Kanskje de bare overnattet der et sted under en fjellknaus. Været var jo fint nok til det.

Mette snudde seg igjen i senga og dro dyna over hodet, men det hjalp ikke stort. Tankene fortsatte bare å kverne. Hun hadde jo avtalt med Arvid at de skulle ta seg en tur dagen etter. Bare de to … alene i fjellet. Han trengte å snakke med henne om alle problemene sine. Skulle bare mangle at hun ikke kunne hjelpe ham i en slik vanskelig situasjon. Men det var nettopp denne tanken som uroet henne. Var det virkelig kun for å hjelpe at hun ble med? Og var det kun for å få hjelp at Arvid hadde foreslått denne turen? Hun hadde kjent spenningen mellom dem der ved hagebordet dagen før, og hun kunne fremdeles merke hvordan hjertet banket fortere når hun tenkte på det.

Men de var jo bare gode venner, og det måtte de da ha lov til å være. Han trengte hjelp. Og det var jo nettopp det som var hennes kall. Hun hadde jo sett det slik, ikke minst gjennom den jobben hun hadde i misjonen. Det var derfor hun hadde tatt så mange kurs i dette med sjeleomsorg. Skulle hun så ikke bruke dette når hun møtte mennesker som trengte hjelp?

Samme hvor mye hun argumenterte med seg selv, så var uroen der like sterk. Et bibelvers kom for henne, men hun husket ikke riktig hvordan det lød. Det var noe med en kappe som var flekket. Hun tok Bibelen fra nattbordet og begynte å lete. Etter en stund fant hun det i Judas brev. Ute i vers 23 sto det: noen skal dere ta dere av … hun stoppet litt der. Det var jo nettopp det. Noen skulle man ta seg av. Her sto jo det helt klart … men der sto visst noe mer. Hun fortsatte å lese: … men vær varsomme så dere til og med avskyr kappen som er flekket av sanselighet.

Et øyeblikk ble hun bare liggende helt stille. Hva betydde det? Jo, hun visste det så altfor godt. Sanselighet … Den sanselige lyst og begjær hadde ikke noe i sjeleomsorgen å gjøre.

Men du verden så lett det kom inn. Mette ynket seg der hun lå. Og så sterke krefter som det var i dette. Hvordan var det mulig å verne seg mot slikt? Når det først tok fatt i en stakkar, så var man jo fullstendig maktstjålen. Følelsene var ikke lette å styre, selv om det sto aldri så klart i Bibelen at det var synd med … Hun fullført ikke tanken. Vred seg bare som i smerte. Hvordan kunne hun komme inn på slike tanker nå, bare få måneder etter at hun ble viet til den vidunderligste mannen i verden? Tanken på fjellturen de hadde hatt den dagen de fikk besøk av saueflokken fra fjellet kom for henne. Så lett man ble dratt med følelsesmessig der i stillheten og ensomheten, og den vidunderlige naturen. Men den gangen hadde det vært gode og trygge følelser. Alt hadde vært fint og vakkert. «Å, Morten, hva er det som skjer?» Et stønn unnslapp henne.

Igjen begynte tankene å arbeide rundt neste dags utflukt. Da skulle hun og Arvid dra av sted … alene … ingen flere skulle være med … hva ville skje? En skjelving gikk gjennom kroppen hennes der hun lå. Igjen så hun for seg øyeblikket da de satt ved hagebordet og holdt hverandre i hendene. Hun kunne ennå kjenne hvordan alle motforestillinger forsvant i følelsen av spenning og indre dragning. «Jeg kommer aldri til å greie å stå imot hvis …» Hun stønnet igjen. Hvorfor skulle alt være så vanskelig? Hva skulle hun gjøre?

Plutselig satte hun seg opp. «Hva er det du ligger der og jamrer for!» skjente hun på seg selv. «Det er da slett ingen grunn til slike bekymringer. Arvid er kun ute etter et menneske å snakke med. Noe mer er det ikke. Nå må det bli slutt på disse fantasiene.» Resolutt snudde hun seg mot veggen og dro dyna opp under haka. Hun ville sove, og det så fort som mulig.

Samme hvor fast bestemt hun var på å skyve tankene og bekymringene vekk, så var de der like fullt. Uroen ville ikke forsvinne, og søvnen ville ikke komme. Svetten begynte å renne ned over panna hennes. De vidåpne, urolige øynene hennes stirret ut i tussmørket. «Holder jeg på å bli tullete?»

Igjen tok hun Bibelen. Det var ennå så pass mye lys i rommet at hun kunne lese uten å tenne lampa. Møysommelig satte hun seg opp og la Bibelen i fanget.

«Hvis det er du, Gud, som uroer meg, så må du si meg hva jeg skal gjøre.» Bønnen kom som et nytt stønn. Litt famlende bladde hun fram og tilbake i den slitte boka. Med ett fanget blikket hennes inn et vers i Jakobs brev. Det var fjerde kapittel og vers åtte. Der sto det: Hold dere nær til Gud, så skal Han holde seg nær til dere. Gjør hendene rene, dere syndere, rens hjertene, dere som har et delt sinn.

Med et sukk sank hun ned på puta igjen. Delt sinn … ja det var jo akkurat slik hun følte seg. Men alt dette som måtte gjøres! Aldri i verden om hun kunne greie det. At hun var en synder, det var hun ikke i tvil om der hun lå, men å «rense hender og hjerte», nei, det greide hun bare ikke.

Hun løftet opp Bibelen og lot blikket gli langs verselinjene igjen. Kunne det stå noe mer som kunne hjelpe henne i denne situasjonen? «Bøy dere da for Gud!» leste hun i verset over, «men stå Djevelen imot, så skal han flykte fra dere.»

At det var Djevelen som var på ferde, det var hun ikke et øyeblikk i tvil om. Men å stå ham imot, det greide hun bare ikke. Dette gikk bare ikke … «jeg greier det bare ikke!» Et hulk unnslapp henne idet Bibelen falt ned på dyna igjen. Hun var fortapt.

Plutselig sto en ny tanke klart for henne. «Det er ikke du som skal greie det. Du skal bare holde deg nær til Gud, og det gjør du ved å søke Ham, slik som du nå har gjort ved å søke hjelp i Hans Ord. Og ved der å erkjenne din egen maktesløshet gir du Gud muligheter til å hjelpe deg.»

Undrende satte hun seg opp igjen. Enda et vers ble fanget inn av blikket hennes, som flakkende søkte over bibelsiden. Gud står de stolte imot, men de ydmyke gir han nåde.

Ydmykhet var det han krevde. Ikke noe annet. Og den som var villig til å vise ydmykhet, den skulle få nåde. Ja, nåde var akkurat det hun nå trengte mest av alt.

En stund ble hun sittende i dype tanker. Så vanskelig som dette var! For ville hun egentlig gi slipp på dette? En hard kamp begynte å rase inni henne. Det var kampen mot lystene i hennes indre. Du verden så sterke krefter dette var. Ja, hun visste det. Det var sterke krefter, for det var Djevelen selv hun kjempet imot.

«Åååå,» stønnet hun, og sank igjen tilbake på puten. «Han greier jeg aldri å stå meg mot. Han er altfor sterk for meg. Herre, hjelp meg!»

I det samme kjente hun en forunderlig fred som begynte å sige innover henne. Det var akkurat som om de vonde følelsene inni henne med ett ble borte. Tankene fortsatt å arbeide, men nå var de mye klarere.

Hold dere nær til Gud, så skal han holde seg nær til dere, sto det. Betydningen sto med ett klart for henne. Den som i ydmykhet søkte Gud og erkjente sitt problem for Ham, den ville få erfare at også Gud holdt seg nær til ham eller henne. Ingen mennesker kan greie å stå seg mot Djevelens lumske angrep i egen kraft. Kanskje de kan greie det en tid, men før eller siden vil de få erfare at de må gi tapt. Djevelens makt er så mye større enn menneskenes makt. Der er kun en makt som er større, og det er Guds makt. Derfor er det kun ved Hans hjelp at et menneske kan seire i kampen og fristelsen.

Denne Guds makt får menneskene del i ved å søke Gud i ydmykhet og ærlighet. Ved å erkjenne sin synd fullt ut for Ham vil de få erfare seier, for da virker det slik at Djevelen møter Jesus når han går til angrep. Og overfor den oppstandne Kristus må han vike. Kampen mot Jesus tapte han den gangen Frelseren utåndet på korset. Det er en sak Den Onde er fullstendig klar over. Det kan ikke nytte for ham å ta opp den kampen på nytt.

En sitrende glede begynte å fylle henne der hun lå. Der var håp. Hun hadde en redningsmann. Det sto også tindrende klart for henne hva hun i dette øyeblikk måtte gjøre. Hun spratt opp av senga og begynte å kle på seg igjen. Det måtte gjøres med det samme. Ventet hun til neste dag, var hun redd for at fristelsen igjen skulle få makt over henne, og da kunne det jo hende at hun valgte den i stedet for denne hjelpen som hun i øye - blikket merket at Gud hadde gitt henne.

Raskt gikk hun ut og bortover mot campingområdet. Luften var kjølig, men klar. Det ville bli ei fin natt. Kanskje neste dag ville bli en ekstra fin dag, kom det for henne...en ekstra fin dag for fjelltur. Men det kom ikke til å bli noen fjelltur på henne. Hun banket forsiktig på døra til Arvids vogn. Det tok litt tid før døra ble åpnet. Antakelig hadde han lagt seg.

Et underlig smil gled over ansiktet hans da han fikk se henne utenfor. «Ser man det,» sa han og åpnet døra helt opp. Ble det for ensomt der inne i dobbeltsenga i kveld?» Blikket han sendte henne, gav tydelig utrykk for hva han mente var årsaken til at hun kom på den tiden av døgnet, og så nettopp en kveld da Morten var bortreist.

En sterk rødme spredte seg over ansiktet til Mette. Stammende begynte hun å forklare, men Arvid avbrøt henne: «Kom inn, kom inn. Her er det da plass nok til to innendørs.»

Mette ristet heftig på hodet. «Nei, jeg kan ikke.»

«Kan ikke? Har du hørt slikt tøys.» Arvid så forundret på henne.

Mette trakk seg et skritt unna og fortsatte: «Jeg kan ikke bli med på den turen i morgen.» Hun skalv litt i stemmen, men hun fortsatte likevel bestemt: «Jeg tror ikke det er rett av oss å dra alene på den turen. Jeg syns heller du skal få med deg Morten. Dere kan jo ta med fiskestengene. Jeg er sikker på at det vil bli en mye finere tur for deg.»

Mørke skygger kom til syne i ansiktet til Arvid. «En mye finere tur?» gjentok han spørrende og snøftet foraktelig. «Du skjønner da at det er deg jeg vil ha med.» Han la ikke lenger skjul på sine hensikter. «Og slik jeg oppfattet det den dagen ved hagebordet, var du ikke så helt uinteressert du heller?» Uttalelsen ble slengt som et spørsmål, og en anklage, rett mot henne.

Mette kjente en gufs langt inn i sitt innerste. Med ett var alle fortryllende følelser og tanker borte. Hva var det hun hadde vært i ferd med å innlate seg på? At hun kunne ha vært så naiv og tro at det bare var for å snakke at Arvid ville ha henne med til fjells. Så nær hun hadde vært en forferdelig ulykke. Hun grøsset og snudde seg halvt.

«Kanskje det kunne oppfattes slik,» sa hun, «men min mening er i hvert fall klar. Dette kan jeg ikke være med på. Så må du bare ha det bra. Jeg må gå nå.»

Før Arvid rakk å si noe mer, løp hun tilbake igjen gjennom det duggvåte gresset. Hun hørte at døra til campingvogna ble slengt igjen med et smell. Enda et grøss gikk gjennom henne ved tanken på hvor nær hun hadde vært et stort feiltrinn. Aldri skulle noen få greie på dette. Hun ville gjemme det i sitt innerste som en vond, men lærerik erfaring.

Søvnen lot fremdeles vente på seg en stund, men Mette hadde fått fred og ro. Hun lå og tenkte på hva hun ville ha møtt om hun hadde blitt med på den turen. Plutselig kunne hun ikke begripe at hun i det hele tatt kunne ha tenkt i slike baner. Du verden så besnærende synden kunne være.

Da Mette kom fra fjøset neste morgen, la hun merke til at det sto ei campingvogn mindre på området. I seterbua lå det en konvolutt med en hyggelig avskjedshilsen til Morten, og penger som oppgjør for leien av plassen han hadde brukt. Arvid var borte. De kom nok aldri til å se ham mer. Hun kjente et vemodig stikk i sitt indre med det samme, men så minnet hun seg selv på at dette nok var det beste for dem alle.

49 • På sykehuset

«Lurer på hvordan det går på setra?» Mette satt og halvdøste i det trange flysetet med hodet hvilende mot Mortens skulder.

«Det går sikkert bra.» Morten var heller ikke mer enn halvvåken. Det hørtes ikke ut til at han bekymret seg stort for verken folk eller dyr som var igjen der hjemme i Gamlelandet. «Tante Anna holder nok kontrollen, og Ellen tar seg av tungarbeidet. Det er jeg helt trygg på.» Han lukket øynene igjen og la hodet mot seteryggen. Mette følte seg også avslappet, men hun kunne ikke fri seg fra å tenke på dem der hjemme. Det var vel ikke akkurat hjemlengsel hun følte. Til det var spenningen foran det de nå skulle ut på for sterk, men setra sto jo hennes hjerte svært nær, så hun greide ikke å få tankene helt vekk fra den.

De siste dagene hadde forresten vært en svært travel tid. Alle forberedelsene til reisen, i tillegg til den hektiske aktiviteten på setra, hadde gjort at hun nå følte det godt å bare kunne sitte der og slappe av. Men tankene var det ikke så lett å koble ut.

Noen seter lenger framme satt Frank sammen med de andre amerikanerne. De hadde ikke oppholdt seg på setra hele tiden. Etter fire dager hadde de dratt videre. Det var mange steder de skulle besøke, så det var først den siste dagen at de hadde kommet tilbake igjen. Da hadde de vært på farten i over en uke.

Planen nå var at de skulle ha følge til Chicago. Der skulle de skilles ad for en stund. Frank og følget hans skulle ta fly videre til Bismarck, mens Morten og Mette skulle reise til Minneapolis. Etter noen dager skulle de komme etter til Bismarck, hvor de skulle møte Frank igjen.

Mette og Morten hadde forberedt seg så godt de kunne til turen. Alt de hadde funnet i de gamle brevene, og som de mente hadde betydning for saken, hadde de notert seg. De hadde også funnet ut hvilket sykehus Robert arbeidet på. Frank hadde hjulpet dem med dette. Han hadde også ordnet med plass på et hotell for dem i byen.

Mette kjente spenningen stige etter hvert som de nærmet seg bestemmelsesstedet. Hun så på klokka. Om ikke lenge var de i «det forjettede landet» som deres slektninger, for så mange år tilbake, hadde oppsøkt for å finne bedre levevilkår. Der hadde muligens slekta fortsatt sin gang, mens kontakten med de der hjemme i Norge ble brutt. Ville de finne noen av dem? Var det en altfor vanskelig oppgave de hadde påtatt seg? De måtte i hvert fall forsøke.

Tunge, grå skyer hang over flyplassen da de landet i Chicago. Det ble med ett en hektisk aktivitet. Følget skulle skille lag, og de måtte få sagt skikkelig farvel til dem som de hadde blitt så godt kjent med denne tiden, og som de ikke kom til å treffe igjen. Men til Frank sa de bare på gjensyn. De fikk telefonnummeret hans i tilfellet de skulle få bruk for hjelp.

Så var det å komme seg på det rette flyet videre. De måtte ta buss over til en annen terminal. Skal si det var en gedigen flyplass de var kommet til!

○ ○ ○

Turen til Minneapolis gikk ganske raskt, og snart kunne de strekke seg ut i hver si seng på hotellrommet. Det var godt å få hvile ut etter den lange reisa.

Selv om de hadde vært trøtte da de kom fram til hotellet, var de lysvåkne tidlig neste morgen. Før klokka fem begynte Mette å vri seg i senga. Det var umulig å få sove lenger. Hun regnet raskt om tiden i hodet og måtte smile for seg selv. Det var nok ikke så rart at hun ikke fikk sove lenger, for hjemme var klokka nesten tolv, og kroppen hennes var nok innstilt på den tiden fremdeles.

Morten våknet også snart. De bestemte seg for å ta en tidlig oppdagelsestur rundt hotellet.

Ute var det en frisk morgenbris, men de forsto at det kom til å bli en fin og varm dag. Trafikken i gatene var i full gang, men butikkene så ennå ut til å sove.

Etter en lang, forfriskende spasertur fant de seg et sted hvor de kunne få seg et tidlig frokostmåltid. Så dro de tilbake til hotellet for å forberede dagens ekspedisjon.

Mette skalv av spenning da de gikk ut for å skaffe seg en taxi. Snart var de på vei til sykehuset. Hun var glad for at de slapp å lete seg fram til bestemmelsesstedet selv. Det gikk gate opp og gate ned. Hun mistet kontrollen på retningen lenge før de var halvveis. Endelig stoppet bilen utenfor en stor bygning.

«Nå gjelder det,» sa Mette med dypt alvor i stemmen da de sto ute på gaten. Morten så på henne og smilte. «Har du det nå klart for deg hva du skal spørre etter?» Han la armen rundt henne og trykket henne inntil seg mens han så henne dypt inn i de lyseblå øynene. Mette måtte også smile av den ertende tonen hans. Han visste jo så godt at hun hadde pugget disse opplysningene opp og i mente, i flere dager.

Da de kom inn gjennom den store hovedinngangen, ble de stående litt og se seg forvirret omkring. Hvor kunne de henvende seg, tro?

«Det er vel best vi forsøker resepsjonen først,» sa Morten og gikk mot en skranke. Dama på den andre siden av glassdøra møtte dem med et vennlig smil.

«Kan du gi oss noen opplysninger?» spurte Morten og så spent på henne. «Vi er fra Norge, og nå er vi kommet hit for lete etter en slektning. Den eneste opplysningen vi har, er at han har jobbet som lege her ved dette sykehuset. Har dere oversikt over dem som har jobbet her tidligere? Navnet hans er Robert Aanensen.»

Kvinnen rynket pannen og begynte å bla i noen papirer. «Det er et fremmed navn for meg,» svarte hun, «men jeg skal se om jeg kan finne ut av det. Bare et lite øyeblikk.» Hun reiste seg og gikk inn i et annet rom.

Etter noen minutter kom hun tilbake igjen. «Jeg kan ikke finne ut at det har arbeidet noen ved det navnet her,» sa hun beklagende.

Mette så skuffet opp på Morten. «Hva gjør vi nå?» Morten tenkte seg om et øyeblikk. «Det kan godt hende at det er en del år siden,» fortsatte han til damen i luka. «Han er sannsynligvis i syttifemårs alderen.»

Igjen forsvant kvinnen. Denne gangen ble hun ganske lenge borte. Da hun kom tilbake til dem igjen, ristet hun fortsatt på hodet. «Det navnet der er helt ukjent for oss. Jeg må bare beklage. Det ser ikke ut til at vi kan hjelpe deg.»

Dypt skuffet ble de stående utenfor sykehuset en stund og diskutere hva de burde gjøre. «Kanskje det er et annet sykehus?» foreslo Mette. Morten rynket pannen og tenkte seg om. «Jeg tror ikke det,» sa han etter en stund. Frank virken svært overbevist da han så hva som sto i de gamle brevene. La oss heller dra tilbake til hotellet. Der må finnes en forklaring på dette. Vi kan jo gå igjennom opplysningene vi har en gang til. Kanskje vi finner ut noe nytt.»

Hele formiddagen ble de sittende på hotellrommet og studere gamle brev. De hadde tatt med seg en god del av dem for å vise til eventuelle slektninger de måtte finne. Over begge de to store sengene hadde Mette brettet dem ut. I dyp taushet satt de og leste begge to.

«Jeg begriper ikke at her kan være noe mer å finne,» sa plutselig Morten oppgitt og kastet fra seg et brev. Mette så fortvilet på ham.«Men vi kan da ikke bare gi opp slik med det samme. Der må da finnes noe mer vi kan gjøre.»

Morten tenkte seg om igjen. «Kanskje jeg skal ringe til Frank. Det er jo mulig at han kan gi oss noen råd.»

«Ja, gjør det.» Mette ble ivrig med det samme.

Fra telefonen på hotellrommet fikk Morten direkte forbindelse med Frank. «Vi finner ikke ut av dette,» sa Morten oppgitt. «Kan du hjelpe oss?» Han forklarte at der ikke var mye hjelp å få på sykehuset.

Det ble stille en stund i den andre enden. Mette satt så nær at hun kunne høre det som ble sagt. «Hva var det du kalte denne mannen?» spurte Frank etter å ha tenkt seg om en stund. «Fornavnet er Robert,» forklarte Morten, «og familienavnet deres var Aanensen.»

«Det er nok lite sannsynlig at denne mannen har fortsatt å kalle seg Aanensen,» sa Frank. «Det er et svært vanskelig navn for amerikanerne. Og fornavnet kan også være forandret. Robert blir gjerne bare uttalt Rob eller Bob, eller noe slikt.»

Morten ble ivrig igjen. «Ja, der har vi kanskje forklaringen. Vi leter etter feil navn. Men hva kan så det rette etternavnet være da?»

«Er der et stedsnavn de kan ha brukt, tror du?» fortsatte Frank. «Eller kanskje han har brukt farens fornavn med å føye son etter?»

«Da måtte det bli for eksempel Bob Nelson?» svarte Morten. «Ja, det er et mye mer amerikansk navn,» sa Frank begeistret. «Jeg foreslår at dere tar dere en tur til, og så tar dere med dere alle de navnealternativene dere kan tenke dere at er aktuelle. Dere må ikke gi dere med dette.»

Situasjonen så med ett atskillig lysere ut for de to på hotellet. Straks forberedte de seg på en ny tur til sykehuset.

Damen ved skranken var særdeles vennlig og tålmodig, syntes Mette, da de på nytt kom med spørsmålene sine. Gang på gang gikk hun igjennom navnelister. Og rett som det var henvendte hun seg til andre kolleger med spørsmål.

«Det eneste vi kan se,» sa hun etter en lang stund med undersøkelser, «er at det arbeidet en Nelson her for en del år siden. En av de eldre legene her husker ham, men han har ingen forbindelse med ham lenger. Han har heller ingen anelse om hvor han bor, eller om han lever lenger i det hele tatt. Dessverre ser det ikke ut til …» Hun ble plutselig avbrutt av en som kom inn og sa noe til henne. Raskt forsvant hun ut igjen, mens Mette og Morten igjen ble stående og vente.

«Dette ser da slett ikke noe lysere ut,» sa Mette og var nesten på gråten. «Tenk den lange veien vi har reist, og så til ingen nytte.»

Morten så også nokså oppgitt ut. «Til ingen nytt kan vi vel ikke si at det har vært.» Hun skjønte at han ville forsøke å trøste henne, men hun var i tvil om det ikke like mye var for å trøste seg selv. Dette var jo tross alt hans slekt. «Vi har jo ennå besøket i Bismarck igjen, og der får vi i hvert fall treffe Frank.»

I det samme kom damen tilbake igjen. «I morgen venter vi en eldre mann her. Han har arbeidet som lege ved dette sykehuset tidligere. Han skal følge en pasient hit, og det er jo mulig at han har noen opplysninger. Hvis dere kommer hit i morgen klokka tolv, så skal vi gi beskjed om at her er noen som vil snakke med ham.»

Morten takket hjertelig for hjelpen, og lovet at de skulle være på plass.

Resten av dagen brukte de til å se seg omkring i byen. Mette var innom en masse butikker hvor hun handlet en del. Så spiste de middag på et «steakhouse» for å få oppleve et skikkelig amerikansk måltid. De fikk servert et digert kjøttstykke med bakte poteter og salat.

«Nå trenger jeg ikke spise mer før jeg er hjemme på setra igjen,» sa Mette og stønnet da de forlot restauranten.

Morten lo og forsikret at også han var blitt mett denne dagen.

Neste dag møtte de på sykehuset presis klokka tolv. De ble henvist til et rom hvor de kunne vente. Den sterke spenningen fikk dem til å sitte i total taushet mens de ventet. Det varte heller ikke lenge før døra gikk opp og en eldre herre kom inn. Han hilste litt spørrende på dem.

Morten begynte å forklare ærendet deres. «Vi kommer fra Norge, og er nå på leting etter slekt som vi går ut fra fremdeles befinner seg her i landet,» begynte han. «Vi har bare gamle brev å holde oss til, så sporene våre er nokså vage. Men vi har funnet ut at en av slektningene våre har arbeidet ved dette sykehuset.»

Mens de snakket, kunne de se både forbauselse og en form for interesse som tegnet seg i øynene hans.

«Navnet til denne personen er vi imidlertid nokså usikre på,» fortsatte Morten, «men vi tenkte at du kanskje kunne hjelpe oss. Kanskje du har arbeidet sammen med denne i din tid som lege?»

Morten forklarte også navneproblemet de hadde i saken.

En stund ble den eldre mannen sittende og tenke. Noe vaktsomt kom over ansiktet hans mens han studerte dem begge med et intenst blikk. Da han endelig begynte å snakke, var det nesten noe avvisende i stemmen. «Der er så mange norskættede her i denne delen landet, og dette er jo så lenge siden. Det er nok ikke lett å finne ut av en slik sak.»

Plutselig ble døren revet opp. En sykepleier kom styrtende inn. «Du må komme,» ropte hun, «det er kritisk …» Mer hørte de ikke, for hun var allerede ute igjen. Mannen reiste seg raskt, men snudde seg mot Morten før han gikk ut døra:

«Jeg skal tenke litt på dette. Hvis dere er her i morgen til samme tid, så kan vi kanskje få snakket litt mer.» Dermed forsvant også han ut av døra.

Det var med nokså blandede følelser de forlot sykehuset den dagen. Det hadde kommet et sterkt glimt av håp da de traff mannen, men da han snakket med dem viste han slett ikke særlig mye entusiasme. Der var heller noe avvisende og tilbakeholdende ved ham. «Han virket nesten litt mystisk,» sa Mette da de sto og ventet på en taxi. «I hvert fall var der ingen tegn å spore på at han ville gjøre for mye for å hjelpe oss.»

«Nå får vi se i morgen,» sa Morten. «Kanskje ser alt lysere ut da.»

«Ja, la oss håpe det,» svarte hun. Men hun begynte allerede å forberede seg mentalt på at dette ikke ville lykkes.

50 • En lidende familie

De fikk se mye av Minneapolis disse dagene. Også til tvillingbyen Saint Paul, som ikke lå langt unna, tok de seg en tur. Men om kvelden dro de tilbake igjen og oppsøkte den norske Minnekirken i byen. Der skulle det være gudstjeneste, og den ville de være med på.

Etter gudstjenesten kom de i snakk med flere der av norsk opprinnelse. Noen av dem snakket til og med ganske bra norsk. Både Mette og Morten var frampå med ærendet sitt. Kanskje noen der kunne hjelpe dem? Men det så ikke ut til at noen av dem kjente mannen de lette etter. «Mange av de norske kommer hit,» var det ei som sa, «men dette er ukjente navn for oss.»

De hadde ikke annet å gjøre enn å fortsette letingen der de hadde begynt. Det kunne jo hende at denne gamle legen hadde noe interessant å komme med neste dag.

Det ble lenger ventetid enn de hadde trodd da de dagen etter igjen trådte opp på sykehuset. De ble vist til et sted hvor de kunne vente, men han de ventet på var opptatt med en pasient. Ingen visste når han var ledig. «Hvis dere sitter her så kommer den eldre legen, og familien til pasienten hans, hit etter hvert,» var det ei sykepleier som forklarte.

Mette satt og betraktet alle menneskene som gikk forbi, eller satt og ventet. «Lurer på hva som har brakt dem hit?» tenkte hun. Kanskje der lå en del tunge skjebner skjult bak de tause maskene. På et sykehus var det ofte mye nød under overflaten.

«Jeg tar meg en tur og ser om jeg kan få skaffet oss et par kopper med kaffe,» sa Morten plutselig og reiste seg.

Mens han var borte, fortsatte Mette å studere menneskene rundt seg. Det var ikke så mange som satt akkurat der hvor de var, men det gikk stadig noen forbi.

Plutselig kom det ei kvinne og satte seg i en stol et lite stykke unna Mette. Hun bar tydelig preg av å ha grått. Over hele det bleke ansiktet lå det et dypt drag av smerte. Mette kjente med det samme en inderlig medlidenhet med denne kvinnen. Hva det enn var som plaget henne, så måtte det være noe svært vondt. Hun krøp nesten helt sammen i stolen sin, mens det rett som det var gikk skjelvinger gjennom kroppen hennes

En plutselig innskytelse fikk Mette til å reise seg og gå bort til henne. «Det ser ut som du har det vondt,» sa hun vennlig til kvinnen. «Er det noe jeg kan hjelpe deg med?»

Hun ristet sakte på hodet mens blikket så ut som det kunne sluke hele Mette. Den dype fortvilelsen som tegnet seg i de store, mørke øynene fikk Mette til å sette seg ved siden av henne.

«Det må nok et under til skal jeg bli hjulpet,» sa hun med et hikst. «Eller rettere sagt,» fortsatte hun, «hvis sønnen min skal bli hjulpet.» Uten nærmere oppfordring begynte hun å snakke. Mette tenkte at slik var det visst amerikanerne var, så mye mer åpne, og lette å få kontakt med, enn folk i Norge. Dette var tydeligvis ei som også hadde et sterkt behov for å utøse sin bekymring for noen.

«Det er sønnen min som har problemer,» begynte hun. «Han var ute for en bil-ulykke for noen måneder siden, og etter det har han for det meste tilbrakt tiden på syke-huset. Til tider ser det også ganske alvorlig ut for ham, slik som det er akkurat nå.» Hun pusset nesen mens et nytt smertedrag gikk over ansiktet hennes. «Det er noe i hodet som nå er problemet. Han har blitt operert flere ganger, men denne gangen ser det ekstra ille ut. Mannen min og svigerfar er hos legen hans akkurat nå. De skal for-berede enda en operasjon. Jeg orker ikke å bli med inn.» Det siste ble sagt med et stønn mens hun sank enda mer sammen.

I det samme kom Morten med kaffen. Han så litt undrende på de to som satt der og snakket, men sa ikke noe. Rakte bare den ene kaffekoppen til Mette. Takknemlig tok hun imot og rakte den videre til kvinnen. «Se her,» sa hun. «Litt kaffe vil sikkert gjøre deg godt.» Takknemlig tok hun imot koppen og nippet til den varme drikken. En stund ble hun sittende der, bare opptatt med kaffen og de bekymrede tankene sine. Mette sa heller ikke noe. Men så begynte hun å snakke igjen:

«Det har vært så vanskelig for oss denne tiden. Mannen min har måttet ta seg fri fra arbeidet i lange perioder for å ta seg av Allan.» Mette skjønte at det var sønnen hun snakket om, men hun sa ikke noe, lyttet bare til den fortvilede kvinnen. «Når han er på sykehuset, trenger han at en av oss er der nesten hele tiden, og når han er hjemme, har han jo enda større behov for vår hjelp. Dette har slitt fælt på oss, ikke minst økonomisk, for vi har ikke forsikringer som dekker alt dette.»

Et øyeblikk ble hun sittende taus før hun igjen begynte å snakke. «Svigerfar har riktignok hjulpet oss godt, men det er jo begrenset hva han kan skaffe av midler. Jeg har forresten en mistanke om at han har tatt opp et lån i banken for å hjelpe oss.» Hun stønnet igjen.

Mette kjente at hun ble rystet langt inn i sitt innerste der hun satt og lyttet. Hadde hun bare kunne vært til noe hjelp for disse menneskene, men der var ikke stort annet hun kunne gjøre enn å sitte der og lytte. Nå forsto hun jo også godt at det slett ikke var for å få hjelp at kvinnen satt der og fortalte henne dette. Det var nok heller et behov hun hadde for å utøse sin fortvilelse for noen. Og hvis det bare var et par åpne ører hun trengte, så var Mette mer enn villig til å lytte.

Minuttene gikk mens de to kvinnene satt der helt oppslukt av den vonde situasjonen. Morten hadde funnet en avis som det så ut til at hadde fanget hele hans oppmerksomhet.

Plutselig rettet kvinnen seg opp og stirret bortover korridoren. Mette fulgte blikket hennes og fikk se to menn som kom gående. Til hennes forbauselse var den ene av dem mannen de hadde snakket med dagen før. De to mennene gikk i heftig samtale, så det var tydelig at de hadde noe med hverandre å gjøre. Denne gamle legen måtte antakelig ha blitt kalt til sykehuset, på tross av at han var pensjonert, for å hjelpe med det vanskelige tilfellet som Allan var, tenkte Mette.

«Hvordan går det?» spurte kvinnen og gikk de to mennene i møte.

En stund ble de tre stående i dyp samtale, men så var det som om legen våknet opp og så bort på Morten. «Ja, det var dere,» sa han og kom nærmere. «Jeg har tenkt på det dere spurte om i går.» Han så på dem begge med et granskende blikk. «Kanskje jeg kan hjelpe dere med opplysninger, men det er nok også det eneste jeg kan hjelpe med.» Det siste ble sagt med ekstra tyngde, mens blikket hans fortsatt var like granskende.

Mette og Morten vekslet blikk. Det var noe underlig med denne mannen. Men så vendte Morten seg mot ham igjen: «Hvis du kan gi oss noen opplysninger, så er det det eneste vi ønsker,» svarte han like bestemt.

Et trett drag kom over den aldrende skikkelsen idet han satte seg i en stol ved siden av Morten. Mette la merke til at de to andre forsvant bortover korridoren i samme retning som de to mennene var kommet fra.

«Det var altså norske slektninger dere var på leting etter.» Han så ut i luften med et fjernt blikk. «Kan dere si litt mer om disse slektningene?» spurte han uten å flytte blikket. Morten begynte å fortelle om de to tantene til hans mor som hadde reist over for mer enn åtti år siden. Han fortalte om Mina som døde ikke lenge etter at de kom til landet, og han fortalte om slekten som Gunhild hadde reist til i Nord Dakota.

Mens han snakket, satt legen taus og lyttet. Da Morten forklarte at de ikke hadde andre spor å lete etter enn dette sykehuset, hvor en av sønnene til Gunhild angivelig skulle ha arbeidet, kremtet tilhøreren og så rett på Morten. Stemmen var en helt annen da han begynte å snakke. Den var rolig, men hadde en trett klang:

«Min mor het Ginni, og min far het Nels. De kom begge fra Norge. Mor fortalte mye om ei tvillingsøster som døde i tuberkulose like etter at de kom til Amerika. Det er nok ingen tvil om at dere er kommet til rett person.»

Mette kjente en dirrende følelse inni seg med det samme. Kunne det være mulig? Var dette den Robert som de lette etter? Men han virket så underlig. Det trette blikket hans flakket fra Mette til Morten.

«Men …» fortsatte han. Plutselig stoppet han og så ned på hendene sine i fanget. Det tok et øyeblikk før han fortsatte: «… der er nok ikke mye å komme etter her.»

Mette og Morten så spørrende på hverandre. Hva var det med denne mannen?

Morten forsøkte seg igjen med et spørsmål: «Hva er egentlig navnet ditt?»

«Jeg heter egentlig Robert, men alle kaller meg Bob. Etternavnet mitt var Aanensen, men jeg måtte forandre det til et lettere navn. Derfor tok jeg min fars fornavn. Det ble altså Nelson.»

«Da var det jo slik som vi trodde,» sa Mette begeistret. «Da har vi jo funnet deg.» Plutselig så det ut som sannheten gikk opp for dem, og begeistringen lyste av dem begge to. Hr. Nelson smilte også, men det bedrøvede utrykket lå der fremdeles.

Morten rynket brynene igjen og så betenkt ut i luften. «Du sa at din mor het Ginni, vi trodde hun het Gunhild?»

«Det er jo slik her,» svarte han, «at navnene ofte blir forkortet, i hvert fall de navnene som er litt tunge og vanskelige. Det er nok derfor hun fikk navnet Ginni. Men hun het jo Gunhild, det har jeg bevis for. Det gamle passet hennes ligger hjemme i ei skuff.»

«Men … er det bare ønsket om å finne fjerne slektninger som har brakt dere hit, denne lange veien, helt fra Norge?» Igjen var det granskende blikket tilbake.

Morten kikket bort på Mette. Det var som han ville spørre om de nå kunne komme med ærendet sitt, eller om de måtte ha flere bevis for at det var den rette personen de hadde funnet. Mette nikket svakt. Det kunne ikke være noen tvil om at dette var den rette personen, men det var bare så underlig at han var så tilbakeholdende.

«Vi kommer egentlig i et spesielt ærend,» sa Morten henvendt til den eldre mannen. Så begynte han å fortelle om onkel Torkel som var død. Han fortalte om brevene de hadde funnet, og som gav dem mistanke om at der kunne være slekt i Amerika, ja, ikke bare slekt, men også slekt som var arveberettiget. Da han fortalte om arven, kunne de se at utrykket forandret seg hos tilhøreren. Først ble han blek, så kom det røde flekker i kinnene før tårene begynte å renne.

«Er dette sant? Dere har ikke misforstått på noen måte?» Stemmen hans var hes og ustø. Morten forsikret at alt var slik som han hadde sagt. Papirene hadde han på hotellet. Dit kunne de jo dra og sjekke det.

«Og jeg som trodde …» han kremtet og begynte på nytt. «Jeg trodde dere kom hit for å få penger av meg. Jeg kunne ikke begripe hvorfor dere ellers skulle oppsøke en fjern slektning etter så lang tid. Så er det altså helt motsatt. Dette er ikke til å begripe.»

Plutselig spratt han opp av stolen. «La oss gå et sted hvor vi kan snakke mer sam-

405

men,» sa han. «Ja, la oss gjøre det,» sa Mette og Morten i munnen på hverandre. Begeistringen lyste av dem alle tre.

De fant en kafé litt lenger nede i gata. Mette registrerte knapt hva det var hun spiste. Gleden over endelig å ha funnet den de lette etter, overveldet henne helt. Bob fortalte ivrig om sin barndom og oppvekst i Nord Dakota. Han fortalte også om hvor vanskelig det hadde vært da faren døde etter en ulykke for mange år siden. Og han fortalte om de to brødrene sine, Willy og Mical, som begge var døde uten at de hadde etterlatt seg noen familie. Men selv hadde han etterkommere.

Han og kona Nancy bodde i et hus i utkanten av byen. De hadde to barn som også begge var gift. Og så hadde de seks barnebarn. «Det var den eldste sønnen min dere så her,» avsluttet han og så sørgmodig ut i lufta.

Morten så forvirret fra Mette til Bob. «Sønnen? Jeg trodde du var her som lege?»

«Å nei.» Den gamle mannen ristet på hodet. Legegjerningen min er jeg ferdig med nå, men de synes likevel det er trygt å ha meg med når han må på sykehus. Han fortalte om gutten som ble utsatt for en bilulykke, og som etter det hadde vært svært dårlig. Mette hadde jo hørt historien før, men at dette var den svigerfaren som kvinnen hadde snakket om, det hadde heller ikke hun forstått.

Med ett gikk det opp for henne hva det måtte bety for disse menneskene å få beskjed om denne arven akkurat nå mens de var i denne vanskelige økonomiske situasjonen. Bob fortalte åpent om det alt sammen. «Jeg har bedt og tryglet Gud om hjelp,» fortsatte han, «men skal jeg være ærlig, hadde jeg nok ingen tro på at jeg skulle få noen slags svar på min bønn.»

Mette kjente at tårene ikke var langt unna. Hun måtte svelge et par ganger før hun greide å snakke. «Ja, det er forunderlig hvilken omsorgsfull Gud vi har.»

«Et klarere bønnesvar kunne jeg da aldri ha fått,» fortsatte Bob. «Og så et slikt mektig under da. Dette skal bli noe å fortelle Tim og Sally.»

Et blikk på klokka fikk ham til å reise seg. Jeg må tilbake til sykehuset, men vi må treffes igjen.» De gjorde en rask avtale før han forsvant ut av døra igjen.

Morten og Mette ble ennå sittende en stund og snakke sammen. Begge var nesten i ekstase over den vendingen saken deres hadde tatt. Og opplysningene om at arven kom til folk som trengte den så sårt, det gjorde det ekstra gledelig. At det på en eller annen måte var en guddommelig styrelse i det hele, det var de ikke i tvil om, uten at de helt kunne greie å forstå det.

«Hvor mye penger dreier det seg egentlig om?» spurte plutselig Mette. Hun hadde aldri hørt den eksakte summen av onkel Torkels formue.

Morten tenkte seg om et øyeblikk før han svarte. «Du vet halvparten av summen faller jo på Bob, og blir eiendommen solgt, så vil det nok dreie seg om en sum på ca en million norske kroner som blir hans part.»

Mette gispet. «Jeg ante ikke at det var slike summer det dreide seg om.» Morten lo litt av det forbausede utrykket hennes. «Men når det gjelder oss,» fortsatte han, «så må jo den andre halvparten deles på tre. Så vi kommer ikke til å bli så styrtrike akkurat av dette.»

Mette måtte også le. «Det er i hvert fall godt at pengene her kommer til folk som virkelig trenger dem,» sa hun, og det var Morten helt enig i.

51 • På prærien

På grunn av den spente situasjonen på sykehuset, ble det ikke anledning til å være sammen med slektningene de nettopp hadde funnet, så mye som de alle ønsket. Men de fikk likevel hilse på kona til Bob, ei yndig kvinne som også så ut til å gjøre hva hun kunne for den syke gutten. Nyheten om arven i Norge kom som et sjokk på dem alle. Ikke minst guttens mor, som viste seg å hete Sally, ble grundig overrasket. Hun strålte mot Mette da de igjen traff hverandre. «Tenk at der satt du med løsningen, og hjelpen for oss alle, uten å vite det.» Mette smilt. Hun var lykkelig over at hun likevel kunne komme med hjelp til dem.

Morten og Mettes opphold i Minneapolis var nesten over. Snart skulle de videre til Bismarck, hvor Frank ventet dem, men de var alle bestemt på at nå måtte kontakten holdes ved like.

Den eneste de ikke fikk anledning til å hilse på, var Ted, den andre sønnen til Bob. Han bodde i New York med sin familie, så det ble for langt unna.

Selv om det ikke ble så langt bekjentskap, og stundene de fikk sammen heller ikke ble så mange, følte de likevel et stort savn da de skulle ta farvel. Mette og Sally hadde blitt ekstra gode venner.

Det var bare Bob som var med og kjørte dem til flyplassen. De andre var på sykehuset. Operasjonen til Allan hadde gått bra, men han var ennå ikke utenfor fare. Spenningen og uroen preget dem fremdeles, så Morten og Mette mente at det ikke var klokt å forlenge oppholdet noe mer. De kunne jo heller komme tilbake en gang senere.

I Bismarck sto Frank og ventet på dem da flyet landet. Gjensynsgleden var stor hos dem alle.

«Jeg har funnet ut litt om slekta deres her,» sa han da de kjørte ut av byen, og tok fatt på de lange, rette vegstrekningene nordover.» De lyttet begge oppmerksomt til det han hadde å fortelle.

«Noen kilometer unna vår farm bor det en familie som jeg kjenner litt til,» fortsatte han. «Etter en del roting i gamle papirer fant jeg ut at også de stammer fra de første settlerne her. Jeg tok en prat med gamlefar i huset der en dag, og han kunne bekrefte at hans bestefar var en av dem som ble tatt hånd om av Sjur, da han kom fra Norge. Etter de opplysningene dere gav meg, fant vi ut at hans bestefar var den Theodor som dere snakket om.»

«Så fantastisk!» Mette og Morten snakket i munnen på hverandre av begeistring. «Da er det kanskje også flere å finne av slekta her i distriktet?»

Frank ristet på hodet. «Nei, jeg tror ikke det. Noen har flyttet vekk til andre steder, mens andre rett og slett må ha dødd ut. Jeg har arbeidet litt med dette disse dagene, men dette er det eneste jeg har funnet.»

Med disse opplysningene økte spenningen enda mer ettersom de beveget seg lenger og lenger nordover. En underlig følelse fylte Mette der hun satt i bilen og fòr bortover de store prærieslettene. Der hadde emigrantene fra deres hjemland, trasket etter ei prærievogn. Hester, eller kanskje bare okser, var det eneste framkomstmiddelet de hadde langs de endeløse stiene, før jernbanen kom.

Hvor ofte hadde hun ikke hørt om de flate og milevide slettene med langt, stritt præriegress duvende i vinden. Nå kunne hun ikke si at hun syntes disse slettene just var så flate som ei pannekake. Hun ville heller beskrive dem som et bølgende hav, for landskapet var utrolig kollete. Noen steder var kollene svært bratte også.

Mette lot blikket gli langs horisonten i vest. Det var som om hun hvert øyeblikk ventet at en indianerflokk skulle dukke opp over en bakkekant. Frank fortalte at det lå et indianerreservat der borte i vest. «Men det er nok ikke lenger malte ryttere med fjær og piler dere vil finne der,» sa han og lo.

Mette smilte for seg selv. Nei, der var nok ikke lenger stort igjen av det eventyrbildet som mange hadde av ville vesten.

Prærien lå heller ikke som ei duvende gresslette. Nesten over alt var det oppdyrkede jorder hvor det ble sådd forskjellige slags vekster. Med spredte mellomrom så de husklynger innimellom trær og busker.

«Trærne er plantet for å gi husene ly for vær og vind,» forklarte Frank.

«Hva slags vekster er det helst som blir dyrket her?» spurte Morten. Han så på de frodige viddene som strakte seg milevidt utover på alle kanter.

«Det er ganske mye forskjellig,» svarte Frank. «Men soyabønner og mais er her mye av. Og så dyrkes det jo mye gressmark, for her finnes også ganske store rancher.»

«Rancher?» Mette stusset litt. «Hva er forskjell på en ranch og en farm?»

Frank forklarte villig: «Ranch er et sted hvor de har dyr. Der dyrkes det mest gress til dyrefôr. Farm er derimot et sted hvor det dyrkes forskjellige slags korn og andre vekster.»

Snart svingte de av fra hovedveien og tok inn på en mindre vei i østlig retning. Ennå kjørte de et godt stykke før Frank stoppet bilen utenfor en enorm uthusbygning. Noen digre traktorer og maskiner sto parkert utenfor.

«Her er det system i sakene,» sa Morten beundrende og gikk ut av bilen. Det varte ikke lenge før han satt høyt oppe i en diger skurtresker. «Denne skulle jeg hatt på setra,» ropte han ned til Mette og lo. Mette krøket seg av latter ved tanken på den lille jordeflekken der hjemme. Denne maskinen hadde aldri en gang greid å snu der.

Snart kom det folk til fra alle kanter. Det viste seg at Frank bodde sammen med sønnen, og familien hans, på denne farmen. Han hadde flyttet sammen med dem da han for noen år siden ble enkemann.

De hilste både på sønnen og kona hans. Barna kom også for å ta utlendingene i nærmere øyesyn. Det var fire stykker av dem. Den eldste var allerede gammel nok til å ta sin tørn i traktoren ute på jordene, men den yngste var bare ti år.

Det ble en usedvanlig hyggelig ettermiddag. Den åpne gjestfriheten de ble møtt med, varmet dem begge.

Selv om farmen var i den aller beste forfatning, og redskapene av beste sort, så var huset og innboet av svært enkel standard. De ble plassert ved kjøkkenbordet til et vel - smakende måltid på den solide voksduken. Gardiner og duker var det ikke akkurat overflod av, men tryggheten ved den vennlige atmosfæren gjorde at de med en gang følte seg som hjemme.

Etter måltidet kom Frank med den gamle dagboken etter Sjur. «Det er jo her jeg har hentet de fleste opplysningene om slekta og Norge,» sa han og la den store, slitte boka på bordet. Forsiktig bladde Mette rundt noen sider. «Hvordan i all verden har du greid å tyde dette?» spurte hun og så på de snirklete gotiske bokstavene. Hun hadde så vidt tittet litt i den da han hadde hatt den med på turen til Norge, og også da hadde Mette undret seg over det.

Frank smilte litt. «Det var ikke så lett til å begynne med, men etter hvert som jeg ble kjent med bokstavene, så gikk det bedre. Det største problemet var faktisk språket til denne mannen. I begynnelsen er det så blandet med norsk at det er vanskelig å forstå sammenhengen. Da jeg begynte å lese måtte jeg rett som det var søke hjelp i ei engelsk –norsk ordbok.»

I dagene som fulgte var de norske gjestene travelt opptatt med å studere alt det en nordamerikansk farm kan være. Spesielt Morten var interessert i å se hvordan de forskjellige maskiner og redskaper virket, og vertsfolket var hele tiden ivrige med å vise og forklare.

Dagen etter ankomst dro de for å besøke dem som de hadde fått greie på var deres slektninger. Igjen ble det velkomst med bortimot tårevåt begeistring. Ekteparet som bodde der, var i sekstiårene. Mette stusset litt med det samme. Kunne det være denne Frank hadde kalt «Gamlefar». Han var da slett ikke så gammel.

Alle barna var imidlertid flyttet vekk, bortsett fra den eldste sønnen. Han var gift og hadde bygd hus i nærheten, men han var ikke hjemme akkurat den dagen.

Praten gikk livlig, og mat manglet det heller ikke på. Også denne farmen var av samme type som farmen til Frank. Maskiner og redskaper sto på rekke og rad ute på den store gårdsplassen.

Mens de satt ved kaffebordet ble det fortalt mange historier fra den første nybyggertiden i distriktet. Kona i huset, som het Martha, var også av norsk opprinnelse. Slekten hennes kom fra Gudbrandsdalen i Norge kunne hun fortelle. De første utvandrerne kom til Amerika allerede på attenhundre tallet en gang. Da slo de seg ned i en by som de kalt Westby i Wisconsien. «Dit skulle dere ha tatt dere en tur,» sa hun begeistret. «Den byen er nesten Norsk fremdeles.»

Ivrig fortalte hun om butikker med håndverk og andre gjenstander som tydelig viste den norske tradisjonen. «Å, tenk om vi kunne ha tatt en tur dit,» sa Mette.

«Ja, det burde da være mulig,» sa Frank og tenkte seg om en stund.

Etter en del diskusjon fram og tilbake ble de enige om at de, i stedet for å ta fly tilbake til Chicago, skulle ta den strekningen i bil. «Det blir mange timer i bil, sa Frank men dere vil få se en masse av det «Norske Amerika». Både Mette og Morten forsikret at de slett ikke gjorde seg noe av litt kjøring. Dette ville bli en sjelden anledning for dem til å oppleve det som tidligere bare hadde vært eventyr for dem. Både Martha og mannen hennes, Simen, bestemte raskt at også de ville være med.

Det ble med ett en ivrig og spent atmosfære der i det gamle præriehuset. De trengte litt tid alle sammen til å forberede reisen, så de ble enige om at avreisen ikke kunne skje før om noen dager. I mellomtiden ville Frank vise gjestene rundt en del i distriktet der de bodde.

Plutselig spratt Martha opp av stolen. «Jeg har noe jeg vil vise dere,» sa hun og forsvant ut av døra. Etter ei lita stund kom hun tilbake med ei pappeske.

«Denne har ligget oppe på loftet,» sa hun og satte eska på bordet. «Jeg hadde helt glemt den vekk. Men etter at Frank kom med opplysningene om de norske slektningene, kom jeg på den igjen. Det var svigerfar som fortalte meg om den. Hans far hadde fått den av Sjur før han døde. Han ville at en nordmann skulle få den, for han mente at hans egen slekt ikke var interessert i det som hadde med Gamlelandet å gjøre. Ikke hadde han noe slekt der hjemme heller, så han ville at vår familie skulle få dette.»

Hun åpnet lokket og tok opp et mørkt tøystykke. Det var vevet i grov ull. «Dette var det eneste Sjur hadde etter sin mor. Det var det sjalet hun var pakket inn i da hun som spedbarn ble fraktet til gården der hun vokste opp, skal Sjur ha forklarte til bestefar.»

Frank reiste seg og gikk bort til sjalet. Med varsomme hender strøk han over det grove tøyet. «Så underlig,» sa han med ærbødighet i stemmen.

«Vi tenkte at dette nå helst tilkom deg,» sa Martha henvendt til Frank. «Hvis du vil ha det da?»

«Vil dere gi det til meg?» sa han med store øyne. «Kan skjønne jeg vil ha det.»

«Vi har aldri tenkt på dette før, siden Sjur sa at ingen av familien hans var interessert i det,» fortsatte hun.

Frank ristet på hodet. «De tenkte vel ikke slik i den tiden, men for meg er dette meget verdifullt.»

Den kvelden ble Mette sittende lenge sammen med Frank og studere det gamle sjalet, mens Morten var med sønnen ute på jordet. De grove trådene var slitt over flere steder.

«Dette er i hvert fall velbrukt,» sa Mette og strøk hånden langs kanten der det en gang i tiden hadde vært knyttede frynser. I det ene hjørnet var det også revet bort et stort stykke.

Mette fant fram fotoapparatet sitt og tok flere bilder av det gamle plagget. Frank ble også fotografert fra alle bauer og kanter. «Jeg skal sende deg et eksemplar, når bildene blir framkalt, så du virkelig skal få se hvilken vakker fotomodell du er,» sa hun muntert. De lo begge to mens de pakket sjalet sammen igjen for å legge det vekk.

52 • Indianernes land

De fikk noen fantastiske dager i Nord Dakota sammen med Frank og familien hans. Rett som det var tok de bilturer rundt i distriktet for å se de stedene hvor deres forfedre hadde slitt og strevd for å skaffe et levebrød for seg og familien. Flere ganger hadde de kontakt med Bob over telefon. Han forklarte hvor han var vokst opp, og hvor de andre slektningene hans hadde bodd. Dit tok de også turer. Det var rart å tenke på at prærien, som de der så foran seg, var dyrket opp av deres egne slektninger. Alle eiendommene, bortsatt fra den hos familien de hadde besøkt, var riktignok på fremmede hender nå, men sporene etter de første settlerne kunne man fremdeles ane. Alle de traff rundt på farmene de besøkte var svært hyggelige og fortalte ivrig om stedet og historien der.

Frank tok dem også med til et sted hvor det for mange år siden hadde vært en stor indianerleir. «Det var Mandan indianere som bodde her,» forklarte Frank da de gikk bortover mot noen store runde jordhytter. «Denne leiren ble utdødd lenge før europeerne kom og slo seg ned i denne delen av landet. Det var en koppeepidemi som gjorde ende på folkene her. Men nå i den senere tid er noen av hyttene deres bygd opp igjen for å vise hvordan det egentlig så ut her i den tiden. Og også for å vise litt om hvordan indianerne levde da.»

De gikk inn i ei av hyttene. Det var et stort åpent rom der inne med mange forskjellige slags redskaper og gjenstander. På gulv og vegger var der vakre flettede matter, og midt i hytta var det et ildsted.

«Her kunne det jammen bo mange så stor som denne er,» sa Mette forbauset. «Ja,» sa Frank, «og rundt i dette området var det flere titals slike hytter, så det var et betydelig samfunn som levde her.»

«Hva er det?» spurte Morten da de kom ut av hytta igjen. Han pekte på noen stokker

410

som var satt ned i jorda slik at de dannet en rund ring. Stokkene sto tett i tett, og var et par meter høye. Et stykke oppe på stokkeringen var det bundet rundt et slags tau av flettet siv eller gress.

«Det var det religiøse senteret i leiren.» svarte Frank. Det var også der alle viktige avgjørelser ble tatt, så det var liksom der «kommunestyret» hadde sine møter,» sa han og lo.

«Men de stokkene der, hva skulle de tjene til?» fortsatt Morten mens han studerte det grovt tilhogde treverket.

«Ja det er en ganske interessant sak,» sa Frank ivrig. «Som jeg sa var dette deres religiøse senter. Og disse stokkene symboliserte en viktig hendelse i deres tro. Deres tradisjon fortalte at det for mange år tilbake hadde hendt en stor katastrofe. Gud måtte straffe folkene på jorden for deres ondskap. Det gjorde han ved å sende en stor vannflom. Da var det at en mann greide å berge seg, og sannsynligvis også familien, ved å sette opp stokker i jorda på denne måten. Han greide å tette dem til slik at vannet ikke rant inn i rommet innenfor. Der oppholdt han seg til vannet sank ned igjen. Sivtauet som er bundet rundt der oppe viser hvor langt opp vannet sto på det høyeste. På den måten mente de at menneskeslekten greide å overleve Guds straff.» Frank smilte litt mens han studerte den lille åpningen innenfor stokkene. Det ble jammen ikke mye plass her, for skulle han berge menneskeslekten så måtte han vel også ha hatt med seg kona si,» sa han.

Mette betraktet det enkle byggverket med stigende undring etter hvert som Frank fortalte. «Men det er jo nesten den samme historien som vi har i Bibelen,» sa hun ivrig. «Det er bare det at der er det snakk om en båt, altså Noa og hans Ark.»

«Ja,» sa Frank. «Jeg mener at det ikke er noen tvil om at der må ha vært en vannflom en gang i tiden. Dette finnes visst i enda flere religiøse tradisjoner rundt om i verden. Så dette med vannflommen, og syndefloden, er ikke Bibelen alene om å beskrive. Men det som er spesielt med Bibelen er at den ikke bare forteller om synd, straff og dom. Den har også med beretningen om en frelsesvei, og en Frelser. Det er det som er enestående med Bibelen.»

«Ja,» sa Morten. «Det er klart at hvis vi skal tro på at det virkelig har funnet sted en vannflom en gang i tiden, så er det noe som er en virkelighet for alle folk, enten de tror på Bibelen eller ikke. Så da er det ikke rart at det finnes slike beretninger i de andre religionene også. Det bekrefter jo bare at Bibelen er sann.»

De ble lenge gående rundt omkring i indianerleiren. Frank hadde god greie på historien og tradisjonene der, så det syntes de lærte utrolig mye om den gamle verden der ute på prærien. Kriger og konfrontasjoner hadde der vært mellom indianer og hvit, men også indianerstammene imellom.

«Denne Mandanstammen var en ganske fredelig stamme,» sa Frank da de gikk tilbake mot bilen igjen. «Men det var nok ikke fritt for at de fikk besøk av mer krigerske stammer, og da kunne det nok gå ganske hardt for seg.» Han stoppet litt og pekte på terrenget rundt leiren. «Dere ser at området her ligger ganske beskyttet til med fjell og kløfter rundt omkring. Leiren ble nok lagt akkurat her for å beskytte seg mot krigerske angrep fra andre stammer.

Dette var forresten en fastboende stamme. De flyttet ikke rundt omkring på prærien slik som vi vet at andre stammer gjorde. Derfor bygde de jordhytter her, og bodde i dem i stedet for å bo i telt.

Det ble rene forelesningen for de to utlendingene da de kjørte tilbake igjen til farmen. Frank fortalte om staten Nord Dakotas historie, og folks levesett der. Det var en forholdsvis ny stat kunne han fortelle. I 1889 ble Dakota delt i Nord og Sør Dakota. Og det var også først etter den tid at landet der begynte å bli befolket for alvor. Det var jo slik at da Sjur kom til Nord Amerika på midten av attenhundretallet slo han seg ned litt vest for Chicago. Der var det en betydelig konsentrasjon av norske immigranter. Men da områdene i Nord Dakota begynte å bli mer bebodd flyttet sønnene hans dit. Og da fulgte også han med.

Mette syntes hun begynte å kjenne dette landet ganske godt etter hvert. Hun gledet seg til turen de skulle ha østover. Da ville de reise i forfedrenes spor, bare i motsatt tetning.

53 • I forfedrenes spor

Da avreisedagen opprant kikket Mette fort ut av vinduet. Hun stønnet litt da hun så den skyfri himmelen og den stekende sola. Det ville bli en het fornøyelse å kjøre så langt i slik en varmen, tenkte hun. Men da de begynte på reisen ble hun gledelig overrasket. Klimaanlegget i bilen virket forbløffende bra, så hun skjønte at de nok ikke kom til å lide så ille som hun hadde fryktet. Disse amerikanske bilene av sannelig utstyrt litt annerledes enn de bilene hun var vant med fra Norge.

Det var Frank som kjørte. Og da de hadde plukket opp Martha og Simen la de i vei østover langs den snorrette highwayen. Både Martha og Simen hadde mye å bidra med når det gjaldt historien om de første emigrantene til distriktet. Spesielt Simens beretning om slekta si vakte interesse hos Morten. Det var jo også hans slekt det da var snakk om.

o o o

Det ble en lang dag på veien. Av og til stoppet de for å se på noe som var av spesiell interesse, eller de stoppet for å få seg noe å spise. Men de tok seg ikke lange pausene. Simen avløste Frank ved rattet etter hvert. De ville helst nå så langt som mulig den første dagen.

Landskapet skiftet av og til litt. Det hendte at de kom forbi steder hvor det var mer skog og bakker, men for det meste var det den bølgete prærien som strakte seg milevidt ut på alle kanter.

Etter hvert gav Frank beskjed om at nå hadde de lagt Nord Dakota bak seg. Fargo var den siste byen de kjørte gjennom før de passerte grensen til Minnesota. «Jeg håper vi skal greie å nå Minneapolise for kvelden,» sa han.

Kanskje vi da kan ta inn hos Bob og kona,» sa Mette ivrig. Alle syntes det var en god ide. Morten slo fort nummeret på mobiltelefonen, men der var ingen Bob å få tak i. Det var kona som svarte, og hun kunne fortelle at han var på sykehuset. Allan hadde blitt dårligere igjen. Det var en slags infeksjon han hadde pådratt seg. Tilstanden var høyst usikker. Morten beklaget bare, og nevnte ikke spørsmålet sitt. Han skjønte at de der hadde mer enn nok å tenke på for øyeblikket. Det var nok best de bare tok inn på et hotell.

Etter at de krysset grensen til Minnesota endret de retningen mer sørover, men landskapet var nokså likt. Mil etter mil la de bak seg.

«Hva er det som dyrkes oppover disse åssidene her?» spurte Morten og pekte mot noen bratte koller. Det var dyrket noe i brede striper på tvers av skråningene. «Det er nok soyabønner og mais som dyrkes der,» svarte Frank. «Solsikker er der jo også innimellom.»

«Men hvorfor dyrker de i slike striper?» Morten betraktet de eiendommelige åkrene med stor undring.

«Det for å beholde jordsmonnet og fuktigheten oppe i skråningene. Så bratt som det er der så vil jorda fort renne ut. Det er derfor de sår i striper på tvers av hellingene, og veksler med forskjellige slags vekster.»

«Det må bli enorme avlinger i distriktene her så vidstrakte som disse åkrene er,» sa Morten. «Det ser jo slett ikke ut til at de tar noen ende i det hele tatt.»

«Ja her blir det avlinger skal jeg si deg,» svarte Simen. «Du bør komme tilbake hit til høsten når innhøstingen begynner. Da kjøres hele trailerne ut på åkrene. Så fylles den ene hengeren etter den andre opp med korn eller de vekster de har, for så å fraktet det av sted til oppsamlingssiloene.»

Iveren lyste av øynene til Morten der han stirret utover viddene fra bilvinduet. «Ja det skulle jeg gjerne ha vært med på. Det blir nok noe helt annet enn de små traktorene og tilhengerne som vi arbeider med på de små gårdlappene hjemme i fjellbygda vår.»

Da de nærmet seg Minneapolis kunne Frank fortelle at de hadde kjørt nærmere åtti norske mil. De var alle slitne etter den lange reisen og gledet seg til å kunne strekke seg ut i ei seng et eller annet sted. De fant et greit Motell, og snart kunne de slappe av hver på sitt rom. Ingen av dem hadde særlige problemer med å få sove den kvelden.

Neste morgen var det like fint vær som det hadde vært dagen før. Mette kjente at hun nå var kommet inn i døgnrytmen, så det var nesten litt tungt å komme ut av senga så tidlig som de hadde avtalt. Men de ville utnytte dagen, så de behøvde ikke å vente på noen da Frank startet opp bilen.

De dro først ut på byen for å finne et sted hvor de kunne spise en god frokost. «Jeg vil ha skikkelig mat til frokost,» sa Frank. Slik Kontinental frokost som hotellet serverer er ikke noe for meg.» De andre var enige. Mette kunne i det hele tatt ikke begripe hvordan amerikanerne kunne spise kun søte muffens og smulteringer til frokost.

Det varte ikke lenge før de igjen var på veien. De dro i sydlig retning, og igjen ble det lange timer i bilen. Frank pekte ut retningen både til området hvor Willian Mobergs «Utvandrere» angivelig skulle ha havnet, og til der hvor Laura Ingels en gang i tiden bodde. Hun som siden skrev bøkene: «Huset på prærien».

Da de krysset Missisippi ved byen La Cross, begynte Marta å bli ivrig. «Nå er det ikke lenge til vi er i Coon Valley,» sa hun, «og da er vi også snart i Westby.»

Westby viste seg å være en liten prærieby med mange tegn på skandinaviske røtter. «Se der!» ropte Mette plutselig. Frank stoppet bilen, og alle betraktet i undring en stor murvegg hvor det hang en diger plakat. På plakaten var det tegnet en hoppbakke. I forgrunnen sto det et stokkebygd stabbur, og nederst i venstre hjørne var det norske flagget reist. Over hele plakaten var det skrevet med stor skrift: Hilsen fra Westby! Kom igjen! Ordene sto på Norsk. Og på plenen foran murveggen sto det et vikinghode, utskåret i tre, på en stubbe.

«Her har det vært nordmenn på ferde, ingen tvil om det,» sa Morten. De trasket en stund langs gatene, og snart fikk de se at Martha slett ikke hadde overdrevet. De fant flere bevis på den norske tradisjonen i byen. Der var suvernibutikker som bar tydelig preg av sin stolthet over den norske opprinnelsen, og det norske flagget var å se mange steder.

De måtte kjøre et stykke ut av byen for å komme til stedet hvor Marta, og slekten hennes, var kommet fra. Da de sto ved oppkjørselen til eiendommen, og så utover de

413

vide viddene, kunne de se at Marta var svært beveget. «Det er svært lenge siden jeg har vært her,» sa hun etter en stund, «for ingen av slektningene mine bor her lenger. Men alt ser nesten ut som det gjorde da jeg var her sist. Åkrene er nok blitt litt annerledes. I hvert fall er det litt andre vekster som dyrkes her nå. Jeg kan husk at min far fortalte om hvordan de dyrket tobakk her da han var liten.»

«Tobakk?!» Mette så overrasket på den ivrige dama. «Dyrket de tobakk …?

«Å ja,» Marta smilte av det overraskede utrykket til Mette. «Det var faktisk en viktig næring for mange folk her i distriktet.»

Mens de gikk omkring på eiendommen fortalte hun det hun visste om de norske emigrantene som hadde slått seg ned der i området. Igjen fikk Mette en intens følelse av å bli satt tilbake minst hundre år i tid. Og igjen måtte hun undre seg over den sterke innflytelsen som nordmennene hadde øvd på samfunnet der. De fikk også greie på at norsk hadde vært talespråket der i distriktet til langt inn i det tjuende århundret. «Men det ble nok etter hvert ganske oppblandet med engelsk,» sluttet hun og smilte.

Plutselig stoppet hun ved noen store trær et stykke fra husene. «Her stor det ei gammel jordhytte. Jeg kan huske at vi barna lekte i den da vi var små. Det var det første huset familien hadde her da de kom fra Norge. Faktisk bodde de i den hytta i flere år før et større trehus ble bygd. Det var ufattelig hvordan de kunne greie seg,» sa hun tankefull og så på de lille området mellom trærne. «De ble jo ganske mange her etter hvert. Min bestemor ble født i denne hytta har jeg hørt.»

Snart vendte hun blikket utover mot de store viddene. I taushet ble hun stående et øyeblikk å speide mot noen koller i vest. Noe dystert og tungt så ut til å sige innover henne der hun sto.

Da hun igjen begynte å snakke var stemmen også preget av et dypt alvor. «Jeg husker bestemor fortalte om broren sin. Han var en del år eldre enn henne. En desemberdag dro han av sted med hest og vogn for å skaffe forsyninger til jul. Men han kom aldri hjem igjen. På tilbakeveien fra byen ble han overrasket av et forferdelig uvær. Snø og vind forblindet helt både han og hesten. De greide ikke å finne retning og vei.

Noen dager senere fant de ham borte bak kollene der.» hun pekte i den retningen som hun hadde stått og speidet. «Både han og hesten var ihjelfrosset. Han satt i vogna, og hesten sto i kjørestillein, som om de bare plutselig hadde forsvunnet ut av denne verden.» Hun ristet bedrøvet på hodet.

Alle sto alvorlige og lyttet til det Martha fortalte. Mette kjente et gufs av uhygge. En vakker sommerdag som denne kunne jammen prærien virke både vakker og forlokkende, men hun skjønte at den hadde en annen side også. Når uvær og stormer raste over disse flate viddene, så kunne naturen være så vill og voldsom at livet bare ble som et pust. Plutselig så var det over og slutt. Ingen muligheter fantes det da til å få hjelp. Avstandene var så enorme, og menneskekreftene så ubetydelige mot de avsindige naturkreftene.

«De Norske emigrantene fikk jammen oppleve villmarkens alvor og krav,» sa Frank. «Det var nok mange som måtte børe med livet i ung alder her i Den Nye Verden.»

Enda en stund ble de stående å snakke om forfedrenes liv og skjebner, før de igjen dro tilbake til bilen.

Etter besøket i Westby fortsatte de reisen sørøst over mot en by som het Madison. «Jeg tror vi overnatter her,» sa Frank da de en stund senere kjørte inn i byen. «Da kan vi få bedre tid til å se oss om i Mt. Horeb og Little Norway i morgen. Og så kan vi få med oss Beloit om ettermiddagen når vi kjører mot Chicago.»

Neste dag ble også en hektisk og begivenhetsrik dag. De måtte kjøre et lite stykke vestover igjen for å komme til Mt. Horeb. Også den lille præriebyen bar sterkt preg av de norske som hadde slått seg ned der. Et yrende gateliv møtte dem da de begav seg på oppdagelsesferd rundt i byen. Mange salgs boder sto ute på fortauene med alle salgs suvernier. Norske lusekofter og duker med hardangersøm kunne de får kjøpt. Troll i alle varianter var der å få. Til og med en treskjærer satt med arbeidet sitt ved et bord. Morten og Mette stoppet for å se på mens han arbeidet. Snart kom de i snakk. Han kunne fortelle at han hadde lært kunstene av sine besteforeldre. Til og med det norske språket kunne han ganske mye av.

De kjøpte seg litt mat på en liten fortausrestaurant, og satte seg for å hvile litt før de dro videre til neste bestemmelsessted. Det var Martha og Simen som la opp reiseruta her.

«Nå skal vi virkelig besøke Norge,» sa Simen da de igjen satt i bilen. Han kjørte et lite stykke videre vestover. Plutselig svingte han av fra hovedveien, og med ett var det som om de beveget seg inn i en annen verden. Der var høye trær og busker på begge sider av veien. Knauser og hellinger gjorde at de følte seg ganske innestengte etter de mange milene langs de vidstrakte prærieviddene. «Man skulle nesten tro at vi var hjemme i Norge igjen nå,» sa Mette og stirret forundret ut av bilvinduet.

«Ja,» sa Martha. «Det var nok slik den første settleren her også opplevde det vil jeg tro.»

Et øyeblikk senere stoppet Simen bilen i nærheten av en mørk trebygning. «Dette er Little Norway, sa han og gikk ut av bilen. De andre fulgte etter. Mette gispet da hun fikk se det utrolig idylliske området som lå der foran henne. Dette var virkelig som å bli satt hundre år tilbake i tiden, ja kanskje enda lenger. Etter at de hadde ordnet med billetter ble de, sammen med en del andre turister, guidet rundt fra hus til hus. Mette ble stående et øyeblikk å ta det hele i nærmere øyesyn. Der lå det ei lita åpen slette omkranset av bratte lier med tett skog. Det var både bartrær og løvtrær. Ved foten av skråningene lå det en mengde små og store tømmerhus og hytter inni mellom trærne. Noen av dem var meget vakkert bygd med utskjæringer og ornamenter av forskjellig slag. Der var stabbur og uthusbygg, setehus og til og med ei stavkirke. Rett over sletta rant det en liten bekk. Stedet var vakkert vedlikeholdt med blomster og busker.

Mens de gikk fra hus til hus fikk de grundig forklaring på alt de så, av guiden. Det var en Norsk settler som hadde slått seg ned i denne lille vakre dalen. Det første huset der ble bygd i 1856.

Etter hvert var stedet blitt omgjort til museum. I hyttene rundt omkring i åskanten ble der samlet gjenstander fra de norske utvandrerne. Noen av gjenstandene var nok blitt fraktet med fra Gamlelandet, mens andre var blitt laget av dem der i det nye landet. En mengde fine rosemalte boller og skåler var å se. Likedan gyngestoler og andre møbler. Kokekar og redskaper for arbeidet på gårdene var også samlet der.

Den vakre lille stavkirken, med de smale buede vinduene og de mange dragepryd-ede gavlene, hadde egentlig aldri vært brukt som kirke, fikk de greie på. Det var kun en kirke som ble bygd til ei utstilling i Chicago i 1893. Den ble bygd i Trondheim, og så fraktet over med skip. Siden hadde den blitt satt opp der i den lille Norske dalen.

En lang stund ble de gående der å betrakte alt det vakre som var samlet fra de norske utvandrerne. Mette la spesielt merke til hjørnene på de mange tømmerhyttene. De var akkurat slik som Frank hadde beskrevet den første dagen han var på setra deres. Hver stokk stakk litt lenger ut i hjørnet. De var ikke skåret rett av slik som på deres seterbu. Men ellers var de nokså like.

Egentlig kunne de ha vært der i den vakre dalen hele dagen. Der var mer enn nok

415

å se på, og mange turister hadde også funnet veien dit den deilige sommerdagen. Mette syntes de måtte dra av sted igjen så altfor snart. Men Simen mente at skulle de rekke å se det andre også, som de hadde planlagt, så kunne de ikke stoppe for lenge.

Reisen videre gikk tilbake igjen til Madison, og så videre østover. «Vi må besøke stedet der den første norske bosetningen i Wisconsin var,» sa Simen. «Faktisk var det den sjette norske kolonien i hele Amerika. Den første nordmannen kom dit i 1838. De bygde straks ei kirke i området. Den gamle kirka står ikke lenger, men nye kirker ble bygd. Den som står der i dag er ei vakker stor arbeidskirke. Den tenkte jeg at vi skulle besøke. Stedet heter Jefferson Prairie.»

«Jefferson Prairie ja!» Frank ble ivrig med det samme. Det var jo det stedet gamle Sjur skrev så mye om i dagboka.

«Ja det gjorde han nok,» sa Simen. «Hvis han bodde i Beloit så hadde han nok kontakt med nordmennene i den kolonien.»

Det var ikke så lang en kjøretur før de var framme ved den vakre kirken. Et majestetisk tårn reise seg mot himmelen, og en mengde tilbygg og utspring var føyd til rundt omkring.

De gikk rundt på kirkegårdene og så på gravstøttene som enda sto der. De norske navnene var mange. «Her har de endt sine dager,» sa hun alvorlig. Det ble nok mye hardt slit og mange stunder med lengting og savn, før de havnet her.»

«Ja,» sa Morten. «Men de fikk nok oppleve framgang og lykke på mange måter også. Det var jo tross alt de som bygde denne delen av landet. Og selv om det var mye slit til å begynne med, så arbeidet de seg jo fram. Generasjonene senere fikk nyte fruktene av deres slit. Det ser vi jo tydelig i dag.»

«Ja.» Mette så drømmende ut i luften. «Det er underlig å tenke på at røttene til disse menneskene som bor rundt omkring her kanskje er de samme røttene som også vi er runnet av. Det får liksom det hele til å virke så nært.»

Morten nikket. De sto en stund i taushet mens tankene tok sine egne veier. Men så kalte Simen til oppbrudd igjen.

Ferden gikk videre sørover mot Beloit. Der hadde de ingen informasjon om hvor verken Sjur, eller andre av de norske slektningene hadde bodd. Men byen var allikevel interessant å se. De stoppet et sted hvor de kunne få seg en skikkelig middag før de dro videre over grensen til Illinois.

«Nå er Chicago neste stopp,» opplyste Simen. Det ble en litt vemodig stemning med det samme. Avskjedens øyeblikk nærmet seg. Likevel måtte både Mette og Morten være enige om at det hadde vært en utrolig begivenhetsrik tur. Aldri hadde de trodd at de skulle få oppleve så mye i Amerika. Mette følte seg stappfull av inntrykk.

Det skulle egentlig bli godt å komme hjem igjen også kjente hun. Faktisk var hun ganske sliten. Men mest av alt gledet hun seg over at de hadde fått så god kontakt med slektningene der på den andre siden av det store havet.

54 • Uventede gjester

«Hva i all verden er det som foregår her?» Mette sto i den åpne døra til seterbua og stirret på et kaos av alt mulig som lå strødd utover gulvet. Tante Anna lå på alle fire og rotet inne i et skap. Hun kvakk til da hun hørte stemmen, og kom seg på bena. «Ja det kan du jammen spørre om,» sa hun forfjamset og forsøkte å få på plass noen viltre hårtuster som hadde falt fram i ansiktet. Hun så helt oppjaget ut. «Jeg begriper ikke dette,» fortsatte hun i en rasende fart. «Døra var jo så godt stengt. Det var denne jentungen, hun ville absolutt at jeg skulle … men jeg skulle ikke ha dratt … hvem kan det være som …»

De usammenhengende setningene fikk Mettes forvirring til å bli total. Plutselig syntes hun inderlig synd på den gamle dama som hadde slitt der på setra mens hun og Morten hadde vært i Amerika. Kvelden før hadde de kommet hjem, men de hadde bare lagt seg i huset nede i bygda for å få sove skikkelig ut. Det var allerede langt på dag før de dro opp til setra.

Synet som møtte dem der, virket absolutt forvirrende. Morten kom også inn i det samme. Etter å ha summet seg et øyeblikk tok han et godt tak rundt skulderen til tante Anna og ledet henne bort til en stol. «Sett deg,» sa han rolig, «så kan du forklare hva som har skjedd her.»

«Det har vært innbrudd her,» sa hun, og så brast hun i gråt. «Jeg skulle ha passet bedre på, men Ellen ville absolutt at jeg skulle dra ned til bygda et par dager. Hun mente at hun kunne klare det som skulle gjøres her oppe alene, men vi ser jo hvordan hun passer på. Jeg tror ikke hun har vært her inne i det hele tatt disse dagene, for hun holder seg jo bare der ute i campingvogna til Marit.»

Endelig gikk det opp for dem hva som hadde skjedd. Mette fikk igjen et stikk av dårlig samvittighet. Det hadde nok blitt mye for tante Anna med alt som skulle gjøres der mens de var bortreist. Det hadde Ellen sett, og så ville hun gi henne litt fri. De visste også at Ellen pleide å bruke Marits campingvogn som losji når hun var på setra. Den sto jo der på campingområdet hele sommeren.

«Når skjedde dette?» spurte Morten mens blikket gled over alle tingene som lå strødd utover. «Jeg vet ikke. Enten i natt eller i går, vil jeg tro,» svarte hun mens tårene fortsatte å strømme.

Mette la armen rundt henne. «Dette skal du ikke bry deg noe om. Vi skal snart få ordnet opp her igjen.»

«Men …» hun hikstet igjen, «jeg skulle ha passet bedre på.»

«Du skal bare være glad for at du ikke var her da dette skjedde,» sa Morten. «Det er aldri godt å vite hva slike folk kunne ha gjort med deg.» Han begynte å se over tingene som lå der. «Er det noe som er blitt borte?»

«Jeg vet ikke,» sa tante Anna og reiste seg. «Det var det jeg holdt på å undersøke da dere kom.» Morten kikket bort på henne med et skøyeraktig smil: «Du tror ikke det var gomen din de var ute etter? Har du undersøkt hvor mye som er borte i kjøleskapet?»

Tante Anna lo mellom tårene. «Det var nok ikke mye å bryte opp ei diger eikedør for,» sa hun og begynte å plukke opp det som lå på gulvet.

Alle skap og skuffer så ut til å ha vært gjennomsøkt, men de kunne ikke se at noe var borte. «Dette var underlig.» sa Morten etter en stund. Det er tydelig at de har lett etter noe, men hva skulle det være? Her finnes det jo ingen andre verdisaker enn de gamle møblene, og de er jo her fremdeles.»

Plutselig kom det et rop fra Mette. Hun sto borte ved det store hjørneskapet. «Skrinet er borte!» De andre to kom styrtende til. «Skrinet!» Tante Anna slo hendene sammen og stirret på den tomme plassen i skapet der det hadde stått. «Det var altså skrinet de var ute etter.»

«Men hvem visste at her fantes et gammelt mystisk skrin i seterbua?» Morten så forundret på henne.

Plutselig ble hun helt stille. Både Mette og Morten så forundret på henne, mest fordi det var så uvanlig å oppleve henne så taus.

«Det må være dem,» kom det stille fra henne etter en stund. «Jeg hadde besøk av noen ungdommer her for noen dager siden,» fortsatte hun. «De holdt seg inne i fjellet med telt og fiskestenger. Men så kom de en dag og spurte om de kunne få kjøpt noe melk. Akkurat da de kom, satt Ellen og jeg og så på det gamle skrinet. Guttene viste stor interesse for det. De forsøkte også om de kunne få det opp, men det greide de selvsagt ikke. Det må være dem, men jeg har jo ingen bevis,» sa hun og så beklagende på Morten.

«Nei,» svarte han. «Det er nok ingenting vi kan gjøre med det nå. Vi vet jo ikke om det er verdifullt. Så det kan nok ikke nytte å melde det savnet.»

Skrinet var borte. Mette kjente at noe begynte å koke inni henne. Det skrinet som hun hadde vært så spent på. Hun hadde vært overbevist om at det inneholdt noe interessant, og at de skulle greie å få det opp, men nå var det borte. Hun forsto hva Morten mente. De kunne nok anmelde innbruddet, men de kunne ikke vente at Politiet skulle bruke tid og krefter på å oppspore en gammal rusten blikkboks som kanskje bare inneholdt en mosedott.

«Vet du hvor i fjellet disse ungdommene holdt til?» spurte Mette. Tante Anna ristet på hodet. «Det eneste jeg vet,» svarte hun, «er at de forsvant opp lia der borte, med melka si.» Hun pekte ut av vinduet mot vest.

Morten sto betenkt og kikket i den retning som hun pekte. Så ristet han på hodet. «Det kan nok ikke nytte å lete etter dem. De er nok over alle hauer nå.»

Dypt skuffet begynte Mette å rydde opp i rotet. Skrinet var borte, og de fikk nok aldri se det mer ... eller var det ennå et håp? Hun ville ikke gi opp ennå. På en eller annen måte måtte det da gå an å finne ut av dette. De ungdommene måtte det da gå an å finne ut hvem var. Hun bestemte seg for å gjøre et forsøk på en eller annen måte.

Tante Anna hjalp også iherdig til med ryddingen, mens Morten undersøkte døra som var blitt brutt opp. Selve døra var ikke så mye ødelagt, men den store slåen på innsiden var bøyd og sprengt ut av festene sine. De brukte ikke alltid låsen på den døra. Som oftest pleide de bare å legge slåen på, og så gå ut bakdøren i melkeboden. Der hadde de også god lås på døra.

∘ ∘ ∘

Snart gikk livet sin vante gang igjen på setra, men Mette hadde ikke glemt sin beslutning om å finne ut hvem de ubudne gjestene var. Et par dager senere måtte de til bygda for å handle. Morten hadde en del å gjøre på gården, så Mette dro alene til butikken. Hun bestemte seg for å spørre der hvor de solgte fiskekort om hvem som hadde kjøpt slike kort i den aktuelle tiden.

Om hun hadde vært optimistisk da hun dro av sted, så ble hennes nysgjerrighet og tålmodighet satt på en sterk prøve. Det eneste svaret hun fikk da hun spurte var at han som hadde jobbet der de dagene, var en ferievikar. Nå hadde han sluttet, og kom ikke tilbake dit igjen. De kunne dessverre ikke hjelpe henne mer.

«Ferievikar!» Mette snøftet halvhøyt for seg selv da hun forlot butikken. Nei, hun kunne nok forstå at det ikke var så lett å ha kontroll med alt som skjedde i ferietiden. Nå var de imidlertid kommet ganske langt ut i august, og livet begynte å komme inn i den vanlige rytmen igjen. Men likevel følte hun en intens skuffelse.

Irritert slengte hun varene sine inn i bilen og kjørte tilbake igjen til gården.

Da hun svingte av fra veien ved huset, ble hun oppmerksom på en fremmed bil som sto parkert i oppkjørselen. «Hvem kan det være som er kommet på besøk nå?» tenkte hun mens hun raskt gikk inn på kjøkkenet. Der satte hun handleposene fra seg på benken før hun nysgjerrig gikk mot stuedøra. Stemmene hun hørte der innefra fortalte at Morten var i dyp samtale med en annen mann.

Plutselig bråstoppet hun. Helt stiv ble hun stående og lytte. Var det ikke noe kjent ved den stemmen der inne? Jo, hun kunne tydelig høre det nå. Skjelvende sank hun ned på en stol som sto der. Det var ingen tvil. Der inne satt Tore og snakket med Morten. I det samme vissheten om det gikk opp for henne, vellet alle de vonde følelsene inn over henne igjen. Hun greide ikke å røre seg. Ble bare sittende der, mens tankene fôr i alle retninger. Og dette vonde som hun trodde at hun på et vis hadde kommet over nå.

Tankene gikk tilbake til tiden da hun jobbet på kontoret i Oslo. Da hadde hun jobbet sammen med Tore, men de gikk ikke så bra sammen. Stadig opplevde hun at han kom med sårende bemerkninger og hint hvis hun gjorde noen feil. Hun prøvde hele tiden å utføre arbeidet sitt så grundig og prikkfritt som mulig, men Tore fant hele tiden noe å sette fingeren på. Sitt eget system og sine egne arbeidsrutiner var han imidlertid slett ikke så nøye med. Det hadde ergret henne grenseløst. Mer enn en gang hadde hun konfrontert ham med det, men det så ikke ut til å hjelpe noe særlig. I stedet ble han bare enda mer irriterende med alle sine overlegne spydigheter og bemerkninger mot henne.

Dette var faktisk noe av grunnen til at hun hadde søkt seg bort fra kontoret for en tid, og tatt jobben der oppe på setra forrige sommer.

Da hun der oppdaget at nettopp Tore var en av Mortens beste venner fra militærtiden, hadde hun nesten fått sjokk. Det hadde utspunnet seg en heftig diskusjon mellom dem. I hvert fall hadde hun vært ganske heftig, husket hun. Morten hadde på sin rolige måte forsøkt å forklare henne at det nok var noe med kjemien mellom dem som ikke stemte, for Tore var egentlig en alle tiders kar.

Etter den samtalen hadde hun bestemt seg for å prøve og møte Tore med vennlighet og respekt. Han hadde også vært i bryllupet deres, og da syntes hun at hun hadde greid det ganske bra. I hvert fall hadde hun ikke opplevd noen vanskeligheter den dagen, så hun trodde at problemet kanskje nå var borte.

Men nå satt hun altså der, bare noen få meter unna ham, og skalv. Alt dette vonde var over henne igjen. Tankene, følelsene … og det før hun hadde snakket med ham i det hele tatt.

Stemmene der inne nådde faktisk ut til henne ganske klart. Hva var det egentlig de snakket om? Hun ble sittende og lytte …

«… jeg vet at dette er vanskelig for deg … ja faktisk for dere begge to.» Det var Mortens stemme. Han virket svært alvorlig. Da Tores stemme brøt inn, virket den nesten desperat: «Jeg vet at jeg ikke duger noe særlig, men det går da an å fungere som menneske om man ikke akkurat er like prikkfri som henne. Man må da kunne ha krav på en smule respekt.» Det siste ble sagt med en stemme full av bitterhet.

Mette stivnet enda mer der hun satt. Hun visste ikke hvem det var de snakket om, men en følelse sa henne at det kanskje var noen kjente … ja, svært kjente. En desperat lyst til å flykte langt vekke kom over henne, men hun våget ikke å røre seg.

«Dere er jo nokså forskjellige av natur, vet du.» Det var Mortens stemme som lød igjen. «Jeg er ikke så sikker på at hun sier slikt til deg for å plage deg. Slike påminnelser og bemerkninger kommer hun stadig vekk med til meg også. Jeg tror det bare er hennes måte å være på … hennes måte å organisere ting på.»

Nå var Mette sikker. Det var henne de snakket om. Dette var en samtale som slett ikke var beregnet for hennes ører. En dyp skamfølelse fylte henne, men hun greide likevel ikke å reise seg fra stolen. De der inne ville da ganske sikkert høre henne, og så skjønne at hun hadde sittet der og lyttet. Det var i det hele tatt ubegripelig at de ikke hadde hørt henne da hun kom inn. Det var jo svært lytt mellom stua og kjøkkenet, det kunne hun jo tydelig høre.

Det var blitt en pause der inne. En trykkende stillhet lå i luften. Mette våget nesten ikke å puste. Tenk om de kom ut og fant henne der! Aldri hadde hun følt seg så ussel som i dette øyeblikket. Hennes desperate ønske om å flykte dirret i hele kroppen. Hun ville ut … løpe … langt bort … Men hun våget det bare ikke. Hun greide simpelthen ikke å bevege seg.

Da Tore igjen begynte å snakke, var stemmen forunderlig anstrengt. Med sjokk forsto hun at den var på grensen til å briste i gråt.

«… Når hun begynner slik …» han brøt seg selv av med et lite snufs. Så var det som om han begynte på nytt igjen. «… Det er som å høre min mor.» Igjen ble det en pause. Morten sa ingen ting. Han ventet nok bare på det denne mannen ville si ham, men som var så vanskelig å få fram.

Tore kremtet litt før han begynte igjen. «Så lenge jeg kan huske, har min mor hakket på meg om hvor udugelig jeg er. Aldri var noe av det jeg gjorde, godt nok. Helt siden jeg var så liten at jeg kunne begynne å gjøre ting på egen hånd, så har hun kritisert alt det jeg har gjort. Det ble etter hvert slik for meg at jeg måtte gå til henne og spørre om den minste ting, hvordan det skulle gjøres. Jeg eide ikke selvtillit i det hele tatt. Etter hvert begynte det å vokse opp en trass i meg. Jeg ville ikke være slave under hennes kritiske blikk resten av livet. Derfor dro jeg inn til Oslo og fikk meg en jobb som medførte mye reising. Det fikk meg bort fra henne så pass mye at jeg greide å opparbeide meg en viss grad av selvrespekt. Men så oppsto altså dette …» Han stoppet opp igjen. Et langt øyeblikk var det helt stille.

Mette følte seg uvel der hun satt. Det var nesten som kvalme som veltet nede i magen, men ikke i avsky for mannen som satt der inne og snakket. Snarere tvert imot. Med ett var det som hun så denne mannen i et helt nytt lys. Den beskrivelsen han hadde gitt av sin mor var slett ikke så langt fra en beskrivelse av hennes egen oppførsel overfor ham, det så hun nå ganske klart. At hun kunne ha oppført seg så motbydelig! Men i det samme kom hennes egen smerte fram. Hun hadde jo gjort dette i et tappert forsøk på selvforsvar. Det var jo han som var den som plaget … eller var det ikke slik? Motstridende følelser raste rundt i henne.

Da Tore begynte å snakke igjen, var stemmen atskillig roligere, men den bar fortsatt preg av smerte. «Det er som om dette skal forfølge meg resten av livet. Jeg begriper ikke hvordan jeg skal greie og takle det.»

I det samme hørtes en skarp skrapelyd der inne fra. Det var nok en av dem som reiste seg fra en stol. Mette benyttet øyeblikket til å smette lynraskt ut av døra. Hun hadde hørt nok … Ja, hun hadde hørt mer enn nok.

Med raske skritt gikk hun mot fjøset. Nå måtte hun være for seg selv en stund, og da var det mest naturlige stedet fjøset. Hun gikk rett bort til Keiseren, som lå i båsen sin og jortet. Den reiste seg momentant da hun kom inn.

Keiseren, som ikke lenger var den lille kalven hun hadde lekt og koset seg med oppe på setra forrige sommer, var likevel alltid like begeistret når hun kom inn, enten for å gi den mat, eller bare for å kose litt med den. Og for Mette var han den hun kunne betro seg til i både glede og tunge stunder. En mer trofast venn hadde hun aldri hatt. «Aldri har du noen gang røpet noen av hemmelighetene våre,» sa hun med et lite vemodig smil og la begge armene rundt den tykke halsen til oksen. Mens tårene rant begynte hun å utøse seg for det rolige og tillitsfulle dyret. Alt sa hun … alt om hvordan hun hadde følt konflikten med Tore, og så nå til sist denne dramatiske vendingen, der saken med ett ble snudd helt på hodet. Det var ikke bare hun som hadde hatt det vondt. Hun hadde altså vært årsak til at også han hadde lidd.

«En ting er å selv ha det vondt,» sa hun inn i øret på Keiseren mens hun klødde ham på halsen, «en annen ting er å være årsak til at andre lider. Og det er faktisk mye verre.» Det siste kom som en dyp erkjennelse.

Følelsene fortsatte å rase inni henne, men hun merket at bitterheten og mindreverdighetsfølelsen, som hadde skapt den anspente holdningen til Tore, var i ferd med å vike plassen for noe annet. Det var en følelse av medlidenhet og ønske om å være med på å rette opp igjen og lege noen av de sårene som var skapt. Så viktig det var å forstå bakgrunnen for andres handlemåter! Så mye vondt som kunne ha vært unngått hvis hun bare hadde visst litt mer om dette før. Og så vondt som han måtte ha hatt det. Kanskje han hadde lidd mer enn henne. Tenk å ha en slik mor. At ikke hun kunne ha vist sønnen sin litt mer forståelse og respekt!

Nei, nå måtte hun ikke skyve skylden over på henne. Hun kjente jo slett ikke Tores mor. Kanskje det også der lå noen skjulte tragedier.

Mette klappet Keiseren noen ganger til, og så gikk hun ut igjen i den friske luften. Hun gikk over jordet bak fjøset mot skogen som sto der med sine ruvende trekroner. Den lette brisen som lekte i håret og klærne hennes ville forhåpentlivis lufte ut det meste av fjøslukten hun hadde pådratt seg der inne hos Keiseren.

Tankene fortsatte å kverne rundt i hodet på henne mens hun gikk. Freden og stillheten der inne mellom bjørketrærne gav henne ro til å tenke gjennom hele saken grundig. Så da hun senere gikk mot huset igjen, bar hun i seg en klar bestemmelse om at denne saken nå måtte være ute av verden. Hun ville gjøre alt som sto i hennes makt for å rette opp igjen det vanskelige forholdet til Tore.

Da hun kom tilbake til gårdsplassen igjen, så hun at bilen til Tore var borte. Inne på kjøkkenbenken fant hun en lapp. Det var Morten som gav beskjed om at de begge to hadde reist opp til setra. Han hadde sett varene der, og bilen hennes utenfor, så han skjønte at hun var i nærheten.

55 • Oppgjør

Det ble en lang prat mellom Mette og Morten oppe på setra den kvelden. Tore hadde dratt innover i fjellet med fiskestanga, og kom ikke tilbake før sent på kveld. Mette var glad for at hun fikk anledning til å snakke med Morten alene først. Hun fortalte alt slik som det var, at hun hadde hørt det de hadde snakket om, og at hun hadde tatt seg en tur i skogen for å tenke gjennom saken. Og så til slutt hvilken beslutning hun hadde tatt.

«Men dette blir nok ikke så lett for meg,» avsluttet hun. «Jeg kommer til å bære med meg mange av følelsene ennå en stund, vil jeg tro, så du må hjelpe meg.» Morten la armen omkring henne og trykket henne inn til seg. «Jeg skal gjøre så godt jeg kan,» svarte han tydelig lettet over at det så ut til at dette vonde problemet hadde fått en positiv løsning.

Tore ble på setra i flere dager. Han fikk bo oppe på hemsen inne i seterbua. Til å begynne med følte Mette en viss anspenthet når han var i nærheten, men etter hvert gikk det bedre. Hun forsøkte å vise Tore vennlighet og respekt. Snart merket hun at også han viste henne en annen holdning. Spenningene svant mer og mer hen.

En dag måtte Morten ned til bygda for å være med på arveoppgjøret etter onkel Torkel. Siri var kommet fra Trondheim, og de regnet med å bruke hele dagen borte i Lia. Han dro ned straks han hadde spist frokost. Mette og Tore ble sittende igjen alene ved frokostbordet. Plutselig begynte de å snakke om det vanskelige forholdet dem imellom. Morten hadde fortalt Tore om at Mette hadde overhørt det de hadde snakket om der nede på gården. Hun skjønte at han opplevde det som en lettelse at hun visste om problemene hans.

Lenge ble de sittende der å snakke. Begge fortalte åpent om sine følelser og vanskeligheter i saken. Og begge skjønte at de hadde mye å be den andre om tilgivelse for. Snart måtte Mette medgi at den beskrivelsen Morten hadde gitt av Tore faktisk var ganske treffende. Han var absolutt en svært hyggelig mann. Tenk at hun hadde arbeidet sammen med ham så lenge uten å legge merke til det. Hun hadde bare vært opptatt av sine egne såre følelser, og ikke i det hele tatt sett de positive kvalitetene hans.

Etter dette ble stemningen dem imellom en helt annen. Mette merket også at hun nå kjente seg mye lettere, og fri i sitt indre. Så deilig det var å få ordnet opp i dette. Tore virket også mye mer avslappet.

Det var ikke så mange turister lenger på setra. Det nærmet seg september og det meste av besøkene de hadde var skoleklasser eller leirskoler. Tore hjalp henne med en del arbeid som hun måtte ha unna før neste ungdomsgruppe kom. De arbeidet i sammen på en helt annen måte enn de hadde gjort tidligere. Mette frydet seg. Praten gikk avslappet og naturlig mellom dem.

«Skal si der et er mye multer i fjellet i år,» sa plutselig Tore. «Jeg tror jeg tar meg en tur innover myrene i ettermiddag. Det hadde vært fint å få med litt dessert tilbake til byen.»

«Å ja, det må du gjøre,» sa Mette ivrig. «Skulle ønske jeg kunne bli med deg, men jeg har dessverre ikke tid i dag. Forresten så har Morten lovet å bli med meg på multetur når han får tid. Håper bare det ikke blir så altfor lenge til.»

Da Tore var dratt ble Mette igjen alene på setra. Hun sto og kikket etter ham der han gikk oppover lia. Tankene hennes gikk til sommerturistene som hadde ligget der oppe i telt. Tro om de hadde greid å få opp skrinet? Og i så fall hva hadde de funne inni det. Hun skulle nesten ha gitt hva som helst for å få greie på det. Ergrelsen satt fremdeles dypt i henne. Men hun ante ikke hva hun mer kunne gjøre for å finne det igjen. Nei, der var nok ingenting annet å gjøre enn å innse at skrinet var borte for alltid, og med det også det hemmelighetsfulle innholdet. Mette sukket og gikk tilbake til melkeboden der en masse fløte sto og ventet på å bli kjernet.

Da Morten kom tilbake utpå kvelden var Mette svært spent på hvordan det hadde gått med arbeidet borte i Lia. Han kunne fortelle at alle eiendelene etter onkel Torkel var delt, og gården bestemt til salg. De hadde hatt kontakt med Bob i Amerika, så alt hadde blitt gjort i tett samarbeid med ham.

«Hvordan går det med dem der borte?» spurte Mette spent. «Ligger Allan fremdeles på sykehuset?»

«Det ser ut til å gå svært bra med ham,» svarte Morten. «Han kom hjem for en stund siden. Infeksjonen fikk de visst raskt bukt med, så nå ser det stadig ut til å gå framover med ham. Og det at de nå ikke lenger behøver å bekymre seg over økonomien har også vært til uvurderlig hjelp for dem.»

«Å … det var godt å høre,» sa Mette. «Jeg har stadig tenkt på Allan. Flere ganger har jeg vurdert å ringe til dem, men så har det ikke blitt noe. Jeg er også så glad for at de pengene etter onkel Torkel ble til slik god hjelp for dem.»

«Ja,» Morten nikket samtykkende. «Hadde det ikke vært så stor en sum å dele så tror jeg nesten at jeg hadde gitt avkall på min del til fordel for dem.» Mette nikket ivrig. «De pengene tror jeg ikke jeg hadde greid å glede meg over hvis jeg visste at de der borte hadde det så vanskelig,» sa hun.

«Forresten,» sa Morten ivrig. «Jeg skulle hilse så mye fra dem alle sammen og si at til neste sommer måtte vi gjøre plass til dem her på setra. Da ville de komme for å besøke oss.»

«Så fantastisk!» Mette jublet av begeistring. «Jeg gleder meg allerede.»

Mens de satt og spiste kvelds kom tante Anna tilbake igjen. Hun hadde vært nede i bygda et par dager. Men neste dag ventet de besøk av en skoleklasse, og da måtte hun være der. Hun ble like begeistret som Mette over nyheten om at de kunne vente amerikabesøk neste sommer.

56 • Nye demonstrasjoner

«Se her, Plomma, nå skal du få noe riktig godt av meg.» Mette gikk inn i båsen til den gamle kua og klødde den bak ørene mens hun holdt noen eplebiter opp foran mulen. Kua jafset godsakene til seg og tygget fornøyd. Epler var noe Plomma likte ekstra godt. Mette hadde kuttet eplene opp i biter slik at de ble lettere for kua å tygge. Hun visste også at den lett kunne sette epler i halsen hvis de spiste dem hele, og det kunne være en ganske alvorlig sak.

Det var deilig å være der hos dyrene. Selv om amerikaturen hadde vært både spennende og begivenhetsrik, så var det likevel fint å komme inn i den daglige rytmen igjen.

Stjerna strakte også hodet bort til henne, så Mette måtte finne noen eplebiter til den også. En lang stund ble hun gående der og stelle rundt dyrene, før hun slapp dem ut på beitet. Det var så godt å kjenne de trygge, varme dyrekroppene, og merke den tillitsfulle oppmerksomheten de gav henne. Hun hadde forresten fått en ny skapning der i fjøset som tok mye av hennes oppmerksomhet. Det var en liten kalv som morgenen før kom ruslende sammen med de andre dyrene da hun gikk til fjøset for å melke. Kviga, som de riktignok ventet at snart skulle kalve, hadde rett og slett gjort unna den jobben i løpet av natta. En riktig trivelig liten kvigekalv var det, som fort fant seg til rette blant de andre dyrene. Mette måtte gi den noen ekstra klapp før hun sendte den ut på beitet sammen med moren og de andre dyrene.

Ute var det varmt og godt, selv om de nok kunne merke at høsten begynte å gjøre seg gjeldende. Oppover lia hadde løvet begynt å vise sin gylne farge på de små buskete trærne, og lyngen sto rødmende og blussende i all sin prakt innover heiene. «Tenk om vi kunne ha tatt en multetur snart,» tenkte Mette der hun sto i fjøsdøra og så etter kyrne som raskt fant sine beiteområder. Morten hadde lovet å bli med henne og vise henne noen steder hvor de alltid pleide å finne godt med bær. «Men,» sa hun til seg selv, «det nytter ikke å tenke på multetur nå, for i dag kommer det jo en flokk med gjester.»

Tante Anna var alt i full gang med forberedelsene. Hun hadde båret rokken sin ut på volle, og flere kurver med ull sto på et bordet. De som skulle få demonstrert karding og spinning av ull, var en videregående skoleklasse fra Kristiansand. Tante Anna hadde også mye av både historier og tradisjoner å by på fra sin allvitende hukommelse.

Mette gikk bort til bordet og så på ulla som lå i kurvene. Der var ull i alle slags farger. Hun husket godt forrige sommer da tante Anna hadde demonstrert plantefarging for et husflidlag. Da hadde alle sammen vært i funksjon for å finne planter og ellers hjelpe med fargingen. Det hadde vært en særdeles interessant dag, syntes Mette.

Denne dagen ble det nok ingen plantefarging, men hun var ikke i tvil om at tante Anna kom til å forklare litt om prosessen.

«Hva et dette?» spurte Mette forundret da tante Anna kom bort til henne og plasserte enda ei kurv på bordet. Det som lå i den, så nesten ut som noe tørt, tynt siv eller gress.

«Det er lin,» svarte den eldre dama begeistret. «Slik ser altså linfibrene ut før de blir spunnet til tråder, og vevd.»

«Skal du spinne dette?» Mette så spent på henne.

Et stort smil bredte seg over det runde ansiktet. «Ja, jeg tenkte at jeg ville forsøke på det. Nå har ikke akkurat jeg drevet så mye med linspinning, men jeg vet i hvert fall hvordan det ble gjort i gamle dager. Så får vi bare se hvordan det går,» sa hun. «Men nå må jeg inn og se til stekepanna.» Hun snudde seg raskt og forsvant inn i seterbua igjen.

De skulle også servere mat til gjestene. Tante Anna hadde tatt med en masse lefser fra lageret sitt nede i bygda. Nå strevde hun med pannekakesteking. Lefser og pannekaker sto på menyen. Mette hadde aldri smakt den kombinasjonen, så hun gledet seg til måltidet. Ikke lenge etter kjente hun den deilige duften av nystekte pannekaker. «Kanskje jeg kan få sneket til meg en bit som sen frokost?» sa Mette til seg selv og gikk etter inn i seterbua.

Tante Anna sto med blussende kinn over den varme stekepanna. Svetten piplet fram i panna. Temperaturen der inne var allerede nådd langt over midtsommersvarme. Et stort glass med en blekhvit væske sto ved siden av henne. Hun treiv glasset og drakk begjærlig. Mette rynket brynene og kom bort til henne. «Er det oppvaskvannet du står her og drikker,» spurte hun forbauset med en liten latter. Tante Anna lo så hun nær hadde sluppet hele glasset i gulvet. «Nei, dette er slett ikke noe oppvaskvann, kan jeg fortelle deg. Dette er «Blånna». Det er kjernemelk som er blandet med vann,» forklarte hun da hun så det spørrende blikket til Mette. «Slik drikk brukte vi mye om sommeren da jeg var barn. Den er så god for tørsten,» sa hun og drakk ut det som var igjen i glasset.

Mette kunne ikke akkurat si at hun syntes drikken fristet noe særlig, men hun sa ikke noe mer om det. Tante Anna fortsatte med stekingen, og før de første bilene begynte å komme, hadde hun en diger stabel med løvtynne pannekaker ved siden av seg på benken.

Det ble en hektisk aktivitet ute på vollen da over tjue ungdommer veltet ut av bilene. Latter og spøk hang i lufta hele tiden. Tante Anna frydet seg. Ungdommene flokket seg rundt henne for å se og høre. Hun begynte med å forklare hvordan ulla ble bearbeidet i gamle dager rundt omkring på gårdene. Vasking og farging ble nøye redegjort for. Så tok hun fram kardene og la ull på dem. Med øvede hender dro hun dem over hverandre til hun hadde laget ei fin og luftig lita pølse.

Mette hadde sett dette flere ganger tidligere, så for henne var det ikke noe nytt, men elevene fulgte interessert med i alt hun gjorde. Snart lå en hel liten stabel med lette ullpølser i kurven ved siden av henne.

Så satte hun seg til rokken. Etter at hun hadde fått skikkelig sving på hjulet, begynte hun å legg pølsene inn mot en tråd som hun allerede hadde spunnet der før. Den snurret rundt i stor fart, og tok lett fatt i den tynne ulla. Tante Anna dro ullpølsa ut mens den snurret rundt der den var festet til tråden. Snart var hele pølsa omdannet til en tynn, fin ulltråd. Så var det å feste på ei ny ullpølse. Farten på hjulet holdt hun jevn og fin ved å trø på en pedal under rokken.

Flere av elevene hadde lyst til å prøve. Tante Anna forklarte og veiledet, men de forsto snart at dette var et arbeid som der trengtes en god porsjon trening for å få til. Tråden gikk rett som det var i surr for dem, og det var heller ikke lett å få den jevn og fin. Enten ble det store klumper på den, eller så slet de den rett av.

Om de ikke fikk det helt til, så syntes de i hvert fall det var moro å forsøke.

Etterpå forklarte hun om linen. Hun tok kurven med linfibrer og holdt den opp slik at alle kunne se. «Dette er bearbeidet lin som ikke er spunnet,» begynte hun. «Jeg skal forsøke å spinne noe av dette, men først vil jeg forklare litt om hvordan linen ble dyrket og bearbeidet i gamle dager.»

Mette sto sammen med ungdommene og lyttet med stor interesse. Dette hadde hun ikke hørt om før. Tante Anna hadde så mye å lære fra seg, at hun skjønte hun måtte være lenge sammen med henne før hun hadde hørt om alt.

«I min ungdom var jeg en tid hos ei tante some bodde i Marnardal på Sørlandet,» fortsatte den ivrige læremesteren. «Hun dyrket lin, så der fikk jeg lære litt om den prosessen. Jeg husker ennå linåkeren hennes. Da den sto i blomst utpå sommeren, var det som et vidunderlig blått teppe som duvet i vinden. Aldri har jeg sett noe så vakkert.» Hun slo ut med hendene mot vollen og speidet ut i lufta med et fjernt blikk. Det var som hun så det hele for seg. Elevene lyttet i intens taushet. Den levende måten hennes å fortelle på fengslet dem helt.

«Det var blå lin hun hadde,» fortsatte hun. «Jeg vet at det også finnes hvit lin, men den blå har nok vært den mest vanlige her.»

Hun vendte igjen oppmerksomheten mot tilhørerne: «Før frøkapslene begynte å dannes, måtte åkeren høstes. Jeg husker ennå hvordan vi strevde med det.» Hun humret og lo. Hele damen levde seg inn i det hun sa. «Linen kunne ikke høstes på samme måte som man høster korn. Den måtte rykkes opp med rot. Linstråene måtte ikke kuttes over. Vi gikk der i åkeren og rykket opp stråene, og så buntet vi dem sammen i mindre bunter. Etter at all linen var buntet sammen slik, måtte neste prosess settes i gang, og det var røytinga.

Hele linen ble lagt i en bekk. Der lå den flere dager. Den skulle gjennomgå en slags forråtnelsesprosess. Jeg husker ennå tante, hvordan hun stadig gikk til bekken for å se om linen var ferdig røytet. Da knakk hun over et strå og så på hvor langt prosessen var kommet. Hun visste akkurat hvordan den måtte se ut når den var ferdig.

Etter røytingen ble den sendt til en fabrikk som gjorde resten av prosessen for henne. Jeg husker da vi fikk linen igjen. Da var den ferdig spunnet. Men hun fikk også noe uspunnet lin som hun selv arbeidet med, og den så slik ut som dette.» Hun holdt opp kurven hun hadde foran seg igjen.

«For å si litt om den prosessen som ble gjort i fabrikken,» fortsatte hun, «så var det en renselsesprosess. Der ble linstråene knekket over. Men det ble gjort svært forsiktig, for det var bare det ytre skallet som skulle knekkes. Den innerste kjernen måtte være hel, for det er det som er linfiberen. I enda eldre tider ble også det gjort hjemme på gårdene. Da ble det brukt noen stokker. Linen ble lagt over dem, og så ble det slått over linstråene med en annen stokk. Slik ble skallet på stråene knekket.

Etter det måtte skallet renses bort. Da ble det dratt gjennom en slags kam. Hekling ble det kalt. Først ble det dratt gjennom noen grove tenner, og så ble det dratt gjennom finere og finere tenner helt til det bare var den fineste kjernen som var igjen. Det var linen som så kunne spinnes til tråd.

Tante vevde mange fine damaskduker av den linen hun selv hadde dyrket. Jeg har en av dem her.» Hun tok opp en lys grå duk fra ei kurv. Den var pent brettet sammen. Mette gispet da hun så det nydelige arbeidet. Tante Anna bredte ut duken så alle kunne få se den nøyere. De ble lenge stående i beundring da de betraktet det fine håndarbeidet. Kunne dette virkelig være hjemmevevd? Mette måtte spørre tante Anna om hun hadde oppfattet rett. Den runde, trivelige kona smilte og nikket begeistret. «Dette er så hjemmegjort som det bare kan,» sa hun. «Og stråene som ble brukt til denne duken, har jeg vært med på å høste.» Hun lo enda mer over de forbausede blikkene rundt seg.

Snart satte hun seg til rokken igjen. Der monterte hun på en rund sylinderliknende tresak i den ene enden. «Dette kalles Rokkehodet,» forklarte hun. Rundt Rokkehodet sveipte hun den linen som hun hadde i kurven. Så begynte hun å trekke ut fibrene. Hun la dem inn til en tråd på rokken mens hjulet surret og gikk. Snart begynte en fin, tynn lintråd å ta form. De rutinerte fingrene strøk fram og tilbake over tråden, mens hun hele tiden passet på at hun trakk ut passe mye av linen på rokkehodet.

Trengselen rundt rokken var stor. Alle ville se. Ikke minst Mette var interessert. «Dette kommer aldri jeg til å få til,» konkluderte hun raskt. Det så mye vanskeligere ut enn å spinne ull.

Det varte ikke så lenge før tante Anna igjen stoppet rokkehjulet. «Nå må dere ha mat,» sa hun bestemt, og reiste seg raskt.

Igjen ble det hektisk aktivitet. Mette hentet maten, men tante Anna ble ennå en stund stående ved rokken. Det var mange som hadde spørsmål å stille henne. Flere av elevene noterte ivrig ned det hun sa.

Maten ble en ny og fremmed opplevelse også for elevene. Pannekaker var alle vant med, og lefser var det også flere som hadde smakt. Men disse to tingene i kombinasjon hadde ingen vært borte i før.

Tante Anna hadde smurt alle lefsene på forhånd med det gode, hjemmekjernede smøret. Så hadde hun brettet hele de store lefsene på midten, og deretter klippet hver av dem i fire snipper. Hver snipp ble nå lagt rundt ei pannekake som også var brettet i to. Og så var det bare å legge i seg.

Alle så ut til å like maten. Mette nøt det deilige måltidet og bestemte seg der og da for at dette skulle hun snart prøve igjen.

Det varte ikke lenge før både pannekakefatet og lefsefatet var tomt. Tante Anna ble litt bekymret, og lurte på om de hadde fått nok. Men alle forsikret henne om at de var mer enn mette.

57 • Se, markene står hvite

Igjen senket stillheten og roen seg over setra. Mette satt på vollen og speidet utover, men det var ikke de vakre høstfargene i liene eller den høye skyfri himmelen hun så. Heller ikke så hun det blanke tjernet som de siste solstrålene speilet seg i. Blikket hennes så en annen mark, en duvende blomstereng ... nei, det var ingen blomstereng, det var en linåker som duvet i sommerens hete. Og den linåkeren lå heller ikke der på vollen. Det var en linåker i et helt annet land. Hun satt der helt oppslukt av sine egne tanker, og de tankene hadde fått frie vinger.

Da tante Anna fortalte om den vakre linåkeren, hadde hun i et glimt sett den for seg. Men nå, etter at alle gjestene var reist og hun bare kunne sitte der og slappe av, hadde det synet igjen dukket opp for henne. Det var samtidig et bibelvers som tonte i hennes indre: Løft blikket og se på markene, de står alt hvite mot høst.

Hvor i Bibelen sto det at det var en kornåker Jesus snakket om der i det fjerde kapittelet av Johannes evangelium? Selv hadde hun alltid tatt det som en selvfølge at det var en åker med korn det var snakk om, men korn var da slett ikke hvitt? Kunne det tenkes at det var en linåker Jesus hadde i tankene? Tante Anna hadde jo sagt at der også fantes hvit lin. Kanskje var det en lintype som ble mer brukt på den tiden. Og linåkrer måtte sikkert være et kjent syn for folk på Bibelens tid, for det var jo mye lin-klær de brukte da. Linen var jo et materiale som både virket kjølig, og som hadde stor evne til å absorbere fuktighet. Det var altså et materiale som egnet seg spesielt godt der sola stekte og svetten rant.

I det samme kom tante Anna ut på vollen. «Hva er det du sitter der og funderer på? Aldri har jeg vel sett et så bortreist blikk.» Hun satte seg i en stol på den andre siden av hagebordet.

Mette skvatt da hun ble snakket til. Litt forvirret så hun bort på tante Anna. «Ja, nå var jeg virkelig langt borte,» sa hun og fortalte hva hun hadde tenkt på. Tante Anna ble også ivrig over de tankene Mette hadde sittet med.

«Du sier noe. Det har jeg aldri tenkt på, men det er klart at det kan være noe i det. Du vet når linen står i blomst, da vet man at nå er det snart høstetid.»

Plutselig tidde hun. Med ett var det tante Anna som forsvant inn i sine egne tanker. Men det varte ikke så lenge før snakketøyet hennes begynte å arbeide igjen. «Det bibelsitatet du henviste til er jo hentet fra beretningen om Jesus som var i samtale med ei samaritansk kvinne. Resultatet av den samtalen ble at kvinnen løp inn i byen og fortalte hva hun hadde hørt, og da var det mange i den byen som kom til tro på Gud. Det ble det vi kaller vekkelse. Men før det skjedde, så var det altså at Jesus snakket med apostlene. Han forberedte dem på en innhøstingstid, og da en innhøsting av mennesker for Himmelen. Åkeren og aksene var altså et bilde på menneskene.»

Igjen tidde hun litt før hun fortsatte. «Det var jammen et talende bilde, det med linen.» Hele bearbeidelsesprosessen kan være et bilde på hva som skjer med et menneske når det blir frelst, og så videre i livet frem mot evigheten.»

Mette så forundret på henne. «Hvordan da, mener du?» Tante Anna smilte, men blikket var blitt fjernt igjen. «Tenk på det jeg fortalte om stråene som ikke måtte skjæres, men som måtte rykkes opp med rot. Slik er det jo også med et menneske som blir en kristen. Der må det skje en fundamental forandring. Det går ikke an å bare forandre litt på det ytre … det på overflaten. Nei, man må «rykkes opp med rot», forandringen må skje helt til bunns av hjertedypet.»

«Å ja.» Mette ble ivrig. Og dette er ikke noe mennesket, eller stråene, kan greie på egen hånd. Der må «høstfolk» til for å få inn avlingen. Det er altså noe som Gud og Hans engler må gjøre.»

«Ja, og så kommer denne Røytingen, også det er noe som Høstens Herre må ta seg av.» Det så ut til at hele kroppen til den store kvinnen fulgte med i de tankene som var satt i sving der mellom dem.

«Hvis de stråene som ble lagt ned der i bekken kunne snakke, hva tror du de hadde sagt? Kanskje de hadde beklaget seg slik: Hva skal dette bety, her ligger jeg henslengt i en bekk, i ferd med å råtne hen. Hvor er det blitt av høstens Herre, og hvor er det blitt av høstfolkene som snakket så fint om et vakkert produkt som skulle lages? Har de glemt meg? Var jeg ikke mer verd? Var jeg ubrukelig? Var dette alt? Her er det jo bare mørkt og trist.»

Mette lo av den ivrige ordflommen til tante Anna. «Jeg skjønner hvor du vil hen. Jeg har også hørt den leksa noen ganger. Mennesker som har tatt imot Jesus, ja også noen som har levd med Ham i lang tid, de har kommet inn i det vi kaller anfektelse. Alt virker mørkt og trist. Gud virker langt borte. De ser ingenting i sitt liv som de mener kan behage Gud. Ja, faktisk kan de oppleve det så sterkt at de er i tvil om de i det hele tatt er et Guds barn lenger.»

«Ja,» sa tante Anna, «anfektelsens dype daler og mørke skygger får vel de fleste kristne oppleve fra tid til annen. Og ofte kan jo slike følelser og tanker komme ikke lenge etter at en bestemmelse om å følge Jesus er tatt. Men det underlige er at nettopp en slik tilstand er et trekk fra Gud selv. Riktignok er det djevelen som herjer og uroer, men det er Gud som lar dette skje. Vi må bearbeides og gjøres i stand for det himmelske bryllupet. Og så trenger vi å lære oss å overlate alt i vår Herres hender. Dette er altså en slags læreprosess.»

«Røyting …» Mette så tankefull på tante Anna. «Det må være ganske ydmykende …»

Hun nikket. «Ja, men skal vi bli foredlet og dyktiggjort, så må det mye ydmykelse til. Det er ydmykende å overlate alt i seg selv til en annen, selv om denne er Gud.»

«Gud har jammen mye arbeid med oss.» Mette sukket. Hele livet er jo egentlig en eneste foredlingsprosess. Det er vel det vi kaller helliggjørelse.»

«Eller heklingen,» skjøt tante Anna inn med et smil. «Hele tiden trenger vi å bli renset for rusk og rask som dette livet påfører oss. Og stadig vil renselsen gå dypere og dypere. Forskjellige slags bindinger må bort. Tanker og holdninger må endres. Synd som kommer på, må ordnes opp i, erkjennes og bekjennes. Hovmod, stolthet og sjalusi må det taes et oppgjør med. Prøvelser kommer på for at vi skal vinne lærdom og erfaring. Gjennom dette styrkes vi i tro og tillit til Gud.»

«Det er litt rart at Gud arbeider på denne måten,» sa Mette.

«Ja.» Tante Anna ristet undrende på hodet. Men så ble hun ivrig igjen. «Der står faktisk noe i Bibelen om akkurat det. Det står også i Johannes evangelium, men i det femtende kapittelet. Der står det i vers to: hver gren som bærer frukt, renser han så den skal bære mer.

Det er altså den grenen som bærer frukt som må renses. Og dette gjøres for at den skal bære mer.

Gud har en plan med hvert eneste menneske. Og det er denne planen han hele tiden handler etter. Han har en plan om å bruke noen i innhøstingsarbeidet, og til det trenger det en spesiell utrustning. Men det overordnede mål med alle er at de skal gjøres i stand for Det Himmelske Bryllupet.

Så en dag skal vi få se det ferdige «teppet» i all sin herlighet, fullkommet, hjemme i Himmelen.» Igjen så hun drømmende ut i lufta.

Mette satt taus og lyttet helt henført av de mektige tankene.

«Hver lintråd som er vevd inn i det,» fortsatte tante Anna, «er av beste kvalitet. Kun de fineste kjernene er blitt med. Ingen skall og rusk er fulgt med i den veven. Og disse linfibrene, det er oss mennesker … gjort i stand og renset av Mesteren selv, ved Hans blod!»

«Det er forunderlig at Gud vil ha så mye bry med oss,» sa Mette.

«Ja,» svarte tante Anna, «men alt dette blir gjort i den inderligste kjærlighet. Selv om vi til tider får oppleve mørke stunder, så fører han oss også ut i lyset igjen. Han er med oss hele tiden. Ingen har noen gang fått oppleve at Gud har forlatt dem der i mørket. Selv om vi ikke ser han, så ser han oss.»

Hun tidde litt igjen. Hele ansiktet hennes lyste der hun satt, syntes Mette. En indre styrke og harmoni syntes å prege hele den kraftige kvinnen.

«Det som jeg synes er det mest fantastiske med det å være et Guds barn,» sa hun etter en liten stund, «det er at vi får eie fred med Han i en god samvittighet.»

«Det er virkelig sant,» svarte Mette. Hun sa ikke mer, men tankene hennes gikk til den tiden da hun planla fjellturen sammen med Arvid. Da opplevde hun at den freden ble borte. Hun var i ferd med å gjøre noe som ikke Gud kunne være med på, og da forsvant også den gode freden.

«Jeg må eie den freden,» sa hun bestemt, og så reiste hun seg.

Sola var gått ned, og det var begynt å bli kjølig. Tante Anna reiste seg også. Ingen av dem hadde registrert at kvelden var i ferd med å senke seg over seterområdet. Noen skarpe ugleskrik kunne høres innimellom trærne på den andre siden av jordet. Der levde naturen sitt eget liv med mang en kamp på liv og død. Men den kampen som raste i menneskenes indre, mellom de onde og de gode kreftene, den var forutsagt på forhånd. Jesus hadde seiret, så den som overlot hele sitt liv i Hans hender, skulle få lov til å skjule seg i Ham. Og derved ville de få den samme freden og seieren som Han hadde vunnet.

58 • Multetur

«**J**eg tror vi klatrer opp skråningen her.» Morten pekte mot en kløft rett foran dem. Det så svært bratt ut, men kløften så ut til å være fin å ta seg fram i. «Det er ganske bratt til å begynne med her, men der er noen fine myrer innover når vi bare kommer opp på toppen.»

Morten gikk foran med ryggsekken, mens Mette fulgte hakk i hæl med bærspannet. Morten hadde også et spann hengende i en stropp bak på sekken.

Endelig hadde de kommet seg av sted på den etterlengtede multeturen. Været hadde vært litt grått fra morgenen av , men det regnet ikke, så de bestemte seg for å dra av sted som planlagt.

Det ble hard klatring en stund, men slitet ble belønnet med en nydelig utsikt da de endelig var oppe. De sto på en høyde med hele fjellheimens majestetiske storhet foran seg. Lave skyer seilte over himmelen og slapp søyler av solstråler ned som mektige spottlighter mot den rødmende lyngmarka. En lett dis hang i lufta og skapte ekstra sterk lyseffekt i det mektige panoramaet. Myrene strakte seg utover mellom høydedrag og knauser, mens bekkefar snodde seg tvers gjennom det hele fra fjellvann til fjellvann.

Mette gispet av det vakre synet. Morten ble også stående en stund i taus beundring. Det eiendommelige lyset, stillheten og de mektige fargene gav dem en følelse av ærefrykt. Langs en dal kunne de se en saueflokk som gikk og beitet.

Morten begynte å gå igjen. «Jeg tror vi prøver de myrene der borte først, sa han og pekte nordover mot et område hvor vegetasjonen så ekstra vakker ut.

«Ja, la oss gå dit,» sa Mette begeistret.

Mens de gikk, så de stadig tettere med multeris. Morten visste tydeligvis hvor han skulle gå for å finne bær. Snart var de inne i et område hvor bærene sto tett i tett. «Her kan det ikke ha vært noen før oss,» sa Mette og plukket ivrig de gylne, deilige bærene. Rett som det var havnet det et i munnen.

«Dette området får vi som regel for oss selv,» svarte Morten. «Det er få som orker å gå opp den bratte kløfta.»

En lang stund var de bare opptatt med bærene der på myra. Mette spratt fra tue til tue og sopte med seg alt hun så av de lysegule bærene. Hun frydet seg der hun gikk. Sola kom også mer og mer til syne. En vakrere dag kunne de ikke ha valgt for bærtur.

Plutselig stoppet hun opp. «Hva er dette?» Under noe kratt fikk hun se noe loddent. Morten kom raskt til. Han dro vekk noen kvister og løv, og der kom en død sau til syne. Han ble mørk i ansiktet. «Her har det vært rovdyr på ferde.» Sauen var tydelig bitt i hjel, og det var også spist en del av den. «Det kan ikke være lenge siden det har skjedd.» Han undersøkte blodet som hadde runnet utover marka. «Antakelig ble den drept i natt.»

Mette grøsset. «Hva slags dyr er det som kan ha gjort dette?»

«Jeg vet ikke helt.» Han undersøkte sauen enda en stund. Så rettet han seg opp og speidet innover i fjellet. «Håper bare ikke der er flere slike kadaver rundt omkring her.»

De fortsatte bortover myren. Morten var hele tiden på utkikk etter flere tegn på herjinger i saueflokkene.

«Så rart,» sa Mette betenkt. «Det så ut som om den sauen var gjemt der. Den var jo dekket til med kvister og rusk. Du tror ikke det kan ha vært mennesker som har gjort det da?»

Morten ristet på hodet. «Nei, det var tydelig at et rovdyr hadde gjort det. Det er en del dyr som gjør det på den måten. De dekker byttet til for å komme tilbake senere og spise mer.»

De fant ikke flere saueskrotter, men multer fant de i massevis. Etter som tiden gikk ble bøttene stadig fullere.

«La oss klatre opp på den høyden der, foreslo Morten og pekte. «Så kan vi sitte der og spise. Der vil vi ha en fin utsikt over fjellet.»

De fulle bøttene med bær satte de fra seg før de begynte klatringen. De måtte jo ned samme vei når de skulle hjem igjen.

Enda en gang ble de belønnet med en utsikt som nesten tok pusten fra dem. Mette gikk nærmere skrenten på den motsatte siden. Der skrånet det bratt ned mot et vann, og flere myrer. Morten fulgte rett bak.

Plutselig skvatt de til. En lys skygge kom opp over fjellskrenten foran dem, og forsvant i lynets fart ned på den andre siden hvor de var kommet opp.

«Hva var det?» Mette sto og så forvirret i den retningen skyggen var forsvunnet. Morten løp mot skråningen, men den var allerede forsvunnet bak knauser og kratt. «Det kan i hvert fall ikke ha vært en rev,» svarte han. «Den ville ikke ha våget å styrte utfor disse bratte skrentene i slik en fart, og en hare kunne det slett ikke være.»

De ble begge gående en stund og studere marka der dyret hadde løpt. «Se her!» ropte Morten. Han pekte på et sted hvor det hadde ligget en vannpytt. Vannet var tørket bort, men en mengde fint slam lå igjen. Der kunne de tydelig se fire fotavtrykk i den bløte leiren.

«Det der ser da ut som store hundespor,» sa Mette. Morten ristet på hodet mens han hele tiden undersøkte fotavtrykkene. «Dette er ikke hund. På hundesporene kan man lett se merke etter kloa her framme.» Han pekte ned i gjørmen. «Her er det ingen klomerke. Dette ser mer ut som kattespor, bare de er mye større.»

Han rettet seg opp og så igjen utover fjellet med et speidende blikk. «Det er nok ingen tvil om hva slags dyr dette er. Og det forklarer også hvem som har vært på ferde i saueflokken. Dette må være ei gaupe.»

Mette gispet. «Gaupe? Men er ikke de farlige da?» Hun stirret på Morten med redsel i blikket. Morten smilte. «Den er ikke farlig for oss. Du så jo at den nok var mye reddere for oss enn vi er for den. Vi kom nok over den mens den lå og koste seg i sola der borte i skråningen. Gaupene pleier gjerne å legge seg til høyt oppe i en skråning om dagen, der de kan ha god utsikt. Og de pleier også å dekke til byttet sitt når de vil spare litt av maten sin til senere,» sa han og mørknet til i blikket. «Nei, det er nok ingen tvil om hvem som er syndebukken her.»

Mens de spiste nisten sin, ble de sittende og snakke om det de hadde sett. Morten var svært bekymret for sauene som gikk rundt omkring i hele området. «Det er ikke så lenge til de skal hentes ned fra fjellet nå,» sa han. «Håper bare ikke denne gaupa greier å ta for mange før det.»

De tok seg god tid med spisingen. Det var ingen plikter som ventet dem på setra før melketid, så de kunne bare slappe av. Mette nøt freden og stillheten der oppe i fulle drag.

De strakte seg ut på fjellet og bevilget seg en ørliten middagshvil før de igjen begynte på nedstigningen.

Da de kom ned, fant de raskt igjen bærbøttene som nesten var breddfulle av deilige multebær. Heldigvis hadde Morten med seg ryggsekken. I den hadde de et par plastposer, så de kunne ennå plukke med seg noen flere bær før de dro hjemover igjen.

«Jeg tror vi går litt bortover i vestlig retning,» sa han etter en stund. Da kan vi komme ned et annet sted, og så havner vi ved lia i vestenden av seterområdet.

Det ble et langt stykke å gå, men Mette frydet seg hele tiden over den herlige turen. Etter en stund stoppet de ved et lite fjellvann for å puste ut litt. Mette satte seg på en stein ved vannet. «Se her,» sa hun og pekte på noe mellom steinene i vannkanten. «Her har det vært folk for ikke så lenge siden.»

Morten kom også bort til henne. «Ja, her har det vært tent opp bål. Og der,» sa han og pekte bortover bredden, «der må det ha stått et telt.» De så tydelige merker etter aktivitet, for gresset var flattrykket og nedtrampet. Her og der lå det også søppel og skrot henslengt.

«Folk bør i hvert fall rydde opp etter seg,» sa Mette ergerlig og begynte å plukke opp det som lå der og flagret.

Plutselig stoppet hun og stirret ned i lyngen. «Se her!» Morten kom styrtende til da han hørte utropet hennes som nesten lød som et skrik. «Hva er det?» Mette svarte ikke, men løftet bare opp noe fra marka. Det var en gammel rusten blikkboks.

«Skrinet!» Morten ble også stående og stirre. Så begynte han å undersøkte det nøyere.

«Det er ikke åpnet,» konstaterte han. «Nei,» sa Mette og pustet lettet ut. «Men de har arbeidet hardt for å få det til.» De kunne se flere skrapemerker i rusten, og en del bulker var der også som tydet på at de hadde slått på det med noe hardt.

«De har nok ikke greid å åpne det, og så har de bare slengt det fra seg her,» sa Morten. «Men nå skal det opp!»

Mette kikket fort bort på han. Der lå et lite smil om munnen hans, men bemerkningen ble sagt med en fasthet som tydet på at dette var noe han ikke ville ha flere vanskeligheter med.

Det ble ingen lang hvilepause der ved vannet. Begge var mest opptatt av skrinet. Nå måtte de finne ut hva det var som skjulte seg så godt der inni.

59 • Høyspenning

Selv om Mette var ganske sliten etter den lange fjellturen, ble fjøsstellet unnagjort på rekordtid. Det ble ingen ekstra kos rundt dyrene, og melka ble bare tømt over i et spann som hun satte i kulpen til kjøling. Alle tankene hennes kretset rundt det gamle skrinet. Morten hadde tatt det med seg bort til hagebordet. Der hadde han funnet noe verktøy, og hele tiden mens hun holdt på med melkingen, arbeidet han med skrinet. Hun var så spent at hun ikke greide å konsentrere seg skikkelig om arbeidet. Heldigvis var hun etter hvert blitt så rutinert at hun kunne greie det meste uten å tenke så mye over hva hun gjorde.

Der var ingen turister på setra for øyeblikket. Så sent på året var det jo mest skoleelever de hadde besøk av. Mette var derfor alene med kveldsstellet i fjøset.

Snart var kyrne ute på beitet igjen. Den lille kalven hoppet og spratt rundt henne. Pia kom også for å få litt ekstra forpleining, men hun klappet dem bare noen ganger. Fingrene hennes fikk den ikke suge på denne kvelden. Det tok hun seg ikke tid til. Så fort hun kunne løp hun bort til Morten for å se hvordan det gikk med «brekket».

«Får du det opp, tror du?» spurte hun spent, og satte seg ved siden av ham på en stol. «Jeg tror nok det skal gå,» svarte han, «men det tar tid. Dette var jammen et seigt materiale å komme gjennom.» Han satt og filte med ei baufil. Hun kunne se at han var svært forsiktig så han ikke skulle ødelegge noe av det som kunne være inni. Sagbladet åt seg inn i det tykke metallet millimeter etter millimeter.

Sola var i ferd med å senke seg ned bak fjellene i vest, men ingen av dem la merke til den vakre, rødmende himmelen. Heller ikke den friske brisen, som etter hvert bare ble friskere og friskere, lot de til å registrere. Hele deres oppmerksomhet var rettet mot den lille saga som trofast kjempet seg videre. Mette strakte hals for å se hvor langt arbeidet var kommet. Det var rett under kanten på lokket at Morten hadde begynt å sage. Systematisk arbeidet han seg rundt langs kantene på skrinet, men det tok tid. Rett som det var måtte han ta en liten pause for å hvile fingrene.

«Nå er det bare denne svingen igjen,» sa han etter en stund, «så kan vi kanskje greie å brekke opp lokket.» Mette var så spent at hun nesten skalv. Hva kunne det være som hadde ligget gjemt der i hulen? Etter hva tante Anna mente, så måtte det ha ligget der svært lenge. Det så slett ikke ut som noe søppel som bare var slengt vekk der, til det var det altfor godt gjemt.

«Der,» sa Morten og la verktøyet fra seg. «Nå må vi se om vi kan greie å brekke opp toppen. Han tok et godt tak i skrinet og dro i lokket, men det rikket seg ikke noe særlig. «Jeg må visst finne noen sterkere hjelpemidler,» sa han og gikk bort til bilen. Etter litt roting i bagasjerommet fant han en del redskaper som han kom tilbake til bordet med. Et langt, kraftig skruejern ble lagt inn i den smale sprekken, og da var det ikke lenge før de kunne se at åpningen begynte å utvide seg. Snart hadde de en åpning som var så stor at de kunne få inn ei smal hånd. Mette var ikke sen om å forsøke seg. Forsiktig stakk hun inn hånden. Hun famlet litt rundt der inne før hun fikk tak i noe som lå på bunnen. Varsomt trakk hun det ut. Snart satt hun med rynkede bryn og så på et gammelt tøystykke.

«Er det denne filla vi har risikert nesten liv og lemmer på?» sa hun og så på de røde fingrene til Morten. Han kom sikkert til å få vannblemmer der. «Og innbruddet. De skulle ha visst hva de risikerte frihet og rulleblad for, disse guttene oppe i fjellet.» Ergerlig slengte hun tøystykket fra seg på bordet.

Morten satte i å le. «Kan du begripe så nysgjerrige vi mennesker er. Hvor mye hadde ikke vi også risikert for å finne ut hva dette skrinet inneholdt?» Mette måtte også le. Hun plukket opp tøystykket igjen og så granskende på det.

Sakte forsvant smilet, mens et utrykk av undring la se over ansiktet hennes. «Dette har jeg da sett før?» Det var ei grov ullfille. I den ene enden hang det ned noen lange tråder. De var tydelig knyttet på der som frynser.

Morten så ikke på Mette. Det var skrinet han var opptatt av. Han hadde snudd det opp ned. Og da falt det ut en gul, morknet papirlapp. Før han rakk å vise den til Mette var hun allerede inne i seterbua. Et øyeblikk etter kom hun tilbake med en bunke foto - grafier.

«Se her,» sa Morten da hun kom ut igjen. «Se hva jeg fant.» Mette stirret på lappen. «Står det noe på den?» «Ja, jeg tror det, men det er nokså utydelig.»

Mette strakte hodet over skulderen hans mens han stirret intenst på de få bokstavene som var skrevet der. «Farvel mit baan,» stavet han seg fram til. Hva slags mening kan du få ut av det?» spurte Mette forvirret. Morten ristet på hodet. «Nei, sannelig om jeg vet.»

«Men hva er det du kommer med?» Han ble i det samme oppmerksom på det hun hadde i hendene.

«Ja, se her,» sa Mette ivrig og la hele bunken på bordet. Det var bildene de hadde tatt på amerikaturen. Raskt bladde hun seg fram til de bildene hun var ute etter.

«Se her.» Hun holdt fram et bilde av Frank. Han satt med det gamle sjalet foran seg. «Denne filla her ligner jo svært på det gamle sjalet vi så i Amerika.»

Morten ble også ivrig med det samme. Han tok bildet og la det på bordet. Så la han det grove lille tøystykket ved siden av.

«Ser du det?» Begeistringen lyste ut av øynene hans. Denne lille tøyfilla passer jo akkurat inn der hvor det var revet bort et stykke i sjalet. Det kan ikke være noen tvil. Dette er den manglende biten der.»

Et øyeblikk ble de bare sittende og måpe. Hva kunne dette bety? Morten tok opp igjen den lille papirlappen. «Dette ser ut til å være en avskjedshilsen, for det første ordet er da tydelig farvel. Men det siste ordet virker mye mer fremmed.»

Plutselig treiv han mobiltelefonen og slo et nummer. Mette kunne lett høre, der hun satt ved siden av ham, at det var tante Anna han snakket med.

En liten stund etter la han mobiltelefonen fra seg igjen. «Tante Anna kunne fortelle at det siste ordet her er bån, som egentlig betyr barn. Det var slik de sa det før i tiden her.»

«Farvel mitt barn!» Mette tygde litt på ordene.

Plutselig smalt Morten hånden i bordet. «Der har vi det. Ja, det er nødt til å være slik. Frank fortalte jo om Sjur som kom fra en gård her i nærheten. Moren hans kom til gården da hun var et spedbarn. Tror du det var Silja som var bestemoren til Sjur?»

Igjen ble de sittende i taushet begge to. Men så brast det ut av Mette. «Selvsagt. Det må jo være slik. Barnet ble tatt fra henne etter fødselen. Det var nok barnefaren som ordnet det. Kanskje det ble kamp da det skjedde, slik at denne fliken ble revet av sjalet i kampen. Så har altså den ulykkelige moren «begravd» det hun hadde igjen av den lille her i dette skrinet før hun selv hoppet i tjernet.»

Et dypt alvor la seg over dem begge der de satt. Sagnet hadde med ett rykket dem helt nær igjen. Kunne det være mulig at det slett ikke bare var et sagn? Jo, der var nok ingen tvil om det. Mette kom også til å huske på hva den gamle kirkegårdsgraveren hadde fortalt den søndagen de hadde gudstjeneste der borte ved tjernet. Det han hadde sagt om kisten til Silja var jo også noe som sterkt bekreftet en slik tanke.

Det var Morten som først brøt tausheten. Han strøk åndsfraværende med hånden over det mørke ullstoffet. «For en tragedie …» Det var som om alvoret i situasjonen med ett gikk opp for ham for fullt. Den ulykkelige jenta som ikke så noen annen utvei enn å gjøre slutt på livet. Kanskje hadde der utspunnet seg dramatiske ting før hun gikk til det drastiske skrittet. Mette så på tøystykket igjen. Det skulle jammen litt krefter til for å greie å rive den av.

«Så annerledes forholdene må ha vært i den tiden,» sa hun og sukket tungt. Morten nikket.

Sola var nå borte bak fjellene, og skumringen begynte å senke seg. Den kjølige brisen trengte helt inn på kroppen til de to som satt der på vollen. Ja, faktisk så var det en kulde som gikk helt gjennom marg og ben på dem ved vissheten om hva den fjellskrenten der borte hadde skjult i så mange år.

Som på kommando reiste de seg begge to og gikk inn i den lune og koselige seterbua. •

434

MATOPPSKRIFTER

• Dravle •

Dette er dravle slik de lager den, og spiser den i Sirdal i Vest-Agder. Dravle måtte aldri mangle på festbordet i gamle dager, enten det var bryllup eller begravelse. Fremdeles i dag er dette en festrett, derfor den store oppskriften.

1 liter råmelk	**1 liter kulturmelk**
6 liter helmelk	**700-800 gram sukker**
10-11 egg	

Kok opp helmelka i ei stor gryte. Råmelk, kulturmelk, egg og sukker vispes sammen i en bolle. Tøm blandingen i den kokende melka. Rør litt rundt i gryta. Etter dette må det ikke røres mer i gryta. Kok det hele forsiktig (trekke) i 7 timer. Ha lokk på gryta, men det kan gjerne være litt trukket til side så det ikke er helt tett. Når dravlen er ferdig kokt, bør den stå i gryta til den er kjølnet godt ned for da er den lettere å behandle. Ostemassen har nå samlet seg til ei tykk og fast kake på toppen av mysen (søen). Tøm forsiktig av mysen. Hvelv oste—"kaka" over på et fat, og dravlen er ferdig. Den serveres oppskåret i centimetertykke skiver til lefse. Da blir gjerne lefsa smurt med smør og strødd med sukker, og så brettet sammen og skåret i mindre stykker. Dravlen spises med skje ved siden av. Man kan også legge dravle rett på lefsa slik som man gjør med eggost.

• Pannekaker •

Dette var festmat i eldre tider. Da ble de gjerne brukt sammen med lefser. En lefsesnipp og en pannekake ble smurt med smør, og brettet sammen på en spesiell måte. Jeg har ikke hørt at denne retten var brukt i så veldig vide kretser. Men den ble i hvert fall brukt oppover i Mandalen, Vest-Agder. Nå er helst pannekaker en rett for barna. Da spises de enten med smør og sukker på, eller smør og syltetøy, og da helst blåbærsyltetøy. Har man ertesuppe ved siden av, blir det en god middagsrett.

1 liter melk (Kan blandes	**50-100 gram sukker**
med litt fløte)	**1 ts. vaniljesukker**
3 egg	**50 gram smeltet smør**
½ ts. salt	**Hvetemel**

Alt blandes godt sammen i en bolle. Ha i så mye hvetemel at det blir ei nokså tynn røre. La røra hvile ca. en halv time før steking. Varm opp ei rund stekepanne, og ha litt smør i slik at ikke pannekakene skal sette seg fast under stekingen. Hell så ca. en dl. av røra i panna. Hell på stekepanna slik at røra flyter helt ut og dekker hele bunnen. Kaka skal være tynn, men allikevel så tykk at den henger sammen når man skal snu den. Den stekes lysebrun på begge sider. Etter hvert som kakene blir ferdigstekt, legges de oppå hverandre på et fat, eller man bretter dem i fire og legger dem i en haug på et fat. Serveres enten varme eller kalde.

435

• Eggost (Søtost) •

Eggosten finnes det flere forskjellige oppskrifter på. Denne oppskriften har jeg etter min svigermor som kommer fra Hægebostad, Vest-Agder. Også svigerfar som er fra Eiken i Vest-Agder, er vant til denne type eggost fra sitt barndomshjem. Men der kaller de den Søtost. Det er fordi de også bruker noe som heter Saltost eller Dravlost. Det er den samme osten, men kun med litt salt i isteden for sukker. Da knaes saltet i ostemassen etter at den er tatt opp av søen (mysen).

| 1 liter melk (kanskje litt mer) | ½ liter sur melk (kulturmelk) |
| ca. 2 dl. sukker | 4 egg |

La melka få et oppkok. Sur melk, egg og sukker blandes sammen i en bolle. Tøm blandingen i den kokende melka. Rør forsiktig rundt et par ganger med ei sleiv. La det hele stå og trekke ca. 20 minutter. (Til ostemassen har skilt seg helt ut og det kun er en nesten klar væske (myse eller sø) igjen rundt og under.) Unngå røring i ostemassen. Osten taes forsiktig opp med ei hullsleiv og legges på et fat. La den renne godt av seg. Det vil trekke ut mer væske mens den ligger på fatet. Tøm det av eller trekk det opp med papirhåndkle. Når osten er avkjølt, strøes det kanel over, og den kan serveres. Eggost brukes som pålegg på lefser, potetkaker (lomper) eller brød (da helst loff).

• Gome •

Der finnes flere forskjellige oppskrifter på Gome, alt etter distriktet man bor i. Detter er den oppskriften jeg bruker, og som min mor og min bestemor brukte.

ca. 4 liter melk	En neve rosiner
ca. 1 liter sur melk (kulturmelk)	1 ts. salt
ca. 3 dl. sukker	1 ss. hvetemel (i surmelka)
1 ts. kardemomme	Hvetemel til jevning
Et par små kanelstenger	

Få melka på kok i ei stor gryte. Ha så i den sure melka som er tilsatt 1 ss. hvetemel. Brun sukkeret i ei stekepanne (rør godt i panna så det ikke brenner) og ha det i den kokende melka. Rør forsikteig til sukkermassen er oppløst, men pass på så ikke osten, som snart vil begynne å skille seg ut, blir helt rørt i stykker. Det brunede sukkeret vil gi gomen en pen brunfarge. Det går også an å bruke mørk sirup i stedet for brunet sukker. La det hele småkoke (trekke) noen timer ... til ostemassen er så nedkokt som man ønsker å ha den. Ca. en halv time før den er ferdig nedkokt, haes rosinene og kanelen i. Når den så er ferdig nedkokt, tar man opp litt av mysen (søen) (det som er flytende) og avkjøler det til å røre ut jevningen i. Salt og kardemomme haes i jevningen. Synes man at gomen er blitt for lite søt, kan man ha i mer sukker i jevningen. Rør så på jevning til den er passe tykk (grøttykkelse). Husk at den tykner mer mens den koker. Det må røres forsiktig i gomen så man ikke rører osteklumpene helt i stykker, men samtidig må man røre så godt at der ikke blir klumper av jevningen. La det hele koke ca. ti minutter. Gomen taes opp og legges i ei skål til avkjøling. Den serveres kald som pålegg på lefser, flatbrød, potetkaker (lomper) eller på brød. Den kan også dypfryses, men da bør den få et oppkok igjen når den tines, og så avkjøles igjen før den serveres.

• Lefse og flatbrød •

I eldre tider var det viktig å lage litt variasjon i kosten med de hjelpemidler de hadde rundt omkring på gårdene. Og da var det helst melk og egg de hadde tilgang på. Vanlig brød ble ikke brukt så mye til hverdags. Det var helst flatbrød de brukte. Og da var det jo viktig å lage noe som man kunne bruke som pålegg til det. Ut fra dette ble også festmaten utviklet. Og de visste hvordan de skulle lage det for å få det godt.

Til lefse og flatbrødbaking trenges det så pass mye ekstrautstyr at man vanskelig kan gi en skikkelig oppskrift. Man er også så avhengig av erfaring for å bake dette at konkret oppskrift nesten ikke kan skrives ned. Men jeg vil likevel si litt om hvordan man baker dette i Vest-Agder. Det finnes forskjellige typer lefser alt etter hvor i landet man befinner seg. Dette er Sørlandslefsen, også kalt potetlefse—potetflatbrød.

Først kokes potetene og skrelles. De avkjøles litt før baking. Noen ganger må de være helt kalde, det avhenger av hva slags potetsort man bruker, og når på året det er vi baker. Om man bruker samme potetsort så kan de likevel være forskjellige på konsistens fra åker til åker. Og potetene mister fuktighet etter hvert under lagring. Det merkes godt ved slik baking.

Potetene males i kjøttkvern. Mal ikke opp for stor porsjon av gangen da lefsedeigen lett bløtner mens den ligger. Kna så i hvetemel til en passe tykk deig som lett kan eltes og kjevles. Til flatbrød kan man også godt bruke litt grovt hvetemel blandet med fint hvetemel. Det er en treningssak å kjenne hvor mye mel man må ha i deigen. For lite mel gjør deigen klissete og vanskelig å kjevle. Det brenner seg også da lettere fast på hella. For mye mel gjør lefsene harde, stive og lite spenstige. Til flatbrød kan man bruke mer mel, for de skal være harde.

Ta et passe emne av deigen (som en tennisballstørrelse) og form den rund, og trykk den flat. Kjevl så emnet ut til en tynn leiv. Når den er halvveis utkjevlet strøes det mel over den, og den snues. Kjevl videre på den andre siden. Vær forsiktig så den ikke henger seg fast til underlaget. Da blir det lett hull i leiven. Strø på mer mel under hvis den begynner å henge ved. Underlaget man kjevler på kan være forskjellig. Vi bruker gjerne en tykk papplate som er klippet på størrelse med hella. Da kan man lett dreie leiven rundt uten å ødelegge den. Man må bruke et kjevle med riller i. Formen på rillene har også stor betydning for å få et fint resultat. Noen bruker også kjevler med ruter.

Så skal leiven stekes. Da rulles den rundt en "Fløy". Det er en lang flat pinne. Det er også en treningssak å få leiven smidig over fra bakebordet, og bort på hella. Hella er ei stor, rund og flat stekeinretning. Nå brukes bare elektriske heller, men i tidligere tider brukte man ei rund, flat jernplate som ble lagt over vedkomfyren (bryggepanna) eller i skorsteinen. Jeg husker at min bestemor stekte lefsene i skorsteinen på ei slik plate.

Når lefsa er lagt til rette på hella, vætes den med en våt klut. Da bruker vi gjerne ei fille som er knyttet fast på en pinne. Den dyppes i ei skål med vann som er tilsatt litt salt. Så strykes filla forsiktig over lefsa. Stekingen går ganske raskt, for til lefser må man ha god varme på. Når den er ferdig stekt på den ene siden, må den snues og stekes på den andre.

Flatbrød blir stekt på samme måte, men da væter man ikke leiven på hella. Man bruker også mindre varme til flatbrød, slik at de tørker mens de steker. Da blir de fine og sprø. Både flatbrød og lefser bør være så tynt kjevlet at man kan skimte underlaget gjennom lefsa når den er ferdig kjevlet.

Lefser kan også stekes med svakere varme, og uten væting. Da blir de harde og må bløtes i vann før de skal smøres for servering. Slike harde lefser kan oppbevares over lengre tid på et tørt sted, på samme måte som flatbrød kan. Men nå som man har dypfryser,

437

blir det helst den myke lefsetypen som lages.

Lefsene kan med fordel smøres og kuttes i passe serveringsstykker før dypfrysing. Da er de ferdig til servering når de taes opp av fryseboksen. De tiner ganske raskt. Man smører da hele lefsen. Så brettes sidene inn slik at det blir til en avlang firkant. Denne brettes igjen på midten slik at det blir en ca. 15 cm. bred, og 40 cm. lang firkant. Denne deles (kuttes eller klippes) i ca. 5 - 7 cm. brede stykker.

Vi bruker også lefser som tilbehør til forskjellige slags middagsretter. Til Torsk eller Lutefisk er det godt med lefser til. Da kuttes lefsene bare i åtte snipper (Slik som man kutter opp et rund kake) og legges i en stabel på et fat (eller i fryseboksen klar til servering). Så smøres snippene med smør, og poteter og fisk legges oppå. Det hele rulles sammen til ei pølse som spises med fingrene.

Det samme gjøres til tørket sauekjøtt, og da helst ribben. Men da smøres ikke lefsen med smør. Den dyppes i ribbefetter. Man kan også steke kjøttet på gloa i peisen eller på et bål, og så pakke det stekte kjøttet inn i lefse sammen med kokte poteter, og så spise det på samme måte. Det kalles "Glosteik. Dette var den gamle julemiddagen i de indre bygder her på Sørlandet.

• Prim •

Prim ble kokt av Mysen (søen). Når man hadde kokt en av disse rettene der ostemassen skulle taes av når den hadde skilt seg, kokte man prim av det som ble igjen. Da måtte man få ut så mye som mulig av ostemassen så det ikke ble klumper i primen. Mysen ble så kokt til den var helt nedkokt. Det kunne ta flere timer alt etter hvor mye myse man hadde. På slutten måtte man røre rundt i primen så den ikke skulle brennes. Da var den blitt til en brun seig masse. Man kunne også ha litt jevning i på slutten for å drøye den, og for å få den tykk og fast fortere. Prim ble servert kald som pålegg på lefser, flatbrød eller brød.

• Kalvedans (Råmelkspudding, Kyrost) •

Dette er en ost som kokes av Råmelk. Råmelk er melk fra ei ku som nettopp har kalvet. Da er melka tykk, fet og gul. De ca. tre første gangene man melker kua etter en kalving, kan den melka som blir igjen etter at kalven har fått sitt, brukes til å koke Kalvedans av. Det er svært forskjellig fra ku til ku hvor tykk melka er. Er melka svært tykk må den blandes med litt vanlig helmelk før koking for at ikke osten skal bli for hard. Er den for tynn kan det bli vanskelig å få den stiv i det hele tatt. Dette er noe man nesten må prøve seg fram med.

Til 1 liter råmelk tilsettes ca. 1 dl. sukker. Melka helles i ei krukke som settes i ei gryte med vann. Vannet må stå like langt opp på krukka som melka inni krukka. Legg lokk over krukka og sett gryta til koking. Det må ikke koke for hardt og voldsomt i gryta. Helst bare trekke på kokepunktet. La det hele koke til råmelka så vidt er stivnet helt gjennom. Prøv med ei skje midt i innholdet. Den vil antakelig være ferdig på under en time. Kalvedans kan serveres lunken eller helt kald. Den kan serveres som dessert med rød saus på, eller som pålegg med kanel og kanskje litt sukker på.

438

• *Lappekaker* •

Lappekaker er nokså like de Amerikanske pannekakene. I eldre tider ble lappekaker brukt som festmat. Til bryllup, begravelser og andre festligheter ble disse kakene alltid servert. Fremdeles er de brukt som festmat enkelte steder. Men stort sett er de nå mer brukt som en hverdagsrett, eller litt knask til kaffen. De har også forskjellige navn etter hvor i landet vi befinner oss. På Nord-Vestlandet kalles de Svele, og i Hallingdal kalles de Kvikaku. Der finnes nok mange andre navn også, men det er Kvikaku fra Hallingdal jeg nå vil gi oppskrift på.

7 dl. sur melk (kan blandes med søt)
3 dl. sur eller søt fløte
(gjerne en blanding)
3 egg

1 dl. sukker
1 ts. natron
½ ts. salt
Hvetemel

Alt blandes godt sammen i en bolle. Ha i så mye hvetemel at det blir ei tykk røre. La røra hvile ca. en halv time før steking. Kakene stekes lysebrune på hver side, i stekepanne eller på helle. Kakene skal være nesten så store som en amerikansk pannekake.

• *Ertesuppe/Kjøttsuppe* •

Tørket sauekjøtt er ekstra godt til kjøttsuppe og ertesuppe. Da skjæres lår og bøger i passe store serveringsstykker, og legges i kokende vann i ei gryte. La kjøttet småkoke/trekke to tre timer—til kjøttet er mørt. Skum av det som under kokingen samler seg på toppen av suppen. Ca. 45 min før kjøttet er ferdig kokt, legges grønsaker i gryta. Oppskåret gulrøtter, kålrot, kål, purre og løk passer bra. Til ertesuppe haes oppbløtte erter i, ca. en halv time før grønsakene legges i. Retten serveres både som suppe og middagsrett med varme poteter til. En god løksaus passer godt til.

• *Løksaus* •

100 gram smør/marg.
100 gram hvetemel
1 litter kraft fra suppen

1 løk, finhakket
1 ss. sukker
1 ss. eddik, 7%

Smelt smøret i en kasserolle, tilsett melet når smøret er helt smeltet. Rør godt. Tilsett kraften og la det hele koke opp under stadig omrøring. Tilsett sukker, eddik og løk. La sausen småkoke 5 - 10 minutter.

• *Lapskaus* •

Til denne retten passer det også bra med tørket sauekjøtt. Men det mest vanlige er nok å bruke lettsaltet svinekjøtt. Lapskaus var kanskje en av de mest vanlige middagsrettene i Norge for en del år siden. Det kan også se ut til at dette var en svært vanlig rett for de som emigrerte over til Amerika for noen generasjoner tilbake.

Til ca. ½ kg kjøtt:
½ kg gulrøtter
100 gram selleri
½ liten purre

½ kg kålrot
½-1 kg poteter
Kjøttkraft eller buljong
Salt og pepper etter smak

Kjøttet skjæres i små terninger og legges i ei gryte med ca. 5 dl. kokende vann. La gjerne kjøttet koke noen minutter før grønsakene legges i. Alle grønsakene skjæres i små stykker eller terninger og haes i gryta. Rør om av og til under kokingen så det ikke brenner i bunnen. La det hele koke en times tid—til det er blitt en grøtaktig masse. Serveres varm som middagsrett, gjerne med litt flatbrød til.

• *Salting og tørking av sauekjøtt* •

Denne oppskriften forklarer hvordan salting og tørking foregår når man bruker en hel sau eller lam. Kjøttet bør ikke være for magert. Det kuttes opp i store stykker. Lår, bøger og ribber er de mest vanlige stykkene som blir brukt til tørking. De må bearbeides hele uten å kuttes i mindre stykker.

Salting: De oppskårede stykkene legges i et stort kar til salting. Hvert stykke gnies godt inn med grovt salt. (Fint salt kan også brukes. Men det trenges mye salt, og det fine saltet er mye dyrere enn det grove, så de fleste bruker grovt salt.) Før kjøttet legges i karet, strøes et godt lag med salt på bunnen. Kjøttstykkene legges ned så tett som mulig, og med et godt lag salt mellom hvert stykke. Skinnsidene på stykkene bør ligge opp. Det kan være en fordel å legge litt trykk på toppen av kjøttet slik at det presses tettere sammen. Dekk karet med plast eller et lokk, og plasser det på et kjølig sted. Etter hvert som saltet begynner å virke på kjøttet, vil det trekke ut væske. De nederste stykkene som blir liggende i denne saltlaken, får de beste forhold. De øverste stykkene bør gnies inn med salt flere ganger i løpet av prosessen, og da kan det være lurt å bruke saltlaken fra bunnen av karet. Man kan også koke en saltlake og helle over hvis man ønsker at alle stykkene skal ligge i lake. Pass da bare på at laken er helt kald før den helles over kjøttet.

Utvanning: Etter ca to uker er ribbesidene og bøgene ferdig saltet. De legges i et kar med rent kaldt vann. Lårene trenger en uke til i salt på grunn av at de er så mye tykkere. Etter ca. 24 timer i vann, kan kjøttet henges opp til tørk. (Lårene trenger ca. 36 timers utvanningstid.) Hvert kjøttstykke må dyppes ned i saltlaken igjen før den henges til tørk. Dette for at kjøttet skal få ei salthinne utenpå. Dette vil forhindre at kjøttet begynner å råtne før det er tørt.

Tørking: Der hvor luftfuktigheten er lav, kan man kaldtørke kjøttet. Da henges det på et kjølig og luftig sted. I eldre tider ble det gjerne hengt opp på et trekkfullt loft, eller i et stabbur. Der hvor det er høy luftfuktighet, må kjøttet henges på et varmt sted, gjerne over en vedovn. I eldre tider hang de det på kroker i taket over ovnen i kjøkkenet eller stuen. Det er viktig at temperaturen er forholdsvis høy til å begynne med slik at det kan danne seg ei fin hinne på kjøttet. Etter hvert kan temperaturen senkes litt. Men det må være jevn varme under hele tørketiden, ellers kan kjøttet begynne å råtne i hulrommene langs hinnene inne i kjøttstykkene. Etter et par uker er de minste stykkene ferdig tørket. Lårene trenger også lenger tørketid. Gjerne tre-fire uker.

Nå er kjøtter ferdig til bruk. Noen tørker kjøttet før de vanner det ut. Da må det vannes før bruk. Det er gjerne tilfellet med det pinnekjøttet som fåes kjøpt i butikken.

I de områder hvor luftfuktigheten er lav, kan tørket kjøtt oppbevares på tørkestedet hele vinteren. Men der hvor det må varmtørkes, er det en fordel å dypfryse kjøttet for lagring.

• *Pinnekjøtt* •

Dette er saue-/lammeribben hvor ribbenene er kuttet fra hverandre. Det brukes ei forholdsvis stor gryte. Et par lag med bjørkepinner legges i bunnen. Herav navnet pinnekjøtt. (Ei stålrist kan også brukes.) Hell på så mye vann at det akkurat når over pinnene. Kok opp vannet. Legg kjøttet over pinnene på kryss og tvers. La kjøttet koke tre – fire timer, til det slipper fra benet. Det må være god kok i gryta så det blir god damp. Etterfyll med vann etter hvert som det damper bort. Når kjøttet er ferdig kokt, kan man legge det over i ei form og sette det inn i en varm stekeovn noen minutter. Da får det en fin sprø overflate. Pinnekjøtt serveres med varme poteter og kålrotstappe. Sausen er det vannet i bunnen av gryta som under kokingen er blitt blandet med fett.

• *Glosteik* •

Dette var en vanlig måte å steke kjøttet på i eldre tider. Kjøttet ble skåret i stykker som til pinnekjøtt, eller stykker ble skåret av lår og bøger. Dette ble stekt på gloa i skorsteinen/peisen eller ovnen. Etter hvert som et stykke var ferdigstekt, ble det pakket inn i lefse, gjerne sammen med varme poteter, og spist med fingrene. En julemiddag kunne da se slik ut: Far satt foran ovnen med et stekespyd. I fanget hadde han en haug lefser. Etter hvert som kjøttet ble oppvarmet, begynte det å renne fett av det. Dette passet han på å samle opp i ei lefse ved å til stadighet ta kjøttet ut og tørke det på lefsa. Etter hvert som kjøttstykkene ble ferdigstekt, pakket ham dem inn i den lefsa som han hadde tørket av fettet på. Dette ble gitt i tur og orden til familiemedlemmene som satt rundt ham, eller ved spisebordet, og ventet må godbitene. Noen pleide også å stekte kjøttet i ei stekepanne på komfyren, eller i stekeovnen. Da ble ribbestykkene lagt i stekepanna eller stekeovnspana etter at fettranden på oversiden av stykket var rutet opp med en skarp kniv. Etter en times steketid (i stekeovnen) ved ca. 170°, var kjøttet ferdig til servering. Det ble spist med lefser og poteter, som ble dyppet i ribbefett.

• *Kvit Steik* •

Til denne retten kuttes tørket sauekjøtt i små, tynne skiver eller stykker. Kjøttet stekes i stekepanna til det er gjennomstekt. Lag en tykk hvit saus av margarin, hvetemel og melk. Hell de ferdigstekte kjøttbitene i sausen sammen med det fettet som har dannet seg under stekingen. Serveres som middagsrett med varme poteter til. •

SIX-GENERATION PEDIGREE CHART – *Descendants of Even and Gunhild Lia*

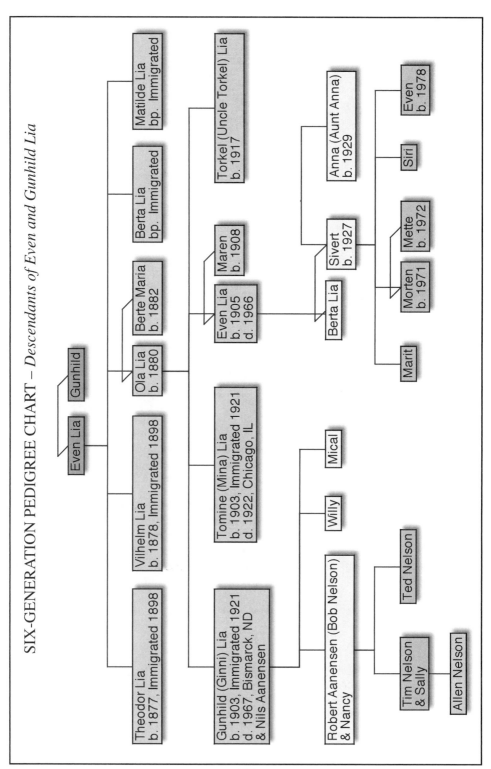